PENGUIN

THE TRU
AND (

DANIEL DEFOE was a London _nes, Cripplegate, the son of James Foe, a tallow-c _member of the Butchers' Company. Daniel began to use t _ne 'De Foe' c. 1695. He was educated for the Presbyterian ministry at Morton's Dissenting Academy at Newington Green, but decided he had no vocation and instead went into the wholesale hosiery business, acquiring premises in Cornhill. In 1685 he participated in Monmouth's unsuccessful rebellion. His business activities were extended into the wine trade and marine insurance, but in 1692 he was declared bankrupt. The consequences of this débâcle pursued him for the rest of his life, though he profited from the experience by becoming an expert in bankruptcy law, which he had some influence in reforming.

Meanwhile, Defoe was becoming a prolific and versatile writer, producing pamphlets and books on a wide variety of topics, including politics, crime, religion, economics, marriage, topography and superstition. His first extant political tract (against James II) was published in 1688. Becoming a staunch supporter of King William, he published early in January 1701 a verse satire, *The True-Born Englishman*, championing William and making merciless fun of English chauvinism, and the poem was an instant and runaway success. Two years later he brought out *The Shortest Way with the Dissenters*, a pamphlet pretending to be by a High Churchman calling for a root-and-branch extirpation of Dissent. It caused the enraged Government to have Defoe committed to Newgate and tried at the Old Bailey, where he was sentenced to stand three times in the pillory. For the following ten years he acted as a personal agent for the Secretary of State, Robert Harley, with whose support he launched an influential periodical, the *Review*.

Defoe turned to fiction relatively late in life and in 1719 published his great imaginative work, *Robinson Crusoe*. This was followed in 1722 by *Moll Flanders* and *A Journal of the Plague Year*, and in 1724 by his last important novel, *Roxana*. Other major works include a *History of the Union* (1709); *The Family Instructor* (1715); *A Tour Through the Whole Island of Great Britain*, a guide-book in three volumes (1724–6;

abridged Penguin edition, 1965); *The Political History of the Devil* (1726); *A Plan of the English Commerce* (1728); and *The Compleat English Gentleman* (not published until 1890). He died on 24 April 1731.

P. N. FURBANK is Emeritus Professor of Literature at the Open University. His books include *E. M. Forster: A Life* (2 vols., 1977–8), *Unholy Pleasure: The Idea of Social Class* (1985) and *Diderot: A Critical Biography* (1992). He is co-author, with W. R. Owens, of *The Canonisation of Daniel Defoe* (1988), *Defoe De-Attributions* (1994) and a *Critical Bibliography of Daniel Defoe* (forthcoming, 1998), as well as numerous articles on Defoe. He has also edited Dickens's *Martin Chuzzlewit* and Kipling's *Life's Handicap* for Penguin Classics.

W. R. OWENS is Staff Tutor and Senior Lecturer in Literature at the Open University. His publications include two volumes in the Clarendon edition of *The Miscellaneous Works of John Bunyan* and a co-edited collection of essays, *John Bunyan and His England 1628–88* (1990). He is founder editor of the periodical *Bunyan Studies*, and he also edited Bunyan's *Grace Abounding to the Chief of Sinners* for Penguin Classics.

DANIEL DEFOE

The True-Born Englishman
and Other Writings

Edited by
P. N. FURBANK AND W. R. OWENS

PENGUIN BOOKS

PENGUIN BOOKS

Published by the Penguin Group
Penguin Books Ltd, 27 Wrights Lane, London w8 5tz, England
Penguin Books USA Inc., 375 Hudson Street, New York, New York 10014, USA
Penguin Books Australia Ltd, Ringwood, Victoria, Australia
Penguin Books Canada Ltd, 10 Alcorn Avenue, Toronto, Ontario, Canada m4v 3b2
Penguin Books (NZ) Ltd, 182–190 Wairau Road, Auckland 10, New Zealand

Penguin Books Ltd, Registered Offices: Harmondsworth, Middlesex, England

This collection first published 1997
1 3 5 7 9 10 8 6 4 2

Introduction and Notes copyright © P. N. Furbank and W. R. Owens, 1997
All rights reserved

The moral right of the editors has been asserted

Set in 9.5/12pt Monotype Ehrhardt
Typeset by Rowland Phototypesetting Ltd, Bury St Edmunds, Suffolk
Printed in England by Clays Ltd, St Ives plc

Contents

Introduction   vii
Further Reading   xxvii
Note on the Texts   xxix

DEFENDER OF KING WILLIAM

An Argument, Shewing, that a Standing Army, with Consent of
    Parliament, is not Inconsistent with a Free Government   5
The True-Born Englishman   26
The Six Distinguishing Characters of a Parliament-Man   60

TRIBUNE OF THE PEOPLE

Legion's Memorial   72
The Original People of England   85

NON-CONFORMING DISSENTER

An Enquiry into the Occasional Conformity of Dissenters   114
The Shortest Way with the Dissenters   132
A Brief Explanation of a Late Pamphlet   146
A Dialogue between a Dissenter and the Observator   150
A Hymn to the Pillory   170

SOCIAL REFORMER

From An Essay upon Projects   186
Giving Alms No Charity   230

POLITICAL ADVISER

From 'Memorandum to Robert Harley'   258

Notes   270
Appendix: A List of Defoe's Published Writings 1688–1704   295

Introduction

For modern readers Daniel Defoe is first and foremost a novelist, but this was by no means his main claim to fame during his own lifetime. To his contemporaries he was known as the author of a memorable and best-selling poem, *The True-Born Englishman*; as the editor of a pioneering political journal, the *Review*; and as the author (or suspected author, for this was a great age of literary anonymity) of a variety of brilliant prose satires, polemics and 'secret histories'. Defoe was, at his best, a most ingenious and farseeing author, with an idiosyncratic ethical and political stance and a most free and inventive prose-style deserving comparison with those of Cobbett, Hazlitt, or George Orwell. Moreover, his life, and especially the earlier part of it, was exceedingly stirring and colourful. Indeed, he touched English life and history at so many different points that he is not easy to get into focus, and all the more so because some of his best writing is not readily available. For all these reasons, it seemed to us that there was a real need for an anthology in which the man and the writer, particularly the 'radical' Defoe of his earlier years, could be seen in the round.

DEFOE'S EARLY LIFE

Daniel Defoe was born in 1660 or thereabouts, the son of James Foe, a City tradesman and member of the Butchers' Company living in the parish of Cripplegate. The year 1660 saw the demise of Oliver Cromwell's Puritan republic and the restoration of Charles II to the throne, and one of the first acts of the restored Parliament was to introduce a series of laws reversing Cromwell's policy of religious toleration. Anglican clergymen who refused to comply with the Act of Uniformity (1662) were ejected from their livings, and Dissenters of all denominations suffered civil and religious persecution and were forced to worship in secret.

Thus, the moment of Defoe's birth was of considerable significance for his family, which was strongly Puritan in character. It worshipped under the celebrated Samuel Annesley, who was ejected from the Church in 1662 and set up a Dissenting meeting-house in Bishopsgate; and Daniel received his later education at Charles Morton's Dissenting Academy at Newington Green. As this implies, he was intended for the ministry, and later he would write that 'it was my disaster first to be set apart for, and then to be set apart from, the honour of that sacred employ'.[1] What exactly deterred him is not clear. At all events, somewhere about 1682, without going through the customary apprenticeship, he set up as a wholesale hosier and general merchant.

In the same year he was courting Mary, the daughter of John Tuffley, a well-to-do cooper and freeman of the City of London, and compiled for her a volume entitled 'Historical Collections'.[2] It is an anthology of memorable anecdotes and sayings, culled from Plutarch, Fuller's *Holy State*, Foxe's *Book of Martyrs* and other such works, and is dedicated to 'Clarinda' by 'The meanest & truest of your adorers & servants, Bellmour'. A manuscript of some pious 'Meditations', accompanying the transcript of a series of sermons, belongs to the same period.[3]

Defoe and Mary Tuffley were married in 1684 and, aided by Tuffley's dowry, he established a warehouse and counting-house in Freeman's Yard on the north side of Cornhill. He traded in woollen goods and wines and brandies and was in correspondence with France, Spain, Portugal and America. A few years later, he was also investing substantial sums in marine insurance, suffering heavy losses during the war with France.

The City of London, where they lived, was a stronghold of Whiggism and Dissent. In 1683, the Whig leaders Lord William Russell and Algernon Sidney were executed for their supposed involvement in the Rye House Plot against the King's life, and the event was a signal for renewed persecution of the Dissenters. Defoe's old tutor Charles Morton had to go into hiding, and many less fortunate Dissenters died in prison. Defoe was especially concerned at the fate of Thomas De Laune, the author of *A Plea for the Nonconformists* (1683), a work which, in Defoe's view, was the best statement of the Dissenters' case ever given. De Laune was tried for libel and fined for his pamphlet and, being unable to pay his fine, died in Newgate – betrayed, so Defoe was to write, not only by his Anglican opponent Benjamin Calamy but by his fellow Dissenters, who were too mean to raise the small sum needed to save his life.[4]

During the last years of Charles's reign, opposition to the Court grouped itself round the figure of the Protestant Duke of Monmouth, Charles's illegitimate son; and, in 1685, when Charles's brother, the avowedly Roman Catholic James, Duke of York, succeeded to the throne, Monmouth led an unsuccessful rising. According to his own account,[5] Defoe took arms under Monmouth, though he escaped the ensuing 'Bloody Assizes', which sent many of the rebels to the scaffold.

Defoe, who was to become such a prolific writer, seems to have begun authorship relatively late. The first published work of his that we hear of came out in 1683, when the Turks were besieging Vienna. Many Whigs, at that time, welcomed the prospect of a defeat for the House of Habsburg, arguing that it would aid the Protestant cause, and Defoe published a pamphlet attacking this attitude as both short-sighted and a betrayal of Christianity.[6] At the time of writing it, he was, he wrote later, 'then but a young man, and a younger author'.[7] He also published another anonymous tract in 1688, *A Letter to a Dissenter from his Friend at the Hague*, designed to persuade his fellow Dissenters not to be fooled by James II's offer to grant them toleration. By the end of the year 1688, there had taken place the 'Glorious Revolution', by which James was forced to quit the throne, and his daughter's husband and cousin, William of Orange, invited to reign in his place. Defoe was always to be a wholehearted admirer of William, and a slashing verse satire on City politics entitled *A New Discovery of an Old Intreague*, which he published anonymously in 1691, ended with a paean of praise to his royal hero.

'A wit, turned tradesman! What an incongruous part of nature is there brought together, consisting of direct contraries!' So wrote Defoe many years later, and one supposes he might have been thinking of himself as a young man and writer. The fate of such a person, he says, is certain: 'As the first part is all comedy, so the last acts are always made up of tragedy.'[8] Whether for the reason he suggests, the next year (1692) certainly saw Defoe in desperate straits as a businessman, struggling to save himself by shady ruses, and paying more than one visit to the Fleet prison; in the end he was bankrupted, with debts amounting to the very large sum of £17,000. The psychology of bankrupts, and the illogicality and inhumanity of the manner of treating bankrupts, would become one of his major themes as a writer. By 1705 he had reduced his debt to £5,000, and there were times, later, when he would enjoy considerable affluence; nevertheless, he would never be entirely free from the effects of this early bankruptcy.

It may be significant, though, that he wrote of a 'wit turned tradesman' and not a 'tradesman turned wit'. Certainly, his next important publication, *An Essay upon Projects* (1697), the Preface to which was signed with his initials 'D.F.', shows him seriously bidding for recognition as a professional writer. We shall come back to this work later.

DEFENDER OF KING WILLIAM

In September 1697, King William's nine-year war against the French ended with the Treaty of Ryswick, and William, on his return to England, received a triumphant welcome. He was, however, by no means the popular figure he had been ten years earlier, as the saviour of England's liberties and victor over King James. His aloofness and coldness were considered offensive, there were rumours and scandals about his Dutch advisers, and he found himself faced with a distinctly hostile Parliament. The attack began on his right to maintain an army in peace time. In October, the Whig polemicists John Trenchard and Walter Moyle published a pamphlet, *An Argument Shewing that a Standing Army is Inconsistent with a Free Government*, calling for the disbanding of all professional troops, leaving the defence of the country to a militia. Only England, they argued, had preserved its freedom 'in this unhappy age, when an universal deluge of tyranny has overspread the face of the whole earth'; and her salvation was owing to her being an island and to resisting, up to now, the lure of a standing army. Their pamphlet was answered by the Whig Lord Chancellor, Lord Somers – the debate was to be almost entirely a Whig affair – and a number of other writers joined in. Meanwhile, a motion was passed in the House of Commons requiring all land forces raised since September 1680 to be disbanded – leaving a force of something under 10,000 men.

It was an opportunity for Defoe to come to the support of the king whom he greatly honoured, and he contributed three times to this standing-army debate – most comprehensively in his *An Argument, Shewing, that a Standing Army, with Consent of Parliament, is not Inconsistent with a Free Government etc.*, published in December 1698. In this, he argued that both sides had fallen into extremes, and that what was wanted was a 'medium' between them. In the hands of a prince as far-seeing as King William, the value of a standing army would be not to enable England to defend herself against the whole world, but to preserve the balance of power in Europe. (The

European powers had been happy to let William lead them while he commanded an army, but would they pay any attention to him without one?) Secondly, it was infinitely desirable that England should fight her wars abroad and not on her own soil, but this entailed a professional army, since a militia could not be commanded to fight abroad. Thirdly, one of the great arguments of the opponents of standing armies was that the only safe system was something like the feudal one, by which the power of the sword lay not in the king's hands but in those of his lords and their vassals: that 'all such Governments where the Prince has the power of the sword, though the people have the power of the purse, are no more monarchies but tyrannies' (p. 13). But this, said Defoe, was simply false. The power of the purse was quite as great as, or greater than, the power of the sword – and especially in England, where the 'purse' was so especially sacred. The reason why Charles I had not managed to destroy English liberties was because, without calling a Parliament, he could pay his army.

Things grew steadily more difficult for William. It was resented that, though he was no longer required to lead armies, he went to Holland again in the summer of 1698 for several months, accompanied by his hated Dutch advisers. During this summer – indeed, in secrecy and quite without the authority of Parliament – he would be engaged in high-level international diplomacy. The ailing and semi-imbecile king of Spain, Carlos II, was plainly near to death, which raised the question: what should be done with his enormous dominions in Spain, Flanders, Italy and South America? There was general agreement that they could not continue in the hands of a single power and, prompted by France, William had taken it on himself to draw up a Treaty of Partition. The terms of the Treaty became known in October 1698, when it had already been signed, and the news caused an outcry.

In the general election during this summer, a new 'Country' party, made up of landowning Tories and discontented Whigs, had won a number of seats, and under its influence the Commons resolved on an even more drastic reduction of the army, also insisting that it must be composed of English-born troops – which meant that William must dismiss his faithful Dutch guards. He was bitterly wounded and contemplated abdication.

Even worse, from his point of view, was to follow. In the summer of 1699, a Parliamentary committee was set up to investigate the lavish grants he had made, to friends and supporters, of forfeited estates in Ireland, and on receiving its report, the House ruled that these grants must be rescinded.

There followed a prolonged and bitter clash between the two Houses of Parliament and a further attack on William's personal entourage. An address was made to the King to appoint no foreigner to his Privy Council, and eventually he had to give way. He then prorogued Parliament, being too angry to make his usual speech from the throne, and set off once more for Holland.

A month later there appeared a vicious verse-attack on him by the Whig journalist John Tutchin. It was entitled *The Foreigners* and related how the 'Israelites' (English) had freed themselves from a tyrant and replaced him by a prince from 'Gibeon' (the United Provinces), but had been mad enough to allow into the country with him a 'boorish' brood, born from bogs and 'nature's excrement', to prey upon the land. What had the 'Israelites' to do with such proud 'vermin' as 'Bentir' (William's favourite, Hans Willem Bentinck), who not only devoured whole provinces in 'Israel' but also presumed to divide the possessions of the unfortunate 'Hiram' (King of Spain)? What had they to do with such as 'Keppech' (another of William's favourites, Arnold van Keppel, Earl of Albemarle), who mounted to high position 'by the usual course/Of whoring, pimping, or a crime that's worse' (i.e. sodomy[9])?

Defoe later described how he read this 'vile abhorred pamphlet, in very ill verse . . . in which the author, who he was I then knew not, fell personally upon the King himself, and then upon the Dutch nation; and after having reproached his Majesty with crimes, that his worst enemy could not think of without horror, he sums up all in the odious name of FOREIGNER'. It filled him, he said, 'with a kind of rage against the book, and gave birth to a trifle which I never could hope should have met with so general an acceptation as it did'.[10] He is referring to his own poem *The True-Born Englishman*, which he published early in January 1701 and which became an instant and amazing success.

The theme of *The True-Born Englishman* is simple but profound. It takes England's behaviour towards her saviour William as a supreme example of her national vice. Other nations have their native vice – for Spain it is pride, for Italy lust, for Germany drunkenness – and in the case of the English it is, beyond dispute, ingratitude: 'An ugly, surly, sullen, selfish spirit,/Who Satan's worst perfections does inherit' (p. 30). What possible right has a race composed of all the offscourings of Europe, Romans, Gauls, Saxons, Danes and Normans – as well as needy Scots – to despise *foreigners*? The idea is grotesque, but, as it expands in the poet's mind, wonderfully funny, giving the poem a quality of joyous exhilaration and genial comic rage. The verse, though in heroic couplets, dispenses with all the cunning Popean devices of the couplet considered as a closed unit. Instead, impelled by a master idea, it runs swiftly and irresistibly on, its gaiety reinforced by bisyllabic rhymes and given cumulative energy by the continual return, swelling each time in irony, of the phrase 'True-Born Englishman'. The poem is a satire and, at the same time, a ballad, complete with refrain, and one can imagine it sung by a street ballad-singer. Over-riding everyday logic, an excuse is found in it to insult everyone: the English for invidiousness towards the 'foreigners' they were themselves a generation or two earlier; foreigners, for being locust-like marauders and invaders; and English women for welcoming them.

If we are to believe his own account, this poem brought Defoe to the attention of William III.[11] The King asked to see him, and the two were soon on terms of intimacy, William discussing affairs of state with him and sometimes taking his advice. This story of his relations with King William was to become a favourite topic with him and he would often air it later in his journal the *Review*. It has to be said, though, that it must be treated with caution, for the evidence for it comes exclusively from Defoe himself, and there are contradictions in his account. Nevertheless, whatever the truth in this matter, Defoe's poem was of enormous value to William's cause, and it transformed Defoe from a relatively obscure pamphleteer to the most famous poet of the moment. The title of his poem was soon on everybody's lips; there were numerous answers to it; and for many years, on title-pages and elsewhere, he would continue to refer to himself as 'The Author of *The True-Born Englishman*'.

The poem came out in the middle of a general election and, side by side with it, Defoe published, in the form of prose pamphlets, various further and effective pieces of Williamite propaganda. In October 1700, Carlos II of Spain finally died and, to the world's astonishment, was found to have left a will bequeathing his entire dominions to Louis XIV's grandson, the young Duke of Anjou – though with a proviso that the crowns of Spain and France must remain separate. This, of course, cut across William's schemes for a partition, and if Louis XIV were to decide to recognize the will, violating his previous renunciations, it could mean his taking over control of Spain, if not actually uniting the two nations.

Defoe drew up a response to the news from Spain (*The Two Great Questions Consider'd*) before it was known what line Louis XIV would take, asking his readers 'calmly' to consider the consequences were Louis to recognize the will. If Louis had had no rivals, he would infallibly, and very reasonably, accept the will and annex Spain to the crown of France. Being a wise prince, however, he might decide he would profit more by outmanoeuvring his neighbours than by directly flouting them. So much for the first 'great question', what will Louis do? The second question is, what ought the English to do? It has to be admitted, writes Defoe, that with the reckless dismantling of its army, England makes 'but a very mean figure abroad'. Still, 'all the world does not yet see our weak side', and William will infallibly be concerting a league with the Dutch and others to preserve the balance of power in Europe. Defoe here proceeds to state a *Realpolitik* view central to his political, as to his ethical, theories:

A just balance of power is the life of peace. I question whether it be in the human nature to set bounds to his own ambition, and whether the best man on earth would not be King over all the rest if he could. Every King in the world would be the universal monarch if he might, and nothing restrains but the power of neighbours.[12]

This is the same sentiment as we find in the famous opening couplet of *Jure Divino* (1706), his verse treatise on the theory of monarchy:

> Nature has left this tincture in the blood,
> That all men would be tyrants if they could.

It is a pessimistic realism based, in good Calvinist fashion, on the doctrine of original sin, and is one of the things that distinguish Defoe as a political thinker from John Locke.

Another of his pamphlets from this time, *The Six Distinguishing Characters of a Parliament-Man*, was direct election propaganda, cunningly designed to counter the stock Tory advice to electors to choose men of 'estate and honour'. This latter was good advice, argued Defoe, when Parliamentary corruption was so rife; for a man of 'estate' would think responsibly before voting taxes, seeing that they would affect him personally. But now that, under the blameless rule of King William, there was so much less corruption, this consideration had less force. Men without estates could be just as good judges of the nation's needs; they might even sometimes be better. For, after all, it might well be that a man of 'estate and honour' was quite unsuitable as a legislator for other reasons – like being a Jacobite, or an atheist, or too young, or immoral, or simply a *fool*.

Defoe's strategy in this pamphlet is to clear the Whigs of the charge of fanaticism or persecution. Jacobites and Papists, he implies, may be perfectly good citizens. It is merely that they are absurdly out of place in the Parliament of a Protestant nation.

TRIBUNE OF THE PEOPLE

Louis XIV, realizing England's worst fears, recognized the late king of Spain's will, and thereupon events moved swiftly. In February 1701, his grandson Philip of Anjou entered Madrid. Meanwhile, the French seized most of the fortresses in the Spanish Netherlands, and there was talk of a French invasion of England. It was a menacing situation, but the new House of Commons – strongly Tory in composition, with a large admixture of Jacobites – seemed unwilling to take retaliatory action. Instead, they devoted their energies to impeaching William's ministers and agents for their part in the Partition treaties, and meanwhile they delayed voting 'supplies'.

Events then took a surprising turn. On 29 April 1701, at the Kent Quarter-Sessions at Maidstone, the Grand Jury, justices and freeholders signed a petition to the Commons about 'the dangerous estate of this kingdom', humbly imploring the House to 'have regard to the voice of the people' and to turn their loyal addresses into votes of supply, so that the King might be 'enabled powerfully to assist his allies before it is too late'. Five Kentish gentlemen were deputed to deliver the petition, which they did on 7 May, and the House, highly incensed, voted it 'scandalous, insolent, and seditious' and threw the petitioners into prison.

This was the cue for Defoe to emerge on the public scene in a new role, as intrepid demagogue and political agitator. A week after the arrest of the 'Kentish Gentlemen', he made an appearance in Westminster, accompanied by a guard of sixteen 'gentlemen of quality', and delivered to the Speaker of the House a paper known as *Legion's Memorial*. It presented, as from 'The People of England', and in the most threatening terms, an 'abridgement' of the nation's grievances against the Commons. The Speaker was commanded 'by two hundred thousand Englishmen' to put the Memorial before the Commons and told that if he refused, he would 'find cause in a short time to repent it'. 'Our name is Legion', the Memorial ended, 'and we are many.'

This really rather astonishing ultimatum appears to have terrified the House. At all events, it seems to have taken no steps to punish the authors. The impeachments of William's ministers dropped; the King eventually got his 'supplies'; and, on the prorogation of Parliament, the Kentish gentlemen were released from prison. Immediately afterwards, they were entertained at a lavish dinner in Mercers' Hall. Defoe sat next to the guests of honour, and – as a Tory journalist remarked – 'one might have read the downfall of parliaments in his very countenance'.[13] The philanthropic projector and amused satirist had become a formidable radical activist and self-appointed spokesman for the 'People'.

In September 1701, the exiled James II died, and Louis XIV declared James's son to be his lawful successor and rightful king of England. These events prompted two more pamphlets from Defoe. In *The Present State of Jacobitism Considered*, he addressed a persuasive and diplomatic argument to Protestant Jacobites, to the effect that the death of James had released them from their vows of loyalty, and they could now honourably 'come into the bosom and protection of the Government'. Their previous commitments, even if foolish, were worthy of respect, and their fellow-citizens would welcome them back. Defoe added (a characteristic touch) that the behaviour of Louis XIV, that wise king, towards the Stuarts, father and son, was a perfectly rational piece of statecraft, and the Jacobites would be fools to take it for more than it was worth.

In the second tract, *Reasons Against a War with France*, he argued that the actions of Louis XIV did not amount to a breach of the Treaty of Ryswick, and if England were to have a war, it should be with Spain, not France. England always did well out of her wars with Spain; and if the French joined in, they would be fighting at a disadvantage.

In these tracts, as during all this year, Defoe had been responding directly to day-to-day events. At the very end of 1701, however, he brought out a pamphlet, *The Original Power of the Collective Body of the People of England*, in which he expounded his underlying theory of sovereignty. It is one of his most important writings, an idiosyncratic statement of an extreme Whig point of view. Framed as a sequence of brief maxims, it is not only an attack on the 'divine right' theory of monarchy, but more particularly on a recent pamphlet by the Tory financier and MP Sir Humphrey Mackworth, entitled *A Vindication of the Rights of the Commons of England* (1701). Mackworth asserted that all political authority in England lay with the King, Lords and Commons. Their respective powers served as checks and balances to one another, but they were 'not to be limited by any authority besides their own', and the ordinary citizen had no right to criticize them. Defoe, by contrast, asserts the 'original right' of the 'People' of England to govern themselves. They may depute this right to a monarch, a nobility and a house of representatives, but if those governors betray the 'public good' their authority ends, and (as he had phrased it in *The True-Born Englishman*) 'power retreats to its original'. There is, and must be, 'some power prior to the power of King, Lords and Commons, from which, as the streams from the fountain, the power of King, Lords and Commons is derived' (p. 92); and if the 'People' cannot retrieve this power from bad governments by peaceful means, they may reasonably resort to force or ask for help from a neighbouring nation. (Reason is the 'test and touchstone of laws'.)

There is, nevertheless, an important qualification. The power or 'original right' that Defoe speaks of belongs essentially to freeholders. They are the proper owners of the country, the other inhabitants, he writes, being merely 'sojourners' or lodgers, who must either accept the laws that the freeholders impose or leave the country. (If any single man in England were to become landlord of the whole freehold of England, he adds with a touch of fantasy, he would be entitled to return himself to Parliament for every county.)

This pamphlet of Defoe's, perhaps the clearest statement of his political theories, was often later quoted both by friends and enemies and would be reprinted half a century later during John Wilkes's struggle over the rights of the citizen *vis-à-vis* Government and Parliament.

THE NON-CONFORMING DISSENTER

We now turn to Defoe's attitude towards religion and towards his fellow Dissenters, and in particular to the practice of 'occasional conformity'. Under the Corporation Act of 1661 and the Test Act of 1673, no one might hold a municipal or national office without first qualifying by taking the sacrament according to the rite of the Church of England. There had thus grown up a practice among Dissenters, when appointed to a municipal office, to take communion in an Anglican church on a single occasion, while continuing their membership of a Dissenting congregation. The matter had not attracted much notice until, upon becoming Lord Mayor

in 1697, the Presbyterian Sir Humphrey Edwin took communion in
St Paul's and, on the same Sunday, attended a Dissenting communion
service at Pinners' Hall in full mayoral regalia, compelling his indignant
sword-bearer to do likewise. His action caused an outcry from the High
Church party, and a good deal of waggishness in ballads and lampoons. It
fell to Defoe, however, to attack Sir Humphrey's action, and with it the
whole practice of occasional conformity, on serious religious grounds.

In a pamphlet *An Enquiry into the Occasional Conformity of Dissenters,
in Cases of Preferment*, published in January 1698, he told Sir Humphrey,
in a Preface, that if the rights of his sword-bearer were infringed by Sir
Humphrey's forcing him to attend a Dissenting meeting-house, his own
liberty of conscience was equally violated by being forced to communicate
at St Paul's. Why did Sir Humphrey put up with it? When we saw him
at St Paul's, Defoe writes ironically, we were in hopes that he had seen
the error of his Dissenting ways. (For to suspect he was doing it to curry
favour with both political parties would be too base: and anyway it would
have had the opposite effect.) But to see him, immediately afterwards,
worshipping in a meeting-house left one simply bewildered. What was
this 'new sort of a religion that looks two ways at once'?

The Dissenters, wrote Defoe, were the heirs of the Puritans, but in
some respect their unworthy heirs. To be a Protestant under Mary Tudor
was a genuine test of conscience, and the debates between the Reformers
in the age of Elizabeth were singularly earnest and devout. Their tone was
very different from later ones. Indeed, the present day offered a unique
spectacle.

There is a sort of truth which all men owe to the principles they profess; and
generally speaking, all men pay it; a Turk is a Turk zealously and entirely; an
idolater is an idolater, and will serve the Devil to a tittle: none but Protestants halt
between God and Baal. (p. 121)

It was, he said, such a 'bantering with religion' and 'playing Bo-peep with
God Almighty' (p. 124) as could not but fill any modest Christian with
horror.

Defoe's opinion about the practice persisted unchanged to the end of
his life, and it lies at the heart of his attitude, perfectly coherent but full
of surprises, towards Dissent and the Dissenters. This attitude was soon
to be severely tested and to bring disaster on his head.

In March 1702 King William died, and it became clear that, with the accession of Queen Anne, the country had taken a swerve towards Tory and High Church views. Thus the Dissenters could expect trouble. Anathemas against them, and hints that it was time to reconsider William's Act of Toleration, were to be heard from Anglican pulpits; and, in a sulphurous sermon, Henry Sacheverell, a fellow of Magdalen College in Oxford, called upon all good sons of the Church to 'hang out the bloody flag, and banner of defiance' against Dissenters and members of the low church. By November a legal blow had been aimed at the Dissenters in the shape of a Parliamentary bill to outlaw the practice of occasional conformity.

Defoe's reaction to this was characteristic and significant. In a pamphlet *An Enquiry into Occasional Conformity, Shewing that the Dissenters are no Way Concern'd in it*, he argued that everybody, in either camp, was strangely mistaken about the Bill – everybody but himself. (It was awkward to say this, 'but if it be so, who can help it?') The fact was, the Bill was thoroughly unjust and malicious, but it could do no possible harm to conscientious Dissenters, who would not dream of practising occasional conformity anyway. It might even strengthen them in their faith; and, if it prompted weaker brethren to desert the Dissenting fold, well, the Church was welcome to them. The Queen had promised to maintain the Act of Toleration, wrote Defoe. The Dissenters deserved more, but this was their essential and precious protection, and they must content themselves with it.

His tract was aimed at his fellow Dissenters, whom he was very happy to enrage. For High Church readers, he was constructing a different engine of war. On 1 December, three days after the Bill passed the Commons, he published an anonymous tract entitled *The Shortest Way with the Dissenters*, in which the imaginary author, in the very accents of Sacheverell and his like, outlined what would really be the simplest solution as regards the Dissenters. For fourteen years (that is to say, since the Revolution), they had bullied the Church with their Act of Toleration, and set up their 'canting-synagogues' at the very church-door. Now, with a new 'royal, English, true' friend of the Church on the throne, it was time for retribution. The Dissenters realized it themselves, crying out self-pityingly as they did about peace, union, forbearance and charity – 'as if the Church had not too long harboured her enemies under her wing, and nourished the viperous brood, till they hiss and fly in the face of the mother that cherished them' (p. 132). The simple answer was that they must be rooted out. The King of France had managed it with his Protestants, and they were more numerous. Moreover, it would be the Dissenters' own fault; for in the days of their ascendancy during the Commonwealth, what charity had they ever showed to their enemies? 'Alas the Church of England! What with Popery on one hand, and schismatics on the other, how has she been crucified between two thieves. – Now let us crucify the thieves' (p. 144).

Defoe's plan was for some at least of his High Church readers to be taken in and believe these very welcome views to come from one of their own number. In this he succeeded magnificently – in fact, far too well for his own comfort. A number of his high-flying readers praised this salutary tract, and when they realized they had been gulled, their fury was intense. But Defoe's Dissenting brethren were almost equally resentful. They smarted at having been fooled (as many were) and told themselves that such terrible things ought not really to be said, even in jest or irony. The Government, for its part, took the matter very seriously, and on 3 January 1703 a warrant was issued for Defoe's arrest. He decided to flee from justice, and a week or so later a proclamation was issued in the Queen's name offering a reward for his capture.

Eventually, in May, he was caught and arrested in Spitalfields, at the house of a friend of his, a silk weaver named Sammen. He was lengthily interrogated by the Secretary of State, was tried at the Old Bailey and was fined and sentenced to imprisonment and to stand three times in the pillory.

This latter event, in fact, turned out to be a personal triumph. The crowd pelted him, not with rotten eggs, but with flowers; and copies of a poem, 'A Hymn to the Pillory', that he had composed for the occasion were handed round and recited by ballad-singers. The theme of this poem, which is in the form of an irregular Pindaric ode, is the rights and grandeur of authorship and its power to turn even the pillory to advantage. By a brilliant succession of conceits, the pillory is made to stand for all the institutions of society: the pulpit, the stage, the bar, the pageants and the 'opening vacancys' (in other words, jobs) of a corrupt state system. The poem even dares to insult the 'mob', whom the powers-that-be intend to pelt the victim with filth, challenging the crowd to act, not as a 'mob', but as the 'people'.

The triumph or débâcle of *The Shortest Way* (however one regards it) brought an end to Defoe's career as public agitator. It also taught him a lesson, though a lesson he would never fully assimilate, i.e. that people either cannot, or deliberately will not, recognize irony. Soon after his arrest he issued *A Brief Explanation of a Late Pamphlet, Entitled The Shortest Way with the Dissenters*, in which he patiently pointed out what should have been obvious: that his *Shortest Way*, according to a perfectly familiar convention, said the opposite of what he meant. Shortly afterwards, no doubt recognizing that nobody listens to patient explanations, he returned to the topic in a cheerfully and impenitently satirical vein, in *A Dialogue between a Dissenter and the Observator, Concerning The Shortest Way with the Dissenters*. But for all this, more than once later in his career he would practise a similar sort of irony, with similar, and nearly as fatal, results.

THE SOCIAL REFORMER

We mentioned earlier that, in 1697, Defoe published a major book called *An Essay upon Projects*. This formed the first of many works he was to write on questions of social reform. It was an age of projects; as a young man, he had become personally involved with a number of 'projectors'. He had, for instance, helped form a company to rescue treasure from shipwrecked vessels by means of a patent diving-bell (it lost him his whole investment and led to a lawsuit). Also, he had dealings with the notorious projector Thomas Neale and acted as a manager for one of his lotteries.

His *Essay* was the fruit of nearly five years' work, and he laments in his Preface that some of the schemes proposed in it had been anticipated in the meantime. He gives a history of 'projecting' and puts forward proposals for country banks and friendly societies, an elaborate scheme for repairing the highways, a Pension Office, a military academy and an academy for women, humane treatment of the mentally handicapped, a reform of the bankruptcy laws, and an improved system for recruiting seamen for the navy. It is an impressive programme, and several of his schemes, when he gave them wider publicity in his journal, the *Review*, actually bore fruit. He was, for instance, partly responsible, in 1706, for a Parliamentary Bill to Prevent Frauds Committed by Bankrupts, and later he was invited to submit proposals for naval recruiting to a Parliamentary committee.

Philanthropic 'projecting' would continue to be one of his interests, and in his old age, in the *persona* of the elderly and curmudgeonly 'Andrew Moreton', he would put forward a further series of reforming schemes: for retirement homes for the elderly, an undenominational university, and protection against street robbery, et cetera.

Another of Defoe's major interests was trade. Unsuccessful as he had been as a merchant, he loved the topics of trade and economic theory; writing about trade, he admitted, was 'the whore I really doted upon'.[14] A good idea of his general theory on trade, and its logical connection with the rest of his outlook, can be gained from the tract entitled *Giving Alms No Charity*. The pamphlet came out in November 1704, as a counterblast to a Bill for the Better Relief, Imployment, and Settlement of the Poor, recently introduced in the Commons and later published in pamphlet form, by Defoe's old opponent Sir Humphrey Mackworth. Mackworth's scheme was to extend the existing workhouse system by authorizing the Overseers of the Poor in every town or group of towns in England to provide the resources, i.e. materials for spinning and weaving, et cetera, to give employment to the destitute poor. Defoe, claiming the right of an English freeholder to address Parliament about a Bill in progress, declares the scheme to be quite fatal, calculated to ruin the English wool trade and liable, rather than to relieve the poor, to add to their number.

The history of the English wool trade, he argues, is a memorable example of the power of Providence to extract good from evil. Queen Elizabeth was clear-sighted in realizing how woollen manufacture might be expanded in England; but it was the blindness of tyranny, the persecution of the Flemings by their Spanish overlords, that was 'the wheel to turn over the great machine of trade from Flanders into England'. 'Tyranny and persecution, the one an oppression of property, the other of conscience, always ruin trade' (p. 232). Here, writes Defoe, is to be found the origin of those 'true-born English families' in Essex and Norfolk, with surnames like DeVink and Rebow and Papillon, from whose skills the English have learned so much (p. 234).

Thanks to the woollen manufacture, argued Defoe, England had grown immensely prosperous. Nevertheless she was overrun by beggars and workless vagrants. What could be the explanation? It was not, he felt certain, because there was no work for them to do. 'There is in England more labour than hands to perform it, and consequently a want of people, not of employment' (p. 235). So what should be the remedy? Not, most emphatically, to try to create work for the workless; but rather to compel them to look for it themselves, by enforcing the laws against beggars.

'Truly the scandal lies on our charity', writes Defoe; 'and people have such a notion in England of being pitiful and charitable, that they encourage vagrants, and by a mistaken zeal do more harm than good' (p. 238). The project of creating work and setting up cloth manufacture in every town was a sure way to wreck the delicate mechanism of English trade. It would not create any new trade or new market: thus, for every skein of worsted spun in a workhouse or the like there must be 'a skein the less spun by some poor family or person that spun it before' (p. 241). Moreover, there were 'arcanas' or secrets explaining why particular manufactures have flourished in particular regions. Again, this regional specialism carried with it all the huge benefits of circulation of trade. Set up the same trades everywhere, and you will ruin all the innkeepers and carters and other intermediaries who serve this circulation and gain their living by it. Defoe's earnestness in this is plain. When Mackworth's scheme came up again in 1706, he wrote in the *Review*: 'I would think myself happy to be led out to immediate execution, rather than to have the curse of a whole nation's poor follow me to a grave more remote, or have it wrote on my grave-stone, that here lies D.F. that projected the destruction of the English manufactures, and ruined the poor of this kingdom'.[15]

Sidney and Beatrice Webb, in their *English Local Government*, are shocked at Defoe's harshness towards the unemployed, and one can well see why. Nevertheless he is so knowledgeable that they are continually forced to quote from him. There is, moreover, a side of him that they miss and that plays its part in *Giving Alms No Charity* – the visionary enthusiasm, very far from just utilitarian, that he brought to the idea of trade. 'An estate is a pond; trade is a spring' was for him a precious truth, suggesting something semi-miraculous in the phenomenon of trade.[16]

POLITICAL ADVISER

Defoe's early career as a merchant had ended in disaster and bankruptcy; and though he had recouped his fortunes since this débâcle, establishing a prosperous brick and tile factory on the Thameside near Tilbury, his imprisonment over *The Shortest Way* wrecked this too. Moreover, from the vantage point of 1703, his career as a writer appeared equally to have ended in disaster. It was evidently the moment for a new start; and providentially one was offered. The ambitious Robert Harley, leader of the new 'Country' party, had realized the potential usefulness of such a skilled writer and propagandist, and, with the assistance of the Lord High Treasurer Godolphin, he secured his release from Newgate and engaged him as an unofficial agent and adviser – also enabling him to launch a tri-weekly political journal, the *Review*. The exalted way in which, at least at the outset, Defoe interpreted his new role can be judged from the remarkable memorandum he drew up for Harley in the summer of 1704, in which he lays down the duties of a Secretary of State, explains the workings of Cabinet government, describes the necessity for a nationwide intelligence-gathering system, and pronounces on the virtues and temptations of statesmanship. It is as if he were picturing himself playing Richelieu to Harley's Louis XIII. He was to perform a variety of services for Harley, including acting as his private agent at the time of the Union with Scotland; and though their association went through various vicissitudes, it continued until 1714 and was the most important political connection of Defoe's life.

DEFOE'S PERSONALITY

The character of this extraordinary man takes a good deal of puzzling out, a process not helped by the mania people have had from his own day to ours for ascribing to him almost any ownerless work.[17] We are inclined to stress two traits in Defoe's character, not always commented on. First, his contrariness or 'cussedness', which amounted to a clear moral principle. It is significant that in the first published piece of his that we know of (the one about the siege of Vienna) he is deliberately separating from his fellow Whigs, and that throughout his career he never tired of teasing or reproaching his fellow Dissenters – initially over occasional conformity, but before long over their political behaviour generally, as well as their educational policy. In letters to Robert Harley, he frequently gives contemptuous advice about how to 'handle' the Dissenters. It is in a way disloyal, but it cannot be called venal or, given his assumptions, in any way inconsistent.

This refusal to be a 'joiner' is reflected in many other spheres. One of his favourite maxims is the saying attributed to Julius Caesar, that one should never despise one's enemies. In writing about England's great enemy Louis XIV, he liked to annoy his readers by insisting on the French king's sagacity and vision. Similarly, the title he chose for his first periodical was *A Review of the Affairs of France* – with the implication, partly, that the English had everything to learn from France. The habit of mind is plainly closely connected with his ironic propensity to impersonate his enemy, as in *The Shortest Way*, or to publish pamphlets with 'scandalous' titles, such as the one he brought out in 1713 entitled *Reasons Against the Hanover Succession*. There is something reckless and self-destroying in this trait of Defoe's. It would help explain his great admiration for the libertine poet Lord Rochester, at first sight a strange enthusiasm for a man of strict Calvinist views. What he liked in Rochester, one feels, was his recklessness and gaiety in putting himself in the wrong.

The other trait we have in mind is intellectual pride, which is very prominent in Defoe. 'Never, ladies, marry a fool', is the heartfelt cry of the heroine of his novel *Roxana* (1724): 'any husband rather than a fool; with some other husbands you may be unhappy, but with a fool you will be miserable; with another husband you *may*, I say, be unhappy, but with a fool you *must*'.[18] One seems to hear Defoe's own voice in this. 'Sir, the Whigs are weak', he tells Harley pityingly in November 1704, after talking to some of Harley's critics; 'they may be managed, and always have been so. Whatever you do, if possible divide them, and they are easy to be divided. Caress the fools of them most, there are enough among them.'[19] The same contempt for fools colours his attitude towards his Dissenting brethren. There is a nice passage in *A Dialogue between a Dissenter and the Observator*, in which the true distinguishing mark of a Dissenter is said to be 'want of brains' (p. 154).

The fools chastised here are ones that might have known better. They are a very different matter from 'fools' in the sense of 'naturals' or the mentally deprived. The distinction is much in Defoe's mind, and in his essay on 'Fools' in *An Essay upon Projects* he speaks very humanely and feelingly of 'fools' in this latter sense. 'They would seem', he says, to be 'a particular rent-charge on the great family of mankind' (p. 191), and it shocks him to see how contemptuously they are treated in England. Why, he wonders, has no refuge been found for them, as for lunatics? To remedy this, he puts forward a scheme for a public 'Fool-House'. But how shall it be financed? Here he is tempted into mild irony, and it is not clear quite how serious he is being. He suggests it might be fitting (since those endowed with 'extraordinary gifts' have a duty to succour those deprived of them) to raise the money by a tax on learning, to be paid by authors. But if such a tax cannot be got through Parliament, then why not 'maintain fools out of our own folly' (p. 194) and raise the money by a lottery (a fool's game if ever there was one)?

These two characteristics were fundamental to Defoe throughout his career. The qualities which made him, briefly, a heroic spokesman for the 'people' were rather less basic. The episode was altogether memorable and picturesque, but it reached not only its climax but its termination in the pillory. During the rest of his political life, as ministerial adviser and secret agent, he would work from behind the scenes, and this was perhaps in some ways better suited to his secretive temperament. One might even say that, in his later career, the 'radical' Defoe got somewhat mislaid, or overlaid, though there were to be other 'Defoes' of equal significance – including, one need hardly say, the novelist. It is with this idea in mind that the present selection was planned.

Further Reading

BIOGRAPHIES

There is at present no entirely satisfactory biography of Defoe. Two nineteenth-century works remain of value: Walter Wilson's *Memoirs of the Life and Times of Daniel De Foe* (3 vols., 1830), and the first volume of William Lee's *Daniel Defoe: His Life, and Recently Discovered Writings* (3 vols., 1869). More recent accounts include James Sutherland, *Defoe* (1937), and F. Bastian, *Defoe's Early Life* (1981). The fullest treatment to date is Paula Backscheider, *Daniel Defoe: His Life* (1989).

TEXTS

There have been many partial editions of Defoe, but no complete one. His letters are excellently edited in *The Letters of Daniel Defoe*, ed. G. H. Healey (1955). A facsimile reprint of his *Review* was edited by A. W. Secord in 22 volumes (1938; reprinted 1965). The best editions of *The True-Born Englishman* and *A Hymn to the Pillory* are the ones by Frank H. Ellis in *Poems on Affairs of State*, vol. 6 (1970).

CRITICISM

The following books and articles have a particular bearing on the writings included in the present selection.

Maximillian E. Novak, *Defoe and the Nature of Man* (1963).

Lois G. Schwoerer, 'The Literature of the Standing Army Controversy, 1697–1699', *Huntington Library Quarterly*, 28 (1965), 187–212.

Maximillian E. Novak, 'Defoe's *Shortest Way with the Dissenters*: Hoax,

Parody, Paradox, Fiction, Irony, and Satire', *Modern Language Quarterly*, 27 (1966), 402–17.

Miriam Lerenbaum, ' "An Irony Not Unusual": Defoe's *Shortest Way with the Dissenters*', *Huntington Library Quarterly*, 37 (1974), 227–50.

Peter Earle, *The World of Defoe* (1976).

Paul Alkon, 'Defoe's Argument in *The Shortest Way with the Dissenters*', *Modern Philology*, 73 (1976), 512–23.

L. S. Horsley, 'Contemporary Reactions to Defoe's *Shortest Way with the Dissenters*', *Studies in English Literature*, 16 (1976), 407–20.

John McVeagh, 'Defoe and the Romance of Trade', *Durham University Journal*, 70 (1978), 141–7.

J. A. Downie, 'Defoe's *Shortest Way with the Dissenters*: Irony, Intention, and Reader-Response', *Prose Studies*, 9 (1986), 120–39.

Michael Seidel, 'Crisis Rhetoric and Satiric Power', *New Literary History*, 20 (1988), 165–86.

J. A. Downie, 'Daniel Defoe: King William's Pamphleteer?', *Eighteenth-Century Life*, 12 (1988), 105–17.

Spiro Peterson, 'Daniel Defoe', in *Eighteenth-Century British Poets*, ed. John Sitter (1990).

Manuel Schonhorn, *Defoe's Politics* (1991).

A Note on the Texts

The texts of published works included here are based on those of the first editions in every instance save one. The exception is *A Hymn to the Pillory*, where the second edition, which we have followed, was extensively corrected and expanded by Defoe. In the case of the 'Memorandum to Robert Harley', which was unpublished in Defoe's lifetime, we have followed the text published by G. F. Warner in the *English Historical Review*, 22 (1907), pp. 132–43, checking this against the text in *The Letters of Daniel Defoe*, ed. George Harris Healey (Oxford, 1955), pp. 29–50.

We have brought use of capitals, italics and spelling into line with modern practice. On the whole, though, we have retained as much of the original punctuation as we could, altering it only where it was obviously wrong. Part of Defoe's rhetorical or dramatic effect as a prose writer depends, often, on his handling of unusually large verbal units. His long, improvisatory sentence-paragraphs, full of interpolations and clauses branching off in unexpected new directions, use colons and semi-colons to mark what are essentially new thoughts, though ones related to what has gone before, and we think that to replace these with full stops does a definite, if subtle, injury to the rhythm and movement of the prose.

In making our selection, we decided as far as possible to present works complete. Obviously we had to break this rule in making extracts from *An Essay upon Projects*, a book-length work, and we decided also to cut the final section from the 'Memorandum to Robert Harley', where Defoe discusses political and military events in Europe. By grouping works under a number of thematic headings we have tried to indicate the extraordinary range of Defoe's interests in this early period of his career, but it should be noted that what is reprinted here is only a fraction of his output during these years. Unfortunately, in our view there is currently no satisfactory bibliography of Defoe's works to which readers can be referred. John Robert Moore's *Checklist of the Writings of Daniel Defoe*, the standard authority since its publication in 1960, is now widely recognized to be seriously flawed in its whole approach. It includes over two hundred titles attributed to Defoe in the nineteenth and twentieth centuries for which no good evidence has ever been presented. For a detailed discussion of this whole problem, see our *The Canonisation of Daniel Defoe* (1988); *Defoe De-Attributions: A Critique of J. R. Moore's 'Checklist'* (1994); and *A Critical Bibliography of Daniel Defoe* (forthcoming, 1998). To give readers a picture of the variety and number of writings from which we have made our selection, we have included as an appendix a list of works published between 1688 and 1704 which are certainly, or probably, by Defoe.

DEFENDER OF
KING WILLIAM

AN
ARGUMENT

Shewing, That a

𝔖𝔱𝔞𝔫𝔡𝔦𝔫𝔤 𝔄𝔯𝔪𝔶,

With Consent of

PARLIAMENT,

Is not Inconsistent with a

Free Government, &c.

---

2 Chron. 9. 25.

And King Solomon had four thousand Stalls for Horses and Chariots, and twelve thousand Horsemen ; whom he bestowed in the Chariot-Cities, and with the King at Jerusalem.

LONDON:

Printed for *E. Whitlock* near *Stationers.* 1698.

The Preface.

The present pen and ink war raised against a standing army has more ill consequences in it than are at first sight to be discerned. The pretence is specious, and the cry of liberty is very pleasing; but the principle is mortally contagious and destructive of the essential safety of the kingdom; liberty and property are the glorious attributes of the English nation; and the dearer they are to us, the less danger we are in of losing them; but I could never yet see it proved, that the danger of losing them by a small army was such as we should expose ourselves to all the world for it. Some people talk so big of our own strength, that they think England able to defend itself against all the world. I presume such talk without book; I think the prudentest course is to prevent the trial, and that is only to hold the balance of Europe as the King now does; and if there be a war to keep it abroad. How these gentlemen will do that with a militia, I should be glad to see proposed; 'tis not the King of England alone, but the sword of England in the hand of the King, that gives laws of peace and war now to Europe; and those who would thus wrest the sword out of his hand in time of peace, bid the fairest of any men in the world to renew the war.

The arguments against an army have been strongly urged; and the authors with an unusual assurance, boast already of their conquest, though their armour is not yet put off. I think their triumph goes before their victory; and if books and writing will not, God be thanked the Parliament will confute them, by taking care to maintain such forces, and no more, as they think needful for our safety abroad, without danger at home, and leaving it to time to make it appear, that such an army, with consent of Parliament, is not inconsistent with a free government, &c.

An Argument, Shewing, that a Standing Army, with Consent of Parliament, is not Inconsistent with a Free Government, &c.

In the great debates about a standing army, and in all the arguments used on one side and 'tother in the case, it seems to me that both parties are guilty of running into the extremes of the controversy.

Some have taken up such terrible notions of an army, that take it how you will, call it what you will, be it raised, paid or commanded by whom you will, and let the circumstances be altered never so much, the term is synonymous, an army is an army; and if they don't enslave us, the thanks is not to our good conduct; for so many soldiers, so many masters: they may do it if they will; and if they do not do it now, they may do it in another reign, when a king shall arise who knows not Joseph,[1] and therefore the risk is not to be run by any means: from hence they draw the consequence, *that a standing army is inconsistent with a free government, &c.* which is the title to the argument.

This we find backed by a *Discourse of Militias*,[2] and by a *Second Part of the Argument*,[3] &c. and all these three, which seem to me to be wrote by the same hand, agree in this point in general, that the war being at an end, no forces at all are to be kept in pay, no men to be maintained whose profession is bearing arms, whose commission is to kill and slay, as he has it in the *Second Part*; but they must be dismissed, as men for whom there is no more occasion against an enemy, and are dangerous to be kept up, lest they find occasion against ourselves.

The advocates for the necessity of a standing army, seem to make light of all these fears and jealousies; and plead the circumstances of the kingdom, with relation to our leagues and confederacies abroad, the strength of our neighbours, a pretender to the crown in being, the uncertainties of leagues, and the like, as arguments to prove an army necessary. I must own these are no arguments any longer than those circumstances continue, and therefore can amount to no more than to argue the necessity of an army for a time, which time none of them has ventured to assign, nor to say

5

how, being once established, we shall be sure to be rid of them, in case a new king should succeed before the time be expired, who may not value our liberty at the rate his present Majesty has done.

I desire calmly to consider both these extremes, and if it be possible, to find out the safe medium which may please us all.

If there be any person who has an ill design in pushing thus against the soldiery, I am not to expect, that less than a disbanding the whole army will satisfy him; but such who have no other end than preserving our liberties entire, and leaving them so to posterity, will be satisfied with what they know is sufficient to that end; for he who is not content with what will fully answer the end he proposes, has some other end than that which he proposes. I make no reflections upon any party, but I propose to direct this discourse to the honest well-meaning English freeholder, who has a share in the *terra firma*, and therefore is concerned to preserve freedom to the inhabitant that loves his liberty better than his life, and won't sell it for money; and this is the man who has the most reason to fear a standing army, for he has something to lose; as he is most concerned for the safety of a ship, who has a cargo on her bottom.

This man is the hardest to be made believe that he cannot be safe without an army, because he finds he is not easy with one. To this man all the sad instances of the slavery of nations, by standing armies, stand as so many buoys to warn him of the rocks which other free nations have split upon; and therefore 'tis to this man we are to speak.

And in order to state the case right, we are to distinguish first between England formerly, and England now; between a standing army able to enslave the nation, and a certain body of forces enough to make us safe.

England now is in sundry circumstances different from England formerly, with respect to the manner of fighting, the circumstances of our neighbours, and of ourselves; and there are some reasons why a militia are not, and perhaps I might make it out cannot, be made fit for the uses of the present wars. In the ancient times of England's power, we were for many years the invaders of our neighbours, and quite out of fear of invasions at home; but before we arrived to that magnitude in the world, 'tis to be observed we were hardly ever invaded, but we were conquered; William the Conqueror was the last, and if the Spaniard did not do the same, 'twas because God set the elements in battle array against them, and they were prevented bringing over the Prince of Parma's army;[4] which if they had

6

done, 'twould have gone very hard with us; but we owe it wholly to Providence.

I believe it may be said, that from that time to this day, the kingdom has never been without some standing troops of soldiers entertained in pay, and always either kept at home or employed abroad; and yet no evil consequence followed, nor do I meet with any votes of the Parliament against them as grievances, or motions made to disband them, till the days of King Charles the First. Queen Elizabeth, though she had no *Guard du Corps*,[5] yet she had her *Guards du Terres*.[6] She had even to her last hour several armies, I may call them, in pay among foreign states and Princes, which upon any visible occasion were ready to be called home. King James the First had the same in Holland, in the service of Gustavus Adolphus King of Sweden, and in the unfortunate service of the King of Bohemia;[7] and that Scotch regiment, known by the name of Douglas's regiment, have been, (they say) a regiment two hundred and fifty years. King Charles the First had the same in the several expeditions for the relief of Rochelle,[8] and that fatal descent upon the Isle of Rhe, and in his expeditions into Scotland; and they would do well to reconcile their discourse to itself, who say in one place, *If King Charles had had five thousand men, the nation had never struck one stroke for their liberties*; and in another, *that the Parliament were like to have been petitioned out of doors by an army a hundred and fifty miles off, though there was a Scotch army at the heels of them*: for to me it appears that King Charles the First had an army then, and would have kept it, but that he had not the purse to pay them, of which more may be said hereafter.

But England now stands in another posture, our peace at home seems secure, and I believe it is so: but to maintain our peace abroad, 'tis necessary to enter into leagues and confederacies: here is one neighbour[9] grown too great for all the rest; as they are single states or kingdoms, and therefore to mate him, several must join for mutual assistance, according to the Scotch law of duelling, that if one can't beat you ten shall. These alliances are under certain stipulations and agreements, with what strength and in what places, to aid and assist one another; and to perform these stipulations, something of force must be at hand if occasion require. That these confederacies are of absolute and indispensable necessity, to preserve the peace of a weaker against a stronger prince, past experience has taught us too plainly to need an argument.

There is another constant maxim of the present state of the war; and that is, *carry the war into your enemy's country, and always keep it out of your own*. This is an article has been very much opposed 'tis true; and some, who knew no better, would talk much of the fruitless expense of a war abroad; as if it was not worth while to defend your confederates' country, to make it a barrier to your own. This is too weak an argument also to need any trouble about; but this again makes it absolutely necessary to have always some troops ready to send to the assistance of those confederates if they are invaded. Thus at the Peace of Nimeguen,[10] six regiments were left in Holland, to continue there in time of peace, to be ready in case of a rupture. To say, that instead of this we will raise them for their assistance when wanted, would be something, if this potent neighbour were not the French king, whose velocity of motion the Dutch well remember in 1672.[11] But then, say they, we may send our militia. First, the King can't command them to go; and secondly, if he could, nobody would accept them; and if they would go, and would be accepted of, they would be good for nothing:[12] if we have no forces to assist a confederate, who will value our friendship, or assist us if we wanted it? To say we are self-dependent, and shall never need the assistance of our neighbour, is to say what we are not sure of, and this is certain it is as needful to maintain the reputation of England in the esteem of our neighbours, as 'tis to defend our coasts in case of an invasion; for keep up the reputation of our power, and we shall never be invaded.

If our defence from insurrections or invasions, were the only necessary part of a future war, I should be the readier to grant the point, and to think our militia might be made useful; but our business is *principiis obsta*,[13] to beat the enemy before he comes to our own door. Our business in case of a rupture, is to aid our confederate princes, that they may be able to stand between us and danger: our business is to preserve Flanders, to garrison the frontier towns, and be in the field in conjunction with the confederate armies: this is the way to prevent invasions, and descents: and when they can tell us that our militia is proper for this work, then we will say something to it.

I'll suppose for once what I hope may never fall out, that a rupture of this peace should happen, and the French, according to custom, break suddenly into Flanders, and over-run it, and after that Holland, what condition would such a neighbourhood of such a Prince, reduce us to? If it be answered again, soldiers may be raised to assist them, I answer, as before, let those who say so, read the history of the French king's irruption into Holland in the year 1672, where he conquered sixty strong fortified towns in six weeks time: and tell me what it will be to the purpose to raise men, to fight an enemy after the conquest is made?

'Twill not be amiss to observe here that the reputation and influence the English nation has had abroad among the Princes of Christendom, has been always more or less according as the power of the prince, to aid and assist, or to injure and offend, was esteemed. Thus Queen Elizabeth carried her reputation abroad by the courage of her English soldiers and seamen; and on the contrary, what a ridiculous figure did King James, with his *beati pacifici,*[14] make in all the courts of Christendom? How did the Spaniard and the Emperor banter and buffoon him? How was his ambassador ashamed to treat for him, while Count Colocedo told Count Mansfield,[15] *That his new master* (meaning King James) *knew neither how to make peace or war?* King Charles the First fared much in the same manner: and how was it altered in the case of Oliver?

> Though his government did a tyrant resemble,
> He made England great, and her enemies tremble.
> *Dialogue of the Horses.*[16]

And what is it places the present king at the helm of the confederacies? Why do they commit their armies to his charge, and appoint the congress of their plenipotentiaries at his court? Why do distressed princes seek his mediation, as the Dukes of Holstein, Savoy, and the like? Why did the Emperor and the King of Spain leave the whole management of the peace[17] to him? 'Tis all the reputation of his conduct and the English valour under him; and 'tis absolutely necessary to support this character which England now bears in the world, for the great advantages which may and will be made from it; and this character can never live, nor these alliances be supported with no force at hand to perform the conditions.

These are some reasons why a force is necessary, but the question is, what force? for I grant, it does not follow from hence, that a great army must be kept on foot in time of peace, as the author of the *Second Part of the Argument* says is pleaded for.

Since then no army, and a great army, are extremes equally dangerous, the one to our liberty at home, and the other to our reputation abroad, and the safety of our confederates; it remains to inquire what medium is to be found out; or in plain English, what army may, with safety to our liberties, be maintained in England, or what means may be found out to make such an army serviceable for the defence of us and our allies, and yet not dangerous to our constitution.

That any army at all can be safe, the *Argument* denies, but that cannot be made out; a thousand men is an army as much as 100,000; as the Spanish Armado is called *An Armado*, though they seldom fit out above four men of war; and on this account I must crave leave to say, I do confute the assertion in the title of the *Argument*, that a standing army is inconsistent with a free government, and I shall further do it by the authority of Parliament.

In the claim of right, presented to the present king, and which he swore to observe, as the *pacta conventa*[18] of the kingdom, it is declared, *in hac verba*,[19] *that the raising or keeping a standing army within the kingdom in time of peace, unless it be by consent of Parliament, is against law*.

This plainly lays the whole stress of the thing, not against the thing itself, a standing army, nor against the season, in time of peace, but against the circumstance, consent of Parliament; and I think nothing is more rational than to conclude from thence, that a standing army in time of peace, with consent of Parliament, is not against law, and I may go on, nor is not inconsistent with a free government, nor destructive of the English monarchy.

There are two distinctions necessary therefore in the present debate, to bring the question to a narrow compass.

First, *I distinguish between a great army and a small army*. And

Secondly, *I distinguish between an army kept on foot without consent of Parliament, and an army with consent of Parliament*.

And whereas we are told, an army of soldiers is an army of masters, and the consent of Parliament don't alter it, but they may turn them out of doors who raised them, as they did the Long Parliament, the first distinction answers that; for if a great army may do it, a small army can't; and then the second distinction regulates the first. For it cannot be supposed, but the Parliament when they give that consent which can only make an army lawful, will not consent to a larger army then they can so master, as that the liberties or people of England shall never be in danger from them.

No man will say this cannot be, because the number may be supposed as small as you please; but to avoid the sophistry of an argument, I'll suppose the very troops which we see the Parliament have not voted to be disbanded; that is, those which were on foot before the year 1680.[20] No man will deny them to be a standing army, and yet sure no man will imagine any danger to our liberties from them.

We are asked, if you establish an army, and a revenue to pay them, how shall we be sure they will not continue themselves? But will any man ask that question of such an army as this? Can six thousand men tell the nation they won't disband, but will continue themselves, and then raise money to do it? Can they exact it by military execution? If they can, our militia must be very despicable. The keeping such a remnant of an army does not hinder but the militia may be made as useful as you please; and the more useful you make it, the less danger from this army: and however it may have been the business of our kings to make the militia as useless as they could, the present king never showed any tokens of such a design. Nor is it more than will be needful, for 6,000 men by themselves won't do, if the invasion we speak of should ever be attempted. What has been said of the appearance of the people on the Purbeck fancied invasion,[21] was very true; but I must say, had it been a true one of forty thousand regular troops, all that appearance could have done nothing, but have drove the country in order to starve them, and then have run away: I am apt enough to grant what has been said of the impracticableness of any invasion upon us, while we are masters at sea; but I am sure the defence of England's peace, lies in making war in Flanders. Queen Elizabeth found it so, her way to beat the Spaniards, was by helping the Dutch to do it. And she as much defended England in aiding Prince Maurice to win the great battle of Newport,[22] as she did in defeating their invincible *Armado*. Oliver Cromwell took the same course; for he no sooner declared war against Spain, but he embarked his army for Flanders: the late King Charles did the same against the French, when after the peace of Nimeguen, six regiments of English and Scots were always left in the service of the Dutch, and the present war is a further testimony: for where has it been fought, not in England, God be thanked, but in Flanders? And what are the terms of the peace, but more frontier towns in Flanders? And what is the great barrier of this peace, but Flanders; the consequence of this may be guessed by the answer King William gave when Prince of Orange, in the late treaty of Nimeguen; when, to make the terms the easier, 'twas offered, that a satisfaction should be made to him by the French, for his lands in Luxemburgh; to which the Prince replied, he would part with all his lands in Luxemburgh to get the Spaniards one good frontier town in Flanders. The reason is plain; for every one of those towns, though they were immediately the Spaniards', were really bulwarks to keep the French the further off from his own country; and thus it is now: and how our militia can have any share in this part of the war, I cannot imagine. It seems strange to me to reconcile the arguments made use of to magnify the serviceableness of the militia, and the arguments to enforce the dread of a standing army; for they stand like two batteries one against another, where the shot from one dismounts the cannon of the other: if a small army may enslave us, our militia are good for nothing; if good for nothing, they cannot defend us, and then an army is necessary: if they are good, and are able to defend us, then a small army can never hurt us, for what may defend us abroad, may defend us at home; and I wonder this is not considered. And what is plainer in the world than that the Parliament of England have all along agreed to this point, that a standing army in time of peace, with consent of Parliament, is not against law. The establishment of the forces in the time of K. Charles II was not as I remember ever objected against in Parliament, at least we may say the Parliament permitted them if they did not establish them: and the present Parliament seems inclined to continue the army on the same foot, so far as may be supposed from their vote to disband all the forces raised since 1680. To affirm then, that a standing army (without any of the former distinctions) is inconsistent, &c. is to argue against the general sense of the nation, the permission of the Parliament for 50 years past, and the present apparent resolutions of the best composed House that perhaps ever entered within those walls.

To this House the whole nation has left the case, to act as they see cause; to them we have committed the charge of our liberties, nay the King himself has only told them his opinion, with the reasons for it, without leading them at all; and the article of the Claim of Right is left in full force: for this consent of Parliament is now left the whole and sole judge, whether an army or no army; and if it votes an army, 'tis left still the sole judge of the quantity, how many, or how few.

Here it remains to enquire the direct meaning of those words, *unless it be by consent of Parliament*, and I humbly suppose they may, among other things, include these particulars.

   1. *That they be raised and continued not by a tacit, but explicit consent of*
      Parliament; or, to speak directly, by an Act of Parliament.

2. *That they be continued no longer than such explicit consent shall limit and appoint.*

If these two heads are granted in the word consent, I am bold to affirm, such an army is not *inconsistent with a free government, &c.*

I am as positively assured of the safety of our liberties under the conduct of King and Parliament, while they concur, as I am of the salvation of believers by the passion of our Saviour; and I hardly think 'tis fit for a private man to impose his positive rules on them for method, any more than 'tis to limit the Holy Spirit, whose free agency is beyond his power: for the King, Lords and Commons, can never err while they agree; nor is an army of 20 or 40,000 men either a scarecrow enough to enslave us, while under that union.

If this be allowed, then the question before us is, what may conduce to make the harmony between the King, Lords and Commons eternal? And so the debate about an army ceases.

But to leave that question, since frailty attends the best of persons, and kings have their *faux pas* as well as other men, we cannot expect the harmony to be immortal; and therefore to provide for the worst, our Parliaments have made their own consent the only clause that can make an army legitimate: but to say that an army directly as an army, without these distinctions, is destructive of the English monarchy, and inconsistent with a free government, &c. is to say then that the Parliament can destroy the English monarchy, and can establish that which is inconsistent with a free government; which is ridiculous. But then we are told, that *the power of the sword was first placed in the Lords or Barons, and how they served the king in his wars with themselves and their vassals, and that the King had no power to invade the privileges of the Barons, having no other forces than the vassals of his own demesnes to follow him*: and this form is applauded as an extraordinary constitution, *because there is no other limitation of a monarchy of any signification than such as places the sword in the hand of the subject: and all such governments where the prince has the power of the sword, though the people have the power of the purse, are no more monarchies but tyrannies: for not only that government is tyrannical which is tyrannically exercised, but all governments are tyrannical which have not in their constitution sufficient security against the arbitrary power of their prince*; that is, which have not the power of the sword to employ against him if need be.[23]

Thus we come to the argument: which is not how many troops may be allowed, or how long; but in short, no mercenary troops at all can be maintained without destroying our constitution, and metamorphizing our government into a tyranny.

I admire how the maintainer of this basis came to omit giving us an account of another part of history very needful to examine, in handing down the true notion of government in this nation, *viz.* of Parliaments. To supply which, and to make way for what follows, I must take leave to tell the reader, that about the time, when this service by villeinage and vassalage began to be resented by the people, and by peace and trade they grew rich, and the power of the Barons being too great, frequent commotions, civil wars, and battles were the consequence, nay sometimes without concerning the King in the quarrel: one nobleman would invade another, in which the weakest suffered most, and the poor man's blood was the price of all; the people obtained privileges of their own, and obliged the King and the Barons to accept of an equilibrium; this we call a Parliament: and from this the due balance we have so much heard of is deduced. I need not lead my reader to the times and circumstances of this, but this due balance is the foundation on which we now stand, and which the author of the *Argument* so highly applauds as the best in the world; and I appeal to all men to judge if this balance be not a much nobler constitution in all its points, than the old Gothic model of government.

In that the tyranny of the Barons was intolerable, the misery and slavery of the common people insupportable, their blood and labour was at the absolute will of the lord, and often sacrificed to their private quarrels: they were as much at his beck as his pack of hounds were at the sound of his horn; whether it was to march against a foreign enemy, or against their own natural prince: so that this was but exchanging one tyrant for three hundred, for so many the Barons of England were accounted at least. And this was the effect of the security vested in the people, against the arbitrary power of the king; which was to say the Barons took care to maintain their own tyranny, and to prevent the king's tyrannizing over them.

But 'tis said, *the Barons growing poor by the luxury of the times, and the common people growing rich, they exchanged their vassalage for leases, rents, fines, and the like.*[24] They did so, and thereby became entitled to the service of themselves; and so overthrew the settlement, and from hence came a

House of Commons: and I hope England has reason to value the alteration. Let them that think not reflect on the freedoms the Commons enjoy in Poland, where the Gothic institution remains, and they will be satisfied.

In this establishment of a parliament, the sword is indeed trusted in the hands of the king, and the purse in the hands of the people; the people cannot make peace or war without the king, nor the king cannot raise or maintain an army without the people; and this is the true balance.

But we are told, *the power of the purse is not a sufficient security without the power of the sword*: What! not against ten thousand men? To answer this, 'tis necessary to examine how far the power of the sword is in the hands of the people already, and next whether the matter of fact be true.

I say the sword is in part in the hands of the people already, by the militia, who, as the *Argument* says, are the people themselves. And how are they balanced? 'Tis true, they are commissioned by the king, but they may refuse to meet twice, till the first pay is reimbursed to the country: and where shall the king raise it without a parliament? that very militia would prevent him. So that our law therein authorizing the militia to refuse the command of the king, tacitly puts the sword into the hands of the people.

I come now to examine the matter of fact, that the purse is not an equivalent to the sword, which I deny to be true; and here 'twill be necessary to examine, how often our kings of England have raised armies on their own heads, but have been forced to disband them for want of moneys, nay, have been forced to call a parliament to raise money to disband them.

King Charles the First is an instance of both these; for his first army against the Scots he was forced to dismiss for want of pay; and then was forced to call a parliament to pay and dismiss the Scots; and though he had an army in the field at the pacification, and a church army too, yet he durst not attempt to raise money by them.

I am therefore to affirm, that the power of the purse is an equivalent to the power of the sword; and I believe I can make it appear, if I may be allowed to instance in those numerous armies which Gaspar Coligny,

Admiral of France, and Henry the Fourth King of Navarre, and William the First P. of Orange brought out of Germany into France, and into the Low Countries, which all vanished, and could attempt nothing for want of a purse to maintain them: but to come nearer, what made the efforts of King Charles all abortive, but want of the purse? Time was, he had the sword in his hand, when the Duke of Buckingham went on those fruitless voyages to Rochelle, and himself afterwards to Scotland, he had forces on foot, a great many more than five thousand, which the *Argument* mentions, but he had not the purse; at last he attempted to take it without a parliament, and that ruin'd him. King Charles the Second found the power of the purse so much out-balanced the power of the sword, that he sat still, and let the parliament disband his army for him, almost whether he would or no.

Besides, the power of the purse in England differs from what the same thing is in other countries, because 'tis so sacred a thing, that no king ever touched at it but he found his ruin in it. Nay, 'tis so odious to the nation, that whoever attempts it, must at the same time be able to make an entire conquest or nothing.

If then neither the consent of Parliament, nor the smallness of an army proposed, nor the power of the sword in the hands of the militia, which are the people themselves, nor the power of the purse, are not a sufficient balance against the arbitrary power of the king, what shall we say? Are ten thousand men in arms, without money, without Parliament authority, hemmed in with the whole militia of England, and damned by the laws? Are they of such force as to break our constitution? I cannot see any reason for such a thought. The Parliament of England is a body, of whom we may say, that no weapon formed against them could ever prosper;[25] and they know their own strength, and they know what force is needful, and what hurtful, and they will certainly maintain the first and disband the last.

It may be said here, 'tis not the fear of ten thousand men, 'tis not the matter of an army, but 'tis the thing itself; grant a revenue for life, and the next king will call it, my revenue, and so grant an army for this king, and the next will say, give me my army.

*

To which I answer, that these things have been no oftener asked in Parliament than denied; and we have so many instances in our late times of the power of the purse, that it seems strange to me, that it should not be allowed to be a sufficient balance.

King Charles the Second, as I hinted before, was very loath to part with his army raised in 1676, but he was forced to it for want of money to pay them; he durst not try whether when money had raised an army, an army could not raise money. 'Tis true, his revenues were large, but frugality was not his talent, and that ruined the design. King James the Second was a good husband,[26] and that very husbandry had almost ruined the nation; for his revenues being well managed, he maintained an army out of it. For 'tis well known, the Parliament never gave him a penny towards it; but he never attempted to make his army raise any money; if he had, 'tis probable his work had been sooner done than it was.

But pray let us examine abroad, if the purse has not governed all the wars of Europe. The Spaniards were once the most powerful people in Europe; their infantry were in the days of the Prince of Parma, the most invincible troops in the world. The Dutch, who were then his subjects, and on whom he had levied immense sums of money, had the 10th penny[27] demanded of them, and the demand backed by a great army of these very Spaniards, which, among many other reasons caused them to revolt. The Duke D'Alva afterwards attempted for his master to raise this tax by his army, by which he lost the whole Netherlands, who are now the richest people in the world; and the Spaniard is now become the meanest and most despicable people in Europe, and that only because they are the poorest.

The present war is another instance, which having lasted eight years, is at last brought to this conclusion, that he who had the longest sword has yielded to them who had the longest purse.

The late King Charles the First, is another most lively instance of this matter, to what lamentable shifts did he drive himself? and how many despicable steps did he take, rather than call a Parliament, which he hated to think of. And yet, though he had an army on foot, he was forced to do it, or starve all his men; had it been to be done, he would have done it.

'Tis true, 'twas said the Earl of Strafford proposed a scheme, to bring over an army out of Ireland, to force England to his terms; but the experiment was thought too desperate to be attempted, and the very project ruined the projector; such an ill fate attends every contrivance against the Parliament of England.

But I think I need go no further on that head: the power of raising money is wholly in the parliament, as a balance to the power of raising men, which is in the King; and all the reply I can meet with is, that this balance signifies nothing, for an army can raise money, as well as money raise an army; to which I answer, besides what has been said already, I do not think it practicable in England: the greatest armies, in the hands of the greatest tyrants we ever had in England, never durst attempt it. We find several kings in England have attempted to raise money without a Parliament, and have tried all the means they could to bring it to pass; and they need not go back to Richard the Second, to Edward the Second, to Edward the Fourth, to Henry the Eighth, or to Charles the First, to remind the reader of what all men who know any thing of history are acquainted with: but not a king ever yet attempted to raise money, by military execution, or billetting soldiers upon the country. King James the Second had the greatest army and the best, as to discipline, that any king ever had; and his desperate attempts on our liberties showed his good will, yet he never came to that point. I won't deny, but that our kings have been willing to have armies at hand, to back them in their arbitrary proceedings, and the subjects may have been awed by them from a more early resentment; but I must observe, that all the invasion of our rights, and all the arbitrary methods of our governors, has been under pretences of law. King Charles the First levied ship-money as his due, and the proclamations for that purpose cite the pretended law, that in case of danger from a foreign enemy, ships should be fitted out to defend us, and all men were bound to contribute to the charge; coat and conduct money[28] had the like pretences; charters were subverted by *quo warrantoes,*[29] and proceedings at law; patriots were murthered under formal prosecutions, and all was pretended to be done legally.

I know but one instance in all our English story, where the soldiery were employed as soldiers, in open defiance of law, to destroy the people's liberties by a military absolute power, and that stands as an everlasting brand of infamy upon our militia; and is an instance to prove, beyond the power of a reply, that even our militia, under a bad government, let them be ourselves, and the people, and all those fine things never so much, are, under ill officers and ill management, as dangerous as any soldiery whatever, will be as insolent, and do the drudgery of a tyrant as effectually.

In the year [1682] when Mr. Dubois and Mr. Papillon, a member of the present parliament, were chosen sheriffs of London, and Sir John Moor, under pretence of the authority of the chair, pretended to nominate one sheriff himself, and leave the City to choose but one, and confirm the choice of the Mayor, the citizens struggled for their right, and stood firm to their choice, and several adjournments were made to bring over the majority of the Livery, but in vain: at length the day came when the sheriffs were to be sworn, and when the livery-men assembled at Guild-hall to swear their sheriffs, they found the hall garrisoned with a company of trained-bands under Lieutenant Col. Quiney, a citizen himself, and most of the soldiers, citizens and inhabitants; and by this force the ancient livery-men were shut out, and several of them thrown down, and insolently used, and the sheriffs thrust away from the hustings, and who the Lord Mayor pleased was sworn in an open defiance of the laws of the kingdom, and privileges of the City.[30] This was done by the militia to their everlasting glory, and I do not remember the like done by a standing army of mercenaries; in this age at least. Nor is a military tyranny practicable in England, if we consider the power the laws have given to the civil magistrate, unless you at the same time imagine that army large enough to subdue the whole English nation at once, which if it can be effected by such an army as the Parliament now seem inclined to permit, we are in a very mean condition.

I know it may be objected here, that the forces which were on foot before 1680 are not the army in debate, and that the design of the court was to have a much greater force.

I do not know that, but this I know, that those forces were an army, and the design of all these opponents of an army is in so many words, against any army at all, small as well as great; a tenet absolutely destructive of the present interest of England, and of the treaties and alliances made by His Majesty with the princes and states of Europe, who depend so much on his aid in guard of the present peace.

The power of making peace or war is vested in the King: 'tis part of his prerogative, but 'tis implicitly in the people, because their negative as to payment, does really influence all those actions. Now if, when the King makes war, the subject should refuse to assist him, the whole nation would be ruined: suppose in the leagues and confederacies his present Majesty is engaged in for the maintenance of the present peace, all the confederates are bound in case of a breach to assist one another with so many men, say ten thousand for the English quota, more or less, where shall they be found? Must they stay till they are raised? To what purpose would it be then for any confederate to depend upon England for assistance?

It may be said indeed, if you are so engaged by leagues or treaties, you may hire foreign troops to assist till you can raise them. This answer leads to several things which would take up too much room here.

Foreign troops require two things to procure them; time to negotiate for them, which may not be to be spared, for they may be almost as soon raised; time for their march from Germany, for there are none nearer to be hired, and money to hire them, which must be had by Parliament, or the King must have it ready: if by Parliament, that is a longer way still; if without, that opens a worse gate to slavery than t'other: for if a king have money, he can raise men or hire men when he will; and you are in as much danger then, and more than you can be in now from a standing army: so that since giving money is the same thing as giving men, as it appeared in the late K. James's reign, both must be prevented, or both may be allowed.

But the Parliament we see needs no instructions in this matter, and therefore are providing to reduce the forces to the same quota they were in before 1680, by which means all the fear of invading our liberties will be at an end, the army being so very small that 'tis impossible, and yet the King will have always a force at hand to assist his neighbours, or defend himself till more can be raised. The forces before 1680 were an army, and if they were an army by consent of Parliament, they were a legal army; and if they were legal, then they were not inconsistent with a free government, &c. for nothing can be inconsistent with a free government, which is done according to the laws of that government: and if a standing army has been in England legally, then I have proved, *that a standing army is not inconsistent with a free government, &c.*

FINIS

THE

True-Born *Englishman.*

A

SATYR.

Statuimus Pacem, & Securitatem, & Concordiam Judicium & Justitiam inter Anglos & Normannos, Francos & Britones, Walliæ, & Cornubiæ, Pictos & Scotos, Albaniæ, *similiter inter Francos & Insulanos Provincias, & Patrias, quæ pertinent ad Coronam nostram, & inter omnes nobis Subjectos, firmiter & inviolabiliter observari.*
Charta Regis Willielmi Conquisitoris de Pacis Publica, *Cap.* 1.

Printed in the Year MDCC.

The Preface.

The end of Satyr is reformation: and the author, though he doubts the work of conversion is at a general stop, has put his hand to the plough.

I expect a storm of ill language from the fury of the town, and especially from those whose English talent it is to rail: and without being taken for a conjurer, I may venture to foretell, that I shall be cavilled at about my mean style, rough verse, and incorrect language; things I might indeed have taken more care in. But the book is printed; and though I see some faults, 'tis too late to mend them. And this is all I think needful to say to them.

Possibly somebody may take me for a Dutchman, in which they are mistaken: but I am one that would be glad to see Englishmen behave themselves better to strangers, and to governors also; that one might not be reproached in foreign countries, for belonging to a nation that wants manners.

I assure you, Gentlemen, strangers use us better abroad; and we can give no reason but our ill nature for the contrary here.

Methinks an Englishman, who is so proud of being called a goodfellow, should be civil: and it cannot be denied but we are in many cases, and particularly to strangers, the churlishest people alive.

As to vices, who can dispute our intemperance, while an honest drunken fellow is a character in a man's praise? All our reformations are banters, and will be so, till our Magistrates and gentry reform themselves by way of example; then, and not till then, they may be expected to punish others without blushing.

As to our ingratitude, I desire to be understood of that particular people, who pretending to be Protestants, have all along endeavoured to reduce the liberties and religion of this nation into the hands of King James and his Popish powers: together with such who enjoy the peace and protection of the present Government, and yet abuse and affront the King who procured it, and openly profess their uneasiness under him: these, by whatsoever names or titles they are dignified or distinguished, are the people aimed at: nor do I disown, but that it is so much the temper of an Englishman to abuse his benefactor, that I could be glad to see it rectified.

They who think I have been guilty of an error, in exposing the crimes of my own countrymen to themselves, may among many honest instances of the like nature, find the same thing in Mr. Cowley,[1] in his imitation of the second Olympick Ode of Pindar: his words are these,

> But in this thankless world, the givers
> Are envied even by th' receivers:
> 'Tis now the cheap and frugal fashion,
> Rather to hide than pay an obligation.
> Nay, 'tis much worse than so;
> It now an artifice doth grow,
> Wrongs and outrages to do,
> Lest men should think we owe.

The True-Born Englishman[2]

THE INTRODUCTION

Speak, Satyr; for there's none can tell like thee,
Whether 'tis folly, pride, or knavery,
That makes this discontented land appear
Less happy now in times of peace,[3] than war:
Why civil feuds disturb the nation more
Than all our bloody wars have done before.
   Fools out of favour grudge at knaves in place,
And men are always honest in disgrace:
The Court-preferments make men knaves in course:
But they which would be in them would be worse.
'Tis not at foreigners that we repine,
Would foreigners their perquisites resign:
The grand contention's plainly to be seen,
To get some men put out, and some put in.
For this our senators make long harangues,
And florid members whet their polished tongues.
Statesmen are always sick of one disease;
And a good pension gives them present ease.
That's the specific makes them all content
With any king, and any government.
Good patriots at Court-abuses rail,
And all the nation's grievances bewail:
But when the sovereign balsam's once applied,
The zealot never fails to change his side.
And when he must the golden key resign,[4]
The railing spirit comes about again.
   Who shall this bubbled[5] nation disabuse,

26

While they their own felicities refuse?
Who at the wars have made such mighty pother,
And now are falling out with one another;   30
With needless fears the jealous nation fill,
And always have been saved against their will:
Who fifty millions sterling have disbursed,
To be with peace and too much plenty cursed.
Who their old monarch eagerly undo,
And yet uneasily obey the new.[6]
Search, Satyr, search, a deep incision make;
The poison's strong, the antidote's too weak.
'Tis pointed truth must manage this dispute,
And down-right English Englishmen confute.   40
    Whet thy just anger at the nation's pride;
And with keen phrase repel the vicious tide.
To Englishmen their own beginnings show,
And ask them why they slight their neighbours so.
Go back to elder times, and ages past,
And nations into long oblivion cast;
To old Britannia's youthful days retire,
And there for true-born Englishmen enquire.
Britannia freely will disown the name,
And hardly knows herself from whence they came: 50
Wonders that they of all men should pretend
To birth and blood, and for a name contend.
Go back to causes where our follies dwell,
And fetch the dark original from hell:
Speak, Satyr, for there's none like thee can tell.

PART I

Wherever God erects a house of prayer,
The Devil always builds a chapel there:[7]
And 'twill be found upon examination,
The latter has the largest congregation:
For ever since he first debauched the mind,   60
He made a perfect conquest of mankind.

With uniformity of service, he
Reigns with a general aristocracy.
No nonconforming sects[8] disturb his reign,
For of his yoke[9] there's very few complain.
He knows the genius and the inclination,
And matches proper sins for every nation.
He needs no standing-army government;
He always rules us by our own consent:
His laws are easy, and his gentle sway
Makes it exceeding pleasant to obey.
The list of his vicegerents and commanders,
Outdoes your Caesars, or your Alexanders.
They never fail of his infernal aid,
And he's as certain never to be betrayed.
Through all the world they spread his vast command,
And death's eternal empire's maintained.
They rule so politicly and so well,
As if they were L[ords] J[ustices][10] of Hell,
Duly divided to debauch mankind,
And plant infernal dictates in his mind.

    Pride, the first peer, and president of Hell,
To his share Spain, the largest province, fell.
The subtle prince thought fittest to bestow
On these the golden mines of Mexico,
With all the silver mountains of Peru,
Wealth which would in wise hands the world undo:
Because he knew their genius was such;
Too lazy and too haughty to be rich.
So proud a people, so above their fate,
That if reduced to beg, they'll beg in state.
Lavish of money, to be counted brave,
And proudly starve, because they scorn to save.
Never was nation in the world before,
So very rich, and yet so very poor.

    Lust chose the torrid zone of Italy,
Where blood ferments in rapes and sodomy:
Where swelling veins overflow with livid streams,
With heat impregnate from Vesuvian flames:

70

80

90

Whose flowing sulphur forms infernal lakes,   100
And human body of the soil partakes.
There nature ever burns with hot desires.
Fanned with luxuriant air from subterranean fires:
Here undisturbed in floods of scalding lust,
Th' infernal King reigns with infernal gust.

    Drunk'ness, the darling favourite of Hell,
Chose Germany to rule; and rules so well,
No subjects more obsequiously obey,
None please so well, or are so pleased as they.
The cunning artist manages so well,   110
He lets them bow to Heaven, and drink to Hell.
If but to wine and him they homage pay,
He cares not to what deity they pray,
What God they worship most, or in what way.
Whether by Luther, Calvin, or by Rome,
They sail for Heaven, by wine he steers them home.

    Ungoverned passion settled first in France,
Where mankind lives in haste, and thrives by chance.
A dancing nation, fickle and untrue:
Have oft undone themselves, and others too: 120
Prompt the infernal dictates to obey,
And in Hell's favour none more great than they.

    The Pagan world he blindly leads away,
And personally rules with arbitrary sway:
The mask thrown off, plain Devil his title stands;
And what elsewhere he tempts, he there commands.
There with full gust th' ambition of his mind
Governs, as he of old in Heav'n designed.
Worshipped as God, his paynim[11] altars smoke,
Embrued with blood of those that him invoke.   130

    The rest by deputies he rules as well,
And plants the distant colonies of Hell.
By them his secret power he maintains,
And binds the world in his infernal chains.

    By zeal the Irish; and the Rush[12] by folly:
Fury the Dane: the Swede by melancholy:
By stupid ignorance, the Muscovite:

The Chinese by a child of Hell, called wit:
Wealth makes the Persian too effeminate:
140 And poverty the Tartars desperate:
The Turks and Moors by Mah'met he subdues:
And God has giv'n him leave to rule the Jews:
Rage rules the Portuguese; and fraud the Scotch:
Revenge the Pole; and avarice the Dutch.

    Satyr be kind, and draw a silent veil,
Thy native England's vices to conceal:
Or if that task's impossible to do,
At least be just, and show her virtues too;
Too great the first, alas the last too few.

150   England unknown as yet, unpeopled lay;
Happy, had she remained so to this day,
And not to every nation been a prey.
Her open harbours, and her fertile plains,
The merchant's glory these, and those the swain's,
To every barbarous nation have betrayed her,
Who conquer her as oft as they invade her.
So beauty guarded but by innocence,
That ruins her which should be her defence.

    Ingratitude, a devil of black renown,
160 Possessed her very early for his own.
An ugly, surly, sullen, selfish spirit,
Who Satan's worst perfections does inherit.
Second to him in malice and in force,
All devil without, and all within him worse.

    He made her first-born race to be so rude,
And suffered her to lie so oft subdued:
By sev'ral crowds of wandering thieves o're-run,
Often unpeopled, and as oft undone.
While every nation that her powers reduced,
170 Their languages and manners introduced.
From whose mixed relics our compounded breed,
By spurious generation does succeed;
Making a race uncertain and unev'n,
Derived from all the nations under Heav'n.

    The Romans first with Julius Caesar came,

Including all the nations of that name,
Gauls, Greeks, and Lombards; and by computation,
Auxiliaries or slaves of every nation.
With Hengist, Saxons; Danes with Sueno[13] came,
In search of plunder, not in search of fame.   180
Scots, Picts, and Irish from th' Hibernian shore:
And conqu'ring William brought the Normans o're.

   All these their barb'rous offspring left behind,
The dregs of armies, they of all mankind;
Blended with Britains[14] who before were here,
Of whom the Welsh ha' blessed the character.

   From this amphibious ill-born mob began
That vain ill-natured thing, an Englishman.
The customs, surnames, languages, and manners,
Of all these nations are their own explainers: 190
Whose relics are so lasting and so strong,
They ha' left a shibboleth[15] upon our tongue;
By which with easy search you may distinguish
Your Roman-Saxon-Danish-Norman English.

   The great invading Norman let us know
What conquerors in after-times might do.
To every musketeer he brought to town,
He gave the lands which never were his own.
When first the English crown he did obtain,
He did not send his Dutchmen home again.[16]   200
No reassumptions[17] in his reign were known,
Davenant[18] might there ha' let his book alone.
No Parliament his army could disband;[19]
He raised no money, for he paid in land.
He gave his legions their eternal station,
And made them all freeholders of the nation.
He cantoned[20] out the country to his men,
And every soldier was a denizen.
The rascals thus enriched, he called them Lords,
To please their upstart pride with new-made words;   210
And Doomsday-book his tyranny records.

   And here begins the ancient pedigree
That so exalts our poor nobility:

'Tis that from some French trooper they derive,
Who with the Norman Bastard did arrive:
The trophies of the families appear;
Some show the sword, the bow, and some the spear,
Which their great ancestor, forsooth, did wear.
These in the Heralds' Register remain,
220 Their noble mean extraction to explain.
Yet who the hero was, no man can tell,
Whether a drummer or a colonel:
The silent record blushes to reveal
Their undescended dark original.

    But grant the best, how came the change to pass:
A True-Born Englishman of Norman race?
A Turkish horse can show more history,
To prove his well-descended family.
Conquest, as by the moderns[21] 'tis expressed,
230 May give a title to the lands possessed.
But that the longest sword should be so civil,
To make a Frenchman English, that's the devil.

    These are the heroes that despise the Dutch,
And rail at new-come foreigners so much;
Forgetting that themselves are all derived
From the most scoundrel race that ever lived.
A horrid medley of thieves and drones,
Who ransacked kingdoms, and dispeopled towns.
The Pict and painted Britain, treach'rous Scot,
240 By hunger, theft, and rapine, hither brought.
Norwegian pirates, buccaneering Danes,
Whose red-haired offspring everywhere remains.
Who joined with Norman-French, compound the breed
From whence your True-Born Englishmen proceed.

    And lest by length of time it be pretended,
The climate may this modern breed ha' mended,
Wise Providence, to keep us where we are,
Mixes us daily with exceeding care:
We have been Europe's sink, the jakes[22] where she
250 Voids all her offal out-cast progeny.
From our fifth Henry's time, the strolling bands

Of banished fugitives from neighb'ring lands,
Have here a certain sanctuary found:
The eternal refuge of the vagabond.
Where in but half a common age of time,
Borr'wing new blood and manners from the clime,
Proudly they learn all mankind to contemn,
And all their race are True-Born Englishmen.

    Dutch, Walloons, Flemings, Irishmen, and Scots,
Vaudois and Valtolins,[23] and Huguenots,   260
In good Queen Bess's charitable reign,
Supplied us with three hundred thousand men.
Religion, God we thank thee, sent them hither,
Priests, Protestants, the Devil and all together:
Of all professions, and of every trade,
All that were persecuted or afraid;
Whether for debt or other crimes they fled,
David at Hackelah[24] was still their head.

    The offspring of this miscellaneous crowd,
Had not their new plantations long enjoyed,   270
But they grew Englishmen, and raised their votes
At foreign shoals of interloping Scots.
The royal branch from Pict-land did succeed,
With troops of Scots and scabs from North-by-Tweed.
The seven first years of his pacific reign,
Made him and half his nation Englishmen.
Scots from the northern frozen banks of Tay,
With packs and plods[25] came whigging[26] all away:
Thick as the locusts which in Egypt[27] swarmed,
With pride and hungry hopes completely armed: 280
With native truth, diseases, and no money,
Plundered our Canaan of the milk and honey.
Here they grew quickly Lords and Gentlemen,
And all their race are True-Born Englishmen.

    The Civil Wars,[28] the common purgative,
Which always use to make the nation thrive,
Made way for all that strolling congregation,
Which thronged in pious Ch[arle]s's restoration.[29]
The royal refugee our breed restores,

290 With foreign courtiers, and with foreign whores:
And carefully repeopled us again,
Throughout his lazy, long, lascivious reign,
With such a blessed and True-Born English fry,
As much illustrates our nobility.
A gratitude which will so black appear,
As future ages must abhor to hear:
When they look back on all that crimson flood,
Which streamed in Lindsey's, and Caernarvon's blood:
Bold Strafford, Cambridge, Capel, Lucas, Lisle,
300 Who crowned in death his father's fun'ral pile.[30]
The loss of whom, in order to supply
With True-Born English nobility,
Six bastard dukes survive his luscious reign,
The labours of Italian C[astlemai]n,
French P[ortsmout]h, tabby S[co]t, and Cambrian.[31]
Besides the num'rous bright and virgin throng,
Whose female glories shade them from my song.
    This offspring, if one age they multiply,
May half the House with English Peers supply:
310 There with true English pride they may contemn
S[chomber]g and P[ortlan]d,[32] new-made noblemen.
    French cooks, Scotch pedlars, and Italian whores,
Were all made Lords, or Lords' progenitors.
Beggars and bastards by his new creation,
Much multiplied the peerage of the nation;
Who will be all, e're one short age runs o're,
As True-Born Lords as those we had before.
    Then to recruit the Commons he prepares,
And heal the latent breaches of the wars:
320 The pious purpose better to advance,
He invites the banished Protestants of France:[33]
Hither for God's sake and their own they fled,
Some for religion came, and some for bread:
Two hundred thousand pair of wooden shoes,[34]
Who, God be thanked, had nothing left to lose;
To Heav'n's great praise did for religion fly,
To make us starve our poor in charity.

34

In every port they plant their fruitful train,
To get a race of True-Born Englishmen:
Whose children will, when riper years they see,   330
Be as ill-natured and as proud as we:
Call themselves English, foreigners despise,
Be surly like us all, and just as wise.

    Thus from a mixture of all kinds began,
That het'rogeneous thing, an Englishman:
In eager rapes, and furious lust begot,
Betwixt a painted Briton and a Scot:
Whose gend'ring offspring quickly learnt to bow,
And yoke their heifers to the Roman plough:
From whence a mongrel half-bred race there came,   340
With neither name nor nation, speech or fame.
In whose hot veins new mixtures quickly ran,
Infused betwixt a Saxon and a Dane.
While their rank daughters, to their parents just,
Received all nations with promiscuous lust.
This nauseous brood directly did contain
The well-extracted blood of Englishmen.

    Which medley cantoned in a heptarchy,[35]
A rhapsody of nations to supply,
Among themselves maintained eternal wars,   350
And still the ladies loved the conquerors.

    The western Angles all the rest subdued;
A bloody nation, barbarous and rude:
Who by the tenure of the sword possessed
One part of Britain and subdued the rest.
And as great things denominate the small,
The conqu'ring part gave title to the whole.
The Scot, Pict, Britain, Roman, Dane submit,
And with the English-Saxon all unite:
And these the mixture have so close pursued,   360
The very name and memory's subdued:
No Roman now, no Britain does remain;
Wales strove to separate, but strove in vain:
The silent nations undistinguished fall,
And Englishman's the common name for all.

Fate jumbled them together, God knows how;
Whate're they were, they're True-Born English now.
    The wonder which remains is at our pride,
To value that which all wise men deride.
370   For Englishmen to boast of generation,
Cancels their knowledge, and lampoons the nation.
A True-Born Englishman's a contradiction,
In speech an irony, in fact a fiction.
A banter[36] made to be a test of fools,
Which those that use it justly ridicules.
A metaphor invented to express
A man akin to all the universe.
    For as the Scots, as learned men ha' said,
Throughout the world their wand'ring seed ha' spread;
380   So open-handed England, 'tis believed,
Has all the gleanings of the world received.
    Some think of England 'twas our Saviour meant,
The gospel should to all the world be sent:
Since when the blessed sound did hither reach,
They to all nations might be said to preach.
    'Tis well that virtue gives nobility,
Else God knows where we had our gentry;
Since scarce one family is left alive,
Which does not from some foreigner derive.
390   Of sixty thousand English gentlemen,
Whose names and arms in registers remain,
We challenge all our Heralds[37] to declare
Ten families which English-Saxons are.
    France justly boasts the ancient noble line
Of Bourbon, Mommorency,[38] and Lorrain.
The Germans too their House of Austria show,
And Holland their invincible Nassau.[39]
Lines which in heraldry were ancient grown,
Before the name of Englishman was known.
400   Even Scotland too her elder glory shows,
Her Gordons, Hamiltons, and her Monroes;
Douglas, Mackays, and Grahams, names well known,
Long before ancient England knew her own.

But England, modern to the last degree,
Borrows or makes her own nobility,
And yet she boldly boasts of pedigree:
Repines that foreigners are put upon her,
And talks of her antiquity and honour:
Her S[ackvi]lles, S[avi]lles, C[eci]ls, De[lame]res,
M[ohu]ns and M[ontag]ues, D[urase]s and V[e]res,   410
Not one have English names, yet all are English Peers.
Your H[oublo]ns, P[api]llons, and L[ethui]lliers,[40]
Pass now for True-Born English knights and squires,
And make good Senate-Members, or Lord-Mayors.
Wealth, howsoever got, in England makes
Lords of mechanics, gentlemen of rakes.
Antiquity and birth are needless here;
'Tis impudence and money makes a Peer.
　Innumerable City-Knights we know,
From Bluecoat Hospitals and Bridewell[41] flow.   420
Draymen and porters fill the City Chair,
And footboys magisterial purple wear.
Fate has but very small distinction set
Betwixt the counter[42] and the coronet.
Tarpaulin Lords,[43] pages of high renown,
Rise up by poor men's valour, not their own.
Great families of yesterday we show,
And Lords, whose parents were the Lord knows who.

PART II

The breed's described: now, Satyr, if you can,
Their temper show, for manners make the man.   430
Fierce as the Britain, as the Roman brave;
And less inclined to conquer than to save:
Eager to fight, and lavish of their blood;
And equally of fear and forecast[44] void.
The Pict has made 'em sour, the Dane morose;
False from the Scot, and from the Norman worse.
What honesty they have, the Saxon gave them,

And that, now they grow old, begins to leave them.
The climate makes them terrible and bold;
440 And English beef their courage does uphold:
No danger can their daring spirit pall,
Always provided that their belly's full.

In close intrigues their faculty's but weak,
For gen'rally whate're they know, they speak:
And often their own councils undermine
By their infirmity, and not design.
From whence the learned say it does proceed,
That English treasons never can succeed:
For they're so open-hearted, you may know
450 Their own most secret thoughts, and others too.

The lab'ring poor, in spite of double pay,
Are saucy, mutinous, and beggarly:
So lavish of their money and their time,
That want of forecast is the nation's crime.
Good drunken company is their delight;
And what they get by day, they spend by night.
Dull thinking seldom does their heads engage,
But drink their youth away, and hurry on old age.
Empty of all good husbandry and sense;
460 And void of manners most, when void of pence.
Their strong aversion to behaviour's such,
They always talk too little, or too much.
So dull, they never take the pains to think;
And seldom are good-natured, but in drink.

In English ale their dear enjoyment lies,
For which they'll starve themselves and families.
An Englishman will fairly drink as much
As will maintain two families of Dutch:
Subjecting all their labours to the pots;
470 The greatest artists[45] are the greatest sots.

The country poor do by example live;
The gentry lead them, and the clergy drive:
What may we not from such examples hope?
The landlord is their God, the priest their Pope.
A drunken clergy, and a swearing bench,

Has giv'n the Reformation[46] such a drench,
As wise men think there is some cause to doubt,
Will purge good manners and religion out.
    Nor do the poor alone their liquor prize,
The sages join in this great sacrifice.   480
The learned men who study Aristotle,
Correct him with an explanation-bottle;
Praise Epicurus rather than Lysander,
And Aristippus more than Alexander.[47]
The doctors too their Galen[48] here resign,
And gen'rally prescribe specific wine.
The graduates' study's grown an easier task,
While for the urinal they toss the flask.
The surgeons' art grows plainer every hour,
And wine's the balm which into wounds they pour.   490
    Poets long since Parnassus have forsaken,
And say the ancient bards were all mistaken.
Apollo's lately abdicate and fled,
And good King Bacchus reigneth in his stead:
He does the chaos of the head refine,
And atom-thoughts jump into words by wine:
The inspiration's of a finer nature;
As wine must needs excel Parnassus water.
    Statesmen their weighty politics refine,
And soldiers raise their courages by wine.   500
Cecilia[49] gives her choristers their choice,
And lets them all drink wine to clear the voice.
    Some think the clergy first found out the way,
And wine's the only spirit by which they pray.
But others less prophane than so, agree,
It clears the lungs, and helps the memory:
And therefore all of them divinely think,
Instead of study, 'tis as well to drink.
    And here I would be very glad to know,
Whether our Asgillites[50] may drink or no.   510
Th' enlight'ning fumes of wine would certainly
Assist them much when they begin to fly:
Or if a fiery chariot should appear,

Inflamed by wine, they'd ha' the less to fear.
    Even the gods themselves, as mortals say,
Were they on earth, would be as drunk as they:
Nectar would be no more celestial drink,
They'd all take wine, to teach them how to think.
But English drunkards, gods and men outdo,
Drink their estates away, and senses too.
Colon's[51] in debt, and if his friends should fail
To help him out, must die at last in gaol:
His wealthy uncle sent a hundred nobles,[52]
To pay his trifles off, and rid him of his troubles:
But Colon, like a True-Born Englishman,
Drank all the money out in bright champagne;
And Colon does in custody remain.
Drunk'ness has been the darling of the realm,
E're since a drunken pilot[53] had the helm.
    In their religion they are so unev'n,
That each man goes his own by-way to Heav'n.
Tenacious of mistakes to that degree,
That every man pursues it sep'rately,
And fancies none can find the way but he:
So shy of one another they are grown,
As if they strove to get to Heav'n alone.
Rigid and zealous, positive and grave,
And every grace, but charity, they have:
This makes them so ill-natured and uncivil,
That all men think an Englishman the Devil.
    Surly to strangers, froward to their friend;
Submit to love with a reluctant mind;
Resolved to be ungrateful and unkind.
If by necessity reduced to ask,
The giver has the difficultest task:
For what's bestowed they awkwardly receive,
And always take less freely than they give.
The obligation is their highest grief;
And never love, where they accept relief.
So sullen in their sorrows, that 'tis known,
They'll rather die than their afflictions own:

And if relieved, it is too often true,
That they'll abuse their benefactors too:
For in distress their haughty stomach's such,
They hate to see themselves obliged too much.
Seldom contented, often in the wrong;
Hard to be pleased at all, and never long.
    If your mistakes their ill opinion gain,
No merit can their favour reobtain:
And if they're not vindictive in their fury,   560
'Tis their unconstant temper does secure ye:
Their brain's so cool, their passion seldom burns;
For all's condensed before the flame returns:
The fermentation's of so weak a matter,
The humid damps the fume, and runs it all to water.
So tho the inclination may be strong,
They're pleased by fits, and never angry long.
    Then if good nature shows some slender proof,
They never think they have reward enough:
But like our modern Quakers of the town,   570
Expect your manners, and return you none.[54]
    Friendship, th' abstracted union of the mind,
Which all men seek, but very few can find:
Of all the nations in the universe,
None talk on't more, or understand it less:
For if it does their property annoy,
Their property their friendship will destroy.
    As you discourse them, you shall hear them tell
All things in which they think they do excel:
No panegyric needs their praise record;   580
An Englishman ne're wants his own good word.
His first discourses gen'rally appear
Prologued with his own wondrous character:
When, to illustrate his own good name,
He never fails his neighbour to defame:
And yet he really designs no wrong;
His malice goes no further than his tongue.
But pleased to tattle, he delights to rail,
To satisfy the lech'ry of a tale.

590   His own dear praises close the ample speech,
Tells you how wise he is; that is, how rich:
For wealth is wisdom; he that's rich is wise;
And all men learned poverty despise.
His generosity comes next, and then
Concludes that he's a True-Born Englishman;
And they, 'tis known, are generous and free,
Forgetting, and forgiving injury:
Which may be true, thus rightly understood,
Forgiving ill turns, and forgetting good.
600   Cheerful in labour when they've undertook it;
But out of humour, when they're out of pocket.
But if their belly and their pocket's full,
They may be phlegmatic, but never dull:
And if a bottle does their brains refine,
It makes their wit as sparkling as their wine.
     As for the general vices which we find
They're guilty of in common with mankind,
Satyr, forbear, and silently endure;
We must conceal the crimes we cannot cure.
610   Nor shall my verse the brighter sex defame;
For English beauty will preserve her name.
Beyond dispute, agreeable and fair;
And modester than other nations are:
For where the vice prevails, the great temptation
Is want of money, more than inclination.
In general, this only is allowed,
They're something noisy, and a little proud.
     An Englishman is gentlest in command;
Obedience is a stranger in the land:
620   Hardly subjected to the Magistrate;
For Englishmen do all subjection hate.
Humblest when rich, but peevish when they're poor;
And think whate're they have, they merit more.
     Shamwhig[55] pretends t' ha' served the Government,
But baulked of due reward, turns malecontent.
For English Christians always have regard
To future recompences of reward.

His forfeit liberty they did restore,
And gave him bread, which he had not before.
But True-Born English Shamwhig lets them know,   630
His merit must not lie neglected so.
As proud as poor, his masters he'll defy;
And writes a piteous Satyr upon Honesty.[56]
    Some think the poem had been pretty good,
If he the subject had but understood.
He got five hundred pence by this, and more,
As sure as he had ne're a groat before.
    In business next some friends of his employed him;
And there he proved that fame had not belied him:
His benefactors quickly he abused,   640
And falsely to the Government accused:[57]
But they, defended by their innocence,
Ruined the traitor in their own defence.
    Thus kicked about from pillars unto posts,
He whets his pen against the Lord of Hosts:
Burlesques his God and King in paltry rhymes:[58]
Against the Dutch turns champion for the times;
And huffs[59] the King, upon that very score,
On which he panegyricked him[60] before.
    Unhappy England, hast thou none but such,   650
To plead thy scoundrel cause against the Dutch?
This moves their scorn, and not their indignation;
He that lampoons the Dutch, burlesques the nation.
    The meanest English ploughman studies law,
And keeps therefore the Magistrates in awe:
Will boldly tell them what they ought to do,
And sometimes punish their omissions too.
    Their liberty and property's so dear,
They scorn their laws or governors to fear:
So bugbeared with the name of slavery,   660
They can't submit to their own liberty.
Restraint from ill is freedom to the wise;
But Englishmen do all restraint despise.
Slaves to the liquor, drudges to the pots,
The mob are statesmen, and their statesmen sots.

Their governors they count such dangerous things,
That 'tis their custom to affront their Kings:
So jealous of the power their Kings possessed,
They suffer neither power nor Kings to rest.
670 The bad with force they eagerly subdue;
The good with constant clamours they pursue:
And did King Jesus reign, they'd murmur too.
A discontented nation, and by far
Harder to rule in times of peace than war:
Easily set together by the ears,
And full of causeless jealousies and fears:
Apt to revolt, and willing to rebel,
And never are contented when they're well.
No Government could ever please them long,
680 Could tie their hands, or rectify their tongue.
In this to ancient Israel well compared,[61]
Eternal murmurs are among them heard.

It was but lately that they were oppressed,
Their rights invaded, and their laws suppressed:
When nicely tender of their liberty,
Lord! what a noise they made of slavery.
In daily tumults showed their discontent;
Lampooned their King, and mocked his Government.
And if in arms they did not first appear,
690 'Twas want of force, and not for want of fear.
In humbler tone than English used to do,
At foreign hands for foreign aid they sue.

William the great successor of Nassau,
Their prayers heard, and their oppressions saw:
He saw and saved them: God and him they praised;
To this their thanks, to that their trophies raised.
But glutted with their own felicities,
They soon their new deliverer despise;
Say all their prayers back, their joy disown,
700 Unsing their thanks, and pull their trophies down:
Their harps of praise are on the willows hung;[62]
For Englishmen are ne're contented long.

The rev'rend clergy too! and who'd ha' thought

That they who had such non-resistance[63] taught,
Should e're to arms against their Prince[64] be brought?
Who up to Heav'n did regal power advance;
Subjecting English laws to modes of France.
Twisting religion so with loyalty,
As one could never live, and t'other die.
And yet no sooner did their Prince design   710
Their glebes and perquisites to undermine,
But all their passive doctrines laid aside;
The clergy their own principles denied:
Unpreached their non-resisting cant, and prayed
To Heav'n for help, and to the Dutch for aid.
The Church chimed all her doctrines back again,
And pulpit-champions did the cause maintain;
Flew in the face of all their former zeal,
And non-resistance did at once repeal.

    The Rabbis say it would be too prolix,   720
To tie religion up to politics:
The Church's safety is *suprema lex*.[65]
And so by a new figure of their own,
Do all their former doctrines disown.
As laws *post facto*[66] in the Parliament,
In urgent cases have obtained assent;
But are as dangerous precedents laid by;
Made lawful only by necessity.

    The rev'rend Fathers then in arms appear,
And men of God became the men of war.   730
The nation, fired by them, to arms apply;
Assault their antichristian monarchy;
To their due channel all our laws restore,
And made things what they should ha' been before.
But when they came to fill the vacant throne,
And the pale priests looked back on what they had done;
How English liberty began to thrive,
And Church of England loyalty out-live:
How all their persecuting days were done,
And their deliv'rer placed upon the throne: 740
The priests, as priests are wont to do, turned tail;

They're Englishmen, and nature will prevail.
Now they deplore the ruins they ha' made,
And murmur for the master they betrayed.
Excuse those crimes they could not make him mend;
And suffer for the cause they can't defend.
Pretend they'd not ha' carried things so high;
And proto-martyrs make for Popery.
　　Had the Prince done as they designed the thing,
Ha' set the clergy up to rule the King;
Taken a Donative[67] for coming hither,
And so ha' left their King and them together,
We had, say they, been now a happy nation.
No doubt we had seen a blessed reformation:
For wise men say 't's as dangerous a thing,
A ruling priesthood, as a priest-rid king.
And of all plagues with which mankind are cursed,
Ecclesiastic tyranny's the worst.
　　If all our former grievances were feigned,
King James has been abused, and we trepanned;[68]
Bugbeared with Popery and power despotic,
Tyrannic government, and leagues exotic:
The Revolution's a fanatic plot,
William a tyrant, Sunderland[69] a sot:[70]
A factious army and a poisoned nation,
Unjustly forced King James's abdication.
　　But if he did the subjects' rights invade,
Then he was punished only, not betrayed:
And punishing of kings is no such crime,
But Englishmen ha' done it many a time.
　　When kings the sword of justice first lay down,
They are no kings, though they possess the crown.
Titles are shadows, crowns are empty things,
The good of subjects is the end of kings;
To guide in war, and to protect in peace:
Where tyrants once commence, the kings do cease:
For arbitrary power's so strange a thing,
It makes the tyrant, and unmakes the king.
If kings by foreign priests and armies reign,

750

760

770

And lawless power against their oaths maintain, 780
Then subjects must ha' reason to complain.
If oaths must bind us when our kings do ill;
To call in foreign aid is to rebel.
By force to circumscribe our lawful prince,
Is wilful treason in the largest sense:
And they who once rebel, most certainly
Their God, and King, and former oaths defy.
If we allow no maladministration
Could cancel the allegiance of the nation;
Let all our learned sons of Levi[71] try, 790
This ecclesiastic riddle to untie:
How they could make a step to call the Prince,
And yet pretend to oaths and innocence.

   By th' first address they made beyond the seas,
They're perjured in the most intense degrees;
And without scruple for the time to come,
May swear to all the Kings in Christendom.
And truly did our Kings consider all,
They'd never let the clergy swear at all:
Their politic allegiance they'd refuse; 800
For whores and priests do never want excuse.

   But if the mutual contract was dissolved,
The doubt's explained, the difficulty solved:
That Kings, when they descend to tyranny,
Dissolve the bond, and leave the subject free.
The government's ungirt when justice dies,
And constitutions are non-entities.
The nation's all a mob, there's no such thing
As Lords or Commons, Parliament or King.
A great promiscuous crowd the Hydra[72] lies, 810
Till laws revive, and mutual contract ties:
A chaos free to choose for their own share,
What case[73] of Government they please to wear:
If to a King they do the reins commit,
All men are bound in conscience to submit:
But then that King must by his oath assent
To *postulatas*[74] of the Government;

Which if he breaks, he cuts off the entail,[75]
And power retreats to its original.[76]

820   This doctrine has the sanction of assent,
From nature's universal parliament.
The voice of nations, and the course of things,
Allow that laws superior are to Kings.
None but delinquents would have justice cease,
Knaves rail at laws, as soldiers rail at peace:
For justice is the end of government,
As reason is the test of argument.

   No man was ever yet so void of sense,
As to debate the right of self-defence;

830 A principle so grafted in the mind,
With nature born, and does like nature bind:
Twisted with reason, and with nature too;
As neither one nor t'other can undo.

   Nor can this right be less when national;
Reason which governs one, should govern all.
Whate're the dialect of courts may tell,
He that his right demands, can ne're rebel.
Which right, if 'tis by Governors denied,
May be procured by force, or foreign aid.

840 For tyranny's a nation's term for grief;
As folks cry Fire, to hasten in relief.
And when the hated word is heard about,
All men should come to help the people out.

   Thus England groaned, Britannia's voice was heard;
And great Nassau[77] to rescue her, appeared:
Called by the universal voice of Fate;
God and the people's legal Magistrate.
Ye Heav'ns regard! Almighty Jove look down,
And view thy injured monarch on the throne.

850 On their ungrateful heads due vengeance take,
Who sought his aid, and then his part forsake.
Witness, ye Powers! it was our call alone,
Which now our pride makes us ashamed to own.
Britannia's troubles fetched him from afar,
To court the dreadful casualties of war:

But where requital never can be made,
Acknowledgment's a tribute seldom paid.
   He dwelt in bright Maria's circling arms,
Defended by the magic of her charms,
From foreign fears, and from domestic harms.   860
Ambition found no fuel for her fire,
He had what God could give, or man desire.
Till pity roused him from his soft repose,
His life to unseen hazards to expose:
Till pity moved him in our cause t'appear;
Pity! that word which now we hate to hear.
But English gratitude is always such,
To hate the hand which does oblige too much.
   Britannia's cries gave birth to his intent,
And hardly gained his unforeseen assent: 870
His boding thoughts foretold him he should find
The people, fickle, selfish, and unkind.
Which thought did to his royal heart appear
More dreadful than the dangers of the war:
For nothing grates a generous mind so soon,
As base returns for hearty service done.
   Satyr be silent, awfully prepare
Britannia's song and William's praise to hear.
Stand by, and let her cheerfully rehearse
Her grateful vows in her immortal verse.   880
Loud fame's eternal trumpet let her sound;
Listen ye distant poles, and endless round.
May the strong blast the welcome news convey
As far as sound can reach, or spirit fly.
To neighb'ring worlds, if such there be, relate
Our hero's fame, for theirs to imitate.
To distant worlds of spirits let her rehearse:
For spirits without the helps of voice converse.
May angels hear the gladsome news on high,
Mixed with their everlasting symphony.   890
And Hell itself stand in suspense to know
Whether it be the fatal blast, or no.

BRITANNIA

The fame of virtue 'tis for which I sound,
And heroes with immortal triumphs crowned.
Fame built on solid virtue swifter flies,
Than morning light can spread my Eastern skies.
The gath'ring air returns the doubling sound,
And loud repeating thunders force it round:
Echoes return from caverns of the deep:
900   Old Chaos[78] dreams on't in eternal sleep.
Time hands it forward to its latest urn,
From whence it never, never shall return,
Nothing is heard so far, or lasts so long;
'Tis heard by every ear, and spoke by every tongue.

My hero, with the sails of honour furled,
Rises like the great genius of the world.
By fate and fame wisely prepared to be
The soul of war, and life of victory.
He spreads the wings of virtue on the throne,
910   And every wind of glory fans them on.
Immortal trophies dwell upon his brow,
Fresh as the garlands he has won but now.

By different steps the high ascent he gains,
And differently that high ascent maintains.
Princes for pride and lust of rule make war,
And struggle for the name of conqueror.
Some fight for fame, and some for victory.
He fights to save, and conquers to set free.

Then seek no phrase his titles to conceal,
920   And hide with words what actions must reveal.
No parallel from Hebrew stories[79] take,
Of God-like kings my similies to make:
No borrowed names conceal my living theme;
But names and things directly I proclaim.
'Tis honest merit does his glory raise;
Whom that exalts, let no man fear to praise.
Of such a subject no man need be shy;

Virtue's above the reach of flattery.
He needs no character but his own fame,
Nor any flattering titles, but his name.   930
    William's the name that's spoke by every tongue:
William's the darling subject of my song.
Listen ye virgins to the charming sound,
And in eternal dances hand it round:
Your early offerings to this altar bring;
Make him at once a lover and a king.
May he submit to none but to your arms;
Nor ever be subdued, but by your charms.
May your soft thoughts for him be all sublime;
And every tender vow be made for him.   940
May he be first in every morning thought,
And Heav'n ne're hear a prayer where he's left out.
May every omen, every boding dream,
Be fortunate by mentioning his name.
May this one charm infernal powers affright,
And guard you from the terrors of the night.
May every cheerful glass as it goes down
To William's health, be cordials to your own.
Let every song be chorused with his name,
And music pay her tribute to his fame.   950
Let every poet tune his artful verse,
And in immortal strains his deeds rehearse.
And may Apollo never more inspire
The disobedient bard with his seraphic fire.
May all my sons their grateful homage pay;
His praises sing, and for his safety pray.
    Satyr return to our unthankful isle,
Secured by Heav'n's regard, and William's toil.
To both ungrateful, and to both untrue;
Rebels to God, and to good nature too.   960
    If e're this nation be distressed again,
To whomsoe're they cry, they'll cry in vain.
To heav'n they cannot have the face to look;
Or if they should, it would but Heav'n provoke.
To hope for help from man would be too much;

Mankind would always tell 'em of the Dutch:
How they came here our freedoms to maintain,
Were paid, and cursed, and hurried home[80] again.
How by their aid we first dissolved our fears,
970 And then our helpers damned for foreigners.
'Tis not our English temper to do better;
For Englishmen think every man their debtor.

   'Tis worth observing, that we ne're complained
Of foreigners, nor of the wealth they gained,
Till all their services were at an end.
Wise men affirm it is the English way,
Never to grumble till they come to pay;
And then they always think their temper's such,
The work too little, and the pay too much.
980   As frighted patients, when they want a cure,
Bid any price, and any pain endure:
But when the doctor's remedies appear,
The cure's too easy, and the price too dear.

   Great Portland[81] ne're was bantered, when he strove
For us his master's kindest thoughts to move.
We ne're lampooned his conduct, when employed
King James's secret Councils to divide:
Then we caressed him as the only man,
Which could the doubtful oracle explain:
990 The only Hushai[82] able to repell
The dark designs of our Ahithophel.
Compared his master's courage to his sense;
The ablest statesman, and the bravest Prince.
On his wise conduct we depended much,
And liked him ne're the worse for being Dutch.
Nor was he valued more than he deserved;
Freely he ventured, faithfully he served.
In all King William's dangers he has shared;
In England's quarrels always he appeared:
1000 The Revolution first, and then the Boyne;
In both his counsels and his conduct shine.
His martial valour Flanders will confess;
And France regrets his managing the peace.[83]

Faithful to England's interest and her King:
The greatest reason of our murmuring.
Ten years in English service he appeared,
And gained his master's and the world's regard:
But 'tis not England's custom to reward.
The wars are over, England needs him not;
Now he's a Dutchman, and the Lord knows what.   1010
   Schonbergh, the ablest soldier of his age,
With great Nassau did in our cause engage:
Both joined for England's rescue and defence;
The greatest Captain and the greatest Prince.
With what applause his stories did we tell?
Stories which Europe's volumes largely swell.
We counted him an army in our aid:
Where he commanded, no man was afraid.
His actions with a constant conquest shine,
From Villa-Vitiosa to the Rhine.   1020
France, Flanders, Germany, his fame confess;
And all the world was fond of him, but us.[84]
Our turn first served, we grudged him the command.
Witness the grateful temper of the land.
   We blame the King that he relies too much
On strangers, Germans, Huguenots, and Dutch;
And seldom does his great affairs of state,
To English counsellors communicate.
The fact might very well be answered thus:
He has so often been betrayed by us,   1030
He must have been a madman to rely
On English gentlemen's fidelity.
For laying other arguments aside,
This thought might mortify our English pride,
That foreigners have faithfully obeyed him,
And none but Englishmen have e're betrayed him.
They have our ships and merchants bought and sold,
And bartered English blood for foreign gold.
First to the French they sold our Turkey-fleet,[85]
And injured Talmarsh[86] next at Camaret.   1040
The King himself is sheltered from their snares,

53

Not by his merit, but the crown he wears.
Experience tells us 'tis the English way,
Their benefactors always to betray.
    And lest examples should be too remote,
A modern Magistrate[87] of famous note,
Shall give you his own history by rote.
I'll make it out, deny it he that can,
His Worship is a True-Born Englishman,
In all the latitude that empty word
By modern acceptation's understood.
The parish-books his great descent[88] record,
And now he hopes e're long to be a Lord.
And truly as things go, it would be pity
But such as he bore office in the City:[89]
While robb'ry for burnt-offering he brings,
And gives to God what he has stole from Kings:[90]
Great monuments of charity he raises,
And good St Magnus[91] whistles out his praises.
To City-gaols he grants a jubilee,[92]
And hires huzza's from his own mobile.[93]
    Lately he wore the golden chain and gown,
With which equipped he thus harangued the town.

SIR CHARLES DUNCOMB'S FINE SPEECH, &C.

With clouted iron shoes and sheepskin breeches,
More rags than manners, and more dirt than riches:
From driving cows and calves to Layton-Market,
While of my greatness there appeared no spark yet,
Behold I come, to let you see the pride
With which exalted beggars always ride.
    Born to the needful labours of the plough,
The cart-whip graced me as the chain does now.
Nature and Fate in doubt what course to take,
Whether I should a Lord or plough-boy make;
Kindly at last resolved they would promote me,
And first a knave, and then a Knight they vote me.

1050

1060

1070

What Fate appointed, Nature did prepare,
And furnished me with an exceeding care.
To fit me for what they designed to have me;
And every gift but honesty they gave me.

    And thus equipped, to this proud town I came,   1080
In quest of bread, and not in quest of fame.
Blind to my future fate, an humble boy,
Free from the guilt and glory I enjoy.
The hopes which my ambition entertained,
Were in the name of foot-boy all contained.
The greatest heights from small beginnings rise;
The gods were great on earth, before they reached the skies.

    Backwell,[94] the generous temper of whose mind,
Was always to be bountiful inclined:
Whether by his ill fate or fancy led,   1090
First took me up, and furnished me with bread.
The little services he put me to,
Seemed labours rather than were truly so.
But always my advancement he designed;
For 'twas his very nature to be kind.
Large was his soul, his temper ever free;
The best of masters and of men to me.
And I who was before decreed by Fate,
To be made infamous as well as great,
With an obsequious diligence obeyed him,   1100
Till trusted with his all, and then betrayed him.[95]

    All his past kindnesses I trampled on,
Ruined his fortune to erect my own.
So vipers in the bosom bred, begin
To hiss at that hand first which took them in.
With eager treach'ry I his fall pursued,
And my first trophies were ingratitude.

    Ingratitude's the worst of human guilt,
The basest action mankind can commit;
Which like the sin against the Holy Ghost,   1110
Has least of honour, and of guilt the most.
Distinguished from all other crimes by this,
That 'tis a crime which no man will confess.

That sin alone, which should not be forgiv'n
On earth, although perhaps it may in heav'n.
    Thus my first benefactor I o'rethrew;
And how should I be to a second true?
The public trust[96] came next into my care,
And I to use them scurvily prepare:
My needy sov'reign lord[97] I played upon,   1120
And lent him many a thousand of his own;
For which, great int'rest I took care to charge,
And so my ill-got wealth became so large.
    My predecessor Judas was a fool,
Fitter to ha' been whipped, and sent to school,
Than sell a Saviour: had I been at hand,
His Master had not been so cheap trepanned;
I would ha' made the eager Jews ha' found,
For thirty pieces, thirty thousand pound.
    My cousin Ziba,[98] of immortal fame,   1130
(Ziba and I shall never want a name:)
First-born of treason, nobly did advance
His master's fall, for his inheritance.
By whose keen arts old David first began
To break his sacred oath to Jonathan:
The good old King, 'tis thought, was very loth
To break his word, and therefore broke his oath.
Ziba's a traitor of some quality,
Yet Ziba might ha' been informed by me:
Had I been there, he ne're had been content   1140
With half th' estate, nor half the government.
    In our late Revolution 'twas thought strange,
That I of all mankind should like the change:
But they who wondered at it, never knew,
That in it I did my old game[99] pursue:
Nor had they heard of twenty thousand pound,
Which ne're was lost, yet never could be found.
    Thus all things in their turn to sale I bring,
God and my master first, and then the King:
Till by successful villanies made bold,   1150
I thought to turn the nation into gold;

And so to forgery[100] my hand I bent,
Not doubting I could gull the government;
But there was ruffled by the Parliament.
And if I 'scaped th' unhappy tree to climb,
'Twas want of law, and not for want of crime.

But my old friend,[101] who printed in my face
A needful competence of English brass,
Having more business yet for me to do,
And loth to lose his trusty servant so,   1160
Managed the matter with such art and skill,
As saved his hero, and threw out the bill.

And now I'm graced with unexpected honours,
For which I'll certainly abuse the donors:
Knighted,[102] and made a tribune of the people,[103]
Whose laws and properties I'm like to keep well:
The *custos rotulorum*[104] of the City,
And Captain of the Guards of their *banditti*.[105]
Surrounded by my catchpoles,[106] I declare
Against the needy debtor open war.   1170
I hang poor thieves for stealing of your pelf,
And suffer none to rob you, but myself.

The King commanded[107] me to help reform ye,
And how I'll do it, Miss [Morgan][108] shall inform ye.
I keep the best seraglio in the nation,
And hope in time to bring it into fashion
No brimstone-whore need fear the lash from me,
That part I'll leave to Brother Jeffery.[109]
Our gallants need not go abroad to Rome,
I'll keep a whoring jubilee at home.   1180
Whoring's the darling of my inclination;
A'n't I a Magistrate for Reformation?[110]
For this my praise is sung by every bard,
For which Bridewell would be a just reward.
In print my panegyrics[111] fill the street,
And hired gaol-birds their huzza's repeat.
Some charities[112] contrived to make a show,
Have taught the needy rabble to do so:[113]

Whose empty noise is a mechanic fame,
1190   Since for Sir Belzebub they'd do the same.

THE CONCLUSION

Then let us boast of ancestors no more,
Or deeds of heroes done in days of yore,
In latent records of the ages past,
Behind the rear of time, in long oblivion placed.
For if our virtues must in lines descend,
The merit with the families would end:
And intermixtures would most fatal grow;
For vice would be hereditary too;
The tainted blood would of necessity,
1200   Involuntary wickedness convey.
    Vice, like ill nature, for an age or two,
May seem a generation to pursue;
But virtue seldom does regard the breed;
Fools do the wise, and wise men fools succeed.
    What is't to us, what ancestors we had?
If good, what better? or what worse, if bad?
Examples are for imitation set,
Yet all men follow virtue with regret.
    Could but our ancestors retrieve their fate,
1210   And see their offspring thus degenerate;
How we contend for birth and names unknown,
And build on their past actions, not our own;
They'd cancel records, and their tombs deface,
And openly disown the vile degenerate race:
For fame of families is all a cheat,
'Tis personal virtue only makes us great.[114]

FINIS.

THE

Six Distinguishing Characters

OF A

Parliament - Man.

Address'd to the Good People of *England*.

—— *And that in Respect of some Matters of the Highest Importance to this our Kingdom, we do intend to give Directions for the calling a new Parliament, which shall begin, and be holden at* Westminster, *on* Thursday *the Sixth Day of* February *next.* Vide Proclamation.

LONDON:
Printed in the Year MDCC.

The Six Distinguishing Characters of a Parliament-Man.

Good People of England,

The disuse, or distrust of parliaments in the four last reigns, was the nation's general grievance; and 'twas but lately that parliaments were consulted in the matters of highest importance to the kingdoms.

This was the destruction of that mutual confidence between king and people, which is so essential to the prosperity of a nation.

Parliaments were called together, a long speech and great pretences for money opened the session; and as soon as the end was answered, they were sent home about their business.

If they began to show their resentments, and appear sensible of their being imposed upon, if they began to search into the intrigues of the court, if they began to question favourites, and ministers, they were equally certain of being dismissed.

Now to show us what kind of a nation we are that (according to the old character of an Englishman) can never tell when we are well, Providence has changed the scene.

Former kings have been addressed by their parliament to make war against the French, and money given by millions to carry it on, and have had their money spent, and no war could be had.

Now we have a king that has fought our battles in person, and willingly run through all the hazards of a bloody war, and has been obliged to use all the persuasions possible to bring us to support him in it.

Former kings would stand still, and see the French over-run Flanders, and ruin our Protestant neighbours, though the parliament and people have entreated them to assist them, and save Flanders from the falling into the hands of the French.

Now we have a king, who solicits the people to enable him to preserve Flanders from falling into the hands of the French, and to stand by and assist our Protestant neighbours. And we on the contrary are willing to see the French and Popish powers, unite and possess Flanders, and every thing else, and glad the Dutch are in danger to be ruined; nay, so willing we are to have the States General destroyed, that *Damn the Dutch* is become a proverb among us.

Formerly we had kings who raised armies in times of peace, and maintained them on sham pretences of a war never designed, and received aids from the parliament three times for the disbanding one army, and having spent the money, left the parliament to do it themselves.

Now we have a king who against his judgment, and, as it now appears, against the nation's interest, consented to disband the army[1] at the first word from his Parliament, though he left all the most powerful of our neighbours with their forces in full pay.

Formerly we had kings who did what they pleased, now we have a king who lets us do what we please.

And yet Englishmen are not contented, but, as it were with our Saviour, when our kings come eating and drinking, they cry, *behold a glutton and a drunkard*;[2] and now they have a king that comes neither eating or drinking, they cry out, *He has a d[evi]l.*[3]

'Tis a vain thing to pretend to open the eyes of the English nation, but by their own immediate danger; any body might have known in former times what the issue of a Popish successor would have been, and some wiser than others told the people of it, and were rewarded with the ax and the halter for their news.

But when that Popish successor came to the crown, and had reduced the liberties and religion of the nation to the last gasp, then those very people, who could not see their danger at a distance, took a fright when it was upon them, and what was the consequence? Nothing but all the blood and treasure of this last war.

Had the nation seen with the same eyes as the late Lord Russell,[4] Earl of Essex,[5] and the Oxford Parliament,[6] did see, could they have been convinced by argument that it was inconsistent with the constitution of this Protestant kingdom to be governed by a Popish prince. Could the b[isho]ps, who threw out that bill,[7] have known that a Popish king would erect a High Ecclesiastic Commission court, and send them to the Tower for refusing him a power to dispense with the laws, this war had been prevented, and the blood of 300,000 English Protestants, who have perished in it, had been saved, all the ships our merchants have lost to the French, had been safe, and the many millions of money, which have been spent, had been in our pockets; all this is owing to the blindness of that age, who could not see the danger of the nation, till it was just upon them.

Now, Gentlemen, this is to give you notice, that the nation is in more danger at this time from abroad, than ever it was then in at home.

The King in his proclamation[8] for the calling a parliament, has done two things which no king his predecessor ever did in our age.

First, he has told us that he has such a confidence in his people, that he is very desirous to meet them, and have their advice in Parliament.

Secondly, he tells us, that what he will advise with them about are matters of the highest importance to the kingdom.

Matters of the highest importance to a kingdom must relate to some of these things, peace and war, the safety of religion, liberty and trade; at least it will be allowed that these are matters of the highest importance to the kingdom.

Now, though I shall not adventure to explain His Majesty's meaning, yet I may be allowed to build the following discourse on the supposition of this explication: and venture to suppose His Majesty had said, that the danger the Protestant religion seems to be in from the formidable appearance of the French power, and the danger our trade is in from the succession of Spain[9] devolving to the House of Bourbon, and the danger of a new flame of war breaking out upon our confederated neighbours, whom our interest, as well as leagues and alliances, oblige us to assist; all these things being matters of the highest importance to the kingdom, he has resolved to call a new parliament, to advise with them about these important things.

And because the circumstances of affairs are such, as may bring us under a necessity of armies, which people are so mightily afraid of; and that the condition the breach of our army has left us in has been such, that if another should be wanting to defend us, 'tis a question where it could be raised.

Wherefore our proper defence, may be one of the important things, for aught we know, about which they are to advise.

And because the debate of an army is a tender nice point, I shall explain myself; I do not mean that a standing army should have been kept up in England in time of peace, but, I say, it had been better for England and all Europe that we had not disarmed ourselves so soon; and if we had disarmed, that we had not so entirely done it all at once; whereby we rendered ourselves so despicable, that the French king has had an opportunity to affront the whole confederacy, in renouncing a league ratified and exchanged, and taking possession of a crown for his grandson, on the new invented title of a last will and testament.

This he would not have adventured to have done, had the English been in a capacity to have possessed Flanders, and to have appeared at sea, to have protected the princes of Italy in their adherence to the Emperor.

But the English having reduced themselves to such a condition, that whenever the French, or anybody else please to quarrel with us, we must be a considerable while before we can be in a posture to act offensively, and the French having so insulted us in the affair of Spain, that it will stand as an effectual proof, whether we are in a capacity to resent an affront or no; His Majesty, who, when in a much lower station, did not use to suffer himself to be so treated, has thought fit to advise with the English parliament in the case.

By advising with the parliament, I understand, informing them of the state of affairs, telling them his own opinion, and asking theirs, proposing the measures he thinks fit to take, and desiring their opinion of the matter, and if they agree with him in the measures which are to be taken, then to propose their making provision in a parliamentary way, for enabling him to prosecute such measures as they agree to.

For to debate and consider matters of so much consequence, the King has directed writs for the calling a new parliament, to meet at Westminster the sixth of February next.

Since then the matter is referred to the people of England, and they are to choose representatives for so great a work, as to advise with a Protestant king about things of the highest importance to the kingdom, give a stander-by leave, Gentlemen, to offer something to the people of England, by way of advice or direction, in the great affair they have before them, and if it be with more freedom than is usual, bear with him for once, because 'tis about matters of the highest importance.

The usual advices given in like cases, formerly (when the elections of members were so corrupted, that indeed advice was necessary, though hopeless) use to be, to choose men that had estates, and men of honesty, men that had interests in the freehold, and in the corporations, and that would not give away their liberties, and the advice was good: and had the country taken that advice, the P[arliament] would not have been huffed by King James into a tacit permission both of a standing army at home, and the dispensing the Popish officers[10] continuing in commission without taking the Test.

But my advice must differ from, though it must include part of, the forementioned particulars; and therefore while I am directing these sheets to the freeholders of England, I beg them to consider in their choice of Parliament-men, that there may be men of estates, and men of honour in the countries,[11] who by some circumstances may not be proper to serve in this parliament, because by prejudice or private principles their judgment may be pre-engaged to the disadvantage of the nation's interest; and since there are such, 'tis necessary, Gentlemen, to caution you,

First, That you be well assured the gentlemen you shall choose are thoroughly engaged with the present circumstances of the nation, and thoroughly satisfied with the present establishment of the government; as Papists are justly excluded by law from coming to parliament because it cannot be expected that a Roman Catholic can be a proper person to consult about the interest of a Protestant kingdom, so it cannot be rational that he who is a declared friend to King James or his interest, can be a proper person to advise with King William about matters of the highest importance to the kingdom; it cannot be rational, that he who would be willing to have this nation return to her obedience to a Popish King, can be a proper person to be consulted with in parliament about securing and defending the Protestant religion; this were to pull down what we intend to build, and would be as proper a way to help us, as a French army maintained in England, would be proper to defend us against Lewis the XIV.

Those men that drink healths to King James, and wish him all manner of prosperity, are they fit men to represent a Protestant nation, and to advise a Protestant prince for the security of the Protestant religion?

Wherefore, Gentlemen, for God's sake, and for your own sakes, take heed, and set a mark on such men; if you choose men disaffected to the present settlement of the nation, friends to the late king, or to his interest, you may be certain, such men will pull back the nation's deliverance, and hinder, not further, that unanimity of councils, which is so much more needful now than ever; can the friends to a Popish prince be fit to represent a Protestant people? I have nothing to say to those we call Jacobites, though I wonder any can be such, and yet be Protestants; but as to their persons I say nothing to them, no, nor to the Papists, provided they keep the peace, but to single such out to serve the nation in a Protestant parliament, and to advise with King William in matters of the highest importance, this is a thing so preposterous, is such a contradiction, that I know not what to say to it; 'tis like going to the Devil with a case of conscience.

Even our adversaries cannot but laugh at the folly of the English nation, that they should choose their enemies to be their counsellors, and think to establish King William, by King James's friends; nothing can sooner complete the ruin of the kingdom, than to fill the House of Commons with Jacobite members, who will be sure to forward anything that tends to division, in order to hinder the nation's happiness; wherefore though I might imagine such advice to be needless, I must insist upon it, that you will avoid such men as either have discovered a disaffection to King William, and the present settlement of the nation, or that have been upheld by that party.

In the next place, Gentlemen, let your eyes be upon men of religion; choose no atheists, Socinians, heretics, Asgillites,[12] and blasphemers.

Had the original of the late war been under the reign of such a body of men, England might have made a will, and given her crown to the Duke d'Berry,[13] as Spain has to the Duke d'Anjou, and have sought protection from the French.

The danger of religion calls for men of religion to consult about it; you can never expect that atheists, Socinians, or Asgillites, will have any tenderness upon their minds for the Protestant religion; Jacobites will as soon support King William, as atheists will preserve the Protestant religion; what concern can they have upon their minds for the Protestant religion, who really are of no religion at all? They'll think it hard to raise any money for the preservation of religion, who fancy all religion to be a trick, and the cheat of the clergy; they can never think the danger of the Protestant religion to signify much, who would not give a shilling to secure it; and they will never give a shilling to secure it, who believe nothing of the matter; besides this, what good laws? what Reformation of Manners?[14] what wholesome orders for the morality of conversation can we expect from men of no religion?

Of all things therefore the members you choose should be men of religion, men of orthodox principles, and moral in practice, and that more especially now, because the security of religion not only here, but over the whole world, may lie before them, and have a great dependance upon their councils.

3. Men of sense; the House of Commons is not a place for fools; the great affairs of the state, the welfare of the kingdom, the public safety, the religion, liberties, and trade, the wealth and honour of the nation, are not things to be debated by green heads; the saying we have, that the House of Commons is a school for statesmen, is an error, in my opinion they

should be all well taught, and thoroughly learned in matters of the highest moment before they come there.

There has always been a sort of Gentlemen in the H[ou]se who use to be called the dead weight, who pass their votes in the House as the poor ignorant freeholders in the country do, just as their landlord, or the justice, or the parson directs; so these gentlemen understanding very little of the matter, give their vote just as Sir such a one does, let it be how it will, or just follow such a party, without judging of the matter.

Pray Gentlemen, if we are ruined, and the Protestant religion must sink in the world, let us do our best to save it; don't let us have cause to say, we sent a parcel of fools about the business that fell into heats and parties, and spent their time to no purpose, for want of knowing better.

Of all employments a fool is the most unfit for a Parliament-man, for there is no manner of business for him; he is capable of saying neither Ay, nor No, but as he is led.

I desire to be understood here what I mean by a fool, not a natural, an idiot, a *Ben* in the *Minories*, a born fool, no, nor a silly, stupid, downright blockheaded fool: but men are fools or wise men, comparatively considered with respect to their several capacities, and their several employments; as he may be a fool of a parson who is a very ingenious artificer; a fool of a clockmaker, and yet be a very good sailor; so a gentleman may be a good horse-racer, a good sports-man, a good swords-man, and yet be a fool of a Parliament-man, therefore so I am to be understood.

That he who is capable to serve his country as a representative in Parliament, ought to be a man of sense, that is, a man of a general knowledge, and receptive of the general notions of things, acquainted with the true interest of his native country, and the general state of it, as to trade, liberties, laws, and common circumstances, and especially of that part of it for which he serves; he ought to know how to deliver his mind with freedom and boldness, and pertinent to the case; and he ought to be able to distinguish between the different circumstances of things, to know when their liberties are encroached upon, and to defend them, and to know how to value a Prince who is faithful to the liberty and interest of his country, and to distinguish such a one from those who have made it their business to oppress and invade the liberties and properties of the people, and betray them and their interest to popish and bloody enemies.

4. Men of years; though 'tis confessed wisdom makes a young man old, yet the House of Commons is not a house for boys; we have seen too many

young men in the House, and rash councils are generally the effect of young heads. Fools and boys would do less harm in the House, and grow wiser by being there, were they but allowed to sit, and not give their votes; but while a boy may do as much mischief as a man, and a fool as a man of sense, 'tis hard the material points of the nation's happiness should be committed either to young or weak heads.

The grandeur of the present French monarchy is not unjustly ascribed to the extraordinary men, who are of the king's council. The parliament of England is the great council of the nation, and on their resolutions depends the prosperity both of king and people. Now if these councils are committed to young heads, the proceedings will be suitable; as he that sends a fool with a message must expect a foolish answer; so he that sends a boy to market, expects to make a child's bargain.

5. Men of honesty. It was formerly said, choose men of estates; the reason was, that they might not be tempted by places and pensions from the Court, to sell the nation's liberties; and indeed the caution was good; but, Gentlemen, the case is altered, the Court and the nation's interest are now all of a side, which they were not then, nor indeed never were since Queen Elizabeth. The King desires we should do nothing but what is for the security and prosperity of religion, and the glory of the nation; the caution about estates can do no harm, but a man's estate does not qualify him at all to judge of the necessity of giving.

The article of estate was only supposed to make a man cautious what he gave, because he was to pay the more of it himself. Now let a man have but sense to know when there is a necessity to give, and that sense backed with honesty, if he has not one groat estate, he will be as cautious of giving away the nation's money, as he would be of his own: to desire men should have estates, that their interest should make them shy, and backward to give money, supposes at the same time they should want both sense and honesty. Sense, that they could not value the nation's money, unless they were to pay part of it themselves; and honesty, that they would not take as much care of giving away the nation's money as their own. Wherefore do but choose men of honesty, and I do not lay so great a stress upon a man's estate. If there was anybody to bribe them, something might be said, but that trade is over, (God be thanked) King William has no need for it, and King James can't afford it, and so that fear ceases.

The last character I shall recommend for your choice is, let them be men of morals.

Rakes and beaus are no more fit to sit in the House of Commons, than fools and knaves. 'Tis hard we should put the work of reformation into the hands of such, whose own conversation is vicious and scandalous. A drunken parson is a very improper agent to reform a parish, a lewd swearing Justice is not likely to reform the country, no more is a vicious immoral parliament likely to reform a nation. Reformation of Manners is an article of the highest importance to the kingdom; the King has recommended it to every parliament, and yet we find it very much retarded; it goes on so heavily, that the proceedings are hardly visible; and till you have a reformed parliament, you cannot expect a parliament of reformers.

Unless our members are men of morals, we must expect very few laws against immorality; and if there should such clean things come out of an unclean, it would be all heterodox, and unnatural; 'twould be like a monstrous birth, the parent would be afraid of it, and it would be ashamed of its parent.

Besides, how can ye expect that God should accept of the offering dedicated by impure hands? The work can never be supposed to prosper while the undertakers plead for God, and at the same time sacrifice to the Devil.

'Tis true, that God oftentimes works by unlikely instruments, but 'tis not often that he works by contraries; Jehu[15] was made use of to bring to pass the ruin God had foretold to the family of Ahab, but 'twas a Josiah and a Jehosaphat,[16] for whom God reserved the work of reformation, and the destruction of idolatry.

But allow that God may make use of improper methods, and unlikely instruments when he pleases to bring to pass what his Providence has designed, yet we are not to confine him to show his power, and oblige him to make use of such instruments, as he can have no pleasure in, least he should think fit to refuse his blessing, and make the work abortive, or at least delay his concurrence to the work of our reformation, till we shall think fit to choose such persons for the carrying it on, as are fit to be employed in so great a work.

FINIS.

TRIBUNE OF THE PEOPLE

Mr. S——R·

THE Enclosed *Memorial you are Charg'd with, in the behalf of many Thousands of the good People of* England.
There is neither **Popish,** Jacobite, Seditious, Court, *or Party Interest concern'd in it ;* but honesty and Truth.

You are commanded by Two Hundred Thousand *Englishmen, to deliver it to the H——e of C——s, and to inform them that it is no Banter, but Serious Truth ; and a Serious Regard to it is expected ; nothing but Justice, and their Duty is required, and it is required by them who have both a Right to Require, and Power to Compel, viz. the people of* England.

We could have come to the House *Strong enough to Obleige them to hear us, but we have avoided any Tumults, not desiring to Embroil, but to Save our Native Country.*

If you refuse to Communicate it to them, you will find cause in a short time to Repent it

To R——t H——y Esq; S——r to the H——e of C——s,
These.

The Memorial.

To the K——s, C——s, and B——s in P——t Assembled.

A Memorial,
From the Gentlemen, Free-holders, and Inhabitants of the Counties of—— in behalf of themselves, and many Thousands of the good people of *England.*

Gentlemen,
It were to be wish'd you were Men of that Temper, and possess'd of so much Honour, as to bear with the Truth, tho' it be against you : Especially from us who have so much Right to tell it you, but since, Even Petitions to you from your Masters, (for such are the people who Chose you) are so Haughtily receiv'd, as with the Committing the Authors to Illegal Custody ; you must give us leave to give you this fair Notice of your Misbehaviour, without Exposing our Names.

If you think fit to rectifie your Errors, you will do well, and possibly may hear no more of us ; but if not, assure your selves the Nation will not long hide their Resentments. And tho' there are no stated Proceeding to bring you to your Duty, yet the great Law of Reason says, and all Nations allow, that whatever Power is above Law, its Burthensom and Ty-rannical ; and may be reduc'd by *Extrajudicial* Methods : You are not above the People's Resentments, they that made you Members, may reduce you to the same Rank from whence they chose you ; and may give you a Tast of their abused kindness, in Terms you may not be pleas'd with.

When the People of *England* Assembl'd in Convention, Presented the Crown to His Pre-sent Majesty, they annexed a Declaration of the Rights of the People, in which was Express-'d what was Illegal and Arbitrary in the former Reign, and what was claim'd as of Right to be done by Succeedings Kings of *England.*

In like manner, here follows, *Gentlemen,* a short abridgment of the Nations Grievances, and of your Illegal and Unwarrantable Practices ; and a Claim of Right which we make in the Name of our Selves, and such of the good People of *England,* as are justly Allarum'd at your Proceedings.

I. To

Legion's Memorial

Begin: Mr. S[peake]r.

The enclosed Memorial you are charged with, in the behalf of many thousands of the good People of England.

There is neither Popish, Jacobite, seditious, court, or party interest concerned in it; but honesty and truth.

You are commanded by two hundred thousand Englishmen, to deliver it to the H[ous]e of C[ommon]s, and to inform them that it is no banter, but serious truth; and a serious regard to it is expected; nothing but justice, and their duty is required, and it is required by them who have both a right to require, and power to compel, *viz.* the People of England.

We could have come to the House, strong enough to oblige them to hear us, but we have avoided any tumults, not desiring to embroil, but to save our native country.

If you refuse to communicate it to them, you will find cause in a short time to repent it.

To R[ober]t H[arle]y, Esq.; S[peake]r to the H[ous]e of C[ommon]s, these

THE MEMORIAL

To the K[night]s, C[ommon]s, and B[urgesse]s in P[arliamen]t assembled.

A Memorial from the gentlemen, freeholders, and inhabitants of the counties of ———— in behalf of themselves, and many thousands of the good People of England.

Gentlemen,

It were to be wished you were men of that temper, and possessed of so much honour, as to bear with the truth, though it be against you; especially

72

from us who have so much right to tell it to you; but since even Petitions to you from your masters (for such are the People who chose you) are so haughtily received, as with the committing the authors to illegal custody;[1] you must give us leave to give you this fair notice of your misbehaviour, without exposing our names.

If you think fit to rectify your errors, you will do well, and possibly may hear no more of us; but if not assure yourselves the nation will not long hide their resentments. And though there are no stated proceeding to bring you to your duty, yet the great law of reason, says, and all nations allow, that whatever power is above law, is burthensome and tyrannical; and may be reduced by extrajudicial methods: you are not above the People's resentments, they that made you Members, may reduce you to the same rank from whence they chose you; and may give you a taste of their abused kindness, in terms you may not be pleased with.

When the People of England assembled in Convention,[2] presented the crown to His present Majesty, they annexed a Declaration of the Rights of the People, in which was expressed what was illegal and arbitrary in the former reign, and what was claimed as of right to be done by succeeding Kings of England.

In like manner, here follows, Gentlemen, a short abridgment of the nation's grievances, and of your illegal and unwarrantable practices; and a claim of right which we make in the name of ourselves, and such of the good People of England, as are justly alarmed at your proceedings.

I. To raise funds, for money, and declare by borrowing clauses, that whosoever advances money on those funds, shall be re-imbursed out of the next aids, if the funds fall short; and then give subsequent funds, without transferring the deficiency of the former, is a horrible cheat on the subject who lent the money; a breach of public faith, and destructive to the honour and credit of Parliaments.

II. To imprison men who are not your own Members, by no proceedings but a vote of your House, and to continue them in custody, *sine die,*[3] is illegal; a notorious breach of the liberty of the People; setting up a dispensing power[4] in the House of Commons, which your fathers never pretended to; bidding defiance to the *Habeas Corpus* Act, which is the bulwark of personal liberty, destructive of the laws, and betraying the trust reposed in you. The King at the same time being obliged to ask you leave to continue in custody the horrid assassinators[5] of his person.

III. Committing to custody those gentlemen, who at the command of the People (whose servants you are) did in a peaceable way put you in mind of your duty, is illegal and injurious; destructive of the subject's liberty of petitioning for redress of grievances, which has by all Parliaments before you, been acknowledged to be their undoubted right.

IV. Voting a petition from the gentlemen of Kent insolent, is ridiculous and impertinent, because the freeholders of England are your superiors; and is a contradiction in itself, and a contempt of the English freedom, and contrary to the nature of Parliamentary power.

V. Voting people guilty of bribery and ill practices, and committing them as aforesaid, without bail, and then upon submission, and kneeling to your House, discharging them; exacting exorbitant fees by your officers is illegal, betraying the justice of the nation, selling the liberty of the subject, encouraging the extortion and villainy of gaolers and officers; and discontinuing the legal prosecutions of offenders in the ordinary course of law.

VI. Prosecuting the crime of bribery in some to serve a party, and then proceed no further, though proof lay before you, is partial and unjust; and a scandal upon the honour of Parliaments.

VII. Voting the Treaty of Partition[6] fatal to Europe, because it gave so much of the Spanish dominions to the French, and not concern yourselves to prevent their taking possession of it all. Deserting the Dutch[7] when the French are at their doors, till it be almost too late to help them; is unjust to our treaties, and unkind to our confederates, dishonourable to the English nation, and shew you very negligent of the safety of England, and of our Protestant neighbours.

VIII. Ordering immediate hearings to trifling petitions, to please parties in elections; and postpone the petition of a widow for the blood of her murthered daughter, without giving it a reading; is an illegal delay of justice, dishonourable to the public justice of the nation.

IX. Addressing the King to displace his friends[8] upon bare surmises, before a legal trial or article proved, is illegal, and inverting the law, and making execution go before judgment; contrary to the true sense of the law, which esteems every man a good man till something appears to the contrary.

X. Delaying proceedings upon capital impeachments, to blast the reputation of the persons, without proving the fact; is illegal and oppressive, destructive of the liberty of Englishmen, a delay of justice, and a reproach to Parliaments.

XI. Suffering saucy and indecent reproaches upon His Majesty's person to be publicly made in your House; particularly by that impudent scandal of Parliaments J[oh]n H[o]w,[9] without shewing such resentments as you ought to do, the said J[oh]n H[o]w saying openly 'That His Majesty had made a felonious treaty to rob his neighbours', insinuating that the Partition Treaty (which was every way as just as blowing up one man's house to save another's) 'was a combination of the King to rob the Crown of Spain of its due'. This is making a Billingsgate[10] of the House, and setting up to bully your Sovereign, contrary to the intent and meaning of that freedom of speech which you claim as a right; is scandalous to Parliaments; undutiful and unmannerly, and a reproach to the whole nation.

XII. Your S[peake]r exacting the exorbitant rate of 10*l. per diem* for the V[ote]s,[11] and giving the printer encouragement to raise it on the People, by selling them at 4*d.* per sheet; is an illegal and arbitrary exaction, dishonourable to the House, and burthensome to the people.

XIII. Neglecting still to pay the nation's debts, compounding for interest, and postponing petitions; is illegal, dishonourable, and destructive of the public faith.

XIV. Publicly neglecting the great work of Reformation of Manners,[12] though often pressed to it by the King, to the great dishonour of God, and encouragement of vice; is a neglect of your duty, and an abuse of the trust reposed in you, by God, His Majesty, and the People.

XV. Being scandalously vicious yourselves, both in your morals and religion; lewd in life, and erroneous in doctrine, having public blasphemers and impudent deniers of the divinity of our Saviour among you, and suffering them unreproved and unpunished, to the infinite regret of all good Christians, and the just abhorrence of the whole nation.

Wherefore, in the said prospect of the impending ruin of our native country, while Parliaments (which ought to be the security and defence of our laws and constitution) betray their trust, and abuse the people whom they should protect: and no other way being left us, but that force which we are very loath to make use of, that posterity may know we did not insensibly fall under the tyranny of a prevailing party, we do hereby claim and declare,

1. That it is the undoubted right of the People of England, in case their representatives in Parliament do not proceed according to their duty, and the People's interest, to inform them of their dislike, disown their actions, and to direct them to such things as they think fit, either by Petition, Address, Proposal, Memorial, or any other peaceable way.

2. That the House of Commons, separately and otherwise than by Bill legally passed into an Act, have no legal power to suspend or dispense with the laws of the land, any more than the King has by his prerogative.

3. That the House of Commons has no legal power to imprison any person, or commit them to custody of serjeants, or otherwise (their own members except) but ought to address the King, to cause any person, on good grounds, to be apprehended; which person so apprehended, ought to have the benefit of the *Habeas Corpus* Act, and be fairly brought to trial, by due course of law.

4. That if the House of Commons, in breach of the laws and liberties of the People, do betray the trust reposed in them, and act negligently or arbitrarily and illegally, it is the undoubted right of the People of England to call them to an account for the same, and by convention, assembly or force, may proceed against them as traitors and betrayers of their country.

These things we think proper to declare, as the unquestioned right of the People of England, whom you serve, and in pursuance of that right (avoiding the ceremony of petitioning our inferiors, for such you are by your present circumstances, as the person sent is less than the sender). We do publicly protest against all your foresaid illegal actions, and in the name of ourselves, and of the good People of England, do require and demand

1. That all the public just debts of the nation be forthwith paid and discharged.

2. That all persons illegally imprisoned, as aforesaid, be either immediately discharged, or admitted to bail, as by law they ought to be; and the liberty of the subject recognized and restored.

3. That J[oh]n H[o]w aforesaid, be obliged to ask his Majesty pardon for his vile reflections, or be immediately expelled the House.

4. That the growing power of France be taken into consideration; the succession of the Emperor to the crown of Spain supported, our Protestant neighbours protected, as the true interest of England, and the Protestant religion requires.

5. That the French King be obliged to quit Flanders, or that his Majesty be addressed to declare war against him.

6. That suitable supplies be granted to his Majesty, for the putting all these necessary things in execution, and that care be taken, that such taxes as are raised, may be more equally assessed and collected, and scandalous deficiencies prevented.

7. That the thanks of the House may be given to those gentlemen, who so gallantly appeared in the behalf of their country, with the Kentish Petition, and have been so scandalously used for it.

Thus, gentlemen, you have your duty laid before you, which it is hoped you will think of; but if you continue to neglect it, you may expect to be treated according to the resentments of an injured nation; for Englishmen are no more to be slaves to Parliaments, than to a King.

Our name is Legion, and we are many.[13]

POSTSCRIPT

If you require to have this Memorial signed with our names, it shall be done on your first orders, and personally presented.

The Original

POWER

OF THE

COLLECTIVE BODY

OF THE

People of England,

Examined and Afferted.

LONDON,

Printed in the Year 1702.

To the King.

SIR,

'Tis not the least of the extraordinaries of your Majesty's character, that as you are king of your people, so you are the people's king.

This title, as it is the most glorious, so is it the most indisputable in the world.

God himself appointed, the prophet proclaimed, but the people's assent was the finishing the royal authority of the first king of Israel.

Your Majesty, among all the blessings of your reign, has restored this, as the best of all our enjoyments, the full liberty of original right in its actings and exercise.

Former reigns have invaded it, and the last thought it totally suppressed, but as liberty revived under your Majesty's just authority, this was the first flower she brought forth.

The author of these sheets humbly hopes, that what your Majesty has so gloriously restored, what our laws and constitution have declared and settled, and what truth and justice openly appears for, he may be allowed to vindicate.

Your Majesty knows too well the nature of government, to think it at all the less honourable, or the more precarious, for being devolved from and centered in the consent of your people.

The pretence of patriarchal authority, had it really an uninterrupted succession, can never be supported against the demonstrated practice of all nations; but being also divested of the chief support it might have had, if that succession could have been proved: the authority of governors *jure divino*[1] has sunk ignominiously to the ground, as a preposterous and inconsistent forgery.

And yet, if the *vox populi* be, as 'tis generally allowed, *vox dei*,[2] your Majesty's right to these kingdoms *jure divino* is more plain than any of your predecessors'.

How happy are these nations, after all the oppressions and tyranny of arbitrary rulers, to obtain a king who reigns by the universal voice of the people, and has the greatest share in their affections that ever any prince enjoyed, Queen Elizabeth only excepted.

And how vain are the attempts of a neighbouring prince, to nurse up a contemptible impostor,[3] upon the pretence of forming a claim on the foundation of but a pretended succession, against the consent of the general suffrage of the nation.

To what purpose shall all the proofs of his legitimacy be, supposing it could be made out, when the universal voice of the people, already expressed in enacted laws, shall answer, we will not have this man to reign.

May this affection of your subjects continue to the latest hour of your life, and may your satisfaction be such as may convince the world, that the chiefest felicity of a crown consists in the affections, as the first authority of it derives from the consent, of the people.

To the Lords Spiritual and Temporal, and the Commons of England.

My Lords and Gentlemen,
The vindication of the original right of all men to the government of themselves, is so far from a derogation from, that it is a confirmation of your legal authority.

Your Lordships, who are of the nobility, have your original right, your titles and dignities from the greatness of your shares in the freeholds of the nation: if merit has raised any of your ancestors to distinguishing honours, or, if the royal favours of Princes has dignified families, it has always been thought fit to bestow or enable them to purchase some portion of the freehold of England to be annexed to the said titles, to make such dignity rational, as well as to support the succession of honour.

From hence you are vested with sovereign judicature, as being the properest to be trusted with the distribution of justice in that country, of which you were supposed to have, and once had, the principal propriety.

From hence you sit in Parliament as a branch of our constitution, being part of the collective body, representing nobody but yourselves; and as a testimony that the original of all power centres in the whole.

The rest of the freeholders have originally a right to sit there with you, but being too numerous a body, they have long since agreed that whenever the King thinks fit to advise with his people, they will choose a certain few out of their great body to meet together with your Lordships.

Here, in short, is the original of parliaments; and here, if power at any time meet with a cest[4] of government, bishops and thrones become vacant, to this original, all power of course returns. This is the happy centre in the great circle of politic order.

From hence at the late Revolution, when the King deserted the administration, and His present Majesty was in arms in England, nature directed the people to have recourse to your Lordships, and to desire your appearance as the heads of the great collective body; and all the champions for the great arguments of divine right could not in that exigence have recourse to one precedent, nor to one rule of proceeding, but what nature would have dictated to the meanest judgment, *viz.* that the nation being left without a governor, the proprietors should meet to consider of another.

And you gentlemen of the House of Commons, who are the representatives of your country, you are this great collective body in miniature, you are an abridgment of the many volumes of the English nation.

To you they have trusted jointly with the King and the Lords, the power of making laws, raising taxes, and impeaching criminals: but how? 'Tis in the name of all the Commons of England, whose representatives you are.

All your power is yours, as you are a full and free representative. I nowhere attempt to prove what powers you have not, possibly the extent of your legal authority was never fully understood, nor have you ever thought fit to explain it. But this I may be bold to advance, that whatever powers you have, or may have, you cannot exercise but in the name of the Commons of England, and you enjoy them as their representative, and for their use.

All this is not said to lessen your authority; nor can it be the interest of any English freeholder to lessen the authority of the Commons assembled in Parliament.

You are the conservators of our liberties, the expositors of our laws, the leviers of our taxes, and the redressors of our grievances, the King's best counsellors, and the people's last refuge.

But if you are dissolved, for you are not immortal; or if you are deceived, for you are not infallible; 'twas never yet supposed, till very lately, that all power dies with you.

You may die, but the People remain; you may be dissolved, and all immediate right may cease; power may have its intervals, and crowns their interregnum; but original power endures to the same eternity the world endures to: and while there is people, there may be a legal authority delegated, though all succession of substituted power were at an end.

Nor have I advanced any new doctrine, nothing but what is as ancient as nature, and born into the world with our reason: and I think it would be a sin against the Parliament of England, to suggest that they would be offended either with the doctrine or with the author, since 'tis what their own authority is built upon, and what the laws of England have given their assent unto by confirming the acts of the last Collective Body[5] of the People, from whence the present settlement of the nation does derive.

Wherefore I make no apology for protection or favour as to the fact; as to errors of language I am ready to ask pardon if I offend, declaring my intention is neither for nor against either person or party. As there is but one interest in the nation, I wish there were but one party, and that party would adhere to unbiased justice, and pursue the honour and interest of the Protestant religion, and the English liberty.

The Original Right[6] of the People of England, Examined and Asserted.

I have observed, when interest obliges any person or party to defend the cause they have espoused, they please themselves with fancying they conceal their private designs, by covering their discourses with gay titles.

Like a late Act of Parliament, which in the preamble calls itself, *An Act for the Relief of Creditors*, but in its effect was really *An Act for the Relief of Debtors*.

Thus some gentlemen place fine specious titles on their books, as *Jure Populi Anglicani*,[7] *A Vindication of the Rights of the Commons of England*,[8] and a *Vindication of the Rights of the Lords*,[9] and the like; and with large and high encomiums upon the excellency of our constitution, treat the levity of some people's judgments with fine notions; whereas the true end and design is defending the interest and party they have espoused.

The defence of the rights of the representative body of the people, understood by the name of the Commons of England in Parliament, is a great point; and so plain are their rights, that 'tis no extraordinary task to defend them: but for any man to advance, that they are so august an assembly that no objection ought to be made to their actions, nor no reflection upon their conduct, though the fact be true; and that it is not to be examined whether the thing said be true, but what authority the person speaking has to say it, is a doctrine wholly new, and seems to me to be a badge of more slavery to our own representatives than ever the people of England owes them, or than ever they themselves expected.

This therefore, together with some invasions of the people's rights made public by several modern authors, are the reasons why I have adventured, being wholly disinterested and unconcerned either for persons or parties, to make a short essay at declaring the rights of the people of England, not representatively but collectively considered.

And with due deference to the representative body of the nation, I hope I may say, it can be no diminution of their rights, to assert the rights of that body from whom they derive the powers and privileges of their House, and which are the very foundation of their being. For if the original right of the people be overthrown, the power of the representative, which is subsequent and subordinate, must die of itself.

And because I have to do rather with reason and the nature of the thing, than with laws and precedents, I shall make but very little use of authors, and quotations of statutes, since fundamentals and principles both in law and argument, are superiour to laws or examples.

To come directly to what I design in the following papers, 'tis necessary to lay down some maxims, other than what a late author has furnished us with.

1. That *salus populi suprema lex*,[10] all government, and consequently our whole constitution, was originally designed, and is maintained, for the support of the people's property, who are the governed.

2. That all the members of government, whether King, Lords or Commons, if they invert the great end of their institution, the public good, cease to be in the same public capacity,

> And power retreats to its original.
> *True-Born Englishman*, l. 819

3. That no collective or representative body of men whatsoever, in matters of politics any more than religion, are or ever have been infallible.

4. That reason is the test and touch-stone of laws, and that all law or power that is contradictory to reason, is *ipso facto* void in itself, and ought not to be obeyed.

These four generals run through the whole following discourse.

Some other maxims less general are the consequence of these; as,

First, that such laws as are agreeable to reason and justice being once made, are binding both to King, Lords and Commons, either separately, or conjunctively, till they are actually repealed in due form.

That if either of the three powers do dispense with, suspend, or otherwise break any of the known laws so made, they injure the constitution; and the power so acting ought to be restrained by the other powers not concurring according to what is lately allowed, *That every branch of power is designed as a check upon each other.*

But if all the three powers should join in such an irregular action, the constitution suffers a convulsion, dies, and is dissolved of course.

Nor does it suffice to say, that King, Lords and Commons can do no wrong, since the mutual consent of parties, on which that foolish maxim[11] is grounded, does not extend to every action King, Lords and Commons are capable of doing.

There are laws which respect the common rights of the people, as they are the parties to be governed, and with respect to these the King can do no wrong, but all is laid upon his ministers — who are accountable.

And there are laws which particularly respect the constitution, the King, Lords and Commons, as they are the parties governing. In this regard each branch may wrong and oppress the other, or all together may do wrong to the people they are made to govern.

The King may invade the people's properties, and if the Lords and Commons omit to defend and protect them, they all do wrong by a tacit approving those abuses they ought to oppose.

The Commons may extend their power to an exorbitant degree, in imprisoning the subjects, dispensing with the *habeas corpus* act, giving unlimited power to their sergeant to oppress the people in his custody, withholding writs of election from boroughs and towns, and several other ways; which if they are not checked either by the King or the Lords, they are altogether parties to the wrong, and the subject is apparently injured.

The Lords may err in judicature, and deny justice to the Commons, or delay it upon punctilios and studied occasions, and if neither the King nor the Commons take care to prevent it, delinquents are excused, and criminals encouraged, and all are guilty of the breach of common justice.

That to prevent this, it is absolutely necessary that in matters of dispute the single powers should be governed by the joint, and that nothing should so be insisted upon as to break the correspondence.

And that the three should be directed by the law; and where that is silent, by reason.

That every person concerned in the law is in his measure a judge of the reason, and therefore in his proper place ought to be allowed to give his reason in case of dissent.

That every single power has an absolute negative upon the acts of the other; and if the people, who are without doors, find reason to object, they may do it by petition.[12]

But because under pretence of petitioning, seditious and turbulent people may foment disturbances, tumults and disorders; the subject's right of petitioning being yet recognized and preserved, the circumstances of such petitions are regulated by laws, as to the numbers and qualities of the persons petitioning.

But the laws have nowhere prescribed the petitioners to any form of words, and therefore no pretence of indecency of expression can be so criminal as to be destructive of the constitution; because, though it may deserve the resentment of the petitioned, yet it is not an illegal act, nor a breach of any law.

And yet the representative body of the people ought not to be bantered[13] or affronted neither, at the will and pleasure of any private person without doors, who finds cause to petition them.

But if any expression be offensive to the House, it seems reasonable that the persons who are concerned therein should be required to explain themselves: and if upon such explanation the House find no satisfaction as to the particular affront, they are at liberty to proceed as the law directs; but no otherwise.

And to me, the silence of the law in that case seems to imply, that rejecting the petition is a contempt due to any indecency of that nature, and as much resentment as the nature of the thing requires: but as to breaking in upon personal liberty, which is a thing the law is so tender of, and has made so strong a fence about, I dare not affirm 'tis a justifiable procedure; no, not in the House of Commons.

It is alleged, that it has been practiced by all parliaments; which is to me far from an argument to prove the legality of it.

I think it may pass for a maxim, that a man cannot be legally punished for a crime which there is no law to prosecute. Now since there is no law to prosecute a man for indecency of expression in a petition to the House of Commons, it remains a doubt with me how they can be legally punished.

Precedents are of use to the Houses of Parliament where the laws are silent, in things relating to themselves, and are doubtless a sufficient authority to act from. But whether any precedent, usage or custom, of any body of men whatever, can make a thing lawful which the laws have expressly forbid, remains a doubt with me.

It were to be wished some of our Parliaments would think fit, at one time or another, to clear up the point of the authority of the House of Commons in case of imprisoning such as are not of their House, that having the matter stated by those who are the only expositors of our laws, we might be troubled with no more *Legion Libels*,[14] to tell them what is, or is not, legal in their proceedings.

The good of the people governed is the end of all government, and the reason and original of governors; and upon this foundation it is that it has been the practice of all nations, and of this in particular, that if the maladministration of governors have extended to tyranny and oppression, to destruction of right and justice, overthrowing the constitution, and abusing the people, the people have thought it lawful to reassume the right of government into their own hands, and to reduce their governors to reason.

The present happy restoring of our liberty and constitution is owing to this fundamental maxim, according to a late author,

> That Kings, when they descend to tyranny,
> Dissolve the bond, and leave the subject free.
> *True-Born Englishman*, ll. 804—5

If the people are justifiable in this procedure against the King, I hope I shall not be censured if I say, that if any one should ask me, whether they have not the same right, in the same cases, against any of the three heads of the constitution, I dare not answer in the negative.

I may be allowed to suppose anything which is possible; and I will therefore venture to suppose, that in the late King's reign the House of

Commons, then sitting, had voted the restoration of Popery in England, in compliance with the King's inclination.

I doubt not but it had been lawful for the Grand Juries, Justices of the Peace, and freeholders of any county, or of every county, to have petitioned the House of Commons not to proceed in giving up their religion and laws.

And in case of refusal there, they might petition the House of Lords not to have passed such a bill.

And in case of refusal there, they might petition the King, and put him in mind of his coronation engagement.

And in case of refusal to that petition, they might petition the King again to dissolve the parliament, or otherwise to protect their liberties and religion.

And if all these peaceable applications failed, I doubt not but they might associate for their mutual defence against any invasion of their liberties and religion, and apply themselves to any neighbouring power or potentate for assistance and protection.

If this be not true, I can give but a slender account of our late Revolution; which nevertheless I think to be founded upon the exact principles of reason and justice.

Nor will the pretence of indecency of expression be any argument to bar the subject of his right of petitioning, or justify the ill treatment of such petitioners: for the case exceedingly differs from the supposed case of the Lord Chancellor, and the complaint which a late author brings,[15] in desiring the Lord Chancellor to turn his plausible speeches into righteous decrees.

First of all, the freeholders of England stand in a different capacity to the members of the House, who are their trustees, their attorneys, their representatives, from that of a complainant in Chancery to the judge of that court.

Secondly, the Lord Chancellor has a right by law to commit for personal affronts offered in court: whether the House of Commons have the same right by law I know not, nor will not undertake to determine; but I do not find that worthy member has yet attempted to prove they have.

Thirdly, this is arguing from the inferior court to the Parliament of England, which is directly against Sir H. M.'s late position, *fol.* 4. where he had, as I suppose, forgot that he had laid us down this rule.

When there is occasion to debate concerning these superior powers of King, Lords and Commons, we must not argue like lawyers in Westminster-Hall, from the narrow foundation of private causes of meum and tuum; but like statesmen and senators, from the large and noble foundation of government, and the general good of the King and people.

Fourthly, but I am also informed, that the case is wrong too, and that even in that instance: the Lord Chancellor had no power to commit to the Fleet,[16] unless it were an affront, *viva voce*,[17] in court.

Nor would it be any argument in the supposed case I am upon, for anybody to say, that the occasion must concern that part of the country[18] from whence such petition is brought: for the introducing of Popery would certainly concern every county of England.

And suppose again, the people thought themselves in danger of an invasion from France, and thereupon the counties of Kent and Sussex should have petitioned the House to take them into consideration, who, in such case, were like to be the seat of the war, and first exposed to the enemy; would anybody say, the occasion did not arise in the county from whence such petition did proceed?

In this universal right of the people consists our general safety: for notwithstanding all the beauty of our constitution, and the exact symmetry of its parts, about which some have been so very elegant, this noble well-contrived system has been overwhelmed; the government has been inverted, the people's liberties have been trampled on, and parliaments have been rendered useless and insignificant: and what has restored us? The last resort has been to the People; *Vox Dei* has been found there, not in the representatives, but in their original the represented.

And what has been the engine that has led the nation to it? The reason and nature of the thing. Reason governs men when they are masters of their senses, as naturally as fire flies upwards, or water descends.

For what is it that King, Lords and Commons assemble? 'Tis to reason together concerning the weighty matters of the state, and to act and do for the good of the people, what shall be agreeable to reason and justice.

I grant 'tis reasonable that every branch should be vested with due powers, and those powers be equally distributed.

But if they must be vested with power, some body must vest them with it: if these powers must be distributed, some body must distribute them. So that:

There must be some power prior to the power of King, Lords and Commons, from which, as the streams from the fountain, the power of King, Lords and Commons is derived.

And what are all the different terms which statesmen turn so often into fine words to serve their ends; as, reason of state, public good, the Commonwealth, the English constitution, the Government, the laws of England, the liberties of England, the fleets, the armies, the militia of England, the trade, the manufactures of England? All are but several terms drawn from and reducible to the great term, the People of England. That's the general, which contains all the particulars, and which had all power before any of the particulars had a being. And from this consideration it is, that some who yet would be opposers of this doctrine, say, when it serves their turn, that all the great offices which have the title of England annexed to them, ought to be nominated and approved by the people of England, as the High Chancellor of England, High Admiral of England, and the like.

That power which is original, is superior; God is the fountain of all power, and therefore is the supreme: and if we could suppose a prior and original of the divine power, that original would be God, and be superior; for all subsequent power must be subject and inferior to the precedent.

The power vested in the three heads of our constitution is vested in them by the people of England, who were a people before there was such a thing as a constitution.

And the nature of the thing, is the reason of the thing: it was vested in them by the people, because the people were the only original of their power, being the only power prior to the constitution.

For the public good of these people, a constitution and government was originally formed; from the mutual consent of these people the powers and authorities of this constitution are derived: and for the preservation of this constitution, and enabling it to answer the ends of its institution in the best manner possible, those powers were divided.

The second maxim is a rational natural consequence of the former, that at the final, casual, or any other determination[19] of this constitution, the powers are dissolved, and all authority must derive *de novo* from the first fountain, original and cause of all constitutions, the governed.

Now it cannot be supposed this original fountain should give up all its waters, but that it reserves a power of supplying the streams: nor has the stream any power to turn back upon the fountain, and invert its own original. All such motions are eccentric and unnatural.

There must always remain a supreme power in the original to supply, in case of the dissolution of delegated power.

The people of England have delegated all the executive power in the King, the legislative in the King, Lords and Commons, the sovereign judicature in the Lords; the remainder is reserved in themselves, and not committed, no, not to their representatives: all powers delegated are to one great end and purpose, and no other, and that is the public good: if either or all the branches to whom this power is delegated desert the design, the end of their power, the right they have to that power ceases, and they become tyrants and usurpers of a power they have no right to.

The instance has been visible as to kings in our days; and history is full of precedents in all ages, and in all nations; particularly in Spain, in Portugal, in Swedeland, in France, and in Poland.

But in England, the late Revolution is a particular instance of the exercise of this power.

King James on the approach of a foreign army, and the general recourse of the people to arms, fled out of the kingdom. What must the people of England do? They had no reason to run after him to be governed there; there was no body to call a parliament, so the constitution was entirely dissolved.

The original of power, the People, assembled in Convention, to consider of delegating new powers for their future government, and accordingly made a new settlement of the crown, a new declaration of right, and a new representative of the people; and some have thought they ought to have given a new sanction to all precedent laws.

It remains to argue from hence, but what course must the people of England take, if their representatives exercise the power intrusted with them, to the ruin of the constitution?

It has been advanced, that every man must submit, and not presume to argue against it upon any supposition of mismanagement.

I can see no reason given to confirm such a position; for unless we will place the original of power in the persons representing, not in the persons represented, it cannot be made out that there ought to be no complaint upon the score of mismanagement.

It is not the design of this discourse to lessen the authority of Parliament: but all power must centre somewhere. If it is in the three branches of the constitution, 'tis there inherently and originally, or it is there by deputation. If it be there by deputation, then there must be a power deputing, and that must be both prior, and consequently superior to the deputed, as before.

If we will come off of this, we must fly to the old weak refuge of a power *jure divino*, a doctrine which the most famed pretenders to, have lived to be ashamed of; and whose foundation is so weak, that 'tis not worth while to expose it.

I should therefore have been very glad, that for the perfecting the defence of the English constitution, the gentlemen who have begun so well, would have gone forward to recognize the power of the people of England, and their undoubted right to judge of the infractions made in their constitution, by either parties abusing the particular powers vested in them; and inverting them, by turning them against the people they are designed to defend.

That they would have stated fairly what the people of England are to do, if their representatives shall hereafter betray the liberties or religion of the people they are intrusted with the defence of.

What by the laws of nature and reason is to be expected, and what by the laws of our constitution are allowed.

To say, it cannot be supposed the House of Commons can ever betray their trust, is a compliment no man is bound to make them, *humanum est errare*.[20] We have seen parliaments err, and do what succeeding parliaments have thought fit to undo: and as that which has been may be, so that may be which never has been before.

We have seen parliaments comply with kings to the ruin of the nation; and we have seen parliaments quarrel with kings, to the overturning of the constitution, dissolving the House of Lords, and suppressing the monarchy.

We have seen parliaments concur so with the fate and fortunes of princes, as to comply backward and forward, in deposing and reinthroning alternately two kings as often as victory put power into their hands, I mean Henry the Sixth, and Edward the Fourth, who were kings and prisoners five or six times, and always the parliament complied with the conquerors.

We have seen a parliament of England confirm the usurpation of Richard the Third, the greatest tyrant and most bloody man that ever England brought forth.

We have seen a parliament confirm Henry the Seventh, who really had no right at all by succession, and rescind all the precedent parliament had done.

Afterwards, in matters of religion, King Henry the Eighth made a popish parliament pull down the supremacy of Rome, and set up the King's; and afterwards suppress all the religious houses in the nation. His son pulled up Popery by the roots, and planted the Reformation, still the parliament complied. Queen Mary re-established Popery, and unravelled both the Reformation of King Edward, and all the acts both of Church and State relating to her mother's divorce, and still the parliament consented. One parliament voted Queen Mary legitimate, and Queen Elizabeth a bastard: another parliament legitimated Queen Elizabeth, and repudiated Queen Mary. Queen Elizabeth undid all her sister had done, and suppressed all the proceedings of Popery; and all was by authority of parliament.

So that this parliamentary branch of power is no more infallible than the kingly.

Had Sir H. M. gone on to have recognized the people's right to preserve their own liberties in case of failure in any, or in all the branches of the constituted power, he had completed his *Vindication of the Commons of England*, which no man could have done better than himself.

If then upon the subversion of the laws, and interruption of common justice, the centre of power is in the people, *a fortiori* the people are also concerned in every degree of such a subversion.

And 'tis the most reasonable thing in the world, that those who upon a total subversion are the sufferers, and have a right to the re-establishment, should have a right to take cognisance of any degree of invasion made upon their right, and which tends to that general subversion.

'Twould be nonsense to suppose, that which has all the greater powers should not have the less.

Can the people's good be the main and only end of government, and the people's power be the last resort when government is overwhelmed by the errors of governors? and have these people no right not so much as to be sensible of the ruin of their liberties, till it is absolutely completed? 'Twould be ridiculous.

The truth is in right reasoning, the first invasion made upon justice, either by the tacit or actual assent of the three heads of our constitution, is an actual dissolution of the constitution; and, for aught I can see, the people have a right to dispossess the incumbent, and commit the trust of government, *de novo*, upon that first act.

But I choose rather to put the argument upon total subversions of right order and defence, and I am sure nobody will dispute it with me there.

And here, if I have any foresight, lies an absolute security for us against that bug-bear, which so many pretend to be frighted at, a Commonwealth.

The genius of this nation has always appeared to tend to a monarchy, a legal limited monarchy; and having had in the late Revolution a full and uninterrupted liberty, to cast themselves into what form of government they pleased: there was not discovered the least inclination in any party towards a Commonwealth, though the treatment they met with from their last two kings, had all in it that could be, to put them out of love with monarchy.

THE ORIGINAL POWER OF THE PEOPLE OF ENGLAND

A Commonwealth can never be introduced, but by such invasions of right as must make our present constituted government impracticable: the reason is, because men never willingly change for the worst; and the people of England enjoy more freedom in our regal, than any people in the world can do in a popular, government.

The people of England can never choose a Commonwealth government, till they come to desire less liberty than they now enjoy; that is, till they come to be blind to their own interest. 'Tis true, example is no argument; but I might freely appeal to the friends of the last republic in England to answer this question.

Whether the people of England, during the short government of Parliament in England, which was erroneously called a Commonwealth, did, or whether they can under any Commonwealth government, founded never so wisely, enjoy greater privileges and advantages than under the present constitution in its full and free exercise, uninterrupted by the excesses of kings' evil counsellors, parties and passions.

If any shall pretend that the late parliament is aimed at in this, I hope I may have as much liberty to suppose they are mistaken; for the days of judging by innuendo are at an end.

If anything seem to lie that way, the error must be theirs who have so mean thoughts of them, as to think the coat will fit them; if it does, they are welcome to wear it. For my part, I declare myself to intend only the bringing things to such a right understanding, as may preserve the balance of power; and, I hope, I cannot offend any free representative of the people of England, in saying, that what power they have they receive from the people they represent; and, that some powers do still remain with the people, which they never neither divested themselves of, nor committed to them.

Nor can I be sensible of offending if I say, that 'tis possible for even a House of Commons to be in the wrong. 'Tis possible for a House of Commons to be misled by factions and parties. 'Tis possible for them to be bribed by pensions and places, and by either of these extremes to betray their trust, and abuse the people who entrust them: and if the people should have no redress in such a case, then were the nation in the hazard of being ruined by their own representatives. And 'tis a wonder to find it

97

asserted in a certain treatise, that it is not to be supposed that ever the House of Commons can injure the people who intrust them. There can be no better way to demonstrate the possibility of a thing, than by proving that it has been already.

And we need go no farther back than to the reign of King Charles the Second, in which we have seen lists of 180 members who received private pensions from the court; and if anybody shall ask whether that parliament preserved the balance of power in the three branches of our constitution, in the due distribution some have mentioned, I am not afraid to answer in the negative.

And why even to this day are gentlemen so fond of spending their estates to sit in that House, that ten thousand pounds has been spent at a time to be chosen, and now that way of procuring elections is at an end, private briberies and clandestine contrivances are made use of to get into the House. No man would give a groat to sit where he cannot get a groat honestly for sitting, unless there were either parties to gratify, profits to be made, or interest to support.

If then these things are possible, it seems to me not so improper for the people, who are the original and end of the constitution, and have the main concern in it, to be very solicitous that the due balance of power be preserved, and decently; and, according to law, always to shew their dislike and resentment at any public encroachment, which either branch of the constitution, shall make on each other, or on the whole, be it by their own representatives or anywhere else.

If it is expected, that I should descend to particular matters, debated between the two Houses in the last session of this present Parliament; such expectants will be deceived: I shall not meddle with a case which appears so difficult to be decided, that the two Houses of Parliament could not agree about.

And since, as I said before, every person who takes upon him to speak to or of the Parliament, ought to have liberty to explain himself; so I have taken that liberty in the preface to this book, to which I refer. But this in general I may say, for I am upon generals, and shall keep to them without any relation to particular cases.

It cannot be that the people of England, who have so much concern in the good agreement of their governors, can see the two Houses of Parliament at any time clash with one another, or with the King, or the King with them; or encroach upon the rights and liberties of the subjects, and be unconcerned and not express their fears.

If any fellow subject be impeached, to see the disputes between the two Houses about punctilios of form, interrupt the due and ordinary course of justice; so that a criminal cannot be detected, nor an innocent man be justified, but such impeachments shall lie as a brand upon the reputation of an innocent person, which is a punishment worse than his crime deserved, if he were guilty: these are injuries to the subject in general, and they cannot be easy to see them.

We have a great cry against an evil ministry, the noise of which is so great, as it drowns the complaints of the people; but I dare say none of the people of England would be against having due resentments shown, and legal punishments inflicted with impartial justice, where the persons appear guilty: but if enquiry after disorders at home should delay taking care of our safety abroad; if private clashings and disputes between parties and interests should take up the hours which are due to the emergency of foreign affairs, the people of England will be very ill served; and the persons, whoever they are concerned, will be able to give but a sorry account to the country that employed them of the trust they had committed to them: not that delinquents should not be punished, or evil ministers impeached, but, as our Saviour says in another case, These things ye ought to have done,[21] and not have the other left undone.

What shall we then say to the manner of fixing guilt upon a person or a party by vote. That the Lords denying a free conference was a delay of justice, and tended to destroy the good correspondence, &c. and refusing to proceed to the trial of one impeached Lord, because another Lord, not impeached, had affronted the House.[22]

Truly I shall venture to say nothing of it but this, that the clashings and disagreement between the two Houses are things our enemies rejoiced at, and the people of England were very sorry for. Who are in the right of it Sir H. M. must answer for me, who says, *It is not to be imagined that a majority of so numerous a body of gentlemen can be influenced against reason and justice.* But at the same time supposes the Lords may, by receiving articles of impeachment today, and appointing to try them forty years hence, or else tomorrow morning at Truro[23] in Cornwall.

If he means that it is not probable, I readily allow it; but if he means that 'tis not possible, I cannot agree, for the reasons and examples aforesaid: and if it be but possible, 'tis not reasonable the liberty and safety of England should be exposed even to a possibility of a disaster; and therefore reason and justice allows, that when all delegated powers fail or expire, when governors devour the people they should protect; and when parliaments, if ever that unhappy time shall come again, should be either destroyed or, which is as bad, be corrupted, and betray the people they represent, the people themselves, who are the original of all delegated power, have an undoubted right to defend their lives, liberties, properties, religion and laws, against all manner of invasion or treachery, be it foreign or domestic; the constitution is dissolved, and the laws of nature and reason act of course, according to the late author quoted before.

> The government's ungirt when justice dies,
> And constitutions are non-entities:
> The nation's all a mob; there's no such thing
> As Lords and Commons, Parliament or King.
> A great promiscuous crowd the Hydra lies,
> Till laws revive and mutual contract ties.
> A chaos free to choose for their own share
> What case of government they please to wear.
> If to a king they do the reins commit,
> All men are bound in conscience to submit:
> But then that king must by his oath assent
> To *postulatas* of the government:
> Which if he breaks he cuts off the intail,
> And power retreats to its original.
>   *True-Born Englishman*, ll. 806–19

It may be objected; but who are these people to whom power must thus retreat? And who have the original right in their hands? It must be the whole people. If there be one negative, every one having an equal right, the real claim of power is imperfect: and since there can be no general collective meeting of the whole community, there can be no execution of their power; and therefore this does not justify a few of that body in the name of the rest, to execute any part of that power.

This may be answered; though upon a dissolution of government all the people collectively cannot be enquired of as to what they will have done, yet one negative ought not to interrupt the whole.

I'll suppose a general dissolution of government in any country, such as was seen in this nation at the last Revolution.

The people assembled in a universal mob to take the right of government upon themselves, are not to be supposed to give their personal suffrages to every article, but they may agree to a convention of such persons as they think fit to intrust, to constitute *de novo*, and may delegate their power, or part of it to such a convention; and in such case a general concurrence is to be supposed, unless there be a public dissent.

Now suppose the general collective body of the people should not unanimously agree, 'tis owned the power could not be universally delegated, and there a division would follow; but in such case, those who dissented from such an agreement, must declare their dissent, and agree to any other form of government for themselves, and so divide from the other body, and if they do not divide, they in effect do not dissent.

But then this division must be before any members are delegated by them to convene.

For example:
Suppose the freeholders in Cornwall in such a case should say, we do not approve of your deputing men to meet and consult of a new government and constitution, we are resolved to be governed by such a man of our own country.

This resolution being against no law, and that county having sent no members to represent them, and to join with the rest of the body, they cannot be legally disturbed, or punished, or forced to unite with the rest of the nation.

Such a division might be looked upon as a misfortune to the general body, and unkind in the county or part dividing from the rest, but in the nature of the thing it could not be unjust.

For as much as any body of men are at liberty, upon the dissolution of former contracts, to be governed by such laws and persons, and in such manner as they shall think fit.

Yet is there no fear of such a division in a country so depending on its several parts as this is, because the rest would render them so uneasy, that interest would compel them to comply.

I do not place this right upon the inhabitants, but upon the freeholders; the freeholders are the proper owners of the country: it is their own, and the other inhabitants are but sojourners, like lodgers in a house, and ought to be subject to such laws as the freeholders impose upon them, or else they must remove; because the freeholders having a right to the land, the other have no right to live there but upon sufferance.

In former days the freehold gave a right of government to the freeholder, and vassalage and villeinage was derived from this right, that every man who will live in my land shall be my servant; if he won't, let him go about his business, and live somewhere else: and 'tis the same still in right reasoning.

And I make no question but that property of land is the best title to government in the world; and if the King was universal landlord, he ought to be universal governor of right, and the people so living on his lands ought to obey him, or go off of his premises.

And if any single man in England should at any time come to be landlord of the whole freehold of England, he could indeed have no right to dispossess the King, till the present legal settlement of the crown failed, because it was settled by those that had then a right to settle it.

But he would immediately be the full representative of all the counties in England, and might elect himself knight of the shire for every county, and the Sheriff of every county must return him accordingly.

He would have all the baronies and titles of honour which are entailed upon estates devolved upon him, and upon any expiration of the settlement would be king by natural right.

And he would be king upon larger terms than ever any man was legally king of England; for he would be king by inherent right of property.

When therefore I am speaking of the right of the people, I would be understood of the freeholders, for all the other inhabitants live upon sufferance, and either are the freeholders' servants, or having money to pay rent live upon conditions, and have no title to their living in England, other than as servants, but what they must pay for.

Upon this foot it is that to this day our law suffers not a foreigner to purchase any of the freeholds of England: for if a foreigner might purchase, your neighbours (having money to spare) might come and buy you out of your own country, and take possession by a legal and indisputable right.

This original right was the first foundation of the several tenures of land in England; some held of the King, some of the Lord, some by knight service, socage,[24] and the like, and some were called freeholds. The lords of manors had their homages and their services from their tenants, as an acknowledgment that the right of the land gave a certain right of government to the possessor over all the tenants and inhabitants.

And as a thing which will put this argument out of all question. The right to lands, manors, and lordships was not originally a right granted by patents from kings or Acts of Parliament, but a natural right of possession handed down by custom and ancient usage, as the inheritance from the still more ancient possessors, and prescription, as the lawyers call it, or usage time out of mind, is to this day allowed to be a sufficient title in several cases, where conveyances, deeds, charters, and writings of estates are silent, especially as to buttings and boundings of land, highways, footpaths, water courses, bridges, and the like.

This right, as all right originally, is founded upon reason. For it would be highly unreasonable, that those people who have no share of the house should live in it whether he that built it will or no. No person has any right to live in England, but they to whom England belongs; the freeholders of England have it in possession; England is their own, and nobody has any thing to do here but themselves.

If they permit other people to live here, well and good, but no man but a freeholder lives here upon any terms but *permissu superiorum*,[25] and he pays rent for his licence to live here.

Thus the liberties and privileges of towns and corporations are founded upon Acts of Parliament to confirm charters or grants from the crown, by which the freeholders give their consent that such and such bodies of men living in such towns, shall enjoy certain privileges in consideration of their being so considerably serviceable to the nation, by paying taxes, maintaining the poor, by manufactures, trade, and the like, notwithstanding they are not possessed of any part of the freehold.

And 'tis observable, the King cannot give this privilege, so as to enable any of these corporations to send representatives to Parliament. None but the freeholders of England (and such towns in conjunction) to whom the freeholders have already granted such privilege, can give a qualification of such a nature, as is a receiving them into an equal state of privilege with a freeholder.

Every man's land is his own property; and 'tis a trespass in the law for another man to come upon his ground without his consent. If the freeholders should all agree, that such a man shall not come upon their land; that they will not let him a house for his money; that whose land soever he sets his foot on, the owner shall indict him for a trespass, as by law he may, the man must fly the nation of course.

Thus the freeholders having a right to the possession of England, the reason must be good that they must have the same right to the government of themselves, that they have to the government of the rest of the inhabitants; and that there can be no legal power in England, but what has its original in the possessors; for property is the foundation of power.

I am not undertaking to find fault with our constitution, though I do not grant neither, that it is capable of no amendment; but I would endeavour to make way, by retreating to originals, for every member to perform its proper function, in order to put the general body into its regular motion.

For as in the natural body, if any member, either by contraction of the organ, dislocation, or other accident, fails in the performance of its proper duty, the locomotive faculty is either interrupted, and the body distorted, or at least the regularity of natural motion is invaded: so in the body politic, if one branch of the general union err, and that error is not corrected, the whole constitution suffers a shock, and there is an infraction of the general order.

The excellency of our constitution consists of the symmetry of parts; and the balance of power; and if this balance be broken, one part grows too great for the other, and the whole is put into confusion.

To give some instances of this, 'twill be needful to enter a little into history, and we need not go far to inform ourselves, that there has been a time when the weakness of our constitution has appeared.

Our constitution, when all the fine things in the world have been said of it, is not impregnable; when power has been thrown wholly into one scale, the other has always been trampled under foot, and overthrown by it.

The regal power under King Charles the First, over-balanced the Lords and Commons, to the invading the right of levying taxes vested wholly in the Parliament, and to the discontinuing Parliaments for fourteen years, and the many convulsions the constitution felt in that time, is too melancholy a subject to reflect upon.

The House of Commons in the next settlement over-balanced the Lords, and power being added to one side, tossed the upper house quite out of the scale, absolutely annihilated the very being of the peers as a House,[26] and voted them out of the constitution.

By the Restoration the constitution returned to its original, and the balance was poised again: what attempts have since been made to overthrow it, are needless to be insisted upon, but the nature of the thing leads me to make one remark, that if the King can do no wrong, nor is not punishable or blameable by our constitution, but the ministry, as a late author[27] has very clearly set down. Then we have acted strangely in the late Revolution; that the ministry of the late reign, for whose misbehaviour we thought we had a just right to call in foreign aid, and to suppress whose exorbitant power we took up arms against our prince, should not only not be punished as they deserved, but be still capable of acting in the ministry again, and of representing in Parliament that very people they had betrayed.

Not that I am of some people's opinion neither, who think the late King had hard measure in being deposed, when he was really not accountable. For I presume I may affirm, that the deposing King James was founded upon his deserting the nation, not his maladministration; for had he continued in England you might possibly have subdued him, and took him prisoner, but there had been no room for transposing the crown while he had been alive.

And 'tis allowed by all, that those persons who advised him to quit the kingdom by flying out of it, either wilfully betrayed him, or very ignorantly gave him the only counsel which could complete his ruin.

How then it comes to pass that those evil ministers have arrived to impunity for what was past, and again to be trusted both in the court and in the Parliament with the people's liberties, is a mystery past our reaches.

If I had no name myself, I would set down theirs; or if I had a press in the clouds to print their practices, the world should not be ignorant; but since 'tis not so, I shall only say as our Saviour said of somebody else, by their works ye shall know them.[28]

These are the men who cry loudest against the present ministry and on all occasions make use of the pretence of liberty to animate the nation against not only the present, but against every ministry by which the public affairs shall be managed, and against the King himself. The same men who in former days cried up a Popish army in a profound peace, the very same now cried down a Protestant army in time of danger. The very same men who could digest the absolute power of ruining our liberty and religion, being vested in a Popish king, were the first and forwardest that durst not trust a Protestant king with forces enough to defend us till peace was better established, but have by that means, according to their hearts' desire, laid us and all Europe under a necessity of arming again to maintain that peace, which 'twas then in our power to have maintained.

For I am free to say 'twas not the Treaty of Partition[29] which so much run the Spaniards upon giving themselves up to the French, as it was the despicable figure the English forces were reduced to, which made the French king bold to take possession of the Spanish monarchy, which had some, I do not say all, our forces been continued but a year or two longer, he would not have ventured to have done.

And yet all these forces might have been subjected so absolutely to parliamentary power, as if they had been their own; for the King never denied them any security they desired, and so they might have been disbanded as easily now as then.

Nor do I think that in this discourse I can be supposed to favour that party, if there be such a party, which indeed I question, who would govern this nation by the help of a standing army; but I must be allowed to lay down this for a maxim, that any force as shall be agreed to by consent of parliament is legal, and some force may at some particular times be necessary, of which the Parliament are the only judges.

Still I allow that of this power so derived from property, the House of Commons are the abridgment; they are the freeholders of England in miniature; to them all needful powers and privileges are committed, to make them capable of acting for the people they represent; and, extremities excepted, they are our last resort: But if they employ those privileges and powers against the people, the reason of those powers is destroyed, the end is inverted, and the powers cease of course.

From hence 'tis reasonable to give them instructions; and though they are not conditionally chosen as to their instructions, yet they ought in honour to think themselves under equal obligation to stand by those instructions.

Instructions to members are like the power given to an arbitrator, in which though he is left fully and freely to act, yet 'tis in confidence of his honour that he will think himself bound by the directions he receives from the person for whom he acts.

If an arbitrator inverts the design of his principal, he destroys the end of his election, and is sure never to be entrusted again.

The House of Commons are our sanctuary against the oppression of princes, the nation's treasurers, and the defenders of their liberties; but all these titles signify, that at the same time they are the nation's servants.

The House of Commons also are mortal, as a House; a king may dissolve them, they may die and be extinct; but the power of the people has a kind of eternity with respect to politic duration: parliaments may cease, but the People remain; for them they were originally made, by them they are continued and renewed, from them they receive their power, and to them in reason they ought to be accountable.

THE CONCLUSION.

The dissolution of the last parliament[30] has been subsequent to the writing these sheets, and two observations fall out so naturally on this occasion, that I cannot but conclude this subject with them.

That both His Majesty and the whole nation have very happily given their approbation to the positions here laid down.

It cannot be doubted but that the language of the addresses of the people presented to his majesty, upon the indignity offered him by the French king[31] has in general a dislike included in them of the management of their late representatives; and though it is a new thing, yet it is plain that their proceedings in general have been disobliging to the nation.

There was no need to express in words at length, before also His Majesty's Intentions were known, that they desire him to dissolve the present parliament. Good manners required, that they should not so plainly lead His Majesty in what he was to be the author of; besides, the parliament was in being, and the illegal arbitrary usage of the Kentish Gentlemen[32] fresh in the memory of the people. But what is the meaning of the following expressions in the addresses? *If Your Majesty please to entrust us with the choice of a new parliament*; *when Your Majesty shall be graciously pleased to call a new parliament*; *in conjunction with a parliament*; and the like. What would the addressors have us, or have the King to understand by these expressions, but that the people finding themselves injured by the proceedings of their representatives, and the nation in danger of being abused and betrayed to the invasions of the French, by the illegal and arbitrary designs of a party in the House, have recourse to his Majesty, to depose for them a power which they saw going to be misapplied to the ruin of those from whom and for whom it was appointed?

Nor was this any thing but what was seen and known before; all those addresses are the legitimate offspring of the Kentish petition; and had not the freeholders been awed by the ill usage of the Kentish Gentlemen, the whole nation had then as unanimously petitioned the House; as they have now addressed His Majesty.

This is evident from the tenor, and yet undiscovered original of the Legion Paper;[33] the contents of which had so much plain truth of fact, and truth of law, that the House stood convicted in the plain consternation the contents of it threw them in; and which I could give a better history of, if it were needed, by which they gave a full assent to the right of the people.

But beyond all this is His Majesty's proclamation, wherein, according to truth, reason, and the nature of the thing, His Majesty has graciously given a sanction to the natural right of his people, proclaiming from the English throne, of which he is the most rightful possessor by the voice of the people, that ever sat on it.

That when the people of England do universally express their resolution to do what should or ought to be desired of good Englishmen and Protestants, *it is reasonable to give them an opportunity to choose such persons to represent them in Parliament, as they may judge most likely to bring to effect their just and pious purposes.*

The words need no comment, they contain in them a glorious recognition from the restorer of English liberty, and an unexampled testimony to the reasonableness of those just rights which, though former kings blinded by ambition have endeavoured to suppress, his present Majesty, according to his first declaration and continued practice, has accounted it his chief honour to preserve, and which we doubt not he will hand down unbroken to our posterity.

D.F.

NON-CONFORMING DISSENTER

AN
ENQUIRY
INTO THE
Occasional Conformity
OF
DISSENTERS,
IN
Cases of Preferment.

WITH A

PREFACE to the LORD MAYOR,
Occasioned by his carrying the
Sword to a CONVENTICLE.

If the Lord be God, follow him: but if Baal, then follow him, 1 Kings 18. 21.

LONDON:
Printed *Anno Dom.* 1697.

The Preface

My LORD,

I know not that the following sheets will at all affect Your Lordship, for I cannot say, that Your Lordship did communicate with the Dissenters before, or does with the Church now; nor does it import much whether you did either. The discourse is not meant for a satyr on Your Lordship, nor upon any man else; neither has it any double aspect, but directly points at the fact, which whether it be a crime or not, let their consciences judge, who know themselves guilty.

My Lord, the step Your Lordship made into the Chair, had something in it of surprize, and your management of it has more. The figure Your Lordship made, when you were the man whom the King delighted to honour, was very magnificent; and we find, that since that, Your Lordship does not bear the sword in vain.

I bear Your Lordship testimony, that I never heard any man reflect, either on Your Lordship's morals or management (since your being Lord Mayor)[1] save only in the matter of Pinners' Hall:[2] and since nobody has opened their mouths on Your Lordship's behalf, I humbly crave leave to be Your Lordship's advocate in one point. One principal allegation against Your Lordship, is, that you forced the pious, conscientious Mr. M[an] to the Meeting-house, and there enclosed him, *nolens volens*,[3] contrary to the true intent and meaning of an Act of Parliament, in that case made and provided, entitled, An Act for Liberty of Conscience,[4] &c. And that at the same time, Your Lordship caused the sword (that very individual sword, that had the honour to be carried so far before the King) even the City sword of state, to be carried to a conventicle or Meeting-house, called Pinners' Hall.

My Lord, I own the fact in Your Lordship's behalf, that Your Lordship's sword and sword-bearer was there; and I can find out but two clauses in which Your Lordship can be charged with a mistake.

One is in forcing that good man against his conscience. Liberty of conscience is a thing, that gentleman, I confess, never was fond of. But since 'tis now become every subject's right, 'tis hard Your Lordship should refuse it Mr. M[an].

But now, My Lord, I must crave the freedom to inform Your Lordship, that Mr. M[an], and Your Lordship, are exactly under the same predicaments as to liberty; for if Your Lordship has, against his will, obliged him to go to Pinners' Hall; Your Lordship seems in as large a measure to be imposed upon, in being obliged to go to the Cathedral worship of St. Paul's.

Till Your Lordship arrived at the magnitude you now sit in, you never suffered yourself to be abridged of your liberty; and shall your power be great in everything, but in the management of yourself?

My Lord, either your profession before was bad or good: if it was bad, Your Lordship does well to alter it, and would do better to do so wholly. If 'twas good, why does Your Lordship alter it at all? But I beg leave of Your Lordship to consider how 'twas possible to be both good and bad too? That Your Lordship should worship God one way in the morning, and another in the afternoon. My Lord, your elevated station places you above the fear of man, and he that is above fear, is above shame. If your former profession was good, Your Lordship need never be ashamed of it: if 'twas bad, you need not be ashamed to mend it, for no wise man is ashamed of growing wiser.

Human politics seldom agree with nice consciences; and if I could entertain such base thoughts, as to believe Your Lordship designs by this to gain parties, and make both your friends, I would think it also needful to assure Your Lordship, that by it you will most effectually lose both parties; but Your Lordship is wiser than to need that admonition. Your Lordship never was a trimmer in your life, and certainly you won't trim it with your maker.

I neither press Your Lordship to go to Church or Meeting, but to use the authority man has given you to procure yourself the freedom of using the judgment God has given you; that honest Mr. Sword-bearer may have his liberty, and Your Lordship your own.

We were in hopes when Your Lordship first appeared in the quire[5] at Paul's, that you were effectually convinced of your former error, as a Dissenter; and that noble quire should have been graced at its first opening with so noble a convert as Your Lordship; but since we find Your Lordship is pleased to practice such latitudinarian principles, as to be a conformist in the morning, and a nonconformist before night; it puts us upon considering what this new sort of a religion that looks two ways at once, means.

The following sheets, if Your Lordship should give yourself the trouble of reading them, will directly point out to Your Lordship what is meant by this blunt preface. In short, that the Church or the Meeting-house is the place where Your Lordship may worship, but that both Church and Meeting-house, at the same time, is preposterous, derogatory to the character of Your Lordship's wisdom, a scandal upon the grandeur of the principal magistrate of the City; and a slight put upon God himself, as if Your Lordship were very indifferent which way you did it, and consequently, whether you did it all, or not.

Your Lordship sits in a chair of great authority, and the respect due to you is great, and your example is very significant. Wherefore 'tis the author's humble request to Your Lordship, that you will be pleased to consider, whether the example Your Lordship now sets us, is such as you would really advise anybody to follow, and if not, I have no more to say to the matter; but that I am,

Your Lordship's
most humble servant,
One, Two, Three, Four.

A Discourse Upon Occasional Conformity.

When I review the past times, and look back upon the various scenes, which they present us as to ecclesiastical transactions within this kingdom, there seems nothing more strange than the turns we have had from Popish to regal supremacy, from the Romish religion to reformed, from reformed back again to Romish, and then to reformed again, and so on through several degrees of reformation, and back again from those degrees to the first steps of reformation, and then forward again.

King Henry the 8th, a prince of a haughty spirit, disdaining the insolence with which his predecessors were treated by the Popes, gave the first shock to the Roman power in these kingdoms. I won't say he acted from any principles of conscience, whatever his ambition and interest led him to pretend; but that, as it is in most cases of public revolutions, was the gloss; however it was, having satisfied his pride by subduing the supremacy of the Pope, and establishing his own; his interest next guided him to the suppression of abbeys and monasteries; the horrible vices which were protected, as well as practised in those nests of superstition, giving his pretence of piety the larger scope; and I'll for once be so free with the character of that prince, as to suppose what to me seems plain, that neither this religion, or that, were of much moment in his thoughts, but his interest, as the sequel made plain, by the seizure he made of the revenues of the Church. And yet the justice of Providence seemed very conspicuous in that point, that those houses who under the specious pretences of religion and extraordinary devotion, had amassed to themselves vast revenues to the impoverishing many families, and in the meantime practised secretly most unheard-of wickedness, should under the same pretence of zeal and piety be suppressed and impoverished by a person, who merely to serve his own glory, triumphed over them, pretending, Jehu-like,[6] *to shew his zeal for the Lord.*

Some do assure us, that the eyes of this prince were really opened as to the point of religion; and that had he lived longer, he would most effectually have established the Reformation in his time; but God, who gave him that light, *if he had it*, however he might accept his intention, as he did that of David's building his house, yet he reserved the glory of the performance to his son.

King Edward the 6th, of whom wondrous things are spoken in all our English writers, and more than we need suppose should be literally true; yet was, without doubt, a prince of the strictest piety, not only that ever reigned, but that ever lived, perhaps, since the days of Josiah,[7] whose parallel our writers say he was.

The Reformation began in his hand; not but that the Protestant religion had been received in England many years before, by the preaching of John Wickliff,[8] William Tindall,[9] and others, and had many professors, and those such, who gallantly offered their lives in defence of the truth.

But it got but little ground; for religion has but few votaries, while all its professors must also be confessors, and while exile or martyrdom is all the present prospect of advantage to be got by it.

None will dare to be Dissenters in times of danger, but such whose consciences are so awakened that they dare not be otherwise.

But in the hands of this young prince, the great work was begun, and in a shorter time than could be imagined, was finished and established; the Romanists fled or conformed; for we find but very few had any inclination to martyrdom if it had been put upon them. Some indeed to show the nature of their religion, pleaded for Baal, and rebelled, stirring up the ignorant people to murther their Gideon[10] for throwing down the Altars of Baal; but like the Ephramites of old, their *shibboleth*[11] was their undoing.

God, who thought fit to discover the levity of those who had only conformed, and not reformed, who, *in exemplum regis*,[12] had took up this as they would have done any religion, and also for the trial and glory of his Church, suffered all this great fabric, however of his own working, to be overthrown at the death of this good king, and a deluge of cruelty and Popery overwhelmed the people in the reign of the Queen, his sister.

But Popery found more Dissenters than the Reformation had done, and the impression religion had made on the minds of those who had sincerely embraced it, was not so easily defaced as the pretended Reformation of others; for the glosses men had put on their actions, only as a cover from common observation, was soon discovered, when the safety of owning their old principles rendered those outsides no longer needful; but where the true religion had got footing in the mind, it was still the same, whatever alterations of times might make it dangerous; and yet all people did not burn; but some being persecuted in one city, fled to another; and Germany especially was a sanctuary for the distressed English Protestants, that country having been before-hand with us in the Reformation.

'Twas here that our exiled clergy having conversed with the learned Reformers abroad, and particularly with John Calvin, found, that though they were reformed indeed from the gross errors of Popery and superstition, there was yet several things which might be further and further reformed; and being willing to arrive to the greatest perfection they were capable of in religion (that as near as possible they might pursue the great example of Christ Jesus, whose name they professed, and for whom they could most gloriously die), they corrected in themselves those things which they saw needful, and by letters to their brethren in England communicated their opinions, with their reasons, exhorting them to go on unto perfection as they had begun.

Some of the most zealous for piety and holiness of life, rejected this motion; and others as zealous and pious, closed with it; and the disputes were carried so far sometimes, as to invade the charity of one another; an humble acknowledgment of which you have in a most Christian reconciling letter from Bishop Ridley[13] to Bishop Hooper,[14] two of the most glorious triumphant martyrs that ever confessed the truth of Christ at the stake.

For the present, the fire of the persecution, (as the greater light obscures the less), extinguished that of dissension. But when Queen Elizabeth rescued the Protestant religion, and the Church enjoyed its peace again, the debate revived: but the first establishment of King Edward obtained so on the minds of men, that the further Reformation was rejected; the other party being not at all convinced, though over-ruled, submitted their persons to the laws, but not their opinion; affirming 'that 'twas the duty of every Christian, to endeavour to serve God with the greatest purity of worship that was possible; and that this was the purest worship which came nearest to the divine institution, which they believed the established liturgy did not, and therefore in conscience they must be Dissenters.'

It must be owned, that the original authors of these disputes were learned, devout, and singularly pious, strict in conversation to excess, if that be possible, and from thence, in a sort of happy derision, were called *Puritans*; of whom I shall say nothing, but leave for a record the last speech of a famous foreigner,[15] who had seen the way of living among those Dissenters, and speaking of the words of Balaam,[16] *Let me die the death of the righteous, and let my latter end be like his,* cried out,

Sit anima mea cum Puritanis Anglicanis.[17]

I shall not take upon me to observe the difference between these primitive Dissenters and our present, which is too plain; nor to dispute the substance of the point in debate between them and the established national Church.

I shall only observe, that the reasons for the present Dissenters' separation from the established Church, are said to be exactly the same they were then; and the present Dissenters are the successors of those first, as the present Conformists are the successors of the first reformers under King Edward the Sixth, and Queen Elizabeth.

I must acknowledge, that it fares with the Church of England, and with the Dissenters both, as it has always fared with Christ's church in the whole world; that while suppressed and persecuted, their professors were few, and their profession more severe; but when a religion comes to be the mode of the country, so many painted hypocrites get into the Church, who are not by their voices to be distinguished, that guile is not to be seen, till it arrive to apostasy. The whole ecclesiastical history, from the first century of the Christian church, is full of instances to confirm this, that the prosperity of the church of Christ has been more fatal to it, than all the persecution of its enemies.

I am now brought down to the present time, when the Dissenting Protestant is sheltered by the laws, and protected from the violence which he suffered in the late reigns, under the arbitrary commands of such state-ministers who strove to dash the whole Protestant interest to pieces by its own weight: and nothing is more apparent to those who are any thing acquainted with the late management of affairs in this land, than that the Court used both parties alternately, as policy and occasion directed, to suppress and destroy one another; that the whole house, *which being so divided, could not stand,*[18] might at last fall of itself.

But our eyes are at last opened, and the name of Protestant is now the common title of an Englishman, and the Church of England extends her protection to the tender consciences of her weaker brethren, knowing that all may be Christians, though not alike informed; and the Dissenter extends his charity to the Church of England, believing that in his due time *God shall reveal even this unto them.* If this is not, I wish this were the temper of both parties; and I am sure it is already the temper of some of each side, and those few are of the wisest, most pious, and most judicious.

But while frailty and infirmity is an essential to humanity, and pride and hypocrisy are the two regnant vices of the Church, this good spirit cannot be universal, and we do not expect it.

But there is a sort of truth which all men owe to the principles they profess; and generally speaking, all men pay it; a Turk is a Turk zealously and entirely; an idolater is an idolater, and will serve the Devil to a tittle: none but Protestants halt between God and Baal; Christians of an amphibious nature, that have such preposterous consciences, that can believe one way of worship to be right, and yet serve God another way themselves; *this is a strange thing in Israel*.[19] The whole history of religions in the world do not shew such a case: 'tis like a ship with her sails haled some back, and some full: 'tis like a workman, that builds with one hand, and pulls down with t'other: 'tis like a fisherman, that catches fish with one hand, and throws them into the sea with another: 'tis like every thing that signifies nothing. To say a man can be of two religions, is a contradiction, unless there be two Gods to worship, or he has two souls to save.

Religion is the sacred profession of the name of God; serving him, believing in him, expecting from him; and like the God it refers to, 'tis in one and the same object, one and the same thing perfectly indivisible and inseparable; there is in it no neuter gender, no ambiguous article, God or Baal; mediums are impossible.

As to the different modes and ways, which are the circumstantials of this sacred thing I call religion; I won't say, but that as ships take different courses at sea, yet to the best of their skill, keeping to the direct rules of navigating by the compass, they may arrive at the same port; so Christians taking different methods in the serving this God, yet going to the best of their judgments by the direct rules of the Scripture, may arrive at the same Heaven; but this is nothing at all to the case; for no ship would arrive at any port, that sailed two ways together, if that were possible; nor no man can serve one God, and at the same time hold two opinions. There is but one best, and he that gives God two bests, gives him the best and the worst, and one spoils t'other, till both are good for nothing.

I have said already, that both the Church of England, and the Dissenter, suffer in their reputation for the mixed multitude of their members, which is occasioned by their present prosperity: if a third party were to tyrannize over them both, we should see then who were professors, and who were confessors; but now it cannot be: wherefore, I think 'twere well to put both sides in mind of one thing, which they are bound mutually to observe; and that is, that the personal miscarriages of any particular person or member, is not really any reflection upon the religion they profess, nor ought not to be so accounted, unless it be where such miscarriages are the direct dictates of the doctrines they teach; and thus I would be understood in the present case. Wherefore I shall give my essay as to what I understand a real Dissenting Protestant is, or ought to be.

He who dissents from an established church on any account, but from a real principle of conscience, is a politic, not a religious, Dissenter. To explain myself; he who dissents from any other reasons, but such as these, that he firmly believes the said established Church is not of the purest institution, but that he can really serve God more agreeable to his will, and that accordingly 'tis his duty to do it so, and no otherwise. Nay, he that cannot die, or at least desire to do so, rather than conform, ought to conform. Schism from the Church of Christ is, doubtless, a great sin, and if I can avoid it, I ought to avoid it, but if not, the cause of that sin carries the guilt with it.

But if I shall thus dissent, and yet at the same time conform; by conforming I deny my dissent being lawful, or by my dissenting I damn my conforming as sinful.

Nothing can be lawful and unlawful at the same time; if it be not lawful for me to dissent, I ought to conform; but if it be unlawful for me to conform, I must dissent; several opinions may at the same time consist in a country, in a city, in a family, but not in one entire person, that is impossible.

To come to the point; there are Dissenters who have separated from the Church of England, and joined in communion with Dissenting churches or congregations. They have appeared zealous, conscientious, and constant; have borne the reproaches and inconveniences of their party, nay, suffered persecution, and loss of estates and liberty for the cause: and who could have so little charity as to doubt the sincerity of their profession? And yet these persecuted, suffering Dissenters, to make themselves room in the public advancements, and glittering gaudy honours of the age, shall conform to that which they refused under all those disadvantages to do before. And which is worse than all this; hear O Heavens! as soon as the present honour is attained, the present advantage made, they return to the former circumstance again, and are freely received, a double crime, as having done no evil.

I know not, I profess, what these persons can say for themselves, and therefore cannot pretend to answer their objections; but I cannot omit one answer which some people give for them, *viz.* that this is no conformity in point of religion, but done as a civil action, in obedience to the laws of the land, which have made it a necessary characteristic quality, for admittance into public employments, which they think it their duty to accept, in order to serve their country, which they doubly perform by executing those offices to the public interest, and by excluding those who would otherwise get into those places, and betray their country and their liberties.

I have never met with any considerable excuse made for this fast and loose game of religion, but this, and this I desire to consider a little particularly.

1. That this is no conformity in point of religion, but done as a civil action. How this can be possible, remains to be determined. 'Tis true, the morality of an action consists in its end; but I cannot conceive that an action purely and originally religious, such as the solemn ordinances of God's worship, can be made civil actions by any end, design, will, or intention of man whatsoever. 'Tis true, an oath, which is a calling God to witness, is an action both civil and religious, but still that was appointed and instituted to that end, as is expressly noted. Naaman's bowing in the house of Rimmon;[20] to which the prophet answered, *Go in peace*, which is understood as a permission, is a thing still different; for Naaman only bowed for the conveniency or state of the king, at the same time publicly disowning the worship, as interpreters are of opinion; besides, bowing the head, though it may be a customary act of worship at that place, yet is no act confined to worship only, and instituted and directed so by the God who is worshipped, but is an act used in common salutations. Thus we kneel to God, and to the King; but sacraments are things appropriated by the divine institution of God himself, as things which have no other signification or import but what is divine: had Naaman desired to be excused in offering sacrifices to the idol Rimmon, the prophet would hardly have bid him go in peace. Some actions are not civil or religious, as they are civilly or religiously performed, but as they are civil or religious in themselves; for some religious actions are so entirely such, that they cannot without a horrid invasion of the sovereignty of the institutor be appropriated

to any other use, and such are in especial manner, the two sacraments instituted by Christ; such was, before Christ, the sacrifices by fire; and the judgments of God on Nadab and Abihu,[21] for attempting to offer sacrifice with strange fire, stands as a terrible instance of what we ought to think is the will of God in this matter.

Further, speaking directly of the sacraments, are they not the same thing, though differently administered in the established church, or in a Dissenting church; and how can you take it as a civil act in one place, and a religious act in another? This is playing Bo-peep with God Almighty, and no man can tell of them when they are about a civil action, and when about a religious. But to answer this pretence at once, sacraments as sacraments are religious acts, and can be no other; if you do not take it as a sacrament, the case differs; but how can you say you do not take it as a sacrament; an oath is to be taken in the sense of the imposer; and a sacrament, which is a recognition of the most sacred of oaths, must be also taken in the sense of the imposer; if the person administring declared at the administration, *he did not give it as a sacrament, but only gave you a bit of bread, and a draught of wine as a friend*, or the like, this was something; but can a minister deliver the bread to you, and say, *The Body of our Lord Jesus Christ, &c.* and you kneeling with reverence take it as such, and repeat the responses at the communion, and say amen to the prayer, and say 'tis a civil action. This is such bantering[22] with religion, as no modest Christian can think of without horror.

2. Another part of the apology is, that without it they cannot be admitted into public places of trust; and if they are not admitted, such will get in as will betray their country and liberties, and they do it purely to secure their country, which they think their duty.

These are patriots that will damn their souls to save their country; a sort of a public spirit hardly to be found in the world, and indeed a non-entity in itself; for 'tis a mistake; the gentlemen who make this answer, put the case wrong. For I would desire such to answer a few questions.

If the service of their country be so dear to them, pray why should they not choose to expose their bodies and estates for that service, rather than their souls; the penalty of the law in accepting the public employments is wholly pecuniary; the difference lies here, they choose the trespassing on their consciences, before the hazard of their estates, as the least evil; for 'tis plain, any man who will suffer the penalty, or run the risk of it, which is all one, may excuse the conformity: for the law does not say you shall so and so conform, but if you do not conform, you shall incur such and such penalties; any man that will incur the penalty, may commit the trespass.

So that all this compliance is not to be admitted to places, that they may be able to serve their country, but to save the five hundred pounds, and other penalties of that Act.

2. Why, if we believe the power of God to be omnipotent, should we imagine that he is not able to protect our country and liberties, without our perpetrating so wicked an act to secure them, as doing evil that good may come, which is expressly forbidden?

But we are told again, this is in itself no sinful act, and therefore it is not doing evil. This is tacitly answered before; though 'tis not a sinful act in itself, yet 'tis either a sinful act in a Dissenter, or else his Dissenting before was a sinful act. For if he is satisfied he does well in conforming now, why did he not before? There is but one answer for that, which is, he is otherwise convinced; to which I reply, if that were true, he would then as a convert continue in this new communion; but 'tis evident the same persons return immediately to the former profession as Dissenters, and they can have no such excuse, unless it be, that they were convinced, and reconvinced, and then convinced again.

Some have the folly to argue against the law itself, as a most notorious imposition upon the consciences of men, by making the sacred institutions of Christ a drudge to secular interest, and a cause of men's sins, by leading them into temptation. I could say enough to vindicate that part, though I am no more reconciled to that law, than other men, but 'tis remote to our argument: 'Tis an act of Parliament, and what is so, is of every man's own doing, and therefore 'tis just every one should comply with the terms, or suffer the penalty; but here is no penalty, if no crime; if no preferments are sought, no honours accepted, there is no crime; if self-denial was as practicable as self-advancement, here is no need of the crime. So that they who do this, seek the crime, that is the first sin; then mortgage their consciences to avoid the penalty, and so add one sin to another. But we are told by some, 'tis not against their consciences, they hope both parties are good Christians; there are differences between them which they don't understand nor meddle with, and their consciences are very well satisfied to communicate with either.

I would ask such, if their consciences would serve to communicate with the Church, why did they separate? For communicating with the Dissenter, is not an occasional or casual thing, but an open declared breaking off from the Church established. Now no man can be said to separate from, and join to a thing at the same time; if your conscience is satisfied in joining, it cannot be satisfied in separating, unless you can suppose your conscience to be satisfied and dissatisfied both together. If you have a conscience of any religion at all, it must be of some religion or other; if of this, it cannot be of that; if of that, it cannot be of this: to dissent and approve, are different acts, and can never be fixed upon the same object at the same time; as for a man, passively religious, that can communicate anywhere, that man may from the same principle, and with far less guilt, communicate nowhere, for such a man, in downright English, has prostituted the little religion he had, if ever he had any, to his interest, and may be Turk, Jew, Papist, or anything.

The latter part of the charge leads me to consider another point, which relates to the assemblies of the Dissenters, who admit, and by consequence approve this way of proceeding. I do not pretend to examine by what methods such particular churches do proceed. And I would be as tender as possible in making reflections. I wish they would be as charitable in censuring this reproof.

I do think, with submission, 'tis impossible to prove that any person, whose case the foregoing paragraph reaches, can be received again into church-communion in a Dissenting assembly upon any other terms, than as a penitent. I have heard of some, who have been said to have leave from their ministers for this matter; if so, they have assumed some dispensing authority, which I believe does not appertain to the ministerial function, nor is not contained in the mission of our Saviour. But I do not affirm that any such thing has been really allowed.

As to the relation of churches, and the members thereof, one to another, as the Dissenters now establish them; I am sure, the allowance of any member in a promiscuous communion with the Church of England and the Dissenter at the same time, is not pretended to be allowed, nor is it consistent with itself. 'Tis preposterous, and eccentric, and is destructive of the very foundation of the Dissenters' principles, as is already noted, concerning schisms in the Church. In this case, charity can heal nothing, nor help nothing; 'tis of absolute necessity that one man be but of one side, at one and the same time. Either the Conformist will mar the Dissenter, or the Dissenter will mar the Conformist. For if I shall be admitted into the communion of the Dissenter, and of the Church together; then the

Dissenter must have some other reason for being a Dissenter than purity of worship.

Methinks men should seem what they are; if a man dissent from the Church, let him do so; and his principle being well grounded for such Dissent, let him hold it; if not well grounded, let him leave it; if he cannot suffer one way, let him suffer another; and why should we not be as honest to God as our country.

The motives to serve our country are strong, but there are ways to do it without such a violation of all our principles and profession; if not, trust God's Providence with the issue, who never wants agents to preserve and deliver his people when his time is at hand; and you can have small hope to expect that the office and trust you shall execute, shall receive any assistance from his Providence, when the first step into it, is made by offering the greatest affront to his honour, and committing the vilest act of perfidy in the world.

But if the gay prospect of a great place, tempt any person beyond the power that God's grace is pleased to assist him with, *in that way let him abide*, and not be re-admitted, because of his gold ring and fine apparel, without a penitent acknowledgment. The Dissenters in England, can never pretend to be Dissenters upon the mere principle of purity of worship, as I have related in the beginning of this discourse, if such shall be received as blameless into their communion, who have deserted them upon the occasion of preferment, and have made the sacred institutions of Christ Jesus, become pimps to their secular interest, and then wipe their mouths, and sit down in the Church, and say, *They have done no evil.*

'Tis also an intolerable affront to the Church of England, reflecting upon its doctrine as well as practice; to make use of the Church for a cover to fence them against the laws, at the same time continuing to disown its communion, as a thing not fit to be continued in.

And yet the Church of England is in the right to receive such of the Dissenters as shall come to them, without the ceremony of recognition, because it is agreeable to the notion of a national church, which they profess to be. But Dissenters are bound to justify their separation from them, or else their whole constitution falls to the ground. Now, how a separation and a conformity are consistent, is to me an inexplicable riddle.

I question not here the lawfulness of the Dissenters' separation; it is not the business of this discourse to define it; and I am as careful as I can in making reflections upon either; but I am bold to affirm, that no Dissenting church can with lawful cause separate from the Church of England, establish private churches or communions, and at the same times allow the members to conform to the established Church too: this is incongruous, and one must destroy the other. From whence I think it becomes the Dissenters, if they would maintain the doctrine they teach; if they would have us believe they dissent purely on the honest principles of conscience, and purity of worship, with such a one, no, not to eat. And it is not sufficient that the offender be a Lord Mayor, or any greater person; unless he would be Lord Mayor without a breach of the sacred relation he had entered into, he should be dealt with in that case, as the meanest member of such a society.

On the other hand, if a man be called upon to be a magistrate, and has courage enough to follow the impartial dictates of his conscience, a query lies before him, what shall he do?

The case is plain: either refuse the honour, or run the risk. The first indeed is the plainest and easiest way, and the ground of it is good, for he whose conscience dictates to him that the terms are sinful, may refuse the call; for preferments and honours are a bait that some have refused on mere points of speculative philosophy; and 'tis hard, Christianity should not carry a man as far. Well, but perhaps a man has a mind to be a Sheriff and Lord Mayor, and is a Dissenter; or perhaps he really thinks 'tis his indispensable duty to serve his country, if he is called to that, or the like office; or perhaps he thinks 'tis a duty he owes his family, to advance his children, and the like, and he is a professed Dissenter; what shall he do? Let him boldly run the risk, or openly and honestly conform to the Church, and neither be ashamed of his honour, nor of his profession; such a man all men will value, and God will own: he need not fear carrying the sword to a conventicle, or bringing the conventicle to his own house. But to make the matter a game, to dodge religions, and go in the morning to Church, and in the afternoon to the meeting; to communicate in private with the Church of England, to save a penalty, and then go back to the Dissenters and communicate again there: this is such a retrograde devotion, that I can see no colour of pretence for in all the Sacred Book.

I have heard, indeed, that some, who are ministers of Dissenting churches do, or did, at the same time communicate with the Church of England. I do not dispute how far a minister may conform as a layman, though he cannot as a clergyman; but how any Dissenting minister can conform as a layman, and at the same time execute a pastoral charge over a congregation, whom he teaches to separate from the Church in a lay-communion, I cannot imagine.

'Tis not, as I have already noted, conformity or nonconformity, that I am discoursing; but 'tis conformity and nonconformity at the same time, in one and the same person, that is the point; and doing this for a secular end, to save a penalty, and privately; and then, as being ashamed of it, to go back and sit down as not having done it at all; and a church society admitting this without taking notice of it. These are the contradictions I insist upon, and rather wish, than expect, to see rectified.

FINIS.

THE
SHORTEST-WAY
WITH THE
DISSENTERS:
OR
PROPOSALS
FOR THE
ESTABLISHMENT
OF THE
CHURCH.

LONDON:
Printed in the Year **MDCCII.**

The Shortest Way with the Dissenters

Sir Roger l'Estrange[1] tells us a story in his collection of fables, of the cock and the horses. The cock was gotten to roost in the stable, among the horses, and there being no racks, or other conveniences for him, it seems, he was forced to roost upon the ground; the horses jostling about for room, and putting the cock in danger of his life, he gives them this grave advice: *Pray gentlefolks let us stand still, for fear we should tread upon one another.*

There are some people in the world, who now they are unperched, and reduced to an equality with other people, and under strong and very just apprehensions of being further treated as they deserve, begin with Aesop's cock, to preach up peace and union, and the Christian duties of moderation, forgetting, that when they had the power in their hands, those graces were strangers in their gates.

It is now near fourteen years,[2] that the glory and peace of the purest and most flourishing Church in the world has been eclipsed, buffeted, and disturbed, by a sort of men, who God in his providence has suffered to insult over her, and bring her down; these have been the days of her humiliation and tribulation: she has borne with an invincible patience the reproach of the wicked, and God has at last heard her prayers, and delivered her from the oppression of the stranger.

And now they find their day is over, their power gone, and the throne of this nation possessed by a royal, English, true, and ever constant member of, and friend to the Church of England. Now they find that they are in danger of the Church of England's just resentments; now they cry out *peace*, *union*, *forbearance*, and *charity*, as if the Church had not too long harboured her enemies under her wing, and nourished the viperous brood, till they hiss and fly in the face of the mother that cherished them.

No gentlemen, the time of mercy is past, your day of grace is over; you should have practised peace, and moderation, and charity, if you expected any yourselves.

We have heard none of this lesson for fourteen years past: we have been huffed and bullied with your Act of Toleration; you have told us that you are the Church established by law, as well as others; have set up your canting-synagogues at our Church-doors, and the Church and her members have been loaded with reproaches, with oaths, associations, abjurations, and what not; where has been the mercy, the forbearance, the charity you have shewn to tender consciences of the Church of England, that could not take oaths as fast as you made 'em; that having sworn allegiance to their lawful and rightful King, could not dispense with that oath, their King being still alive, and swear to your new hodge-podge of a Dutch-government. These have been turned out of their livings, and they and their families left to starve; their estates double taxed, to carry on a war they had no hand in, and you got nothing by: what account can you give of the multitudes you have forced to comply, against their consciences, with your new sophistical politics, who like the new converts in France, sin because they can't starve. And now the tables are turned upon you, you must not be persecuted, 'tis not a Christian spirit.

You have butchered one King, deposed another King, and made a mock King of a third; and yet you could have the face to expect to be employed and trusted by the fourth; anybody that did not know the temper of your party, would stand amazed at the impudence, as well as folly, to think of it.

Your management of your Dutch monarch, whom you reduced to a mere King of Cl[out]s, is enough to give any future Princes such an idea of your principles, as to warn them sufficiently from coming into your clutches; and God be thanked, the Queen is out of your hands, knows you, and will have a care of you.

There is no doubt but the supreme authority of a nation has in itself a power, and a right to that power, to execute the laws upon any part of that nation it governs. The execution of the known laws of the land, and that with but a weak and gentle hand neither, was all that the fanatical party of this land have ever called persecution; this they have magnified to a height, that the sufferings of the Huguenots in France were not to be compared with —— Now to execute the known laws of a nation upon those who transgress them, after having first been voluntarily consenting to the making those laws, can never be called persecution, but justice. But justice is always violence to the party offending, for every man is innocent in his own eyes. The first execution of the laws against Dissenters in

England, was in the days of King James the First; and what did it amount to, truly, the worst they suffered, was at their own request, to let them go to New England, and erect a new colony, and give them great privileges, grants, and suitable powers, keep them under protection, and defend them against all invaders, and receive no taxes or revenue from them. This was the cruelty of the Church of England, fatal lenity! 'Twas the ruin of that excellent Prince, King Charles the First. Had King James sent all the Puritans in England away to the West-Indies, we had been a national unmixed Church; the Church of England had been kept undivided and entire.

To requite the lenity of the father, they take up arms against the son; conquer, pursue, take, imprison, and at last put to death the anointed of God, and destroy the very being and nature of Government, setting up a sordid impostor,[3] who had neither title to govern, nor understanding to manage, but supplied that want with power, bloody and desperate councils and craft, without conscience.

Had not King James the First witheld the full execution of the laws; had he given them strict justice, he had cleared the nation of them, and the consequences had been plain; his son had never been murthered by them, nor the monarchy overwhelmed; 'twas too much mercy shewn them, was the ruin of his posterity, and the ruin of the nation's peace. One would think the Dissenters should not have the face to believe that we are to be wheedled and canted into peace and toleration, when they know that they have once requited us with a civil war, and once with an intolerable and unrighteous persecution for our former civility.

Nay, to encourage us to be easy with them, 'tis apparent, that they never had the upper hand of the Church, but they treated her with all the severity, with all the reproach and contempt as was possible: what peace, and what mercy did they shew the loyal gentry of the Church of England in the time of their triumphant Commonwealth? How did they put all the gentry of England to ransom, whether they were actually in arms for the King or not, making people compound for their estates, and starve their families? How did they treat the clergy of the Church of England, sequestered the ministers, devoured the patrimony of the Church, and divided the spoil, by sharing the church-lands among their soldiers, and turning her clergy out to starve; just such measure as they have mete, should be measured to them again.[4]

Charity and love is the known doctrine of the Church of England, and 'tis plain she has put it in practice towards the Dissenters, even beyond what they ought, till she has been wanting to herself, and in effect, unkind to her own sons; particularly, in the too much lenity of King James the First, mentioned before, had he so rooted the Puritans from the face of the land, which he had an opportunity early to have done, they had not the power to vex the Church, as since they have done.

In the days of King Charles the Second, how did the Church reward their bloody doings with lenity and mercy, except the barbarous regicides of the pretended Court of Justice; not a soul suffered for all the blood in an unnatural war: King Charles came in all mercy and love, cherished them, preferred them, employed them, witheld the rigour of the law, and oftentimes, even against the advice of his Parliament, gave them liberty of conscience; and how did they requite him with the villainous contrivance to depose and murther him and his successor at the Rye-Plot.[5]

King James, as if mercy was the inherent quality of the family, began his reign with unusual favour to them: nor could their joining with the Duke of Monmouth[6] against him, move him to do himself justice upon them; but that mistaken Prince thought to win them by gentleness and love,[7] proclaimed an universal liberty to them, and rather discountenanced the Church of England than them; how they requited him all the world knows.

The late reign is too fresh in the memory of all the world to need a comment; how under pretence of joining with the Church in redressing some grievances, they pushed things to that extremity, in conjunction with some mistaken gentlemen, as to depose the late King, as if the grievance of the nation could not have been redressed but by the absolute ruin of the Prince: here's an instance of their temper, their peace, and charity. To what height they carried themselves during the reign of a King of their own; how they crept into all places of trust and profit; how they insinuated into the favour of the King, and were at first preferred to the highest places in the nation; how they engrossed the Ministry, and above all, how pitifully they managed, is too plain to need any remarks.

But particularly, their mercy and charity, the spirit of union they tell us so much of, has been remarkable in Scotland, if any man would see the spirit of a Dissenter, let him look into Scotland; there they made an entire conquest of the Church, trampled down the sacred orders, and suppressed the Episcopal government, with an absolute, and as they suppose, irretrievable victory, though, 'tis possible, they may find themselves mistaken: now 'twould be a very proper question to ask their impudent advocate, the *Observator*,[8] pray how much mercy and favour did the members of the Episcopal Church find in Scotland, from the Scotch Presbyterian-government; and I shall undertake for the Church of England, that the Dissenters shall still receive as much here, though they deserve but little.

In a small treatise[9] of the sufferings of the Episcopal clergy in Scotland, 'twill appear, what usage they met with, how they not only lost their livings, but in several places, were plundered and abused in their persons; the ministers that could not conform, turned out, with numerous families, and no maintenance, and hardly charity enough left to relieve them with a bit of bread; and the cruelties of the party are innumerable, and not to be attempted in this short piece.

And now to prevent the distant cloud which they perceived to hang over their heads from England; with a true Presbyterian policy, they put in for a union of nations, that England might unite their Church with the Kirk of Scotland, and their Presbyterian Members sit in our House of Commons, and their Assembly of Scotch canting long-cloaks in our Convocation; what might have been, if our fanatic, Whiggish statesmen had continued, God only knows; but we hope we are out of fear of that now.

'Tis alleged by some of the faction, and they began to bully us with it, that if we won't unite with them, they will not settle the Crown with us again, but when her Majesty dies, will choose a King for themselves.[10]

If they won't, we must make them, and 'tis not the first time we have let them know that we are able: the Crowns of these kingdoms have not so far disowned the right of succession, but they may retrieve it again, and if Scotland thinks to come off from a successive to an elective state of government, England has not promised not to assist the right heir, and put them into possession, without any regard to their ridiculous settlements.

These are the gentlemen, these their ways of treating the Church, both at home and abroad. Now let us examine the reasons they pretend to give why we should be favourable to them, why we should continue and tolerate them among us.

First, they are very numerous, they say, they are a great part of the
nation, and we cannot suppress them.

To this may be answered 1. They are not so numerous as the Protestants
in France, and yet the French King effectually cleared the nation of them[11]
at once, and we don't find he misses them at home.

But I am not of the opinion they are so numerous as is pretended; their
party is more numerous than their persons, and those mistaken people of
the Church, who are misled and deluded by their wheedling artifices, to
join with them, make their party the greater; but those will open their
eyes, when the Government shall set heartily about the work, and come
off from them, as some animals, which they say, always desert a house
when 'tis likely to fall.

2dly. The more numerous, the more dangerous, and therefore the more
need to suppress them; and God has suffered us to bear them as goads in
our sides, for not utterly extinguishing them long ago.

3dly. If we are to allow them, only because we cannot suppress them,
then it ought to be tried whether we can or no; and I am of opinion 'tis
easy to be done, and could prescribe ways and means, if it were proper,
but I doubt not but the Government will find effectual methods for the
rooting the contagion from the face of this land.

Another argument they use, which is this, that 'tis a time of war, and
we have need to unite against the common enemy.

We answer, this common enemy had been no enemy, if they had not
made him so; he was quiet, in peace, and no way disturbed, or encroached
upon us, and we know no reason we had to quarrel with him.

But further, we make no question but we are able to deal with this
common enemy without their help; but why must we unite with them
because of the enemy, will they go over to the enemy, if we do not prevent
it by a union with them ——— we are very well contented they should;
and make no question, we shall be ready to deal with them and the common
enemy too, and better without them than with them.

Besides, if we have a common enemy, there is the more need to be
secure against our private enemies; if there is one common enemy, we
have the less need to have an enemy in our bowels.

'Twas a great argument some people used against suppressing the old money,[12] that 'twas a time of war, and 'twas too great a risk for the nation to run, if we should not master it, we should be undone; and yet the sequel proved the hazard was not so great, but it might be mastered; and the success was answerable. The suppressing the Dissenters is not a harder work, nor a work of less necessity to the public; we can never enjoy a settled uninterrupted union and tranquillity in this nation, till the spirit of Whiggism, faction, and schism is melted down like the old money.

To talk of the difficulty, is to frighten ourselves with chimeras and notions of a powerful party, which are indeed a party without power; difficulties often appear greater at a distance, than when they are searched into with judgment, and distinguished from the vapours and shadows that attend them.

We are not to be frightened with it; this age is wiser than that, by all our own experience, and their's too; King Charles the First had early suppressed this party, if he had took more deliberate measures. In short, 'tis not worth arguing, to talk of their arms, their Monmouths, and Shaftesburys,[13] and Argylls[14] are gone, their Dutch sanctuary is at an end, Heaven has made way for their destruction, and if we do not close with the divine occasion, we are to blame ourselves, and may remember that we had once an opportunity to serve the Church of England, by extirpating her implacable enemies, and having let slip the minute that Heaven presented, may experimentally complain, *post est occasio calvo*.[15]

Here are some popular objections in the way.

> As first, the Queen has promised them, to continue them in their tolerated liberty; and has told us she will be a religious observer of her word.

What her Majesty will do we cannot help, but what, as the Head of the Church, she ought to do, is another case: her Majesty has promised to protect and defend the Church of England, and if she cannot effectually do that without the destruction of the Dissenters, she must of course dispense with one promise to comply with another. But to answer this cavil more effectually: her Majesty did never promise to maintain the toleration, to the destruction of the Church; but it is upon supposition that it may be compatible with the well-being and safety of the Church, which she had declared she would take especial care of: now if these two interests clash, 'tis plain her Majesty's intentions are to uphold, protect, defend, and establish the Church, and this we conceive is impossible.

Perhaps it may be said, that the Church is in no immediate danger from the Dissenters, and therefore 'tis time enough: but this is a weak answer.

For first, if a danger be real, the distance of it is no argument against, but rather a spur to quicken us to prevention, lest it be too late hereafter.

And 2dly, here is the opportunity, and the only one perhaps that ever the Church had to secure herself, and destroy her enemies.

The representatives of the nation have now an opportunity, the time is come which all good men have wished for, that the gentlemen of England may serve the Church of England; now they are protected and encouraged by a Church of England Queen.

What will ye do for your sister in the day that she shall be spoken for.[16]

If ever you will establish the best Christian Church in the world.

If ever you will suppress the spirit of enthusiasm.[17]

If ever you will free the nation from the viperous brood that have so long sucked the blood of their mother.

If you will leave your posterity free from faction and rebellion, this is the time.

This is the time to pull up this heretical weed of sedition, that has so long disturbed the peace of our Church, and poisoned the good corn.

But, says another hot and cold objector, this is renewing fire and faggot, reviving the Act *De Heret. Comburendo*:[18] this will be cruelty in its nature, and barbarous to all the world.

I answer, 'tis cruelty to kill a snake or a toad in cold blood, but the poison of their nature makes it a charity to our neighbours, to destroy those creatures, not for any personal injury received, but for prevention; not for the evil they have done, but the evil they may do.

Serpents, toads, vipers, &c. are noxious to the body, and poison the sensitive life; these poison the soul, corrupt our posterity, ensnare our children, destroy the vitals of our happiness, our future felicity, and contaminate the whole mass.

Shall any law be given to such wild creatures: some beasts are for sport, and the huntsmen give them advantages of ground; but some are knocked on head by all possible ways of violence and surprise.

I do not prescribe fire and faggot, but as Scipio said of Carthage, *Dilenda est Carthago*;[19] they are to be rooted out of this nation, if ever we will live in peace, serve God, or enjoy our own: as for the manner, I leave it to those hands who have a right to execute God's justice on the nation's and the Church's enemies.

But if we must be frighted from this justice, under the specious pretences, and odious sense of cruelty, nothing will be effected: 'twill be more barbarous and cruel to our own children, and dear posterity, when they shall reproach their fathers, as we do ours, and tell us, 'You had an opportunity to root out this cursed race from the world, under the favour and protection of a true English Queen; and out of your foolish pity you spared them, because, forsooth, you would not be cruel, and now our Church is suppressed and persecuted, our religion trampled under foot, our estates plundered, our persons imprisoned and dragged to jails, gibbets, and scaffolds; your sparing this Amalakite race is our destruction, your mercy to them proves cruelty to your poor posterity.

How just will such reflections be, when our posterity shall fall under the merciless clutches of this uncharitable generation, when our Church shall be swallowed up in schism, faction, enthusiasm, and confusion; when our government shall be devolved upon foreigners, and our monarchy dwindled into a republic.

'Twould be more rational for us, if we must spare this generation, to summon our own to a general massacre, and as we have brought them into the world free, send them out so, and not betray them to destruction by our supine negligence, and then cry it is mercy.

Moses was a merciful meek man, and yet with what fury did he run through the camp, and cut the throats of three and thirty thousand[20] of his dear Israelites, that were fallen into idolatry; what was the reason? 'twas mercy to the rest, to make these be examples, to prevent the destruction of the whole army.

How many millions of future souls we save from infection and delusion, if the present race of poisoned spirits were purged from the face of the land.

*

'Tis vain to trifle in this matter, the light foolish handling of them by mulcts, fines, &c. 'tis their glory and their advantage; if the gallows instead of the counter,[21] and the gallies instead of the fines, were the reward of going to a conventicle, to preach or hear, there would not be so many sufferers, the spirit of martyrdom is over; they that will go to Church to be chosen Sheriffs and Mayors, would go to forty Churches rather than be hanged.

If one severe law were made, and punctually executed, that whoever was found at a conventicle, should be banished the nation, and the preacher be hanged, we should soon see an end of the tale, they would all come to Church; and one age would make us all one again.

To talk of 5 s. a month[22] for not coming to the sacrament, and 1 s. per week for not coming to Church, this is such a way of converting people as never was known, this is selling them a liberty to transgress for so much money: if it be not a crime, why don't we give them full licence? And if it be, no price ought to compound for the committing it, for that is selling a liberty to people to sin against God and the Government.

If it be a crime of the highest consequence, both against the peace and welfare of the nation, the glory of God, the good of the Church, and the happiness of the soul, let us rank it among capital offences, and let it receive a punishment in proportion to it.

We hang men for trifles, and banish them for things not worth naming, but an offence against God and the Church, against the welfare of the world, and the dignity of religion, shall be bought off for 5 s. This is such a shame to a Christian Government, that 'tis with regret I transmit it to posterity.

If men sin against God, affront his ordinances, rebel against his Church, and disobey the precepts of their superiors, let them suffer as such capital crimes deserve, so will religion flourish, and this divided nation be once again united.

And yet the title of barbarous and cruel will soon be taken off from this law too. I am not supposing that all the Dissenters in England should be hanged or banished, but as in cases of rebellions and insurrections, if a few of the ring-leaders suffer, the multitude are dismissed, so a few obstinate people being made examples there's no doubt but the severity of the law would find a stop in the compliance of the multitude.

To make the reasonableness of this matter out of question, and more unanswerably plain, let us examine for what it is that this nation is divided into parties and factions, and let us see how they can justify a separation, or we of the Church of England can justify our bearing the insults and inconveniencies of the party.

One of their leading pastors,[23] and a man of as much learning as most among them, in his answer to a pamphlet, entitled, *An Enquiry into the Occasional Conformity*, hath these words, p. 27: *Do the religion of the Church and the Meeting-houses make two religions? Wherein do they differ? The substance of the same religion is common to them both; and the modes and accidents are the things in which only they differ.* P. 28: *Thirty-nine Articles are given us for the summary of our religion, thirty-six contain the substance of it, wherein we agree; three the additional appendices,[24] about which we have some differences.*

Now, if as by their own acknowledgment, the Church of England is a true Church, and the difference between them is only a few modes and accidents, why should we expect that they will suffer gallows and gallies, corporeal punishment and banishment for these trifles; there is no question but they will be wiser; even their own principles won't bear them out in it, they will certainly comply with the laws, and with reason, and though at the first, severity may seem hard, the next age will feel nothing of it; the contagion will be rooted out; the disease being cured, there will be no need of the operation, but if they should venture to transgress, and fall into the pit, all the world must condemn their obstinacy, as being without ground from their own principles.

Thus the pretence of cruelty will be taken off, and the party actually suppressed and the disquiets they have so often brought upon the nation, prevented.

Their numbers, and their wealth, makes them haughty, and that is so far from being an argument to persuade us to forbear them, that 'tis a warning to us, without any more delay, to reconcile them to the unity of the Church, or remove them from us.

At present, Heaven be praised, they are not so formidable as they have been, and 'tis our own fault if ever we suffer them to be so; Providence, and the Church of England, seems to join in this particular, that now the destroyers of the nation's peace may be overturned, and to this end the present opportunity seems to be put into our hands.

To this end her present Majesty seems reserved to enjoy the crown, that the ecclesiastic as well as civil rights of the nation may be restored by her hand.

To this end the face of affairs have received such a turn in the process of a few months, as never has been before; the leading men of the nation, the universal cry of the people, the unanimous request of the clergy, agree in this, that the deliverance of our Church is at hand.

For this end has Providence given us such a Parliament, such a Convocation,[25] such a gentry, and such a Queen as we never had before.

And what may be the consequences of a neglect of such opportunities? The succession of the crown has but a dark prospect, another Dutch turn may make the hopes of it ridiculous, and the practice impossible: be the house of our future princes never so well inclined, they will be foreigners; and many years will be spent in suiting the genius of strangers to the crown, and to the interests of the nation; and how many ages it may be before the English throne be filled with so much zeal and candour, so much tenderness, and hearty affection to the Church, as we see it now covered with, who can imagine?

'Tis high time then for the friends of the Church of England, to think of building up, and establishing her, in such a manner, that she may be no more invaded by foreigners, nor divided by factions, schisms, and error.

If this could be done by gentle and easy methods, I should be glad, but the wound is corroded, the vitals begin to mortify, and nothing but amputation of members can complete the cure: all the ways of tenderness and compassion, all persuasive arguments have been made use of in vain.

The humour of the Dissenters has so increased among the people, that they hold the Church in defiance, and the House of God is an abomination among them: nay, they have brought up their posterity in such prepossessed aversions to our holy religion, that the ignorant mob think we are all idolaters, and worshippers of Baal; and account it a sin to come within the walls of our Churches.

The primitive Christians were not more shy of a heathen temple, or of meat offered to idols, nor the Jews of swine's flesh, than some of our Dissenters are of the Church, and the divine service solemnized therein.

This obstinacy must be rooted out with the profession of it, while the generation are left at liberty daily to affront God Almighty, and dishonour his holy worship, we are wanting in our duty to God, and our mother the Church of England.

How can we answer it to God, to the Church, and to our posterity, to leave them entangled with fanaticism, error, and obstinacy, in the bowels of the nation; to leave them an enemy in their streets, that in time may involve them in the same crimes, and endanger the utter extirpation of religion in the nation.

What's the difference betwixt this, and being subjected to the power of the Church of Rome, from whence we have reformed? If one be an extreme on one hand, and one on another, 'tis equally destructive to the truth, to have errors settled among us, let them be of what nature they will.

Both are enemies of our Church, and of our peace, and why should it not be as criminal to admit an enthusiast as a Jesuit? Why should the Papist with his seven sacraments be worse than the Quaker with no sacraments at all? Why should Religious houses be more intolerable than Meeting-houses—— Alas the Church of England! What with Popery on one hand, and schismatics on the other, how has she been crucified between two thieves.

Now let us crucify the thieves. Let her foundations be established upon the destruction of her enemies: the doors of mercy being always open to the returning part of the deluded people: let the obstinate be ruled with the rod of iron.

Let all true sons of so holy an oppressed mother, exasperated by her afflictions, harden their hearts against those who have oppressed her.

And may God Almighty put it into the hearts of all the friends of truth, to lift up a standard against pride and Antichrist, that the posterity of the sons of error may be rooted out from the face of this land for ever ——.

FINIS.

A BRIEF
EXPLANATION
Of a Late Pamphlet,
ENTITULED,
The Shortest Way with the
DISSENTERS.

THe Author professes he thought, when he wrote the Book, he shou'd never need to come to an Explication, and wonders to find there should be any reason for it.

If any man take the pains seriously to reflect upon the Contents, the Nature of the Thing and the Manner of the Stile, it seems impossible to imagine it should pass for any thing but an Irony.

That it is free from any Seditious design, either of stirring up the Dissenters to any evil practice by way of prevention; much less of animating others to their destruction. will be plain, I think, to any man that understands the present Constitution of *England,* and the nature of our Government.

But since Ignorance, or Prejudice has led most Men to a hasty Censure of the Book, and several poor People are like to come under the displeasure of the Government for it, in justice to those who are in danger to suffer for it; in Humble submission to the Parliament and Council, who may be offended at it; and in Courtesse to all mistaken People, who it seems have not penetrated into the real design: The Author presents the World with the

A   Native

A Brief Explanation of a Late Pamphlet, Entitled, The Shortest Way with the Dissenters.

The author professes he thought, when he wrote the book, he should never need to come to an explication, and wonders to find there should be any reason for it.

If any man take the pains seriously to reflect upon the contents, the nature of the thing and the manner of the style, it seems impossible to imagine it should pass for any thing but an irony.

That it is free from any seditious design, either of stirring up the Dissenters to any evil practice by way of prevention; much less of animating others to their destruction, will be plain, I think, to any man that understands the present constitution of England, and the nature of our Government.

But since ignorance, or prejudice has led most men to a hasty censure of the book, and several poor people[1] are like to come under the displeasure of the Government for it; in justice to those who are in danger to suffer for it; in humble submission to the Parliament and Council, who may be offended at it; and in courtesy to all mistaken people, who it seems have not penetrated into the real design: the author presents the world with the native genuine meaning and design of the paper, which he hopes may allay the anger of the Government, or at least satisfy the minds of such as imagine a design to inflame and divide us.

The paper, without the least retrospect to, or concern in the public bills in Parliament, now depending; or any other proceedings of either House, or of the Government relating to the Dissenters, whose occasional conformity the author has constantly opposed, has its immediate original from the virulent spirits of some men who have thought fit to express themselves to the same effect, in their printed books, though not in words so plain and at length, and by an irony not unusual, stands as a fair answer to several books published in this liberty of the press; which, if they had been handed to the Government with the same temper as this has, would, no question have found the same treatment.

The sermon preached at Oxford,[2] the *New Association*,[3] the *Poetical Observator*, with numberless others; have said the same thing, in terms very little darker, and this book stands fair to let those gentlemen know that what they design can no farther take with mankind than as their real meaning stands disguised by artifice of words; but that when the persecution and destruction of the Dissenters, the very thing they drive at, is put into plain English, the whole nation will start at the notion, and condemn the author to be hanged for his impudence.

The author humbly hopes he shall find no harder treatment for plain English without design, than those gentlemen for their plain design in duller and darker English.

Any gentlemen who have patience to peruse the author of the *New Association*, will find gallows, galleys, persecution and destruction of the Dissenters, as directly pointed at, as fairly intended, and designed in this shortest way, as, had it been real, can be pretended; there is as much virulence against a Union with Scotland, against King WILLIAM's Government, and against the line of Hanover, there is as much noise and pains taken in Mr S[acheverell]'s sermon to blacken the Dissenters, and thereby to qualify them for the abhorrence of all mankind, as is possible.

The meaning then of this paper is in short to tell these gentlemen,

1. That 'tis nonsense to go round about, and tell us of the crimes of the Dissenters, to prepare the world to believe they are not fit to live in a humane society, that they are enemies to the Government, and law, to the QUEEN, and the public peace, and the like; the shortest way, and the soonest, would be to tell us plainly that they would have them all hanged, banished and destroyed.

2. But withal to acquaint those gentlemen who fancy the time is come to bring it to pass, that they are mistaken, for that when the thing they mean, is put into plain English, the whole nation replies with the Assyrian Captain, *Is thy servant a dog, that he should do these things?*[4] The gentlemen are mistaken in every particular, it will not go down, the QUEEN, the Council, the Parliament are all offended, to have it so much as suggested, that such a thing was possible to come into their minds; and not a man, but a learned mercer, not far from the corner of Fanchurch-street, has been found to approve of it.

Thus a poor author has ventured to have all mankind call him villain and traitor to his country and friends, for making other people's thoughts speak in his words.

From this declaration of his real design, he humbly hopes the Lords of her Majesty's Council, or the House of Parliament, will be no longer offended, and that the poor people in trouble on this account shall be pardoned or excused.

He also desires that all men who have taken offence at the book, mistaking the author's design, will suffer themselves to think again, and withhold their censure till they find themselves qualified to make a venture like this for the good of their native country.

As to expressions which seem to reflect upon persons or nations; he declares them to be only the cant of the non-juring party exposed, and thinks it very necessary to let the world know that 'tis their usual language with which they treat the late KING, the Scotch Union, and the line of Hanover.

'Tis hard, after all, that this should not be perceived by all the town, that not one man can see it, neither Churchman nor Dissenter.

That not the Dissenters themselves can see that this was the only way to satisfy them, that whatever the Parliament might think fit to do to restrain occasional communion, persecution and destruction was never in their intention, and that therefore they have nothing to do but to be quiet and easy.

For anything in the manner of the paper which may offend either the Government, Parliament, or private persons, the author humbly begs their pardon, and protesting the honesty of his intention, resolves, if the poor people now in trouble may be excused, to throw himself upon the favour of the Government rather than others shall be ruined for his mistakes.

POSTSCRIPT.

The scandal of the Observator's charging[5] the author of this book, with being the author of the *Black List*,[6] the *Kentish Feast*,[7] the *Legion Paper*,[8] and a world of other things, which he knows nothing of, is a baseness peculiar to himself. The author challenges the said Observator to make out so much as the least shadow of any part of his charge to be truth, and till he does, his character speaks for itself.

A

DIALOGUE

BETWEEN

A

DISSENTER

AND THE

OBSERVATOR,

CONCERNING

The Shortest Way with the DISSENTERS.

LONDON,
Printed in the Year, MDCCIII.

A Dialogue Between a Dissenter
and the Observator

Diss. Pray Sir, are you the author of the *Observator*?[1]

Obs. Suppose it Sir, what then?

Diss. Nay don't be angry, are you the reputed author?[2] Come off, you taught me in one of your papers about Mr. F.

Obs. And what then?

Diss. Why I wanted a little civil discourse with you.

Obs. If it be civil, as you say, you are welcome, but you begin but oddly.

Diss. My questions may be blunt, but you are not bound to answer them, but let that be as you like 'em.

First, pray who do you reckon is the author of this devilish book, called, *The Shortest Way*?

Obs. I shall answer most of your questions with a question, I believe, and begin with you here.

Do you think my name is Mr. Bellamy,[3] that you take me for an informer? read the *Gazette*, there you have the man with the *sharp chin*,[4] and a *Dutch nose*.

Diss. Ay, but Sir, we begin to doubt that is not the true author, that he has been only made the tool of some other party, who now they find the world exasperated at it, have slipped out of the noose, and left him in it; we begin to be afraid the thing is a reality, and there is such a design on foot.

Obs. Your answer, like Parson Jacob's text,[5] ought to be taken a pieces and explained.

1. If you are not sure he is the author, you Dissenters have done him a great deal of wrong, for you have railed at him more than all the rest of the world, and charged him with more crimes than 'tis well possible for one man to be guilty of.

2. And yet by supposing him not to be the author, you suppose him to be very honest to his friends, that he bears all this without discovering them.

3. As for your fears of a real design, to put *The Shortest Way* in practice upon you, no question there are abundance of people in the world, who would be glad there was not one of you left; I believe nobody doubts it.

Diss. Pray who do you think they are?

Obs. Sir your humble servant; no Bellamy, I tell you, not I, Sir; if I were in a plot with the Devil, I'll never turn evidence, besides Sir, I have no mind to have my nose and chin described, but if you please I'll answer you negatively, who I believe are not concerned in it.

Diss. That may be some satisfaction, Sir.

Obs. Not the Queen, Sir, not the Parliament, not the Council, not the Army, not the Ministers of State, not the Government.

Diss. Thou art a safe man, thoul't never go to Newgate for negatives.

Obs. No Sir, nor for positives neither, if I can help it; but you have had your will at catechising, and I ought to have my turn, let me ask you a few questions too.

Diss. You are welcome.

Obs. Pray why are you Dissenters angry at the book called *The Shortest Way*, 'tis a little mysterious, Sir, that the Church men are affronted because t'was writ against them, and the Dissenters are affronted because 'tis wrote against them too, I don't well understand it, one sort must be fools, that's certain.

Diss. I don't care whether I understand it or no, he is a rogue, a villain, and I wish the Government had him, if I knew where he was, I'd deliver him up and abate them the 50*l.*

Obs. Spoken like a Dissenter truly, so that I find you are angry at him because you don't understand him, and the Government because they do.

Diss. You are so sharp upon me, I do understand a little too, I understand he meddled with that he had nothing to do with, and he is the man they say who has been the occasion of all this persecution which is coming upon us, by railing at Occasional Conformity.

Obs. If he exposed you for Occasional Conformity, 'tis what you ought to have rectified yourselves, that you need not have been exposed for it; and in that he was your friend; for had you took the hint and exploded the practice, there had been no need of an Act of Parliament[6] to force you to it.

Diss. But what had he to do with that?

Obs. Nay, what had Mr. How[7] to do to meddle with it afterward, I'll assure you his name is down in my pocket book, and when any man in

England defends a cause worse, I'll put his name out, and put t'other's name in: but pray Sir, why do you call this bringing persecution upon you; do you suppose the Occasional Bill will be a persecution?

Diss. Without doubt it will.

Obs. What sort of persecution can you call it? it can't be a persecution for conscience sake.

Diss. Why so Sir?

Obs. Why, pray, Sir, suppose one of your brethren Dissenters, who can go to the Meeting today, and to the Church tomorrow; take the Sacrament today, sitting, and tomorrow to get a good place, go to Church, and take it kneeling, wipe his mouth and go home to dinner, and so to the Meeting again; suppose this gentleman should be put up for Sheriff, or Lord Mayor, can this man pretend conscience not to conform? I tell you Sir, Mr. How must make a better answer to the matter before I can be convinced, you may call it persecution but it can never be for conscience sake.

Diss. Persecution is persecution, let it be for what sake it will, every man ought to be at liberty.

Obs. Ay that is true, I am for liberty for every man to serve God as is most agreeable to his conscience: but this is not serving God at all: besides Sir, I could easily make it appear, this Act is for your advantage, if ye were a sort of people were to be convinced.

Diss. Pray, how Sir?

Obs. Why Sir, it will purge you of all your half in half professors. That's one thing; then it will put all those gentlemen into a capacity of being in places and Parliaments, who though by this Act they are separated from you, and rejoined to the Church because they can conform, will still be friends to your interest in all public concerns; and therefore had I been to word the Bill so as to have done most harm, it should have excluded all that ever were Dissenters, and have forced you to continue so, and not have accepted your return to the Church without a public repentance.

Diss. Well, well, you may persuade us 'tis for our advantage, but we don't like it, and therefore we hate him for meddling with it; for what had he to do with it?

Obs. About as much as you and I have to do with him; if a man meddles with what does not concern him, that's his fault, and if we who really have nothing to do with him, meddle with him, that is our fault, let the Government alone with him, have you nothing else to talk on?

Diss. Why all the town has talked of him as well as we.

Obs. Yes, and reckoned up all his faults, all the sins that ever he committed in his life, and abundance more; be the man who he will, and what he will, I don't see but the best of us would be loth all the faults we have should be reckoned up and writ in our foreheads, as his are..

Diss. Oh, he has been a most wicked wretch.

Obs. You force a man to be an advocate for one he has no kindness for; a wicked wretch you say; why what, has he been a thief, a murderer?

Diss. No no, I don't mean that way.

Obs. What, has he been a clipper or coiner?

Diss. No no, nor that neither.

Obs. Has he been a whoremaster or a drunkard, or a swearer?

Diss. No, I can't say so neither, but he broke and can't pay his debts.

Obs. If you had said he had broke and won't pay his debts, you had said more to the purpose.

But I must do one piece of justice to the man, though I love him no better than you do, that is this: that meeting a gentleman in a coffee-house, where I and everybody else was railing at him, the gentlemen took us up with this short speech.

Gentlemen, said he, I know this D. Foe as well as any of you, and I was one of his creditors, and I compounded with him, and discharged him fully; and several years afterward he sent for me, and though he was clearly discharged, he paid me all the remainder of his debt voluntarily, and of his own accord: and he told me, that as fast as God should enable him he intended to do so with everybody; when he had done, he desired me to set my hand to a paper to acknowledge it, which I readily did, and found a great many names to the paper, before me, and I think myself bound to own it, though I am no friend to the book he has wrote, no more than you. What do you think of this story?

Diss. Think of it, I don't believe it!

Obs. I can't help that, nor I care not whether you do or no, but I assure you after I heard it, I never railed at him any more.

Diss. Ay, but I'll rail at him for all that.

Obs. You Dissenters are in something like case with the Pharisees;[8] when the question was put to them by our Saviour about John's baptism, whether it was from heaven or of men. If a man should ask you of *The Shortest Way*, was it wrote for you or against you? If you should say for us, you would be asked why then are you so mad with the author? And if you should say against you, the people would laugh at you; for all men but you see into it, and that a Dissenter wrote it; you must say therefore, we cannot tell, and consequently, that you rail at the author for you can't tell what.

Diss. But we don't count him a Dissenter.

Obs. He has all the marks of a Dissenter upon him, but want of brains.

Diss. Why are we so empty of brains pray?

Obs. There's reason for it, God has given you equivalents.

Diss. I don't understand you.

Obs. That's a further testimony of your being a Dissenter; why if you will have it, take it, I say, God Almighty would have seemed unkind to you, if he had not given you a great deal of grace; for he has given you but little wit.

Diss. Well, I hope they'll take him still, I should be glad to see him hanged for it, I am sure he deserves it; I heard one met him a little while ago, would I had been there.

Obs. Alone, do you mean Sir, or to have helped the other?

Diss. Any how, so I could but have taken him.

Obs. 'Twas in Hackney Fields, was it not?

Diss. Yes, I think so.

Obs. Ay, and they say 'twas one of your own party too, and one that would fain have got the 50 *l.* but that he drew upon him, frighted him out of his wits, and made him down of his knees and swear that if ever he met him again, he should shut his eyes till he was half a mile off him.

Diss. I don't think he's such a fighting fellow.

Obs. Do you know him?

Diss. No not I.

Obs. So I thought by your charity and good nature; I know him not neither; but the man has the Government upon his back already, and if they take him they'll avenge your quarrel for you. Let him alone, 'tis ungenerous, as I said before in print,[9] to triumph over a man in his affliction; 'twas but a little while ago he wrote a book that pleased you, and then you cried him up as much as now you cry him down.

Diss. What book pray?

Obs. Why the *New Test of Church of England Loyalty*.[10]

Diss. Did he write that book?

Obs. I told you I was no informer, go ask Mr. Bellamy.

Diss. Why truly that was a good thing, I liked it fully. 'Twas well done, but this cursed *Shortest Way* is the devil, he must be turned rogue now, whatever he was then.

Obs. Why, this 'tis to oblige a Dissenter, if you serve them a hundred times 'tis well, but once get your head in the pillory for them, and they'll be the first to pelt you with rotten eggs; what, can't you set down one good thing and one bad, and balance with him: you understand accompts well enough; but you Dissenters are like a shopkeeper I knew, who having traded 20 year with a gentleman, and served all his family and gotten a great deal of money by him, at last the poor gentleman fell to decay, and owing him 40 s. the shopkeeper abused him, and called him all the knaves and rogues for cheating of him of 40 s.

Diss. No, no, this has spoiled all.

Obs. Well, but we'll go back further with you, there's the *Reformation of Manners*,[11] and the *True-Born Englishman*; there he pleased you for certain, for he is for reforming your magistrates.

Diss. I don't understand them, I am for reformation as much as anybody.

Obs. But what say you to the *Legion Paper*?

Diss. Ay that was a good thing indeed.

Obs. Well, but if he had been taken in doing that, would you not have called him as many rogues then as you do now?

Diss. No indeed, should I not?

Obs. But I don't find you call him one rogue the less for it now, and that's hard.

Diss. Well, but you see he denies it,[12] and challenges you to prove it.

Obs. Ay, deny it, I told you he was no fool, indeed I am not glad I printed it, for though it is charged upon him by common fame, I am not for hanging men upon suppositions as you do.

Diss. Well, you do well, and I think 'tis a little hard, the man is gone, and though he has done ill, he might mean no harm, and so let him alone, I reckon you won't be long before you follow him.

Obs. And when I am gone, you'll call me as many rogues as you do him, won't you?

Diss. No, it may be I shan't, but I can tell you of some that do already.

Obs. It's all one to me, common fame like a common strumpet, jilts everybody, but methinks slander and reproach, out of the mouth of a Dissenter comes with some more than common ill savour.

Diss. They think they have good reason for it upon you.

Obs. And I think not, pray what are their good reasons?

Diss. For abusing your friends?

Obs. My friends, prithee who are they? I know but very few I have, and I am very sure I never abused them.

Diss. They all agree you would not be permitted to write so long, but the party would have ruffled you before now, only you court them and please them by a side-wind, with your railing at King William's friends[13] sometimes.

Obs. King William's enemies you mean; look, Sir, I have as much veneration for the memory of King William as any of you, and do but once prove them to be King William's friends, and I'll own all you say, and recant all I have wrote.

Diss. It's easy to prove they were his friends.

Obs. Pray Sir, don't you tax me with abusing King William, and abuse him yourself, I have proved sufficiently they were the nation's enemies: now if you can prove the nation's enemies were King William's friends, you'll make a fine spot of work on't indeed.

Diss. The nation's enemies! That is, because being in great places, they got as much money as they could, and so would you do, and so have all the favourites that ever were or will be.

Obs. Whenever favourites did, do or shall get money by rapine or injustice, and oppression of the subject, they were and will be the nation's enemies and their sovereign's too.

Diss. But what have you to do with it? 'tis none of your business.

Obs. 'Tis every man's business to discover mischief, fraud and ill design, as much as every man who first spies fire has a duty upon him to raise the neighbours: I am a subject, and am cheated among the rest.

Diss. You cheated, why what have you to lose?

Obs. Why, my liberty, which you said but now, every man had a right to, and my money when I have it; what's that to you, how little, or much I have, and how do you know how much I may have hereafter.

Diss. Nay, they say you get money by railing, and so you may soon be rich.

Obs. Then I rail for something, and you get none, and yet you rail; pray who has the best excuse for it?

Diss. He that has the best reason for it, not he that gets the most money by it.

Obs. I believe if you could get money by railing, you would count it the best reason in the world.

Diss. Why so?

Obs. Because you are so willing to rail at anybody, when you know not for what, nor why, and charge people with crimes they never committed; of all your Christian duties, you make the least use of your charity.

Diss. Why, since you put so hard, I can tell the time when you abused King William himself, as openly as you durst speak it, or anybody dare print, particularly in a poem of yours, called the *Foreigners*.[14]

Obs. How do you prove 'twas mine?

Diss. Nay, they say 'twas yours, you were the reputed author, as you said in another case.

Obs. I tell you, there's no people in the world so forward to condemn a man upon hearsay, as the Dissenters, when they have a mind to slander a man, they take everything upon trust, 'tis their *Shortest Way*.

Diss. These scribbling people are always meddling with things they have nothing to do with; what have you to do with Kings and favourites, or that t'other fellow with the *Shortest Way*: you pamphleteers are always quacking with[15] the State.

Obs. Come let's turn the tables, now it's my play, what have you to do with Acts of Parliaments; you Dissenters are always thrusting in your oar too; what have you to do to talk of persecution and Acts against Occasional Conformity, you are mountebanking with[16] the State too in every coffee-house, pray meddle with your own business.

Diss. We shall have to do with it, when we feel it.

Obs. I am persuaded if you were put to it severally, few of you would stay to feel it, at least few of your wealthy members, few of Mr. How's mind, few of such Dissenters as go from Meeting to Church, and can back-stroke and fore-stroke, communicate on both sides.

Diss. I wish they may not, but we are afraid 'twill not only be a persecution, but a very long one.

Obs. Why then you are beholding to the author we talked of, for you see he is for putting you out of your pain, but I am of a different opinion from you in several of your darkest thoughts about persecution.

Diss. Pray what is your opinion?

Obs. 1. I am of opinion that if your enemies were true masters of politics, they would not persecute you at all, I take you to be a declining party, toleration will be your ruin; and if God in mercy to you don't send a persecution among you, you are lost, you will all dwindle back into the

Church again; your old stock of ministers die off, your Owens, Mantons, Charnocks, Clarksons, Baxters, and Bates's[17] are gone, and pray what can you name out of the new generation of your Leyden Doctors fit to succeed them.

2. The Occasional Bill at once carries off your wealthy members, who are the support of your clergy, and as Mr. Williams very well observed at Salters' Hall,[18] *If the rich ones forsake you, the party will be weakened so as to make you fear the dissolution of the whole.* Indeed the gentleman was in the right, if the wealthy members quit the congregations, 'twill make poor work for the ministers, and they like other people generally do their work best where they have best wages.

Diss. I thought you had loved the Dissenters better, than to abuse them at this rate.

Obs. I don't abuse them, I wish them clear of all their hypocrites, and that there were none among them but what were Dissenters for mere conscience: if that were so, 'twould make their enemies at peace with them, they'd never be persecuted; the Government would cherish them, and be as tender of them as they would desire. But to be plain with you, 'tis your own pride and pushing at great things has made you obnoxious, and withal your discovering by an alternate double-faced conscience, that while you pretend to Dissent, and to have tender consciences, you can nevertheless conform, if you please; this makes your enemies suspect your honesty, and apprehend more trick and design in you, than I hope they need. Nay this gives your enemies such advantage against you, as you can never answer.

Diss. I do not think any man ought to be confined by laws and Acts of Parliaments about his religion.

Obs. It may be I think so too; but men ought to be honest to their own principles, whether there were laws or no; and if I see a man pretend he can't conform, and upon occasion I find he can, it makes me suspect his honesty, and if I once think a man a knave, I am not to blame to fence myself against him by laws: I tell you an Act of Parliament to keep you honest, can never be called persecution.

Diss. Ay, if there was no more in it.

Obs. If there be any more in it, I wish there was not, I'm sure I know not what is in it, and I believe you don't neither; pray have you seen the Bill?

Diss. No not I, but I hear 'tis a very terrible Bill.

Obs. True to the old way still, always to judge before you hear. Indeed

I forgot to ask you, but on my conscience I don't believe you ever read the book of the *Shortest Way*; come, be honest.

Diss. Read it, why the very outside of that is enough for any man to read; I thank God I spend my time better.

Obs. I think you ought to spend your time better too, than to give your verdict upon anything before you read it.

Diss. You are a strange man, why everybody says 'tis a horrible book, and not fit to be read, but what's that to this Act of Parliament?

Obs. Why thus much 'tis, that you cry out persecution from this Act of Parliament, and there's not a word of persecution in it.

Diss. I think 'tis persecution, if I must not be at liberty to worship God as I think fit.

Obs. Still you are without book, why you may be a Dissenter all the days of your life, and go to Meetings as long as you live, and never be troubled by this Act.

Diss. I can't imagine what you mean, why, I must pay, God knows what, if I am seen at a Meeting.

Obs. Ay, Sir, that's after you have strained your conscience from the Meeting to the Church; after you have bobbed your religion to be Sheriff of London, or the like; and then want to go back again; but if you, to keep your conscience, can be content to be without these gay things called places, you may be a Dissenter to the end of the chapter: so that this will only be a persecution for honour's sake, not for conscience's sake, and never fall upon you neither, till you bring it upon yourself.

Diss. Well, I hope it won't pass for all that.

Obs. I hope so too, but if it don't, it must be *the Lord's doing, and it will be marvellous in our eyes.*[19]

Diss. The House of Lords you mean, I suppose.

Obs. I must mean as you will have me, let it be how it will, but if I hope it will not pass, it's from different reasons with you.

Diss. Pray, your reasons?

Obs. Because I am against (and ever shall be) imposing any religious ordinance or part of worship as a qualification for any temporal employment. Let the Princes be at full liberty to employ who, or what sort of their subjects they see cause. 2. Such impositions are a bait to people to banter their consciences, and to comply with that for a preferment, which otherwise they would not, and so seem to lead them into temptation: but I don't know the contents of the Bill, therefore I'll say no more.

Diss. And I would not have it pass, because I take it to be a foundation of persecution; 'tis but pulling down the Toleration next, and then we are all undone.

Obs. You faithless and perverse generation![20] Has not the QUEEN promised to maintain your Toleration? Besides, what's that to the Bill?

Diss. Why should not we be afraid of it, as well as some of the Church-party have the confidence to hope it? Nay, to condemn the Toleration as antichristian, and threaten us with the having it overthrown.

Obs. Why these are for *the shortest way*; you ought to rail at them as much as you do at the man with the hook nose, and sharp chin, and more too; and no doubt if you would but turn informer, you might hook their noses into the *Gazette* too; to be sure the Government would not allow of it; they would never suffer the QUEEN to be so affronted.

Diss. I don't know how 'tis, such things are suffered daily. I heard our parson t'other day say at a public dinner 'twould never be well with England till some course was taken to reconcile all Dissenters to the Church, longest way or shortest, 'twas all one to him; he said he hoped to see the Church flourish without them; and a great deal more, and worse than this.

Obs. That was a topping high-flying gentleman indeed, and why did you not acquaint the Government with it?

Diss. What do you think I am an informer? My name is not Bellamy any more than yours, but pray why do you make so strange of it? Don't we hear daily people expressing their high-flying hopes that a Parliament in Scotland will restore Episcopacy there, and yet has not the QUEEN given her word, and published it in our *Gazette*, that she will maintain the Presbyterian Government there.

Obs. Has she so? Then though they have the impudence to hope, you ought not to have the ignorance to fear it. The QUEEN gave her word to maintain it! be not slow of heart to believe. She has taken up the famous motto of Q. Elizabeth, *semper eadem*,[21] and can you so much as doubt she will deface it, for a few Scotch Bishops.

Diss. I am sorry for my fears, I beg her Majesty's pardon, there are so many turns and windings in law and State matters, that we know not what to say to things.

Obs. Say! Why a promise is a promise, and you may depend upon it, she has never broke her word with us yet.

Diss. Ay, but what if the Parliament should do it?

Obs. Nay, if the Parliament does it, we do it ourselves.

Diss. Very good, so that we may be undone, and the Toleration Bill taken away; and yet the QUEEN be as good as her word still.

Obs. Yes Sir, so you may, whenever an Act of Parliament becomes so without the Royal assent, and when do you think that can be?

Diss. Why then these high-flying Churchmen are very impudent fellows, to suggest such things of the QUEEN, and to bully us with overturning the Toleration, and put us in such fears of what they will do to us, when it can never be done without the QUEEN's acting so directly against her royal promise.

Obs. Well, and what then.

Diss. Why I think they ought to be used as they used the author of the *Shortest Way*, *Gazetted* and a reward for the discoverer.

Obs. Or as you have used him rather, *viz.* rail at them, for being of your own side: you Dissenters are rare fellows for punishments, if God should have no more mercy on you, than you shew to all men that offend you, we should have plagues, pestilence and famine every year upon us; so now you are come about again, these high-flying Church Men have bullied you with the fears of losing your Toleration, come confess.

Diss. Yes.

Obs. And made you distrust the QUEEN's veracity.

Diss. Yes, GOD and the QUEEN forgive us.

Obs. And have terrified you with what things they'll do when they have pulled down your antichristian toleration, have they not?

Diss. Ay, Ay.

Obs. And so you thought the *Shortest Way* was wrote to make a beginning with you, and to set the dragoons of the Church upon your backs; did you not?

Diss. 'Tis very true.

Obs. And continued of the same mind like an ignoramus, though you heard 'twas wrote by one of your own party.

Diss. Indeed I did.

Obs. Now pray, after so much patience as I have had with you, have a little with me; and if I can, I'll set you right in your thoughts of these things.

There are a sort of people among the Dissenters who can either Dissent or Conform, as they find their inclinations or interest rather directs them, these by their wealth and interest have always put themselves into good

places, and qualified themselves for that purpose, by taking the sacrament:
of these people, even the most moderate Churchmen have an ill opinion,
and truly so have two thirds of your own friends, for it looks as if they
were men of no principles at all.

Against these men the Act against Occasional Conformity is principally
designed, and if there was nothing else in the Bill, I believe no good man
would be against it.

Concerning these things, two sorts of people have been very grossly
mistaken, and upon their mistakes have proceeded to act very foolishly.

First, the high-flying Church party begun to think, all was a-going their
own way, and that the Government would fall in with them, and do your
business for you, and away they run with the notion, and preach you down,
and print you down, and talk you down like mad men; there is sermon
upon sermon, pamphlet upon pamphlet: one says you are all rogues and
hypocrites, another says you are enemies to the Government; one flies at
the Toleration, and tells the world 'tis destructive to the nation's happiness,
and the politicians must pull it down, another says 'tis antichristian, and
we cannot be true sons of the Church of England, if we don't pull it down;
others like hare-brained huntsmen that overrun the hounds, roar you down
with full cry, till they run themselves out of breath; others are for having
you deprived of voices in elections of Parliament, in hopes of arriving to
that blessed day, when they shall have a Parliament of their own mind;
and thus they run before they are sent, and without reflecting upon their
ill-grounded zeal, without examining any authorities, other than their
passions, without regard to good manners, taking no notice of the preamble
of the Act of Parliament, which declares against persecution, or the honour
and sacred promise of Her MAJESTY, given to make her subjects
easy, they blow up the fire of persecution and destruction, whether the
Government will or no.

You are the next sort of people, who are mistaken, for being naturally a
little hypish,[22] as the *beaus* call it, troubled with the spleen, and hypochondriac
vapours, this cloud of raillery so darkened your understanding, that you
presently take these people and the QUEEN, these people and the Government, these people and the Parliament, to be all of a mind; and the QUEEN
having displaced all your friends, as 'tis but just, that all Princes should
employ who they please: and the Parliament falling on your Occasional
Conformers, and this book of *The Shortest Way* coming out altogether,
the High Church party thundered at you from the press and the pulpit:

away you run with the notion that you are all to be blown up, that all these things aimed at your destruction, and that fire and faggot was at the door.

But the Government is steady, and the QUEEN still has maintained her motto, the Parliament steers in the middle way, going about to restrain, but not to destroy you; and taking no notice either of the heat of one party, or folly of the other, they hold the balance of your liberty between your own exorbitant license, and the other party's unchristian fury; and in my opinion, thus far are you safe.

Diss. But then why has not the Government thought fit to disown the zeal of these High-flyers, by punishment, and make examples of some of them?

Obs. I told you, the Dissenters were all for punishments and examples, for the same reason that they have not punished you for suspecting the QUEEN's honesty to her word, charging the Parliament with going about to persecute you, and the like; for this reason, because they are more merciful than both parties deserve.

Diss. 'Twould have convinced us very plainly of two very significant things. First, that there is such a design, and then that the authors of it received no countenance from Court.

Obs. Good manners and common justice ought to have convinced you of the last, and your author of *The Shortest Way*, to his cost, opened your eyes in the first, if you had not wilfully shut them against the light.

1. Good manners would inform you, not to doubt the word of your Prince, till you had some reason from her MAJESTY herself.

2. Common justice commands us to suppose every person just and honest, till something appears to the contrary; and it is a very unchristian, uncharitable way of treating the QUEEN, that because some of the High Churchmen have had the indiscretion, without her authority, to swagger you out of your senses; therefore you must suppose her promise broken, and her word of no value.

The author of *The Shortest Way* comes with a lanthorn for you, and he sums up all the black things this High party had published, into one general, and if you had any eyes, you might learn two things from him, while he is like to pay dear enough for teaching you.

First, from the general abhorrence mankind shewed of the book, you might learn that the destruction of your party is a cruelty not to be found in the English nature.

Secondly, from the outcry made against it by that party in particular, you might learn who they were that were touched in the book, and where the design against them lay.

As to the quarrel you Dissenters have at the book that's a mystery no man can unriddle but yourselves. 'Tis like Mr. Mead's wheel within a wheel,[23] and a further testimony to the world that you are a most unaccountable people whose ways are past finding out.

Diss. So that you would go about to persuade me the book was writ of our side.

Obs. First, Sir, 'tis hard to know what side you are of, and

Secondly, Sir, I know you too well to go about to persuade you to anything, whose peculiar talent is to be unpersuadable; but if you will please to answer me a few questions you may perhaps persuade yourself of something or other.

Diss. What questions?

Obs. Why are the High Churchmen angry with him, while at the same time they openly declare 'tis the only way to deal with you, and what they would feign be at?

Diss. Truly you puzzle me a little there.

Obs. They are angry, because they take the book as the author meant it, and you, because you take it as he wrote it; they as he meant, *viz.* to expose them, and though they are heartily willing to do you a kindness that way, and have shewn their good will by their words, yet knowing they wanted power to execute it, and being conscious to themselves that the Government was not of their opinion; they are enraged to have all their designs laid open in miniature, and an abridgment communicated to the world in true Billingsgate.[24]

Diss. There may be some truth in this, but pray why then is the Government so angry with him? I believe I have puzzled you now.

Obs. No, no, the Government may have reasons to be angry that you nor I know not of, nor have nothing to do with: but what if I should suppose that the Government not thinking any person could be so barbarous as to harbour such a villainous design as the book suggests, are displeased at it as an affront done to the Church of England to father principles of cruelty and destruction upon her members, which they are not guilty of; I say, if I suppose this to be a reason, I believe you cannot suppose a better.

Diss. I confess, I begin to have better thoughts of the Government than I had.

Obs. I'm glad of that.

Diss. I begin to hope they won't persecute us now, and as for Occasional Conformity what care I? I shall never be Lord Mayor or Common Council man; if I am called to it, 'tis time enough to come off then.

Obs. God Almighty is wonderfully beholden to you; when he calls you from a middle state to a good place, you'll take it for granted He calls you from the Meeting to the Church, and you'll be sure to come. But I tell you, you ought to be so far from the fear of a persecution, that if you have any respect to your party, you ought to pray for a persecution upon them or ye are all undone.

Diss. Why thou art mad, thou art for the *shortest way*.

Obs. No, no, I an't for such persecution neither, but I told you my mind before, I am sure you have received more damage in your interest as Dissenters, and more weakened your reputation as well as your number, since the late Toleration, than ever your enemies did for you by all the penal laws, informers, fines, and prisons of the last persecution.

Diss. Well, but here's another danger upon us that we han't talked of yet, and fear it will come upon us too.

Obs. Pray what's that?

Diss. We are afraid that this restless party will overthrow our Settlement, for they do not stick to talk that way.

Obs. We afraid, who do you mean by we? Are not the Church of England as much concerned in the Settlement as you and more too, as they are the major part of the nation? and we (if you will give me leave to talk your way) we Protestants fear nothing for our Settlement, and for this, I'll give you a quotation[25] from the man with the hook nose and sharp chin, it may be you won't like it because of the author, but his words are these.

The Settlement of the Crown (says he) is the basis of our religion, laws and liberties. This is the solid bottom on which we all stand, and of which, with respect to civil right, may be said *Other foundation can no man lay than that which is laid.* 'Tis the rock on which we are all built, and that stone of which, according to the Scripture, it may without profaneness be said, *Whosoever it falls upon, he will be broken to pieces, but on whomsoever it shall fall, it will grind him to powder.*[26]

'Tis the last thing the People of England will part with after all their estates, wives and children, churches and houses are destroyed.

'Tis the pledge of the Divine goodness to the nation, which they purchased at the expense of 50 millions of money, and the blood of above 100,000 English men in eleven years war.

'Twas one of the great things King WILLIAM did for us, and the treasure GOD and his MAJESTY left in our hands in trust for our posterity; which if we part with, our children will curse our memory and dig us out of our graves.

'Tis a thing so sacred the dissolving of it cannot be mentioned without a crime, nor so much as intended without being guilty of treason in the most intense degree.

'Tis the solid prop upon which stands her present MAJESTY'S throne, and the right and just title she has to govern us.

'Tis like the two pillars in the house of Dagon:[27] whoever pulls them down will, like Samson, be buried in the ruins, and pull the whole nation upon their heads.

I fear nothing for this Settlement; the Parliament of England are the trustees for the seeing it forthcoming to the People of England, and a Parliament of England will never betray their trust.

The Parliament will not, and all the rest of human power dare not attempt to dissolve it, no weapon formed against it can prosper.

Diss. Is this done by our *Shortest Way* man?
Obs. The very same.
Diss. Well, I shall love him the better for it: but there's one thing more still, what say you to the Prince of Wales?[28] If ever he comes again you'll be hanged, that's for certain.
Obs. And if ever we let him come we ought all to be hanged. I can do no better than refer you to the same author.

The Act of Settlement (says he) and the Prince of Wales are the two buckets, keep one but up and the other must be down, and put the one down and the other comes up of course: there can be no pretence made to alter or dispose the Settlement, but the bringing in the Prince of Wales; therefore whoever they are that mention it, we ought to suppose they would be so understood.

Diss. So that you are of opinion we are in no danger of our Settlement.
Obs. Indeed I am of the opinion your fears both of the Prince of Wales, and of altering the Settlement, and of persecution, are all groundless and equally so. I would only advise the Dissenters to be honest to their own

principles; if they can conform they ought to do it, if they cannot, nobody forces them; let them dissent, and not for the desire of preferment bring such a scandal upon their integrity, as if they were men of no principles. 'Tis scandalous to the very name of a Dissenter and injurious to all the rest of that body who are honest and conscientious.

And so I bid you farewell.

A

HYMN

TO THE

PILLORY.

The *Second Edition Corrected,* with *Additions.*

LONDON:
Printed in the Year. MDCCIII.

A Hymn to the Pillory

Hail! hieroglyphic[1] state machine,
Contrived to punish fancy in:
Men that are men, in thee can feel no pain,
And all thy insignificants[2] disdain.
  Contempt, that false new word for shame,
  Is without crime, an empty name,
  A shadow to amuse[3] mankind,
But never frights the wise or well-fixed mind:
  Virtue despises human scorn,
  And scandals innocence adorn.
  Exalted on thy stool of state,
What prospect do I see of sov'reign fate;
How the inscrutables of Providence,
  Differ from our contracted sense;
  Here by the errors of the town,
  The fools look out, the knaves look on.
Persons or crimes find here the same respect,
  And vice does virtue oft correct,
The undistinguished fury of the street,
  With mob and malice mankind greet:
  No bias can the rabble draw,
But dirt throws dirt without respect to merit, or to law.

Sometimes the air of scandal to maintain,
Villains look from thy lofty loops in vain:[4]
But who can judge of crimes by punishment,
Where parties rule, and l[aw']s subservient.
Justice with change of int'rest learns to bow,
And what was merit once, is murther now:

Actions receive their tincture from the times,
And as they change are virtues made or crimes.   30
  Thou art the state-trap of the law,
But neither can keep knaves, nor honest men in awe;
    These are too hardened in offence,
    And those upheld by innocence.

How have thy opening vacancys received,
In every age the criminals of state?
    And how has mankind been deceived,
    When they distinguish crimes by fate?
Tell us, great engine, how to understand,
Or reconcile the justice of the land;   40
How Bastwick, Prynne, Hunt, Hollingsby and Pye,[5]
    Men of unspotted honesty;
    Men that had learning, wit and sense,
    And more than most men have had since,
    Could equal title to thee claim,
With Oates and Fuller,[6] men of later fame:
    Even the learned Selden[7] saw,
    A prospect of thee, through the law:
He had thy lofty pinnacles in view,
But so much honour never was thy due: 50
Had the great Selden triumphed on thy stage,
    Selden the honour of his age;
    No man would ever shun thee more,
Or grudge to stand where Selden stood before.

Thou art no shame to truth and honesty,
Nor is the character of such defaced by thee,
    Who suffer by oppressive injury.
    Shame, like the exhalations of the sun,
    Falls back where first the motion was begun:
And he who for no crime shall on thy brows appear,   60
    Bears less reproach than they who placed him there.

But if contempt is on thy face entailed,
    Disgrace itself shall be ashamed;

Scandal shall blush that it has not prevailed,
   To blast the man it has defamed.
Let all that merit equal punishment,
Stand there with him, and we are all content.

   There would the famed S[achevre]ll[8] stand,
With trumpet of sedition in his hand,
70   Sounding the first crusado in the land.
He from a Church of England pulpit first
   All his Dissenting brethren cursed;
   Doomed them to Satan for a prey,
   And first found out *the shortest way*;[9]
With him the wise Vice-Chancellor o'th' press,
Who, though our printers' licences defy,
   Willing to show his forwardness,
   Blessed it with his authority;[10]
He gave the Church's sanction to the work,
80   As Popes bless colours for troops which fight the Turk.
   Doctors in scandal these are grown
For red-hot zeal and furious learning known:
Professors in reproach and highly fit,
For Juno's Academy, Billingsgate.[11]
   Thou like a *True-born English* tool,
   Hast from their composition stole,[12]
And now art like to smart for being a fool:
And as of English men, 'twas always meant,
They're better to improve than to invent;
90   Upon their model thou hast made
   A monster makes the world afraid.[13]

   With them let all the statesmen stand,
   Who guide us with unsteady hand:
   Who armies, fleets, and men betray;
   And ruin all *the shortest way*.
   Let all those soldiers stand in sight,
Who're willing to be paid and not to fight.
Agents, and Colonels, who false musters bring,
To cheat their country first, and then their King:

Bring all your coward Captains of the Fleet;   100
Lord! What a crowd will there be when they meet?
   They who let Pointi 'scape to Brest,
Whom all the Gods of Carthagena blessed.[14]
   Those who betrayed our Turkey fleet;
Or injured Talmash sold at Camaret.[15]
   Who missed the squadron from Thoulon,[16]
And always came too late or else too soon,
All these are heroes whose great actions claim,
Immortal honours to their dying fame;
   And ought not to have been denied,   110
On thy great counterscarp, to have their valour tried.

Why have not these upon thy spreading stage,
Tasted the keener justice of the age;
If 'tis because their crimes are too remote,
Whom leaden-footed justice has forgot?
   Let's view the modern scenes of fame,
If men and management are not the same,
When fleets go out with money, and with men,
Just time enough to venture home again?
Navys prepared to guard th' insulted coast,   120
And convoys settled when our ships are lost.
   Some heroes lately come from sea,
If they were paid their due, should stand with thee;
   Papers too should their deeds relate,
   To prove the justice of their fate:
Their deeds of war at Port Saint Mary's done,
And set the trophies by them, which they won:
Let Or[mon]d's Declaration there appear,
He'd certainly be pleased to see 'em there.
   Let some good limner represent,   130
   The ravished nuns, the plundered town,
   The English honour how misspent;
The shameful coming back, and little done.[17]

   The Vigo men should next appear,
   To triumph on thy theatre;

They, who on board the great galoons had been,
Who robbed the Spaniards first, and then the Queen:
Set up the praises to their valour due,
How eighty sail, had beaten twenty-two.
    Two troopers so, and one dragoon,
Conquered a Spanish boy in pantaloon.
    Yet let them O[rmon]d's conduct own,
Who beat them first on shore, or little had been done:
    What unknown spoils from thence are come,
How much was brought away, how little home.[18]
If all the thieves should on thy scaffold stand
    Who robbed their masters in command:
    The multitude would soon outdo,
    The city crowds of Lord Mayor's show.

    Upon thy penitential stools,
    Some people should be placed for fools:
As some for instance who while they look on,
See others plunder all, and they got none.
    Next the Lieutenant General,[19]
To get the devil, lost the de'l and all;
    And he some little badge should bear,
Who ought, in justice, to have hanged 'em there:
    This had his honour more maintained,
    Than all the spoils at Vigo gained.

    Then clap thy wooden wings for joy,
    And greet the men of great employ;
The authors of the nation's discontent,
And scandal of a Christian government.
Jobbers, and brokers of the City stocks,
With forty thousand tallies[20] at their backs;
Who make our banks and companies obey,
    Or sink 'em all *the shortest way*.
    Th' intrinsic value of our stocks,
Is stated in their calculating books;
Th' imaginary prices rise and fall,
    As they command who toss the ball;

140

150

160

170

Let 'em upon thy lofty turrets stand,
With bear-skins[21] on the back, debentures[22] in the hand,
  And write in capitals upon the post,
    That here they should remain,
    Till this enigma they explain,
  How stocks should fall, when sales surmount the cost,
    And rise again when ships are lost.

  Great monster of the law, exalt thy head;
    Appear no more in masquerade,   180
  In homely phrase express thy discontent,
  And move it in th' approaching Parliament:
  Tell 'em how paper went instead of coin,
  With int'rest eight per cent and discount nine.[23]
    Of Irish transport debts[24] unpaid,
  Bills false endorsed,[25] and long accounts unmade.
  And tell them all the nation hopes to see,
    They'll send the guilty down to thee;
  Rather than those who write their history.

  Then bring those Justices upon thy bench,   190
  Who vilely break the laws they should defend;
    And upon equity intrench,
  By punishing the crimes they will not mend.
    Set every vicious Magistrate,
  Upon thy sumptuous chariot of the state;
    There let 'em all in triumph ride,
  Their purple and their scarlet laid aside.
  Let none such Bridewell Justices protect,
  As first debauch the whores which they correct:
    Such who with oaths and drunk'ness sit,   200
  And punish far less crimes than they commit:
    These certainly deserve to stand,
With trophies of authority in either hand.

  Upon thy pulpit, set the drunken priest,
  Who turns the gospel to a bawdy jest;
  Let the fraternity degrade him there,
    Lest they like him appear:

There let him, his *memento mori* preach,
And by example, not by doctrine, teach.
210   Next bring the lewder clergy there,
Who preach those sins down, which they can't forbear;
Those sons of God who every day go in,
Both to the daughters and the wives of men;[26]
There let 'em stand to be the nation's jest,
And save the reputation of the rest.

A[sgi]ll[27] who for the gospel left the law,
And deep within the clefts of darkness saw;
Let him be an example made,
Who durst the parson's province so invade;
220   To his new ecclesiastic rules,
We owe the knowledge that we all are fools:
Old Charon[28] shall no more dark souls convey,
A[sgi]ll has found *the shortest way*:
Vain is your funeral pomp and bells,
Your grave-stones, monuments and knells;
Vain are the trophys of the grave,
A[sgi]ll shall all that foppery save;
And to the clergy's great reproach,
Shall change the hearse into a fiery coach:
230   What man the learned riddle can receive,
Which none can answer, and yet none believe;
Let him recorded, on thy lists remain,
Till he shall heav'n by his own rules obtain.

If a poor author has embraced thy wood,
Only because he was not understood,[29]
They punish mankind but by halves,
Till they stand there,
Who false to their own principles appear:
And cannot understand themselves.
240   Those Nimshites,[30] who with furious zeal drive on,
And build up Rome to pull down Babylon;
The real authors of *The Shortest Way*
Who for destruction, not conversion pray:

There let those sons of strife remain,
  Till this Church riddle they explain;
How at Dissenters they can raise a storm,
  But would not have them all conform;
For there their certain ruin would come in,
And moderation, which they hate, begin.
  Some Churchmen next should grace thy pews,   250
Who talk of loyalty they never use;
Passive obedience[31] well becomes thy stage,
For both have been the banter of the age.
  Get them but once within thy reach,
Thou'lt make them practice what they used to teach.

  Next bring some lawyers to thy bar,
By innuendo they might all stand there;
  There let them expiate that guilt,
And pay for all that blood their tongues ha' spilt;
  These are the mountebanks of state,   260
Who by the slight of tongue can crimes create,
And dress up trifles in the robes of fate.
  The mastiffs of a government,
To worry and run down the innocent;
  The engines of infernal wit,
  Covered with cunning and deceit:
Satan's sublimest attribute they use,
  For first they tempt, and then accuse;
No vows or promises can bind their hands,
  Submissive law obedient stands: 270
When power concurs, and lawless force stands by,
He's lunatic that looks for honesty.

  There sat a man of mighty fame,[32]
Whose actions speak him plainer than his name;
In vain he struggled, he harangued in vain,
To bring in whipping sentences again:
And to debauch a milder government,
With abdicated kinds of punishment.
  No wonder he should law despise,
  Who Jesus Christ himself denies;[33]   280

His actions only now direct,
What we when he is made a J[udg]e, expect:
   Set L[ove]ll[34] next to his disgrace,
With Whitney's horses[35] staring in his face;
There let his cup of penance be kept full,
Till he's less noisy, insolent and dull.

When all these heroes have passed o'er thy stage,
And thou hast been the Satyr of the age;
Wait then a while for all those sons of fame,
Whom present pow'r has made too great to name:
Fenced from thy hands, they keep our verse in awe,
Too great for satyr, and too great for law.
   As they their commands lay down,
They all shall pay their homage to thy cloudy throne:
     And till within thy reach they be,
     Exalt them in effigy.

The martyrs[36] of the by-past reign,
For whom new oaths have been prepared in vain;
She[rloc]k's disciple first by him trepanned,
He for a k[nave] and they for f[ool]s should stand.
Though some affirm he ought to be excused,
   Since to this day he had refused;
And this was all the frailty of his life,
He damned his conscience, to oblige his wife.[37]
But spare that priest, whose tottering conscience knew
That if he took but one, he'd perjure two:
Bluntly resolved he would not break 'em both,
And swore by God he'd never take the Oath;
   Hang him, he can't be fit for thee,
   For his unusual honesty.

Thou speaking trumpet of men's fame,
   Enter in every court thy claim;
Demand 'em all, for they are all thy own,
Who swear to three Kings,[38] but are true to none.
   Turn-coats of all sides are thy due,
And he who once is false, is never true:

Today can swear, tomorrow can abjure,
For treachery's a crime no man can cure:
Such without scruple, for the time to come,
May swear to all the Kings in Christendom;   320
    But he's a madman will rely
    Upon their lost fidelity.

They that in vast employments rob the state,
Let them in thy embraces meet their fate;
Let not the millions they by fraud obtain,
Protect 'em from the scandal, or the pain:
    They who from mean beginnings[39] grow
    To vast estates, but God knows how;
    Who carry untold sums away,
From little places, with but little pay: 330
    Who costly palaces erect,
    The thieves that built them to protect;
The gardens, grottos, fountains, walks, and groves
Where vice triumphs in pride, and lawless loves:
Where mighty luxury and drunk'ness reigned,
Profusely spend what they prophanely gained:
Tell 'em their Mene Tekel's[40] on the wall,
Tell 'em the nation's money paid for all:

    Advance thy double front and show,
And let us both the crimes and persons know: 340
    Place them aloft upon thy throne,
Who slight the nation's business for their own;
Neglect their posts, in spite of double pay,
And run us all in debt *the shortest way*.

    Great pageant, change thy dirty scene,
For on thy steps some ladies may be seen;
When beauty stoops upon thy stage to show,
She laughs at all the humble fools below.
Set Sappho there, whose husband paid for clothes
Two hundred pounds a week in furbulos: 350
There in her silks and scarlets let her shine,
She's beauteous all without, all whore within.

Next let gay Urania ride,
Her coach and six attending by her side:
    Long has she waited, but in vain,
    The city homage to obtain:
The sumptuous harlot longed t' insult the chair,
And triumph o'er our city beauties there.
Here let her haughty thoughts be gratified,
360   In triumph let her ride.

    Let Diadora next appear,
And all that want to know her, see her there.
What though she's not a *True-Born English* whore?
    French harlots have been here before;
Let not the pomp nor grandeur of her state
    Prevent the justice of her fate,
But let her an example now be made
To foreign wh[ore]s who spoil the English trade.

Let Flettumacy with his pompous train,
370   Attempt to rescue her in vain;
    Content at last to see her shown,
Let him despise her wit, and find his own:
Though his inheritance of brains was small,
Dear-bought experience will instruct us all.

    Claim 'em, thou herald of reproach,
Who with uncommon lewdness will debauch;
Let C[risp] upon thy borders spend his life,
'Till he recants the bargain with his wife:
    And 'till this riddle both explain,
380   How neither can themselves contain;
How Nature can on both sides run so high,
As neither side can neither side supply:
    And so in charity agree,
He keeps two brace of whores, two stallions she.

What need of Satyr to reform the town?
    Or laws to keep our vices down?
    Let 'em to thee due homage pay,
This will reform us all *the shortest way*.

Let 'em to thee bring all the knaves and fools,
 Virtue will guide the rest by rules;   390
They'll need no treacherous friends, no breach of faith,
No hired evidence with their infecting breath;
 No servants masters to betray,
 Or knights o'th' post,[41] who swear for pay;
No injured author'll on thy steps appear,
Not such as won't be rogues, but such as are.

 The first intent of laws
Was to correct th' effect, and check the cause;
 And all the ends of punishment,
Were only future mischiefs to prevent.   400
 But justice is inverted when
  Those engines of the law,
 Instead of pinching vicious men,
  Keep honest ones in awe;
 Thy business is, as all men know,
To punish villains, not to make men so.

 Whenever then thou art prepared,
 To prompt that vice thou should'st reward,
And by the terrors of thy grisly face,
 Make men turn rogues to shun disgrace;   410
The end of thy creation is destroyed,
Justice expires of course, and law's made void.
What are thy terrors? That for fear of thee,
Mankind should dare to sink their honesty?
He's bold to impudence, that dare turn knave,
The scandal of thy company to save:
He that will crimes he never knew confess,
Does more than if he knew those crimes transgress:
And he that fears thee more than to be base,
May want a heart, but does not want a face.   420
 Thou like the devil dost appear
 Blacker than really thou art by far:
A wild chimeric notion of reproach,
Too little for a crime, for none too much:

Let none th' indignity resent,
For crime is all the shame of punishment.

Thou bug-bear of the Law stand up and speak,
    Thy long misconstrued silence break,
Tell us who 'tis upon thy ridge stands there,
430   So full of fault, and yet so void of fear;
        And from the paper in his hat,[42]
        Let all mankind be told for what:

Tell them it was because he was too bold,
And told those truths, which should not ha' been told.
    Extol the justice of the land,
Who punish what they will not understand.
        Tell them he stands exalted there,
        For speaking what we would not hear;
        And yet he might ha' been secure,
440   Had he said less, or would he ha' said more.[43]
        Tell them that this is his reward,
        And worse is yet for him prepared,
Because his foolish virtue was so nice
As not to sell his friends, according to his friends' advice;
        And thus he's an example made,
        To make men of their honesty afraid,

        That for the time to come they may,
        More willingly their friends betray,
Tell 'em the M[agistrates] that placed him here,
450   Are sc[anda]ls to the times,
        Are at a loss to find his guilt,
            And can't commit his crimes.

SOCIAL REFORMER

A N

ESSAY

UPON

Projects.

LONDON:

Printed by *R. R.* for *Tho. Cockerill*,
at the *Three Legs* in the *Poultrey*.
MDC XC VII.

Introduction.

Necessity, which is allowed to be the mother of invention, has so violently agitated the wits of men at this time, that it seems not at all improper, by way of distinction, to call it, The Projecting Age. For though in times of war and public confusions, the like humour of invention has seemed to stir; yet, without being partial to the present, it is, I think, no injury to say, the past ages have never come up to the degree of projecting and inventing, as it refers to matters of negoce,[1] and methods of civil polity, which we see this age arrived to.

Nor is it a hard matter to assign probable causes of the perfection in this modern art. I am not of their melancholy opinion, who ascribe it to the general poverty of the nation; since I believe 'tis easy to prove, the nation itself, taking it as one general stock, is not at all diminished or impoverished by this long, this chargeable war;[2] but on the contrary, was never richer, since it was inhabited.

Nor am I absolutely of the opinion, that we are so happy as to be wiser in this age, than our forefathers; though at the same time I must own, some parts of knowledge in science as well as art, has received improvements in this age, altogether concealed from the former.

The art of war, which I take to be the highest perfection of human knowledge, is a sufficient proof of what I say, especially in conducting armies, and in offensive engines; witness the new ways of mines, fougades,[3] entrenchments, attacks, elodgments, and a long *et cetera* of new inventions which want names, practised in sieges and encampments; witness the new sorts of bombs and unheard-of mortars, of seven to ten ton weight, with which our fleets standing two or three miles off at sea, can imitate God Almighty himself, and rain fire and brimstone out of Heaven, as it were, upon towns built on the firm land; witness also our new-invented child of Hell, the machine, which carries thunder, lightning, and earthquakes in its bowels, and tears up the most impregnable fortifications.

But if I would search for a cause, from whence it comes to pass that this age swarms with such a multitude of projectors more than usual; who besides the innumerable conceptions which die in the bringing forth, and (like abortions of the brain) only come into the air, and dissolve, do really every day produce new contrivances, engines, and projects to get money, never before thought of; if, I say, I would examine whence this comes to pass, it must be thus:

The losses and depredations which this war brought with it at first, were exceeding many, suffered chiefly by the ill conduct of merchants themselves, who did not apprehend the danger to be really what it was: for before our Admiralty could possibly settle convoys, cruisers, and stations for men of war all over the world, the French covered the sea with their privateers, and took an incredible number of our ships. I have heard the loss computed by those who pretended they were able to guess, at above fifteen millions of pounds sterling, in ships and goods, in the first two or three years of the war: a sum, which if put into French, would make such a rumbling sound of great numbers, as would fright a weak accomptant out of his belief, being no less than one hundred and ninety millions of *livres*. The weight of this loss fell chiefly on the trading part of the nation; and amongst them, on the merchants; and amongst them again upon the most refined capacities, as the insurers, &c. And an incredible number of the best merchants in the kingdom sunk under the load; as may appear a little by a bill which once passed the House of Commons, for the relief of merchant-insurers,[4] who had suffered by the war with France. If a great many fell, much greater were the number of those who felt a sensible ebb of their fortunes, and with difficulty bore up under the loss of great part of their estates. These, prompted by necessity, rack their wits for new contrivances, new inventions, new trades, stocks, projects, and any thing to retrieve the desperate credit of their fortunes. That this is probable to be the cause, will appear further thus; France, though I do not believe all the great outcries we make of their misery and distress, if one half of which be true, they are certainly the best subjects in the world; yet without question has felt its share of the losses and damages of the war; but the poverty there falling chiefly on the poorer sort of people, they have not been so fruitful in inventions and practices of this nature, their genius being quite of another strain. As for the gentry and more capable sort, the first thing a French man flies to in his distress, is the army; and he seldom comes back from thence to get an estate by painful industry, but either has his brains knocked out, or makes his fortune there.

If industry be in any business rewarded with success, 'tis in the merchandizing part of the world, who indeed may more truly be said to live by their wits than any people whatsoever. All foreign negoce, though to some 'tis a plain road by the help of custom, yet it is in its beginning all project, contrivance, and invention. Every new voyage the merchant contrives, is a project; and ships are sent from port to port, as markets and merchandizes differ, by the help of strange and universal intelligence; wherein some are so exquisite, so swift, and so exact, that a merchant sitting at home in his counting-house, at once converses with all parts of the known world. This, and travel, makes a true-bred merchant the most intelligent man in the world, and consequently the most capable, when urged by necessity, to contrive new ways to live. And from hence, I humbly conceive, may very properly be derived the projects, so much the subject of the present discourse. And to this sort of men 'tis easy to trace the original of banks, stocks, stock-jobbing, assurances, friendly societies, lotteries, and the like.

To this may be added, the long annual enquiry in the House of Commons for ways and means, which has been a particular movement to set all the heads of the nation at work; and I appeal, with submission, to the gentlemen of that honourable House, if the greatest part of all the ways and means, out of the common road of land-taxes, polls, and the like, have not been handed to them from the merchant, and in a great measure paid by 'em too.

However I offer this but as an essay at the original of this prevailing humour of the people; and as 'tis probable so, 'tis also possible to be otherwise; which I submit to future demonstration.

Of the several ways this faculty of projecting has exerted itself, and of the various methods, as the genius of the authors has inclined, I have been a diligent observer, and in most an unconcerned spectator; and, perhaps, have some advantage from thence more easily to discover the *faux pas* of the actors. If I have given an essay towards anything new, or made discovery to advantage of any contrivance now on foot, all men are at the liberty to make use of the improvement; if any fraud is discovered, as now practiced, 'tis without any particular reflection upon parties or persons.

Projects of the nature I treat about, are doubtless in general of public advantage, as they tend to improvement of trade, and employment of the poor, and the circulation and increase of the public stock of the kingdom; but this is supposed of such as are built on the honest basis of ingenuity and improvement; in which, though I'll allow the author to aim primarily at his own advantage, yet with the circumstances of public benefit added.

Wherefore 'tis necessary to distinguish among the projects of the present times, between the honest and the dishonest.

There are, and that too many, fair pretences of fine discoveries, new inventions, engines, and I know not what, which being advanced in notion, and talked up to great things to be performed when such and such sums of money shall be advanced, and such and such engines are made, have raised the fancies of credulous people to such height, that merely on the shadow of expectation, they have formed companies, chose committees, appointed officers, shares, and books, raised great stocks, and cried up an empty notion to that degree, that people have been betrayed to part with their money for shares in a new-nothing; and when the inventors have carried on the jest till they have sold all their own interest, they leave the cloud to vanish of itself, and the poor purchasers to quarrel with one another, and go to law about settlements, transferrings, and some bone or other thrown among 'em by the subtlety of the author, to lay the blame of the miscarriage upon themselves. Thus the shares at first begin to fall by degrees, and happy is he that sells in time; till like brass money it will go at last for nothing at all. So have I seen shares in joint-stocks, patents, engines, and undertakings, blown up by the air of great words, and the name of some man of credit concerned, to 100 *l.* for a 500*th.* part, or share, some more, and at last dwindle away, till it has been stock-jobbed down to 10, 12, 9, 8 *l.* a share, and at last no buyer; that is, in short, the fine new word for nothing-worth, and many families ruined by the purchase. If I should name linen-manufactures, saltpetre-works, copper-mines, diving-engines, dipping, and the like, for instances of this, I should, I believe, do no wrong to truth, or to some persons too visibly guilty.

I might go on upon this subject to expose the frauds and tricks of stock-jobbers, engineers, patentees, committees, with those exchange-mountebanks we very properly call brokers; but I have not gall enough for such a work; but as a general rule of caution to those who would not be tricked out of their estates by such pretenders to new inventions, let them observe, that all such people who may be suspected of design, have assuredly this in their proposal, your money to the author must go before the experiment: and here I could give a very diverting history of a patent-monger,[5] whose cully[6] was nobody but myself; but I refer it to another occasion.

But this is no reason why invention upon honest foundations, and to fair purposes, should not be encouraged; no, nor why the author of any such fair contrivances should not reap the harvest of his own ingenuity; our Acts of Parliament for granting patents[7] to first inventors for fourteen years, is a sufficient acknowledgment of the due regard which ought to be had to such as find out any thing which may be of public advantage; new discoveries in trade, in arts and mysteries,[8] of manufacturing goods, or improvement of land, are without question of as great benefit, as any discoveries made in the works of nature by all the academies and Royal Societies in the world.

There is, 'tis true, a great difference between new inventions and projects, between improvement of manufactures or lands, which tend to the immediate benefit of the public, and employing of the poor; and projects framed by subtle heads, with a sort of a *deceptio visus*,[9] and legerdemain, to bring people to run needless and unusual hazards: I grant it, and give a due preference to the first, and yet success has so sanctified some of those other sorts of projects, that 'twould be a kind of blasphemy against fortune to disallow 'em; witness Sir William Phips's voyage[10] to the wreck; 'twas a mere project, a lottery of a hundred thousand to one odds; a hazard, which if it had failed, everybody would have been ashamed to have owned themselves concerned in; a voyage that would have been as much ridiculed as Don Quixote's adventure upon the windmill: bless us! that folks should go three thousand miles to angle in the open sea for pieces of eight! why, they would have made ballads of it, and the merchants would have said of every unlikely adventure, 'twas like Phips his wreck-voyage; but it had success, and who reflects upon the project?

> Nothing's so partial as the laws of fate,
> Erecting blockheads to suppress the great.
> Sir Francis Drake the Spanish plate-fleet won,
> He had been a pirate if he had got none.
> Sir Walter Raleigh strove, but missed the plate,
> And therefore died a traitor to the state.
>
> Endeavour bears a value more or less,
> Just as 'tis recommended by success:
> The lucky coxcomb every man will prize,
> And prosp'rous actions always pass for wise.

However, this sort of projects comes under no reflection as to their honesty, save that there is a kind of honesty a man owes to himself and to his family, that prohibits him throwing away his estate in impracticable, improbable adventures; but still some hit even of the most unlikely, of which this was one, of Sir William Phips, who brought home a cargo of silver of near 200,000 *l.* sterling, in pieces of eight, fished up out of the open sea remote from any shore, from an old Spanish ship which had been sunk above forty years. [. . .]

OF FOOLS

Of all persons who are objects of our charity, none move my compassion, like those whom it has pleased God to leave in a full state of health and strength, but deprived of reason to act for themselves. And it is, in my opinion, one of the greatest scandals upon the understanding of others, to mock at those who want it. Upon this account, I think the hospital we call Bedlam,[11] to be a noble foundation; a visible instance of the sense our ancestors had of the greatest unhappiness which can befall human kind: since as the soul in man distinguishes him from a brute, so where the soul is dead (for so it is as to acting) no brute so much a beast as a man. But since never to have it, and to have lost it, are synonymous in the effect, I wonder how it came to pass, that in the settlement of that hospital they made no provision for persons born without the use of their reason, such as we call fools, or, more properly, naturals.

We use such in England with the last contempt, which I think is a strange error, since though they are useless to the commonwealth, they are only so by God's direct Providence, and no previous fault.

I think 'twould very well become this wise age to take care of such: and perhaps they are a particular rent-charge on the great family of mankind, left by the Maker of us all; like a younger brother, who though the estate be given from him, yet his father expected the heir should take some care of him.

If I were to be asked, who ought in particular to be charged with this work? I would answer in general, those who have a portion of understanding extraordinary: not that I would lay a tax upon any man's brains, or discourage wit, by appointing wise men to maintain fools: but some tribute is due to God's goodness for bestowing extraordinary gifts; and who can it be better paid to, than such as suffer for want of the same bounty?

For the providing therefore some subsistence for such, that natural defects may not be exposed:

It is Proposed,

That a Fool-House be erected, either by public authority, or by the City, or by an Act of Parliament; into which, all that are naturals, or born fools, without respect or distinction, should be admitted and maintained.

For the maintenance of this, a small stated contribution, settled by the authority of an Act of Parliament, without any damage to the persons paying the same, might be very easily raised, by a tax upon learning, to be paid by the authors of books.

Every book that shall be printed in folio, from 40 sheets and upwards, to pay at the licensing, (for the whole impression)	5 *l.*
Under 40 sheets,	40 *s.*
Every quarto,	20 *s.*
Every octavo of 10 sheets and upward,	20 *s.*
Every octavo under 10 sheets, and every bound book in 12,	10 *s.*
Every stitched pamphlet,	2 *s.*

Reprinted copies the same rates.

This tax to be paid into the chamber of London[12] for the space of twenty years, would without question raise a fund sufficient to build and purchase a settlement for this House.

I suppose this little tax being to be raised at so few places as the printing presses, or the licensers of books, and consequently the charge but very small in gathering, might bring in about 1,500 *l. per annum*, for the term of twenty years, which would perform the work to the degree following.

The House should be plain and decent (for I don't think the ostentation of buildings necessary or suitable to works of charity); and be built some-where out of town, for the sake of the air.

The building to cost about 1,000 *l.* or if the revenue exceed, to cost 2,000 *l.* at most, and the salaries mean in proportion.

In the House,

A steward	30 *l. per ann.*
A purveyor	20
A cook	20
A butler	20
Six women to assist the cook, and clean the House, 4 *l.* each }	24
Six nurses to tend the people 3 *l.* each }	18
A chaplain	20
	152
A hundred alms-people, at 8 *l. per ann.*, etc., etc. }	800
	952
The table for the Officers, and contingencies, and clothes for the alms-people, and firing put together, }	500

An auditor of the accounts, a committee of the Governors and two clerks.

Here I suppose 1,500 pounds *per ann.* revenue, to be settled upon the House, which 'tis very probable might be raised from the tax aforesaid. But since an Act of Parliament is necessary to be had for the collecting this duty, and that taxes for keeping of fools would be difficultly obtained, while they are so much wanted for wise men; I would propose to raise the money by voluntary charity, which would be a work would leave more honour to the undertakers, than feasts and great shows, which our public bodies too much diminish their stocks with.

But to pass all suppositious ways, which are easily thought of, but hardly procured; I propose to maintain fools out of our own folly: and whereas a great deal of money has been thrown about in lotteries,[13] the following proposal would very easily perfect our work.

A CHARITY-LOTTERY

That a lottery be set up by the authority of the Lord-Mayor and Court of Aldermen, for a hundred thousand tickets, at twenty shillings each, to be drawn by the known way and method of drawing lotteries, as the million-lottery[14] was drawn; in which no allowance to be made to any body; but the fortunate to receive the full sum of one hundred thousand pounds put in, without discount; and yet this double advantage to follow:

(1.) That an immediate sum of one hundred thousand pounds shall be raised and paid into the exchequer for the public use.

(2.) A sum of above twenty thousand pounds be gained, to be put into the hands of known trustees, to be laid out in a charity for the maintenance of the poor.

That as soon as the money shall be come in, it shall be paid into the exchequer, either on some good fund, if any suitable, or on the credit of exchequer; and that when the lottery is drawn, the fortunate to receive tallies[15] or bills from the exchequer for their money, payable at four years.

The exchequer receives this money, and gives out tallies according to the prizes, when 'tis drawn, all payable at four years; and the interest of this money for four years is struck in tallies proportioned to the time, and given to the trustees; which is the profit I propose for the work.

Thus the fortunate have an immediate title to their prizes, at four years, without interest; and the hospital will have also an immediate title to 6,000 *l. per ann.* for four years, which is the interest at 6 *per cent. per ann.*

If any should object against the time of staying for their prizes, it should be answered thus, that whoever did not like to stay the time for the money, upon discounting four years' interest at 8 *per cent.* should have their money down.

I think this specimen will inform anybody what might be done by lotteries, were they not hackneyed about in private hands, who by fraud and ill management put them out of repute, and so neither gain themselves, nor suffer any useful handsome design to succeed.

'Twould be needless, I suppose, to mention, that such a proposal as this ought to be set on foot by public approbation, and by men of known integrity and estates, that there may be no room left for a suspicion of private advantage.

If this or any equivalent proposal succeeded to raise the money, I would have the House established as aforesaid, with larger or smaller revenues, as necessity obliged; then the persons to be received should be without distinction or respect, but principally such as were really poor and friend-less; and any that were kept already by any parish-collection, the said parish should allow forty shillings yearly towards their maintenance; which no parish would refuse that subsisted them wholly before.

I make no question but that if such an Hospital was erected within a mile or two of the City, one great circumstance would happen, (viz.) that the common sort of people, who are very much addicted to rambling in the fields, would make this house the customary walk, to divert themselves with the objects to be seen there, and to make what they call sport with the calamity of others; as is now shamefully allowed in Bedlam.

To prevent this, and that the condition of such, which deserves pity, not contempt, might not be the more exposed by this charity, it should be ordered, that the steward of the House be in Commission of the Peace[16] within the precincts of the house only, and authorized to punish by limited fines, or otherwise, any person that shall offer an abuse to the poor alms-people, or shall offer to make sport at their condition.

If any person at reading of this, should be so impertinent as to ask, to what purpose I would appoint a chaplain in an hospital of Fools? I could answer him very well, by saying, for the use of the other persons, officers and attendants in the House.

But besides that, pray, why not a chaplain for Fools, as well as for knaves, since both, though in a different manner, are uncapable of reaping any benefit by religion, unless by some invisible influence they are made docible; and since the same secret power can restore these to their reason, as must make the other sensible; pray, why not a chaplain? Idiots indeed were denied the communion in the primitive churches, but I never read they were not to be prayed for, or were not admitted to hear.

If we allow any religion, and a Divine Supreme Power, whose influence works invisibly on the hearts of men (as he must be worse than the people we talk of, who denies it), we must allow at the same time, that power can restore the reasoning-faculty to an idiot; and 'tis our part to use the proper means of supplicating Heaven to that end, leaving the disposing-part to the issue of unalterable Providence.

The wisdom of Providence has not left us without examples of some of the most stupid natural idiots in the world, who have been restored to their reason, or as one would think, had reason infused after a long life of idiotism; perhaps, among other wise ends, to confute that sordid supposition, that idiots have no souls.

OF BANKRUPTS

This chapter[17] has some right to stand next to that of fools; for besides the common acceptation of late, which makes every unfortunate man a fool, I think no man so much made a fool of as a bankrupt.

If I may be allowed so much liberty with our laws, which are generally good, and above all things are tempered with mercy, lenity, and freedom, this has something in it of barbarity; it gives a loose to the malice and revenge of the creditor, as well as a power to right himself, while it leaves the debtor no way to show himself honest: it contrives all the ways possible to drive the debtor to despair, and encourages no new industry, for it makes him perfectly incapable of anything but starving.

This law, especially as it is now frequently executed, tends wholly to the destruction of the debtor, and yet very little to the advantage of the creditor.

(1.) The severities to the debtor are unreasonable, and, if I may so say, a little inhuman; for it not only strips him of all in a moment, but renders him for ever incapable of helping himself, or relieving his family by future industry. If he 'scapes from prison, which is hardly done too, if he has nothing left, he must starve, or live on charity; if he goes to work, no man dare pay him his wages, but he shall pay it again to the creditors; if he has any private stock left for a subsistence, he can put it nowhere; every man is bound to be a thief, and take it from him: if he trusts it in the hands of a friend, he must receive it again as a great courtesy, for that friend is liable to account for it. I have known a poor man prosecuted by a statute to that degree, that all he had left was a little money, which he knew not where to hide; at last, that he might not starve, he gives it to his brother, who had entertained him; the brother, after he had his money, quarrels with him to get him out of his house; and when he desires him to let him have the money lent him, gives him this for answer, I cannot pay you safely, for there is a statute against you; which ran the poor man to such extremities, that he destroyed himself. Nothing is more frequent, than for men who are reduced by miscarriage in trade, to compound and set up again, and get good estates; but a statute,[18] as we call it, for ever shuts up all doors to the debtor's recovery; as if breaking were a crime so capital, that he ought to be cast out of human society, and exposed to extremities worse than death. And, which will further expose the fruitless severity of this law, 'tis easy to make it appear, that all this cruelty to the debtor is so far (generally speaking) from advantaging the creditors, that it destroys the estate, consumes it in extravagant charges, and unless the debtor be consenting, seldom makes any considerable dividends. And I am bold to say, there is no advantage made by the prosecuting of a statute with severity, but what might be doubly made by methods more merciful. And though I am not to prescribe to the legislators of the nation, yet by way of essay I take leave to give my opinion and my experience in the methods, consequences, and remedies of this law.

All people know, who remember anything of the times when that law was made, that the evil it was pointed at, was grown very rank, and breaking to defraud creditors so much a trade, that the Parliament had good reason to set up a fury to deal with it; and I am far from reflecting on the makers of that law, who, no question, saw 'twas necessary at that time: but as laws, though in themselves good, are more or less so, as they are more or less reasonable, squared, and adapted to the circumstances and time of the evil they are made against; so 'twere worth while (with submission) for the same authority to examine:

(1.) Whether the length of time since that Act was made, has not given opportunity to debtors,

　1. To evade the force of the Act by ways and shifts to avoid the power of it, and secure their estates out of the reach of it?

　2. To turn the point of it against those whom it was made to relieve? Since we see frequently now, that bankrupts desire statutes, and procure them to be taken out against themselves.

(2.) Whether the extremities of this law are not often carried on beyond the true intent and meaning of the Act itself, by persons, who besides being creditors, are also malicious, and gratify their private revenge, by prosecuting the offender, to the ruin of his family.

If these two points are to be proved, then I am sure 'twill follow, that this Act is now a public grievance to the nation; and I doubt not but will be one time or other repealed by the same wise authority which made it.

(1.) Time and experience has furnished the debtors with ways and means to evade the force of this statute, and to secure their estate against the reach of it; which renders it often insignificant, and consequently, the knave, against whom the law was particularly bent, gets off; while he only who fails of mere necessity, and whose honest principle will not permit him to practice those methods, is exposed to the fury of this Act: and as things are now ordered, nothing is more easy, than for a man to order his estate so, that a statute shall have no power over it, or at least but a little.

If the bankrupt be a merchant, no statute can reach his effects beyond the seas; so that he has nothing to secure but his books, and away he goes into the Friars.[19] If a shopkeeper, he has more difficulty; but that is made easy, for there are men (and carts) to be had, whose trade it is, and who in one night shall remove the greatest warehouse of goods, or cellar of wines in the town, and carry them off into those nurseries of rogues, the Mint[20] and Friars; and our constables and watch, who are the allowed-Magistrates of the night, and who shall stop a poor little lurking thief, that it may be has stole a bundle of old clothes, worth 5 s. shall let them all pass without any disturbance, and see a hundred honest men robbed of their estates before their faces, to the eternal infamy of the justice of the nation.

And were a man but to hear the discourse among the inhabitants of those dens of thieves, when they first swarm about a newcomer, to comfort him; for they are not all hardened to a like degree at once.———Well, says the first, Come, don't be concerned, you have got a good parcel of goods away, I promise you; you need not value all the world. Ah! would I had done so, says another, I'd a'laughed at all my creditors. Ay, says the young proficient in the hardened trade, but my creditors! Damn the creditors, says a third, why, there's such a one and such a one, they have creditors too, and they won't agree with them, and here they live like gentlemen, and care not a farthing for them. Offer your creditors half a crown in the pound, and pay it them in old debts, and if they won't take it, let them alone, they'll come after you, never fear it. O! But a statute, says he again. O! But the Devil, cries the Minter. Why, 'tis the statutes we live by, say they: why, if 'twere not for statutes, creditors would comply, and debtors would compound, and we honest fellows here of the Mint would be starved. Prithee, what need you care for a statute? A thousand statutes can't reach you here. This is the language of the country, and the newcomer soon learns to speak it; (for I think I may say, without wronging any man, I have known many a man go in among them honest, that is, without ill design, but I never knew one come away so again.)———Then comes a graver sort among this black crew (for here, as in Hell, are fiends of degrees, and different magnitude) and he falls into discourse with the newcomer, and gives him more solid advice. Look you, Sir, I am concerned to see you melancholy, I am in your circumstance too, and if you'll accept of it, I'll give you the best advice I can; and so begins the grave discourse.

The man is in too much trouble, not to want counsel, so he thanks him, and he goes on: Send a summons to your creditors, and offer them what you can propose in the pound (always reserving a good stock to begin the world again), which if they will take, you are a free man, and better than you were before; if they won't take it, you know the worst of it, you are on the better side of the hedge with them: if they will not take it, but will proceed to a statute, you have nothing to do, but to oppose force with force; for the laws of nature tell you, you must not starve; and a statute is so barbarous, so unjust, so malicious a way of proceeding against a man, that I do not think any debtor obliged to consider anything but his own preservation, when once they go on with that.———For why, says the old studied wretch, should the creditors spend your estate in the commission, and then demand the debt of you too? Do you owe anything to the commission of the statute? (No, says he); Why then, says he, I warrant their charges will come to 200 *l.* out of your estate, and they must have 10 *s.* a day for starving you and your family. I cannot see why any man should think I am bound in conscience to pay the extravagance of other men. If my creditors spend 500 *l.* in getting in my estate by a statute, which I offered to surrender without it, I'll reckon that 500 *l.* paid them, let them take it among them; for equity is due to a bankrupt as well as to any man; and if the laws do not give it us, we must take it.

This is too rational discourse not to please him, and he proceeds by this advice; the creditors cannot agree, but take out a statute; and the man that offered at first, it may be, 10 *s.* in the pound, is kept in that cursed place till he has spent it all, and can offer nothing, and then gets away beyond sea, or after a long consumption gets off by an Act of Relief to poor debtors, and all the charges of the statute falls among the creditors. Thus I knew a statute taken out against a shopkeeper in the country, and a considerable parcel of goods too seized, and yet the creditors, what with charges, and two or three suits at law, lost their whole debts, and 8 *s. per* pound contribution-money for charges; and the poor debtor, like a man under the surgeon's hand, died in the operation.

(2.) Another evil that time and experience has brought to light from this Act, is, when the debtor himself shall confederate with some particular creditor to take out a statute; and this is a masterpiece of plot and intrigue: for perhaps some creditor honestly received in the way of trade a large sum of money of the debtor for goods sold him when he was *sui juris*;[21] and he by consent shall own himself a bankrupt before that time, and the statute shall reach back to bring in an honest man's estate, to help pay a rogue's debt. Or a man shall go and borrow a sum of money upon a parcel of goods, and lay them to pledge; he keeps the money, and the statute shall fetch away the goods to help forward the composition. These are tricks I can give too good an account of, having more than once suffered by the experiment. I could give a scheme of more ways, but I think 'tis needless to prove the necessity of laying aside that law, which is pernicious to both debtor and creditor, and chiefly hurtful to the honest man who it was made to preserve.

The next enquiry is, whether the extremities of this law are not often carried on beyond the true intent and meaning of the act itself, for malicious and private ends, to gratify passion and revenge?

I remember the answer a person gave me, who had taken out statutes against several persons, and some his near relations, who had failed in his debt; and when I was one time dissuading him from prosecuting a man who owed me money as well as him, I used this argument with him; You know the man has nothing left to pay. That's true, says he, I know that well enough. To what purpose then, said I, will you prosecute him? Why, revenge is sweet, said he.———Now a man that will prosecute a debtor, not as a debtor, but by way of revenge, such a man is, I think, not intentionally within the benefit of our law.

In order to state the case right, there are four sorts of people to be consider'd in this discourse; and the true case is how to distinguish them.

(1.) There is the honest debtor, who fails by visible necessity, losses, sickness, decay of trade, or the like.

(2.) The knavish, designing, or idle, extravagant debtor, who fails because either he has run out his estate in excesses, or on purpose to cheat and abuse his creditors.

(3.) There is the moderate creditor, who seeks but his own, but will omit no lawful means to gain it, and yet will hear reasonable and just arguments and proposals.

(4.) There is the rigorous severe creditor, that values not whether the debtor be honest man or knave, able, or unable; but will have his debt, whether it be to be had or no; without mercy, without compassion, full of ill language, passion, and revenge.

How to make a law to suit to all these, is the case: that a necessary favour might be shown to the first, in pity and compassion to the unfortunate, in commiseration of casualty and poverty, which no man is exempt from the danger of: that a due rigour and restraint be laid upon the second, that villainy and knavery might not be encouraged by a law: that a due care be taken of the third, that men's estates may, as far as can be, secured to them: and due limits set to the last, that no man may have an unlimited power over his fellow-subjects, to the ruin of both life and estate.

All which I humbly conceive might be brought to pass by the following method; to which I give the title of

A Court of Enquiries.

This court should consist of a select number of persons, to be chosen yearly out of the several wards of the City, by the Lord-Mayor and Court of Aldermen; and out of the several Inns of Court, by the Lord Chancellor, or Lord Keeper, for the time being, and to consist of,

A president,
A secretary,   } To be chosen by the rest, and named
A treasurer,   every year also.

A judge of causes for the proof of debts.

Fifty-two citizens, out of every ward two; of which number to be twelve merchants.

Two lawyers (barristers at least) out of each of the Inns of Court.

That a commission of enquiry into bankrupts' estates be given to these, confirmed and settled by Act of Parliament, with power to hear, try, and determine causes as to proof of debts, and disputes in accounts between debtor and creditor, without appeal.

The office for this court to be at Guildhall, where clerks should be always attending, and a *quorum* of the commissioners to sit *de die in diem*,[22] from three to six o'clock in the afternoon.

To this court every man who finds himself pressed by his affairs, so that he cannot carry on his business, shall apply himself as follows:

He shall go to the Secretary's office, and give in his name, with this short petition:

To the Honourable the President and Commissioners of His Majesty's Court of Enquiries. The humble Petition of *A.B.* of the Parish of   in the   Haberdasher.

Sheweth,

That your Petitioner being unable to carry on his business, by reason of great losses and decay of trade, and being ready and willing to make a full and entire discovery of his whole estate, and to deliver up the same to your honours upon oath, as the law directs for the satisfaction of his creditors, and having to that purpose entered his name into the books of your office on the   of this instant:

> Your Petitioner humbly prays the Protection
> of this Honourable Court.

> And shall ever pray, etc.

The Secretary is to lay this petition before the Commissioners, who shall sign it of course; and the petitioner shall have an officer sent home with him immediately, who shall take possession of his house and goods, and an exact inventory of every thing therein shall be taken at his entrance by other officers also, appointed by the court; according to which inventory the first officer and the bankrupt also shall be accountable.

This officer shall supersede even the Sheriff in possession, excepting by an extent for the King; only with this provision;

That if the Sheriff be in possession by warrant on judgment, obtained by due course of law, and without fraud or deceit, and, *bona fide*, in possession before the debtor entered his name in the office, in such case the plaintiff to have a double dividend allotted to his debt; for it was the fault of the debtor to let execution come upon his goods before he sought for protection; but this not to be allowed upon judgment confessed.

If the Sheriff be in possession by *fieri facias*[23] for debt immediately due to the King, the officer however shall quit his possession to the

Commissioners, and they shall see the King's debt fully satisfied, before any division be made to the creditors.

The officers in this case to take no fee from the bankrupt, nor to use any indecent or uncivil behaviour to the family (which is a most notorious abuse now permitted to the Sheriff's officers), whose fees I have known, on small executions, on pretence of civility, amount to as much as the debt, and yet behave themselves with unsufferable insolence all the while.

This officer being in possession, the goods may be removed, or not removed, the shop shut up, or not shut up, as the bankrupt upon his reasons given to the commissioners may desire.

The inventory being taken, the bankrupt shall have fourteen days' time, and more if desired, upon showing good reasons to the Commissioners, to settle his books, and draw up his accounts; and then shall deliver up all his books, together with a full and true account of his whole estate, real and personal; to which account he shall make oath, and afterwards to any particular of it, if the Commissioners require.

After this account given in, the Commissioners shall have power to examine upon oath all his servants, or any other person; and if it appears that he has concealed anything, in breach of his oath, to punish him, as is hereafter specified.

Upon a fair and just surrender of all his estate and effects, *bona fide*, according to the true intent and meaning of the Act, the commissioners shall return to him in money, or such of his goods as he shall choose, at a value by a just appraisement, 5 *l. per cent.* of all the estate he surrendered to him, together with a full and free discharge from all his creditors.

The remainder of the estate of the debtor to be fairly and equally divided among the creditors, who are to apply themselves to the Commissioners. The Commissioners to make a necessary enquiry into the nature and circumstances of the debts demanded, that no pretended debt be claimed for the private account of the debtor: in order to which enquiry, they shall administer the following oath to the creditor, for the proof of the debt.

I A.B. do solemnly swear and attest, that the account hereto annexed is true and right, and every Article therein rightly and truly stated and charged in the names of the persons to whom they belong: and that there is no person or name named, concealed, or altered in the said account by me, or by my knowledge, order, or consent: and that the said does really and *bona fide* owe and stand indebted to me for my own proper account, the full Sum of   mentioned in the said account, and that for a fair and just value made good to him, as by the said account expressed; and also that J have not made or known of any private contract, promise, or agreement between him the said   (or any body for him) and me, or any person whatsoever.

So help me God.

Upon this oath, and no circumstances to render the person suspected, the creditor shall have an unquestioned right to his dividend, which shall be made without the delays and charges that attend the commissions of bankrupts. For,

(1.) The goods of the debtor shall upon the first meeting of the creditors, be either sold in parcels,[24] as they shall agree, or divided among them in due proportion to their debts.

(2.) What debts are standing out, the debtors shall receive summonses from the Commissioners, to pay by a certain time limited; and in the mean time the Secretary is to transmit accounts to the persons owing it, appointing them a reasonable time to consent or disprove the account.

And every six months a just dividend shall be made among the creditors of the money received: and so if the effects lie abroad, authentic procurations shall be signed by the bankrupt to the Commissioners, who thereupon correspond with the persons abroad, in whose hands such effects are, who are to remit the same as the commissioners order; the dividend to be made, as before, every six months, or oftener, if the court see cause.

If any man thinks the bankrupt has so much favour by these articles, that those who can dispense with an oath have an opportunity to cheat their creditors, and that hereby too much encouragement is given to men to turn bankrupt; let them consider the easiness of the discovery, the difficulty of a concealment, and the penalty on the offender.

(1.) I would have a reward of 30 *per cent.* be provided to be paid to any person who should make discovery of any part of the bankrupt's estate concealed by him; which would make discoveries easy and frequent.

(2.) Any person who should claim any debt among the creditors, for the account of the bankrupt, or his wife or children, or with design to relieve them out of it, other or more than is, *bona fide*, due to him for value received and to be made out; or any person who shall receive in trust, or by deed of gift, any part of the goods or other estate of the bankrupt, with design to preserve them for the use of the said bankrupt, or his wife or children, or with design to conceal them from the creditors, shall forfeit for every such act 500 *l.* and have his name published as a cheat, and a person not fit to be credited by any man. This would make it very difficult for the bankrupt to conceal anything.

(3.) The bankrupt having given his name, and put the officer into possession, shall not remove out of the house any of his books; but during the fourteen days' time which he shall have to settle the accounts, shall every night deliver the books into the hands of the officer; and the Commissioners shall have liberty, if they please, to take the books the first day, and cause duplicates to be made, and then to give them back to the bankrupt to settle the accounts.

(4.) If it shall appear that the bankrupt has given in a false account, has concealed any part of his goods or debts, in breach of his oath, he shall be set in the pillory at his own door, and be imprisoned during life, without bail.

(5.) To prevent the bankrupt concealing any debts abroad, it should be enacted, that the name of the bankrupt being entered at the office, where every man might search *gratis*, should be publication enough; and that after such entry, no discharge from the bankrupt should be allowed in account to any man, but whoever would adventure to pay any money to the said bankrupt or his order, should be still debtor to the estate, and pay it again to the Commissioners.

And whereas wiser heads than mine must be employed to compose this law, if ever it be made, they will have time to consider of more ways to secure the estate for the creditors, and, if possible, to tie the hands of the bankrupt yet faster.

This law, if ever such a happiness should arise to this kingdom, would be a present remedy for a multitude of evils which now we feel, and which are a sensible detriment to the trade of this nation.

(1.) With submission, I question not but it would prevent a great number of bankrupts, which now fall by divers causes: for,

1. It would effectually remove all crafty designed breakings, by which many honest men are ruined. And

2. Of course 'twould prevent the fall of those tradesmen who are forced to break by the knavery of such.

(2.) It would effectually suppress all those sanctuaries and refuges of thieves, the Mint, Friars, Savoy,[25] Rules, and the like; and that these two ways;

1. Honest men would have no need of it, here being a more safe, easy, and more honourable way to get out of trouble.

2. Knaves should have no protection from those places, and the Act be fortified against those places by the following clauses, which I have on purpose reserved to this head.

Since the provision this Court of Enquiries makes for the ease and deliverance of every debtor who is honest, is so considerable, 'tis most certain that no man, but he who has a design to cheat his creditors, will refuse to accept of the favour; and therefore it should be enacted.

That if any man who is a tradesman or merchant shall break or fail, or shut up shop, or leave off trade, and shall not either pay or secure to his creditors their full and whole debts, twenty shillings in the pound, without abatement or deduction; or shall convey away their books or goods, in order to bring their creditors to any composition; or shall not apply to this office as aforesaid, shall be guilty of felony, and upon conviction of the same, shall suffer as a felon, without benefit of clergy.

And if any such person shall take sanctuary either in the Mint, Friars, or other pretended privilege-place, or shall convey thither any of their goods as aforesaid, to secure them from their creditors, upon complaint thereof made to any of His Majesty's justices of the peace, they shall immediately grant warrants to the constable, &c. to search for the said persons and goods, who shall be aided and assisted by the trained-bands,[26] if need be, without any charge to the creditors, to search for and discover the said persons and goods; and whoever were aiding in the carrying in the said goods, or whoever knowingly received either the goods or the person, should be also guilty of felony.

For as the indigent debtor is a branch of the commonwealth, which deserves its care, so the wilful bankrupt is one of the worst sort of thieves. And it seems a little unequal, that a poor fellow, who for mere want steals from his neighbour some trifle, shall be sent out of the kingdom, and sometimes out of the world; while a sort of people who defy justice, and violently resist the law, shall be suffered to carry men's estates away before their faces, and no officers to be found who dare execute the law upon them.

Any man would be concerned to hear with what scandal and reproach foreigners do speak of the impotence of our constitution in this point: that in a civilized government, as ours is, the strangest contempt of authority is shown, that can be instanced in the world.

I may be a little the warmer on this head, on account that I have been a larger sufferer by such means than ordinary: but I appeal to all the world as to the equity of the case; what the difference is between having my house broken up in the night to be robbed, and a man coming in good credit, and with a proffer of ready money in the middle of the day, and buying 500 *l.* of goods, and carry them directly from my warehouse into the Mint, and the next day laugh at me, and bid me defiance; yet this I have seen done: I think 'tis the justest thing in the world, that the last should be esteemed the greater thief, and deserves most to be hanged.

I have seen a creditor come with his wife and children, and beg of the debtor only to let him have part of his own goods again, which he had bought, knowing and designing to break: I have seen him with tears and entreaties petition for his own, or but some of it, and be taunted and swore at, and denied by a saucy insolent bankrupt: that the poor man has been wholly ruined by the cheat. 'Tis by the villainy of such, many an honest man is undone, families starved and sent a-begging, and yet no punishment prescribed by our laws for it.

By the aforesaid Commission of Enquiry, all this might be most effectually prevented, an honest, indigent tradesman preserved, knavery detected, and punished; Mints, Friars, and privilege-places suppressed, and without doubt a great number of insolencies avoided and prevented; of which many more particulars might be insisted upon, but I think these may be sufficient to lead anybody into the thought; and for the method, I leave it to the wise heads of the nation, who know better than I how to state the law to the circumstances of the crime.

OF ACADEMIES

We have in England fewer of these than in any part of the world, at least where learning is in so much esteem. But to make amends, the two great seminaries we have, are without comparison the greatest, I won't say the best in the world; and though much might be said here concerning universities in general, and foreign academies in particular, I content myself with noting that part in which we seem defective. The French, who justly value themselves upon erecting the most celebrated academy of Europe, owe the lustre of it very much to the great encouragement the Kings of France have given to it. And one of the members making a speech at his entrance, tells you, that 'tis not the least of the glories of their invincible monarch, to have engrossed all the learning of the world in that sublime body.

The peculiar study of the Academy of Paris, has been to refine and correct their own language; which they have done to that happy degree, that we see it now spoken in all the courts of Christendom, as the language allowed to be most universal.

I had the honour once to be a member of a small society, who seemed to offer at this noble design in England. But the greatness of the work, and the modesty of the gentlemen concerned, prevailed with them to desist an enterprise which appeared too great for private hands to undertake. We want indeed a Richlieu to commence such a work: for I am persuaded, were there such a genius in our kingdom to lead the way, there would not want capacities who could carry on the work to a glory equal to all that has gone before them. The English tongue is a subject not at all less worthy the labour of such a society than the French, and capable of a much greater perfection. The learned among the French will own, that the comprehensiveness of expression is a glory in which the English tongue not only equals but excels its neighbours; Rapin, St. Evremont, and the most eminent French authors have acknowledged it: and my Lord Roscommon,[27] who is allowed to be a good judge of English, because he wrote it as exactly as any ever did, expresses what I mean, in these lines:

> For who did ever in French authors see
> The comprehensive English energy?
> The weighty bullion of one sterling line,
> Drawn to French wire would through whole pages shine.

And if our neighbours will yield us, as their greatest critic has done, the preference for sublimity and nobleness of style, we will willingly quit all pretensions to their insignificant gaiety.

'Tis great pity that a subject so noble should not have some as noble to attempt it: and for a method, what greater can be set before us, than the Academy of Paris? Which, to give the French their due, stands foremost among all the great attempts in the learned part of the world.

The present King of England, of whom we have seen the whole world writing panegyrics and encomiums, and whom his enemies, when their interest does not silence them, are apt to say more of than ourselves; as in the war he has given surprising instances of a greatness of spirit more than common; so in peace, I dare say, with submission, he shall never have an opportunity to illustrate his memory more, than by such a foundation: by which he shall have opportunity to darken the glory of the French King in peace, as he has by his daring attempts in the war.

Nothing but pride loves to be flattered, and that only as 'tis a vice which blinds us to our own imperfections. I think princes as particularly unhappy in having their good actions magnified, as their evil actions covered: but King William, who has already won praise by the steps of dangerous virtue, seems reserved for some actions which are above the touch of flattery, whose praise is in themselves.

And such would this be: and because I am speaking of a work which seems to be proper only for the hand of the King himself, I shall not presume to carry on this chapter to the model, as I have done in other subjects. Only thus far:

That a Society be erected by the King himself, if his Majesty thought fit, and composed of none but persons of the first figure in learning; and 'twere to be wished our gentry were so much lovers of learning, that birth might always be joined with capacity.

The work of this Society should be to encourage polite learning, to polish and refine the English tongue, and advance the so much neglected faculty of correct language, to establish purity and propriety of style, and to purge it from all the irregular additions that ignorance and affectation have introduced; and all those innovations in speech, if I may call them such, which some dogmatic writers have the confidence to foster upon their native language, as if their authority were sufficient to make their own fancy legitimate.

By such a Society I dare say the true glory of our English style would appear; and among all the learned part of the world, be esteemed, as it really is, the noblest and most comprehensive of all the vulgar languages in the world.

Into this Society should be admitted none but persons eminent for learning, and yet none, or but very few, whose business or trade was learning: for I may be allowed, I suppose, to say, we have seen many great scholars, mere learned men, and graduates in the last degree of study, whose English has been far from polite, full of stiffness and affectation, hard words, and long unusual coupling of syllables and sentences, which sound harsh and untuneable to the ear, and shock the reader both in expression and understanding.

In short, there should be room in this Society for neither clergyman, physician, or lawyer. Not that I would put an affront upon the learning of any of those honourable employments, much less upon their persons: but if I do think that their several professions do naturally and severally prescribe habits of speech to them peculiar to their practice, and prejudicial to the study I speak of, I believe I do them no wrong. Nor do I deny but there may be, and now are among some of all those professions, men of style and language, great masters of English, whom few men will undertake to correct; and where such do at any time appear, their extraordinary merit should find them a place in this Society; but it should be rare, and upon very extraordinary occasions, that such be admitted.

I would therefore have this Society wholly composed of gentlemen; whereof twelve to be of the nobility, if possible, and twelve private gentlemen, and a class of twelve to be left open for mere merit, let it be found in who or what sort it would, which should lie as the crown of their study, who have done something eminent to deserve it. The voice of this Society should be sufficient authority for the usage of words, and sufficient also to expose the innovations of other men's fancies; they should preside with a sort of judicature over the learning of the age, and have liberty to correct and censure the exorbitance of writers, especially of translators. The reputation of this Society would be enough to make them the allowed judges of style and language; and no author would have the impudence to coin without their authority. Custom, which is now our best authority for words, would always have its original here, and not be allowed without it. There should be no more occasion to search for derivations and constructions, and 'twould be as criminal then to coin words, as money.

The exercises of this Society would be lectures on the English tongue, essays on the nature, original, usage, authorities and differences of words, on the propriety, purity, and cadence of style, and of the politeness and manner in writing; reflections upon irregular usages, and corrections of erroneous customs in words; and in short, everything that would appear necessary to the bringing our English tongue to a due perfection, and our gentlemen to a capacity of writing like themselves; to banish pride and pedantry, and silence the impudence and impertinence of young authors, whose ambition is to be known, though it be by their folly.

I ask leave here for a thought or two about that inundation custom has made upon our language and discourse by familiar swearing; and I place it here, because custom has so far prevailed in this foolish vice, that a man's discourse is hardly agreeable without it; and some have taken upon them to say, *It is pity it should not be lawful, 'tis such a grace in a man's speech, and adds so much vigour to his language.*

I desire to be understood right, and that by swearing I mean all those cursory oaths, curses, execrations, imprecations, asseverations, and by whatsoever other names they are distinguished, which are used in vehemence of discourse, in the mouths almost of all men more or less, of what sort soever.

I am not about to argue anything of their being sinful and unlawful, as forbid by divine rules; let the parson alone to tell you that, who has, no question, said as much to as little purpose in this case as in any other: but I am of the opinion, that there is nothing so impertinent, so insignificant, so senseless and foolish, as our vulgar way of discourse, when mixed with oaths and curses; and I would only recommend a little consideration to our gentlemen, who have sense and wit enough, and would be ashamed to speak nonsense in other things, but value themselves upon their parts; I would but ask them to put into writing the commonplaces of their discourse, and read them over again, and examine the English, the cadence, the grammar of them; then let them turn them into Latin, or translate them into any other language, and but see what a jargon and confusion of speech they make together.

Swearing, that lewdness of the tongue, that scum and excrement of the mouth, is of all vices the most foolish and senseless; it makes a man's conversation unpleasant, his discourse fruitless, and his language nonsense.

It makes conversation unpleasant, at least to those who do not use the same foolish way of discourse; and indeed, is an affront to all the company who swear not as he does; for if I swear and curse in company, I either presume all the company likes it, or affront them who do not.

Then 'tis fruitless; for no man is believed a jot the more for all the asseverations, damnings and swearings he makes: those who are used to it themselves, do not believe a man the more, because they know they are so customary, that they signify little to bind a man's intention; and they who practise them not, have so mean an opinion of those that do, as makes them think they deserve no belief.

Then, they are the spoilers and destroyers of a man's discourse, and turn it into perfect nonsense; and to make it out, I must descend a little to particulars, and desire the reader a little to foul his mouth with the brutish, sordid, senseless expressions, which some gentlemen call polite English, and speaking with a grace.

Some part of them indeed, though they are foolish enough, as effects of a mad, inconsiderate rage, are yet English; as when a man swears he will do this or that, and it may be adds, *God damn him he will*; that is, *God damn him if he don't*: this, though it be horrid in another sense, yet may be read in writing, and is English: but what language is this?

Jack, *God damn me* Jack, *how dost do, thou little dear son of a whore? How hast thou done this long time, by God?*————And then they kiss; and the t'other, as lewd as himself, goes on:

Dear Tom, *I am glad to see thee with all my heart, let me die. Come, let us go take a bottle, we must not part so; prithee let's go and be drunk by God.*————

This is some of our new florid language, and the graces and delicacies of style, which if it were put into Latin, I would fain know which is the principal verb.

But for a little further remembrance of this impertinence, go among the gamesters, and there nothing is more frequent than, *God damn the dice*, or *God damn the bowls*.

Among the sportsmen 'tis, *God damn the hounds*, when they are at a fault; or *God damn the horse*, if he balks a leap: they call men *sons of bitches*, and *dogs*, *sons of whores*: and innumerable instances may be given of the like gallantry of language, grown now so much a custom.

'Tis true, custom is allowed to be our best authority for words, and 'tis fit it should be so; but reason must be the judge of sense in language, and custom can never prevail over it. Words, indeed, like ceremonies in religion, may be submitted to the magistrate; but sense, like the essentials, is positive, unalterable, and cannot be submitted to any jurisdiction; 'tis a law to itself, 'tis ever the same, even an Act of Parliament cannot alter it.

Words, and even usages in style, may be altered by custom, and proprieties in speech differ according to the several dialects of the country, and according to the different manner in which several languages do severally express themselves.

But there is a direct signification of words, or a cadence in expression, which we call speaking sense; this, like truth, is sullen and the same, ever was and will be so, in what manner, and in what language soever 'tis expressed. Words without it, are only noise, which any brute can make as well as we, and birds much better, for words without sense make but dull music. Thus a man may speak in words, but perfectly unintelligible as to meaning; he may talk a great deal, but say nothing. But 'tis the proper position of words, adapted to their significations, which makes them intelligible, and conveys the meaning of the speaker to the understanding of the hearer; the contrary to which we call nonsense; and there is a superfluous crowding in of insignificant words, more than are needful to express the thing intended, and this is impertinence; and that again carried to an extreme, is ridiculous.

Thus when our discourse is interlined with needless oaths, curses, and long parentheses of imprecations, and with some of very indirect signification, they become very impertinent; and these being run to the extravagant degree instanced in before, become perfectly ridiculous and nonsense; and without forming it into an argument, it appears to be nonsense by the contradictoriness; and it appears impertinent, by the insignificancy of the expression.

After all, how little it becomes a gentleman to debauch his mouth with foul language, I refer to themselves in a few particulars.

This vicious custom has prevailed upon good manners too far; but yet there are some degrees to which it is not yet arrived.

As first, the worst slaves to this folly will neither teach it to, nor approve of it in their children: some of the most careless will indeed negatively teach it, by not reproving them for it; but sure no man ever ordered his children to be taught to curse or swear.

2. The grace of swearing has not obtained to be a mode yet among the women; *God damn ye*, does not sit well upon a female tongue; it seems to be a masculine vice, which the women are not arrived to yet; and I would only desire those gentlemen who practice it themselves, to hear a woman swear: it has no music at all there, I am sure; and just as little does it become any gentleman, if he would suffer himself to be judged by all the laws of sense or good manners in the world.

'Tis a senseless, foolish, ridiculous practice; 'tis a mean to no manner of end; 'tis words spoken which signify nothing; 'tis folly acted for the sake of folly, which is a thing even the Devil himself don't practice: the Devil does evil, we say, but it is for some design, either to seduce others, or, as some divines say, from a principle of enmity to his maker: men steal for gain, and murther to gratify their avarice or revenge; whoredoms and ravishments, adulteries and sodomy, are committed to please a vicious appetite, and have always alluring objects; and generally all vices have some previous cause, and some visible tendency; but this, of all vicious practices, seems the most nonsensical and ridiculous, there is neither pleasure nor profit; no design pursued, no lust gratified, but is a mere frenzy of the tongue, a vomit of the brain, which works by putting a contrary upon the course of nature.

Again, other vices men find some reason or other to give for, or excuses to palliate; men plead want, to extenuate theft; and strong provocations, to excuse murthers; and many a lame excuse they will bring for whoring; but this sordid habit, even those that practise it will own to be a crime, and make no excuse for it; and the most I could ever hear a man say for it, was, that he could not help it.

Besides, as 'tis an inexcusable impertinence, so 'tis a breach upon good manners and conversation, for a man to impose the clamour of his oaths upon the company he converses with; if there be any one person in the company that does not approve the way, 'tis an imposing upon him with a freedom beyond civility; as if a man should fart before a Justice, or talk bawdy before the Queen, or the like.

To suppress this, laws, Acts of Parliaments, and Proclamations, are baubles and banters, the laughter of the lewd party, and never had, as I could perceive, any influence upon the practice; nor are any of our Magistrates fond or forward of putting them in execution.

It must be example, not penalties, must link this crime; and if the gentlemen of England would once drop it as a mode, the vice is so foolish and ridiculous in itself, 'twould soon grow odious and out of fashion.

This work such an academy might begin; and I believe nothing would so soon explode the practice, as the public discouragement of it by such a Society, where all our customs and habits both in speech and behaviour, should receive an authority. All the disputes about precedency of wit, with the manners, customs, and usages of the theatre would be decided here; plays should pass here before they were acted, and the critics might give their censures, and damn at their pleasure; nothing would ever die which once received life at this original: the two theatres[28] might end their jangle, and dispute for priority no more; wit and real worth should decide the controversy, and here should be the infallible judge.

> The strife would then be only to do well,
> And he alone be crowned who did excel.
> Ye call them Whigs, who from the Church withdrew,
> But now we have our Stage-Dissenters too;
> Who scruple ceremonies of pit and box,
> And very few are sound and orthodox:
> But love disorder so, and are so nice,
> They hate conformity, though 'tis in vice.
> Some are for patent-hierarchy; and some,
> Like the old Gauls, seek out for elbow-room;
> Their arbitrary governors disown,
> And build a conventicle-stage o' their own.
> Fanatic beaus make up the gaudy show,
> And wit alone appears incognito.
> Wit and religion suffer equal fate;
> Neglect of both attends the warm debate.
> For while the parties strive and counter-mine,
> Wit will as well as piety decline.

Next to this, which I esteem as the most noble and most useful proposal in this book, I proceed to academies for military studies; and because I design rather to express my meaning, than make a large book, I bring them all into one chapter.

I allow the war is the best academy in the world, where men study by necessity, and practise by force, and both to some purpose, with duty in the action, and a reward in the end, and 'tis evident to any man who knows the world, or has made any observations on things, what an improvement the English nation has made, during this seven years' war.

But should you ask how dear it first cost, and what a condition England was in for a war at first on this account; how almost all our engineers and great officers were foreigners, it may put us in mind how necessary it is to have our people so practised in the arts of war, that they may not be novices when they come to the experiment.

I have heard some, who were no great friends to the Government, take advantage to reflect upon the King in the beginning of his wars in Ireland, that he did not care to trust the English, but all his great officers, his generals, and engineers were foreigners. And though the case was so plain as to need no answer, and the persons such as deserved none, yet this must be observed, though 'twas very strange, that when the present King took possession of this kingdom, and seeing himself entering upon the bloodiest war this age has known, began to regulate his army, he found but very few among the whole martial part of the nation fit to make use of for general officers; and was forced to employ strangers, and make them Englishmen; as the Counts Schomberg, Ginkel, Solms, Ruvigny,[29] and others: and yet it is to be observed also, that all the encouragement imaginable was given to the English gentlemen, to qualify themselves, by giving no less than sixteen regiments to gentlemen of good families, who had never been in any service, and knew but very little how to command them: of these several are now in the army, and have the rewards suitable to their merit, being Major-Generals, Brigadiers, and the like.

If then a long peace had so reduced us to a degree of ignorance that might have been dangerous to us, had we not a King, who is always followed by the greatest masters in the world, who knows what peace and different governors may bring us to again?

The manner of making war differs perhaps as much as anything in the world; and if we look no further back than our Civil Wars; 'tis plain a General then would hardly be fit to be a Colonel now, saving his capacity of improvement. The defensive art always follows the offensive; and though the latter has extremely got the start of the former in this age, yet the other is mightily improving also.

We saw in England a bloody Civil War, where, according to the old temper of the English, fighting was the business. To have an army lying in such a post, as not to be able to come at them, was a thing never heard of in that war; even the weakest party would always come out and fight; Dunbar fight,[30] for instance; and they that were beaten today, would fight again tomorrow, and seek one another out with such eagerness, as if they had been in haste to have their brains knocked out. Encampments, intrenchments, batteries, counter-marchings, fortifying of camps, and cannonadings, were strange, and almost unknown things, and whole campaigns were passed over, and hardly any tents made use of. Battles, surprises, storming of towns, skirmishes, sieges, ambuscades, and beating up quarters, was the news of every day. Now 'tis frequent to have armies of fifty thousand men of a side stand at bay within view of one another, and spend a whole campaign in dodging, or as 'tis genteely called, observing one another, and then march off into winter quarters. The difference is in the maxims of war, which now differ as much from what they were formerly, as long perukes do from piqued beards;[31] or as the habits of the people do now, from what they then wore. The present maxims of the war are:

> *Never fight without a manifest advantage.*
> *And always encamp so as not to be forced to it.*

And if two opposite generals nicely observe both these rules, it is impossible they should ever come to fight.

I grant that this way of making war spends generally more money and less blood than former wars did, but then it spins wars out to a greater length; and I almost question whether if this had been the way of fighting of old, our Civil War had not lasted till this day. Their maxim was,

> *Whenever you meet your enemy, fight him.*

But the case is quite different now, and I think 'tis plain in the present war, that 'tis not he who has the longest sword, so much as he who has the longest purse, will hold the war out best. Europe is all engaged in the war, and the men will never be exhausted while either party can find money; but he who finds himself poorest, must give out first; and this is evident in the French King, who now inclines to peace, and owns it, while at the same time his armies are numerous and whole; but the sinews fail, he finds his exchequer fail, his kingdom drained, and money hard to come at: not that I believe half the reports we have had of the misery and poverty of the French are true; but 'tis manifest the King of France finds, whatever his armies may do, his money won't hold out so long as the Confederates'; and therefore he uses all the means possible to procure a peace, while he may do it with the most advantage.

There is no question but the French may hold the war out several years longer; but their King is too wise to let things run to extremity; he will rather condescend to peace upon hard terms now, than stay longer, if he finds himself in danger to be forced to worse.

This being the only digression I design to be guilty of, I hope I shall be excused it.

*

The sum of all is this, that since 'tis so necessary to be in a condition for war in a time of peace, our people should be inured to it. 'Tis strange that everything should be ready but the soldier: ships are ready, and our trade keeps the seamen always taught, and breeds up more; but soldiers, horsemen, engineers, gunners, and the like, must be bred and taught; men are not born with muskets on their shoulders, nor fortifications in their heads; 'tis not natural to shoot bombs, and undermine towns: for which purpose I propose,

A Royal Academy for Military Exercises.

The founder the King himself; the charge to be paid by the public, and settled by a revenue from the crown, to be paid yearly.

I propose this to consist of four parts.

(1.) A college for breeding up of artists[32] in the useful practice of all military exercises; the scholars to be taken in young, and be maintained, and afterwards under the King's care for preferment, as their merit and His Majesty's favour shall recommend them; from whence His Majesty would at all times be furnished with able engineers, gunners, fire-masters, bombardiers, miners, and the like.

The second college for voluntary students in the same exercises; who should all upon certain limited conditions be entertained, and have all the advantages of the lectures, experiments, and learning of the college, and be also capable of several titles, profits, and settlements in the said college, answerable to the Fellows in the Universities.

The third college for temporary study, into which any person who is a gentleman, and an Englishman, entering his name, and conforming to the orders of the house, shall be entertained like a gentleman for one whole year *gratis*, and taught by masters appointed out of the second college.

The fourth college, of schools only, where all persons whatsoever for a small allowance shall be taught and entered in all the particular exercises they desire; and this to be supplied by the proficients of the first college.

I could lay out the dimensions, and necessary incidents of all this work; but since the method of such a foundation is easy and regular from the model of other colleges, I shall only state the economy of the house.

The building must be very large, and should rather be stately and magnificent in figure, than gay and costly in ornament: and I think such a house as Chelsea College, only about four times as big, would answer it;

and yet I believe might be finished for as little charge as has been laid out in that palace-like hospital. [. . .]

In the first of these colleges should remain the governing part, and all the preferments be made from thence, to be supplied in course from the other; the General of the first to give orders to the other, and be subject only to the Founder.

The government should be all military, with a constitution for the same regulated for that purpose, and a Council to hear and determine the differences and trespasses by the college laws.

The public exercises likewise military, and all the schools be disciplined under proper officers, who are so in turn, or by order of the General, and continue but for the day.

The several classes to perform several studies, and but one study to a distinct class, and the persons as they remove from one Study to another, to change their classes, but so as that in the general exercises all the scholars may be qualified to act all the several parts, as they may be ordered.

The proper studies of this college should be the following:

Geometry	Bombarding
Astronomy	Gunnery
History	Fortification
Navigation	Encamping
Decimal Arithmetic	Entrenching
Trigonometry	Approaching, Attacking
Dialing	Delineation
Gauging	Architecture
Mining	Surveying.
Fireworking	

And all arts or sciences appendixes to such as these.

With exercises for the body, to which all should be obliged, as their genius and capacities led them. As,

(1.) Swimming; which no soldier, and indeed no man whatever ought to be without.

(2.) Handling all sorts of firearms.

(3.) Marching and countermarching in form.

(4.) Fencing, and the long staff.

(5.) Riding and managing, or horsemanship.

(6.) Running, leaping, and wrestling.

And herewith should also be preserved and carefully taught all the customs, usages, terms of war, and terms of art, used in sieges, marches of armies, and encampments; that so a gentleman taught in this college, should be no novice when he comes into the King's armies, though he has seen no service abroad. I remember the story of an English gentleman, an officer at the siege of Limerick in Ireland, who though he was brave enough upon action, yet for the only matter of being ignorant in the terms of art, and knowing not how to talk camp-language, was exposed to be laughed at by the whole army, for mistaking the opening of the trenches, which he thought had been a mine against the town.

The experiments of these colleges would be as well worth publishing, as the Acts of the Royal Society. To which purpose the house must be built where they may have ground to cast bombs, to raise regular works, as batteries, bastions, half-moons, redoubts, horn-works, ports, and the like; with the convenience of water to draw round such works, to exercise the engineers in all the necessary experiments of draining, and mining under ditches. There must be room to fire great shot at a distance, to canonade a camp, to throw all sorts of fire-works and machines, that are or shall be invented; to open trenches, form camps, &c.

Their public exercises will be also very diverting, and more worth while for any gentlemen to see, than the sights or shows which our people in England are so fond of.

I believe, as a constitution might be formed from these generals, this would be the greatest, the gallantest, and the most useful foundation in the world. The English gentry would be the best qualified, and consequently, best accepted abroad, and most useful at home of any people in the world; and His Majesty should never more be exposed to the necessity of employing foreigners in the posts of trust and service in his armies.

And that the whole kingdom might in some degree be better qualified for service, I think the following project would be very useful.

When our military weapon was the long-bow, at which our English nation in some measure excelled the whole world, the meanest country-man was a good archer; and that which qualified them so much for service in the war, was their diversion in times of peace; which also had this good effect, that when an army was to be raised, they needed no disciplining:

and for the encouragement of the people to an exercise so publicly profitable, an Act of Parliament was made, to oblige every parish to maintain butts for the youth in the country to shoot at.

Since our way of fighting is now altered; and this destructive engine, the musket, is the proper arms for the soldier, I could wish the diversion also of the English would change too, that our pleasures and profit might correspond. 'Tis a great hindrance to this nation, especially where standing armies are a grievance, that if ever a war commence, men must have at least a year before they are thought fit to face an enemy, to instruct them how to handle their arms; and new-raised men are called raw soldiers. To help this, at least in some measure, I would propose, that the public exercises of our youth should by some public encouragement (for penalties won't do it) be drawn off from the foolish boyish sports of cocking, and cricketing, and from tippling, to shooting with a firelock; an exercise as pleasant, as 'tis manly and generous; and swimming, which is a thing so many ways profitable, besides its being a great preservative of health, that methinks no man ought to be without it. [. . .]

Under this head of Academies, I might bring in a project for

An Academy for Women.

I have often thought of it as one of the most barbarous customs in the world, considering us as a civilised and a Christian country, that we deny the advantages of learning to women. We reproach the sex every day with folly and impertinence, while I am confident, had they the advantages of education equal to us, they would be guilty of less than ourselves.

One would wonder indeed how it should happen that women are conversable at all, since they are only beholding to natural parts for all their knowledge. Their youth is spent to teach them to stitch and sew, or make baubles: they are taught to read indeed, and perhaps to write their names, or so; and that is the height of a woman's education. And I would but ask any who slight the sex for their understanding, what is a man (a gentleman, I mean) good for, that is taught no more?

I need not give instances, or examine the character of a gentleman with a good estate, and of a good family, and with tolerable parts, and examine what figure he makes for want of education.

The soul is placed in the body like a rough diamond, and must be polished, or the lustre of it will never appear: and 'tis manifest, that as the rational soul distinguishes us from brutes, so education carries on the distinction, and makes some less brutish than others: this is too evident to need any demonstration. But why then should women be denied the benefit of instruction? If knowledge and understanding had been useless additions to the sex, God Almighty would never have given them capacities; for he made nothing needless: besides, I would ask such, what they can see in ignorance, that they should think it a necessary ornament to a woman? Or how much worse is a wise woman than a fool? Or what has the woman done to forfeit the privilege of being taught? Does she plague us with her pride and impertinence? Why did we not let her learn, that she might have had more wit? Shall we upbraid women with folly, when 'tis only the error of this inhuman custom, that hindered them being made wiser?

The capacities of women are supposed to be greater, and their senses quicker than those of the men; and what they might be capable of being bred to, is plain from some instances of female wit, which this age is not without; which upbraids us with injustice, and looks as if we denied women the advantages of education, for fear they should vie with the men in their improvements.

To remove this objection, and that women might have at least a needful opportunity of education in all sorts of useful learning, I propose the draught of an academy for that purpose.

I know 'tis dangerous to make public appearances of the sex; they are not either to be confined or exposed; the first will disagree with their inclinations, and the last with their reputations; and therefore it is somewhat difficult; and I doubt a method proposed by an ingenious lady, in a little book, called, *Advice to the Ladies*,[33] would be found impracticable. For, saving my respect to the sex, the levity, which perhaps is a little peculiar to them, at least in their youth, will not bear the restraint; and I am satisfied, nothing but the height of bigotry can keep up a nunnery: women are extravagantly desirous of going to Heaven, and will punish their pretty bodies to get thither; but nothing else will do it; and even in that case sometimes it falls out that nature will prevail.

When I talk therefore of an academy for women, I mean both the model, the teaching, and the government, different from what is proposed by that ingenious lady, for whose proposal I have a very great esteem, and also a great opinion of her wit; different too from all sorts of religious confinement, and above all, from vows of celibacy.

Wherefore the academy I propose should differ but little from public schools, wherein such ladies as were willing to study, should have all the advantages of learning suitable to their genius.

But since some severities of discipline more than ordinary would be absolutely necessary to preserve the reputation of the House, that persons of quality and fortune might not be afraid to venture their children thither, I shall venture to make a small scheme by way of essay.

The House I would have built in a form by itself, as well as in a place by itself.

The building should be of three plain fronts, without any jettings,[34] or bearing-work,[35] that the eye might at a glance see from one coign to the other; the gardens walled in the same triangular figure, with a large moat, and but one entrance.

When thus every part of the situation was contrived as well as might be for discovery, and to render intriguing dangerous, I would have no guards, no eyes, no spies set over the ladies, but shall expect them to be tried by the principles of honour and strict virtue.

And if I am asked, *why*, I must ask pardon of my own sex for giving this reason for it:

I am so much in charity with women, and so well acquainted with men, that 'tis my opinion, there needs no other care to prevent intriguing, than to keep the men effectually away: for though inclination, which we prettily call love, does sometimes move a little too visibly in the sex, and frailty often follows; yet I think verily, custom, which we miscall modesty, has so far the ascendant over the sex, that solicitation always goes before it.

> Custom with women 'stead of virtue rules;
> It leads the wisest, and commands the fools:
> For this alone, when inclinations reign,
> Though virtue's fled, will acts of vice restrain.
> Only by custom 'tis that virtue lives,
> And love requires to be asked, before it gives.
> For that which we call modesty, is pride:
> They scorn to ask, and hate to be denied.
> 'Tis custom thus prevails upon their want;
> They'll never beg, what asked they easily grant.
> And when the needless ceremony's over,
> Themselves the weakness of the sex discover.

If then desires are strong, and nature free,
Keep from her men, and opportunity.
Else 'twill be vain to curb her by restraint;
But keep the question off, you keep the saint.

In short, let a woman have never such a coming-principle, she will let you ask before she complies, at least if she be a woman of any honour.

Upon this ground I am persuaded such measures might be taken, that the ladies might have all the freedom in the world within their own walls, and yet no intriguing, no indecencies, nor scandalous affairs happen; and in order to this, the following customs and laws should be observed in the colleges; of which I would propose one at least in every county in England, and about ten for the City of London.

After the regulation of the form of the building as before;

(1.) All the ladies who enter into the House, should set their hands to the orders of the House, to signify their consent to submit to them.

(2.) As no woman should be received, but who declared herself willing, and that it was the act of her choice to enter herself, so no person should be confined to continue there a moment longer than the same voluntary choice inclined her.

(3.) The charges of the House being to be paid by the ladies, everyone that entered should have only this encumbrance, that she should pay for the whole year, though her mind should change as to her continuance.

(4.) An Act of Parliament should make it felony without clergy,[36] for any man to enter by force or fraud into the House, or to solicit any woman, though it were to marry, while she was in the House. And this law would by no means be severe; because any woman who was willing to receive the addresses of a man, might discharge herself of the House when she pleased; and on the contrary, any woman who had occasion, might discharge herself of the impertinent addresses of any person she had an aversion to, by entering into the House.

In this House,

The persons who enter, should be taught all sorts of breeding suitable to both their genius and their quality; and in particular, music and dancing, which it would be cruelty to bar the sex of, because they are their darlings: but besides this, they should be taught languages, as particularly French and Italian; and

I would venture the injury of giving a woman more tongues than one.

They should, as a particular study, be taught all the graces of speech, and all the necessary air of conversation; which our common education is so defective in, that I need not expose it: they should be brought to read books, and especially history, and so to read as to make them understand the world, and be able to know and judge of things when they hear of them.

To such whose genius would lead them to it, I would deny no sort of learning; but the chief thing in general is to cultivate the understandings of the sex, that they may be capable of all sorts of conversation; that their parts and judgments being improved, they may be as profitable in their conversation as they are pleasant.

Women, in my observation, have little or no difference in them, but as they are, or are not distinguished by education. Tempers indeed may in some degree influence them, but the main distinguishing part is their breeding.

The whole sex are generally quick and sharp: I believe I may be allowed to say generally so; for you rarely see them lumpish and heavy when they are children, as boys will often be. If a woman be well-bred, and taught the proper management of her natural wit, she proves generally very sensible and retentive: and without partiality, a woman of sense and manners is the finest and most delicate part of God's creation; the glory of her Maker, and the great instance of his singular regard to man, his darling creature, to whom he gave the best gift either God could bestow, or man receive: and 'tis the sordidest piece of folly and ingratitude in the world, to withhold from the sex the due lustre which the advantages of education gives to the natural beauty of their minds.

A woman well bred and well taught, furnished with the additional accomplishments of knowledge and behaviour, is a creature without comparison; her society is the emblem of sublimer enjoyments; her person is angelic, and her conversation heavenly; she is all softness and sweetness, peace, love, wit, and delight: she is every way suitable to the sublimest wish; and the man that has such a one to his portion, has nothing to do but to rejoice in her, and be thankful.

On the other hand, suppose her to be the very same woman, and rob her of the benefit of education, and it follows thus;

If her temper be good, want of education makes her soft and easy.

Her wit, for want of teaching, makes her impertinent and talkative.

Her knowledge, for want of judgment and experience, makes her fanciful and whimsical.

If her temper be bad, want of breeding makes her worse, and she grows haughty, insolent, and loud.

If she be passionate, want of manners makes her termagant, and a scold, which is much at one with lunatic.

If she be proud, want of discretion (which still is breeding) makes her conceited, fantastic, and ridiculous.

And from these she degenerates to be turbulent, clamorous, noisy, nasty, and the Devil.

Methinks mankind for their own sakes, since say what we will of the women, we all think fit one time or other to be concerned with 'em, should take some care to breed them up to be suitable and serviceable, if they expected no such thing as delight from 'em. Bless us! What care do we take to breed up a good horse, and to break him well! and what a value do we put upon him when it is done, and all because he should be fit for our use! and why not a woman? Since all her ornaments and beauty, without suitable behaviour, is a cheat in nature, like the false tradesman, who puts the best of his goods uppermost, that the buyer may think the rest are of the same goodness.

Beauty of the body, which is the women's glory, seems to be now unequally bestowed, and nature, or rather Providence, to lie under some scandal about it, as if 'twas given a woman for a snare to men, and so make a kind of a She-Devil of her: because they say exquisite beauty is rarely given with wit; more rarely with goodness of temper, and never at all with modesty. And some, pretending to justify the equity of such a distribution, will tell us 'tis the effect of the justice of Providence in dividing particular excellencies among all his creatures, share and share alike, as it were, that all might for something or other be acceptable to one another, else some would be despised.

I think both these notions false; and yet the last, which has the shew of respect to Providence, is the worst; for it supposes Providence to be indigent and empty; as if it had not wherewith to furnish all the creatures it had made, but was fain to be parsimonious in its gifts, and distribute them by piece-meal, for fear of being exhausted.

If I might venture my opinion against an almost universal notion, I would say, most men mistake the proceedings of Providence in this case, and all the world at this day are mistaken in their practice about it. And because the assertion is very bold, I desire to explain myself.

That Almighty First Cause which made us all, is certainly the fountain of excellence, as it is of being, and by an invisible influence could have diffused equal qualities and perfections to all the creatures it has made, as the sun does its light, without the least ebb or diminution to himself; and has given indeed to every individual sufficient to the figure his Providence had designed him in the world.

I believe it might be defended, if I should say, that I do suppose God has given to all mankind equal gifts and capacities, in that he has given them all souls equally capable; and that the whole difference in mankind proceeds either from accidental difference in the make of their bodies, or from the foolish difference of education.

1. From accidental difference in bodies. I would avoid discoursing here of the philosophical position of the soul in the body: but if it be true as philosophers do affirm, that the understanding and memory is dilated or contracted according to the accidental dimensions of the organ through which 'tis conveyed; then though God has given a soul as capable to me as another, yet if I have any natural defect in those parts of the body by which the soul should act, I may have the same soul infused as another man, and yet he be a wise man, and I a very fool. For example, if a child naturally have a defect in the organ of hearing, so that he could never distinguish any sound, that child shall never be able to speak or read, though it have a soul capable of all the accomplishments in the world. The brain is the centre of the soul's actings, where all the distinguishing faculties of it reside; and 'tis observable, a man who has a narrow contracted head, in which there is not room for the due and necessary operations of nature by the brain, is never a man of very great judgment; and that proverb, a great head and little wit, is not meant by nature, but is a reproof upon sloth; as if one should, by way of wonder, say, Fye, fye, you that have a great head, have but little wit, that's strange! that must certainly be your own fault. From this notion I do believe there is a great matter in the breed of men and women; not that wise men shall always get wise children; but I believe strong and healthy bodies have the wisest children; and sickly weakly bodies affect the wits as well as the bodies of their children. We are easily persuaded to believe this in the breeds of horses, cocks, dogs, and other creatures; and I believe 'tis as visible in men.

But to come closer to the business; the great distinguishing difference which is seen in the world between men and women, is in their education; and this is manifested by comparing it with the difference between one man or woman, and another.

And herein it is that I take upon me to make such a bold assertion, that all the world are mistaken in their practice about women: for I cannot think that God Almighty ever made them so delicate, so glorious creatures, and furnished them with such charms, so agreeable and so delightful to mankind, with souls capable of the same accomplishments with men, and all to be only stewards of our houses, cooks and slaves.

Not that I am for exalting the female government in the least: but, in short, I would have men take women for companions, and educate them to be fit for it. A woman of sense and breeding will scorn as much to encroach upon the prerogative of the man, as a man of sense will scorn to oppress the weakness of the woman. But if the women's souls were refined and improved by teaching, that word would be lost; to say, the weakness of the sex, as to judgment, would be nonsense; for ignorance and folly would be no more to be found among women than men. I remember a passage which I heard from a very fine woman, she had wit and capacity enough, an extraordinary shape and face, and a great fortune, but had been cloistered up all her time, and for fear of being stolen had not had the liberty of being taught the common necessary knowledge of women's affairs; and when she came to converse in the world, her natural wit made her so sensible of the want of education, that she gave this short reflection on herself: *I am ashamed to talk with my very maids*, says she, *for I don't know when they do right or wrong: I had more need to go to school, than be married*. I need not enlarge on the loss the defect of education is to the sex, nor argue the benefit of the contrary practice; 'tis a thing will be more easily granted than remedied: this chapter is but an essay at the thing, and I refer the practice to those happy days, if ever they shall be, when men shall be wise enough to mend it. [. . .]

Giving Alms no Charity,

And Employing the

POOR

A Grievance to the

NATION,

Being an

ESSAY

Upon this

Great Question,

Whether Work-houses, Corporations, and Houses of
Correction for Employing the Poor, as now pra-
ctis'd in *England* ; or Parish-Stocks, as propos'd in
a late Pamphlet, Entituled, *A Bill for the better Re-*
lief, Imployment and Settlement of the Poor, &c. Are
not mischievous to the Nation, tending to the Destruction of our Trade, and to Encrease the Number and Misery of the Poor.

Addressed to the Parliament of England.

LONDON:
Printed, and Sold by the Booksellers of *London* and *West-*
minster. MDCCIV.

To the Knights, Citizens and Burgesses in Parliament Assembled.

Gentlemen,

He that has truth and justice, and the interest of England in his design, can have nothing to fear from an English Parliament.

This makes the author of these sheets, however despicable in himself, apply to this Honourable House, without any apology for the presumption.

Truth, Gentlemen, however meanly dressed, and in whatsoever bad company she happens to come, was always entertained at your bar; and the Commons of England must cease to act like themselves, or which is worse, like their ancestors, when they cease to entertain any proposal, that offers itself at their door, for the general good and advantage of the people they represent.

I willingly grant, that 'tis a crime in good manners to interrupt your more weighty councils, and disturb your debates, with empty nauseous trifles in value, or mistaken schemes; and whoever ventures to address you, ought to be well assured he is in the right, and that the matter suits the intent of your meeting, *viz.* to dispatch the weighty affairs of the Kingdom.

And as I have premised this, so I freely submit to any censure this Honourable Assembly shall think I deserve, if I have broke in upon either of these particulars.

I have but one petition to make with respect to the author, and that is, that no freedom of expression, which the arguments may oblige him to, may be construed as a want of respect, and a breach of the due deference every Englishman owes to the representing power of the nation.

It would be hard, that while I am honestly offering to your consideration something of moment for the general good, prejudice should lay snares for the author, and private pique make him an offender for a word.

Without entering upon other parts of my character, 'tis enough to acquaint this assembly, that I am an English freeholder, and have by that a title to be concerned in the good of that community of which I am an unworthy member.

This Honourable House is the representative of all the freeholders of England; you are assembled for their good, you study their interest, you possess their hearts, and you hold the strings of the general purse.

To you they have recourse for the redress of all their wrongs, and if at any time one of their body can offer to your assistance, any fair, legal, honest and rational proposal for the public benefit, it was never known that such a man was either rejected or discouraged.

And on this account I crave the liberty to assure you, that the author of this seeks no reward; to him it shall always be reward enough to have been capable of serving his native country, and honour enough to have offered something for the public good worthy of consideration in your Honourable Assembly.

Pauper ubique jacet,[1] said our famous Queen Elizabeth, when in her progress through the kingdom she saw the vast throngs of the poor, flocking to see and bless her; and the thought put her Majesty upon a continued study how to recover her people from that poverty, and make their labour profitable to themselves in particular, and the nation in general.

This was easy then to propose, for that many useful manufactures were made in foreign parts, which our people bought with English money, and imported for their use.

The Queen, who knew the wealth and vast numbers of people which the said manufactures had brought to the neighbouring countries then under the King of Spain, the Dutch being not yet revolted,[2] never left off endeavouring what she happily brought to pass, *viz.* the transplanting into England those springs of riches and people.

She saw the Flemings prodigiously numerous, their cities stood thicker than her people's villages in some parts; all sorts of useful manufactures were found in their towns, and all their people were rich and busy, no beggars, no idleness, and consequently no want was to be seen among them.

She saw the fountain of all this wealth and workmanship, I mean the wool, was in her own hands, and Flanders became the seat of all these manufactures, not because it was naturally richer and more populous than other countries, but because it lay near England, and the staple[3] of the English wool which was the foundation of all their wealth, was at Antwerp in the heart of that country.

From hence, it may be said of Flanders, it was not the riches and the number of people brought the manufactures into the Low Countries, but it was the manufactures brought the people thither, and multitudes of people make trade, trade makes wealth, wealth builds cities, cities enrich the land round them, land enriched rises in value, and the value of lands enriches the Government.

Many projects were set on foot in England to erect the woollen manufacture here, and in some places it had found encouragement, before the days of this Queen, especially as to making of cloth, but stuffs,[4] bays,[5] says,[6] serges,[7] and such like wares were yet wholly the work of the Flemings.

At last an opportunity offered perfectly unlooked for, *viz.* the persecution of the Protestants, and introducing the Spanish Inquisition into Flanders, with the tyranny of the Duke D'Alva.[8]

It cannot be an ungrateful observation, here to take notice how tyranny and persecution, the one an oppression of property, the other of conscience, always ruin trade, impoverish nations, depopulate countries, dethrone Princes, and destroy peace.

When an Englishman reflects on it, he cannot without infinite satisfaction look up to Heaven, and to this Honourable House, that as the spring, this as the stream from and by which the felicity of this nation has obtained a pitch of glory, superior to all the people in the world.

Your councils especially, when blest from Heaven, as now we trust they are, with principles of unanimity and concord, can never fail to make trade flourish, war successful, peace certain, wealth flowing, blessings probable, the Queen glorious; and the people happy.

Our unhappy neighbours of the Low Countries were the very reverse of what we bless ourselves for in you.

Their Kings were tyrants, their governors persecutors, their armies thieves and blood-hounds.

Their people divided, their councils confused, and their miseries innumerable.

D'Alva the Spanish Governor, besieged their cities, decimated the inhabitants, murthered their nobility, proscribed their Princes and executed 18,000 men by the hand of the hang-man.

Conscience was trampled under foot, religion and reformation hunted like a hare upon the mountains, the Inquisition threatened, and foreign armies introduced.

Property fell a sacrifice to absolute power, the country was ravaged, the towns plundered, the rich confiscated, the poor starved, trade interrupted, and the 10th. penny[9] demanded.

The consequence of this was, as in all tyrannies and persecutions it is, the people fled and scattered themselves in their neighbours' countries, trade languished, manufactures went abroad, and never returned, confusion reigned, and poverty succeeded.

The multitude that remained, pushed to all extremities, were forced to obey the voice of nature, and in their own just defence to take arms against their governors.

Destruction itself has its uses in the world, the ashes of one city rebuilds another, and God Almighty, who never acts in vain, brought the wealth of England, and the power of Holland into the world from the ruin of the Flemish liberty.

The Dutch in defence of their liberty revolted, renounced their tyrant Prince, and prospered by Heaven and the assistance of England, erected the greatest Commonwealth in the world.

Innumerable observations would flow from this part of the present subject, but brevity is my study. I am not teaching, for I know who I speak to, but relating and observing the connection of causes, and the wondrous births which lay then in the womb of Providence, and are since come to life.

Particularly how Heaven directed the oppression and tyranny of the poor should be the wheel to turn over the great machine of trade from Flanders into England.

And how the persecution and cruelty of the Spaniards against religion should be directed by the secret over-ruling hand, to be the foundation of a people, and a body that should in ages then to come, be one of the chief bulwarks of that very liberty and religion they sought to destroy.

To this general ruin of trade and liberty, England made a gain of what she never yet lost, and of what she has since increased to an inconceivable magnitude.

As D'Alva worried the poor Flemings, the Queen of England entertained them, cherished them, invited them, encouraged them.

Thousands of innocent people fled from all parts from the fury of this merciless man, and as England, to her honour has always been the sanctuary of her distressed neighbours, so now she was so to her special and particular profit.

The Queen who saw the opportunity put into her hands which she had so long wished for, not only received kindly the exiled Flemings, but invited over all that would come, promising them all possible encouragement, privileges and freedom of her ports and the like.

This brought over a vast multitude of Flemings, Walloons, and Dutch, who with their whole families settled at Norwich, at Ipswich, Colchester, Canterbury, Exeter, and the like. From these came the Walloon church at Canterbury, and the Dutch churches at Norwich, Colchester and Yarmouth; from hence came the true born English families[10] at those places with foreign names; as the DeVinks at Norwich, the Rebows at Colchester, the Papillons, &c. at Canterbury, families to whom this nation are much in debt for the first planting those manufactures, from which we have since raised the greatest trades in the world.

This wise Queen knew that number of inhabitants are the wealth and strength of a nation; she was far from that opinion we have of late shown too much of in complaining that foreigners came to take the bread out of our mouths, and ill treating on that account the French Protestants who fled hither for refuge in the late persecution.[11]

Some have said that above 50,000 of them settled here, and would have made it a grievance, though without doubt 'tis easy to make it appear that 500,000 more would be both useful and profitable to this nation.

Upon the settling of these foreigners, the scale of trade visibly turned both here and in Flanders.

The Flemings taught our women and children to spin, the youth to weave, the men entered the loom to labour instead of going abroad to seek their fortunes by the war, the several trades of bayes at Colchester, sayes and perpets,[12] at Sudbury, Ipswich, &c. stuffs at Norwich, serges at Exeter, silks at Canterbury, and the like, began to flourish. All the counties round felt the profit, the poor were set to work, the traders gained wealth, and multitudes of people flocked to the several parts where these manufactures were erected for employment, and the growth of England, both in trade, wealth and people since that time, as it is well known to this Honourable House, so the causes of it appear to be plainly the introducing of these manufactures, and nothing else.

Nor was the gain made here by it more visible than the loss to the Flemings; from hence, and not as is vainly suggested from the building the Dutch Fort of Lillo on the Scheld, came the decay of that flourishing city of Antwerp. From hence it is plain the Flemings, an industrious nation, finding their trade ruined at once, turned their hands to other things, as making of lace, linen, and the like, and the Dutch to the sea affairs and fishing.

From hence they become poor, thin of people, and weak in trade, the flux both of their wealth and trade, running wholly into England.

I humbly crave leave to say, this long introduction shall not be thought useless, when I shall bring it home by the process of these papers to the subject now in hand, *viz.* the providing for and employing the poor.

Since the times of Queen Elizabeth this nation has gone on to a prodigy of trade, of which the increase of our customs from 400,000 crowns to two millions of pounds sterling, *per ann.* is a demonstration beyond the power of argument; and that this whole increase depends upon, and is principally occasioned by the increase of our manufacturers is so plain, I shall not take up any room here to make it out.

Having thus given an account how we came to be a rich, flourishing and populous nation, I crave leave as concisely as I can to examine how we came to be poor again, if it must be granted that we are so.

By poor here I humbly desire to be understood, not that we are a poor nation in general; I should undervalue the bounty of Heaven to England, and act with less understanding than most men are masters of, if I should not own, that in general we are as rich a nation as any in the world; but by poor I mean burthened with a crowd of clamouring, unemployed, unprovided for poor people, who make the nation uneasy, burthen the rich, clog our parishes, and make themselves worthy of laws, and peculiar management to dispose of and direct them: how these came to be thus is the question.

And first I humbly crave leave to lay these heads down as fundamental maxims, which I am ready at any time to defend and make out.

1. There is in England more labour than hands to perform it, and consequently a want of people, not of employment.
2. No man in England, of sound limbs and senses, can be poor merely for want of work.
3. All our work-houses, corporations[13] and charities for employing the poor, and setting them to work, as now they are employed, or any Acts of Parliament to empower overseers of parishes, or parishes themselves, to employ the poor, except as shall be hereafter excepted, are, and will be public nuisances, mischiefs to the nation which serve to the ruin of families, and the increase of the poor.

4. That 'tis a regulation of the poor that is wanted in England, not a setting them to work.

If after these things are made out, I am enquired of what this regulation should be, I am no more at a loss to lay it down than I am to affirm what is above; and shall always be ready, when called to it, to make such a proposal to this Honourable House, as with their concurrence shall for ever put a stop to poverty and beggary, parish charges, assessments[14] and the like, in this nation.

If such offers as these shall be slighted and rejected, I have the satisfaction of having discharged my duty, and the consequence must be, that complaining will be continued in our streets.

'Tis my misfortune, that while I study to make every head so concise, as becomes me in things to be brought before so honourable and august an assembly, I am obliged to be short upon heads that in their own nature would very well admit of particular volumes to explain them.

1. I affirm, that in England there is more labour than hands to perform it. This I prove,

1st. From the dearness of wages, which in England outgoes all nations in the world; and I know no greater demonstration in trade. Wages, like exchanges, rise and fall as the remitters and drawers, the employers and the work-men, balance one another.

The employers are the remitters, the work-men are the drawers, if there are more employers than work-men, the price of wages must rise, because the employer wants that work to be done more than the poor man wants to do it, if there are more work-men than employers the price of labour falls, because the poor man wants his wages more than the employer wants to have his business done.

Trade, like all nature, most obsequiously obeys the great law of cause and consequence; and this is the occasion why even all the greatest articles of trade follow, and as it were pay homage to this seemingly minute and inconsiderable thing, the poor man's labour.

I omit, with some pain, the many very useful thoughts that occur on this head, to preserve the brevity I owe to the dignity of that assembly I am writing to. But I cannot but note how from hence it appears, that the glory, the strength, the riches, the trade, and all that's valuable in a nation, as to its figure in the world, depends upon the number of its people, be they never so mean or poor; the consumption of manufactures increases the manufacturers; the number of manufacturers increases the consumption; provisions are consumed to feed them, land improved, and more hands employed to furnish provision: all the wealth of the nation, and all the trade is produced by numbers of people; but of this by the way.

The price of wages not only determines the difference between the employer and the work-man, but it rules the rates of every market. If wages grows high, provisions rise in proportion, and I humbly conceive it to be a mistake in those people, who say labour in such parts of England is cheap because provisions are cheap, but 'tis plain, provisions are cheap there because labour is cheap, and labour is cheaper in those parts than in others; because being remoter from London there is not that extraordinary disproportion between the work and the number of hands; there are more hands, and consequently labour cheaper.

'Tis plain to any observing eye, that there is an equal plenty of provisions in several of our South and Western counties, as in Yorkshire, and rather a greater and I believe I could make it out, that a poor labouring man may live as cheap in Kent or Sussex as in the Bishopric of Durham; and yet in Kent a poor man shall earn 7 s. 10 s. 9 s. a week, and in the North 4 s. or perhaps less; the difference is plain in this, that in Kent there is a greater want of people, in proportion to the work there, than in the North.

And this on the other hand makes the people of our Northern countries spread themselves so much to the South, where trade, war and the sea carrying off so many, there is a greater want of hands.

And yet 'tis plain there is labour for the hands which remain in the North, or else the country would be depopulated, and the people come all away to the South to seek work; and even in Yorkshire, where labour is cheapest, the people can gain more by their labour than in any of the manufacturing countries of Germany, Italy or France, and live much better.

If there was one poor man in England more than there was work to employ, either somebody else must stand still for him, or he must be starved; if another man stands still for him he wants a day's work, and goes to seek it, and by consequence supplants another, and this a third, and this contention brings it to this; no says the poor man, that is like to be put out of his work, rather than that man shall come in I'll do it cheaper; nay, says the other, but I'll do it cheaper than you; and thus one poor man wanting but a day's work would bring down the price of labour in a whole nation, for the man cannot starve, and will work for anything rather than want it.

It may be objected here, this is contradicted by our number of beggars.

I am sorry to say I am obliged here to call begging an employment, since 'tis plain, if there is more work than hands to perform it, no man that has his limbs and his senses need to beg, and those that have not ought to be put into a condition not to want it.

So that begging is a mere scandal in the general, in the able 'tis a scandal upon their industry, and in the impotent 'tis a scandal upon the country.

Nay, the begging, as now practiced, is a scandal upon our charity, and perhaps the foundation of all our present grievance———How can it be possible that any man or woman, who being sound in body and mind, may as 'tis apparent they may, have wages for their work, should be so base, so meanly spirited, as to beg an alms for God-sake———.Truly the scandal lies on our charity; and people have such a notion in England of being pitiful and charitable, that they encourage vagrants, and by a mistaken zeal do more harm than good.

This is a large scene, and much might be said upon it; I shall abridge it as much as possible———. The poverty of England does not lie among the craving beggars but among poor families, where the children are numerous, and where death or sickness has deprived them of the labour of the father; these are the houses that the sons and daughters of charity, if they would order it well, should seek out and relieve; an alms ill directed may be charity to the particular person, but becomes an injury to the public, and no charity to the nation. As for the craving poor, I am persuaded I do them no wrong when I say, that if they were incorporated they would be the richest society in the nation; and the reason why so many pretend to want work is, that they can live so well with the pretence of wanting work, they would be mad to leave it and work in earnest; and I affirm of my own knowledge, when I have wanted a man for labouring work, and offered 9 s. per week to strolling fellows at my door, they have frequently told me to my face, they could get more a begging, and I once set a lusty fellow in the stocks for making the experiment.

I shall, in its proper place, bring this to a method of trial, since nothing but demonstration will affect us, 'tis an easy matter to prevent begging in England, and yet to maintain all our impotent poor at far less charge to the parishes than they now are obliged to be at.

When Queen Elizabeth had gained her point as to manufactories in England, she had fairly laid the foundation, she thereby found out the way how every family might live upon their own labour, like a wise princess she knew 'twould be hard to force people to work when there was nothing for them to turn their hands to; but as soon as she had brought the matter to bear, and there was work for everybody that had no mind to starve, then she applied herself to make laws to oblige the people to do this work, and to punish vagrants, and make everyone live by their own labour; all her successors followed this laudable example, and from hence came all those laws against sturdy beggars,[15] vagabonds, strollers, &c. which had they been severely put in execution by our magistrates, 'tis presumed these vagrant poor had not so increased upon us as they have.

And it seems strange to me, from what just ground we proceed now upon other methods, and fancy that 'tis now our business to find them work, and to employ them rather than to oblige them to find themselves work and go about it.

From this mistaken notion come all our work-houses and corporations, and the same error, with submission, I presume was the birth of this Bill now depending, which enables every parish to erect the woollen manufacture within itself, for the employing their own poor.

'Tis the mistake of this part of the Bill only which I am enquiring into, and which I endeavour to set in a true light.

In all the Parliaments since the Revolution, this matter has been before them and I am justified in this attempt by the House of Commons having frequently appointed Committees to receive proposals upon this head.

As my proposal is general, I presume to offer it to the general body of the House; if I am commanded to explain any part of it I am ready to do anything that may be serviceable to this great and noble design.

As the former Houses of Commons gave all possible encouragement to such as could offer, or but pretend to offer at this needful thing, so the imperfect essays of several, whether for private or public benefit I do not attempt to determine, which have since been made, and which have obtained the powers and conditions they have desired, have by all their effects demonstrated the weakness of their design; and that they either understood not the disease, or know not the proper cure for it.

The imperfection of all these attempts is acknowledged, not only in the preamble of this new Act of Parliament, but even in the thing, in that there is yet occasion for any new law.

And having surveyed, not the necessity of a new Act, but the contents of the Act which has been proposed as a remedy in this case; I cannot but offer my objections against the sufficiency of the proposal, and leave it to the consideration of this wise assembly, and of the whole nation.

I humbly hope the learned gentleman, under whose direction this law is now to proceed, and by whose order it has been printed,[16] will not think himself personally concerned in this case; his endeavours to promote so good a work, as the relief, employment, and settlement of the poor merit the thanks and acknowledgment of the whole nation, and no man shall be more ready to pay his share of that debt to him than myself. But if his scheme happen to be something superficial, if he comes in among the number of those who have not searched this wound to the bottom, if the methods proposed are not such as will either answer his own designs or the nation's, I cannot think myself obliged to dispense with my duty to the public good, to preserve a personal value for his judgment, though the gentleman's merit be extraordinary.

Wherefore, as in all the schemes I have seen laid for the poor, and in this Act now before your honourable House; the general thought of the proposers runs upon the employing the poor by Work-houses, Corporations, Houses of Correction, and the like, and that I think it plain to be seen, that those proposals come vastly short of the main design. These sheets are humbly laid before you, as well to make good what is alleged, *viz.* that all these Work-houses, &c. tend to the increase, and not the relief of the poor, as to make an humble tender of mean, plain, but I hope, rational proposals for the more effectual cure of this grand disease.

In order to proceed to this great challenge, I humbly desire the Bills already passed may be reviewed, the practice of our Corporation Work-houses, and the contents of this proposed Act examined.

In all these it will appear that the method chiefly proposed for the employment of our poor, is by setting them to work on the several manufactures before mentioned; as spinning, weaving, and manufacturing our English wool.

All our Work-houses, lately erected in England, are in general thus employed, for which without enumerating particulars, I humbly appeal to the knowledge of the several members of this honourable House in their respective towns where such Corporations have been erected.

In the present Act now preparing, as printed by direction of a Member of this Honourable House, it appears, *that in order to set the poor to work, it shall be lawful for the Overseers*[17] *of every town, or of one or more towns joined together, to occupy any trade, mystery, &c. and raise stocks*[18] *for the*

carrying them on for the setting the poor at work, and for the purchasing wool,
iron, hemp, flax, thread, or other materials for that purpose. Vide the Act
published by Sir Humphrey Mackworth.

And that charities given so and so, and not exceeding 200 *l. per annum*
for this purpose, shall be incorporated of course for these ends.

In order now to come to the case in hand, it is necessary to premise,
that the thing now in debate is not the poor of this or that particular town.
The House of Commons are acting like themselves, as they are the
representatives of all the commons of England, 'tis the care of all the poor
of England which lies before them, not of this or that particular body of
the poor.

In proportion to this great work, I am to be understood that these
Work-houses, Houses of Correction, and stocks to employ the poor may
be granted to lessen the poor in this or that particular part of England;
and we are particularly told of that at Bristol, that it has been such a terror
to the beggars that none of the strolling crew will come near the city. But
all this allowed, in general, 'twill be felt in the main, and the end will be
an increase of our poor.

1. The manufactures that these gentlemen employ the poor upon, are
all such as are before exercised in England.

2. They are all such as are managed to a full extent, and the present
accidents of war and foreign interruption of trade considered rather beyond
the vent of them than under it.

Suppose now a Work-house for employment of poor children, sets them
to spinning of worsted.—For every skein of worsted these poor children
spin, there must be a skein the less spun by some poor family or person
that spun it before; suppose the manufacture of making bays to be erected
in Bishopsgate-street, unless the makers of these bays can at the same time
find out a trade or consumption for more bays than were made before, for
every piece of bays so made in London there must be a piece the less made
at Colchester.

I humbly appeal to the honourable House of Commons what this may
be called, and with submission, I think it is nothing at all to employing
the poor, since 'tis only the transposing the manufacture from Colchester
to London, and taking the bread out of the mouths of the poor of Essex
to put it into the mouths of the poor of Middlesex.

If these worthy gentlemen, who show themselves so commendably
forward to relieve and employ the poor, will find out some new trade,

some new market, where the goods they make shall be sold, where none of the same goods were sold before; if they will send them to any place where they shall not interfere with the rest of that manufacture, or with some other made in England, then indeed they will do something worthy of themselves, and may employ the poor to the same glorious advantage as Queen Elizabeth did, to whom this nation, as a trading country, owes its peculiar greatness.

If these gentlemen could establish a trade to Muscovy for English serges, or obtain an order from the Czar, that all his subjects should wear stockings who wore none before, every poor child's labour in spinning and knitting those stockings, and all the wool in them would be clear gain to the nation, and the general stock would be improved by it, because all the growth of our country, and all the labour of a person who was idle before, is so much clear gain to the general stock.

If they will employ the poor in some manufacture which was not made in England before, or not bought with some manufacture made here before, then they offer at something extraordinary.

But to set poor people at work, on the same thing which other poor people were employed on before, and at the same time not increase the consumption, is giving to one what you take away from another; enriching one poor man to starve another, putting a vagabond into an honest man's employment, and putting his diligence on the tenters[19] to find out some other work to maintain his family.

As this is not at all profitable, so with submission for the expression, I cannot say 'tis honest, because 'tis transplanting and carrying the poor people's lawful employment from the place where was their lawful settlement, and the hardship of this our law considered is intolerable. For example:

The manufacture of making bays is now established at Colchester in Essex; suppose it should be attempted to be erected in Middlesex, as a certain worthy and wealthy gentleman near Hackney once proposed, it may be supposed, if you will grant the skill in working the same, and the wages the same, that they must be made cheaper in Middlesex than in Essex, and cheapness certainly will make the merchant buy here rather than there, and so in time all the bay making at Colchester dies, and the staple for that commodity is removed to London.

What must the poor of Colchester do, where they buy a parochial settlement;[20] those that have numerous families cannot follow the manufacture and come up to London, for our parochial laws empower the church-wardens to refuse them a settlement, so that they are confined to their own country, and the bread taken out of their mouths, and all this to feed vagabonds, and to set them to work, who by their choice would be idle, and who merit the correction of the law.

There is another grievance which I shall endeavour to touch at, which every man that wishes well to the poor does not foresee, and which, with humble submission to the gentlemen that contrived this Act, I see no notice taken of.

There are *arcanas*[21] in trade, which though they are the natural conse-quences of time and casual circumstances, are yet become now so essential to the public benefit, that to alter or disorder them, would be an irreparable damage to the public.

I shall explain myself as concisely as I can.

The manufactures of England are happily settled in different corners of the kingdom, from whence they are mutually conveyed by a circulation of trade to London by wholesale, like the blood to the heart, and from thence disperse in lesser quantities to the other parts of the kingdom by retail. For example:

Serges are made at Exeter, Taunton, &c.; stuffs at Norwich; bays, says, shaloons,[22] &c. at Colchester, Bocking, Sudbury, and parts adjacent; fine cloth in Somerset, Wilts, Gloucester and Worcestershire; coarse cloth in Yorkshire, Kent, Surry, &c.; druggets[23] at Farnham, Newbury, &c. All these send up the gross of their quantity to London, and receive each others sorts in retail for their own use again. Norwich buys Exeter serges, Exeter buys Norwich stuffs, all at London; Yorkshire buys fine cloths, and Gloucester coarse, still at London; and the like, of a vast variety of our manufactures.

By this exchange of manufactures abundance of trading families are maintained by the carriage and re-carriage of goods, vast number of men and cattle are employed, and numbers of innholders, victuallers, and their dependencies submitted.

And on this account I cannot but observe to your honours, and 'tis well worth your consideration, that the already transposing a vast woollen manufacture from several parts of England to London, is a manifest detriment to trade in general; the several woollen goods now made in Spittlefields, where within this few years were none at all made, has already visibly affected the several parts, where they were before made, as Norwich,

Sudbury, Farnham, and other towns, many of whose principal tradesmen are now removed hither, employ their stocks here, employ the poor here, and leave the poor of those countries to shift for work.

This breach of the circulation of trade must necessarily distemper the body, and I crave leave to give an example or two.

I'll presume to give an example in trade, which perhaps the gentlemen concerned in this bill may, without reflection upon their knowledge, be ignorant of.

The city of Norwich, and part adjacent, were for some ages employed in the manufactures of stuffs and stockings.

The latter trade, which was once considerable, is in a manner wholly transposed into London, by the vast quantities of worsted hose wove by the frame,[24] which is a trade within this 20 years almost wholly new.

Now as the knitting frame performs that in a day which would otherwise employ a poor woman eight or ten days, by consequence a few frames performed the work of many thousand poor people; and the consumption being not increased, the effect immediately appeared; so many stockings as were made in London, so many the fewer were demanded from Norwich, till in a few years the manufacture there wholly sunk, the masters there turned their hands to other business; and whereas the hose trade from Norfolk once returned at least 5,000 *l. per* week, and as some say twice that sum, 'tis not now worth naming.

'Tis in fewer years, and near our memory, that of Spittlefields men have fallen into another branch of the Norwich trade, *viz.* making of stuffs, druggets, &c.

If any man say the people of Norfolk are yet full of employ, and do not work; and some have been so weak as to make that reply, avoiding the many other demonstrations which could be given, this is past answering, *viz.* that the combers of wool in Norfolk and Suffolk, who formerly had all, or ten parts in eleven of their yarn manufactured in the country, now comb their wool indeed, and spin the yarn in the country, but send vast quantities of it to London to be woven; will any man question whether this be not a loss to Norwich? Can there be as many weavers as before? And are there not abundance of work-men and masters too removed to London?

If it be so at Norwich, Canterbury is yet more a melancholy instance of it, where the houses stand empty, and the people go off, and the trade die, because the weavers are following the manufacture to London; and whereas there was within few years 200 broad looms at work, I am well assured there are not 50 now employed in that city.

These are the effects of transposing manufactures, and interrupting the circulation of trade.

All methods to bring our trade to be managed by fewer hands than it was before, are in themselves pernicious to England in general, as it lessens the employment of the poor, unhinges their hands from the labour, and tends to bring our hands to be superior to our employ, which as yet it is not.

In Dorsetshire and Somersetshire there always has been a very considerable manufacture for stockings, at Colchester and Sudbury for bays, says, &c. most of the wool these counties use is bought at London, and carried down into those counties, and then the goods being manufactured are brought back to London to market; upon transposing the manufacture as before, all the poor people and all the cattle who hitherto were employed in that *voiture*[25] are immediately disbanded by their country, the innkeepers on the roads must decay, so much land lie for other uses, as the cattle employed, houses and tenements on the roads, and all their dependencies sink in value.

'Tis hard to calculate what a blow it would be to trade in general, should every county but manufacture all the several sorts of goods they use; it would throw our inland trade into strange convulsions, which at present is perhaps, or has been, in the greatest regularity of any in the world.

What strange work must it then make when every town shall have a manufacture, and every parish be a warehouse; trade will be burthened with corporations, which are generally equally destructive as monopolies, and by this method will easily be made so.

Parish stocks, under the direction of justices of peace, may soon come to set up petty manufactures, and here shall all useful things be made, and all the poorer sort of people shall be awed or biased to trade there only. Thus the shop-keepers, who pay taxes, and are the support of our inland circulation, will immediately be ruined, and thus we shall beggar the nation to provide for the poor.

As this will make every parish a market town, and every hospital a storehouse, so in London, and the adjacent parts, to which vast quantities of the woollen manufacture will be thus transplanted thither, will in time too great and disproportioned numbers of the people assemble.

Though the settled poor can't remove, yet single people will stroll about and follow the manufacturer; and thus in time such vast numbers will be drawn about London, as may be inconvenient to the government, and especially depopulating to those countries where the numbers of people, by reason of these manufactures are very considerable.

An eminent instance of this we have in the present trade to Muscovy,[26] which however designed for an improvement to the English nation, and boasted of as such, appears to be converted into a monopoly, and proves injurious and destructive to the nation. The persons concerned removing and carrying out our people to teach that unpolished nation the improvements they are capable of.

If the bringing the Flemings to England brought with them their manufacture and trade, carrying our people abroad, especially to a country where the people work for little or nothing, what may it not do towards instructing that populous nation in such manufactures as may in time tend to the destruction of our trade, or the reducing our manufacture to an abatement in value, which will be felt at home by an abatement of wages, and that in provisions, and that in rent of land; and so the general stock sinks of course.

But as this is preparing, by eminent hands, to be laid before this House as a grievance meriting your care and concern, I omit insisting on it here.

And this removing of people is attended with many inconveniencies which are not easily perceived, as

1. The immediate fall of the value of all lands in those countries where the manufactures were before; for as the numbers of people, by the consumption of provisions, must wherever they increase make rents rise, and lands valuable; so those people removing, though the provisions would, if possible, follow them, yet the price of them must fall by all that charge they are at for carriage, and consequently lands must fall in proportion.

2. This transplanting of families, in time, would introduce great and new alterations in the countries they removed to, which as they would be to the profit of some places, would be to the detriment of others, and can by no means be just any more than it is convenient; for no wise government studies to put any branch of their country to any particular disadvantages, though it may be found in the general account in another place.

If it be said there will be manufactures in every parish, and that will keep the people at home.

I humbly represent what strange confusion and particular detriment to the general circulation of trade mentioned before it must be, to have every parish make its own manufactures.

1. It will make our towns and counties independent of one another, and put a damp to correspondence, which all will allow to be a great motive of trade in general.

2. It will fill us with various sorts and kinds of manufactures, by which our stated sorts of goods will in time dwindle away in reputation, and foreigners not know them one from another. Our several manufactures are known by their respective names; and our serges, bays and other goods, are bought abroad by the character and reputation of the places where they are made; when there shall come new and unheard of kinds to market, some better, some worse, as to be sure new undertakers will vary in kinds, the dignity and reputation of the English goods abroad will be lost, and so many confusions in trade will follow, as are too many to repeat.

3. Either our parish-stock must sell by wholesale or by retail, or both; if the first 'tis doubted they will make sorry work of it, and having other business of their own, make but poor merchants; if by retail, then they turn pedlars, will be a public nuisance to trade, and at last quite ruin it.

4. This will ruin all the carriers in England, the wool will be all manufactured where it is sheared, everybody will make their own clothes, and the trade which now lives by running through a multitude of hands, will go then through so few, that thousands of families will want employment, and this is the only way to reduce us to the condition spoken of, to have more hands than work.

'Tis the excellence of our English manufacture, that it is so planted as to go through as many hands as 'tis possible; he that contrives to have it go through fewer, ought at the same time to provide work for the rest; as it is it employs a great multitude of people, and can employ more; but if a considerable number of these people be unhinged from their employment, it cannot but be detrimental to the whole.

When I say we could employ more people in England, I do not mean that we cannot do our work with those we have, but I mean thus:

First, it should be more people brought over from foreign parts. I do not mean that those we have should be taken from all common employments and put to our manufacture; we may unequally dispose of our hands, and so have too many for some works, and too few for others; and 'tis plain, that in some parts of England it is so; what else can be the reason, why in our southern parts of England, Kent in particular borrows 20,000 people of other counties to get in her harvest.

But if more foreigners came among us, if it were 2 millions, it could do us no harm, because they would consume our provisions, and we have land enough to produce much more than we do, and they would consume our manufactures, and we have wool enough for any quantity.

I think therefore, with submission, to erect manufactures in every town, to transpose the manufactures from the settled places into private parishes and corporations, to parcel out our trade to every door, it must be ruinous to the manufacturers themselves, will turn thousands of families out of their employments, and take the bread out of the mouths of diligent and industrious families to feed vagrants, thieves and beggars, who ought much rather to be compelled, by legal methods, to seek that work which it is plain is to be had; and thus this Act will instead of settling and relieving the poor, increase their number, and starve the best of them.

It remains now, according to my first proposal, page 235, to consider from whence proceeds the poverty of our people, what accident, what decay of trade, what want of employment, what strange revolution of circumstances makes our people poor, and consequently burthensome, and our laws deficient, so as to make more and other laws requisite, and the nation concerned to apply a remedy to this growing disease. I answer:

1. Not for want of work; and besides what has been said on that head, I humbly desire these two things may be considered.

First, 'tis apparent, that if one man, woman, or child, can by his, or her labour, earn more money than will subsist one body, there must consequently be no want of work, since any man would work for just as much as would supply himself rather than starve. What a vast difference then must there be between the work and the workmen, when 'tis now known that in Spittlefields, and other adjacent parts of the City, there is nothing more frequent than for a journeyman weaver, of many sorts, to gain from 15 s. to 30 s. per week wages, and I appeal to the silk throwsters,[27] whether they do not give 8 s., 9 s., and 10 s. per week to blind men and cripples, to turn wheels, and do the meanest and most ordinary works.

Cur moriatur homo, &c.[28]

Why are the families of these men starved, and their children in work-houses, and brought up by charity? I am ready to produce to this honourable

House the man who for several years has gained of me by his handy labour at the mean scoundrel employment of tile-making[29] from 16 s. to 20 s. *per* week wages, and all that time would hardly have a pair of shoes to his feet, or clothes to cover his nakedness, and had his wife and children kept by the parish.

The meanest labours in this nation afford the workmen sufficient to provide for himself and his family, and that could never be if there was a want of work.

2. I humbly desire this honourable House to consider the present difficulty of raising soldiers in this kingdom; the vast charge the kingdom is at to the officers to procure men; the many little and not over honest methods made use of to bring them into the service, the laws made to compel them; why are gaols rummaged for malefactors, and the Mint and prisons for debtors, the war is an employment of honour, and suffers some scandal in having men taken from the gallows, and immediately from villains and house-breakers made gentlemen soldiers. If men wanted employment, and consequently bread, this could never be; any man would carry a musket rather than starve, and wear the Queen's cloth, or anybody's cloth, rather than go naked, and live in rags and want; 'tis plain, the nation is full of people, and 'tis as plain, our people have no particular aversion to the war, but they are not poor enough to go abroad; 'tis poverty makes men soldiers, and drives crowds into the armies, and the difficulties to get English men to list[30] is, because they live in plenty and ease, and he that can earn 20 s. *per* week at an easy, steady employment, must be drunk or mad when he lists for a soldier, to be knocked o'th'head for 3 s. 6 d. *per* week; but if there was no work to be had, if the poor wanted employment, if they had not bread to eat, nor knew not how to earn it, thousands of young lusty fellows would fly to the pike and musket, and choose to die like men in the face of the enemy, rather than lie at home, starve, perish in poverty and distress.

From all these particulars, and innumerable unhappy instances which might be given, 'tis plain, the poverty of our people which is so burthensome, and increases upon us so much, does not arise from want of proper employments, and for want of work, or employers, and consequently:

Workhouses, corporations, parish stocks, and the like, to set them to work, as they are pernicious to trade, injurious and impoverishing to those already employed, so they are needless, and will come short of the end proposed.

The poverty and exigence of the poor in England, is plainly derived from one of these two particular causes,

Casualty or Crime.

By casualty, I mean sickness of families, loss of limbs or sight, and any, either natural or accidental impotence as to labour.

These as infirmities merely providential are not at all concerned in this debate; ever were, will, and ought to be the charge and care of the respective parishes where such unhappy people chance to live, nor is there any want of new laws to make provision for them, our ancestors having been always careful to do it.

The crimes of our people, and from whence their poverty derives, as the visible and direct fountains are,

1. Luxury.
2. Sloth.
3. Pride.

Good husbandry is no English virtue; it may have been brought over, and in some places where it has been planted it has thriven well enough, but 'tis a foreign species, it neither loves, nor is beloved by an Englishman; and 'tis observed, nothing is so universally hated, nothing treated with such a general contempt as a rich covetous man, though he does no man any wrong, only saves his own, every man will have an ill word for him, if a misfortune happens to him; hang him a covetous old rogue, 'tis no matter, he's rich enough; nay when a certain great man's house was on fire, I have heard the people say one to another, let it burn and 'twill, he's a covetous old miserable dog, I won't trouble my head to help him, he'd be hanged before he'd give us a bit of bread if we wanted it.

Though this be a fault, yet I observe from it something of the natural temper and genius of the nation; generally speaking, they cannot save their money.

'Tis generally said, the English get estates, and the Dutch save them; and this observation I have made between foreigners and Englishmen, that where an Englishman earns 20 s. per week, and but just lives, as we call it, a Dutchman grows rich, and leaves his children in very good condition; where an English labouring man with his 9 s. per week lives wretchedly and poor, a Dutchman with that wages will live very tolerably well, keep the wolf from the door, and have everything handsome about him. In short, he will be rich with the same gain as makes the Englishman poor, he'll thrive when the other goes in rags, and he'll live when the other starves, or goes a begging.

The reason is plain: a man with good husbandry, and thought in his head, brings home his earnings honestly to his family, commits it to the management of his wife, or otherwise disposes it for proper subsistence, and this man with mean gains lives comfortably, and brings up a family, when a single man getting the same wages, drinks it away at the ale-house, thinks not of tomorrow, lays up nothing for sickness, age, or disaster, and when any of these happen he's starved, and a beggar.

This is so apparent in every place, that I think it needs no explication; that English labouring people eat and drink, but especially the latter, three times as much in value as any sort of foreigners of the same dimensions in the world.

I am not writing this as a satyr on our people, 'tis a sad truth, and worthy the debate and application of the nation's physicians assembled in Parliament; the profuse extravagant humour of our poor people in eating and drinking, keeps them low, causes their children to be left naked and starving, to the care of the parishes, whenever sickness or disaster befalls the parent.

The next article is their sloth.

We are the most lazy diligent nation in the world; vast trade, rich manufactures, mighty wealth, universal correspondence and happy success have been constant companions of England, and given us the title of an industrious people, and so in general we are.

But there is a general taint of slothfulness upon our poor; there's nothing more frequent, than for an Englishman to work till he has got his pocket full of money, and then go and be idle, or perhaps drunk, till 'tis all gone, and perhaps himself in debt; and ask him in his cups what he intends, he'll tell you honestly, he'll drink as long as it lasts, and then go to work for more.

I humbly suggest this distemper's so general, so epidemic, and so deep rooted in the nature and genius of the English, that I much doubt its being easily redressed, and question whether it be possible to reach it by an Act of Parliament.

This is the ruin of our poor; the wife mourns, the children starve, the husband has work before him, but lies at the ale-house, or otherwise idles away his time, and won't work.

'Tis the men that won't work, not the men that can get no work, which makes the numbers of our poor; all the work-houses in England, all the overseers setting up stocks and manufactures won't reach this case; and I humbly presume to say, if these two articles are removed, there will be no need of the other.

I make no difficulty to promise on a short summons, to produce above a thousand families in England, within my particular knowledge, who go in rags, and their children wanting bread, whose fathers can earn their 15 to 25 s. per week, but will not work, who may have work enough, but are too idle to seek after it, and hardly vouchsafe to earn anything more than bare subsistence, and spending money for themselves.

I can give an incredible number of examples in my own knowledge among our labouring poor. I once paid six or seven men together on a Saturday night, the least 10 s. and some 30 s. for work, and have seen them go with it directly to the ale-house, lie there till Monday, spend it every penny, and run in debt to boot, and not give a farthing of it to their families, though all of them had wives and children.

From hence comes poverty, parish charges, and beggary; if ever one of these wretches falls sick, all they would ask was a pass to the parish they lived at, and the wife and children to the door a-begging.

If this honourable House can find out a remedy for this part of the mischief; if such Acts of Parliament may be made as may effectually cure the sloth and luxury of our poor; that shall make drunkards take care of wife and children; spend-thrifts lay up for a wet day; idle, lazy fellows diligent; and thoughtless sottish men, careful and provident.

If this can be done, I presume to say there will be no need of transposing and confounding our manufactures, and the circulation of our trade; they will soon find work enough, and there will soon be less poverty among us, and if this cannot be done, setting them to work upon woollen manufactures, and thereby encroaching upon those that now work at them, will but ruin our trade, and consequently increase the number of the poor.

I do not presume to offer the schemes I have now drawn of methods for the bringing much of this to pass, because I shall not presume to lead a body so august, so wise, and so capable as this honourable assembly.

I humbly submit what is here offered, as reasons to prove the attempt now making insufficient; and doubt not but in your great wisdom, you will find out ways and means to set this matter in a clearer light, and on a right foot.

And if this obtains on the house to examine farther into this matter, the author humbly recommends it to their consideration to accept, in behalf of all the poor of this nation, a clause in the room of this objected against, which shall answer the end without this terrible ruin to our trade and people.

POLITICAL ADVISER

I allow That in Our Constitucion we admit of No Supreme Ministry.

That ye Nacon is Particularly Jealous of Favourites.

These are ye Two Chief Observacons in ye way of a Refin'd and Lifting Statesman and These are ye Two Reasons why we have had No Capitall Men in ye Civill Administracon No <u>Richlieus</u> <u>Mazarines</u> or Colberts in ye State

But I must Go Back for a Reason for These two Principles. and Must Say
1. It wou'd be best to have a Supreme Ministry
2. The Nacon May Easily be reconcil'd to it

Twill be Needless to prove ye Advantage of a Chief Ministry. Our Confusions in Council Our Errors in Executing and Unwariness in Directing from ye Multitude and Bad conduct of Ministers make it too Plain

To Prove ye Nacon May be Easily reconcil'd to it; Twill be Needfull to go back for ye reasons why Former Favourites have so ill Pleas'd ye Nacon, and how Others have dis: charg'd Themselves wth Honour

The Spencers ye Gavestones of Former Reigns are too Remote ye Prime Ministers of Modern Times have been Principally, ye Earle of Leicester ye Somersett Buckingham the

These all Incurr'd ye Displeasure of ye people by One Crime. Pursueing their Private Intrest En: riching and Aggrandizing themselves and Familyes. and raising Vast Estates Out of ye Spoils of ye Publick. and by their Princes favour Leaping up Honors and Titles to themselves from Mean Originalls

I Need Not Search History for ye Particulars, ye fact is too Plain
The Consequences of this Spirit of Covetousness were allways Extorcions Oppression Bribe Sale of Publick Employments Intrenchments on ye Publick Moneys Exorbitant Grants & Rapa

Bowent

Memorandum to Robert Harley

I allow that in our constitution we admit of no supreme ministry;[1] that the nation is particularly jealous of favourites. These are the two chief obstructions in the way of a refined[2] and rising statesman, and these are the two reasons why we have had no capital men in the civil administration, no Richlieus,[3] Mazarines[4] or Colberts[5] in the state. But I must go back for a reason for these two principles, and must say: 1. It would be best to have a supreme ministry; 2. The nation may easily be reconciled to it. 'Twill be needless to prove the advantage of a chief ministry; our confusions in council, our errors in executing and unwariness in directing from the multitude and bad conduct of ministers make it too plain. To prove the nation may be easily reconciled to it, 'twill be needfull to go back for the reasons why former favourites have so ill pleased the nation, and how others have discharged themselves with honour. The Spencers, the Gavestones[6] of former reigns are too remote; the prime ministers of modern times have been principally the Earl of Leicester,[7] the [Dukes] of Somerset,[8] Buckingham,[9] etc. These all incurred the displeasure of the people by one crime: pursuing their private interest, enriching and aggrandizing themselves and families, and raising vast estates out of the spoils of the public, and by their Prince's favour heaping up honours and titles to themselves from mean originals. I need not search history for the particulars, the fact is too plain. The consequences of this spirit of covetousness were always extortions, oppressions, bribes, sale of public employments, intrenchments on the public moneys, exorbitant grants of royal bounty, and the like. If any man will show me the man that served the state abstracted from his own interest, I'll show them the man who was as much the people's favourite as the king's. Thomas Lord Cromwell[10] was such a one, and, though he fell, as who in the reign of that fickle, unconstant king could stand, he fell a sacrifice to the Protestant party, universally beloved and lamented of the people. Sir Francis Walsingham,[11] though not a prime minister, yet, if we read his story, the ablest statesman and the longest employed, the most employed in difficult cases and the greatest master of intelligence in the age, [was such another]. Both these died poor, they spent their whole time in the service of their country, and no man would have repined at their enjoying their Prince's favour longer.

This premised I bring home the matter to the case in hand. How shall you make yourself Prime Minister of state, unenvied and unmolested, be neither addressed against by Parliament, intrigued against by parties, or murmured at by the mob? With submission 'tis very feasible with an accurate conduct. They say those designs require most policy which have least of honesty; this design must be honest, because it must be honest to serve our country. If it be objected, 'But I would not be Prime Minister,' I return, 'Then you can not be Secretary of State.' The Secretary's office well discharged makes a man Prime Minister of course;[12] and you must be Prime Minister with applause, or you will be Secretary with disgrace. Popular fame never thinks a man too high; popular hate never thinks him too low. A generous, free, noble, uncontracted conduct as effectually secures the affection of the people, as a narrow, covetous, craving spirit effectually engages their mortal aversion. 'Tis certainly a noble design to be popular from a principle of real merit. I observe when all our people clamoured at Dutchmen, and even the King could not please them, because he was a foreigner, no man ever had a bad word for Monsieur Overkirk.[13] Nothing wins this nation like generous, free, open-handed courtesy. The King of Sweden[14] in his German wars always employed trusty persons in the towns and cities he reduced, to inform themselves of any known case where one was oppressed, or any family that had the general pity; and unlooked for, unasked, he would send for, right, and relieve them. Sir, that noble soul is a rare pattern; he gained his very enemies by surprising acts of bounty. In your new post,[15] joined with the influence you have on the royal hand, you will have infinite opportunities to fix an invulnerable reputation. May not these heads be proper?

1. To keep a set of faithful emissaries selected by your own judgement; let them be your constant intelligencers of private affairs in the Court.

2. Set your friends by, if they are such they'll wait, but surprise your enemies, if you have any, with voluntary kindness.

3. Communicate your favours with unbiased hand, that all parties may court you.

4. You have estate enough, and honour enough. Let the world know you covet nothing; all men then will covet you.

Let no man under you make a profit of your favours. One Gehezai[16] in your attendants, will undo the merit of all your actions; he will get the money, and you the curse of the person that pays it. 'Tis absolutely necessary to be popular. The people's darling may be a few men's envy, but the people's hate is a statesman's ruin. This opinion of the people is easily gained at first, and if lost at first, never re-established. 'Tis gained by little acts of courtesy; one generous man obliged, one oppressed man relieved, does a man of trust more honour than twenty ill tongues can blot out. In order to this, your trusty servants will enquire you out occasions enough: a general forwarding and dispatch of petitions, and a thousand things which a man in such a post, with such a soul, never wants opportunity for. In the old Prince of Orange's[17] army a captain that had long served in the wars, talking to a friend, was heard to say he would give 10,000 guilders for such a regiment, the colonel being newly dead. 'Why do you not put in for it,' says his friend. 'Because,' says he, 'the Prince has no kindness for me, and I know he will deny me.' The Prince, knowing him to be a man of merit, sends the person who told him this story with orders to take his bond for the 10,000 guilders upon condition that he procured him the regiment, which he did accordingly. The next day the Prince sends for him, gives him the regiment, and as he was going out, 'Here,' says the Prince, 'and here's something for your equipage,' and threw him his bond. The man was so surprised with the generosity of it, he turned from a prejudiced person to the greatest admirer the Prince had.

Sir, this proposal of a generous bounty and courtesy is not directed because you want it, but because you have it. To suppose you want it would first be an insolence unpardonable, as it would propose your feigning it, and so make a virtue of hypocrisy; but, as I have more than ordinary proofs of your being master of the quality, I take the freedom to hint the uncommon advantage it gives you, to make yourself truly great and have all men pleased with it. Envy always goes with her mouth open, and you are not to expect that an advanced post will shut it; but there is a secret in management that checks it effectually, *viz.* a general, unaffected goodness of temper. Julius Caesar was remarkable for it, and conquered more enemies in the forum than in the field. A man can never be great that is not popular, especially in England. 'Tis absolutely necessary in the very nature of our constitution, where the people have so great a share in the government.

Besides, the people here, in recovering their just rights, have usurped some that are not their due, *viz.* censuring their superiors. But the government is bound to submit to the grievance, because 'tis incurable. 'Tis true a wise man will slight popular reproach, but no wise man slights the general approbation, because nothing but virtue can obtain it. 'Tis therefore absolutely necessary for a statesman to be popular. A statesman once in the people's favour has a thousand opportunities to do with freedom what in a contrary circumstance he would not dare to attempt; for as the people often condemn hastily, they approve with more blindness than they censure, and yet, generally speaking, the common people have been always in the right. A statesman envied dares not attempt a thing which he knows is for the public service, lest the miscarriage falls upon himself. Cardinal Richlieu supplied the want of the people's favour by mere force and so ruined those that opposed him, as in the case of the Duke de Momorency[18] and a multitude of others. Though this would be impracticable here, it shows the absolute necessity of the king, *or of an equivalent*. And yet we find this Cardinal strove hard for the public voice and used a thousand artifices to obtain it; among which this was one, that he never appeared to his own resentments and, though a multitude of persons of all ranks were sacrificed to his politic interest, yet he never would be seen in a matter of punishment. If a pardon was to be granted, he took care the debt should be to the Cardinal, but, if justice was to be done, that was in the King. A popular statesman should have the obtaining all the favours and let others have the management of offences and the distribution of justice.

In your particular case, Sir, you have but one public misfortune, *viz.* that your friends for want of judgement are afraid of you, not afraid you'll hurt them but yourself. 'Twould be necessary to confirm them in the belief of all they hope to find.

No. 1. A particular step will absolutely effect it—of which by itself.

No. 2. A scheme of what I mean by popularity in your own particular, and how to be both obtained and improved for the public service, shall be drawn, if you please to admit it.

No. 3. Also a method to make the office of Secretary of State an inner cabinet, and execute necessary parts of private affairs without the intervention of the Privy Council, and yet have their concurrence as far as the law requires.

When a Prince is to act anything doubtful or anything likely to be disputed either at law or in Parliament, the Council is a necessary screen to the Secretaries of State. But in matters of war, treaties, embassies, private instructions, expeditions, how many such has the delay, the hesitations, the ignorance, or something worse, of Privy Councillors overthrown! Matters maturely advised, deliberately concerted, and absolutely resolved require but two qualifications to legitimate their execution, (1) that they are legal, (2) really for the public good. Such need no Council table to screen them, fear no Parliamentary enquiry, and yet the authors are not answerable for the success. Cabinet Councils in England are modern and eccentric, and I question whether an action which is not justifiable unless transacted in Council is justified by being so in the Cabinet. But Cabinets of ten or fourteen are monsters and useless. If her Majesty leaves the course of things to follow the nature and custom of English Kings, her Privy Council should take cognisance of all needful affairs, but her Treasurer and Secretary of State should be all her Cabinet, unless she had a well qualified Chancellor to add to them. Six sorts of great officers are the moving springs of the state, and I cannot but own without flattery England was never capable of being better supplied, I do not say is fully supplied: a Lord Chancellor, a High Admiral, a Generalissimo, a Lord Treasurer, a Secretary of State, an Archbishop, who perhaps might expect to be put first, but not by me. Of these the first should be a good lawyer, the second a good sailor, the third a good soldier, the last a good divine. But the Treasurer and the Secretary ought to be good statesmen. The weight of all the public affairs lies on their shoulders—one for managing the revenues, providing needful funds, maintaining public credit, and regulating abuses and exactions, etc.; the other for foreign intelligences, correspondence with the courts abroad, managing settling and obtaining confederates, observing and suiting affairs with the circumstances and interest of princes.

Intelligence[19] is the soul of all public business. I have heard that our Secretary's office is allowed 12,000 *l. per annum* for this weighty article, and I am credibly informed the King of France has paid 11 millions in one year for the same article, and 'tis allowed he never spares his money on that head, and thereby outdoes all the world in the knowledge of his neighbours. How much of the 12,000 *l.* allowed for intelligence is expended in our Secretary's office, I will not guess at; but this I presume, that, such a sum being so vastly disproportioned to the necessary expense, the work is not done, and consequently the money that is given for it is lost. Our statesmen have been so far from acquainting themselves with other countries that they are strangers to their own, a certain token that they have sought their private advantage not the public service. The Secretary's office should be an abridgement of all Europe. Her Majesty's Secretary of State ought to have tables of all the following particulars to refer to, stated so regularly that they might have recourse to any particular immediately. They ought to have, 1st, a perfect list of all the gentry and families of rank in England, their residences, characters, and interest in the respective counties; 2nd, of all the clergy of England, their benefices, their character and morals, and the like of the Dissenters; 3rd, of all the leading men in the cities and boroughs, with the parties they espouse. They ought to have a table of parties, and proper calculations of their strength in every respective part, which is to be had by having the copies of the polls sent up on all elections, and all the circumstances of such elections historically collected by faithfull hands and transmitted to the office. They should know the names of all the men of great personal estates, that they may know how and when to direct any occasional trust; they should have the special characters of all the justices of the peace and men of note in every county, to have recourse to on all occasions. Two trusty agents would easily direct all this, so if their hands are not too much tied up as to money, and yet the persons entrusted not know who they serve nor for what end. The Secretary of State should have a table of all the ministers of state, lists of the households, the privy councils, and favourites of every court in Europe, and their characters, with exact lists of their forces, names of the officers, state of their revenue, methods of government, etc., so just and authentic and regularly amended as alterations happen that by this he may duly estimate their strength, judge of their interests and proceeding, and treat with them accordingly. He should keep a correspondence of friendship in all courts with ministers of like quality, as far as may be honourably obtained and without prejudice carried on. Mr. Milton[20] kept a constant epistolary conversation with several foreign ministers of state and men of learning abstracted from affairs of state, but so woven with political observations that he found it as useful as any part of his foreign correspondence. A hundred thousand pounds *per annum* spent now for 3 year in foreign intelligences might be the best money ever this nation laid out, and I am persuaded I could name two articles where, if some money had been well applied, neither the insurrection in Hungary[21] nor the war in Poland[22] should have been so fatal to the confederacy as now they are. If it may be of service, I shall give a scheme for the speedy settling those two uneasy articles, and consequently bringing down such a force on the French as should in all probability turn the scale of the war on the Danube and the Po.

A settled intelligence in Scotland, a thing strangely neglected there, is without doubt the principal occasion of the present misunderstandings between the two kingdoms;[23] in the last reign it caused the King to have many ill things put upon him, and worse are very likely to follow. I beg leave to give a longer scheme of thoughts on that head than is proper here, and a method how the Scots may be brought to reason. There is a large article of spies abroad among the enemies. This I suppose to be settled, though by our defect of intelligence, methinks it should not; but it reminds me of a book in eight volumes published in London about 7 or 8 years ago called *Letters Writ by a Turkish Spy*.[24] The books I take as they are a mere romance, but the moral is good. A settled person of sense and penetration, of dexterity and courage, to reside constantly in Paris, though, as 'tis a dangerous post, he had a larger allowance than ordinary, might by one happy turn earn all the money and the charge be well bestowed. There are 3 towns in France where I would have the like, and they might all correspond, one at Thoulon, one at Brest, one at Dunkirk. They three might trade together as merchants, and the fourth also with them. As intelligence abroad is so considerable, it follows in proportion that the most useful thing at home is secrecy; for, as intelligence is the most useful to us, so keeping our enemies from intelligence among us is as valuable a head. I have been in the Secretary's office of a post night when, had I been a French spy, I could have put in my pocket my Lord N[ottingha]m's[25] letters directed to Sir George Rook[26] and to the Duke of Marlbrough laid carelessly on a table for the doorkeeper to carry to the post. How many miscarriages have happened in England for want of silence and secrecy! Cardinal Richlieu was the greatest master of this virtue that ever I read of in the world, and, if history has not wronged him, has sacrificed many a faithful agent after he had done his duty, that he might be sure he should not be betrayed. He kept three offices for the dispatch of his affairs, and one was so private that none was admitted but in the dark, and up a pair of back remote stairs, which office being at the apartments of his niece made room for a censure passed upon her character, which the Cardinal chose to suffer, that he might have the liberty to transact affairs there of much more moment. This is a principal reason why I object against bringing all things before the Council, for I will not affirm that the minutes of our Privy Council have not been read in the Secretary's office at

Versailles. 'Tis plain the French outdo us at these two things, secrecy and intelligence, and that we may match them in these points is the design of the proposal.

Further schemes as to trade funds for taxes, etc., relating to the Lord Treasurer's share in the public administration I omit, having taken up too much room with this.

No. 1. What I mean by a step to confirm your friends in the belief of what they hope for from you cannot be explained without filling your ears with some of those ill-natured things they take the freedom to say, *viz.* that you are a man wholly resolved to make your fortunes and to bring it to pass will sacrifice your judgement as well as your friends to your interest; that you gave proofs of this in embracing the party of those people who pleased themselves and strove to be popular at the expense of King William; that you forsook the king, who treated you kindly, and that his Majesty spoke of it in very moving terms, as what he was concerned for; that now you have forsaken the Dissenters and fallen in with their enemies and promoted the first Occasional Bill;[27] *cum multis aliis*, etc.[28] Sir, it is not that I suppose the Dissenters ought to be deceived, or that you will deceive them, that I repeat it again, *they are to be pleased with words*. But, Sir, as good words are useful in their place, so when not spoken with design [they] are honourable in themselves. There is no immediate action by which you can demonstrate you will serve them. Only let some proper persons carefully inform them that on all occasions they may depend on your good offices with the Queen, and give them some notices by such hands as may be trusted that you are their friend. Particularly it may be very easy to possess the Dissenters that they owe the change of her Majesty's sentiments with relation to the Occasional Bill to your management and councils, and that her Majesty's changing sides was, together with the measures you prescribed, the only reason of the majority obtained in the House of Lords against the said Bill. To effect this a short paper shall be handed about among the Dissenters only, giving them a pretended view of the measures taken by some persons, naming none, to convince the Queen of the unreasonableness of this Bill. It cannot fail to open their eyes that you are their friend, and yet, if your affairs should require you to disown such a paper, it shall easily be true that you had no knowledge of it, for you may really know nothing of it. If my service in another case is accepted, I shall take care to make such a paper be read in all parts of the kingdom. I allow the particular steps mentioned in such a paper may not be fact, yet, if it

[be] really fact that you have appeared against the Bill, that you have
influenced and advised her Majesty in favour of the toleration, etc., the
general is truth and therefore the design just. This is part of the particular
step marked No. 1.

No. 2. Of popularity.

That which I call popularity may a little differ from the thing which
goes by that name in the general opinion, and therefore 'tis needful to
distinguish the term. Popularity in general is the general esteem of the
people; but the popularity I mean must have an adjunct, *viz.* a general
esteem founded on good actions, truly meriting the love of the people.
'Tis true the people are not so apt to love as to hate, and therefore, when
the former is fixed on a person, it ought to imply some merit. But this is
not universally true, for the people sometimes love by antithesis, and show
a general affection for one person to show their dis-esteem of his enemy,
and this may be visible in the case of the Duke of Monmouth, who really
had not a great deal of personal merit. We say happiness consists in being
content; but I must deny it, unless the contentment be fixed on a centre
of virtue, for a vicious man may so be more happy than a virtuous, and a
mad man than both. So here a man may be popular without merit, but
that popularity will neither be useful nor serviceable:

> For though by wicked acts men gain applause,
> The reputation's rotten, like the cause.

A wise man is willing to be popular, and a wise statesman will be so, but
it is such a popular esteem as rises from acts of virtue, bounty, and noble
principles. 'Tis my opinion, Sir, as to yourself, and I speak it with the
same plainness as I do things less smooth, that I ought to use more
arguments with you to persuade you to desire this popular esteem than to
deserve it. And therefore, Sir, I leave the philosophy of the argument to
your own speculation, and go on to the present case. The popularity I
mean now is—a political conduct of your self, between the Scylla and the
Charybdis[29] of parties, so as to obtain from them all a general esteem.
Though this part of conduct is called dissimulation, I am content it shall
be called what they will, but, as a lie does not consist in the indirect position
of words but in the design by false speaking to deceive and injure my
neighbour, so dissembling does not consist in putting a different face upon
our actions but in the further applying that concealment to the prejudice
of the person. For example, I come into a person's chamber who on a

surprize is apt to fall into dangerous convulsions; I come in smiling and pleasant, and ask the person to rise and go abroad, or any other such question, and press him to it till I prevail, whereas the truth is I have discovered the house to be on fire, and I act thus for fear of frighting him. Will any man tax me with hypocrisy and dissimulation? In your particular post, Sir, you may so govern as that every party shall believe you their own. I think I may answer for one side, and shall think very meanly of my own designs if I do not bring the Dissenters to believe it firmly, if you please to give me leave to act as effectually as I may convince you will be needful. The Dissenters, Sir, may be brought: 1, To believe better of past actions, of which I mean in the scheme no. 1; 2, They shall always believe you their friend with the Queen; 3, Take you for their advocate and apply to you on all occasions; 4, Freely acquaint you of all circumstances relating to what they desire or fear; 5, If ever you find occasion, you may be the head of the whole party, and consequently influence them as you please; 6, You will have the opportunity upon all occasions both to represent them right to the Queen, and the Queen right to them, the want of which has been injurious to both; 7, You will caution them against indiscretions, and anything that may be to their disadvantage; 8, You may at second hand acquaint them of the designs of a party against them, and have the honour of saving them from the mischief intended. The influence your office, as well as personal merit, gives you on the Queen will give you opportunities either to bring off many of the hot men on the other side or to discourage them that they may cease to disturb; and as to the moderatest of them, you will often by serving them oblige them to acknowlege you. Of the moderate men you are secure, and they cannot but both approve your conduct, as they see it moves towards the real happiness of us all. This is the dissimulation I recommend, which is not unlike what the Apostle says of himself becoming all things to all men, that he might gain some. This hypocrisy is a virtue, and by this conduct you shall make yourself popular, you shall be faithful and useful to the Sovereign and beloved by the people.

No. 3. Of making the Secretaries of State an inner cabinet to the Queen.

If the Secretaries of State have a right understanding and act entirely in concert, it will forward it exceedingly. The Secretaries should have a set of able heads, under a secret management, with whom to make general calculations, and from whom to receive such needful informations as by other agents under them may be obtained in all necessary or difficult cases, and yet these secret heads need not correspond. From this fund of advice

all things needful to be concerted for the occasions of state may be formed
into schemes and come out perfect. The proposals made by the Secretaries
shall no more be embryos, and be brought before the Council to be argued
and amended, but shall be born at once and come before them whole and
complete, and the Council have little to do but to approve a thing as it is
proposed. If all the proposals relating to public matters were thus digested,
her Majesty would find there was a secret sufficiency somewhere in her
Secretary's office that in time would bring both herself and Council to
depend upon the Secretaries of State for all models of action, as well as
the management, and thus, Sir, I have brought out what I affirmed at first,
that the Secretary of State must of course be Prime Minister. An essay or
two of this nature shall be made when you please.

I acknowlege the conjunction of the Lord Treasurer for the time being
would make a complete conduct, because 'tis impossible but his Lordship
must be furnished with such helps as may finish things with less difficulty.
In this concert all the great actions of state, all orders given to admirals
and generals, all foreign treaties, and foreign intelligences, would receive
their last turns, be digested, and finished, and the Queen see herself
mistress of the most capital part of her affairs before they come before the
Council. All funds for taxes, ways and means, projects of trade, etc., shall
be here formed into heads, and either be fitted for execution or laid aside
as impracticable, and my Lord Treasurer be eased of the intolerable
impertinence of fund makers and projectors. Secret matters relating to
parties, to private persons, home management, etc., will here be settled,
determined, and prepared for execution. Here all the business of the
Crown, the affairs of law only excepted, will centre, and the Secretary's
office be thus the only Cabinet. This would make our actions uniform, our
councils secret, our orders regular and practicable, and the execution
punctual. This would bring the Secretary's office, and above all the Secretary, into such reputation that orders issued would have more regard, since
resentments of misconduct would lie in the breast of the Secretary and be
very certain and severe. Here would be a Prime Ministry without a
grievance, the people pleased, the government served, envy ashamed,
intrigues fruitless, enterprises successful, and all our measures be both
better directed and better executed. At home parties would be suppressed,
furious tempers on all sides checked and discountenanced, peace promoted
and union obtained. All the leading men of all sides would be influenced
here, by a rare and secret management; they should never stir nor speak

as a party but it should be known. Not a Mayor or an Alderman in any corporation, not a Sheriff of a county, not a Member of Parliament or Convocation, could be elected, but the Government should know who to oppose and how to do it, if they saw fit. This would be the wheel of all public business, and all the other business must of course depend on the management of this office. [. . .]

Notes

Introduction

1. *Review*, 22 October 1709 (VI, 341).
2. It was believed to be lost, but in 1982 the manuscript was discovered by Maximillian E. Novak in the William Andrews Clark Memorial Library (MS H6735M3).
3. This manuscript is in the Henry E. Huntington Library (HM 26613); see *The Meditations of Daniel Defoe*, ed. G. H. Healey (Cummington, Mass., 1946).
4. See the 'Preface', first published in 1706, that Defoe wrote for *De Laune's Plea for the Nonconformists* (1683).
5. In his autobiographical *An Appeal to Honour and Justice* (1715), p. 28. It is confirmed by the fact that, two years later, he received a pardon for doing so; see F. Bastian, *Defoe's Early Life* (1981), p. 112.
6. It has not survived.
7. *An Appeal to Honour and Justice* (1715), p. 51.
8. *The Complete English Tradesman* (1726 [for 1725]), II, 58.
9. William's enemies accused him of a sexual relationship with van Keppel.
10. *An Appeal to Honour and Justice* (1715), p. 6.
11. In *An Appeal to Honour and Justice* (1715), p. 6, he writes of 'how this poem was the occasion of my being known to his Majesty; how I was afterwards received by him; how employed; and how, above my capacity of deserving, rewarded.' Elsewhere, though, he claimed to have witnessed the drafting of William's First Partition treaty, which took place at least a year before the appearance of *The True-Born Englishman*; see, for example, *Review*, 6 November 1711 (VIII, 391), and 14 March 1713 ([IX], 140).
12. *The Two Great Questions Consider'd* (1700), p. 15.
13. See *An Account of Some Late Designs to Create a Misunderstanding Betwixt the King and his People* (1702), pp. 16–18.
14. *Review*, 11 June 1713 ([IX], 214).
15. *Review*, 22 February 1707 (IV, 21).

16. *The Complete English Tradesman* (1726 [for 1725]), I, 375–6. See John McVeagh, 'Defoe and the Romance of Trade', *Durham University Journal*, 70 (1978), pp. 141–7.
17. On the whole extraordinary process by which the Defoe 'canon' has been constructed, see P. N. Furbank and W. R. Owens, *The Canonisation of Daniel Defoe* (London and New Haven, 1988); *Defoe De-Attributions: A Critique of J. R. Moore's 'Checklist'* (London and Rio Grande, 1994).
18. *Roxana*, ed. David Blewett (Penguin, 1982), p. 40.
19. *The Letters of Daniel Defoe*, ed. George Harris Healey (Oxford, 1955), p. 68.

DEFENDER OF KING WILLIAM

An Argument, Shewing, that a Standing Army, with Consent of Parliament, is not Inconsistent with a Free Government, &c.

This was probably published early in 1698; it was advertised as published 'this day' in the *Flying Post* for 1–4 January. It was, mainly, an answer to *An Argument Shewing that a Standing Army is Inconsistent with a Free Government*, by John Trenchard and Walter Moyle, published in October 1697.

1. *knows not Joseph*: See Exodus 1:8.
2. *Discourse of Militias*: i.e. Andrew Fletcher's *A Discourse Concerning Militias and Standing Armies* (1697).
3. *Second Part of the Argument*: A continuation of the Trenchard and Moyle pamphlet, published in December 1697.
4. *Prince of Parma's army*: The military organization of the Spanish Armada in 1588 was in the hands of Philip II's minister Alexander Farnese, Prince of Parma.
5. *Guard du Corps*: Life guards.
6. *Guard du Terres*: Yeomanry.
7. *unfortunate service of the King of Bohemia*: In August 1619, James I's son-in-law Frederick of the Palatinate accepted the crown of Bohemia. A year later, however, after his defeat at the battle of White Mountain, a Spanish army invaded the Palatinate, and James was compelled to come to Frederick's rescue.
8. *relief of Rochelle*: In 1627, Charles I despatched a fleet to relieve the Huguenots, besieged in La Rochelle. When, however, the expedition arrived at the Isle de Ré, just off La Rochelle, the Rochellese proved unwilling to throw in their lot with their would-be deliverers.
9. *one neighbour*: i.e. France.
10. *Peace of Nimeguen*: A treaty of peace between France and the United Provinces, signed at Nimeguen in 1678.
11. *1672*: France and England declared war on the Dutch in 1672, and the French army quickly overran the Netherlands.

12. *they would be good for nothing*: As early as his first poem, *A New Discovery of an Old Intreague* (1691), Defoe was highly satirical about the militia.

13. *principiis obsta*: Stop things in their beginning.

14. *beati pacifici*: 'Blessed are the peacemakers', James I's well-known motto.

15. *Count Colocedo . . . Count Mansfield*: Count Don Carlos Coloma was Spanish ambassador to England during the reign of James I. Count Ernst von Mansfeld was a German soldier of fortune who served as a general under James I's son-in-law Frederick; see n. 7 above. In 1624, he was brought to England to command the army then being prepared for intervention in Europe, an appointment which enraged the professional soldiers.

16. *Though his government . . . Horses*: From a poem once attributed to Andrew Marvell.

17. *the peace*: A peace between England, France, Spain and the United Provinces was signed at Ryswick in October 1697.

18. *pacta conventa*: Agreements between William and the Convention parliament, the body which offered him the crown.

19. *in hac verba*: (Properly *haec*), 'in these very words'.

20. *the year 1680*: At the motion of the moderate Tory leader Robert Harley, the Commons voted in December 1697 to disband all troops raised since September 1680.

21. *Purbeck fancied invasion*: The *Second Part of an Argument* (p. 21) refers to 'the Purbeck invasion, which was so private that it was seen only by an old man and a boy: and yet though the country thought the Government against them, we had above forty thousand volunteers in arms in two or three days time'.

22. *battle of Newport*: Maurice of Nassau defeated the Austrians at Nieuwpoort on 2 July 1600.

23. *the power of the sword . . . him if need be*: In the passages in italics, Defoe seems to be giving a close paraphrase of Andrew Fletcher's *A Discourse Concerning Militias and Standing Armies* (1697), p. 6.

24. *the barons growing poor . . . the like*: A close paraphrase of Fletcher's *Discourse*, p. 10.

25. *no weapon . . . could ever prosper*: See Isaiah 54:17.

26. *good husband*: Frugal manager.

27. *the 10th penny*: The tyrannical Duke of Alva attempted to impose a 10 per cent sales tax on the Netherlanders, but without success.

28. *coat and conduct money*: A tax levied on the counties to pay the cost of clothing troops and their travelling expenses.

29. *quo warrantoes*: A *quo warranto* was a writ against a defendant, whether an individual or a corporation, calling on him or it to show by what right he or it laid claim to something. In October 1683, by a *quo warranto* judgment, Charles II deprived the City of its liberties and the Livery Companies of their charters.

30. *In the year [1682] . . . privileges of the City*: At the swearing-in of the new City sheriffs on 28 September, Lieutenant Colonel Adrian Quiney pulled a Whig councillor down off the hustings and threw another, Henry Cornish, out of the hall. A number of suits were brought against him for this behaviour. There is a good account of the event in M. E. Campbell, *Defoe's First Poem* (Bloomington, Indiana, 1938), pp. 122–3.

The True-Born Englishman

The date of publication of Defoe's most famous poem has not been established with certainty; early editions are dated 1700, but it may not have appeared until early January 1701. Something like fifty editions were published before 1750, many of them pirated. In editions after the first, Defoe removed the passage attacking Tutchin as 'Shamwhig', and in an edition of 1716 he added 59 lines. These have not been included here.

1. *Mr. Cowley*: Abraham Cowley (1618–67).
2. *Title*: Perhaps an allusion to *Richard II*, II. iii. 309.
3. *times of peace*: Nine years of war with France had come to an end with the Treaty of Ryswick, signed in September 1697.
4. *golden key resign*: The symbol of office of the Lord Chamberlain is a golden key. The Whig Duke of Shrewsbury resigned as Lord Chamberlain on 23 June 1700 and was immediately replaced by the Tory Edward Villiers, Earl of Jersey.
5. *bubbled*: Cheated.
6. *old monarch . . . new*: James II deserted the kingdom on 11 December 1688, and was replaced on the throne by William and Mary on 13 February 1689.
7. *Wherever God . . . chapel there*: Defoe added a note, 'An English proverb'.
8. *uniformity . . . nonconforming sects*: By the Act of Uniformity of 1662, it became unlawful to worship outside the Church of England, and those who refused to conform ('nonconformists') were subject to severe penalties.
9. *his yoke*: See Matthew 11:39.
10. *Lords Justices*: During William III's visits to the Netherlands each year, Lords Justices were appointed to govern the country.
11. *paynim*: Heathen.
12. *Rush*: i.e. Russian.
13. *Hengist . . . Sueno*: Hengist, one of the leaders of the Jutes, came with the Saxons to England in 449 and became the progenitor of a line of Kentish kings. 'Sueno', or Sweyn, King of Denmark (d. 1014), led numerous invasions of England, and his son, Canute, became King of England.
14. *Britains*: i.e. Britons.
15. *shibboleth*: The Gileadites, to test their captives' origin, made them say the

word 'Shibboleth', which Ephraimites were unable to pronounce correctly. See Judges 12:6.

16. *send his Dutchmen home again*: William was forced by Parliament to disband his Dutch guards regiments; they returned to Holland in March 1699.

17. *reassumptions*: A Bill for the resumption of King William's grants of forfeited estates in Ireland was passed, after much wrangling, in April 1700.

18. *Davenant*: Charles Davenant, political economist, whose book, *A Discourse upon Grants and Resumptions*, appeared in November 1699 (though dated 1700).

19. *Parliament . . . disband*: See n. 16 above.

20. *cantoned*: Divided.

21. *the moderns*: Defoe glosses this 'Dr. Sher[lock] De Facto'. William Sherlock, the prominent non-juring clergyman, in his *The Case of the Allegiance Due to Soveraign Powers* (1691), explained that he had taken the oath of allegiance to William and Mary since they were *de facto* rulers.

22. *jakes*: Latrine.

23. *Vaudois and Valtolins*: The Vaudois, or Waldenses, were a sect which flourished throughout Europe but particularly in Italy. The Valtolins, Protestant inhabitants of Valtellina in Switzerland, were victims of a massacre by Catholics in 1620.

24. *David at Hackelah*: See I Samuel 23:9–19, which relates how David fled to the hill of Hachilah to escape from Saul.

25. *plods*: Plaids? (The OED cites 'plodan' as a variant spelling of 'plaiding'.)

26. *whigging*: Jogging along (It is also, of course, a pun.)

27. *locusts . . . in Egypt*: See Exodus 10:3–20.

28. *Civil Wars*: i.e. The wars between Parliament and Charles I, 1642–8.

29. *Ch[arle]s's restoration*: The restoration of Charles II to the throne in 1660.

30. *Lindsey's . . . fun'ral pile*: Defoe lists notable Royalists who lost their lives during the Civil Wars.

31. *Six bastard dukes . . . Cambrian*: The illegitimate sons of Charles II by his various mistresses. The Dukes of Southhampton, Grafton and Northumberland were born to Barbara Villiers, Countess of Castlemaine; the Duke of Richmond to Louise Renée de Keroualle, Duchess of Portsmouth; the Duke of St Albans to Nell Gwyn ('tabby Scot'); and the Duke of Monmouth to Lucy Walter ('Cambrian' because of her Welsh origins).

32. *S[chomber]g and P[ortlan]d*: Friedrich Herman von Schonberg, one of William III's most trusted generals, was created Earl of Brentford and Duke of Schomberg in 1689. Hans Willem Bentinck, one of William's favourites, who accompanied him to England, was raised to the peerage as Earl of Portland in 1689.

33. *banished Protestants of France*: French Huguenots fled to England in increasing numbers in the years leading up to the Revocation of the Edict of Nantes in 1685.

34. *wooden shoes*: A reference to the sabots, or wooden shoes, worn by French peasants.

35. *heptarchy*: The Angles and Saxons established seven kingdoms in England.

36. *banter*: Jest.

37. *Heralds*: The College of Heralds is the repository for registers of coats of arms.

38. *Mommorency*: The Montmorency family was one of the oldest and greatest of the noble houses of France.

39. *Nassau*: William III inherited the title of Orange-Nassau from his great-grandfather William the Silent, the founder of the Dutch republic.

40. *H[oublo]ns . . . L[ethui]lliers*: Sir John Houblon, the first Governor of the Bank of England, was Lord Mayor of London in 1695. Thomas Papillon was a Whig Member of Parliament between 1673 and 1700. Sir John Lethuillier served as Sheriff in 1674 and as an alderman in 1676, being succeeded in both offices by his younger brother Sir Christopher Lethuillier.

41. *Bluecoat Hospitals and Bridewell*: The orphans and children of the poor who were sent to Christ's Hospital (a school founded in 1552) wore a uniform of blue coats and yellow stockings. The Bridewell Royal Hospital, later to become a prison, was originally a workhouse where homeless apprentices were set to trades.

42. *counter*: A prison for debtors, also known as a 'compter'.

43. *Tarpaulin Lords*: A 'tarpaulin' was a naval officer who had worked his way up through the ranks.

44. *forecast*: Forethought.

45. *artists*: Artisans.

46. *Reformation*: During William III's reign, there was a great campaign against public profanity and immorality. The Society for the Reformation of Manners was founded in 1690, drawing members from various religious denominations.

47. *Epicurus . . . Alexander*: The Greek philosophers Epicurus and Aristippus taught that pleasure was the highest good. Lysander was the Spartan naval commander during the Peloponnesian war, i.e. a famous warrior, like Alexander the Great.

48. *Galen*: The writings of the Greek physician (AD 129–99).

49. *Cecilia*: Saint Cecilia, patron saint of music.

50. *Asgillites*: In July 1700, John Asgill published a pamphlet arguing that it was possible to be translated straight to heaven without dying. Defoe wrote a refutation, *An Enquiry into the Case of Mr Asgil's General Translation*, though this was not published until 1703.

51. *Colon*: A young man up from the country (from the Latin *colonus* meaning farmer).

52. *nobles*: English gold coins.

53. *drunken pilot*: Charles II.

54. *Quakers . . . return you none*: Quakers refused to conform to social courtesies, such as raising the hat.

55. *Shamwig*: John Tutchin. See Introduction, p. xii. This 'character' of Tutchin was cut in all authorized editions of the poem after the first.

56. *Satyr upon Honesty*: Tutchin published *A Search after Honesty* in 1698.

57. *benefactors . . . accused*: Tutchin was dismissed from a clerkship in the Victualling Office after accusing the commissioners of fraud.

58. *paltry rhymes*: Tutchin's poem *The Foreigners*.

59. *huffs*: Attacks.

60. *panegyricked him*: In 1689 Tutchin had published *An Heroick Poem upon the Late Expedition of His Majesty to Rescue England from Popery, Tyranny, and Arbitrary Government*, in which he praised William as 'a Godlike Hero', 'our other Moses', etc.

61. *to ancient Israel well compared*: In *The Foreigners*, Tutchin compares the English to the Israelites, and the Dutch to the Gibeonites of the Old Testament, imitating the method of John Dryden's famous political satire, *Absalom and Achitophel*.

62. *harps . . . hung*: cf. Psalm 137:2.

63. *non-resistance*: Throughout the seventeenth century, Anglican clergy taught that the monarch should never be actively resisted, even if breaking the law, since he or she has divine authority to rule. The teaching was often referred to as the doctrine of 'passive obedience'.

64. *their Prince*: James II.

65. *suprema lex*: Supreme law.

66. *post facto*: Retrospective.

67. *Donative*: Gift, reward.

68. *trepanned*: Tricked, ensnared.

69. *Sunderland*: Robert Spencer (1640–1702), second Earl of Sunderland. While holding office as Lord President of the Council under James II, Sunderland was secretly in touch with William to bring about the Revolution.

70. *sot*: Drunkard, or possibly simply blockhead.

71. *sons of Levi*: Clergy.

72. *Hydra*: In Greek myth, the Hydra was a many-headed serpent.

73. *case*: Form.

74. *postulatas*: Requirements, demands.

75. *entail*: Succession.

76. *original*: i.e. The people; cf. Defoe's *The Original Power of the Collective Body of the People of England*, pp. 80–109.

77. *great Nassau*: See n. 39 above.

78. *Old Chaos*: In Greek mythical cosmogony, Chaos was the first created being.

79. *parallel from Hebrew stories*: See n. 61 above.

80. *hurried home*: See n. 16 above.

81. *Great Portland*: Hans Willem Bentinck, Duke of Portland, served as William's envoy to England before the Revolution. He accompanied William to England, led a regiment of dragoons at the Battle of the Boyne in 1690, and fought in various campaigns against the French in Flanders.

82. *Hushai*: In 2 Samuel 15–17, Hushai is the friend of David who warns Absalom against Ahithophel.

83. *managing the peace*: Portland was involved in the negotiations which led to the Treaty of Ryswick in 1697.

84. *Schonbergh . . . but us*: Friedrich Herman von Schonberg (1615–90), one of the greatest military commanders of his day, volunteered his services to William in 1668. He commanded William's armies in Ireland, and died at the Battle of the Boyne. Among his earlier military exploits was a famous victory over the Spanish at Villa Viciosa in 1665. See also n. 32 above.

85. *Turkey-fleet*: In May 1693, a fleet of nearly 400 merchant ships sailing to the Mediterranean under the protection of the English and Dutch navies was attacked by the French. About 100 ships were lost, at an estimated value of over one million pounds. A parliamentary committee of inquiry blamed the naval commanders for treacherous mismanagement.

86. *injured Talmarsh*: In 1694, Thomas Tollemache, who had replaced Marlborough as Lieutenant-General of the English army, led an attack on the French at Camaret Bay (near Brest). The plan was known to the French, and the attack failed completely. Tollemache, who was fatally wounded, believed that he had been betrayed by William's English ministers.

87. *a modern Magistrate*: Sir Charles Duncombe, an immensely rich goldsmith and banker and Tory Member of Parliament.

88. *great descent*: Duncombe came from a lowly background.

89. *office in the City*: In September 1700, Duncombe failed to be elected Mayor.

90. *stole from Kings*: It was alleged that Duncombe, while serving as a receiver of the customs, had kept back a large sum which he claimed the King owed him.

91. *St Magnus*: In 1700, Duncombe gave an expensive clock to the re-built church of St Magnus Martyr.

92. *City-gaols . . . a jubilee*: While he was Sheriff, Duncombe released many debtors from prison.

93. *mobile*: Mob.

94. *Backwell*: Duncombe began his career as an apprentice to Alderman Edward Backwell, a leading city goldsmith and one of the first public bankers in England.

95. *betrayed him*: Backwell was ruined when Charles II ordered a stop on exchequer payments in 1672, but Duncombe had been forewarned and managed to avoid the same fate.

96. *public trust*: Duncombe was appointed to a post as Receiver of the Customs under Charles II.

97. *sov'reign lord*: Charles II.

98. *Ziba*: For the story of Ziba's betrayal of his master, Mephibosheth, the son of Jonathan, and of David's conflicting oaths to Ziba and Jonathan which were only resolved by dividing Mephibosheth's estate with Ziba, see 2 Samuel 9; 16; 19.

99. *old game*: In 1696 and 1697, it was rumoured that Duncombe was lending money to King William.

100. *forgery*: In February 1698, Duncombe had been expelled from the House of Commons and imprisoned in the Tower, charged with forging endorsements to treasury bills. A bill to confiscate two-thirds of his estate was narrowly defeated in the Lords, and an attempt to prosecute him in the law courts failed on a legal technicality.

101. *old friend*: Probably Charles Paulet, sixth Marquis of Winchester and first Duke of Bolton, who spoke in Duncombe's defence in the House of Lords.

102. *Knighted*: Duncombe was knighted on 20 October 1699.

103. *tribune of the people*: In June 1699, only a week after his acquittal by the King's Bench, Duncombe was elected High Sheriff of London.

104. *custos rotulorum*: The *custos rotulorum* was the principal Justice of the Peace in a county, who had custody of the rolls and records of the sessions of the peace.

105. *banditti*: Bandits, i.e. the London trained bands.

106. *catchpoles*: Sheriff's officers, especially bum-bailiffs (officials empowered to collect debts or arrest debtors for non-payment).

107. *The King commanded*: In 1698, William issued a proclamation ordering magistrates to prosecute and punish severely anyone guilty of 'dissolute, immoral, or disorderly practices'.

108. *Miss [Morgan]*: Nothing is known of her.

109. *Jeffery*: Sir Robert Jeffries (or Geffrey) was elected Sheriff of London in 1673. He made a point of presiding at the flogging of prostitutes, who were stripped to the waist for this purpose.

110. *Reformation*: See n. 46 above.

111. *panegyrics*: A number of pamphlets singing Duncombe's praises were published in 1699 and 1700.

112. *charities*: In the run-up to the elections for Mayor in September 1700, there were many rumours of the great charitable works Duncombe would carry out if elected.

113. *to do so*: To shout huzzas, like the gaol-birds.

114. *'Tis personal virtue only makes us great*: A translation from Juvenal, *Satires*, VIII, 20: *Nobilitas sola est atque unica virtus*.

The Six Distinguishing Characters of a Parliament-Man

This was advertised in the *Post Man* for 2–4 January 1701. The title-page reproduces part of the King's proclamation of December 1700 calling for elections to a new Parliament, to meet on 6 February, 'in respect of some matters of the highest importance to this our kingdom'.

1. *consented to disband the army*: See Introduction above, p. x.
2. *behold a glutton and a drunkard*: See Luke 7:34.

3. *He has a d[evi]l*: See Matthew 11:18.

4. *Russel*: William Russell (1639–83), third son of the fifth Earl of Bedford. He was accused of participating in the Rye House plot against Charles II's life and was executed for high treason.

5. *Essex*: Arthur Capel, Earl of Essex (1631–83). He was committed to the Tower for complicity in the Rye House plot and was found there with his throat cut, possibly by his own hand.

6. *Oxford Parliament*: Charles II's fourth and last Parliament was convened in Oxford in late March 1681.

7. *b[isho]ps, who threw out that bill*: The second Exclusion Bill, intended to prevent the Roman Catholic Duke of York from succeeding to the throne, was defeated in the Lords in November 1680, all the bishops present voting against it.

8. *his proclamation*: See headnote above.

9. *succession of Spain*: See Introduction above, p. xiii–xiv.

10. *dispensing the Popish officers*: In November 1685, both houses of Parliament objected to the employment of Roman Catholic officers in the Army, since this contravened the Test Act. King James, however, prorogued Parliament before any action could be taken.

11. *countries*: i.e. Counties.

12. *Asgillites*: See n. 50 (p. 275).

13. *Duke d'Berry*: Younger brother of the Duke d'Anjou, to whom Charles II of Spain bequeathed his dominions.

14. *Reformation of Manners*: See n. 46 (p. 275).

15. *Jehu*: See 2 Kings 10:18–28. The son of Jehoshaphat, Jehu seized the throne and secured it by the wholesale slaughter of the house of Ahab, as foretold by Elijah.

16. *a Josiah and a Jehosaphat*: Biblical kings of Judah.

TRIBUNE OF THE PEOPLE

Legion's Memorial

This was delivered to the House of Commons on 14 May 1701, so was presumably published that day. It was immediately, and widely, attributed to Defoe, though for obvious reasons he never openly admitted authorship.

1. *illegal custody*: A reference to the arrest of the five 'Kentish Gentlemen'; see Introduction above, p. xv.

2. *assembled in Convention*: The body that offered William the crown called itself a 'Convention', though it subsequently assumed the style of a 'Parliament' without resort to a general election.

3. *sine die*: A legal term meaning 'without date', or 'indefinitely'.

4. *dispensing power*: James's use of the royal 'dispensing power' to suspend laws was one of the leading constitutional crimes of which he was accused, and it was specifically condemned in William III's Bill of Rights (1689).

5. *horrid assassinators*: Presumably some of the participants in the plot against the King's life in February 1696.

6. *Treaty of Partition*: See Introduction above, p. xi.

7. *Deserting the Dutch*: On 8 February 1701, the King laid before the Commons a memorial from England's ally the Dutch, appealing for help against the French, who had occupied all the barrier fortresses between Ostend and Luxembourg. The House was, however, reluctant to take action.

8. *to displace his friends*: On 24 March 1701, the Commons passed a vote condemning William's second Partition Treaty. By mid-April, they began proceedings to impeach the negotiators of the treaty, Portland, Somers, Orford and Halifax, but eventually the impeachments lapsed, through disagreement between the two Houses.

9. *J[ohn] H[o]w*: Jack Howe, as he was known, made these remarks in the Commons on 11 February 1701. He was a fierce Tory, with a slashing mode of oratory. William was so outraged by this reference to his 'felonious treaty' that he said he wished he could challenge Howe to a duel.

10. *Billingsgate*: Billingsgate fish-market was proverbially a place for foul language.

11. *V[ote]s*: i.e. The 'Votes and Proceedings' of Parliament, published from the minutes of the clerks-at-the-table.

12. *Reformation of Manners*: See n. 46 (p. 275) above.

13. *Our name . . . many*: The words of the 'man with an unclean spirit' in Mark 5:9.

The Original Power of the Collective Body of the People of England, Examined and Asserted

This was advertised as published 'this day' in the *Post Man* for 25–27 December 1701. Defoe signed his initials at the end of the tract.

1. *jure divino*: 'By divine right'. Defoe would in 1706 publish a poem in twelve Books entitled *Jure Divino*, attacking the 'divine right' theory of sovereignty.

2. *vox populi . . . vox dei*: The voice of the people . . . the voice of God.

3. *contemptible impostor*: In September 1701, Louis XIV endorsed the claims of the Old Pretender to the English throne.

4. *cest*: Cessation (?).

5. *last Collective Body*: Defoe presumably means the 'Convention Parliament' (not strictly a Parliament) which offered the throne to William III.

6. *Original Right*: It will be noticed that the title is here reworded.

7. *Jure Populi Anglicani*: Or rather *Jura Populi Anglicani; or the Subject's Right to*

Petition set forth, occasioned by the Case of the Kentish Petitioners (1701), by Lord Somers.

8. *A Vindication of the Rights of the Commons of England*: The title of a tract by the high Tory Sir Humphrey Mackworth (1701).

9. *Vindication of the Rights of the Lords*: i.e. *A Vindication of the Rights and Prerogatives of the Right Honourable the House of Lords* (1701), sometimes attributed to Lord Somers.

10. *salus populi suprema lex*: The welfare of the people is the supreme law.

11. *that foolish maxim*: Mackworth writes (p. 5, see n. 8 above) that '. . . the several and respective powers vested in the King, Lords and Commons, are mutual checks and mutual boundaries to one another, but are not to be limited by any authority besides their own.'

12. *by petition*: On 8 May 1701, a petition, calling on the House of Commons to grant the King adequate supplies to preserve the kingdom and assist his European allies, was presented to the House by five Kentish gentlemen. They were immediately taken into the custody of the Sergeant-at-Arms and on 13 May were committed to the Gate-House prison, where they remained till 24 June.

13. *bantered*: Mocked.

14. *Legion Libels*: A reference to *Legion's Memorial*, see above, p. xv.

15. *the complaint which a late author brings*: Mackworth writes (p. 40, see n. 8 above) that if a subject, in a petition to the Lord Chancellor, should presume 'to desire the Lord Chancellor to turn his plausible speeches into just and righteous decrees, I presume his Lordship might legally commit him to the Fleet for such an indignity to the court.'

16. *the Fleet*: The Fleet prison and its liberties, off Farringdon Street. It was by this time mainly a debtors' prison. Defoe himself spent several brief spells in it.

17. *viva voce*: By word of mouth.

18. *must concern that part of the country*: Mackworth writes (p. 38, see n. 8 above): 'It can never . . . be admitted as legal, or so much as consistent with the interest and safety of England, for the Freeholders of any particular place or country, to direct the proceedings of Parliament . . .'

19. *determination*: i.e. termination.

20. *humanum est errare*: It is human to err.

21. *these things ye ought to have done*: See Matthew 23:23.

22. *Lords denying . . . the House*: On 13 June 1701, during the conflict between the two Houses of Parliament over the impeachment of William's ministers, the Commons withdrew from a 'free conference' with the Lords, preliminary to the trial of Lord Somers, because of offensive remarks by Lord Haversham.

23. *forty years hence . . . at Truro*: Mackworth says (p. 20, see n. 8 above) that the Lords might be tempted to frustrate a general impeachment by timetabling it for an absurdly near or an absurdly distant date, and that, though this is a very remote possibility, a wise constitution should guard against it.

24. *socage*: A form of tenure without knight-service.

25. *permissu superiorum*: By permission of his superiors.

26. *annihilated . . . the peers as a House*: In 1649, immediately after the execution of Charles I, the Rump Parliament abolished the House of Lords.

27. *a late author*: i.e. Mackworth, see n. 8 above.

28. *by their works ye shall know them*: 'Wherefore by their fruits ye shall know them', Matthew 7:20.

29. *Treaty of Partition*: See Introduction above, p. xi.

30. *dissolution of the last parliament*: William dissolved Parliament on 11 November 1701.

31. *indignity . . . French king*: In September 1701, upon the death of James II, Louis XIV declared the Pretender to be the rightful king of England.

32. *Kentish Gentlemen*: Defoe gives a vivid account of the episode in his *History of the Kentish Petition* (1701).

33. *Legion Paper*: i.e. *Legion's Memorial* (1701).

NON-CONFORMING DISSENTER

An Enquiry into the Occasional Conformity of Dissenters, in Cases of Preferment

This was first advertised in the *Post Man* for 8–11 January 1698. In the second edition (1701), the Preface to the Lord Mayor was replaced by one to John Howe, a leading Presbyterian divine, and this led to an exchange of pamphlets between Howe and Defoe.

1. *Lord Mayor*: Upon being elected Lord Mayor in September 1697, Sir Humphrey Edwin (1642–1707), a Presbyterian, took the sacrament according to the Anglican rite in St Paul's, as required under the Corporation and Test Acts, but then twice attended the Dissenting meeting at Pinners' Hall in full mayoral regalia, compelling his sword-bearer, named Daniel Man, to accompany him. A court of aldermen, convened to consider Man's complaint about this, ordered Sir Humphrey not to repeat the offence.

2. *Pinners' Hall*: The hall of the Pinmakers' Company, in Broad Street, which was let out as a Dissenting meeting-house.

3. *nolens volens*: Willy-nilly.

4. *Act for Liberty of Conscience*: The Toleration Act, passed in the first year of King William's reign.

5. *quire*: Choir.

6. *Jehu-like*: See 2 Kings 10:16.

7. *Josiah*: King of Judah and suppressor of idolatry.

8. *John Wickliff*: Or Wycliffe (*c.* 1324–84), religious reformer whose followers became known as 'Lollards'.

9. *William Tindall*: Or Tyndale (*c.* 1495–1536), Protestant reformer and translator of the Bible, burnt as a heretic in the Netherlands.

10. *murther their Gideon*: See Judges 6.

11. *shibboleth*: See n. 15 (p. 273).

12. *in exemplum regis*: Following the king's example.

13. *Ridley*: Nicholas Ridley (*c.* 1500–55), Bishop of Rochester, burnt for heresy in the reign of Queen Mary.

14. *Hooper*: John Hooper (*c.* 1495–1555), Bishop of Gloucester, burnt for heresy in the reign of Queen Mary.

15. *famous foreigner*: Defoe means Erasmus; but see n. 17 below.

16. *words of Balaam*: See Numbers 23:10.

17. *Sit anima mea . . . Anglicanis*: 'May my soul be with the English Puritans.' Defoe also attributes this saying to Erasmus in the *Review* for 19 and 2 April 1707, but he must be in some confusion, since it is chronologically impossible for Erasmus to have referred to the Puritans.

18. *which being so divided . . . stand*: See Mark 3:25.

19. *a strange thing in Israel*: See Hosea 8:12.

20. *bowing in the house of Rimmon*: Paltering with one's conscience, an allusion to Naaman obtaining Elisha's permission to worship Rimmon when with his master. See 2 Kings 5:18.

21. *Nadab and Abihu*: See Leviticus 10:1.

22. *bantering*: Playing, trifling.

The Shortest Way with the Dissenters

This was published in early December 1702.

1. *Sir Roger l'Estrange*: Royalist journalist and pamphleteer (1616–1704). He published a translation of Aesop's *Fables* in 1692.

2. *near fourteen years*: i.e. Since the Toleration Act of 1690.

3. *sordid impostor*: Oliver Cromwell.

4. *measured . . . again*: Matthew 7:2.

5. *Rye-Plot*: (Or Rye-House Plot) a plot to seize and possibly kill Charles II and the Duke of York on their way home from Newmarket in 1673. The Whig leaders Lord Russell and Algernon Sidney were executed for their supposed complicity in the conspiracy.

6. *Duke of Monmouth*: A large proportion of Monmouth's followers in the rebellion of 1685 were Dissenters.

7. *gentleness and love*: In April 1687, James II issued a Declaration of Indulgence granting liberty of conscience to Dissenters and Roman Catholics alike.

8. *the Observator*: A bi-weekly Whiggish journal conducted from April 1702 until his death in 1707 by John Tutchin. It always took the form of a dialogue between the 'Observator' and the 'Countryman'.

9. *a small treatise*: In 1707, Defoe would publish a tract ironically entitled *An Historical Account of the Bitter Sufferings . . . of the Episcopal Church in Scotland.*

10. *choose a King for themselves*: The succession to the throne, fixed in England by the Act of Settlement of 1701, was as yet undecided in Scotland.

11. *cleared the nation of them*: In 1685, Louis XIV revoked the Edict of Nantes, causing a large-scale exodus of Huguenots from France.

12. *suppressing the old money*: A grand recoinage, replacing bad and clipped money, took place in 1696. It caused a standstill of trade for several months but not the long-term disturbance that had been feared.

13. *Shaftesburys*: The 1st Earl of Shaftesbury (1621–83) was one of the most prominent opponents of Charles II's pro-Catholic and unconstitutional policies.

14. *Argylls*: Archibald Campbell, 9th Earl of Argyll (1629–85), was a leading opponent of James II and was executed for his part in Monmouth's rebellion.

15. *post est occasio calvo*: (Properly *calva*), opportunity is bald behind (i.e. needs to be taken by the forelock), a well-known Latin proverb.

16. *What will ye do . . . spoken for*: See Song of Solomon 8:8.

17. *enthusiasm*: Over-heated religious excitement, such as the Dissenters were often accused of.

18. *Act De Heret. Comburendo*: The medieval writ *de heretico comburendo* punishing heresy by burning was repealed in 1677.

19. *dilenda est Carthago*: (Properly *delenda*) 'Carthage must be destroyed', the words with which Cato the Elder ended every speech in the Roman Senate, after visiting Carthage in 157 BC and observing her prosperity.

20. *three and thirty thousand*: According to Exodus 32:28, the number was three thousand, and according to Numbers 25:9 it was twenty-four thousand. The imaginary author is evidently exaggerating.

21. *Counter*: i.e. the Compter, or debtors' prison. There was a Compter in the City of London and another in Southwark.

22. *5 s. a month*: The Elizabethan Act for the Uniformity of Common Prayer and Service in the Church (1 Eliz. I c. 2) required all citizens to attend a Church of England place of worship, on penalty of a fine of twelve pence for each violation. Under the Toleration Act of 1689, Dissenters were exempted from this statute on condition of taking the oaths of Allegiance and Supremacy and the Declaration against transubstantiation.

23. *One of their leading pastors*: John Howe (1630–1705); the passage quoted is from his *Some Consideration of a Preface to an Enquiry* (1701).

24. *the additional appendices*: Under the Toleration Act, Dissenters were not obliged

to subscribe to Articles 34, 35, 36, on tradition, the homilies and bishops respectively.

25. *such a Convocation*: When, at the end of 1700, King William invited members of the Tory and high-church party into his government, part of the bargain was that Convocation, a body which had been dormant for many years, should be convened.

A Brief Explanation of a Late Pamphlet

This was discussed in the *Observator* for 6–9 January 1703.

1. *several poor people*: Defoe presumably means his printers.
2. *sermon preached at Oxford*: The famous sermon preached by Dr Henry Sacheverell on 31 May 1702.
3. *New Association*: The title of a pamphlet attack on the Dissenters by the High Church polemicist Charles Leslie, published in 1702.
4. *Is thy servant . . . things*: See 2 Kings 8:13.
5. *the Observator's charging*: The accusation appears in *Observator*, 30 December 1702 – 2 January 1703.
6. *Black List*: In December 1701 the Whigs published a 'Black List' attacking 167 Tory members of the last Parliament.
7. *Kentish Feast*: i.e. Defoe is being accused of organizing the dinner for the 'Kentish Gentlemen' in Mercers' Hall. See Introduction above, p. xvi.
8. *Legion Paper*: i.e. *Legion's Memorial*. Despite the fact that, for very understandable reasons, Defoe here denies it, there is much evidence to suggest that he was the author.

A Dialogue between a Dissenter and the Observator

This was probably published in January 1703.

1. *the Observator*: See n. 8 (p. 284).
2. *reputed author*: In an earlier altercation Tutchin, in the *Observator* for 6–9 January 1703, had denied that he had accused Defoe of being the author of *Legion's Memorial* and other works. He had, he said, merely called him the 'reputed author'.
3. *Bellamy*: Defoe was betrayed to the authorities, at the time of *The Shortest Way*, by Edward Bellamy, who had delivered his manuscript to the printer.
4. *sharp chin*: When Defoe was in hiding during the hue and cry over *The Shortest Way*, the *London Gazette* for 10 January 1703 printed a proclamation offering a reward for his discovery, describing him as: '. . . a middle-sized spare man, about forty years old, of a brown complexion, and dark-brown coloured hair, but wears a wig; a hooked nose, a sharp chin, grey eyes, and a large mole near his mouth'.
5. *Parson Jacob's text*: The *Observator* for 6–9 January 1703 carried a satirical

account of a sermon preached at Turners' Hall on 10 September 1702 by one Joseph Jacob, 'a strange sort of enthusiast', whose followers were 'obliged to wear whiskers'.

6. *Act of Parliament*: In November 1702, the Tories brought in a Bill to prohibit Occasional Conformity, the first of several, which was passed in the Commons but thrown out by the Lords.

7. *Mr. How*: See n. 9 (p. 280).

8. *the Pharisees*: See Mark 11:30.

9. *as I said before in print*: See *Observator* for 16–20 January 1703.

10. *the New Test of Church of England Loyalty*: Defoe's *A New Test of the Church of England's Loyalty* was published in June 1702.

11. *Reformation of Manners*: A poem by Defoe, published in 1702.

12. *he denies it*: Presumably a reference to Defoe's retort at the end of *A Brief Explanation*; see p. 148 above.

13. *railing at King William's friends*: The *Observator*, round about January 1703, had several articles on William's grants to his favourites.

14. *the Foreigners*: See Introduction above, p. xii.

15. *quacking with*: Offering quack remedies to.

16. *mountebanking with*: Pretending to knowledge about.

17. *Owens . . . Bates's*: John Owen (1616–83), Thomas Manton (1620–77), Stephen Charnock (1628–80), Richard Baxter (1615–91), and William Bates (1625–99), eminent Puritan divines.

18. *Salters' Hall*: A weekly lecture at Salters' Hall was founded in 1694, when Daniel Williams was voted out of the Pinners' Hall lecture.

19. *the Lord's doing . . . eyes*: See Matthew 21:42, Mark 12:11.

20. *You faithless and perverse generation*: See Matthew 17:17, Luke 9:41.

21. *semper eadem*: Always the same.

22. *hypish*: Short for hypochondriacal.

23. *Mr. Mead's wheel within a wheel*: In 1689, the nonconformist Matthew Mead had published an exposition of Ezekiel 10:13 entitled *The Vision of the Wheels*.

24. *true Billingsgate*: See n. 10 (p. 280).

25. *a quotation*: We have been unable to trace the source of this quotation.

26. *Whosoever . . . to powder*: See Matthew 21:44; Luke 20:18.

27. *house of Dagon . . . their heads*: See Judges 16:25–30.

28. *Prince of Wales*: i.e. The Pretender.

A Hymn to the Pillory

This was published on 29 July 1703, the first of the three days in which Defoe stood in the pillory. Shortly afterwards a 'second edition, corrected' appeared, which included about twenty new lines, and it is this edition that we have reproduced.

1. *hieroglyphic*: Symbolic, holding a secret meaning.

2. *insignificants*: Trivial significations.

3. *amuse*: Deceive.

4. *Sometimes . . . vain*: This rather obscure couplet seems to be saying that sometimes putting villains in the pillory does nothing to uphold the laws against *scandalatum magnum* (i.e. libelling the great).

5. *Bastwick . . . Pye*: John Bastwick (1593–1654) and William Prynne (1600–69) were famous Puritan pamphleteers, punished in 1637 by having their ears cut off and being made to stand in the pillory. The other three are much less well known.

6. *Oates and Fuller*: Titus Oates (1649–1705), inspirer of the 'Popish Plot' agitation in the late 1670s, was convicted of perjury in 1685, condemned to life imprisonment, and ordered to stand in the pillory five times a year. William Fuller (1670–1733) was twice sentenced to the pillory for perjury.

7. *Selden*: John Selden (1584–1654), famous historian and lawyer, imprisoned in 1629 for his opposition to Charles I's policies.

8. *S[achevre]ll*: See Introduction above, p. xix.

9. *the shortest way*: The work which led to Defoe appearing in the pillory was, of course, *The Shortest Way with the Dissenters*.

10. *Vice-Chancellor . . . authority*: Roger Mander (1649–1704), Vice-Chancellor of Oxford University, gave his imprimatur to the publication of Sacheverell's sermon, even though in fact the requirement for works to be licensed before publication had ceased in 1696.

11. *Juno's Academy, Billingsgate*: See n. 10 (p. 280).

12. *their composition stole*: Defoe adopted the persona of a High-churchman like Sacheverell in his *Shortest Way*.

13. *A monster makes the world afraid*: A reference to the consternation with which *The Shortest Way* was received.

14. *Pointi . . . blessed*: The French naval commander Baron de Pointis (1645–1707) plundered Cartagena in 1697, and managed to get back to Brest before an English fleet could prevent him.

15. *Turkey . . . Camaret*: See nn. 85, 86 (p. 277).

16. *missed the squadron from Thoulon*: In 1695, the English navy under the command of Admiral Edward Russell failed in an attempt to prevent the French grand fleet returning to Toulon.

17. *Some heroes . . . little done*: In August 1702, English troops under the command of the Duke of Ormonde who had been sent to take Cadiz attacked instead the undefended villages of Rota and El Puerto de Santa Maria, where they raped women, including nuns, and looted buildings.

18. *The Vigo men . . . home*: On the way back from the disastrous Cadiz expedition, the English destroyed a fleet of French-protected Spanish treasure galleons at Vigo Bay in northern Spain. Much of the treasure sank, or was stolen.

19. *Lieutenant General*: Lieutenant-General Sir Henry Bellasis, one of Ormonde's

officers, was charged with taking part in the looting at El Puerto de Santa Maria, and subsequently dishonourably discharged from the army.

20. *tallies*: One of the ways in which governments raised money was by issuing 'tallies', the two most important being Tallies of Pro and Tallies of Sol. The system was very liable to corruption. (Originally, a tally was a notched rod, split in half, with one half being given to the creditor, the other to the debtor, as a record of a financial transaction.)

21. *bear-skins*: A bearskin jobber on the stock exchange was one who speculated in expectation of a fall.

22. *debentures*: Government bonds.

23. *paper . . . nine*: Exchequer bills, though used as currency, were traded at less than their nominal value.

24. *Irish transport debts*: Government loans raised to finance William's Irish expeditions, 1689–91.

25. *Bills false endorsed*: See n. 100 (pp. 277–8).

26. *sons of God . . . wives of men*: See Genesis 6:4.

27. *A[sgi]ll*: See n. 50 (p. 275).

28. *Charon*: In Greek mythology, Charon ferried the souls of the dead to the underworld.

29. *not understood*: See Defoe's *Brief Explanation* of *The Shortest Way*, above, p. 146–8.

30. *Nimshites*: i.e. The high-flying clergy, so named by Defoe in reference to Nimshi, the father of Jehu who 'driveth furiously'. See 2 Kings 9:20.

31. *Passive obedience*: See n. 63 (p. 276).

32. *man of mighty fame*: Sir Simon Harcourt, the Solicitor General, who led for the prosecution at Defoe's trial.

33. *Jesus Christ himself denies*: In another poem, *Reformation of Manners* (1702), Defoe referred to 'Socinian Harcourt'.

34. *L[ove]ll*: Sir Salathiel Lovell (1619–1713), Recorder of London, one of the judges who presided at Defoe's trial.

35. *Whitney's horses*: In a much ridiculed speech in 1693, sentencing to death the famous highwayman Captain James Whitney, Lovell was supposed to have warned him that 'the blood of the horses he had slain . . . would rise up in judgement against him'.

36. *martyrs*: i.e. Those Anglican clergy and bishops, known as 'non-jurors', who refused to take the oath of allegiance to William and Mary.

37. *Sherlock's . . . wife*: William Sherlock, Dean of St Paul's, was frequently accused of having abandoned his non-juring principles at the instigation of his wife.

38. *swear to three Kings*: Take the oaths to Charles II, James II, and William III.

39. *mean beginnings*: A reference to Sir Charles Duncombe; see n. 88 (p. 277).

40. *Mene Tekel's*: See Daniel 5:25.

41. *knights o'th' post*: Professional perjurers.

42. *paper in his hat*: The judgement sentencing Defoe to the pillory stipulated that he should stand there 'with a paper on his head on which his offences are written'.

43. *would he ha' said more*: While in Newgate, Defoe was questioned by the Earl of Nottingham, Secretary of State, and the Duke of Buckinghamshire and Normanby, Lord Privy Seal.

SOCIAL REFORMER

An Essay upon Projects

This was advertised as published 'this day' in the *Flying-Post* for 19–21 January 1697.

1. *negoce*: Mercantile trade.

2. *this long . . . war*: The War of the League of Augsburg began in 1688, though England did not join the League till 1689. The war lasted until 1697.

3. *fougades*: Small underground explosives.

4. *bill . . . for the relief of merchant-insurers*: On 13 December 1693, a Bill was presented to the Commons to give 'Merchants Insurers', i.e. merchants ruined by insuring vessels during the present war, relief against their creditors. In February 1694, Defoe, who had recently been bankrupted, petitioned to have his name included in it, and this was done, but the Bill was rejected in the Lords.

5. *history of a patent-monger*: In 1691, a Cornishman named Joseph Williams patented a diving bell and Defoe invested £200 in the company formed to promote it, also being appointed secretary-treasurer. The venture failed, and Defoe lost not only his £200 but some further money he had advanced on Williams's behalf, Williams having repaid it in worthless notes.

6. *cully*: Dupe.

7. *patents*: A statute of the reign of James I provided that the Crown might grant letters patent for fourteen years or under reserving 'the sole working or making of any manner of new manufactures within this realm to the true and first inventor'.

8. *mysteries*: Crafts.

9. *deceptio visus*: Optical illusion.

10. *Sir William Phips's voyage*: In 1687, Sir William Phipps salvaged over £200,000 in gold and silver from a Spanish vessel sunk off the Bahamas.

11. *Bedlam*: Properly Bethlehem Hospital, a madhouse in Moorfields. The spectacle of its inmates was a popular entertainment.

12. *Chamber of London*: An apartment in Guildhall where the City money was kept.

13. *lotteries*: In October 1695, Defoe himself became a manager-trustee of one of Thomas Neale's lotteries. It is not quite clear whether in his censorious remark on p. 194 about lotteries 'hackney'd about in Private Hands' he has Neale in mind.

14. *the million-lottery*: This was a Government loan, with a lottery element thrown in. Thomas Neale was one of the Commissioners in charge of it, and Dalby Thomas played a prominent part in organizing it.

15. *tallies*: See n. 20 (p. 288).

16. *be in Commission of the Peace*: i.e. Have the powers of a magistrate.

17. *This chapter*: Defoe quoted long extracts from this essay in the *Review* for 12 and 14 February 1706, when a Bill for Preventing Frauds Committed by Bankrupts was going through Parliament, and he claimed to have had a share in the designing of the Bill.

18. *a statute*: Legal instrument by which a person might be declared a bankrupt.

19. *Friars*: A Carmelite monastery founded on the south side of Fleet Street gave its name to a district known as Whitefriars and Alsatia, for long a sanctuary for criminals and debtors. It was abolished by Act of Parliament in April 1697.

20. *Mint*: A place of privilege in Southwark, near the King's Prison, where people sheltered from justice on the pretext that it was an ancient royal palace. It was suppressed in 1723.

21. *sui juris*: Legally his own master.

22. *de die in diem*: From day to day.

23. *fieri facias*: A writ of execution to a sheriff to levy a sum from a debtor by seizure of his goods.

24. *parcels*: Lots.

25. *Savoy*: Originally a palace built by the Earl of Savoy in 1245, then a royal hospital, it had by Defoe's time become a warren of lodgings with right of sanctuary for debtors.

26. *trained-bands*: 'Trained-bands' (or 'train-bands') was, from the sixteenth century, the name given to the militia. By an Act of 1662, the system was discontinued in the shires, but the City train-bands survived until 1794.

27. *Lord Roscommon*: Wentworth Dillon, 4th Earl of Roscommon (1637–85). The lines quoted come from 'An Essay on Translated Verse'.

28. *the two theatres*: The two theatres granted a 'patent' by Charles II were Drury Lane and Dorset Garden.

29. *Schomberg, Ginkel, Solms, Ruvigny*: For Schom[n]berg, see nn. 32 and 84 (pp. 274 and 277). Godart Ginkell, later Earl of Athlone, was a Dutch general who fought under William in Ireland. Heinrich Maastricht, Count of Solms-Braunfels, was a Dutch general and relation of William III. Henri de Massue, second Marquis de Ruvigny, later Viscount Galway, was a Huguenot emigré who fought with William and was appointed Lord Justice of Ireland in 1697.

30. *Dunbar fight*: Cromwell's victory over the Scots at Dunbar, on 3 September 1650.

31. *piqued beards*: Pointed beards of the kind fashionable in the seventeenth century.

32. *artists*: Technicians.

33. *Advice to the Ladies*: Mary Astell's *A Serious Proposal to the Ladies, for the Advancement of their True and Greatest Interest* (1694).

34. *jettings*: Defoe perhaps means 'juttings' or protrusions.

35. *bearing-work*: Corbels or buttresses.

36. *felony without clergy*: Presumably short for 'felony without benefit of clergy'. Benefit of clergy was a privilege enjoyed by the clergy and the literate generally not to be tried for certain offences by a regular court; but here no more is meant than 'a heinous offence'.

Giving Alms no Charity (1704)

This was advertised in the *Review* for 18 November 1704.

1. *Pauper ubique jacet*: Paupers are to be found everywhere.

2. *the Dutch being not yet revolted*: The Netherlands declared their freedom from Spanish rule in 1581.

3. *staple*: Principal centre from which a commodity is distributed.

4. *stuffs*: Woollen fabric.

5. *bays*: i.e. Baize.

6. *says*: A distinct two-and-two twill with a single weft.

7. *serges*: A very durable twilled cloth of worsted.

8. *Duke D'Alva*: Fernando, Duke of Alva (1508–83), appointed Governor of the Netherlands in 1567.

9. *10th. penny*: See n. 27 (p. 272).

10. *true born English families*: cf. *The True-Born Englishman*, above, lines 412–14.

11. *late persecution*: There was a flood of French Protestant refugees to England at the time of the revocation of the Edict of Nantes in October 1685.

12. *perpets*: i.e. Perpetuanas, a light, smooth, inexpensive fabric.

13. *corporations*: The setting up of a Corporation of the Poor in Bristol in 1696 was quickly imitated in a number of other towns. It essentially was a method of transferring responsibility for poor-relief from the parish to the city as a whole, under the surveillance of a body of 'Guardians of the Poor', and was the origin of the eighteenth-century workhouse system.

14. *parish charges, assessments*: Assessments for the poor-rate were a constant source of local controversy. Defoe discusses the matter in his 'Andrew Moreton' pamphlet *Parochial Tyranny* (1727).

15. *laws against sturdy beggars*: The laws against vagabonds and 'sturdy beggars' were made harsher under Queen Elizabeth, though the same period saw the setting-up of a system of poor-relief, based on a parish rate.

16. *the learned gentleman ... been printed*: Sir Humphrey Mackworth's Bill was introduced in the Commons on 2 November 1704 and was passed there, but was thrown out by the Lords. He published it as *A Bill for the Better Relief, Imployment, and Settlement of the Poor* (1704).

17. *Overseers*: Officers appointed annually to oversee poor relief.

18. *raise stocks*: The Webbs, in their *English Local Government*, Part 1 (1927), p. 9, mention entries in parish records concerning the 'Church Stock' or 'Parish Stock' – in some cases a flock of sheep, in others a herd of cattle – maintained to yield an annual revenue for the common purposes of the parish.

19. *on the tenters*: On the stretch. (A tenter was a wooden framework on which cloth was stretched to dry.)

20. *buy a parochial settlement*: In the *Review* for 22 March 1707, Defoe repeats this passage, but with the amendment 'have' for 'buy', so the word 'buy' may have been an error.

21. *arcanas*: (Trade) secrets.

22. *shaloons*: Says woven from line yarns, often glazed.

23. *druggets*: A loosely woven plain cloth.

24. *the frame*: The iron knitting-machine or stocking-frame was a remarkable piece of pre-industrial revolution technology, invented in 1589 by William Lee.

25. *voiture*: Carriage.

26. *present trade to Muscovy*: Defoe makes the same criticism of the trade with Russia in the *Review* for 25 March 1707.

27. *silk throwsters*: Operatives who twisted silk fibres into raw silk or raw silk into thread.

28. *Cur moriatur homo*: Why does a man languish and die?

29. *tile-making*: Defoe in 1694 set up what was for several years a prosperous business in brick- and tile-making on the Thameside near Tilbury.

30. *list*: Enlist.

POLITICAL ADVISER

Memorandum to Robert Harley

This memorandum can be dated to between July and August 1704 on internal grounds. It was first published by G. F. Warner in *English Historical Review*, 22 (1907), and is included in *The Letters of Daniel Defoe*, ed. G. H. Healey (Oxford, 1955), pp. 29–50.

1. *supreme ministry*: i.e. Prime Minister.

2. *refined*: Subtle.

3. *Richlieus*: Cardinal Richelieu (1585–1642) was chief minister during the reign of Louis XIII of France and a leading architect of absolute monarchy in that country. Defoe was reading a biography of Richelieu at this time and repeatedly refers to it in the *Review*. He perhaps to some degree pictured himself in the role of a Richelieu, or at all events emulated Richelieu's *Realpolitik*.

4. *Mazarines*: Cardinal Jules Mazarin (1602–61) was chief minister during the minority of Louis XIV.

5. *Colberts*: Jean Baptiste Colbert (1619–83), controller-general of finance, was one of Louis XIV's greatest ministers. He helped found the Académie des Inscriptions et Belles-Lettres and the Académie des Sciences and did much to build up the French navy.

6. *Spencers. . . Gavestones*: Hugh Despenser, Earl of Winchester, and Piers Gaveston, Earl of Cornwall, were favourites of Edward II.

7. *Leicester*: Robert Dudley, Earl of Leicester, was a favourite of Queen Elizabeth.

8. *Somerset*: The Duke of Somerset became Protector after the death of Henry VIII.

9. *Buckingham*: The Duke of Buckingham was a favourite of James I.

10. *Lord Cromwell*: Thomas Cromwell, Earl of Essex, held many high offices under Henry VIII.

11. *Sir Francis Walsingham*: Secretary of State under Queen Elizabeth.

12. *of course*: In the natural course of things.

13. *Overkirk*: Dutch general who gave important support to Marlborough during the War of the Spanish Succession.

14. *The King of Sweden*: Gustavus Adolphus II (1594–1632), King of Sweden: champion of Protestantism during the Thirty Years War.

15. *new post*: Harley became Secretary of State on 18 May 1704.

16. *Gehezai*: The untrustworthy servant of Elisha, see 2 Kings 5:20–27.

17. *old Prince of Orange's*: Maurice, Prince of Orange (*d.* 1625), Stadholder of the Dutch Republic.

18. *Momorency*: Henry II, Duke of Montmorency (1595–1632), revolted against Richelieu but was defeated and executed.

19. *Intelligence*: Secret-service information.

20. *Milton*: The poet Milton acted as Latin Secretary to Cromwell's Council of State and was continued in the post after the Restoration.

21. *insurrection in Hungary*: Hungarian rebels were ravaging the territory of England's ally Austria.

22. *war in Poland*: Sweden had invaded the Polish territories of Augustus II, King of Poland and Saxony, thus incapacitating him from helping in the conflict with France.

23. *misunderstandings between the two kingdoms*: The Scottish Act of Security, passed in 1703, reserved Scotland's right, should Anne die without a surviving heir, to choose a different monarch from England. The resulting tension nearly led to war and was a decisive factor in bringing about the Union of 1707.

24. *Letters Writ by a Turkish Spy*: Famous fictitious and satirical memoirs of a Turkish spy at Paris, published in seven volumes from 1687 onwards and attributed to the Genoese Giovanni Paolo Marana. A *Continuation* of these Letters, published in 1718, is probably by Defoe himself.

25. *Lord N[ottingha]m's*: i.e. Daniel Finch, 2nd Earl of Nottingham (1647–1730), who was Secretary of State 1702–1704. Defoe visited his office in 1703, when under interrogation over his *The Shortest Way with the Dissenters*.

26. *Sir George Rook*: Admiral of the Fleet Sir George Rooke (1650–1709).

27. *first Occasional Bill*: A Bill against occasional conformity (the first of several) was introduced in Parliament in November 1702 but defeated in the Lords.

28. *cum multis aliis*: With many others.

29. *Scylla and . . . Charybdis*: A rock and a whirlpool on opposing sides of the Straits of Messina, hence a proverbial expression for alternative dangers.

Appendix

A LIST OF DEFOE'S PUBLISHED WRITINGS 1688–1704

A Letter to a Dissenter from his Friend at the Hague [1688]. Probably by Defoe

A New Discovery of an Old Intreague (1691)

'To the Athenian Society' [1692]

An Essay upon Projects (1697)

The Character of the Late Dr. Samuel Annesley (1697)

Some Reflections on a Pamphlet . . . Entitled, An Argument Shewing, that a Standing Army is Inconsistent with a Free Government (1697)

An Enquiry into the Occasional Conformity of Dissenters, in Cases of Preferment (1697 [for 1698])

An Argument, Shewing, that a Standing Army, with Consent of Parliament, is not Inconsistent with a Free Government, etc. (1698)

The Poor Man's Plea (1698)

A Brief Reply to the History of Standing Armies in England (1698). Probably by Defoe

Lex Talionis (1698). Probably by Defoe

'An Encomium upon a Parliament' [1699]. Probably by Defoe

The Pacificator (1700)

The Two Great Questions Consider'd (1700)

The Two Great Questions Further Considered (1700)

The Six Distinguishing Characters of a Parliament-Man (1700 [for 1701])

The True-Born Englishman (1700 [for 1701?])

The Danger of the Protestant Religion Consider'd (1701)

The Free-Holders Plea Against Stock-Jobbing Elections of Parliament Men (1701)

A Letter to Mr Howe (1701)

APPENDIX

The Livery Man's Reasons (1701). Probably by Defoe
The Villainy of Stock-Jobbers Detected (1701)
The Succession to the Crown of England Considered (1701)
Legion's Memorial [1701]
'Ye True-Born Englishmen Proceed' [1701]. Probably by Defoe
The History of the Kentish Petition (1701)
The Present State of Jacobitism Considered (1701)
Reasons Against a War with France (1701)
Legion's New Paper (1702 [for 1701]). Probably by Defoe
The Original Power of the Collective Body of the People of England (1702
  [for 1701])
The Mock Mourners (1702)
A New Test of the Church of England's Loyalty (1702)
Reformation of Manners (1702)
*An Enquiry into Occasional Conformity, Shewing that the Dissenters are No
  Way Concern'd in it* (1702)
The Opinion of a Known Dissenter (1703 [for 1702]). Probably by Defoe
The Spanish Descent (1702)
The Shortest Way with the Dissenters (1702)
*A Brief Explanation of a Late Pamphlet, Entitled The Shortest Way with the
  Dissenters* [1703]
*A Dialogue Between a Dissenter and the Observator, Concerning The Shortest
  Way with the Dissenters* (1703). Probably by Defoe
More Reformation (1703)
A True Collection of the Writings of the Author of the True-Born Englishman
  (1703)
The Shortest Way to Peace and Union (1703)
A Hymn to the Pillory (1703)
The Sincerity of the Dissenters Vindicated (1703). Probably by Defoe
A Hymn to the Funeral Sermon (1703). Probably by Defoe
An Enquiry into the Case of Mr. Asgil's Translation (1704)
A Challenge of Peace (1703)
Peace Without Union (1703)
Some Remarks on the First Chapter in Dr. Davenant's Essays (1704 [for
  1703])
The Dissenters Answer to the High-Church Challenge (1704)
An Essay on the Regulation of the Press (1704). Probably by Defoe

A Serious Inquiry into this Grand Question (1704)

To the Honourable the C[ommon]s of England . . . Relating to the Bill for Restraining the Press [1704]

The Parallel [1704?]

The Lay-Man's Sermon upon the Late Storm (1704). Probably by Defoe

Royal Religion (1704)

More Short-Ways with the Dissenters (1704)

'*The Address*' (1704). Probably by Defoe

A New Test of the Church of England's Honesty (1704)

The Storm (1704)

An Elegy on the Author of the True-Born Englishman. With an Essay on the Late Storm (1704)

A Hymn to Victory (1704)

Giving Alms No Charity (1704)

Queries Upon the Bill Against Occasional Conformity (1704)

Visit Penguin on the Internet
and browse at your leisure

- ◆ preview sample extracts of our forthcoming books
- ◆ read about your favourite authors
- ◆ investigate over 10,000 titles
- ◆ enter one of our literary quizzes
- ◆ win some fantastic prizes in our competitions
- ◆ e-mail us with your comments and book reviews
- ◆ instantly order any Penguin book

and masses more!

'To be recommended without reservation ... a rich and rewarding on-line experience' – Internet Magazine

www.penguin.co.uk

READ MORE IN PENGUIN

In every corner of the world, on every subject under the sun, Penguin represents quality and variety – the very best in publishing today.

For complete information about books available from Penguin – including Puffins, Penguin Classics and Arkana – and how to order them, write to us at the appropriate address below. Please note that for copyright reasons the selection of books varies from country to country.

In the United Kingdom: Please write to *Dept. EP, Penguin Books Ltd, Bath Road, Harmondsworth, West Drayton, Middlesex UB7 0DA*

In the United States: Please write to *Consumer Sales, Penguin USA, P.O. Box 999, Dept. 17109, Bergenfield, New Jersey 07621-0120*. VISA and MasterCard holders call 1-800-253-6476 to order Penguin titles

In Canada: Please write to *Penguin Books Canada Ltd, 10 Alcorn Avenue, Suite 300, Toronto, Ontario M4V 3B2*

In Australia: Please write to *Penguin Books Australia Ltd, P.O. Box 257, Ringwood, Victoria 3134*

In New Zealand: Please write to *Penguin Books (NZ) Ltd, Private Bag 102902, North Shore Mail Centre, Auckland 10*

In India: Please write to *Penguin Books India Pvt Ltd, 706 Eros Apartments, 56 Nehru Place, New Delhi 110 019*

In the Netherlands: Please write to *Penguin Books Netherlands bv, Postbus 3507, NL-1001 AH Amsterdam*

In Germany: Please write to *Penguin Books Deutschland GmbH, Metzlerstrasse 26, 60594 Frankfurt am Main*

In Spain: Please write to *Penguin Books S. A., Bravo Murillo 19, 1° B, 28015 Madrid*

In Italy: Please write to *Penguin Italia s.r.l., Via Felice Casati 20, I–20124 Milano*

In France: Please write to *Penguin France S. A., 17 rue Lejeune, F–31000 Toulouse*

In Japan: Please write to *Penguin Books Japan, Ishikiribashi Building, 2–5–4, Suido, Bunkyo-ku, Tokyo 112*

In South Africa: Please write to *Longman Penguin Southern Africa (Pty) Ltd, Private Bag X08, Bertsham 2013*

READ MORE IN PENGUIN

A CHOICE OF CLASSICS

Armadale Wilkie Collins

Victorian critics were horrified by Lydia Gwilt, the bigamist, husband-poisoner and laudanum addict whose intrigues spur the plot of this most sensational of melodramas.

Aurora Leigh and Other Poems Elizabeth Barrett Browning

Aurora Leigh (1856), Elizabeth Barrett Browning's epic novel in blank verse, tells the story of the making of a woman poet, exploring 'the woman question', art and its relation to politics and social oppression.

Personal Narrative of a Journey to the Equinoctial Regions of the New Continent Alexander von Humboldt

Alexander von Humboldt became a wholly new kind of nineteenth-century hero – the scientist–explorer – and in *Personal Narrative* he invented a new literary genre: the travelogue.

The Pancatantra Visnu Sarma

The Pancatantra is one of the earliest books of fables and its influence can be seen in the *Arabian Nights*, the *Decameron*, the *Canterbury Tales* and most notably in the *Fables* of La Fontaine.

A Laodicean Thomas Hardy

The Laodicean of Hardy's title is Paula Power, a thoroughly modern young woman who, despite her wealth and independence, cannot make up her mind.

Brand Henrik Ibsen

The unsparing vision of a priest driven by faith to risk and witness the deaths of his wife and child gives *Brand* its icy ferocity. It was Ibsen's first masterpiece, a poetic drama composed in 1865 and published to tremendous critical and popular acclaim.

READ MORE IN PENGUIN

A CHOICE OF CLASSICS

Sylvia's Lovers Elizabeth Gaskell

In an atmosphere of unease the rivalries of two men, the sober tradesman Philip Hepburn, who has been devoted to his cousin Sylvia since her childhood, and the gallant, charming whaleship harpooner Charley Kinraid, are played out.

The Republic Plato

The best-known of Plato's dialogues, *The Republic* is also one of the supreme masterpieces of Western philosophy, whose influence cannot be overestimated.

Ethics Benedict de Spinoza

'Spinoza (1632–77),' wrote Bertrand Russell, 'is the noblest and most lovable of the great philosophers. Intellectually, some others have surpassed him, but ethically he is supreme.'

Virgil in English

From Chaucer to Auden, Virgil is a defining presence in English poetry. Penguin Classics' new series, Poets in Translation, offers the best translations in English, through the centuries, of the major Classical and European poets.

What is Art? Leo Tolstoy

Tolstoy wrote prolifically in a series of essays and polemics on issues of morality, social justice and religion. These culminated in *What is Art?*, published in 1898, in which he rejects the idea that art reveals and reinvents through beauty.

An Autobiography Anthony Trollope

A fascinating insight into a writer's life, in which Trollope also recorded his unhappy youth and his progress to prosperity and social recognition.

PENGUIN AUDIOBOOKS

A Quality of Writing That Speaks for Itself

Penguin Books has always led the field in quality publishing. Now you can listen at leisure to your favourite books, read to you by familiar voices from radio, stage and screen. Penguin Audiobooks are produced to an excellent standard, and abridgements are always faithful to the original texts. From thrillers to classic literature, biography to humour, with a wealth of titles in between, Penguin Audiobooks offer you quality, entertainment and the chance to rediscover the pleasure of listening.

You can order Penguin Audiobooks through Penguin Direct by telephoning (0181) 899 4036. The lines are open 24 hours every day. Ask for Penguin Direct, quoting your credit card details.

A selection of Penguin Audiobooks, published or forthcoming:

Little Women by Louisa May Alcott, read by Kate Harper

Emma by Jane Austen, read by Fiona Shaw

Pride and Prejudice by Jane Austen, read by Geraldine McEwan

Beowulf translated by Michael Alexander, read by David Rintoul

Agnes Grey by Anne Brontë, read by Juliet Stevenson

Jane Eyre by Charlotte Brontë, read by Juliet Stevenson

The Professor by Charlotte Brontë, read by Juliet Stevenson

Wuthering Heights by Emily Brontë, read by Juliet Stevenson

The Woman in White by Wilkie Collins, read by Nigel Anthony and Susan Jameson

Nostromo by Joseph Conrad, read by Michael Pennington

Tales from the Thousand and One Nights, read by Souad Faress and Raad Rawi

Robinson Crusoe by Daniel Defoe, read by Tom Baker

David Copperfield by Charles Dickens, read by Nathaniel Parker

The Pickwick Papers by Charles Dickens, read by Dinsdale Landen

Bleak House by Charles Dickens, read by Beatie Edney and Ronald Pickup

PENGUIN AUDIOBOOKS

The Hound of the Baskervilles by Sir Arthur Conan Doyle, read by Freddie Jones

Middlemarch by George Eliot, read by Harriet Walter

Tom Jones by Henry Fielding, read by Robert Lindsay

The Great Gatsby by F. Scott Fitzgerald, read by Marcus D'Amico

Madame Bovary by Gustave Flaubert, read by Claire Bloom

Mary Barton by Elizabeth Gaskell, read by Clare Higgins

Jude the Obscure by Thomas Hardy, read by Samuel West

Far from the Madding Crowd by Thomas Hardy, read by Julie Christie

The Scarlet Letter by Nathaniel Hawthorne, read by Bob Sessions

Les Misérables by Victor Hugo, read by Nigel Anthony

A Passage to India by E. M. Forster, read by Tim Pigott-Smith

The Iliad by Homer, read by Derek Jacobi

The Dead and Other Stories by James Joyce, read by Gerard McSorley

On the Road by Jack Kerouac, read by David Carradine

Sons and Lovers by D. H. Lawrence, read by Paul Copley

The Prince by Niccolò Machiavelli, read by Fritz Weaver

Animal Farm by George Orwell, read by Timothy West

Rob Roy by Sir Walter Scott, read by Robbie Coltrane

Frankenstein by Mary Shelley, read by Richard Pasco

Of Mice and Men by John Steinbeck, read by Gary Sinise

Kidnapped by Robert Louis Stevenson, read by Robbie Coltrane

Dracula by Bram Stoker, read by Richard E. Grant

Gulliver's Travels by Jonathan Swift, read by Hugh Laurie

Vanity Fair by William Makepeace Thackeray, read by Robert Hardy

Lark Rise to Candleford by Flora Thompson, read by Judi Dench

The Invisible Man by H. G. Wells, read by Paul Shelley

Ethan Frome by Edith Wharton, read by Nathan Osgood

The Picture of Dorian Gray by Oscar Wilde, read by John Moffatt

Orlando by Virginia Woolf, read by Tilda Swinton

BY THE SAME AUTHOR

Moll Flanders *Edited with an introduction by David Blewett*

Moll Flanders, Defoe's irresistible and notorious heroine, attacks life with all the confident genius of her creator. Born in Newgate prison, Moll's drive to find a secure place in society propels her through incest, adultery, bigamy, prostitution and a resourceful career as a thief. On one level a Puritan's tale of sin and repentance, the rich subtext of *Moll Flanders* conveys all the paradoxes of the struggle for property and power in Defoe's newly individualistic society.

A Journal of the Plague Year
with an introduction by Anthony Burgess

A Journal of the Plague Year (1722), like so much of his work, is a fictional reconstruction based on true accounts. It is the prototype of every account of great cities in times of epidemic, siege, or occupation.

Roxana *Edited by David Blewett*

Roxana charts the moral deterioration and ultimate defeat of the heroine. The story of a woman who wilfully chooses the glamorous but immoral life of a courtesan over the honourable but duller life of a married woman.

A Tour Through the Whole Island of Great Britain
Edited by Pat Rogers

Defoe's Tour (1724–6) was described by G. M. Trevelyan as 'a treasure indeed' and by Dorothy George as 'the best authority for early eighteenth-century England'. But the *Tour* is something more than an invaluable source of social and economic history: Defoe's unfailing sense of process and of the mutability of things raises the work to the level of imaginative literature.

Robinson Crusoe, *read by Tom Baker, and* Moll Flanders, *read by Frances Barber, are also available as Penguin Audiobooks.*

also published:

Robinson Crusoe

BULLETS IN THE SAND

BULLETS IN THE SAND

AJ ABERFORD

This edition produced in Great Britain in 2022

by Hobeck Books Limited, Unit 14, Sugnall Business Centre, Sugnall, Stafford, Staffordshire, ST21 6NF

www.hobeck.net

A CIP catalogue for this book is available from the British Library.

ISBN 978-1-913-793-73-9 (pbk)

ISBN 978-1-913-793-72-2 (ebook)

Cover design by Spiffing Covers

www.spiffingcovers.com

Printed and bound in Great Britain

PRAISE FOR THE GEORGE ZAMMIT CRIME SERIES

BODIES IN THE WATER – BOOK ONE IN THE GEORGE ZAMMIT CRIME SERIES

'I thought I knew everything about murders in the Med – not so – this series is a fantastic read!' Robert Daws, bestselling author of the *Rock* crime series

'What a fantastic debut thriller from AJ Abeford! *Bodies in the Water* gives the real lowdown about crime and corruption in the Mediterranean, in an adventure that ranges from the tourist enclaves of Malta to the war-torn deserts of Libya and weaves together an intricate tale of murder, human trafficking, money laundering, terrorism and organised crime. In the centre of it all is Detective George Zammit, an intriguing new character on the crime thriller scene who is sure to become an instant fan favourite. Meticulously researched by someone who clearly has a deep understanding of the subject matter, *Bodes in the Water* rattles on at a supercharged pace, leaving the reader waiting expectantly for the next novel in what is destined to be a hugely popular new series.'
J.T. Brannan, bestselling thriller and mystery author

'I am definitely a fan of George and 100% will look forward to reading the next in the series.' Alex Jones

'… a cracker. Organised crime, people smuggling, run ins with ISAL and the hapless Detective George Zammit. Tricksy as a Zen novel.' Pete Fleming

'Highly emotive and gripping.' Louise Cannon

'I really enjoyed it. The writing was crisp and flowed well. The characters were strong and it was interesting how their paths crossed. The pace was excellent.' ThrillerMan

'I enjoyed this book immensely … very exciting and unpredictable.' Sarah Leck

'What started as a cross between *The Godfather* and *Midsomer Mysteries* soon developed into a twisty thriller, full of humour and coincidence where you can't help but root for unlikely hero, Inspector George Zammit.' Angela Paull

AUTHOR'S NOTE

Although the plot points are inspired by the political circumstances and certain events at the time of writing, the story is the product of my imagination and not intended to be an accurate account of any such real-life events or a comment on any of the people who may have been involved in them.

Malta is a small island and three-quarters of the population share the same one hundred most common surnames. As a result, there's a chance I have inadvertently given a character the same name as someone alive or maybe dead. If that is the case, I apologise. The events, dialogue and characters in this book were created for the purposes of fictionalisation. Any resemblance of any character or corporation to any entity, or to a person, alive or dead, is purely coincidental.

ARE YOU A THRILLER SEEKER?

Hobeck Books is an independent publisher of crime, thrillers and suspense fiction and we have one aim – to bring you the books you want to read.

For more details about our books, our authors and our plans, plus the chance to download free novellas, sign up for our newsletter at **www.hobeck.net**.

You can also find us on Twitter **@hobeckbooks** or on Facebook **www.facebook.com/hobeckbooks10**.

To my family and my wife's family, who stuck close and tight during the pandemic, helping us to bear our losses and keep our hope.

PROLOGUE

SANT'AGATA PRISON, AVELLINO, ITALY

THE CORRECTIONAL FACILITY of Sant'Agata was hidden away in a wooded area of Avellino province, in the Campania region of Southern Italy. As it accommodated a good number of senior organised-crime figures, and other wealthy white-collar prisoners, its governor and his crew provided a menu of special privileges, on a pay-to-stay basis, to help their guests pass the time more comfortably.

Over the previous four years Sergio Rossi had enjoyed the full range of these concessions, from specially prepared meals to, initially at least, fortnightly visits from his girlfriend, Carlita. His wife, when she was inclined, only visited on his name day and religious holidays. He received an ample supply of cigarettes, DVDs, and even had access to a sports streaming package, direct to the TV in his cell. It was true, he had it better than most, but other more important promises had been broken and that had gradually eaten away his trust in his former associates, to such a point that he now harboured feelings of profound illwill towards them.

He had been sentenced over four years ago. This morning, his term was up. At 08:00, he was free to go. He had paid the price, and anger at his treatment by those he had trusted had helped him survive the physical confinement. During that time there had been plenty of opportunity for him to plan how to avenge himself on those associates who had persuaded him to take the fall for their criminal enterprise, only to abandon him once he was inside.

The buzzer sounded and the steel gate swung open – he was free. Before he crossed the threshold to freedom, he spat on the floor in front of him. Unless a person had survived confinement, they could never understand that no revenge would ever be sweet enough to compensate for the loss of four years of normal life. No revenge would ever be harsh enough to redress the humiliation and insult of standing trial, displayed in a glass box. All because of what had turned out to be a misplaced sense of loyalty. Sergio had agreed to accept sole responsibility for an oil-smuggling conspiracy so that others could remain free.

The prison was set in open countryside. A double wire fence separated the inmates from the fields and forests beyond. Sergio walked out into the sunlit car park and paused to view the facility from an outsider's perspective. It was a stylish three-storey building, with tasteful grey and brown cladding on its lower faces. Only the undersized windows spoke of its true purpose. It looked more like a heavily protected junior school than a prison. Turning his back on Sant'Agata, he immediately spotted the immaculately clean black saloon with heavily tinted windows, parked at the edge of the car park.

Sergio was short, with a barrel chest and long grey hair that he wore swept back behind his ears. The time inside had taken its toll, but he still looked good for a man in his mid-fifties. The occupants of the car recognised him and the doors swung open. Two men got out. Both were wearing black suits, white open-necked shirts and sunglasses. One was holding a silver tray, with a glass and a bottle of champagne on it. Sergio walked towards them, pinning a big Sicilian smile to his sallow face.

"Signor Rossi, Salvatore Randazzo sends his regards and is looking forward to meeting you." The man held out a brimming glass as he spoke and gestured to the back seat while his companion, smiling broadly, bowed slightly and held the door open for Sergio.

He hesitated, one hand on the door, the other around the stem of the glass. He drank some and felt the entire four-year experience begin to recede. He allowed himself to smile, as some of the accumulated anger and hurt started to subside, but his words were still pointed.

"So, he couldn't be bothered to come himself? A big man now, *sì*?"

"Please, Signor Rossi." The driver bobbed his head and waved him into the back of the car.

When it had become apparent that someone would need to go to jail and Sergio had been informed that he should be that person, Salvatore Randazzo had replaced him as head of operations within the Family. Though the Wise Men of their organisation favoured Randazzo, who was clever, good looking and hungry for success, Sergio had found him arrogant and disrespectful. Salvatore had never visited him once in the four years he had been inside, preferring to send messages through intermediaries and grudgingly conduct the occasional brief conversation with Sergio by mobile phone, until it seemed he started to find even these irksome and left further calls unanswered. It had been agreed that Sergio would be *distanced* during his time inside. Nevertheless, it still hurt his pride and he thought the behaviour of the younger man at best, discourteous, at worst, insolent and short-sighted.

The rear passenger door shut behind him, with a solid clunk; the driver and his partner got into the front seats. He sank back into the comfortable leather upholstery, taking another long swallow from his glass. As he refilled it from the bottle left in a wine cooler beside him, he noticed a glass screen between the front and rear seats and rapped on it.

"Where're we going – what's the plan?"

To his surprise, the men did not drop the screen, but

continued to look straight ahead, while the one in the passenger seat replied through an intercom.

"We're going to Naples, Signore. It'll take an hour, so relax, drink champagne and enjoy the journey. There, we'll meet Signor Randazzo."

Sergio realised his phone was in his bag, which the guys had put into the boot of the car. He banged on the screen again.

"Hey!"

"Signore?"

"I need my phone, it's in the boot. Pull over."

There was no reply from the men in front, who continued to stare at the road ahead. The intercom went dead. The car rolled on, with no change of pace. Sergio banged on the window again.

"Hey, pull over, I want my phone!"

The silence from the front started to unnerve him. He tried once more, banging frantically on the glass.

"I'm telling you, *stronzi*, pull over – now!"

He put his hand on the door handle and was not entirely surprised to find it locked. Starting to feel uneasy, he sank back in the soft leather seat.

"Listen, you dickheads – let me out now. You don't know who you're messing with."

The intercom crackled.

"Signor Rossi, we know exactly who you are and we've got our instructions. Please, sit back. Everything is fine. There's nothing to be concerned about."

There was nothing dignified Sergio could do in response, other than set his jaw and stay silent. His body tensed, his heart rate began to race. He acknowledged to himself that he was afraid. The only weapon to hand was the champagne bottle. He put it to his mouth, half-full, and took a long draught.

The single carriageway road from the prison ran through countryside for a while, before it joined the state highway to Naples. After only ten minutes, however, the car slowed. To Sergio's increasing alarm, it pulled off onto a rough, unmade track, leading up a gentle slope bordered by a thick scrub of willows and poplars. Beyond this, they found themselves in an area of reforested pines and cypresses. Not that Sergio noticed the details clearly – his mounting sense of unease was now verging on panic. His breath was coming in short sharp bursts, sweat beading on his brow and upper lip.

He shouted and swung at the glass screen with the base of the champagne bottle. It bounced back at him each time he lashed out until, with a gasp of despair, he realised the screen was not glass, but a thick sheet of acrylic – probably designed to be bullet-proof. The car turned off the track and slowly edged its way towards a small clearing amongst the trees. He could not believe what was happening. This was it. The Family wanted him dead. The intercom came on. The man in the passenger seat turned to look at Sergio. His face was completely calm and relaxed, no sign of tension.

"Signore, they told us you'd be a fighter, so we can do this in one of two ways. We're professionals. It can be handled quickly, with respect and without pain. Please, consider that option. It's the best way. Or you can fight and we'll keep you in the car, with the doors locked. We have ten litres of petrol stored behind those bushes and we'll use it to burn you alive. That won't be so quick and there'll be much pain. It's up to you. Either way, the end will be the same."

These chilling words put the matter beyond any doubt. Sergio slumped back in the seat and took a very deep breath. Despite his efforts to appear calm, his voice was shaky and his words garbled.

"I've got money. More money than you can ever imagine. I'll pay you both and then I'll disappear. Tell them it's done and there'll be no trouble. You'll be rich. We're all businessmen, *yes*?"

"I'm sorry, Signore. I have to deliver proof of death, otherwise it'll be me in the back of the car next time. Now, which way is it going to be?"

Sergio was not going down without a fight. There was no

way he was going to sit there and allow the Family to arrange his disappearance. He had one last play left and nothing to lose.

"Do what you have to do."

The men got out of the car and stood well back. With a remote, the driver unlocked the rear doors. After a second, the one behind the driver's seat flew open and Sergio leaped out, head lowered, and charged like a bull towards the men in black suits, champagne bottle in hand. Anticipating exactly that response, the assassins were ready. One raised his Russian PSS silent pistol.

CHAPTER 1
SUPERINTENDENT
GEORGE ZAMMIT

ST JULIAN'S POLICE STATION,
SPINOLA, MALTA

IT WAS 11 a.m. on a Wednesday morning in early May and Spinola Bay was looking its best: bright sunshine, good-humoured people circulating around the bars and restaurants, the traffic moving smoothly. Superintendent George Zammit, of the Malta Pulizija, was being jostled in a queue by a group of over-excited students from a nearby language school, all clamouring to buy ice cream or soft drinks.

He tried to impose some order.

"Hey, hey! *Mela*, get in line. Come on now!"

A tall Eastern European boy, with blond hair and good teeth, smiled at him and squeezed his shoulder firmly in front of George, blocking his way.

"No time, sir. Only ten minutes for break. I am sorry."

The boy turned away to chat to the two girls he had ushered in ahead of him.

George sighed.

Hands thrust money towards the high counter of the shop front, where a server called Roberto dispensed cones and cans of drink to the crowd of youngsters. He spotted the policeman's reproachful face in the throng below him and shrugged his shoulders.

"Be with you in a minute, George! What can you do?"

He stood his ground, but somehow seemed to move backwards in the queue. He had known Roberto for years; they might even have been at school together, though George could not quite remember. Malta was like that – small enough for everybody to know everybody else.

Feeling the heat of the spring morning sun on his neck, the superintendent put on his sunglasses and loosened his tie. Spring was his favourite time of year. A gentle heat warmed both him and the early-season tourists. Sunlight lit up the brightly coloured fishing boats that rocked on the water, gently stirred by the onshore breeze. At the head of the bay, hotels, apartment blocks and restaurants pressed close to the road that hugged the promenade. It was a colourful and vibrant scene. It was also congested, over-developed and noisy.

Valletta was the island's old-town capital, home to politicians and public officials, but the commercial world revolved around St Julian's. It was here, and in the seedy neighbouring area of Paceville, that the gaming companies and small banks proliferated. It was also in St Julian's that the businessmen and women of the island congregated, meeting in the international hotels and better restaurants, extorting favours, moving money, greasing palms and slowly cementing Malta's reputation as the EU's dirty little sister.

George had been visiting the local police station, where a Latvian croupier was being held. He said he had information about a money-laundering ring operating at a large casino. It transpired the Latvian had a grudge against his manager, who had fired him for signalling hit-or-stand instructions to a longstanding accomplice in blackjack games. George had taken him to one side to tell him his work permit had been revoked. If he did not want to be re-arrested and prosecuted, he must stay away from the casino and leave the island before the weekend.

The Economic Crime Command was already aware of money laundering at the casino, but the time was not quite right for them to act against those involved. A group of Albanians was buying one thousand euro casino cheques from the tellers for one thousand-two hundred euros in cash. He did not want the dealer returning to the casino and upsetting the police surveillance operation before they had finished covertly filming the scam.

George had only just made the front of the icecream queue when the explosion happened. It was a loud, dull crump, unlike any sound he had heard since a trip to Libya four years earlier, when he had encountered hostile militia groups. After his experiences there, he was familiar with the sound of gunfire, grenade and mortar rounds. He instantly knew this sound was no daytime firework, chasing away evil spirits before a religious festival, or noise from a construction site. When he saw a plume of black smoke rising from a residential area a few streets behind him, he knew at once something bad had happened.

He hurried to his car, parked outside the police station, and drove around the corner into The Gardens, an upmarket residential district. It did not take him long to find the source of the trouble.

Along one of the streets of expensive whitewashed villas, smoke billowed high into the clear blue sky. Several agitated people stood outside a house, trying to peer over its high boundary wall. A white metal garage door, that opened onto the street, had been blown off and lay on the road, buckled and twisted. Flames and black oily fumes came gushing across the pavement from the burning vehicle inside the garage.

George drove as near as he could to the house, while phoning the Civil Protection Department HQ in Siġġiewi, telling them to send a fire tender and an ambulance. Then he jumped out of the car and shouted at the bystanders: "Pulizija, stand back, stand back!"

Once the onlookers had retreated, he went up close to the three-metre-high frontage and realised he would have to get over this to see what was happening inside the house. The wall was high and his short, corpulent stature was not made for feats of athleticism such as this. But by using the next-door neighbour's wrought-iron gate as an improvised ladder, he managed to get himself to the top of the wall and look down at the scene of the explosion.

The front of the house had been partially blasted away and was now a pile of stone blocks and rubble. Lying still, on a pile of loose dirt was a small girl, probably six or seven years old. Her arms and legs were in unnatural positions and she was covered in white dust from the blast.

George turned and shouted at the nearest spectator: "There's a child inside. When Civil Protection arrive, tell them I'll get that gate open and bring a medic. I'm going in!"

He swung a leg over and tried to lower himself gently down. The girl was wearing a torn school uniform and her bag lay on the ground nearby. There was a gash on her forehead, presumably from flying debris, but no other visible injuries although one pigtail was bloodstained. George went to kneel down beside her and gently touched her shoulder. She stirred and coughed and looked at him blankly. Then an expression of utter terror took over.

"Thank God! Are you OK? Where does it hurt? Don't be afraid, I'm a policeman."

The girl appeared not to hear and George realised she was deafened by the noise of the explosion. She muttered a few words but they didn't make much sense although he did catch the words 'Mum' and 'Dad'.

"It's OK, help is coming."

Still no response, just a blank look. She stared around her, then seemed to smell the burning rubber and acrid smoke. She visibly tensed, realising something awful had happened. George gently put a hand on her chest to stop her getting to her feet.

"Stay still, don't move. Let's wait for the doctor."

He turned his head back towards the wall and shouted as loudly as he could.

"I need a blanket in here! Please, quickly!"

George had done his first aid course and knew he had to keep her still, awake and warm.

He said, as gently as he could: "You shouldn't really move but you're safe now – is there anybody else inside the house? Who was with you? Do you remember?"

There was no point asking her questions, the girl was dazed and shocked. He saw her looking over towards the blazing vehicle in the shell of the garage. George noticed the side door to the street. He reassured the girl he wasn't leaving and went and opened it. A woman was waiting with a brightly patterned cover from a sofa, that they laid gently over the child. The neighbour stayed with the girl and George went out into the street to be greeted by a silent crowd that had now swollen in numbers. Suddenly, a large black SUV, with American diplomatic plates, came speeding around the corner and screeched to a halt in front of the burning house. Three men jumped out of the vehicle. Two of them ran past George, and through the open side door, into the burning house while the third approached George, waving his arms and shouting.

"Hey, you, come here!"

This man was older than the others, black, with short wiry grey hair and a carefully trimmed beard.

"You!" The man had an American accent and a very bad attitude. He pointed at George and snarled, "Who the fuck are you and what's happened here?"

Feeling all eyes on him, George fronted up to the challenge. He did not like pulling rank, but it seemed it was all this man understood.

"Excuse me, I'm a superintendent of police here and there is no need to talk to me like that. My name is George Zammit and, as you can see, we've got a hell of a problem here. First, let me get some of my men to secure this site. Then you can tell me who you are and what the hell is going on."

"Yeah, OK, OK, sounds good. Sorry, I'm just freaked out by this. Name's Mike Lloyd, Head of Security at the Embassy. The

US Charges d'Affaires lives here, with his wife and daughter. Didn't mean to come across like that." He clenched his teeth and quickly surveyed the scene. "Where's your fire tender? There'll be nothing left in there if it doesn't show up soon!"

George took a deep breath.

"It's on its way. I think there is a body in the car, in the driver's seat and there is a child, who seems shocked, only minor injuries. She's with a neighbour, inside. We're waiting for an ambulance."

"Holy shit! Annie. The girl's called Annie. Poor kid."

George did not reply, he was puzzled by something.

"How d'you get here so quickly? You did it in minutes."

"Look, we know what's happening on this island before it even happens. It's our business after all."

On cue, the fire tender appeared around the corner and Lloyd turned his attention to barking instructions at the bemused fire chief. An ambulance was close behind. The crew took some extinguisher cylinders from the tender and set about spraying the flames, covering the car in a thick layer of foam. Then, unfurling a polyester fire hose, they doused the buildings with water, steam and smoke mingling and drifting in a thick, noxious cloud down the street. Water ran into the gutter, carrying dirt from the explosion and black ash from the fire. The smell of burning rubber and acrid soot hung in the air.

George and Mike Lloyd led the paramedics through the side door and the men in green knelt beside Annie and started to unpack their large medical bags. The American left them to it and began picking around the scene, showing particular interest in the smouldering car, now covered with foam. George, happy Annie was in safe hands. went back out into the street to make a call to Pulizija HQ in Floriana, to let his superiors know what had happened.

In fact, Mike Lloyd had a paygrade well above Head of Security at the Embassy, but the title provided him with the cover he needed for the duration of his stay on Malta. It was twenty minutes before the American came back from inside the wrecked garage and announced: "What d'you know – it's a freakin' car bomb? I thought you guys saved those for your journalists?"

George was surprised by the certainty in his voice.

"How d'you know that – you can't be sure?"

"Three tours in Afghanistan, four years in Iraq – I know a car bomb when I see one, possibly triggered by a motion sensor, don't know yet. Big explosion. No local hoodlum put this together."

"Who was in the car?"

"Definitely Annie's dad, Jim Baxter, our Chargé d'Affaires – number one at the US Embassy. State Department's going to be very pissed. Better tell your guys."

"Who would do this?"

George looked around incredulously.

"Well, there's one helluva question, Superintendent. At the moment, I've got no idea and, even if I had, I wouldn't say. We're gonna crawl all over this. When we're done, we'll let you know what we've found. This ain't a pissing competition, we're going to lead the scene-of-crime stuff. Interfere and I'll have you down at the docks, documenting migrants. Sound fair?"

George pulled himself up to his full height of one and three-quarter metres.

"Have it your way, Mr Lloyd, but you'll need us on the streets to follow through on what you find, so don't get high-handed with me."

"George, come on! This is a diplomatic incident. It's my job to be all over it. And, please, call me Mike – we're all friends here, right?"

He looked at George closely, face breaking into a knowing smile.

"OK, now I've sussed you out. Made a call while I was inside – it pays to know who you're dealing with on this island. You're the Libya hero guy, who machine-gunned those Islamic State dudes and swam back to Malta! All this is pretty weird, 'cos we've been meaning to talk to you."

Four years earlier, George had found himself embroiled in a major criminal conspiracy with its centre of operations in Malta. He had discovered that his superior officer, Assistant Commissioner Gerald Camilleri, had become involved with a shady organised-crime group, known as the Family, who were planning a complex oil-smuggling deal out of war-torn Libya. Camilleri had blackmailed George to go to Tripoli, ostensibly to attend a crime-fighting conference, in reality to smuggle in a briefcase of gold. It was meant as a pay-off to a militia leader, Abdullah Belkacem, who was at the centre of the Libyan end of the arrangements.

George had made contact with Abdullah, but both men nearly lost their lives when they were double-crossed by the Family and ambushed by an extremist Islamic militia, keen to move in on the spoils of the deal.

George and Abdullah escaped and, during their journey to Malta, across desert and sea, forged an unlikely partnership: policeman and people smuggler. It had grown into a friendship that continued to this day. Finding courage, he never knew he had, George had confronted his boss and negotiated a deal. He had used his knowledge of Camilleri's own criminal activities to get Abdullah into the country without being locked up in a camp like the other migrants who ended up on the island. The deal had also secured George's future security. As a newly promoted superintendent in Camilleri's Economic Crime Command, he enjoyed an uneasy peace with his boss, but was aware that he and Abdullah were never far from Camilleri's thoughts and watchful eyes.

"Oh, yes? What do you want to talk to me about?" George asked the American, warily.

"Not about this." Lloyd waved his arm at the car smouldering behind him. "About something else entirely. That Libyan militia guy you brought back in tow, he still around?"

George said nothing, but smiled politely. The conversation went no further. Mike's wife Daisy turned into the street and came running up, bursting through the yellow scene-of-crime tape, like a winning marathon runner.

"Mike – where's Annie?"

"Safe – don't worry, the medics are checking her out. You find Suzanne?"

Daisy drew in her breath sharply and nodded her head.

"Yeah, she's at a gym class. We've sent someone to get her. Where's Jim?"

Mike Lloyd glanced over his shoulder at the blackened wreck of the car, then back at his wife to make sure she understood.

Daisy put her hands over her mouth and her knees buckled slightly. Quickly, she pulled herself together and took a deep breath, saying only: "Oh, sweet Jesus!"

"Will you be here for them? I'm going to be working late. I need to get on top of this."

"Sure, I'll take them home with me, once the medics are done. They'll probably take her over to Mater Dei for a check-up."

Mike nodded grimly in thanks to his wife, who turned away to go and comfort the shell-shocked child while Lloyd stared into the middle distance for a moment, deep in thought.

George stood still, looking on, as Mike Lloyd's private grief almost overwhelmed him. The American allowed himself a pause for private reflection before he spoke again.

"This is a bad day for the Baxter family." He paused before adding menacingly, "And for whichever bastard did this to them."

CHAPTER 2
ARTICLE IN MALTA
TELEGRAPH

REPORTER: *Amy Halliday*

22 May 2019

ISIL Kill Ten in Attack on Libyan Gas Plant

The Libyan-Italian joint venture running the VertWay gas pipeline took another blow last week when its facility in Marsabar, western Libya, was taken over for five days by a militia affiliated to Islamic State.

Italian oil company Italbenzina confirmed six Italian engineers and four Libyan workers were killed in an execution-style shooting. There was substantial damage to the gas-compressor facility and also a stretch of the pipeline.

The 540-kilometre VertWay pipeline was inaugurated in 2004 by Silvio Berlusconi and Muammar Gaddafi, and delivered gas from Marsabar to Gela, Sicily. Gas supplies from the Bouri and Wafa fields on the

Algerian border are frequently interrupted by terrorist activity, but this is the first attack on the oil and gas complex itself.

It is believed to have been made by an extreme Islamist militia, led by Abu Muhammad al-Najafi, which has been active in the area for some years. Attacks and kidnapping of industry personnel as well as blackmail are common and hamper the exploitation of Libya's extensive oil and gas resources.

The Libyan Resources Corporation (LRC) in Tripoli say Italbenzina, who operated the gas facility, has terminated its contract and withdrawn its personnel, due to the deterioration in the security situation.

This ends the supply of gas from Libya to Europe and is a blow to the Government of National Accord in Tripoli (GNA), which is engaged in a long-running civil war against the rebel strongman, General Boutros, based in Tobruk in eastern Libya.

The LRC has said that VertWay, which at its peak carried eleven billion cubic metres of gas per annum, has become unviable due to the threat of terrorist attacks. The facility and the pipeline have been sold to Euromasio, a Russian energy company, and the pipeline is to be salvaged for reuse in a carbon-capture project in the Black Sea. The sale includes a provision prohibiting the Russian company from using VertWay to bring gas ashore in Italy, so as to prevent future sales into the protected European market.

CHAPTER 3
YAROSLAV BUKOV

MARSABAR OIL AND GAS INDUSTRIAL COMPLEX, EASTERN LIBYA

YAROSLAV BUKOV KNEW all about oil and gas. He was born thirty-five years before in a small village on the Russian side of the Northern Caucasus, a few hundred kilometres across the border from Baku, Azerbaijan, where there was always talk of the money to be made in oil and gas on the shores of the Caspian Sea.

Yaroslav's father had set him to work in the family business when he was a young boy, repairing and maintaining cars and trucks. As a teenager, he graduated to maintaining the massive Kirovet tractors used in the local logging industry, as well as gaining notoriety for the speed of his fists and his willingness to use them.

Although there was a living to be made from his father's garage, it was always clear to Yaroslav that this was not the life for him. Ever since he had seen pictures of the brightly coloured domes of St Basil's, he had wanted to venture north and try his luck in Moscow.

He had no fear of hard work and made the most of the limited education available to him at the under-resourced local school. Afterwards, persuading his father to part with his hard-earned savings, Yaroslav had finally managed to secure a coveted place at the Gubkin Russian State University of Oil and Gas, in Moscow, where he had studied for another five years.

During that time, his keen intelligence and prowess in the mixed martial arts clubs, and underground street fighting scene, brought the well-built and formidable young man to the attention of the security services, who scouted the universities for talent. He was introduced to an officer in the KGB, later known as the FSB, where he was eventually employed looking at the new oil and gas technologies in the West, surreptitiously bringing useful knowledge, or sometimes people, back home, bypassing the problems of sanctions and embargos.

Yaroslav had developed his twin-track career in security and engineering, being placed into large infrastructure projects such as the Druzhba pipeline, which took crude oil 5,000 kilometres from Tatarstan to refineries in Eastern Europe. There, he had learned what was involved in moving huge volumes of oil and gas over enormous distances, in terrain that was hostile, both physically and politically.

Over the years, the FSB developed his practical skills in exploiting the Republic's resources, usually for those citizens most favoured by the higher echelons of the party. He became a wellknown and trusted operator in Russia's highly valued energy sector. His technical abilities were matched by his absence of scruples and willingness to adopt the more ruthless practices of the FSB.

He reported to a high-placed official within the energy department of Russia's Duma, Valentin Petrov. Like Yaroslav, Petrov operated between the spheres of state and so-called private enterprise. He made sure all the money flowed in the right direction – and that was not always towards the Federal Treasury.

That was how Yaroslav Bukov found himself stepping out of an armoured transport helicopter onto the car park of the Marsabar Oil and Gas Industrial Complex, in western Libya, the first Russian to visit their newly acquired gas distribution facility.

As the helicopter engines fell silent and the dust storm cleared, six heavily armed Volunteers, private contractors from the Russkaya Volonterskaya Gruppa, jumped out of the machine and formed a perimeter, their automatic weapons sweeping the car park.

Yaroslav saw the complex had sustained physical damage from the recent terrorist attack. Twisted pipework and scorch marks on some of the plant spoke of RPGs and mortar explosions. He was making a mental note of the damage when he noticed a portly figure, in black trousers and a white short-sleeved shirt, walking across the car park towards him.

Adel Abu Khader ran the complex. His political bosses had asked him to give Yaroslav a tour of the site and walk him around the gas facility Euromasio had acquired from the Italians. Yaroslav wanted his visit to be as brief as possible. He did not trust Abu Muhammad's militia, nor anyone else in Libya. The fact that it was he himself who had arranged for the Islamist militia to attack the refinery did not necessarily guarantee his safety.

He had commissioned a show of force as the last act in a campaign to frighten the Italians out of their deal with the LRC to operate the pipeline. The death of the Italbenzina engineers and the locals had not been part of the arrangement and Yaroslav saw their execution as gratuitous and unnecessary, but it had taught him that Abu Muhammad was not afraid to follow his own agenda. At least the murders had been effective in hastening the sale of the facility to the Russian state-owned company Euromasio.

The men introduced themselves and shook hands. Yaroslav looked around the massive complex, with its towering stacks and tank farms. Kilometres of stainless-steel pipework looped and stretched through manifolds and pump systems, spreading their tendrils to every corner of the plant.

"How big?"

"The site is four hundred hectares; three hundred for refinery and storage, and the rest, your gas facility."

Yaroslav looked towards some fire-damaged tanks, on the edge of the car park.

"Was there much damage to the refinery?"

"Not too much, but with gas plant any damage is bad news ..." Khader shrugged. "They don't usually come into the refinery. They must have wanted the Italians and the VertWay pipeline for some reason."

"How many dead?"

"The militia were here five days. They killed six Italians and four local workers, destroyed the stabilisation and compression facility and pumped concrete down the pipeline. They took a barge and ripped up more pipe – how far out, I don't know. The VertWay pipeline is fucked and the Italians have gone. Too dangerous for them."

"Five days? Why did no one come and stop them?"

"If there was a firefight, Tripoli was worried they might do more damage to the oil refinery. That's more important, both to Tripoli and Abu Muhammad. Gas is no use to the militias; they can't easily move it or sell it, but they can move oil, in road and sea tankers. Gas is not so easy for them."

"So why did ISIS kill the Italians?"

Khader smiled and raised his eyebrows.

"Well, first, it wasn't ISIS, it was the ISIL break-off group, Islamic State-in-Libya. Still ISIS, but they make their own agenda. Secondly, militias usually attack the pipelines in the desert. It's safer for them and just as bad for us. This time, they hit the gas facility itself. They scared off the Italians – and then you arrive and buy the place for a few dinars. Forgive me, but I find that a big coincidence."

Yaroslav looked the man straight in the eye and did not comment.

"OK, let me see the damage," was all he said.

Khader was still curious.

"Why have you bought a wrecked gas terminal, a damaged pipeline, and also agreed not to send gas to Europe? It makes no sense."

"We need pipes for carbon-capture project in Black Sea. Simple."

Khader looked at Yaroslav and caught the slight smile at the corners of his mouth. He did not believe a word of it.

The Russian spent the next two hours filming and exploring the wrecked gas plant, making a careful inventory of the damage. When he had finished, he took a walk down the two-kilometre-long finger of jetty, extending into the gentian waters of the Mediterranean, where the tankers came to load the refined oil. Once satisfied he was beyond earshot, Yaroslav took out a satellite phone from his rucksack and rang Petrov in Moscow.

"It's a mess, but we can do something with it. I'll send you the report and photos once I get back to Malta."

"OK, so now we start the next part of the project? Finding some friends there to help us."

"Yes, I've been asking around. There're a few people I can talk to. You won't remember, but a few years ago there was a high-profile oil-smuggling racket, broken up by the Italian Guardia di Finanza. A group of big European players was behind it. This could be right up their street."

CHAPTER 4
ABDULLAH BELKACEM
ABDULLAH'S HARDWARE STORE, BIRKIRKARA, MALTA

BIRKIRKARA HARDWARE STORE was a successful little enterprise. It opened at 06:30 in the morning and did not close until 20:00 in the evening. It was a Mecca for the many local builders and tradesmen, who were busy making money from the Malta property boom. When Abdullah had originally bought the business, he knew nothing about ironmongery and, to make a sale, had to get the customers to point to what they needed and then tell him, in English and Maltese, the name of each item. It greatly amused the buyers who, in exchange for helping him learn his trade, blatantly cheated him on the prices.

He had bought the shop soon after he had arrived in Malta, after his and George's escape from Libya. Abdullah's migrant-trafficking and oil-smuggling days were over and his brother Tareq lay buried in a field, not far from the scene of their gunfight with the same Islamic State militia that had recently attacked the Marsabar Industrial Complex. To Abdullah's relief, his remaining family lived hidden deep in the Nafusa Hills on the border with Tunisia.

Once it was clear he would gain the protection of the Maltese state and, in time, a red EU passport, thanks to Camilleri's intervention, he had to find a way to house and feed himself. He was determined not to end up marooned in one of the open camps to the south of the island, along with hundreds of other exploited maritime migrants, begging for day work. A small shop, with a flat above, seemed the perfect arrangement.

Despite his humble shopkeeper status, Abdullah had arrived in Malta with the fortune in gold that George had been forced by Assistant Commissioner Camilleri to deliver to him in Libya. This was downpayment for Abdullah's part in an oil-smuggling operation. Fortunately, he had managed to hang onto it when the smuggling ring decided to double-cross him and George and he had been forced to flee Libya, pursued by Abu Muhammad and his Islamic State-in-Libya militia.

Hard work took Abdullah's mind off the enforced separation from his family, distracting him from brooding on the revenge he had promised to take on Abu Muhammad. As time passed, he had come to accept the loss of his home, brother and a large part of his wealth, doubtless looted from his stronghold by the enemy, but the estrangement from his wife and sons still chewed him up inside.

His eldest boy, Jamal, was sixteen already – nearly a man. Abdullah had not seen him for four years. But until he could find a way to return to Libya, strong enough to challenge Abu Muhammad and make things right, he had to bide his time in Malta, selling lengths of guttering, tap fittings and brushes, while learning to laugh along with his thieving customers.

Abdullah had been busy ordering stock when he received a call from George.

"Abdullah, I'm confused. Why would the Head of Security for the American Embassy be asking about you? I'm sure it's not for home improvements. Is there something I should know? Something you haven't been telling me?"

"My friend, you worry me by asking this question! I do not know any Americans and I have upset no Americans. That does not mean they will not poke their noses into my business. All I know about Americans is that they cause much trouble, wherever they go."

"*Mela*, that's true, but it bothers me there's this big explosion in St Julian's and, straight afterwards, they want to talk to you."

"*Wallah*, I swear to God, it will be a short conversation. I know nothing of that."

"OK, I believe you, but keep your eyes open. I suspect you'll have visitors very soon."

That very night, Abdullah was closing his shop, taking the display of hardware in from the pavement, when a large black car with tinted windows drove slowly down the road and parked opposite the shop. He was nervous after the conversation with George and did not want to risk being dragged off to Cuba or somewhere, so quickly went inside, locked the door and pulled the shutters down. He was upstairs in his flat, checking out the vehicle through the window, when his phone rang in his pocket.

It was George.

"Abdullah, it's me. I can see you peering through the upstairs blinds! Come down and open the door. We need to talk to you."

"Who are you with in that big black car? I do not know why I ask … I know the answer already!"

"Don't worry, come down. All will become clear."

Abdullah went down, raised the shutters and cracked open the door. George was there, together with the tall policeman Camilleri, immaculate, as always in a navy double-breasted pinstripe suit. Abdullah could also see a medium-built black man, with grey hair and a close-cropped beard. He wore tan chinos, with a thick brown belt and a white polo shirt. The casual look was completed with a pair of bright blue trainers. Flanking the door, facing the street, were two heavy-set men in black suits, their earpieces visible.

"Hah!" Abdullah said, smiling and pushing the door wide open. "The mysterious Americans have arrived. Tell those two to sit in the car. The neighbours will think I am being arrested. It is hard enough being a Muslim in a Catholic country, without security people outside my door!"

The older American called to the men.

"Go sit in the car, guys. You're scaring the locals."

Abdullah turned and gave a nod to George, then tentatively shook Camilleri's long smooth fingers. He remembered the senior policeman preferred to avoid firm handshakes.

"So, Mr Chief Policeman, this is my shop. It is good, is it not? You see, I am a Berber, we know what it is to work. I have made much money. *Inshallah!*"

Assistant Commissioner Camilleri could hardly get into the shop for the piles of stock. Lengths of guttering were racked from the ceiling, lowering its height, so that he had to stoop to avoid causing an avalanche of grey plastic. The floors were littered with ladders, plastic boxes and buckets, which were usually stacked outside on the pavement when the shop was open. Although it appeared to be chaos, Abdullah now boasted he could find any item requested within seconds.

"Yes, a great success obviously." The Assistant Commissioner faked a smile.

Abdullah knew Camilleri was a manipulative, two-faced viper. His arrival with the American was interesting, but also unsettling.

"So, gentlemen, have you come to buy a coil of wire? Some tubs of silicone maybe? There is always a good discount for my policemen friends."

George stopped him with a wave of his hand.

"There's no room to talk, can we go up to the flat? I'll make tea and the Assistant Commissioner will explain why we're here."

The party climbed the narrow stone staircase, the American looking around to make a full assessment of his surroundings. George had been there many times and expertly weaved his way around the piles of stock that had been stashed to one side of the staircase. He went to the kitchen unit in the corner of the living room, put the kettle on and got out the small glasses they used for mint tea. Abdullah shuffled the three chairs around. George leaned against the sink and raised his hand, letting his friend know he was happy to stand.

Camilleri sat and watched. When the three of them were seated with a glass of tea in their hand, he closed his eyes and started to speak.

"Abdullah Belkacem, let me tell you a story. Let us see if you recognise the person I speak of. There is a man who has been badly wronged and who yearns for revenge. He has not seen his family for over four years; his children have forgotten what he looks like. His brother lies unavenged in a grave in the desert. All that he once had – money, respect, power, a good family life – is now gone. Once, he had a vision for the future of his town, his district, maybe even his country. But now he is just an Arab … sorry, a Berber, selling brushes and bags of plaster to ungrateful Maltese. They show him none of the respect he deserves; they laugh at his accent and his religion; they cheat and steal from him, when his back is turned. Do you recognise this man?"

Abdullah said nothing, but glanced at the American sitting across the table from him, whose name he still did not know. He had sunk back into his chair and the tightness of his frown had bunched his features together.

Camilleri continued talking, unperturbed.

"This can all be fixed. How would you like to go back to Libya, with weapons, intelligence support, protection, enough money to buy yourself an army? You can fight the Islamic State barbarians on your own soil and Boutros's militia from the east. You can restore your prosperity and become the man you once were – and more besides. If the years in Malta have not softened you, and if you can still raise men to support you, my friend here can organise that and give you all the help you need."

He nodded at the grey-haired American, who frowned and flared his nostrils, considering his words before he spoke.

"Maybe I can," the American said, running his hand across

his beard. "I'm Mike Lloyd. I fix things. I have everything the Assistant Commissioner mentioned – and some. I have drones, satellite imagery, special forces, artillery. All that you need to wage a war.

"We want the Russian advisers and mercenaries out of western Libya – and with bloody noses. We want the IS jackals to back off the western oil fields, and we want Khalifa Boutros back in Tobruk, or, better still, dead with his army in the dust.

"And another thing – we believe the Russians working out of Libya, busy killing your people by the hundreds, came over to Malta and, for some reason, blew up a good friend of mine. If they wanted to provoke me, they've succeeded.

"It can't be done in a weekend, but we'd like to make a start now before it gets too late. They tell me you're our man."

Abdullah looked at George, still leaning against the sink, keeping a poker face. Abdullah relaxed and sat forward, on the edge of his chair, a half-smile on his face.

He turned to George and said: "What exactly have you been saying to your friends? I do not know who they think I am! Is there more of that tea? This could be thirsty work. I have some questions I would like to ask."

On the way out, two hours later, Camilleri lingered to commandeer Mike Lloyd, taking him aside so they could speak discreetly.

"I hope you have authority for this project and all those promises you made, because a mere Embassy Head of Security would certainly not."

"Well, same, same, Assistant Commissioner. One day you gotta tell me where your authority to act in this venture comes from – 'cos I'm willing to bet the Police Department knows diddly squat about it!"

CHAPTER 5
ARTICLE IN MALTA TELEGRAPH

REPORTER: Amy Halliday

27 May 2019

Fight for Tripoli Enters New Phase

Reports of rocket attacks on the outskirts of Tripoli have spread alarm, as General Boutros's Libyan National Army (LNA) advances towards the capital. The Government of National Accord (GNA)in Tripoli has appealed to the UN to intervene and negotiate a ceasefire, as civilian casualties mount.

The LNA is supported by the United Arab Emirates and Egypt, who see Boutros as a trusted partner, capable of curbing the spread of political Islam in Libya. The GNA in Tripoli have strong ties to the Muslim Brotherhood, who believe the Islamic Sharia should be the basis for organising the affairs of state and society.

The UAE has supplied the LNA with air support, Chinese-made Wing Loong II drones and weapon systems for the advance. They also have funding from Saudi Arabia, the support of at least 1,000 Sudanese troops and the presence of a similar number of Russian mercenaries from Russkaya Volonterskaya Gruppa. Russia is bidding to become a power-broker in the oil-rich North African country.

The incumbent GNA in Tripoli, on the other hand, has the backing of Turkey, who say they have sent drones and troops, 'not to fight, but to support the legitimate government and avoid a humanitarian tragedy'. Qatar, which is more tolerant of the Islamist elements in Tripoli's government, has also provided funds and military resources to the GNA.

So far, the United States has refused to become involved, but recent comments from the White House suggest that some form of intervention may be necessary if Libya is not to become another Syria.

Meanwhile, the UN's efforts to achieve a ceasefire continue, General Boutros's advance on Tripoli progresses and casualties mount.

CHAPTER 6

YAROSLAV BUKOV
PHARAOH'S CASINO, MALTA

On first arriving in Malta, Yaroslav had taken stock of the island. As a former British colony, 300 kilometres off the North African coast, things looked to be in decent shape. The roads were in serviceable condition, health care was good, tourism was booming and Malta had established itself as a financial services centre. Just as the Caymans, Jersey and Mauritius operated as a back door for money to creep in and out of the US, UK and India, so Malta did for the EU.

He found there were a good many Russians already on the island. Specialist shops sold food from home and quality vodka; tall blonde Slavic-faced beauties, with hard, tanned bodies, jogged up and down the Sliema promenade; and over a thousand Russian 'entrepreneurs' had bought Maltese passports, allowing them easy access, in and out of the EU.

Yaroslav was aware of the recent case of attempted oil smuggling from Libya. While, as an oil man, he found such activities irritating, he felt a grudging admiration for the scale of the operation and the ambition of those who had organised it. He thought, if he could meet them in person, he would be able to judge at once whether they would be of use to him.

After a few false starts, a Russian banker told him he had

found those Yaroslav needed to speak to. The banker described
an old and respected Maltese family, with extensive connections
across the island and Europe. It had international business interests, deep pockets, was highly secretive and, if so inclined, could
get any deal here completed. It had been rumoured they had
been involved in the ill-fated oil-smuggling venture a few years
previously, but following its collapse, had withdrawn from the
commercial life of the island. The banker thought, if the deal was
attractive enough, the time might be right to lure them back into
the open.

Making contact with them had proved difficult – Yaroslav
had needed a middle man to meet a middle man! The person
who finally agreed to see if a meeting could be arranged was an
Assistant Commissioner in Malta's police force, one Gerald
Camilleri.

It had taken several days of talks to confirm his credentials,
but eventually Yaroslav had met with a member of the Family.
She turned out to be a striking, tall woman with long dark hair,
who spoke English with a faint Italian accent. She was in her
early-thirties, olive-skinned, with the indefinable air of a person
who had always had everything they wanted as by right. When
they met in the casino, she looked stunning, in a long, sparkling,
high-necked black evening dress that hugged her figure. She
introduced herself as Natasha Bonnici.

After the introductions, she casually played a few spins of the
roulette wheel, taking low-denomination chips from a small
black clutch bag. After a few minutes, she took her modest
winnings, pushed a chip towards the croupier as a tip and they
went to a secluded table at the back of the gaming floor. Her
security sat at the bar, a discreet distance away, but not so far that
Yaroslav did not notice. The woman did not indulge in small
talk.

"Let me tell you, we don't do business with Russians because
it always ends badly," she began. "That's been our experience
over the course of the last two hundred years."

Yaroslav laughed briefly.

"As a Russian businessman, what can I say? But, believe me, I work very hard to find you. Finally, I understand – if there is big pan-European project, with need of patience, resources, connections and vision, your organisation is one of few who can do it. What my project is? I tell you more about it."

She said: "You understand, I'm just a messenger. Tell me what you can. You've got my full attention and an hour of my time. I can't promise you anything in advance. Unless you persuade me there's something of interest to us here, I'll tell you nothing about us. It's not meant to be discourteous, just how we prefer to operate."

What Yaroslav had subsequently learned was that Natasha Bonnici not only had a day job as CEO of a major i-Gaming business, but was also part of a very old organisation, which she referred to simply as the Family, based in Milan. Historically, they had traded across Europe as a financial guild, but the collapse of the Hapsburg Empire and two world wars had taken their toll on the wealth so far accumulated. These days, the Family had interests in commercial property, construction, banking and insurance. More recently, their focus had shifted to energy.

That was how it had started.

CHAPTER 7

NATASHA BONNICI

PIPO'S BAR, ST PAUL'S, MALTA

ON THE SURFACE, BetHi was a hugely successful company, raking in cash and Bitcoin through its virtual casino, sports betting and live gaming lounges. What was not apparent was that it was also one of the most successful money-laundering operations in Europe, washing the ill-gotten gains from the Family's many international enterprises. It had previously traded under the name BetSlick, but Camilleri advised the company to close and reappear under a different name, so he could protect the business from further police enquiries, following the collapse of the oil-smuggling plan.

That afternoon, Natasha hurried out of her office, well before her normal departure time, shouting over her shoulder that she had a meeting and would not be back. She drove her two-seater sports car out of the underground garage and took the coast road north, towards the resort town of St Paul's, but instead of heading inland towards the family home in the hills, she drove down to the sea front and parked alongside Pipo's Bar, a small place with dated illuminated plastic signage, more frequented by locals than the tourists.

She watched the door for a few moments and then looked up and down the promenade. Seeing nothing amiss, she quickly slipped off her heels and took some flipflops from her gym bag. She grabbed her hair, twisted it into a rough ponytail and pushed it through the back of a Yankees baseball cap. A baggy, light-grey hooded top covered her Italian silk blouse, which completed the deconstruction of her classy and glamorous work persona. Natasha covered the upper part of her face with some large, cheap sunglasses, hunched her shoulders, plunged her hands deep into the pockets of the hoody and, deliberately altering her gait, slouched into the bar. Over the last four years, magazine articles and TV appearances had brought the young, good-looking female CEO of one of the island's biggest leisure industries into the public eye. Now, she doubted she would be recognised.

Il-Barri, or The Bull, sat at one end of the bar, his dead eyes staring vacantly into space. The nickname perfectly suited the middle-aged, short, flat-faced barrel of a man, who was a small-time fisherman by day but, when ashore, would use his strength to break fingers and arms for a few euros – or, for a few more, necks. Few would join *Il-Barri* on his brightly painted open boat as it was known the catch was always poor. They said his mere presence was enough to send the shoals diving for deep waters.

He did not move or cast a sideways glance as Natasha sat beside him and reached into her gym bag. She noticed the faint smell of the sea about him and recoiled slightly from the sight of a smattering of fish scales that glistened on his temple. She slipped him an A4 envelope with six photographs inside, given to her by Camilleri. These were the brashly dressed young Albanian blades who had had the cheek, stupidity or ignorance to use the Family-owned casino for their own amateur, unauthorised money-laundering operation.

A second envelope was stuffed with fifty-euro notes. *Il-Barri* reached out, sensing the money, pulled it across the bar top and weighed it in his meaty fist. He said nothing, but turned his head to look at her for the first time. Natasha said: "For that amount of money, you know what I want."

He remained silent, continuing his study of the middle distance ahead.

She knew she should not get personally involved in this sort of thing; she had a host of security people who could take care of business. But she enjoyed it! On the way home, she entertained herself by thinking what misery *Il-Barri* would inflict on the hapless Albanians. When the stupid girls at the cashdesk, who had facilitated the scheme realised what had happened to their clients, she would let them fret and panic for a week or so. Then, just when they thought they had avoided any punishment, she would give *Il-Barri* another envelope of fifty-euro notes. The casino could not afford to get a reputation for being a soft touch.

'Albanians,' she thought, 'always trouble.' She wondered if her father had forgotten, or forgiven her, for the incident with Elbasan, another Albanian. She had used him to set up Nick Walker, her predecessor as CEO at BetSlick, as the business had then been called, and her boyfriend at the time. Nick had held the position she coveted, so Natasha had worked with Elbasan to frame him for the theft of several hundred thousand euros.

All things considered, it had worked out well, given she had been able to step into the job she had wanted so badly. What had not gone so well was the violent quarrel that had blown up between her and Nick. It had resulted in her being injured with a blow from a heavy Murano glass vase, when Nick believed she was about to fire a gun at him. Her lover had left her lying on the floor of his villa, in a pool of blood, and fled the country, with her father, Marco Bonnici, and her Uncle Sergio in hot pursuit.

It had not gone so well for Elbasan, either. He had known too much about Natasha's part in framing Nick and, soon afterwards, had been found dead in the car park of Malta's Aquarium, killed by a vehicle that had repeatedly driven back and forth over his body. Her father had made the connection and been horrified.

Once the business in St Paul's was finished, Natasha turned out of town and up towards the small hilltop hamlet of Il-

Wardija. She felt a keen sense of anticipation as she drove down the narrow, stone-walled lanes on the approach to the family *castello*. Today was special. Her father was coming home!

Whether Marco Bonnici was quite as thrilled to be reunited with his daughter again remained to be seen. Following the unravelling of their oil-smuggling scheme, and the winding up of BetSlick's original money-laundering operation, Marco had felt it best to drop out of the commercial and social life of the island for a few years.

Assistant Commissioner Camilleri had told him he had nothing to fear. The Family's sacrifice and the subsequent conviction of his cousin and best friend, Sergio Rossi, would be sufficient to satisfy the Maltese and Italian authorities that justice had been done. Nevertheless, Marco was tired, stressed and troubled. So he had taken a sabbatical on a secluded estate he owned in western Serbia.

Before Marco had left Malta, he had confessed to Natasha that he was actually fearful of what she had become. For that reason, he felt he had to put some distance between them. Time had helped to soothe his concern and disappointment in her, but he still approached their reunion with a degree of wariness.

Natasha had no such reservations about his return. As far as she was concerned, the past was the past and she had long since set those unpleasant incidents aside. In fact, she rarely thought about them at all.

Her father's return now was a matter of expediency; she needed his help. The conversation with Yaroslav had been more than interesting – it had been exciting. It was many years since an opportunity with such potential had presented itself to the Family, let alone to the Bonnicis.

Petrov, Yaroslav's boss, had planned all along to find a way to bring the Libyan gas through VertFlow and then, via a short spur, into Malta. There was then nothing to stop a Maltese-owned company from piping the gas the hundred kilometres or so to

Sicily, so as to achieve wider European distribution. After all, Malta was in the EU and had access to all its markets.

In the great game of exploiting global energy resources, Russia had made a play to get cheap African gas into Europe, picking up a major pipeline for a few kopeks, and Natasha had managed to win the Bonnicis a seat at the table. This opportunity could help her advance her ultimate personal ambition to occupy an even more prominent seat, heading the *Familia con pane*, or Family for short.

But, for all this to work, she knew she needed her father's connections, wisdom, reputation and support. The Libya deal was potentially massive for a small island like Malta – or 'transformational', as Salvatore would say.

Then there was Salvatore Randazzo himself, the new broom who had replaced Uncle Sergio, following his imprisonment and then shocking murder shortly after leaving Sant'Agata. Salvatore had stepped into his shoes, as the link between the Bonnicis and the Family's Wise Men in Milan. Things between Natasha and Salvatore had soon become difficult.

Salvatore's charm, his crystal blue eyes and dark good looks, were self-evident; he was an attractive man. More out of curiosity than any real affection for him, Natasha had succumbed to a brief affair. She had quickly discovered it had been a mistake. Salvatore Randazzo was an individual with an iron will and a highly developed need for control. For all his easy manners, he was, at heart, as cold as ice, and just as hard. She had continued with the relationship for as long as she had dared, to see how it would play out. He was one of the Family's foremost protégés, a favoured son, so Natasha had been keen to take his measure. If her long-term plans were successful, they would find themselves in competition for power within the Family one day. What better way to prepare for this eventuality than to stay close to him, while she had the chance?

His violent temper had showed itself on several occasions and Natasha had mentally stood back and studied him when he tried to threaten and even physically intimidate her. She was not frightened, but found it interesting to see there was violence in him.

During their last argument, when Natasha had had enough of his behaviour, she had told him that, if his manners continued to be a problem, she would ask the Wise Men to intervene – a scenario she knew he would find deeply humiliating.

It was a low blow, but one she had not been able to resist. She had stood in front of him, smiling, and threatened to tell the Wise Men he had been abusive and about his 'unnatural inclinations'. 'No smoke without fire, Salvatore!' She could tell he was mortified and had secretly rejoiced while she needled his pride and revealed herself to him as a dangerous adversary.

Natasha knew that, one day, the rift between them would have to be allowed to reach its natural conclusion. But, in the meantime, an uneasy truce prevailed, each of them watching the other closely. Natasha was always prepared to play the long game.

CHAPTER 8
SUPERINTENDENT
GEORGE ZAMMIT
POLICE HEADQUARTERS,
FLORIANA, MALTA

OVER THE LAST FEW YEARS, George had found working for Assistant Commissioner Camilleri quite tolerable. He had never crossed his boss, did exactly what was asked of him and looked the other way when required. Camilleri had also got to know George well enough to be confident he would not knowingly disrupt the smooth running of the AC's lucrative sidelines and that, whenever there was a choice, his superintendent would always opt for a quiet life.

Camilleri acted as a one-man regulator. As with much of the southern Mediterranean, crime and corruption were a fact of life in Malta and, rather than try to fight this, he worked with it, curbing excess and limiting the damage to uninvolved civilians. An upper class of politically connected businessmen plundered government revenues, while a cadre of East European and Asian immigrants based themselves on the island, to enjoy the benefits of an EU passport and Malta's flexible financial regulation. Camilleri knew most of the prominent players and, as long as their activities remained within limits and they observed certain proprieties, he allowed them to operate.

George had managed to avoid becoming involved in anything too distasteful. As he had suspected, his accelerated promotion to superintendent had been mainly so that Camilleri could keep a close eye on him and make sure he continued to appreciate the benefits of remaining silent about the Assistant Commissioner's role as facilitator for the Family, as well as Malta's wider commercial and political fraternity. That did not mean George had stopped mistrusting him, or that he was not still a little afraid of his superior.

The day after meeting Abdullah in his shop, George was summoned to Camilleri's office. Although this no longer filled him with dread, he was always suspicious of what Camilleri might be up to and whether it would upset the equilibrium of his superintendent's uneventful life. That day, he guessed the AC merely wanted to follow up on the meeting with Abdullah and there seemed no undue reason to be concerned.

As George was walking out of the shop the previous evening, his friend had looked at him with his eyebrows raised, making a telephone sign with his thumb and little finger. Later that evening, they had spoken.

"So, my friend, you are now a spy, as well as a policeman! Indeed, you have many talents."

"*Mela*, what do you think? Do you really want to do this?"

"I have been waiting four years. The old policeman is right – he knows who I am and I must trust in Allah and follow his plan, *Inshallah.* I will go back with the Americans."

"Do you trust him?"

"You brought him to me, my friend. If you trust him, who am I to doubt you?"

"Don't put this on me! It's your neck on the line, not mine. You could just stay here, bring your family over, educate your sons and have a good life – safe and free. Think carefully, Abdullah.

"You're not as young as you were. You haven't held a gun for four years. The Americans have big plans. They want war in your country. It mightn't be what you expect."

"You are right. I would lie if I said I did not feel this in my stomach. But there is work to be done, my friend. I would be a coward if I did not take this chance. Allah has smiled on me and brought me good friends who will help me. I will go back."

George did not think too hard about who those *good friends* were. With hindsight, he should have paid more attention.

So, today he approached Camilleri's lair cautiously, but with few real misgivings. The Assistant Commissioner's office was an austere, uncluttered corner room in the stone-built Victorian police headquarters. There was a single pile of papers on the desk before him, no family photographs or career trophies, and no potted plants. Instead, the large office benefited from spectacular views down onto the Msida Marina and over to the high rises of Sliema. George could picture Camilleri sitting at the huge oval rosewood conference table that occupied half the room, deep in thought, like a chess-playing spider, mapping the moves ahead and setting traps for the unwary.

His boss had already taken a seat at the head of the table and George sat to one side of him, at a strategic distance. Camilleri placed his elbows on the shining wood. George could smell the lemon-scented polish on it. He also noticed Camilleri had his palms together, fingers steepled, as if in prayer. It was always a sure sign he was about to embark on a difficult conversation. George went onto full alert.

"Well, your friend Abdullah is happy to exchange his life as an ironmonger for a return to being a warlord – this time, a very powerful warlord indeed. Chances are, he will be dead in a matter of months, of course. There is no guarantee of longevity, doing what he is going to do." Camilleri paused, his creepy, trademark mirthless smile spreading across his face. "I really hope you last longer than he does."

In the past, George would have spluttered and claimed he did not understand, but he had learned such a reaction only played into the Assistant Commissioner's hands. He was obviously intent on following a script he had prepared before they had even sat down. George remained silent.

"You must be a very loyal friend to Mr Belkacem. I do not know the full details of what you got up to on your last adventure, but he sees you as a very different person from the one I have come to know."

Abdullah held to a mistaken notion that George was a soldier, a born warrior. Circumstances had cast him in a heroic light while he was in Libya. They had twice been forced to fight the Islamic State–in-Libya militia and Abdullah had seen George kill several of their fighters; some in reaction to the desperate situation, some by accident and some out of blind panic. However, it was also true that George had, in the past, been a champion huntsman and a medallist in both the bullseye and rapid-fire competitions, on the police range at Pembroke. His marksmanship had undoubtedly saved Abdullah's life when they had been ambushed; his friend's brother, Tareq, had been less fortunate.

It was something Abdullah never forgot and never stopped alluding to. He would point to himself and say: '*I saw it with my own eyes. These eyes do not lie.*'

"Anyway," said Camilleri, "you know how keen we are to develop our people, and nowhere more so than in the Economic Crime Command. So, a development opportunity has arisen and I expect you to grasp it with both hands."

George's eyes widened and his mouth went dry. Last time a *development opportunity* had presented itself, it had led to George's nearly being murdered in Libya. All he could do was stare blankly at Camilleri and wait for him to continue.

"Not surprisingly, your friend Abdullah has accepted the Americans' offer of a return to Libya, in order to embark on a suicide mission against Islamic State-in-Libya, while also trying to prevent the militias in the east from gaining Tripoli. I hope Marianna can afford to do without you for a few weeks ... well, months, possibly ... because your friend wants you to accompany him to Libya, as his special adviser. How is that for a show of trust, George? You should be flattered."

George's mind started racing but words were beyond him.

After a few speechless seconds, he stammered: "*M-m-mela*, I can't. It's my daughter's engagement p-party in two weeks!"

It was true. Gina was getting engaged to Giorgio, a presentable local boy who worked at Mifsud's, the butcher on Birkirkara High Street. George's wife, Marianna, was delighted by the whole affair and the engagement party, to be held in their house, had been her only topic of conversation for the last month. Her husband's absence was unthinkable – but, looking at Camilleri, George realised such an excuse would not be good enough to get him out of whatever had been arranged.

The last time Abdullah and George had been thrown together in Libya it had been a nightmare from which George had only just managed to escape with his life. He did not want to repeat the experience.

"Assistant Commissioner, what use would I be in Libya? I'm a policeman, not a soldier. I haven't fired a gun in months. I've got duties here. I'm needed at home. Please, you can't ask me to do this, especially not there!"

He realised he was whining, and it was unbecoming of a senior officer in the Pulizija to behave like that, but he could not help himself. A feeling of desperation engulfed him. It was all starting again. Camilleri was sitting back in his chair, face inscrutable. It seemed to George that his boss was actually enjoying watching him squirm.

"Well, George, I do not think Abdullah wants you there for your military prowess or your leadership capabilities. I agree, you need to develop your skills in these departments. He obviously wants you there as a guarantor, so that he is not abandoned should things go wrong. If you like, I see your role as that of willing hostage. He saw how you secured his safety, and his asylum case, on the last occasion you decided to meddle in affairs well above your rank. So, I can see why he is keen for you to accompany him this time.

"Anyway, there is not a lot I can do about it as our American friends are insisting that all his conditions are met. They feel he and, by association, you, are crucial to their venture. Geopolitics, George – you are playing in the big league now! If only I were a few years younger …"

George was beyond words. He could barely stand to listen to what Camilleri had to say next. The Assistant Commissioner dropped the faintly mocking tone and switched back to business.

"You fly out next week, to the American Al-Udeid Air Base in Qatar. Apparently, it is the biggest in the Middle East and home to their Special Operations Command. It is a very impressive set-up, I am told. They run an induction course for desert warfare. I believe it is run by the Green Berets, or Commandos, something like that, very competent people. You will be perfectly safe! Anyway, that is where the whole thing is being managed from. So do your best, fly the flag for the Pulizija. I know you will not let us down. I will try to arrange a hardship allowance for you. Something to cheer you up if things get uncomfortable at home. Marianna will be pleased about that, at least."

CHAPTER 9

MARCO BONNICI
CASTELLO BONNICI

It was late afternoon when Marco heard Natasha's car crunching on the gravel, under the portico that sheltered the double front doors. He rose from his easy chair in the library to go and meet her. Despite his reservations about returning to Malta, Natasha was his only child and he could not help but smile as he watched her step out of the car into the bright afternoon sunlight. He jogged down the short flight of entrance stairs to hug her tightly.

"Welcome home, Natasha!"

"You're the one who's been away," she replied. "How's everything here? I hope it's to your satisfaction. I broke all my nails for you yesterday, cleaning this place!"

"I noticed the smell of polish – but I did not think it would be you, down on your hands and knees, scrubbing floors. Things have changed!"

"OK, you're right, I got some contractors in."

The *castello* was a large, fortified limestone building with crenellated towers to each corner. It stood inside a substantial estate, with olive groves and vineyards planted in narrow terraces that stepped down the valley sides, towards the coast.

As a home, the *castello* had a somewhat gloomy atmosphere

with its heavy, dark antique furniture, long stone corridors, hall-ways hung with tapestries, and suits of armour standing to atten-tion. But, to Natasha, it was what she knew and she had spent many happy times here while being brought up by her father. Her mother had died in a freak accident, falling on the main staircase, to which Natasha had been the only witness when she was just five years old.

Marco looked around the cavernous hallway, breathing in deeply, taking in the ancient, musty aromas of smoke, leather and tobacco.

"The house is the house, I am sure it has not changed from one century to the next, but the garden is a bloody mess!" he said.

"That's down to you, Dad. Nobody dares mess with your garden."

They went through the house and outside onto the rear terrace. Natasha sat in one of the wicker armchairs and took in the view over the resort of St Paul's. To the north, across the channel, she could clearly see the grey limestone cliffs of the island of Gozo, whose bells, when the wind was right, could be heard here even though they were ten kilometres away. The familiarity of the view comforted her. Marco appeared with a bottle of their own wine, from the fridge in the breakfast room, and pulled the cork. He poured two glasses, then dipped his nose to take in the aroma.

"This is last year's; young, probably a little sweet, but quite palatable. Well, to Sergio." He raised the glass. "He always hated our wine. Maintained it bore no comparison to the Sicilian stuff. Stubborn to the end."

It was the first time they had been together and able to speak properly since his death.

"I'm sorry about Sergio, Dad. I know how close you were to him. What happened? Tell me what you heard."

Marco sighed deeply.

"I rang Salvatore as soon as I could and he told me very little. Later, he conceded Sergio had become a loose cannon, forever making a nuisance of himself. It seems, rather than acting contrite for the mess in Libya and doing his time quietly, he developed a sense of entitlement. Started to make demands for the future, which others found unreasonable." Marco paused, rolling the wine around his mouth, savouring the developing citrus flavours.

"Apparently, he wanted the Family to give him a sizeable stake and set him up in Argentina. Imagine how that went down!"

Marco smiled at the thought.

"Sergio was always headstrong – it got him into trouble all the time. He never cared or watched what he said. Apparently, he made some threats about what he might do if he did not get his way, which was the last straw. He threatened Signor Bruno directly. Well, even Sergio should have known you cannot go around threatening the Wise Men. Prison brought out his Sicilian side and Signor Bruno, in particular, did not like that. The Milanese have firm views about good breeding and manners. Ever since he was young, Sergio was always a bit of an outsider. That is what I liked about him."

Marco sighed.

"But then they murdered him, Natasha. Shot him down, in cold blood, and burned his body. They have never done that to one of our own before. I will never forgive them for it."

They both sat in silence for a few seconds.

"Are we tainted by association?" Natasha asked.

Marco laughed.

"No, they will not bother us. Malta is regarded as an outpost. I make sure I do not get too involved in the Family's internal politics. But do not underestimate the importance of this gas deal. It has certainly raised your profile. It is massive, even by the standards of the Family. How is Signor Bruno, by the way? He must be getting on these days."

Natasha had done a post-graduate business degree in California and then worked for an American bank in London, before returning to Malta. Then, she had caught the eye of Signor Bruno, a former assistant governor of the Banca d'Italia and now the most senior of the Family's Wise Men, or governing body. She currently worked for him two days a week, helping him to look after the trusts and corporate structures that the Family used to conceal its less legitimate business affairs, as well as managing its complex banking and accounting operations. It was tricky to combine her job at BetHi with the work for Signor Bruno, but Natasha was not afraid of hard work and long hours. Nor would she have missed the opportunity to learn as much as she could about the internal affairs of the Family.

"Signor Bruno's much the same. I keep watching and learning. I do exactly what he asks and still make the fortnightly trip to Milan, to report direct to him. I'm not sure how much he trusts me; he seems to be closer to Salvatore. Maybe he doesn't like women?" She shrugged. "When I mentioned the approach from the Russians, the first thing he asked me was whether I had told Salvatore."

"Had you?"

"No way! He would probably have spun it as his idea all along."

Marco smiled. He knew Natasha had a plan to ingratiate herself with the old man and, for the time being, was being outplayed by Salvatore.

"Well, do not let Salvatore Randazzo get under your skin. If you can bring this deal home, you will be well thought of for years to come and this generation of the Family will feel it has acquitted itself well. Legacy is important to old men, remember."

Marco cradled the cold glass between his hands.

"We have to be careful, Natasha … or rather, you have to be careful. I am yesterday's man; they will not bother about me. But you? You are pushing yourself forward and that gets noticed. People will be watching you closely."

He looked over the valley at the olive groves below. It was early evening and the cicadas were rattling away, like high-speed maracas. Years ago, his father had planted a small orchard of orange trees, just below the terrace, so the fragrant smell of the blossom and fruit would be caught by the onshore breeze that blew up the hill. He inhaled the scent and confessed to himself he had missed it all: a glass of wine, the company of his daughter, the warmth and scents of a Maltese afternoon. He turned his attention back to Natasha.

"Speaking of which, Salvatore telephoned me in Serbia, you know, before all this business. I got the feeling you and he were getting on much better then than you are now. It set my antennae twitching. Is there something I should know?"

He smiled and sat back in his chair.

She lowered her eyes to show him there was nothing she could keep secret from her father – except everything of real importance, she reflected.

"Hmmm ... you guessed! Well, OK, we'd a thing going at the end of last year. It was lovely, but not long-lived. We went on trips to Venice and Scotland, but I realised he's a strange man – and not for me. He needs a nice Milanese wife who will shut up, do what she's told and not ask too many questions. I told him things wouldn't work out between us and he didn't take it well. He's been in a sulk ever since."

Marco understood and nodded along with her words.

He looked at his daughter, sitting there in front of him, smiling, relaxed, beautiful. He hated the way he always doubted her, but could think of no good reason why she should involve herself with a duplicitous snake like Salvatore, other than to further some agenda of her own.

"Well, the best thing we can do is keep pressing forward and get this gas deal finalised."

"Well, yeah," said Natasha, "but I've got some concerns about it. We've got a lot of work to do. Signor Bruno has split the deal in two. At the Malta end, we've got to work with the Russians, get the gas onshore and organise all the construction, as well as lay a new underwater pipeline from Malta to Sicily. Salvatore is then going to buy the gas from us in Sicily and organise its onward sale into the wider European transmission network. Oh, and I nearly forgot – we also need a programme of works to pipe the gas to every house on the island. Sounds simple, doesn't it? Well, it's not!"

Marco pondered and said: "It seems everything hangs on the cheaper gas from Libya that the Russians have promised. But when all is said and done, this *is* the Russians and the Libyans we are talking about ..."

"True, but they've never reneged on a deal like this. It would send a terrible signal to the markets if they did. The Libyans need the money and the Russians claim they and their allies can manage security."

"OK, maybe you are right. I hope so. What about our friends in Castille – are they on board?"

The Auberge de Castille housed the office of the Maltese Prime Minister, from which his advisers and favoured ministers ran the country in the traditional southern Mediterranean way.

"That's one of the reasons I need you back. They smell money. The conversion of the island to natural gas is a huge political deal. Brussels is talking about a fortune in grants to support the idea. You can imagine the opportunities in construction!"

"But the Russians are not in control of western Libya yet. Or am I wrong? And we are gambling ... what? Two hundred million?"

"There are considerable financial risks, yes."

"Have you met these Russians? What are they like?"

"The lead is an oil and gas guy, in his late-thirties, Yaroslav Bukov. He's worked pipelines all over Europe and knows the technical stuff backwards. He's nobody's fool – smiles a lot, but is as arrogant as hell! I suspect he's tied in with Russian security services. He's on the island now. I thought we could meet him tomorrow and I will introduce you. Let you get a feel for him."

"OK, sounds sensible."

Marco heaved himself out of the chair and pushed his glasses up onto his greying, wiry hair. He looked tired already and he had only been back a couple of hours.

CHAPTER 10
SUPERINTENDENT GEORGE ZAMMIT'S HOUSE

SUPERINTENDENT GEORGE
ZAMMIT'S HOUSE

GEORGE NEEDED to tell Marianna about his conversation with Camilleri. There seemed no right time to approach the subject, as party planning was all she and Gina talked about. Excitement crackled through the house like a charge of static. When things were going her way, Marianna was a delight to be around but, when they were not, there was usually trouble.

At the end of dinner, two nights after his meeting with Camilleri, he thought he had caught her in an exceptionally good mood. Responses to their invitation to celebrate the engagement were flooding in and she had just got him to agree to hire a traditional accordion player to entertain the guests while the buffet was being served.

George decided to seize the moment.

"*Mela*, I've got some news of my own. I had a meeting with Camilleri and he's got a job for me, outside the country. I'm not sure how long I'll be gone. It's all a bit hush-hush."

"Well, that's exciting. How many shirts will you need?"

"It's not exactly like that."

"Well, what exactly is it like?"

"The dates are, sort of, flexible. I mean … I don't really know when I'll be back."

"How can you not know when you'll be back? How long is this going to be for? One or two days ... a week?"

"*Mela*, as I said, Camilleri wasn't sure – he said it could be up to a month."

George clenched his teeth and tensed his body. That was it, the touchpaper had been lit. It took a while for her to realise the enormity of what had just been said. She was humming a tune while wiping the dinner dishes. The humming suddenly stopped and her whole body went rigid. Marianna turned to look at him, her face twisted with disbelief.

"A month? No, that's impossible."

"I'm afraid it isn't. I've tried everything I can to get out it – but I just can't."

"You know what that means?"

"Yes, I'm sorry."

He saw the tears welling up in her eyes. Marianna threw down the tea towel and started to cry – not out of sorrow, but pure frustration. Within moments, this turned to rage and she was shaking with it. Gina came rushing into the kitchen to see what the commotion was about, and her mother told her, through sobs: "Your father has said he doesn't want to come to your party and would rather work!"

"Gina love, that's not true. I've been told I have to go away for work. I can't help it."

His daughter looked at him in disbelief.

"No, Dad, no! That can't be true! Let someone else go."

"I'm sorry, I've tried, but it has to be me."

Her wailing soon joined that of her mother, which brought Denzel, George's eldest child, rushing into the kitchen. He had graduated from the Police Cadets and was now working as a constable in the Immigration section of the Pulizija, George's old department. He looked at the wailing women and his hapless father, cowering by the sink.

"What the hell's going on?"

Marianna rounded on her son.

"I suppose you've got some lame excuse not to come to the party as well? You men – you just please yourselves and don't care about all the effort we put into things. Neither of you cares about anything!" She turned to George. "How can I invite the Assistant Commissioner, if you're not going to be here?"

Denzel was confused.

"What's this got to do with anything? Is Assistant Commissioner Camilleri coming to the engagement party?"

"No," George shouted, "he's not!" The thought of his conniving boss here in their home, patronising George's friends and family, made him shudder. Then it dawned on him – he should have paid more attention to the guest list. "Who else have you invited that I need to know about?"

The tears abruptly stopped and his wife looked at him sheepishly, with a sideways glance, her head held low. George knew immediately there was more to come.

"*Mela*, tell me who else. Tell me!"

Marianna had an incredible ability to infuriate him. He knew there was something she was hiding behind the tears and swollen eyes. She often got carried away, over-excitable even, and, when that happened, was capable of extraordinary errors of judgement. He feared this was one such occasion. What he heard next beggared belief.

"I wrote to the President to tell her it was Gina's engagement. I know she'll probably be too busy, but I thought she'd like to know, seeing as we all met her when you got your medal."

On his return from Libya, four years before, he had received the Police Medal for Bravery, from the President of the Republic, in the Grandmaster's Palace. After the presentation, they had been served refreshments and the President had briefly spoken to the family. How this gave Marianna licence to ask her to an engagement party at their house, George had no idea! The thought of Camilleri turning up made his blood run cold as it was, but this was off-the-scale lunacy.

"Are you completely insane? How can you make a fool of me

like this?"

His wife gulped and the sobbing started again.

"I thought she might like to know. She has met Gina, after all. I just wanted the party to be a success. It doesn't matter now, it's all ruined."

At this, the sobbing stopped and the wailing resumed. Denzel looked askance at his father.

"Has everyone gone mad? Where're you going anyway?"

"I can't say. Abdullah and I have been asked to sort out some police business."

Marianna leaped off the chair she had slumped into. Reinvigorated by the mention of this name, she launched back onto the attack.

"Abdullah? Where're you going with that awful man? You're never away from him. You two should just move in together! You're missing Gina's party to go gallivanting around with him? You're going to Libya again, aren't you? Oh my God, I don't believe it! Libya, with that Arab! What will Father Borg say?"

George was confused as to what any of this had to do with Father Borg. The views attributed to the Catholic priest by Marianna were often her own, introduced into their arguments as the ultimate authority on whatever was being discussed.

"He says we shouldn't spend too much time with them – you know, the migrants. It's not good for our faith."

Denzel spun on his heel.

"I can't listen to this anymore. I'm going out." He flicked Gina's hair and said: "Text me when things are back to normal."

His sister screeched after him: "Things'll never be back to normal now. My whole marriage is doomed!"

That had been just the start of it. The atmosphere in the house immediately turned ice cold. Preparations for the party continued, with Gina and Marianna ignoring George and talking about him in the third person, as if he was not even in the room. Denzel became even more elusive, missing meals and drifting in and out as he pleased. He often worked odd shifts, for the overtime.

When not at work, he played top-level amateur football and was active in the local Labour Party. George felt he might as well be living alone.

Marianna loved the status conferred on her by being the wife of a Pulizija superintendent. She loved the senior officers' garden party, the civic receptions she was invited to attend and the more glamorous social invitations that came to an officer of George's rank. She had been a poor fit at first, unpolished and lacking not just in her wardrobe, but also in the social graces of the middle-class wives. In time, her sense of humour, and propensity to say the first thing that come into her head, had gained her access to a group of the less snobby wives whom she now counted as her friends. Still, George tried to keep an eye on her as much as possible at such events, to save her from herself more than anything else.

At home, in the unpretentious suburb of Birkirkara, he feared she had turned into a shameless snob and serial namedropper. He heard her talking to neighbours in the shops and on the local high street, and often wondered what people really thought of her. Underneath the gossip and posturing, George knew Marianna was a good wife and a good person, but she had the capacity to drive him to distraction.

The day after his argument with her, he went to see Abdullah at his shop. He needed to have it out with his friend, understand why he had dragged George into this fool's errand. When he arrived, Abdullah was in a state of high excitement while in the process of handing over the care of the shop to Abeao and Mobo.

Abdullah and George had made the crossing from Libya, after their encounter with Abu Muhammad's militia, with these two Nigerian brothers. They were formerly desperate migrants who had paid to make the crossing to Malta in one of Abdullah's inflatable rafts. Abdullah had never expected to need to escape his own country in the same way, but had been glad of the former fishermen's expertise once he and George were at sea. Afterwards, the brothers had kept the secret of Abdullah's history as a trafficker and he had repaid them by giving them jobs in the shop and setting them up as small-time builders.

There were lists of suppliers, invoices, bills, orders and piles of paper all over the countertop. George looked at them. He was not sure whether the brothers could even read, let alone manage business accounts.

It was pointless mentioning it, as Abdullah was not thinking straight these days. He was too excited by the prospect of returning to Marsabar, armed with the hellfire of American weaponry. There, he would unleash his vengeance on his enemy, Abu Muhammad, who, in one cruel afternoon, had effectively ruined Abdullah's life.

The brothers stood looking at him, nodding sagely as he rambled from one aspect of the ironmongery business to the next. They paid no attention to the mounting pile of papers on the counter to which Abdullah enthusiastically pointed and waved.

Suddenly, with a loud "Hah!", he threw a pile of them up into the air.

"Papers! What good are they, eh? They will learn from day to day. These men are honest and good workers. We have more important things to do. We must go training, no?"

George scowled at his friend.

"No! No training."

Abdullah had been watching the Green Beret boot camp films on YouTube and had texted George that they needed to start a fitness campaign before meeting the American Special Forces people.

"First, I'm very pissed off that you told Camilleri I have to come with you to Libya. Why me? What business is this of mine? I have a family and Gina's engagement party is only a couple of weeks away. Marianna's furious. She's not even talking to me," George said bitterly.

"Ah, the lady wife is not pleased." Abdullah pulled a mock-despondent expression, before realising George was genuinely angry. "That is not good, I am sorry. And you will miss your daughter's party – that also is not good. But you will soon be back and she can chide you all the more then, no? I say we buy her and the beautiful Gina a big present and make them happy again!"

He beamed at George and opened his arms in an expansive gesture. Abeao and Mobo beamed too, nodding enthusiastically.

"Abdullah, you're selfish and think of no one but yourself. Fighting Abu Muhammad and retaking Marasbar has nothing to do with me. I don't want to be involved. You're going to tell Camilleri you've changed your mind and don't need me."

George made to reach for his phone. Abdullah's sinewy hand swiftly grasped his wrist. There was strength and resolution in that grip.

"Look, my brother Tareq is dead. He was my help in all things. My general. I need someone to take his place. I cannot do this alone, do you not see that? Who else can I trust with my life? Allah has given me you. What can I do? This is the will of Allah – not Abdullah!"

"*Mela*, I'm not Tareq! I'm not a soldier. I'm a pen-pushing policeman. I don't want to fight IS, radicals, extremists, jihadis or anybody else! Can't you understand? This is not my fight and I don't want to go to the desert – I hate it!"

George slapped his hand down on the counter, more loudly than he had intended. He was upset. Abeao and Mobo looked on, confused.

Mobo suddenly said: "If you want good soldiers, take us. We hate Boko Haram and all Islamic State people. They kill our parents and burn our village. We happy to kill them."

"Oh, for God's sake," George exclaimed, shaking his fists in front of him with frustration. "I think I'm going insane!"

The three of them looked at him, then at each other, confused and concerned, wondering what could possibly be wrong. At that moment George realised he would definitely be going to Libya, like it or not.

CHAPTER 11
ARTICLE IN MALTA
TELEGRAPH

Reporter: Amy Halliday

28 June 2019

Malta on Verge of Libyan Gas Deal

Sources close to Castille have confirmed that Malta could soon become reliant on gas from war-torn Libya!

In a secret deal, they say a new Maltese energy company, part- owned by the Department of Energy, has agreed terms with the Russian company Euromasio, to import billions of cubic metres of Libyan gas a year.

The deal would involve a huge project to supply gas to every home on the country's islands, significantly reducing domestic energy costs. The Russian company recently purchased the VertWay pipeline, which formerly ran from Libya to Sicily, but the terms of that agreement prohibited them from exporting gas via Italy.

Sources suggest the new deal creates a loophole by which surplus gas can then be exported to Europe, via a second pipeline to be laid between Malta and Sicily.

MEP Gianluca Borg said: "We are most concerned about a state-owned Russian energy company taking a dominant position in the supply of energy to Malta."

Mariella Gera of the Malta Green Party said: "The last thing Malta needs is to increase its consumption of fossil fuels. As a Mediterranean island, we have access to abundant wind and solar power that is chronically underdeveloped. I am also alarmed that Malta is being used as a back door, through which the Russians can undermine the EU's energy market."

The Department of Energy has not replied to our request for comment.

In related news, a Russian security company has sent over 1,000 'security advisers' to assist General Boutros's Libyan National Army, which is advancing towards Tripoli in a bid to wrest control away from the UN-backed Government of National Accord.

Unconfirmed security sources claim US-led investigations into the car bomb, that killed the US Chargé d'Affaires in St Julian's, have discovered evidence of Russian involvement. An apartment with a line of sight to the scene of the bombing was leased by a company fronted by two Russian 'businessmen', and materials found abandoned inside suggest it was from there that the bomb was triggered. It is believed the men left the island shortly after the explosion. A Pulizija spokesman declined to comment.

CHAPTER 12

YAROSLAV BUKOV
ST GEORGE'S BAY, MALTA

THE NEXT MORNING, Natasha and Marco drove the short distance to one of the large five-star hotels on St George's Bay, where they were meeting Yaroslav Bukov. They found him already seated at a shaded table on one of the wide terraces that overlooked the narrow inlet. The late-June sunshine could be intense, even by midmorning. At the head of the bay, the faint beat of music could be heard from the many outdoor bars and cafés. The narrow patch of sand that served as the only local beach was already thronged with a colourful crowd of clubbers and partygoers, relaxing and sleeping off the previous night's excesses in Paceville's club land.

Yaroslav had made an effort for the meeting, discarding his usual designer leisure wear for a blue-and-white-striped business shirt and light grey suit. He took off his sunglasses and rose politely to greet Natasha and Marco.

She had decided to take a back seat during the meeting, to let her father and Yaroslav try to establish some sort of relationship.

The Russian was speaking.

"Now, we replace a large section of the VertWay pipeline from Libya, and we survey route for new spur to Malta. So, we're ready for starting to lay pipe. Moscow tells me assault on

Tripoli is beginning and our advisers and Volunteers say the city will soon be ours. Then, we have access to gas plant and oil fields!"

Marco nodded and said: "Still, that is a big concern. You are promising something that is not yet yours."

He remembered Natasha's description of the man's arrogance as the Russian dismissed this fundamental problem with a wave of his hand.

"Not to worry about that. Big problem is here, in Malta. You need to build many things and it is complicated work."

Yaroslav sat back in his chair, pausing the conversation, while he appraised Marco.

"So, who is this 'Family'? One person tell me the Family is masonic lodge, with Pope for boss; another, he say Family is worldwide Mafia!" Yaroslav rolled his eyes dramatically. "Then, a very intelligent man say to me, no, none of these. You are state within state, like Putin, but better, as very private! So, yes, my question to you is, 'Who is Family?'"

Marco studied Yaroslav, his expression unchanging.

"You are right – and, if it helps, over the centuries we have been all of those things. Today we are just a private consortium of old families who jointly do business."

Marco smiled serenely.

"I can say no more."

Yaroslav sat back in his chair.

"I like to know who we do business with."

"Would you like to see a bank statement?"

There was silence for several seconds as the men scrutinised each other. Finally, Yaroslav shook his head and said: "No. It's OK you don't tell me. All is OK as long as the money is good and ready, and I can trust your word. If that is not how it is, then I get on plane for Moscow – no questions."

"I would expect nothing less."

"So, Miss Natasha tells me Salvatore speaks with Italian operators who own pipelines in Italy, taking our gas all over Europe.

That is going good. But I worry there's not good progress in Malta. How do you make all this happen?"

Marco looked at him with the patience of an understanding father, indulging a misbehaving teenager.

"Yaroslav, this is my territory. I am not a technical man, but I know my countrymen. At heart, they are small-island people in a big bad world. If you bully them, they will back away and close themselves off. Then you will get nowhere.

"If you do it my way, the deal will happen because everybody wants it to happen – because there is money to be made. Lots of money. There is a man who helps me with this sort of thing very close to the seat of power, but not hampered by it. He is a practical man who sees the big picture, a businessman in a politician's suit. He will work with me. Not us – me. I prefer to stay one step back. It is better that way."

Yaroslav smiled. He liked Marco. He was a different proposition altogether from his nose-in-the-air daughter.

"Ah, now we have it. I can tell that is good. You see, Natasha, your father knows how to make things happen. But you need to start the works. We will be old men soon! So, I am going away – for maybe one month – I have work to do abroad. Always work. *Yaroslav, go here; Yaroslav, go there*! You do your work, with your politician who is not politician, on buildings, tariffs and the concessions. If there is not good progress when I come back, well, people will not be happy. OK?"

Natasha listened to Yaroslav, with his bad manners and loud mouth, his voice carrying indiscreetly around the terrace. She started to think there had to be a better way of doing this deal than committing themselves to a partnership with these people. Her own words came back to haunt her. *'We don't do business with Russians because it always ends badly. That's been our experience over the course of the last two hundred years.'*

Then she thought about the bomb in St Julian's. The island was awash with rumours about who was behind that but, thinking about it, there could only be one answer. The Americans were very pissed off and she wondered who would dare twist their tail. She smiled to herself – there was something in that line of thought …

Marco's voice broke in.

"So, your partners in the LNA – I suppose with sanctions and Tripoli controlling the oil money, the eastern militias must have funding problems. Who are the biggest supporters? It costs money to wage a war, even a civil war. If we are going into business with you, we need to know your commitment to their cause."

"Ah! You don't answer my question about who is Family, yet you ask me about our money. Not a fair question, is it?"

"It is. It is directly related to your ability to do the deal. We do not want it to fail because the LNA run out of money and Tripoli kick you out of the Marsabar refinery and gas plant."

Yaroslav smiled broadly and wagged a finger at Marco.

"No, very good thinking. So, the Saudis, Egyptians and French all give money to the General Boutros. But we also give much cash, to pay for government, soldiers, fuel, weapons and so on. Big bundles of Libyan dinars, printed in Moscow."

Marco leaned forward, obviously interested.

"You have been supplying cash?" He was more than surprised. "So how much are we talking about?"

Yaroslav was a shameless show off, a dangerous trait for a man in his position.

"Well, last shipment filled two shipping containers. It was one billion Libyan dinars. And that was not first shipment."

Marco was doing the mental arithmetic. He looked at Natasha.

"That is about three-quarters of a billion US dollars! In cash!"

"A lot of money, no? Russian Mint prints the money. We move it by train from Moscow to Novorossiysk, a container port on Black Sea, and then to main shipping hub in Istanbul, then into Benghazi. We expect next shipment to leave last week of next month. I go to Libya myself to organise handover and try to stop too much stealing by LNA. You put cash in warzone – what happens?"

"What, you just send it though standard shipping channels? That much money?"

"Yes, it's OK. It's tracked every mile of journey, but really it's worth nothing, only its weight in blended cotton and linen. Who wants Libyan dinars except for Libyans? General Boutros wants payment in cash, so every time he can be first to steal some, yes? It is always the same, all over the world."

With a smile, Yaroslav gathered his cigarettes and threw a fifty-euro note on the table.

"Good meeting. It is nice to talk to you, Marco, and to see you again, Natasha."

They stood and he shook Marco's hand, then turned to leer at Natasha and gently press her fingers with his. She fought an urge to physically recoil.

She had been sitting back and listening carefully. She was now certain this was her chance to do something that would have a real impact on the Family in Milan, but could not see it happening with this uncultured lech and his fellow Russians.

The gas project was a golden opportunity, and the idea of billions of dinars floating down the Bosphorus a fascinating prospect. If they were to deliver this project without the Russians, they would need to snare another partner with the money, muscle, technical capabilities and motivation to step into their shoes. Realistically speaking, there was only one option.

CHAPTER 13
YAROSLAV BUKOV
SIRTE BASIN, LIBYA

BAYDA LIES ON A HIGH RIDGE, thirty kilometres from the Mediterranean and 600 metres above it. They call it the White City, not because of its white-plastered buildings but because, uniquely in Libya, it occasionally gets snowfall in winter.

In 1960 it was a new town, built by the recently installed monarchy as the future capital city of an emerging, independent, oil-rich Libya. However, things did not turn out that way. Following Gaddafi's coup in 1969, the business of state remained in Tripoli.

That left Bayda with its glossy white Parliament building and a newly built central bank that was supposed to run the finances of the upstart government in the east. All well and good but, if you went inside the bank, you would not see any desks, computers or people. Tripoli kept the oil, so Tripoli kept the money.

Yaroslav had arrived in Libya a week ago, leaving Malta the day after his meeting with Marco and Natasha. He had flown from Malta to Cairo and then driven west for thirteen hours, to Benghazi, where he met Lev Artamonov. He led a group of approximately one hundred volunteers, part of Russkaya Volonterskaya Gruppa – a well-funded security company that had furthered Russian interests in the Ukraine, Syria, the Congo and elsewhere around the globe. The Kremlin was frequently called upon to deny any association with this well-equipped, private army of ex-special forces soldiers.

While Marco politicked in Malta, Yaroslav had been asked by Valentin Petrov to check out their plan to increase output from the oil fields in the Sirte Basin, a place rich in hydrocarbons, some 200 miles inland from the 'Oil Crescent' on the Libyan Coast. He could do the surveys and be back in time to meet the container of cash due to be off-loaded in Benghazi at the end of the month.

The desktop work on the oil fields all spoke of impressive and accessible reserves, but nobody really knew what the situation was like on the ground, at the sites and plants. In the late-1960s, the Sirte Basin had produced more oil than Saudi Arabia, but nationalisation, the war with Chad, embargos, Gaddafi and now the civil war had all reduced output to a fraction of what it had been and what it could be again.

The biggest problem was security – production was frequently halted due to strikes over safety concerns and the difficulty of recruiting skilled workers into an area where kidnaps, shootings and harassment were commonplace.

Yaroslav filled in Lev on the purpose of his visit.

"So, a trip south should be a welcome change for you. I've got a list of seven sites I want to visit, mainly in the Sirte Basin. Security OK down there?"

"It depends. IS-in-Libya come up from Chad and Western Sudan, drive around, make trouble, upset everybody, then disappear. They want us to give up trying to run the fields, so they can just walk in. If they did, they wouldn't have a clue what to do. Ignorant bastards!"

Yaroslav knew differently. Islamic State groups in Iraq did have the knowhow and the logistics, but whether those capabilities had survived the defeats in that country and Syria was anyone's guess.

Lev continued: "At the moment, recon says a handful of technicals have been seen in the area, but nothing we can't handle. They look like they run with the Islamist group led by Abu Muhammad al-Najafi. He's mostly been active in the west but now he's showed up down here."

'Technicals' was army slang for the thousands of Toyota flatbed trucks and other pickups that sped around the deserts and plains of Africa and the Middle East, fitted out with machine guns, rocket launchers or cannons. Compared to armoured military equipment, they were cheap to buy, run and repair, and agile enough to outsmart most heavy motorised weaponry. They were the ideal weapon for hit-and-run militias.

Yaroslav said nothing to Lev, but he was surprised to hear the name Abu Muhammad. It was his militia that had been paid to make the attack on the Marsabar oil and gas complex in the west of the country, to scare off the Italians. Yaroslav thought it strange Abu Muhammad was now operating as far east as the Sirte Basin.

———

Their trip was uneventful. After two days, the convoy reached Jalu, about 200 kilometres south of the coast, the area where the Islamic State-in-Libya militia had last been sighted. Lev had ordered a stop just outside the town, so he could send some pickups to find fuel, before hitting the desert further south.

Yaroslav had climbed onto the roof of the Land Cruiser and spread his jacket over the white-hot metal, flopping down onto it to enjoy the sun, but still catch such breeze as there was. He was in that far-away state that came from hours of driving down long, straight, hypnotic desert roads, with nothing to see but endless, colourless scrub, set against clear blue skies. All conversation had long since dried up and the group in the vehicle had become locked into the torpor of the journey. Yaroslav had just shut his eyes when he became aware of one of Lev's officers running across the scrub towards them. He was shouting as he sprinted away from the command truck.

"We've got two militia vehicles, six kilometres south but coming north on the desert road, moving fast. They're heading towards one of the Waha oil fields. If we're quick, we can intercept them – or we can radio in and let the drone take them."

"Let's not waste drone missiles! The boys could do with some action. It'll wake them up. Take two personnel carriers, the ones with autocannons. Ask for a grid reference for the intercept and get to it. Can we get a visual on this?"

Yaroslav listened to the orders being shouted and watched the men spring into action. He had instantly become fully alert and could sense excitement rising around him as the Volunteers organised themselves, strapping on body armour and tactical belts, then throwing ammunition and supplies between the vehicles.

Within minutes, the two armoured personnel carriers revved their engines and trundled off, amidst a cloud of dust. After twenty minutes of anxious waiting, Lev shouted at Yaroslav and he joined Lev and two others around the laptop on a bench in the back of the command truck. Yaroslav felt his heart beating fast. It had been a while since he had been involved in any combat action, so he had forgotten the thrill of an attack and the energy radiating from pumped-up professional soldiers.

They watched the lead armoured personnel carrier drive out of a side gully straight into the path of the first IS pick-up truck. The IS technicals slid to a halt, throwing a cloud of dust and gravel into the air. From their silent drone feed, they saw a fighter jump out of the rear door and leap behind, onto the deck of the truck, to start readying the twin-barrelled machine gun.

Before the fighter could fire a shot, the personnel carrier opened up with its twin-barrelled autocannon. It fired explosive shells into both pickups at an alarming rate. On the screen, it looked like jets of flame were spurting between the two vehicles. The first IS truck was pushed around the road by the impact of the shells and was soon in flames. The doors had been flung open and two bodies were lying on the road.

There were shouts and yells of excitement from the Russians watching inside the truck. Yaroslav found himself joining them and excitedly banging his fist on the roof above him.

The grainy picture on the laptop screen showed the second vehicle trying to turn away from the clash, but its engine seemed to be running out of power. Its machine gun was manned and flickers of light and a jolting movement told them it was returning fire.

The second personnel carrier drove through the burning wreckage of the first pickup and blasted the fleeing vehicle from behind. Bullets from the mounted machine gun bounced off the carrier's thick armour plating. The hydraulic ramps at the rear of the personnel carriers were lowered and a team of Volunteers quickly jumped out of each vehicle.

There were more cheers and shouts from inside the truck as they watched aerial footage of the Russians finishing off lightly armed militia fighters who tried to flee across the rough scrubland. The Volunteers in the truck were cheering on their comrades in pursuit of the fleeing men and no one was shouting more loudly than Yaroslav.

Lev was watching intently. Yaroslav heard him say to the sergeant on the radio: "Don't kill them all. We need at least one of them to get back and tell them we're onto them!"

Just then, they heard what sounded like an explosion outside. At first, Yaroslav thought it had come from the drone feed, but then he felt the blast waves and everyone inside the comms vehicle instantly fell silent. They stood looking at each other, registering the shock of what they feared had happened. Before anybody could say a word, the rear door was swung open by the tip of an automatic weapon.

A voice speaking perfect English said: "Gentlemen, please put down any weapons. It would be a shame to have to clear you out with a grenade."

Yaroslav, who was probably the most fluent English speaker present, felt his stomach sink as the excitement of the attack was suddenly replaced by hard-biting fear. The voice belonged to a young, heavily built man with a bushy black beard, wearing a brown shirt buttoned to the neck and a green and brown camouflage jacket, a stained pakol beret perched on his head. Sweat was running down his face and he was breathing heavily. Outside, the chatter of automatic weapons and shouts of guttural Arabic voices could be heard.

The Englishman kept smiling, observing the drone feed they had been watching.

"When you charge out of the front door, always make sure the back door's locked. You never know who might come in! Who's the oil man?"

Lev involuntarily glanced towards Yaroslav. It was enough.

"Good," said the bearded man, "now we're getting somewhere. You! Out, now!"

He pointed his gun at Yaroslav and motioned for him to move. Yaroslav looked to Lev for help, but he just stared back blankly, keeping his hands raised in front of him. Yaroslav jumped out of the shaded rear of the truck into the desert light. There were four Volunteers lying on the ground, brown blood soaking into the dirt around them. The fighters were stripping them of weapons, ammunition and other gear.

They herded the remaining dozen Volunteers, as well as some LNA militia who had accompanied them, against a low rocky outcrop on the side of the road. The other personnel carrier was lying idle, black smoke pouring from the windows. It had been hit by armour-piercing shells from the cannons on one of the five IS technicals that had surrounded them.

It had been a carefully executed trap. The IS militia had seen the drone over the desert road and come out to tempt them to split their forces. The decoy had worked. They had correctly guessed expensive missiles would not be wasted on a couple of technicals. Once they knew the Volunteers were distracted, watching the action in the next valley, they had struck. It was typical of the ruthlessness of Abu Muhammad that he was prepared to sacrifice his own men in the ambush, to win the bigger prize.

The Englishman walked towards Yaroslav, gun loosely held but pointing directly at him. The Russian desperately tried to control the fit of shaking that had taken hold of him. He knew he could be minutes away from death.

"Get in the truck. Put your hands on the dash."

The inside of the truck was filthy, every surface thick with desert grit, and cigarette packets and plastic bottles in the footwells. The windscreen was caked in dust and insects, apart from two scallop shell shapes made by the windscreen wipers. The Englishman got into the driver's side of the truck, kicking the litter to one side, took a cable tie from the glove compartment and slipped it around Yaroslav's wrists, pulling it tight, making him wince as the nylon strap dug into his flesh. The fighter then fastened Yaroslav's arms above the level of his shoulders with a second tie attached to the grab bar over the door. Satisfied that the prisoner was secured inside the vehicle, the Englishman got out of the truck and shouted in Arabic towards the rest of the fighters who were making their way back to the pickups.

Yaroslav allowed himself to breathe out. It sounded like a whimper. They were not going to kill him just yet. Then he saw one of the fighters peel off and walk back towards the Comms truck. He took something from a cloth bag that was slung across one shoulder. He fiddled with it and threw it into the back of the truck. There was some shouting, followed by a dull blast. The truck bounced up into the air and smoke streamed out of the rear of the vehicle.

Yaroslav could not believe what he had just seen. There were cries and screams. Lev tumbled out and fell flat onto the scrubby ground. He rolled once, his arms around his head, then lay still, smoke slowly rising from his body. Yaroslav twisted against the tie to see half a dozen fighters start to fire their automatic weapons at the dozen Volunteers and LNA militia fighters standing against the rocks. Some fell and some ran, but the result was the same in every case. The Englishman stood by the open driver's door, calmly smoking a cigarette and watching. He glanced down to see how Yaroslav was taking it all.

"This is war, Russian. I thought you would've known that."

Yaroslav was numb with shock and the shaking made him incapable of speech. He could only look at the Englishman, wide-eyed in disbelief.

Many were not killed outright but died as the IS fighters wandered around between the prone bodies, despatching them with head shots and bursts of automatic fire. Yaroslav felt the bile rise from deep in his stomach and, to find relief, had to bend, as best he could, and retch.

With that, the fighters lit more cigarettes, laughed and chatted between themselves, before making ready to leave. One came and slipped onto the back deck of their vehicle and the Englishman fired the engine. They headed south at speed, the third man sitting out on the bed of the truck, using binoculars to scour the sky for the returning drone. Yaroslav figured the plume of dust from the speeding vehicles would be visible for miles. He shuddered at the irony of being killed by a missile from their own aerial spy.

After thirty minutes of being bounced around inside the speeding truck, they came to the junction of two dirt tracks and the Englishman peeled off to the left, while the main convoy raced south towards the border with Chad. Some hundred yards later, they bumped into a rough camp and drove under a roof of camouflage netting, held up with scaffold poles embedded in concrete blocks. The nets concealed the makeshift camp from drones and satellites, but also provided some shade from the intense afternoon sun. The Englishman killed the engine.

"So, we wait here till dark. Your drone can chase the others, if they think it's worth it."

With that, he got out of the Toyota and went to a small shipping container, hidden under more nets, in a low gully. From there he fetched two small bottles of water. He threw one to the fighter who had been on the back of the truck and returned to the vehicle. He leaned on the roof and pushed his head through the window, looking at Yaroslav. He drank the water, beads of moisture spilling down his thick black beard. His dark brown eyes never left Yaroslav's. Putting the top back on, he grinned and threw the half-full bottle onto the driver's seat.

"Go on, oil man. Have a drink! It's five hours till sundown. There's some shade, but I think it'll get warm in there!" With that, he laughed and turned away.

With his hands bound to the grab bar, there was no way Yaroslav could get to the water. He slumped against the door and rested his head against the window. Fear and shock finally found release in the tears that ran down his cheeks, leaving streaks through the film of fine desert dust that had covered his face.

CHAPTER 14

ARTICLE IN MALTA TELEGRAPH

REPORTER: *Amy Halliday*

17 July 2019

EU Cautions Against Gas Deal with Russia

The Department of Energy has confirmed that negotiations are progressing well to allow Euromasio, a Russian state-owned company, to become the supplier of Libyan gas to Malta. The department is set to grant concessions to MalTech Energy, the mysterious new energy company that will have a monopoly on the gas supply to Maltese homes, as well as exporting Libyan gas into Europe.

EU officials have voiced concern over the lack of transparency of MalTech Energy, owned by a British Virgin Island trust. This arrangement hides the true beneficial ownership of the company and its sources of funding. Representatives from the Department of Energy said they have completed their due diligence into these matters and are satisfied with the explanations they have received, but refused to answer further questions.

Opposition MP Carmelo Gauci said: "It is bad enough allowing the Russians to hold the country hostage, but now we are handing over the profits to a group of shareholders who hide in the shadows of a complex offshore trust. The Panama Papers showed us how they work! It is not only we Maltese who will be the losers, we are also giving these people a back door to sell gas into Europe."

There have been objections from Brussels to MalTech Energy's plans to build a pipeline to Pozzallo, Sicily, giving access to Europe's independent energy transmission networks. These networks had previously been national assets of individual member states, until the EU ordered their privatisation to boost competition. There are fears that cheap Libyan gas will destabilise existing supply arrangements, as well as increasing dependence on the capricious Russian government and a politically unstable regime in Libya.

Sources inside the Prime Minister's Office in Castille said there was growing concern that the project was proceeding so quickly, despite the fact it relied on General Boutros Boutros's rival Libyan National Army deposing the Government of National Accord in Tripoli. The Tripoli government is recognised as the legitimate authority in Libya by the UN, the EU, and has many friends in Malta.

CHAPTER 15

NATASHA BONNICI
CASTELLO BONNICI, MALTA

CASTELLO BONNICI SAT on top of a long ridge that bisected the island at its narrowest part. From here you could look both east and west and see twin flashes of deep blue as the Mediterranean Sea lapped against the two coastlines. Like most Maltese buildings, the *castello* was constructed from local limestone which, in the flat winter light, could look drab and uninviting. It came alive in the summer sunshine when the stone took on the warm hue of Gozitan honey.

The *castello*'s extensive flagged terrace overlooked Marco's formal gardens and stretched the length of the house, on the north-eastern side. For most of the year, this was where the Bonnicis spent their time. Weather permitting, breakfast was always taken in the gentle morning sunshine, and it was their custom also to meet there for pre-dinner drinks. This evening they had turned their table to face west and were watching the sun going down behind the Marfa escarpment, together with their guest, Assistant Commissioner Gerald Camilleri.

It had come as a surprise to receive Camilleri's call. Strictly speaking, he was not a friend of theirs, but was retained by the Family to look after their interests on his territory. He knew everybody and everything that happened on the island so, when he said he had some urgent business to discuss, the Bonnicis were intrigued.

Although Camilleri seemed at ease, lounging back in his high-backed wicker chair, his long spider-like legs were crossing and uncrossing like those of an agitated marionette. Natasha could tell he was nervous. As always, his formality made no concessions to the beautiful spring evening. He was wearing his usual garb – a grey double-breasted pinstripe suit, with a white shirt and unassuming navy tie.

Marco poured him some sparkling water and topped up Natasha's wine. Camilleri took a pack of cigarettes and a lighter from his jacket pocket and started smoking. Then they got down to business.

"So, Gerald, we are curious. To what do we owe this pleasure?"

Camilleri clasped his hands together, narrowing his eyes as he stared at them. His speech was measured and, most likely, carefully rehearsed.

"I hope I can speak both as an old friend of yours and a servant of Malta? I know that sounds pompous, but I am worried by the current turn of events concerning the gas supply arrangements with Libya."

Marco nodded. "Go on, Gerald. Anybody who fails to listen when you express concern is a fool. You have our attention."

"I fear the current direction of travel may not be in your long-term best interests. I might be wrong and, please, if I speak out of turn, just raise a hand and I will stop immediately. We can forget this conversation ever took place.

"I am aware of your arrangements with the Russians – who is not? Also, that you have commissioned Edward Refalo to help you negotiate with Castille."

Refalo was an old acquaintance of Marco's and a former minister whose connections with the current administration ran deep. He was an operator in the private sector now because, while in public office, he had seemed incapable of recognising a conflict of interest if it bit him on the nose.

Marco and Refalo were currently busy all over the island, negotiating concessions, construction permits, distribution agreements and more. They were establishing the physical and commercial arrangements necessary to bring the gas ashore and construct the new pipeline to Sicily.

Camilleri continued speaking.

"There can be no doubt that Libyan gas is a good thing for the island. It is an excellent opportunity to become a player in the European energy markets and, make no mistake, I am fully supportive of the Family's efforts to acquire an interest in it.

"But I am also worried about the articles in the *Malta Telegraph*. They seem to be very accurate and the journalist, Amy Halliday, must have an inside source who keeps on giving. People are becoming concerned and that will be a problem for you, Marco. You understand me?"

"I have read the pieces – some are true and some are wide of the mark."

"Marco, it does not matter what is true and what is not. People believe what she says and there is certainly no love felt for the Russians on this island. You know that. The idea that we should tie the country's energy supply to them is unacceptable in many quarters, especially when there is an alternative. It cannot be good for the project and we do not wish this opportunity to slip through your fingers."

Marco was intrigued.

"An alternative?"

"Yes."

"Go on."

Camilleri shifted in his chair, crossing and uncrossing his spindly shins.

"My investigators tell me the bombing of the American Chargé d'Affaires' residence was the work of the Russians. The Americans have been watching the disruptive Russian involvement in Libya closely and they do not like what they see. In fact, I am told they are on the verge of entering the conflict themselves, and soon. I do not know any details, but you can see how this reflects on your arrangements. In short, I am worried you may be backing the wrong horse."

Marco was shocked. He picked up his glass of wine and glanced at Natasha as he took a sip. After a few moments, he sighed and said: "Hmmm … well, Gerald, that is worrying news indeed."

Marco looked again at his daughter, sitting perfectly still, with a neutral expression on her face.

The Assistant Commissioner continued speaking.

"Once the Americans enter the Libyan theatre, political and commercial pressure will be exerted by the EU to support US efforts, in both the commercial and military spheres, you know that. Western powers have always used Malta in their military and commercial operations in North Africa."

Marco replied, "But we are not even a member of NATO and, technically, non-aligned to it. We refuel the Russian Navy, for God's sake!"

"Come on, Marco, you have to agree, the EU, the US and NATO itself would not countenance Malta becoming an ally of the Russian Federation, even in the most notional sense. This is bigger than a few cubic metres of gas.

"I do not wish to interfere in your business affairs, but there is certainly a feeling you are helping the Russians into Europe by stealth, which is going to make it difficult to get the support you need to deliver the project. Or, at least, that is what I am hearing on the ground."

Marco stood up and paced across the terrace, taking up position next to one of the *castello*'s life-size Neoclassical marble statues.

He looked at Camilleri.

"May I ask how close you are to those who think this way?"

"Since the murder of the Chargé d'Affaires, I have been

working with American security and have been brought into their circle. The Russians organised the St Julian's bomb, to mark their turf and deter the US from getting involved in Libya. I am afraid it has backfired badly on them. Also, I like my friends to be winners, not losers."

Natasha put down her glass and, with a nod to Camilleri, said: "Dad, I hear what Gerald's saying and I think he's right. Amy Halliday's articles have certainly had an impact. Maybe that's why it's proving such a struggle to get the agreements we need here. But if it's not the Russians we partner with, then who?"

Camilleri said, "I think the Americans have one or two ideas about who might step into those big boots. The US administration and their international energy companies have strong ties."

"You are suggesting that the Americans will offer themselves as an alternative partner?" Marco asked.

Camilleri nodded his head very slightly in confirmation.

"Well, we cannot do anything until I have spoken to the Wise Men. And I will also have to find a way of stalling our friend Yaroslav Bukov when he gets back."

Camilleri smiled and said: "I think you may find your Mr Bukov has other things on his mind at the moment. My American friends tell me he is being held by an Islamic State militia in southern Libya."

It was Natasha's turn to express shock.

"Really? What was he doing there?"

"Apparently, he went to survey some oil fields needed to provide the gas and crude for the project, and got himself captured in the southern desert. An Islamic State militia is trailing him round the oil fields, using him as a consultant. When they have finished with him, they will either ransom or kill him."

Natasha tried to supress a short laugh that turned into a snort.

Her father glared at her.

"I'm sorry, but he isn't one of my favourite people, although I wouldn't wish that fate on anyone. Poor Yaroslav!"

Camilleri looked at her mirthlessly, thinking her remark in poor taste.

"Well, Gerald, as always, our meeting has been illuminating and thought provoking," her father said.

"One last thing, Marco: an ironic twist that may amuse you. The Americans are building a militia around Abdullah Belkacem – you recall, the warlord from Marsabar who caused so much trouble with our oil deal a few years ago? Mr Belkacem has insisted on taking my very own Superintendent George Zammit with him, as a special adviser. Small world, is it not?"

Marco nearly choked on his wine.

"What! Gerald, nothing about that time amuses me, although maybe sending Belkacem back is not such a bad idea … I hear he was quite somebody back in his day. But what on earth is your officer going for?"

"Good question, Marco. A very good question."

With that, Camilleri stood, shook hands, politely kissed Natasha on both cheeks and left.

Marco returned from walking the Assistant Commissioner to his car and slumped into a chair. He grabbed his glass and leaned back, legs extended in front of him. A thought had occurred to him while he walked back onto the terrace.

"You have never liked our Russian involvement, have you?"

"I've made no secret of it, I suppose."

"But you are happier now the Americans might step up?"

"Yes, I definitely am."

"I suppose we should be grateful for Amy Halliday's articles, then?"

There was a pause.

"Yep," Natasha admitted. "I mean, we would've realised it ourselves at some point. It's true, I never liked dealing with the Russians, and especially not Bukov. He was a bully and a thug and too used to getting his own way. He was also a lech. The thought of doing business with him for years to come … Well, it wasn't a pleasant prospect."

Marco looked carefully at this daughter. Something here did not feel quite right. She had taken the proposed change of tack in her stride and seemed unnaturally calm and composed. He could not put his finger on it, but it was almost as though she had expected it …

Marco dismissed such a thought from his mind.

"Well, setting personal antipathies aside, we do not have to worry about him now. I am not sure Salvatore will be supportive of a change of plan at this stage. I doubt he is particularly sensitive to geopolitical considerations. Only the Family's views count for him."

"So, you're going to tell him?"

"Well, yes. And the sooner the better. I will play the 'what is best for Malta, is best for the Family' card. We will see what happens."

CHAPTER 16
SUPERINTENDENT GEORGE ZAMMIT

SUPERINTENDENT GEORGE
ZAMMIT

GEORGE WAS MISERABLE. Even his departure from home had not gone well. He had decided to play it cool, given that Marianna and Gina were still not talking to him. On the day itself, he had taken his pick from a pile of newly ironed clothes and quietly packed his suitcase. Then he had gone to see his daughter, who stood stony-faced, peeling vegetables in the kitchen.

"I have to go, Gina. Official business. I'm sorry I can't be at the party but I don't have any choice in the matter. I've got to work. One day you'll understand. Have a lovely time and I'll make it up to you once I'm back and we're all talking to each other again. OK?"

No reply.

"Where's your mother?"

Her bottom lip had protruded, but her stare remained fixed on the courgette she was destroying. She had said nothing but pointed towards the corridor leading to the bedrooms. Marianna was nowhere to be seen.

George had shouted: "I'm off then. See you in a couple of weeks."

Then he paused. Still no reply. Denzel had been waiting in the hall, in uniform, jangling his car keys.

"Come on, Dad. You know what they're like. They'll both be in tears as soon as you close the door."

George had checked his pockets to make sure he had his passport and tickets, slid into Denzel's Subaru and they had set off for the airport.

To George, that all seemed such a long time ago, even though they had only been on the base for ten days. It was a six-hour direct flight from Malta to Doha and the Americans had booked them into business class. Abdullah had never enjoyed such luxury, although he looked disapproving as George accepted a gin and tonic, followed by an endless supply of red wine.

"Enjoy it, my friend. Where we go now, it is water, tea or fruit juice only!"

George did not normally drink a lot, but had become more and more nervous as the flight progressed. He had no idea what they were heading into. He was also slightly unnerved by the change in Abdullah's behaviour. He had pulled back, no longer his chatty and friendly self, and become withdrawn; he, too, seemed anxious. His expression had hardened and his smile was more tense. George understood. Much was expected of him and he expected much of himself. Happily, George was not burdened with such high expectations.

It was only later that Abdullah confided he had never been in an aeroplane before and the experience had terrified him.

On arrival, they had been met and taken by a military SUV on the thirty-minute drive from Hamad International Airport to the Al-Udeid US Air Base. Once inside, they had both been amazed by the sheer scale of it.

The buildings were all camouflaged against the desert sand and rock. They were largely prefabricated units, with rusted air-conditioning systems protruding like ugly tumours. The planes, dozens of them in all shapes and sizes, nestled under large tented structures, to protect them from the scorching sun. Where the fabric was torn or frayed, the canopies fluttered in a stiff breeze, heavy with dust. Even the cheerful branding of the Pizza Hut and Coffee Beanery could not lift the desolate mood of the place.

Abdullah had given George a grim nod before he was directed to his room, up a short, galvanised-steel staircase and into a grimy building, carrying his personal possessions in a red and yellow Birkirkara FC sports bag. George's accommodation was no better. It was dark and at the end of a corridor. It held a bed, a desk and a wardrobe. The window was shuttered and there was a sign saying it was to remain closed at all times. The air conditioner rattled and clattered incessantly, as if a refrigerated truck had been reversed into the wall.

The driver had given him a map of the site, a security pass on a lanyard, and directions for where and when to show up for an orientation meeting. He had also passed over a thick envelope addressed to 'Superintendent George Zammit – Recruit 008/9765'. It had contained a set of instructions headed: 'The Basics of Desert Warfare – Induction Course'. It told George where to collect his equipment, where to attend for a haircut and a description of what was to come. A handwritten amendment then instructed him he was not after all required to attend the barber's as he was 'assuming an Arab identity'.

The advance materials had been blunt and to the point. The focus of the course was to teach the skills necessary to survive in the 'blistering hot sun and frigid nights of desert climates', as well as training in 'direct action combat skills at team and squad levels'.

George had tried to imagine what that might involve. He had not liked the sound of it at all.

Outside the airfield perimeter, the US Army had access to one million acres of desert, where the battlefield training took place. 'This involves a live-fire exercise and hand to hand combat skills,' he read on.

They were to be dumped in the middle of this nothingness, with a compass and a protractor, no GPS or support, and would then be required to find their way back. All George had been able to think was that a person could die out there.

After that, the document said they would spend two days on 'desert survival training: building shelters; starting fires; finding, collecting and filtering water; and setting snares and traps to catch food'. Then, they were expected to put this all into practice with a 72–hour field exercise, where trainees would be divided into squads for 'clashes' with an opposing force of troops, selected from the Green Berets stationed on the base!

By the time he had finished reading the file, he had been panic-stricken. He had to find Abdullah straightway and get him to explain there had been some terrible misunderstanding. This was not what George had signed up for. But he never seemed to get to see his friend, who was busy with the senior Ranger officers, planning strategy and logistics.

George was placed in the care of Sergeant Mario Barrasso, a small squat man with a shaved head and no eyebrows. He was a veteran of the Iraq Wars and had been training what he considered to be 'idiots like you' for too long to stay sane. He ran with the troops, carrying a full twenty-kilo pack, trained with the troops and shouted at the troops. The young guys loved him. George was terrified of him and he did not think much of George, either.

Barrasso and the other trainers soon realised George's limitations, after he collapsed during a twenty-kilometre forced march around the base perimeter. George thought it was barbaric to force people to walk that distance in late July, when it was nearly 40 degrees outside. To his relief, Barrasso told him that, given he was not a genuine recruit to the Army Rangers or the Green Berets, he could sit out some of the rough stuff. He was appointed squad medic and for two days attended a hands-on class in basic battlefield medical techniques, using the US Army's latest *Tactical Combat Casualty Care* protocols.

He was fascinated to learn how to stop traumatic bleeding from gunshot and knife wounds, using the latest pressure bandages and tourniquets. He studied field-fracture immobilisation, clearing airways, wound-cleaning and disinfection, the injection of local anaesthesia and wound closures. When he returned from the course, George actually felt a sense of achievement. He was quickly called into action, to tend a broken arm after a soldier fell out of the back of a moving truck.

He had always had a good eye on the police range so, when it came to marksmanship and the live firing exercises, he excelled. He enjoyed handling the military-grade weapons and could keep a steady aim, despite their weight and powerful recoil. He fired battle rifles, automatic weapons and even a fully automatic SAM machine gun. Sergeant Barrasso looked twice at him when George told him he had already used a mounted Browning machine gun, fighting Islamic State militia in Libya.

"Well, hear that, soldiers. Stay close to Zammit, he's the man. He shot up the ISILs!"

At the end of the day on the range, Sergeant Barrasso even complimented him when he addressed the squad, saying: "In this team, everyone has a role – you may not believe it, but even Special Agent Zammit has his uses!"

By the end of the ten days, George was starting to enjoy himself. He could light fires, catch and skin small mammals, and filter dirty water. He was always a good sleeper and a night in the desert, in a military sleeping system bag, did not prevent him from enjoying hours of solid sleep. He only woke up when Barrasso shook him and told him there were complaints about his snoring from downtown Doha.

All that changed the next day, during the seventy-two-hour field training exercise, when twenty Green Berets rushed the recruits' camp in the middle of the night, hitting them with batons and tearing down their rough shelters. George was so shocked at the screaming, shouting and fighting that he leaped out of his sleeping bag, only to be lashed across the back of the head with a wooden truncheon. Dazed and bleeding, he fell semi-conscious into a gully.

His squad scattered and, conceding defeat, some made their way back to the Al-Udeid base, whilst others were held 'captive' by the Green Berets. As a result, a full head count was never taken. It was only when the two groups were reconciled in the morning that they realised they were a man down.

As the freezing night turned into the blazing heat of day, George awoke from a deep sleep in the wrecked camp, miles away from the airfield, nursing the cut on the back of his head and feeling sorry for himself. He restored one of the shelters they had built, to protect himself from the sun, and started a fire, as instructed, making as much smoke as possible, in the hope someone would eventually come looking for him. Smoke from the dried sticks and bits of leaf rose vertically in a thin thread into the sky of a perfect desert morning.

After thirty minutes or so his head was really hurting, so he decided to lie down on his bag, in the shade of his shelter, as the night's excitement began to catch up with him.

What seemed like an age later, he woke with a start and saw there were two soldiers kneeling over him, in full combat gear, staring at him intently.

"OK, buddy, where're you hurt? We've got a head injury here," one of them observed.

The other had a small laminated sheet in his hand and was reading from it.

"I think he's a Priority 3 casualty. There's no imminent risk to life, so we progress to examine the patient's wounds."

"Yeah, I can go with that."

They were both peering at George's head.

"Any immediate treatment necessary?"

George saw Sergeant Barrasso, standing a little apart, arms folded, staring down at him.

George was a little dazed and still half asleep.

"He's catching some Zs, you dummies!" the sergeant roared. "Zammit, get up, it's nearly lunchtime!"

George raised himself on one elbow and smiled at the sergeant in recognition.

"Good timing, sir. I could do with a bite to eat!"

Sitting in the back of the personnel carrier, a bandage wrapped around his head, avoiding poisonous looks from the sergeant, George was feeling pretty pleased with himself. He had completed the course – it was over – but now that he was officially ready for desert warfare, he began to worry about what Abdullah might expect of him.

CHAPTER 17
ARTICLE IN MALTA TELEGRAPH

REPORTER: *Amy Halliday*

27 July 2019

US Ultimatum to Russia on Libya

The US Secretary of State, Mike Phelps, today told the Russian Ambassador in Washington that the US was no longer prepared to tolerate Russia's blatant intervention in the Libyan conflict.

The Secretary of State accused Russia of deploying a dozen fourth-generation warplanes to Libya in support of private military contractors known as the Russkaya Volonterskaya Gruppa. Such a deployment must have been made with the full knowledge of the Kremlin.

In a statement to the press, he said: "For too long, Russia has denied the full extent of its involvement in the ongoing Libyan conflict. This week, we watched every step of the way as Russia flew jet fighters to Libya."

The American response has so far been confined to a war of words with the Kremlin, but there are growing signs that an American intervention is now a real possibility.

What this means for the gas supply deal with MalTech is unknown. Sources in the Department of Energy said the company will find few friends in Castille, or Brussels, if it aligns itself with Russian interests in Libya, when the West is falling into line behind the US.

Sources in Castille went further, saying that, given the level of investment required from the government, it might be unwise to proceed further with the project just when Libya could be plunged into deeper turmoil, thereby increasing the associated risks.

The situation in Tripoli remains tense, with gunfire and shelling now reaching the outskirts of the city. Turkish efforts to broker a ceasefire are making slow progress, with General Boutros not prepared to make concessions from what he perceives to be a position of strength.

CHAPTER 18

MARCO BONNICI

NATASHA AND MARCO had flown into Milan together. At the request of the Wise Men, Marco was reluctantly meeting with Salvatore to talk about bringing the Americans into the gas deal, while Natasha had her regular meeting with Signor Bruno. The taxi had cruised down the toll road from Malpensa Airport, hitting the outskirts of north-west Milan when, for old times' sake, Marco asked the driver to go past the San Siro stadium.

"Slow down," he shouted, "let me get a look at it! You see, Natasha, don't you think the spiralling ramps look like giant bed springs?" Her father laughed. "You know, when Sergio and I were at university, we came here as often as we could. It was a three-hour drive from Bologna, in Sergio's beat-up Alfa. He was mad about Inter and, just to wind him up, I supported Juventus. They were good days, we had passion to burn."

She smiled at him.

"I wish I could've seen the pair of you then!"

"When we both first came to Milan, before term started, we stayed with Zio Nico, my father's cousin. I had not seen Sergio since he was a young boy, but we were thrown together in Milan when his mother died. Uncle Nico arranged for members of the Family, including your Signor Bruno, to meet us individually, at their grand Croce Bianca club. They set us tasks, sort of an assessment. We were told to go away, earn some money and do something that would impress them. That was all they said. Hilarious when you think about it."

Natasha laughed.

"What did you do?"

"Ah! That is another story. I will tell you some other time, we are nearly there now, but ask Signor Bruno if he remembers the tasks!"

"He doesn't really go in for small talk."

"No, I don't think he ever did."

The taxi slowed down outside a nondescript parade of shops.

Marco said: "Yes, yes, this is the place."

He paid and then asked the driver to wait for a moment at the curbside. He grabbed Natasha's arm and pointed out of the window.

"You see the office up there, on the first floor, above the dry cleaner's? It has no broadband or WiFi, no telephone, and we sweep it for bugs monthly. I use it whenever I am in Milan, for meetings. I took the lease when I was twenty years old so as to have somewhere to work on my VAT scam – my response to Signor Bruno's challenge. More importantly, it has a parking space round the back, so Sergio and I could park the Alfa there before going to the San Siro. Happier days, Natasha. Anyway, I cannot keep Salvatore waiting. Self-important prig! Good luck with Signor Bruno."

"And you, Dad. Give him what for!"

Marco got out and the taxi pulled away. He waved and walked towards the door to the stairs that led up to the office. He punched in the code for the lock, twice, before realising it had been changed. He took out his phone and sent a text to Salvatore.

Outside.

With a loud buzz, the door lock was released and Marco climbed the stairs. As usual, there was coffee waiting on the table, from the café down the street.

"Salvatore, you have changed the entry code?"

They did not bother with the charade of a formal embrace or handshake. It was just the two of them.

"A lot has changed, Marco. You've been gone four years. Things don't stand still."

"Indeed they do not."

Marco looked around the office, noting nothing much had changed in the furnishings.

Salvatore watched him closely.

"Does his ghost still haunt you, Marco?"

He was surprised by the younger man opening the conversation in this way.

"Whose – Sergio's? No. Why would it? I did not kill him. But if you are interested in hearing whether I miss him, the answer is yes. I do not want you to explain why things had to happen like that, because I will never understand. The best I can do is try to put it behind me and forget that people I trusted and liked could do such a thing."

"I see."

They sat down and then spoke at length about Camilleri's briefing. Marco had already discussed it in outline over the phone with Salvatore and it soon became clear that he had been busy sounding out the Wise Men in the interim. Marco let Salvatore talk and work his way towards presenting their conclusion.

"The feeling is, the Russians are more flexible in their approach. I mean, like it or not, we've more in common with them than we do with the Americans.

"You've got to agree, as partners, the Russians will be more willing to let us seize opportunities, as they arise. The Americans will be all red-tape and they'll want to run the show. Also, the big 'if' is whether they have the commitment to get the job done, scare off the LNA, the Russian Volunteers and the rest?"

Marco exhaled loudly.

"Salvatore, the decision here is whether the Family wants to align itself with a volatile and provocative partner that only wants to be a disruptive influence in North Africa. This is why we never do business with the Russians. You cannot trust them."

"Well, Marco, if you put it like that, you've obviously made up your mind! The Wise Men see it differently, and that's what counts. They're keen on the Russian deal. There're too many unknowns in changing now."

"OK, I hear you, but I do not agree with you. Listen, I have one final thought. What is good for Malta, is good for the Family. It is easier for me to make things happen, at a government level, if what is good for us, is also good for the country. Once the American option is understood, and gets EU backing – which it will – the Russian deal will become toxic. When that happens, our plans for European distribution go out of the window. Just remember that. I am warning you – when the Americans go into Libya, I cannot promise to get the Russian deal through."

"Marco, look, the Wise Men have asked me to ask you to have faith. We push on with the Russians. That's the end of it."

Marco shook his head in frustration. Salvatore went on: "And before we finish, if you know who's leaking information to the *Malta Telegraph* and stirring things up, I urge you to stop them, now."

There it was again, the question of who was leaking to the journalist. Marco was shocked by the insinuation that it might be him.

"How dare you suggest that I might know? Here I am, telling you what I think is in the Family's long-term interests. I do *not* go leaking to the press. You should know me better than that! So, is that it then? Your final word? Push on with the Russians?"

Salvatore looked at him in silence.

Marco decided to bite his tongue and moved to end the conversation.

"OK then, I disagree with you. I reserve my right to have my own conversation with the Wise Men on this one. I think they are making a big mistake and I am not certain you have tried your best to represent my point of view."

He could see he had riled Salvatore, who had clenched his jaw. Anger was reflected in every part of him and Marco wondered if Natasha had ever seen that side of him.

"It's not for you to second guess the Wise Men, Marco. Like me, you follow instructions, whether you like them or not. I thought you would've understood that by now? Be careful. People are aware you were close to Sergio and, for you, what happened to him remains a problem. They're watching you and expect you to toe the line."

Marco had held himself in check for long enough; he could not stop the words spilling out of him. As he spoke, tears of anger welled in his eyes.

"Do not threaten me, you upstart! I am proud to say Sergio was my friend. And you, you little shit, had him imprisoned and killed. Do you know what? You will never be a fraction of the man he was. While people might go along with you for now, there are others in the Family who know what you have done and consider it a black stain on your character. They will never trust you again. You have screwed up your own future, you arrogant young prick, and it is *you* who had better be careful!"

With that, Marco turned his back on Salvatore, staggered down the stairs and out into the street. The world had certainly changed and he was no longer sure of his place in it.

Meanwhile, in central Milan, in Signor Bruno's *palazzo* just off via Brera, Natasha was working her way through a pile of papers involving the purchase of some mining leases in South Africa. The palazzo was a small Neoclassical masterpiece, originally built as a Jesuit college in the seventeenth century, with wide galleries around a quiet central courtyard. It had been in Signor Bruno's family for centuries. He had been born here and declared he would probably die here too.

They worked in his book-lined study and Natasha had to concentrate to be sure she did not test his limited reserves of patience. Although Signor Bruno must have been in his late seventies, and seemed the embodiment of a courtly, elderly gentleman, Natasha knew there was a steel core behind his mild retiring manner. She had already experienced the merciless grip of those heavily veined, liver-spotted hands, when he had once grasped her arm while uttering the warning '*never underestimate me*'.

Natasha always focused on her work, but was also trying to get a sense of the old man, to understand his motivations, to find an angle to latch onto – or a weakness. As far as she could make out, the only family he had, or at least ever mentioned, was his mother, with whom he had shared the *palazzo* until her death, some years before.

He was Natasha's sole direct connection with the Wise Men and, so far, was proving totally inscrutable. At the end of their session, when he had declared himself satisfied with her work, she dared to initiate a conversation.

"My father was meeting Salvatore today at his old office, near the San Siro. He told me he took the lease thirty years or so ago, while he worked on a project to try and impress you. That's all he would say. I was wondering what it was?"

"Well, if he will not tell you, then he must have his reasons. But I remember that time well. He was introduced to me at the club, the Croce Bianca, by your great-uncle Nicodemo – as was Sergio." Signor Bruno paused for a moment while his mind travelled back to that time. "Both such fine boys." Suddenly, he snapped out of his reverie. "Anyway, if that is all?"

Natasha took her leave, frustrated as always by her failure to make progress with him, when usually any man to whom she paid attention was instantly won over. But there had been something there today, something she had noticed for the first time about this man who had lived with his mother, never married and whose only non-work-related comment to her, ever, was: 'Both such fine boys.'

It was not much, but it was a start. On the way to the airport, Natasha placed a call to an ultra-discreet private investigator who occasionally did jobs for her.

CHAPTER 19
ABDULLAH BELKACEM
AL-UDEID US AIR BASE, QATAR

ABDULLAH FOUND WORKING with the Americans difficult. He did not have the patience for it. The preparations were extensive and Abdullah understood little of what they were talking about. Like all soldiers, they spoke in acronyms and military slang, which left him feeling confused and excluded. Whatever was being planned was codenamed 'Operation Establish Freedom', which would involve an initial force of 'contractors', followed by a company of 130 Rangers, organised into four platoons.

They told him the aim was 'joint forcible entry' into Marsabar, and then on into Tripoli. The Rangers involved were an elite light infantry force, whose proud history went from the D-Day landings, to fighting Iranian-backed Shi'ite militias in Syria, as well as clearing out ISIL units near the Turkish border.

They planned to land the company at a secure airfield in the southern desert, where vehicles and supplies would be brought in later, by helicopter and larger C130 cargo planes, from the Bizerte-Sidi Ahmed Air Base in north-west Tunisia.

Abdullah was to go into Libya some weeks ahead and prepare the ground. He had to establish a local militia of at least one hundred fighters, loyal to him and ready to execute the plan.

He had also to find an area where they could set up a preliminary base, which meant he had to identify a village where they would be welcome or which they could take by force. They were going to give him one hundred thousand Libyan dinars, about seventy thousand dollars, to help him buy the support of the people and prepare a camp.

No one had asked him, but Abdullah had a plan of his own. Regardless of what was said to him, he was going to return to the Nafusa Hills, a ridge some fifty miles south of Tripoli, reaching six hundred and fifty metres high and stretching all the way west into Tunisia. If George and he were going to reach Tunisia, which he thought likely, he would be able to find his way through the concealed, twisting valleys into western Libya. There he would find his family. He had not seen his wife and sons for four years. It was long enough. The Americans could strategise and plan all they liked, but this was what he was going to do.

Abdullah was from a Berber tribe and his family had lived in those hills for generations. When he had moved to the coast, with his wife Rania and his brother Tareq, his wife's family had stayed behind in the hills. They continued living in the traditional way, raising goats and sheep, and cultivating small fields of wheat and barley for bread. Once Abdullah had seen his family, he would go to Marsabar and contact those he thought might still be loyal to him. Four years was a long absence, though, and he was worried that he might not be as well remembered as he was hoping.

The soldiers never asked him for his thoughts as they continued on their steady route, oblivious to the fact that he had already decided on his plan of action. After many hours and days, they suddenly seemed satisfied. They piled several large binders of papers onto a line of desks and stood to attention when a group of older senior officers arrived to review their work.

The senior officers listened, looked at maps and read papers. One, older than the rest, with sunken cheeks, walnut skin and white spiked hair, asked Abdullah if he agreed with the plan and if he had anything to add.

Abdullah said: "Sir, thank you for your help. This is your plan and I am sure it is a very good one. All I ask is that you take me to western Libya and give me a month, then we can speak again and I will tell you what can be done. This is my country and these are my people; they will tell me. Until I speak to them and see the way it is, all this writing on paper makes no sense to me."

The colonel laughed.

"Well said! When do we deploy him?"

A lieutenant, who had been doing all the writing, replied: "Well, it's him and a Maltese adviser. They're good to go any time. He's as ready as he'll ever be. The adviser is a disaster. He flunked basic desert warfare training in the first week."

"Really? Mr Belkacem, did you hear that? Your friend is a disaster. You still want to take him?"

"Hah! Sir, the most important thing is, he is my friend and," Abdullah wagged a finger, "he is more dangerous than you think. He has fought alongside me before. I know this man. I am happy with him."

The white-haired old man laughed again.

"How do we infiltrate them?"

"We fly them into Tunis on a commercial flight. We've got an agent who'll take them to the border and give them ID, transport, cash, basic weapons. Then he'll set them off and we'll see what happens."

"Hmm." The colonel did not seem too impressed. "Sounds kinda vague to me."

The lieutenant looked at Abdullah and shrugged.

"We work with what we've got, sir."

The colonel turned back to Abdullah and said: "So, what do you say? You think this will all work out?"

Again, Abdullah smiled broadly. Then he dropped the smile

and hardened his expression. He had to show he was a serious man.

"Colonel, I said put me on the ground in western Libya and give me a month." He swept his hand contemptuously towards the piles of printouts, maps and flip-chart pages. "All this is useless.

"Four years ago, nothing happened in north-west Libya without my knowledge and permission. I had a militia of over one hundred men, full-time fighters, loyal to me alone. If we needed to go into action, I could rely on five hundred more. We had vehicles, arms, communication systems, all bought and paid for by me. I fought Gaddafi's soldiers three times, and won; I fought militias and jihadis from Iraq and Syria, and won. Your lieutenant says he does not know what he has got. But he will soon find out, eh?"

"I've read your file. I know who you are."

"No, sir. This is not true. You do not know who I am. You see, four years ago I had a brother, a family home, gold, a place in a good community, respect … I even had an oil tanker. I was robbed of all this, and the chance to see my sons become men. They grew up without me. My wife tells me her hair has become grey. All the while, I sold hardware in another country. I am the man who has waited four years to put all this right. That is who I am."

"Mr Belkacem, I hope you do put all that right, but listen to me carefully."

The colonel walked over to Abdullah and held his face very close. He talked softly but there was menace in his words and fire in his eyes. He was an experienced soldier and had seen it all before.

"You are going back to Libya to help fix your mess of a country and your mess of a life. I get that. Shortly, there will be American lives at stake and I will *not* be fucked about. We will kick back Boutros, destroy the Islamic State-in-fucking-Libya and watch the Russians take their shit back home. *That* is what we are going to do.

"I hope you get your revenge, find your family and recover what you lost. But if I ever think my priorities and yours are in conflict, I will pull the support so fast you will not see it go. If I think you are using us for your own ends, then I will send a message to Abu Muhammad, with your last known coordinates. No warnings. Can I be any clearer?"

Abdullah understood the colonel. He bowed his head.

"You are most clear, sir."

"OK." He offered his hand. "Good luck to you – and remember this conversation."

"It is all in the hands of Allah now, *Inshallah*."

"Not if we have anything to do with it, it isn't!"

They shook hands.

"Lieutenant, send them on their way."

Abdullah watched the officers climb into a large SUV. The heat was searing, but he knew the desert awaited and he had better get used to it again. So he walked the kilometre to George's building. He wound between the low, drab prefabricated buildings and did not see a single other person on foot.

He looked around him at the coffee shops, the runways and the billions of dollars' worth of airplanes. All of it could vanish in a matter of weeks. Once the people and the planes had gone, the desert would strip back the fencing, the sand would cover the runway, the buildings and canvas canopies would be burned up by the sun and blasted by the wind. In a short time, it would be as if they had never been there.

He asked himself what the Americans were really doing? They did not like the country, they did not like the people and they certainly did not understand Islam. Why did they not just go home?

Cars and SUVs rolled past him and, in the distance, he heard the engine pitch of an F-22 Raptor turn into a scream as it blazed down the runway, filling the air with the aroma of its light, sweet exhaust. Off it flew to do harm to some unsuspecting Syrians, Iranians or Kurds. But, all things considered, Abdullah was in an upbeat mood. He wanted to tell George the good news that they were finally leaving for Libya the day after next. He was going home.

When he reached George's room, the noise from the TV was deafening. The policeman was lying on the bed, in baggy white shorts and a vest. Dirty clothes were piled on the bed and there were fast-food takeaway boxes all over the floor. He was watching a baseball game and eating icecream. The room smelled of stale food and unwashed bodies.

"I see military life is suiting you well, my friend. I must tell your lady wife that, without her to look after you, you turn into a goat. And smell like one also."

George got off the bed and used the remote to turn down the sound on the television. He was listening out for something.

"Thank God that rap music has stopped! Fourteen days of it. It's been hell! *Mela,* I can tell you all the words."

"Be quiet, do not make chatter. I bring good news! We leave for Libya in thirty-six hours!"

"What?" George stood, icecream spoon in hand and the residue thickening on his moustache and beard. "Is that all the training we get? I'm not sure I'm ready yet."

"You are ready, my friend. An M-16 in your arms, the sand beneath your boots and the sound of a Toyota engine. It will all come back to you soon."

"That's exactly what I'm afraid of!"

"We meet at Building 34-12, sixteen hundred hours, for equipment checks and final briefing. We fly from Doha, direct to Tunis. It is only six hours in the plane and then we cross the border. Maybe we fly over Malta and you can wave to your lady wife?"

George turned away from him, head down. Abdullah realised why he looked a little sad.

"Tonight is the party night, yes? Do not be sad, my friend.

Think, when you return, you will be a hero again! Maybe there will be more medals?"

George looked at him with raised eyebrows. The thought did not seem to cheer him up.

"You must telephone them before the party – wish them a happy time."

Abdullah was worried. His friend had not phoned his wife or daughter since he had arrived at the camp. He had spoken to his son at work, who had said he tried to spend as little time as possible at the house, due to all the crying. But it seemed nobody wanted to be the first to end the quarrel. Indeed, George was becoming a true Berber.

CHAPTER 20
ASSISTANT COMMISSIONER GERALD CAMILLERI

PRESIDENTIAL GARDENS, ATTARD, MALTA

MIKE LLOYD HAD TELEPHONED Assistant Commissioner Camilleri and suggested it might be an idea if they met up to chew the fat. Camilleri had suggested they take a walk in the San Anton Gardens, part of the Presidential Palace, in central Malta. Although the palace's architecture was unremarkable, its public gardens, with graceful shaded walkways, sculptures and ornamental ponds, made for a good place to relax and hold private conversations.

It was a midweek morning and the gardens were not busy. A mother with a pushchair bumped her child towards the play park, and one or two people with time to spare found cool spots under the palms, jacarandas and cypress trees, to read or study their phones. A man in a cream cardigan and English brogues sat on a bench, reading the *Malta Telegraph*. In front of him, a fountain splashed water, playing games with the reflections on a pond, vivid green with lily pads and aqueous growth.

Mike Lloyd came bustling into the gardens with two security types. They were all dressed in plain white shirts, grey trousers and dark sunglasses, walking at top speed, three abreast, the ripples of their haste immediately disturbing the calm of the gardens. Gerald Camilleri wondered why he had bothered to choose such a discreet and tranquil venue. He should have known better – Americans!

Camilleri sighed. The three of them came thundering towards him. The two security men peeled off, turned their backs and started a visual sweep of the gardens.

"Mike, good of you to meet me here. Lovely day, is it not? I thought we could enjoy some of the morning, while we talked."

"Gerald, yeah, I suppose so. What gives?"

"What gives? You asked me to meet you. I have no idea *'what gives'*."

"OK. In plain English – is Marco Bonnici onside? Are they with us or against us? That's what gives."

"Ah! Well, it is complicated."

Camilleri had already spoken to Mike and told him that the Bonnicis might be prepared to review their arrangements with Euromasio.

"I would say they could be persuaded. Whether their larger organisation can, I am not so sure," the policeman added.

"Hmm, I see. Do we need the larger organisation or can we get what we want from the Bonnicis acting alone?"

"Again, it is complicated. Splitting the Bonnicis from the Family is not something to be undertaken lightly. The Family dynasty, I use the word advisedly, goes back hundreds of years. Although the Bonnicis' links to them run deep, they have good standing in their own right. Marco's father, Franco, was a cousin of Nico Rossi. The pair of them salvaged the Family fortunes after World War Two by rebuilding the infrastructure of Italy and Malta, and by constructing half the hotels on the Mediterranean coast."

"Look, Gerald, I don't want a history lesson. Are they with us or not? You know how pissed we are right now. The Russians at best connived to kill our Chargé d'Affaires, at worst actually did it. It's tantamount to a declaration of war! We're not going to take it lying down. I am asking you to use your famous charm to get the Bonnicis to play ball. So, how's it going to go down?"

"Goodness, we are in a hurry this morning. You will have to learn to employ a little patience, Mike, especially in Malta. It works wonders."

"Gerald, don't fuck with me! I'm not in the mood."

"Well, I am trying to help you and some better manners on your part would go a long way. I have spoken to the Bonnicis and I believe they have some sympathy with your point of view. It might take time to bring them round, but I think it can be done. What exactly do you want them to do?"

"Cancel their deals with the Russians. Sign new deals with us or our proxies. Get the permits and finish all the other stuff they're doing so that, when our militia kick the Libyan National Army of General Boutros all the way back to Egypt and we bring in Exxon and Total to finish the job, it's all good to go."

"And they will want to know, what is in it for them? If they go breaking their very lucrative prior arrangements, there had better be adequate compensation. It is a reasonable position to take, is it not?"

"I don't know about the money and I don't give a rat's ass. I'm security, not finance. Ask them what they want. We do deals. I'll find someone who can make them happy."

"Good. Have you ever met Marco Bonnici? He is a very agreeable chap."

Mike Lloyd shook his head.

"Can't say I've had the pleasure."

"Well, we can put that right. He is sitting over there by the fountain. Would you like to go across and say hello?"

Mike Lloyd was taken aback. After a few seconds, he looked over at his security guys and nodded in Marco's direction. He let Camilleri lead the way to the bench, where Marco sat in his cream cardigan and oxblood English brogues.

Camilleri made the introductions. Mike Lloyd was tense and unsmiling, whilst Marco was relaxed and his usual charming self.

"Beautiful gardens are they not, Mr Lloyd? We do not have

many such places in Malta. Not enough spare land and the climate is too intense. It's such a shame. I always think you can judge a country by the quality of its parks and public spaces. That being so, we in Malta have a lot of work to do."

Marco paused for a moment.

"Did you know, it is customary for every visiting head of state to plant a tree in these gardens, as a symbol of the long and mutually beneficial relationship they hope both countries will enjoy?"

"No, Marco, if I may call you that, I didn't know, but the symbolism of the story doesn't escape me. I don't believe in signs or omens. I'm more the pragmatic type. I'm all for mutually beneficial relationships, but I ain't planting any trees. Is a 'mutually beneficial relationship' something you're interested in?"

"That is a good start to the conversation. To get to the point, we Bonnicis are happy to talk to you. But my associates are cautious people and I am still trying to persuade them to review their arrangements. I hope I will be successful in bringing them round to my point of view.

"You must know, that cannot and will not come cheaply. We believe, if the Americans can secure gas from North Africa through VertWay and feed it into the European transmission system, at the expense of the current Russian supplies, you could transform the economic landscape of Europe by reducing its reliance on Russian gas.

"I do not need to tell you, Russia's GDP, including its energy revenues, is smaller than Italy's. Without its energy revenues, it falls to below that of the Netherlands. It would be interesting to see how it would maintain its defence spending, if that came about."

Mike Lloyd grunted. Marco smiled at him and continued.

"So, you could say there is much to play for? We are prepared to let you into the game, but we want a reasonable share of the upside."

"I hear you, Marco, but seriously, a lot of this I've got to take back home. I'm sure it can all be arranged. We know what's at stake here, but I can't make you any promises, here and now. Gerald, thank you for arranging this, it was a good idea."

Mike Lloyd took off his sunglasses and met Marco's eyes as he spoke.

Marco was folding his paper, ready to leave. He paused.

"Oh, Mike, as a gesture of our goodwill, how would you like to get hold of three-quarters of a billion dollars, cash, in Libyan dinars, to help fund your efforts on the ground? Currently, it is due to be put into a shipping container and moved by standard freight to Istanbul. From there, it goes on to Benghazi and ends up in the clutches of General Boutros, and his Libyan National Army. I can provide more information, if you think it would be helpful."

Marco smiled and slid his newspaper under his arm. He clapped Camilleri on the shoulder, nodded at Mike Lloyd and slowly wandered away through the gardens, stopping to inspect a bed of roses, a variety that was unfamiliar to him.

Mike Lloyd sat in the back of the black SUV as it drove the three kilometres from the San Anton Gardens to the embassy buildings. It was an interesting conversation. Maybe there was something in it or maybe it was what the Russians wanted him to think. Either way, if the money did exist, he did not want it finding its way to Boutros's rebels. Not if he could help it.

CHAPTER 21
SUPERINTENDENT
GEORGE ZAMMIT
TOZEUR, TUNISIA

LEAVING the debris of the business-class flight littered around their seats, George and Abdullah collected their small sports bags, then transferred from the luxury of the international carrier to the local, one-hour flight to Tozeur.

Stepping out into the searing white light of the desert, George realised they were on the edge of the Sahara. Tozeur lies due south of Tunis and is as near to the Libyan border as can be reached by a commercial flight. It was in that crumbling, desert oasis town that they were due to meet the fixer who would take them across the border. Like many travellers before them, who had assembled for the camel-train journeys to Mali, Niger and beyond, George felt that he was standing at the end of the world.

South of this point was dangerous country. Not only were there a thousand kilometres of inhospitable desert, but across the sand was the Sahel. If the Sahara was a sea, then the Sahel was the beach. The strip of scrub that ran from the Atlantic Coast, south of Morocco, through Mali, Niger, Chad and the Sudan, all the way to the Red Sea. Not only was it home to violent tribes, such as the Tuareg and the Fulani, but also to a large number of Islamic State splinter groups, who followed their own agenda, stealing, murdering and kidnapping, on a daily basis. Meanwhile, coming north were the waves of refugees, heading for the coasts of Tunisia and Libya, trying to escape the chaos brought about by the incessant violence in their home countries and the hunger caused by drought and climate change. In their desperation, they could be equally dangerous.

Tozeur was once a classic oasis, the 'go to' location for any desert movie, from *Star Wars* to *The English Patient*. The thousands of palm trees still marked the town out as having an abundant water supply but, over the years, mismanagement and increasing population had led to a general air of poverty and decay. Not even the highly decorated yellow and orange, clay and sand-brick buildings could hide the fact that the town was losing its charm.

Abdullah was in high spirits, however. He was back in North Africa and heading home.

"It is a beautiful place, yes, my friend? Look, try one of these – they are the best! Tozeur is famous for them."

He had insisted on buying dates, a local speciality, farmed in the palmeries on the outskirts of the town. Afterwards, they had made their way to the centre, eventually sitting down at the roadside, their battered sports bags beside them, to eat the fruit. Abdullah draped a newspaper over his head to shield him from the worst of the sun. In Al-Udeid, they had been supplied with locally made clothing and the sports bags, which contained their carefully curated possessions. They would collect more equipment when they met their contact but, for the time being, had only what they carried.

Over the last three weeks, George had let his beard grow and acquired an acceptable moustache. It was now turning from a thick stubble into something recognisable as a full set of whiskers. His hair was getting long at the back and the wisps across his brow were wild and untamed. The time spent in the desert in Qatar had tanned his skin and, with his sandals, cheap baggy jeans, worn T-shirt and unkempt appearance, he fitted comfortably into the street scene of the North African town.

He squatted on the kerbside, his feet in the gutter, kicking the plastic and litter to one side. Rivulets of sweat ran from his hairline, down past his ears. He did not bother to wipe them away.

He thought about what might be happening at home. Before he had left Al-Udeid, he had phoned Camilleri and told him the whole thing was all taking much longer than expected and that he wanted to come home. Camilleri acknowledged that it was 'a difficult and onerous' assignment but said George's commitment to his duty would not be forgotten and would serve him well in the future.

George had mustered as much sarcasm as he had dared and asked him: "How, exactly?"

He was told to stop whining, but Camilleri promised to visit Marianna and make sure she was aware that her sacrifice was being appreciated at the highest levels. The family would start receiving hardship payments, in recognition of their contribution to the wellbeing and security of the state of Malta.

George acknowledged that would help – his wife would no doubt be happy about the increase in the household income. However, it did nothing to lift his own failing spirits.

George kept in touch with Denzel, who told him the crying had stopped and Marianna was now telling neighbours that her husband was on a secret mission, at the request of the President herself! The President had, in fact, sent Gina a card congratulating her on her engagement – something that George could scarcely believe, but which no doubt had thrilled Marianna, who had framed it and had Denzel hang it opposite the photograph of the Holy Father.

While he was pondering affairs back in Malta, he noticed Abdullah was talking to a young teenager wearing a Barcelona football shirt and a Star Wars-branded baseball cap. Abdullah pulled George to his feet.

"Let's go! The boy will take us on the first stage of our journey!"

"*Mela*, how did he recognise us?"

Abdullah pointed behind him to a high stone arch that bridged the street, with tiling across the top, adorned with Arabic script.

"The western gate of the Medina! It was arranged we meet at this time and place."

"Thanks for telling me!" George was miffed. "I hope it's not going to be like this all the rest of the way?"

"My friend, I will tell you what you need to know. Why tell you more? It will only make you worry. You must be happy – it is my job to keep you happy, eh!"

With a laugh, Abdullah set off after the youth.

After winding through the narrow streets, dodging and weaving past the teeming life of the old town, they turned down a lane an arm's-reach wide and ended up in front of a traditional orange-coloured, brick-built house, deep in the Medina. Inside, the rooms were beautifully tiled with patterned ceramics and the inner courtyard was calm, quiet and deep in shade. The only sound was the cooling water that flowed through terracotta channels, which irrigated an array of palms, flourishing in large earthenware pots.

They sat on a low sofa and were served tea in small green glasses while traditional Arabic-Andalusian music played from a radio in another room. After half an hour, just as Abdullah was getting impatient, a bespectacled, white-haired man in his sixties appeared, dressed in a long pastel *jebba*, with baggy pants and an embroidered waistcoat.

"Sorry, sorry, I am Edal Essa, I have been to a wedding!" he announced, holding out his arms to indicate his costume. "Please, five minutes for me to change. Then we go. We will be on the road for some time, so be sure now to be clean and comfortable."

His pickup was in a garage, under a nearby shop, with locked steel boxes bolted to the floor of the flatbed. They set off, driving up the steep concrete ramp, working their way past the narrow streets of the old town and out onto the state highway. They drove south, through the night, across the huge dry salt lake of Chott el-Djerid, until they reached the Jebil National Park, where the scrub gave way to rolling mounds of sand and tracts of exposed rock. They were on the most eastern side of Tunisia, on the north-eastern edges of the Grand Erg Oriental, the vast sea of sand dunes.

Edal drove his 4x4 twin-cabbed Toyota with skill and ease. The route he had chosen was longer, he had said, but safer – fewer smugglers, militants and less security. George slept for long parts of the journey, feet stretched across the back seat, head bouncing back and forth against the window pillar, while Abdullah talked endlessly with Edal, sitting alongside him in the front.

Looking at the map, George knew they were heading south, away from the coastline and from the Nafusa Hills, behind them. They would have to turn east, to cross from Tunisia into Libya. Edal told them he was heading for a crossing point near the Libyan town of al-Nalut. Officially, all the borders were closed, to prevent the passage of smugglers and the Islamic militias, and many of the roads had checkpoints manned by government soldiers. The crossing was a danger point so Abdullah decided they would wait for nightfall the next day. He knew the old smuggler roads well and, once inside Libya, he boasted he would not need a map or GPS, he could find his way home by sense of smell alone!

Edal was a relaxed companion and, although George could not follow all of the conversation, he could tell Abdullah and he were engaged in long and earnest discussions about tribal politics, the strength of the militias and the appetite for change. From time to time, Abdullah would pull a small notebook from his sports bag and make notes, or copy phone numbers from the directory on Edal's phone. George did not want to interrupt; he could sense this was serious business.

After about twenty hours of continuous driving, they arrived at an isolated, single-storey, concrete-block building, with a boundary marked by old tyres, once painted white, now half-buried in the sand. It was dusk. Edal explained this was an abandoned checkpoint, scene of a massacre of Tunisian soldiers by the Islamic extremists who came north from Chad, shortly after the Arab Spring uprising in 2011. The rear wall had mostly collapsed and he drove the truck into what was once a room, to conceal it from view.

Edal jumped out, stretched, urinated and announced that now he needed to sleep. He pulled some filthy foam mats from the back room of the building, shook off some of the straw and dust, checked for scorpions and promptly lay down, closing his eyes.

Abdullah took George to one side to tell him what he had learned. Edal was a Tuareg, from Ubari in the south-west of Libya. He had been helping the Americans for the past two years. The Tuaregs were looking for allies in the north and he believed they would give men and support, in exchange for a promise of autonomy in the south. Abdullah knew they were good and committed fighters who hated Islamic State as much as he did. They had been betrayed by Gaddafi and everyone who came after him. Edal had promised to speak to the leaders, to explain they had Americans behind them and that change was coming.

"This is a good start. And there is better news! Tomorrow is a happy day. We will find my family – I will enjoy a little time with them; then we will decide where fortune takes us next. The Americans have served us well so far."

Early the next morning, a battered, ancient lorry pulled up. The sun and the wind had stripped most of the colour from its paintwork and a thick coating of dust gave a near-perfect camouflage effect. Edal told Abdullah to relax. He lowered the Uzi machine pistol he had taken from the truck's lockbox. Edal chatted with the driver, then went to the rear of the truck and took out a box of food and a dozen bottles of water, which he gave to Abdullah.

"I leave you now but we meet again soon. From now on, it is your country. Travel at night. There are checkpoints, smugglers and the roads are not safe."

"May the road be kind to you, my friend. I do not worry about bandits and terrorists. I have George to defend me!" Abdullah said.

George shook his head.

They all embraced and then Edal climbed into the lorry and, with a brief wave, left them alone in the desolation of the desert.

Abdullah seemed happier by the hour.

"He is right, we must wait till dark. I have not got so close to my family only to stumble into a nest of Muhammad's killers or greedy militia. We leave at dusk and arrive late in the village. It is not far away now."

The daylight hours were interminable. They lay in the shade of the ruined building, to avoid the scorching sun. In the early afternoon, the heat made it difficult to breathe. The flies soon found them and attacked their exposed skin, desperate in their search for drops of perspiration. If they swatted them from their arms and faces, the insects made for their eyes, trying to steal minuscule drops of moisture. A wind had started to blow and the sand soon found its way into their hair, their pants, their mouths, so that every movement became an abrasive torture.

Abdullah lay still and stared at the ceiling. George could not tell whether he was awake or asleep. He tried talking, sleeping, scratching, pacing around the building. He longed to be in Edal's truck, where the air rushing in through the open windows provided some relief at least. By mid afternoon, Abdullah gave in and let George sit in the pickup for thirty minutes, with the air-con running. As his core temperature reduced, he found he could breathe more easily again.

"The desert is a cruel place, no? I have been away too long and grown soft."

"How much time will we spend in it?" George asked, fearful

of the answer. He found the environment taxing and longed to be back home, swimming in the fresh blue waters of Balluta Bay.

"I fear Allah's will means we will return this way before too long." Abdullah pulled at his black beard, straightening it. "We must go south, to Ubari. It is a long journey but we must meet Edal again and talk to the Tuareg leaders about what must be done."

The thought of another long journey, crossing the Grand Erg in the truck, made George feel ill.

"I don't know why you need me here – I'm doing nothing to help!"

Abdullah pondered.

"You have seen *Top Gun*? It is my favourite film. I know they are Americans – for that we must forgive them. So, I am 'Maverick' and you are 'Goose' – my wingman. See? That is how it is."

"*Mela*, I've seen that film; it's good. But doesn't Goose die in *Top Gun*?"

"Well – ummm, yes, that is true and it is very sad. But it is the fault of Iceman, no? And," Abdullah glanced around the shimmering flat lands surrounding them, "there is no Iceman here. It is too hot, eh?"

He laughed, very amused by his own joke, as usual. George shook his head with resignation.

"We must rest, for tonight we do the final part of the first journey."

They set off a little before seven, just as the sun was fast disappearing below the bright orange horizon. Abdullah drove with confidence. After a couple of hours, the moon was nearly full and they could drive without headlights. Once, when he saw another vehicle's lights approaching in the distance, Abdullah pulled off the road. He got out of the truck and waited for the vehicle to pass, hidden from sight, on the opposite side of the road. He cradled the Uzi.

Soon they were in the winding valley roads of the Nafusa Hills, the dunes of the Erg behind them. They could make out enclosed fields, and the straggling bushes on the roadside had become taller and more imposing. They slowed down through the small isolated ribbons of housing that occasionally abutted the roads, even though all the villages were in darkness.

"Here, they sleep when it becomes dark and rise with the sun. It is a sin to waste Allah's sunlight!"

Eventually, they stopped at the head of a long valley, where rocky bluffs rose to each side of them. There were a few isolated farmhouses and the small fields of wheat or barley were bordered by outcrops of rock on the valley sides. From what George could see in the moonlight, the village centre comprised a dusty square with two petrol pumps, a small green and white mosque and a single minimarket. There was blue fluorescent light coming from inside the shop. Abdullah left the truck, ignoring the barking dogs that had gathered outside the shop's front door, and banged on the window.

The door opened a fraction and an elderly man peered out. They spoke briefly and then suddenly the man rushed out, threw himself to his knees and grabbed Abdullah around the ankles. George found it hard to swallow when Abdullah raised the man and they put their arms around each other. Abdullah was home.

With that, the men went inside the shop, leaving George in the lorry. After ten minutes, he noticed car lights coming over the ridge at the head of the valley. The vehicle snaked down the side of the incline, making its way towards the village. As it approached the square, George crouched low in the footwell, unsure whether this was friend or foe. He had his answer soon enough, when the doors flew open and a tall youth in a white singlet and jeans jumped out, closely followed by a plump middle-aged woman in a blue *jilbāb* that covered her head and fell all the way to her feet.

The shop door flew open and Abdullah strode out towards them, arms outstretched. In the moonlight, with tears in his eyes, George watched Abdullah's reunion with Rania, his wife, and their eldest son, Jamal. After embraces and some short but earnest conversations, where no one let go of anybody else, Abdullah turned towards the lorry and beckoned George to join them. As he approached, Abdullah came towards him and pulled him into the family huddle. George's tears joined those already flowing freely.

That night, he insisted on staying with the shopkeeper, who was only too honoured to show him hospitality. Abdullah was able to return to Rania's brother's farm for a full reunion. He was beside himself with excitement at the prospect and the three of them rushed off to exchange news and for Abdullah to see the younger children, who had been told to wait until it was confirmed that the unimaginable had actually happened!

George lay on the low cot in the rear of the shop. The large chest freezer shook and rattled, the mosquitoes buzzed around his head and a mangy shop dog snuffled and farted at his feet, but he was the happiest he had been in many weeks, until he started thinking about his own family back in Malta. He missed them and cursed himself for the manner of his departure.

CHAPTER 22

ARTICLE IN THE MALTA TELEGRAPH

Reporter: Amy Halliday

31 July 2019

US Calls for Ceasefire in Libya

The US Ambassador to the UN, Sally Di Canio, today called for an immediate ceasefire in Libya and urged those involved to respect calls from the UN-backed Government of National Accord (GNA) in Tripoli to lay down arms.

The Ambassador regretted that recent Turkish efforts to agree a ceasefire had failed and said the situation in Libya was becoming increasingly unstable, with the country at risk of deteriorating into a full-scale civil war.

This instability has given rise to increased activity by ISIS-affiliated terrorist groups while production from the once fruitful oil fields has reduced alarmingly.

The Ambassador was critical of Russia, the United Arab Emirates and Egypt, who are all actively supporting General Boutros's Libya National Army with the supply of weapons, advisers and money.

The Government of National Accord was formed under the terms of a United Nations–led initiative in 2015, unanimously endorsed by the United Nations Security Council and recognised as the sole legitimate executive authority in Libya. It was unconscionable, the Ambassador said, that UN members were actively involved in operations to undermine the lawful government.

The Ambassador urged the Security Council to condemn the fighting and redouble its efforts to negotiate a ceasefire and send peacekeepers to enforce it. She said the lessons of Syria had been learned and the point had been reached when the US could no longer stand by and watch one of Europe's near neighbours descend into chaos.

The Russians continue to deny any involvement in the conflict in Libya and are on the verge of signing a strategic energy agreement to use Malta as a staging post to bring Libyan gas into Europe.

Natasha was sitting on the terrace, browsing the Al-Jazeera website on her phone, feeling the spring breeze coming in off the sea. It was getting warm in the evenings and outdoor dining was only a few weeks away.

Marco had told her about his meeting in Milan and what had happened with the American in the San Anton Gardens. Natasha was careful to conceal her satisfaction that her father had reached the conclusion he had and that the Americans had taken the bait, as she had planned all along.

She had not planted the stories with Amy Halliday herself, but fed them through an old friend with whom she had gradually reconnected over the past few months. When she had first rung Nick Walker, he had understandably been reticent to engage with her, suspicious of her motives. Before making the call, she had had to work hard to convince herself that she had no underlying reason for it, other than an innocent curiosity about how he was doing and what he was up to.

Natasha had few, if any, close friends and, in those rare moments when she thought about such things, Nick was the only person, outside of her immediate family, with whom she had ever had a proper relationship. However, her feelings towards him were not exclusively sympathetic in nature. There were times when she also deeply resented the fact that he had assaulted her, nearly killed her, in fact, then fled, leaving her behind without a word. She had never taken rejection well; it ate away at her. The feeling that there was unfinished business between them fortified her resolve not to let him slip away from her again.

Nick was no fool and set a high value on the fact he had escaped from Natasha's orbit and extricated himself from the clutches of the Family, with his life intact and no criminal prosecution for his time spent running BetSlick's money-laundering operation. However, he remained fascinated by Natasha and knew he would never again meet anyone quite like her.

The memory of their relationship lingered for both of them and, while there were many sound reasons for them never to speak to each other again, they found their guarded conversations edged them ever closer together. They circled each other like boxers, each nervous about making the first move. In Nick's mind, another impediment to the relationship going any further than the occasional telephone call, was the fact that he owed Marco a million euros in recompense for the boat he'd stolen, and later sold, to make his escape from Malta. Natasha had promised him that problem would go away if Nick helped her on a small project with which she was having difficulties.

She had asked if he would contact a Maltese journalist with the *Malta Telegraph* and periodically, and anonymously, pass on some information. There seemed no harm in it, although Nick knew he could never be certain whether this was the real reason Natasha had got back in touch with him in the first place. Nevertheless, he went along with the request. A million euros was a million euros and he would be glad to be out of Marco's debt.

Natasha placed her phone down on the table as her father wandered onto the terrace, filthy in corduroy garden pants and an old checked shirt. He plonked himself down in one of the chairs and reached for the wine bottle in the ceramic cooler.

"You always look happiest when you're covered in filth and rooting around in the garden."

Marco smiled at her.

He was a gardener – or rather, a horticulturist – of some renown. During his stay in Serbia, he had used the time to write a couple of well-received books on the succulents of the Mediterranean. They would never be bestsellers, but were the sort of reference books that would stay on specialists' bookshelves for years.

"Give me another year or so and I will have this place looking as it was before I went away. Anyway, I have good news. I've just spoken to Signor Bruno and he says the Wise Men are now convinced we should do business with the Americans. So, they are prepared to let us tell the Russians the deal is off and see what we can put together with Mike Lloyd. I knew they would see sense in the end."

"Really?"

"Yes, it is great news and one in the eye for Salvatore! The only proviso is that the Americans have to prove they can get control of VertWay by buying it from Euromasio. That is for them to sort out, we stay out of it."

"OK. So far, so good. What happened with Salvatore? I can't imagine he took that decision well?"

"I do not care about Salvatore. I told Signor Bruno what I thought of him about what had happened to Sergio. I said I had to get it off my chest. I said I could not, would not, forgive Salvatore, but I would try to be civil towards him in future, in the interests of the Family as a whole."

"Wow!"

"Yes, wow! The phone went very quiet. Signor Bruno thanked me for my candour and said he totally understood my position, wished me a good morning, and that was that!"

"My God, those people …"

"I know, unbelievable." Marco paused for a moment and took a swig of his wine. "So, while I am clearing the air, I want to ask you about those articles in the *Telegraph*. On the one hand, they really helped. They changed the mood in Castille. But, on the other, I would like to know who the source was."

Marco watched her face carefully, but Natasha gave nothing away. He sighed. His tone hardened.

"Tell me, please. Do you know who was behind them? Because I have my suspicions. I have had for a while."

Natasha pondered while studying her glass of wine. It was pointless lying.

"It worked, didn't it? I'm really sorry. I wanted to tell you, but I couldn't before now."

Marco's eyes flashed at her, but he kept his anger under control.

"Of course you could not. You could not tell me because it was a despicable and deceitful thing to do. You could not tell me, because you were playing games with Yaroslav and Salvatore, probably two of the most dangerous men you are ever likely to meet. Because you knew it would scare me to death. There are a million reasons why you chose not to tell me."

"Doesn't the result count for something?"

"When it comes to matters of trust between us, no, it does not. I have known for weeks, but I could not bring myself to believe it. So, you were the source and no one else?"

"There was someone else, who was the actual source, but I'd rather not say. It's not important. It'll just annoy you even more."

"Really? Is that even possible? Spill it."

She had no choice.

"OK, it was Nick Walker."

Marco sat quietly and tried to absorb what Natasha was telling him.

"That man again? But he nearly killed you! He is a loathsome individual. He still owes me a million euros for stealing the *Blue Cascade*, which he has not paid yet, by the way. My God, I do not believe it!"

And there was one more thing that Natasha needed to say.

"Now we're getting it all out on the table, there's something else you should know."

"Oh, fantastic! You have been busy. I had no idea – what now?"

"Well, I needed some leverage to persuade Nick to be the source, so I told him if he helped us, you'd forgive him the debt he owes you for stealing the boat. I mean, you never really expected him to repay it, did you?"

———

Conveniently, at that moment, Natasha's phone rang and she glanced at the screen, excused herself and left her father sitting on the terrace, quietly fuming.

It was her contact in Milan who had being making some enquiries on her behalf. She held the phone close to her ear.

"Well, there's definitely life in our elderly gent yet! He lunches punctually at 13:20 …"

"I know that. Tell me something I don't know."

"Well, after lunch he goes to Orto Botanico di Brera for a constitutional, then home for a nap and then …"

"Yes?"

"Then, on a Monday and a Thursday, his trusted servant, Toni the Sicilian, opens the side door to the palazzo and admits a young *raggazo* for the Signore to enjoy."

Natasha let out a low whistle.

"Oh, dear, Signor Bruno. Shame on you! And how old are these boys?"

"Varies, from fifteen through to late teens. The younger, the better, I suspect."

"Is it always the same boy or do his tastes vary?"

"Signor Bruno seems to like variety. I get the feeling he loses interest quickly and feels the need to … regularly refresh his appetite. "

"How very interesting."

THE SOUTH of Malta was one of Mike's least-favourite parts of the island. He was not a fan of the island generally, but he thought the south, with its broken roads, quarries, small dusty fields and dry-stone walls, was underdeveloped and backward.

If anyone flying into Malta kept an eye out, just before the wheels touched down at Malta's international airport, they would see a rough track, running east to west, leading to a remote farmhouse two hundred metres from the end of the runway. It belonged to one of Mike's 'informal' contractors, a young man called Saviour Azzopardi.

Saviour's father had farmed the small sandy fields that lay to the south of the main runway until his death, a few years before. His son, Savi, declined to follow the family farming tradition and, after a period doing IT for a small startup bank, decided to make a career out of farming people's personal data from the internet instead, selling lists to unscrupulous buyers in eastern Europe and Asia. It was not as backbreaking as scraping a living from the small plots of land his father had once worked and it certainly paid better.

Mike Lloyd had been tipped off by a colleague that when he

needed some off the books work doing, this guy could be useful. Savi had unwisely tried to hack the embassy systems for information about the arrival of an American movie star who was due to start filming on the island. He had nearly succeeded, a fact that impressed those in the embassy's cyber-security team. From that point on, the embassy's Head of Security had Savi's name in his contacts.

For certain projects Mike would rather not have to seek clearance. Planning to steal a billion Libyan dinars from the Russians was one of them. The other benefit of using Savi was that he had connections at Freeport Malta and understood the systems that moved thousands of containers through the dock there every month.

One of the downsides of visiting Savi was that his house was a health risk. His kitchen was a source of all manner of infections, waiting to leap right at you. His living room stank of stale dog and sweet rotting food. Despite the smell, which stuck in his throat and threatened to make bile rise, Mike Lloyd was pressing on with the conversation. He was talking in general terms, trying to avoid telling Savi what they were up to. Unfortunately, he was failing miserably.

"So, say I wanted a container to leave a cargo ship at a certain place – how would I do that?"

"You'd just change the EDIFACT message features. You've got access to an EDI terminal, yeah?"

"Maybe."

"There's no room for 'maybe'. Without EDIFACT messages, nothing moves. But that's easy enough.

"You send a COSTOR message, asking a for a packing facility to stuff a shipping container with goods; a COPARN message to make it available; a COREOR message to …"

"OK, OK, I get it. Say I don't have access to the EDI stuff, but I still want to get the container from A, not to B, but say to C?"

"And you don't want whoever is waiting for the cargo at B to know it has gone to C?"

"Hell, you're sharp. Now we're getting somewhere."

"OK, so you want me to hack the EDIFACT system and divert a container?"

"I do."

"Where's this container coming from and where's it going to?"

"I don't know but, for instance, let's say it's leaving from Novorossiysk, on Russia's Black Sea, and it arrives in Istanbul for transhipment to Benghazi."

"Right!" Savi paused, wondering what he was getting himself into. "All nice places, I'm sure. So, where d'you want to heist it? Istanbul or Benghazi?"

"Probably Istanbul."

"What's the cargo?"

"Stuff, Savi! Stuff! It doesn't matter."

"Russian stuff. That's great. How pissed off will the shippers be when it goes missing?"

"Oh, I'd say pretty pissed."

"Good to know! I'm assuming this 'stuff' is an ambient load, not refrigerated or anything?"

"Yeah, yeah, it's just normal stuff."

"Normal stuff? It's not weapons, toxics or nuclear stuff, is it?"

"I said, normal stuff!"

"Not drugs or human cargo, or anything really nasty – because, I'm telling you, that's not my thing."

"Don't worry – it's just stuff! So, can you heist it or not?"

"Well, sure. But I don't want to end up being the fall guy here."

"Not a chance. We look after those who look after us."

"OK, you better promise me that. I'm just a civilian."

"Uncle Sam promises."

"Well, you could send a COPRAR message to have the container offloaded at a different port and, if you want to do the business at Istanbul, send a COPINO message to alert the container terminal that a land-based carrier, your truck, will be arriving at a certain time to collect the container. All you have to do is get there ahead of the owner's haulier."

Savi was lost in thought.

"The other thing is, at most larger ports they operate a system of PIN authorisations, which the driver will need to get the cargo released. He enters the PIN at the gate, then the port automatically releases the container.

"You can usually get access to the EDI stuff, if you can identify the agent who does the shipping. A bit of phishing and you'd be surprised what people give you."

Mike was getting impatient.

"Yeah, yeah, whatever – can you do it?"

"Well, the PIN to get the haulier into the port and trigger the movement of the container, is given by the carrier to the haulier and he gets it from the person receiving the goods. It operates as the release authority under the bill of lading. That's a bit trickier. Do you know who's going to receive the goods?"

Mike smiled. He certainly did, but there was no need to give the boy all the information in one go.

"So, am I right that you can do all this shit?"

Mike looked at Savi with his most innocent expression.

Savi suddenly clicked this was not a hypothetical conversation.

"Whoa – steady, tiger! If we're really going to do this, I need to know a lot more about what the fuck's going on here and who's involved."

"Trust me, the last thing you need to know is what's going on here! You do me a list of all the details you need and we'll see what we can do. I've got no timescale for this yet. But when I say move, you've got to be ready. It could all kick off tomorrow, for all I know. So get doing your homework."

"How much are you paying for this operation? And, if I get involved, I don't want any blowback to me!"

"You'll be happy. Just get on with it. By the way, did you ever get to see Angelina Jolie in *By the Sea*?"

Savi had a thing for Angelina and it was details of her arrival on Malta that he had tried to hack.

The geek looked at him with a furrowed brow. Mike grinned. "No? It was a really shit film."

CHAPTER 25
ABDULLAH BELKACEM
GHAT, SOUTH-WESTERN LIBYA

ABDULLAH SPENT four days in the village, talking to an endless stream of relatives, friends and well-wishers, who had come from near and far to welcome him home. They sat in the main room of Rania's brother's large stone-built farmhouse, which nestled below a ridge some way above the valley floor. This allowed a cool, clean breeze to sweep through the open windows. A wide loggia ran along the front of the house. This not only provided deep shade, but also gave a great view of the winding valley road, down which any traffic from the north would have to approach.

Abdullah listened wearily to the same stories he had heard before the fall of Gaddafi. Nothing here had changed. The oil revenues in Tripoli were much reduced due to civil war and sanctions but, even so, Libya should have been one of the wealthiest countries in Africa and it rankled with him that it was not.

All the visitors pledged their allegiance to a fight for a new Libya and Abdullah gave his thanks, although he knew these were not the people he needed to win over. There was a family from Marsabar who had heard of his return and travelled for several hours to meet with him. Razan was a carpenter and had made the journey with his brother and their two cousins. All had served with Abdullah previously and they had fought together to push Gaddafi's troops out of Marsabar, down the Coastal Road back to Tripoli, in 2011. He charged them with contacting as many of his former comrades as still lived and breathed, to prepare for his return.

He was shocked by how fast news of his arrival had travelled. It made him realise he needed to leave the village quickly, before he put his family in danger. He knew not everybody would welcome him back. He spoke to George, who had been idling away the days on a low sofa at the back of the room eating, sleeping and watching Abdullah's earnest discussions. At the end of the fourth day, when the farmhouse was quiet, Abdullah told him of his plans.

"Well, my friend, the time of rest is over. Now the hard part begins. Tomorrow morning, I must say goodbye to my family again, and then I will meet you at the shop in the village. You must be ready for a long journey south."

"Are we going to meet Edal Essa?"

"Yes. Can you speak like a Frenchman?"

"No."

"A pity. We go through Algeria for maybe ten hours of driving. In Algeria, they speak the French. I understand only a little. Then we go across the Tassili Mountains. Very high. I have been, it is like driving on the moon! All rocks, no shrubs or sand. The wind has blown them into shapes, so they look like trees! I do not lie, you will see. Rocks shaped like trees. It is a fine sight."

"It sounds like a long way. Can't the Americans help – fly us or something?"

"Hmm. No! These early days, we must be as clever and sly as the fox. Nobody will expect us to go to the south! I told Razan I was coming back north to Marsabar; that is as good as having the Imam announce it at Friday prayers. The man's heart is big, but his mouth is bigger!"

Early the next morning, Abdullah collected George and they set off for the drive south. Abdullah was in a sombre mood and not inclined to talk. George guessed his departure had been painful. The Toyota held additional fuel in twenty-litre plastic jerry cans and two cool boxes of food and water, all concealed under a blue plastic sheet tied down with old nylon rope. Rakes, hoes and other pieces of farming equipment were thrown on top of the sheeting to make the truck look like a local farm vehicle.

Abdullah had wrapped George's head in a long, deep blue turban or *cheche*, in the Tuareg style, with the loose ends wrapped round his neck. The cloth was about three metres in length and Abdullah showed him how to tie the ends around the lower half of his face, so just his sunglasses showed, to protect him from the dust and from suspicion, should they be stopped. It was said that the Tuareg often had a blue tinge to the skin on their faces. The reason lay in the indigo they used to roughly dye the cloth, which combined with the action of sweat and the desert wind.

Rania's brother had given George some battered and torn khaki cargo pants, which were tied with a length of rope, in place of a belt. He offered one of his own long, well-worn cotton tunics, which nearly reached to George's knees, to complete the look.

Abdullah had laughed at the overall effect.

"Mr Policeman, if the lady wife could see you now, I think she would scream! If we are stopped, all you have to do is be quiet and it will be fine. We have the American papers and passports. I have looked at them and they are not so good. The Americans are not good with Arabic script. There are mistakes. But no worries, because I have this. Now we are at war!"

With relish, Abdullah produced a pistol that he had taped to the underside of the driver's sun visor.

"You look under your dashboard, my friend."

George felt the cool butt of a hand gun.

"Is it loaded?"

"Oh, yes! Allah will understand, if you need to use it, eh?"

George looked at his friend to see if he was joking. The set of Abdullah's jaw gave him his answer.

The drive was unremarkable, other than that it took twenty hours and the monotony of the long flat desert roads was only surpassed by the anxiety George felt at the two border crossings. As Abdullah had promised, the road across the Tassili plateau was spectacular and they forgot their weariness as they marvelled at the two thousand metre peaks and the weirdly eroded sandstone boulders, blasted over time into strangely shaped mounds and hollows. The area had not always been a desert. A mere 8,000 years ago it bore the name Plateau of the Rivers. The last echo of those fertile times was in the scattered groves of cypress trees.

Soon, the mountains fell away. After driving east and re-entering Libya, on an unmarked track, they arrived at the town of Ghat, where they were to meet Edal.

It was an old walled frontier town of 22,000 inhabitants, some 700 kilometres south of Marsabar. Inside its walls, the narrow alleys and tightly clustered, irregular white housing made it look like an attractive oasis in the arid sandstone landscape. On getting out of the truck, they found a cruel hot wind was blow-ing, thick with dust, making its inhabitants draw their scarves across their faces and hurry about their business, heads down to protect their eyes.

Ghat lay on the border with Algeria and on the route north from Niger and Chad. Originally a Tuareg slave-trading town, it was still a transit point, with dozens of migrants sitting listlessly on the roadside. It was clear from the numbers of people making their way north that the borders were wide open. Resources and the will to stem the tide were in short supply.

On a hill high above the town stood a large red sandstone fortress, originally built by the Italians in the 1930s, at the height of their imperial ambitions. Just as the French had waged war against the Tuareg across the border in Algeria, so the Italians in Libya had tried to protect their colonial borders. However, lines on a map in Rome went largely unrecognised by the nomadic

Tuareg and those who used the age-old migratory routes from Mali and Niger to the northern coast.

After many stops and requests for directions, Abdullah found the address Edal had given him and they parked at a distance from a small, flat-roofed house. It had a metal gate over the front door and heavy bars protecting the windows. A number of well-worn old cars were scattered in front of it. Abdullah and George eased their stiff limbs out of the truck. George stretched his arms above his head, yawning wearily.

"So, my friend, today we meet Edal Essa and the elders of the Tuareg. There will be much talking," Abdullah announced.

George sighed wearily.

"Fantastic. I could do with a sleep."

"You should try to listen, there is much for you to learn, my friend. I am hoping that they will help us. For many years, the Tuareg have fought the Tebu, another tribe, for control of the trade routes in the south. There was peace for some years, but Boutros stirred the pot and there was war over control of Ubari, a desert town four hours away."

"Why would anyone want to fight over a place like that?"

"Ah! I tell you! Ubari is at the south of the Sharara oil field, so it is very important. He who has Ubari, is in a good place to make the security. There is money to guard the oil from the Islamist gangs who come up from Mali and Niger. That is worth many dinars.

"Also, all the good, sweet water we drink in the north, in the coastal towns, comes from wells in Ubari! And that is not all. In the middle of town is something even more important."

Here, Abdullah allowed himself a dramatic pause and looked at George to make sure he had his attention.

"*Mela*, what's so very important?"

"In the centre of town is a three thousand metre runway, long enough for very big aeroplanes." Abdulla nodded his head enthusiastically and smiled broadly. "This is what the Americans like."

"Right, I see. And who controls Ubari now?"

"Nobody can tell me that. But we will help the Tuareg take it, yes?"

As Abdullah's eyes flashed with excitement, the door and security gate creaked open and the heavily lined, smiling face of Edal Essa emerged, looking up and down the empty street, before then hastily beckoning them inside.

The US PR machine had started to plant stories that the Sharara oil field was at risk from Islamic State terrorists from the Sahel and Boutros in the east, which was partly true. They claimed US and EU interests were being threatened. The message was that patience had run out with Egypt, the UAE and Russia, whose covert actions were destabilising the fragile UN-supported Government of National Accord in Tripoli. Ominously, they argued that steps needed to be taken to establish some order in the country. Those stories had not gone unnoticed in Libya.

Inside the house, the front room held a fug of cigarette smoke as twenty men crammed around the table to hear Abdullah outline his plan. He moved glasses, sugar bowls and ornaments, positioning them around the table, to illustrate his points.

"... then the drones fly in from US Incirlik airbase in Turkey." A salad spoon swooped in from the sky to land alongside the folded headscarf that was acting as the runway. "And, to destroy Boutros's aircraft, the Americans send Reaper drones from Kuwait and ... booom!" A salt cellar dived up and down, the elders' heads bobbing along with the action.

Before this, Abdullah had placed two candle holders, together representing several hundred Tuareg militia, alongside a small group of US contractors, who would be first to arrive at Ubari. They would set up the desert base within easy reach of the strategic oil facilities. It would then be safe for the main body of US Rangers to fly in and train the militia on American-supplied weaponry.

The elders craned over each other's shoulders to see the battlefield before them. Abdullah continued.

"Then, an army of Tuareg, US Rangers and contractors move north, to Marsabar, to meet my militia. We will be even more magnificent!" His hand slapped the table; the cutlery rattled and one of the candlesticks fell over. "With American drones and planes above us, we go down the Coastal Road towards the Az-Zawiyah refinery, west of Tripoli, leaving the Sharara oil fields safely protected."

Abdullah lit a cigarette and stood back.

"Boutros will run back to Egypt and the IS dogs will be at our mercy. We will make sure the oil flows and there will be jobs, money for schools, health … and a place for the Tuareg to live freely.

"It is a good plan, no?"

There were enthusiastic murmurs around the table

"So, I hear you ask me, if you do help us, what does the Tuareg get, eh? What is in it for them from the Americans?"

The elders all fell silent. The only thing that moved were the columns of cigarette smoke that unfurled and spiralled upwards, towards the ochre-stained ceiling.

"The Tuareg will have their own lands, as it was before. Azawad lands, in northern Mali, the Azger confederacy land in Libya and Algeria. All the Tuareg tribes will be recognised."

The was an outburst of excited murmuring around the table.

"The Americans say Tuareg are 'indigenous people' and will go to UN to get proper status and, also, the Americans and French will make it that Tamezgda and Tkerekrit Sultanates in Niger are also autonomous. Tuareg will rule Tuareg. There can be peace in the Sahel. It is good, no?"

A voice spoke from the back.

"All this is good, certainly, but will there be money also?"

"Ah! Yes, there is also money. To get all this, you must be police for national borders. Tuareg will have vehicles and weapons and you will stop the migration into Libya and Algeria from Niger, Mali, Chad and Sudan. You close borders except for proper trade. You keep these people off your land. If IS come, you fight them and the Americans will help. It will be known that to come north is to meet the Tuareg, a thing nobody wants."

Abdullah paused. He had saved the best bit until last. He raised one finger and wagged it in the air to quell the chatter.

"Also, you will provide the security to Wada and Sharara oil fields and for this you will be paid well!"

Many cigarettes were smoked and copious amounts of tea drunk. An atmosphere of excitement built up as it dawned on the elders that they could be on the cusp of reversing the post-colonial losses of the nineteen sixties.

Abdullah was especially pleased as he had achieved all this without touching the one hundred thousand dinars in the lockbox of the truck. He now considered that money his fee for making such excellent arrangements.

Outside, guarding the 'fee', was George, who had left the room, after listening bemused to the first two hours of the debate, and retreated to the truck for a nap, his feet sticking out of a rear window as the wind gradually filled the interior with fine desert dust.

NATASHA WAS SITTING in her favourite wicker chair on the terrace of the *castello*, feeling energised and excited. She was sipping iced coffee in the company of her father and Assistant Commissioner Camilleri. They had been discussing Maltese politics and the progress being made by Marco and Refalo in getting the permits and concessions they needed to bring the gas ashore. All was going well, but there was another matter that Natasha was interested in, which had yet to be raised.

"So, Gerald, what's happening with the Americans and the cash? Are they planning to heist it or not? D'you know?"

Camilleri was a little put out by the bluntness of the question, but could not find a reason to avoid answering her.

"I think they are planning something. I confess, I do not know any details – but it is not our business really. I heard they have some freelance hacker type who lives on a farm in the south of the island. He is putting together a scheme that allows the Americans to walk in and lift the container once it reaches Istanbul. How, I really do not know."

Marco said: "Yes, the Americans' intentions are important. At a local level, in Libya, that amount of cash can accomplish a great deal. We would like to be kept in the loop, if that is possible."

Camilleri replied, "I do not think the Americans are short of money. They are only intercepting it to stop it from getting into the hands of the LNA rebels in the east of the country. They were talking about destroying the cash."

"D'you know the name of this hacker?" Natasha enquired. "Maybe we could try and get some information from him? Spare you having to go and make enquiries."

"No, not his full name. They referred to him as Savi – short for Saviour. I am afraid that is all I know. I have seen him, though, in the back of Mike Lloyd's car. I think I would recognise him again."

Marco and Gerald continued talking while Natasha was engrossed with her phone. After a few minutes, she held the screen in front of Camilleri.

"Is this him?"

They both looked at her.

"How on earth did you do that?" Camilleri asked.

Natasha winked at him.

"Tinder. Look it up, Gerald! His name is Savi Azzopardi. He likes pizza, conspiracy theories and computer games. Just my type!"

At that moment her phone pinged.

"Well, I'd better decide what to wear, I've got myself a date!"

Later that evening, Natasha appeared, dressed for her date, and Marco was surprised to see her wearing a pair of jeans, some white trainers and a T-shirt. Her gold Omega watch had been replaced by a large pink affair, with a plastic wrist strap.

"Where on earth are you going, dressed like that?"

She looked in the hallway mirror to check her lipstick.

"I don't want to scare him, do I? We're going to Pretty Bay promenade, for an ice cream. He doesn't like travelling to the north of the island, says he gets lost easily."

"Jesus! Tell me, why exactly are you meeting him?"

"We want to know what the Americans are up to, don't we? He'll tell me."

"We could just ask them, can't we?"

"We could, but it's better to hear it from the horse's mouth. Oh, one more thing. You needn't worry, Simon is coming with me, just in case there's any funny business. See you later."

She smiled, ran her tongue over her teeth to clear any lipstick marks and left through the huge double doors studded with ancient iron nails.

Marco watched her go and wondered why Simon, his head of security, was going with her on the date. By the look of the lad, Natasha could eat him alive. Then, it belatedly occurred to him what she might have meant about hearing it from the horse's mouth.

CHAPTER 27

GEORGE ZAMMIT AND ABDULLAH BELKACEM

UBARI, LIBYA

EDAL ESSA HAD BEEN as good as his word. The Tuareg elders had agreed that the proposal was a rare opportunity to remedy some historic wrongs, be granted the right to manage their own affairs in the traditional ways – and receive a consignment of free weaponry from the United States into the bargain!

George, however, was bored and feeling useless. He had had little to do since arriving in Ghat and did not see why he could not just go home.

He had raised the issue again with Abdullah, the previous day, when they had taken a break from their discussions, sitting on the roof of the Toyota in the car park of the Old Fortress, high above the town. Abdullah had been in high spirits.

"It is going well, my friend. I could not have wished for a better start. These are good men and I hear that all of Marsabar is ready for me to return and give that dog Abu Muhammad a kicking! Now, we need the Americans to come and deliver what they have promised."

"*Mela*, Abdullah, all this is good, I agree. But I don't understand why I'm here. I wish you well and hope you give Abu Muhammad a good kicking, but do you really need me here?"

"Ah! Of course, yes! Maverick needs his Goose! Where would he be without Goose?"

"Problem is, Goose wants to fly off home, Abdullah. Goose is fed up."

"Hah, Goose wants to get into action, eh? War is like this. Much waiting and little fighting. You must be patient. There will be fighting soon and then you will be happy. I cannot wait to see you again with a gun in your hands and a smile on your face!"

George moaned quietly. The last thing he was looking forward to was actual fighting. In fact, he had no intention of being involved in any at all.

A week later, they were standing at Ghat's small airport, twenty kilometres to the north of the town, in the gathering dusk. Abdullah was excited, talking to Essa and some of the Tuareg elders on a small viewing platform on the flat roof of the one-storey air terminal. George was loitering at a distance. Eventually, his attention was caught by a wave of excitement that spread across the deck as a speck appeared in the distant sky, flying low over the black-silhouetted hills.

"Is this it?" George shouted to Abdullah.

"Yes, I have kept my word to them and the Americans have kept their word to me!" He shook his fist in the air.

They watched the speck form into a massive plane that seemed to hang in the sky, barely moving. Abdullah's eyes were wide in amazement.

"It is a wonder it can fly at all! It is a bigger plane than I thought and it looks heavy."

Abdullah stroked his beard, a look of concern spreading across his face. He put his hand to his mouth and whispered to George.

"I told them the runway was a little longer than is the truth! That will not make problems, eh?"

"You didn't, surely?"

Abdullah looked sheepish.

"We will rely on Allah; he will provide. *Inshallah!*"

They watched spellbound as the giant plane seemed to make a sudden dive for the runway and fall towards the earth.

"Look!" Abdullah grabbed George's arm hard. "The propellers have stopped and are going backwards!"

The plane skimmed the boundary fence and actually touched down on a concrete pad before the runway proper, plumes of smoke blazing from its wheels. The engines screamed as the reverse thrust from the counter-clockwise motion of the props rapidly slowed the plane. At one point, it seemed it would burst through the boundary fence at the far end of the runway but, just in time, it slowed and the pilot forced the turn, dipping the wings as the plane swung off the runway to make its way back towards the apron.

Abdullah looked at George, who puffed out his cheeks and blew a sigh of relief.

"I told you, unbeliever, it is the will of Allah!"

With that, they all ran down the stairs and out onto the apron, forming a small crowd to greet the whale of a machine. George hung back a little, unwilling to be swept up in all the excitement.

An airport worker waved his jacket in the air to guide the plane forwards. When its nose was nearly in the building, he jumped up and down frantically and the plane came to rest. The props stopped turning, the strobes stopped flashing and the rear of the fuselage dropped open. A loadmaster appeared at the head of the ramp, shouting instructions to the waiting crowd, who approached with two forklifts and six flatbed trucks.

The loadmaster quickly winched off ten pallets of assorted weaponry and an armoured personnel carrier, which was to be the transport for a team of six private military contractors. They would give the Tuareg instructions on how to use the new weaponry and then travel to join the fifty other special forces soldiers already on their way to Ubari by road, to establish a perimeter around the airfield.

Within thirty minutes, it was all over and the giant plane, several thousand kilos lighter, trundled to the very end of the runway, spun round, gunned the engines and crawled off, finally inching up into the air, its retracting wheels clearing the boundary fence by a matter of centimetres.

The next day, Abdullah asked George to help unpack the weapons and assist in training the Tuareg. He happily went to the homemade range, in a disused quarry outside of town, glad to make himself useful. He was competent around firearms and his time on the range at the Al-Udeid Air Base in Doha had made him familiar with the M-16 rifle and basic US Army small arms.

The American contractors were a rough bunch, who postured, spat, swore and generally strutted about, wearing wraparound sunglasses, their tactical vests stuffed with more equipment than they could ever have need for. They treated the Tuareg with contempt, speaking to them as though they were a squad of grunts who had never set foot in the desert before.

It took the Tuareg a while to learn how to set up the M-16, zeroing the sights, adjusting the windage drum and elevation settings, but eventually they all became confident and the range rang with the crack of rifle shots. Tuareg learn to fire rifles when they are still children. Soon, they were shredding the paper targets with volleys of measured, accurate shots, impressing their tutors, who started to realise this militia had potential as a powerful fighting force.

When George arrived on the range, he had made himself known to Sam, the platoon leader. The contractors had not known what to make of Abdullah's adviser. George's stubble had now grown out into a proper beard and his indigo *cheche*, expertly tied over his ragged hair, revealed only the upper half of his desert-tanned face. His dusty, worn clothing was being washed, so he had been given a light *bubus*, a traditional long gown worn by many of the older men. He had swapped his heavy, scuffed boots for a pair of sandals and looked every inch a desert nomad.

Sam, the heavily tattooed Texan platoon commander, had

watched him handling the M-16 and sidled over to him afterwards, thumbs tucked into the shoulder pads of his tactical vest.

"So, what's the fucking deal with you?"

George was wary of these hired mercenaries, masquerading under corporate branding.

"No deal. I'm with the Maltese Police, here as an adviser."

"Maltese Police? Dude, you're totally lost!"

"I know. It's not my idea of a great assignment."

"I don't usually ask questions but – how d'you know how to handle the M-16? You ex-military?"

"No, but I've had some experience of desert warfare. I've trained with the Green Berets and the Rangers at Al-Udeid."

"No fucking shit?"

George knew this boast was a mistake, as soon as he'd broadcast it, but there was no way of taking it back.

"Tell you what, have you ever fired an SAW? An M249 squad machine gun?"

"Er, yes, a few rounds on the range at Al-Udeid. I've also fired twin Brownings mounted on a technical."

George could not stop himself from bragging to the big, well-muscled Texan about the time he had closed his eyes, pulled the twin triggers on the Brownings and unleashed mayhem onto Abu Muhammad's men at Abdullah's compound in Marsabar.

"OK! Well, you're the man! We'll fire some bursts this afternoon, but once we get to Ubari, if we get hit, we'll need someone who can handle a squad machine gun, to help in one of the crews. We need four crews covering the perimeter, but we're a bit short of hands. So great, you've got the job! What's your name?"

"George."

Sam looked puzzled.

"George? That's not an Arab name?"

"I'm not an Arab. I told you, I'm Maltese."

"Yeah, cool. I thought you spoke OK English for an Arab."

The night after, Abdullah and George were sitting in their Toyota pickup, their flatbed loaded with boxes of automatic rifles, mortars, ammunition, military ration packs and spare wheels for the technicals. The convoy of nearly twenty vehicles had left Ghat around midnight, to try and cover the 370 kilometres to Ubari before sunrise, so they could arrive in the town undetected.

They drove on at speed through the night, luckily without incident, and reached the town in the half light of early morning. The convoy roared through the streets, causing lights to turn on and citizens to go to their windows, to see what new evil had arrived.

They drove straight into the airport dropoff area. There two contractors, in the by now familiar black personal body armour, waved torches to guide them through a security fence and onto the airside apron. The larger unit of contractors had arrived the day before, from Tunisia, in their own fleet of technicals and trucks.

They had told the few Libyan Air Force personnel stationed at the airport they had an hour to clear the two antique government MiG fighters off the apron, otherwise they would be destroyed. As it turned out, there was only one pilot in the area capable of flying a MiG and the second jet was not in service. So the solitary pilot had quickly got the first plane airborne and headed off to Tripoli, while the second aircraft lay smouldering on the concrete, after the contractors had fired a few grenade rounds into it.

The government in Tripoli had received twenty-four hours' advance warning of US intentions, but knew they could only raise token objections. They had told Libyan Air, the sole commercial operator at the airport, to cancel all forthcoming commercial flights.

A giant C17 Globemaster had landed shortly afterwards, depositing its cargo of bobcat diggers, personnel carriers and a tracked battlefield air-defence system.

The bobcat diggers were scooping buckets of loose rubble and sand from the edges of the runway to fill several lines of Hesco gabions that were to form a defensive perimeter around the entrance to the airport terminal. The Hescos were square, wire-mesh containers, with heavy-duty fabric liners that were filled with dirt and rubble to form instant defensive walls. They littered the warzones of the Middle East, evidence of past conflicts, often piled one on top of another, forming flat-topped modern-day pyramids, in memory of failed ventures and fruit-less conflicts.

CHAPTER 28
YAROSLAV BUKOV
ABU MUHAMMAD'S CAMP,
NORTHERN CHAD

Yaroslav had already survived several weeks as a prisoner of Abu Muhammad's Islamic State-in-Libya. Abu Muhammad had been in Libya since 2014, when ISIS leader Abu Bakr al-Baghdadi dispatched a group of jihadis from Syria to Libya to establish a new branch of the terrorist group. They had set up a base in Darnah, in the east of the country, and soon after announcing they would accept oaths of allegiance from fighters in Libya, had mustered a force of several hundred men.

The Russian was shackled to a hasp, set firmly in the stone floor of what was basically a concrete box. During the first few days, he had chafed, cut and eventually rubbed the skin off his wrist, trying to work the steel hasp from the floor. The design of the restraint was simple and effective, so he was forced to concede defeat, not something that came easily to him.

There was a small, high-level window that indicated the passing of night and day. Occasionally, there was the sound of a voice, or the revving of a motor vehicle outside, but mainly all he could hear was the rasping of the wind as it blew sand and dust against the structures of the camp. He sensed he was still somewhere deep in the southern desert of Libya, or Chad, or Sudan – who knew where? There was nothing he could do except wait.

Food and water were brought daily, but the extremes of hot and cold were a torture in themselves. For a few hours in the early morning and early evening, his body achieved some measure of equilibrium. Other than that, he spent the sweltering July days in his concrete shed, bathed in sweat, the air around him thick and cloying, praying for the cool of the night. The hours of darkness he spent shivering, curled into a ball and dreaming of the heat to come.

He had a thin, soiled mattress to sit or lie on and a bucket, for his toilet. He had been given so little to eat and drink, eventually he had no use for it.

The bulky young Englishman, who called himself Raheem Green, was the only person Yaroslav saw in the first two weeks of his captivity. Raheem spoke to him sparingly. He told Yaroslav he had taken his first name after the footballer and his second from the colour associated with paradise, as foretold in the Quran. Raheem was born and bred in North London and had come to Chad from Iraq. Other than explaining the provenance of his taken name, he told Yaroslav nothing more that might yield a clue as to why he was being held.

For the first few days he had exercised, using various Pilates moves to stretch and maintain his muscle tone. As the heat, physical weakness, depression and the hopelessness of captivity descended on him, this had ceased to be of interest and, despite his efforts, the lethargy of confinement had taken over. He had been at a low point when, three weeks in, Raheem had entered with a younger man and, instead of leaving some flat bread and a bowl of lentils, his companion started fiddling with the locks on the shackle and the hasp.

He beckoned Yaroslav to his feet and placed an oily black hood over his head. He was too weak to cause any trouble, but saw Raheem was holding a semi-automatic rifle. He also noticed he stood far enough away to avoid any sudden lunges.

"Come," Raheem said, "they want to speak to you."

"Who do? What for?"

"Just come. There is no problem."

Yaroslav was no coward, but his throat was dry and his knees were shaking as he shuffled out, cringing away from the full glare of the sunlight that penetrated the hessian hood. He walked maybe one hundred metres and caught the smells of cooking; the harsh guttural tones of the Arab tongue; the sounds of large diesel engines ticking over. He concluded it was a sizeable camp but, by sound alone, could only guess at the numbers of men present.

Eventually, he felt a coolness on his neck and head as he entered deep shade. He was pushed into a structure and the hood removed. He was in a large tan-coloured tent of heavy-duty vinyl. Where the window covers had been rolled back, he could see a further black coating, designed to frustrate heat-sensitive surveillance. To his surprise, he realised the coolness had not come from entering the shade of the tent, but from air-conditioning units attached to the rear fabric wall. He smelled cigarettes, sweat and his own fear.

The command centre was three large integrated tent units. A sophisticated communication setup occupied one corner. Yaroslav quickly assessed the level of organisation and resources. This was no squalid temporary camp.

A small, plump, middle-aged man in camo fatigues got up from a folding chair and walked over to Yaroslav. He had a long grey beard, but no moustache; the left side of his beard was stained yellow from years of heavy smoking. There were half a dozen others in the tent: some working on laptops, others lounging in camping chairs, weapons at their side. A tall, thin man in baggy grey trousers, sandals and a long sleeveless quilted jacket stood up and came across to join them. He had a long, greying beard, but his black eyes remained hard and the intensity of his stare told Yaroslav it was he who shouldered the responsi-bility for whatever was going on here.

The shorter man pointed to a cluster of chairs in the corner of the adjacent tent. He shouted something in Arabic and a youngster appeared with a bottle of ice-cold water, which he gave to Yaroslav. He greedily opened it and poured a huge measure of the icy liquid into his mouth, immediately causing every nerve in his jaw and forehead to jangle in pain. He gasped.

"Slowly, friend. I have seen horses become ill drinking cold water that way." The plump man laughed. "You can call me Faysal."

Yaroslav sat and breathed out heavily. The pain subsided.

"So, you are a Russian Volunteer? Arrived in this faraway country to help Boutros in his good works?" Faysal smiled.

"I am a Russian civilian, here to survey oil fields."

"Then it was not you in the convoy of armed Russians? It was not you who attacked our comrades on the desert road and gunned down six men while they fled? And I suppose it was not you who paid us in weapons to attack the Italians at the Marsabar gas terminal, so you could take it for yourselves?"

The tall man with the black eyes, who sprawled, long-limbed, across a flimsy canvas chair, turned to Faysal and said: "Well, you have got the wrong man. We must let him go."

Faysal looked at him and said in a mocking tone: "Abu Muhammad, please forgive the mistake. It was honestly made."

Abu Muhammad gazed at Yaroslav, his dark eyes and fixed expression giving no clue to his deliberations. Nevertheless, Yaroslav knew his life hung by a thread.

"You would be dead, Russian, if I did not have need of you. I will know what you know, about the oil fields and how they can be used. I need to get the crude refined at the wellheads or send it to refineries on the coast or else Egypt. I need to avoid Boutros in Benghazi and the thieves in Tripoli. I have road transport. I need you to show us the best sites for this and help us make arrangements. I want all your ideas. If you mislead or trick me, there is only one outcome."

Yaroslav understood.

"So, you know I am oil man and not soldier?"

Abu Muhammad was impassive.

"I know you are a Russian and no friend of mine."

"What will you do with me?"

"I will free you from the chain. For thirty minutes in the morning and in the evening, you may leave the house to exercise. If you wander into the desert, we will see which way you choose. Likely, we would let you go, because there is nothing around for a hundred kilometres and you will soon die. If you take a vehicle, I will launch a drone. My men will fight for the pleasure of hunting you down.

"You will work with Faysal and Raheem. When we are happy, we will exchange you for money or for prisoners. If your Volunteers will not trade you, we will kill you. I will decide.

"You can say now that you do not want this work and Faysal will take you outside and it can all be over. No more heat, no more cold, and no more hunger or thirst. Is that what you want?"

Yaroslav looked into the face of the tall man with the black eyes and realised there was only one answer.

"I work."

He racked his brain for what he knew of Abu Muhammad. He knew the name and that he led an IS-affiliated group in Libya. They usually operated further to the west, near to the Sharara oil field and had bases around Marsabar, where they had control of the refinery and port. That was why the Russians had paid them for the raid to scare off the Italians.

After the meeting, things improved dramatically. He was given a camp bed with a fitted mattress and blankets to keep him warm at night. He had a bucket of water every morning, as well as a supply of cold bottled water. He even had a daily allowance of fruit, to help relieve the skin complaint he had developed during his weeks of confinement.

He received a wooden table and a couple of chairs. In the morning and late afternoons, they would work. He told Raheem what he needed.

"I need, how is this called, 'exploration software' to tell me where are good deposits. If deposits are good and well is working, we make arrangements for photographs to see site layout and security.

"I need all geological maps of Sirte Basin. You buy online from Centre of Industrial Studies in Tripoli. They are old maps, from nineteen sixties surveys, when times were good. Things are different now. This is a shit country.

"I want all maps you find. Economic maps, population, transport, climate maps, all maps."

Raheem had a degree in Applied Science from London Metropolitan University and proved able to access a lot of the technical information Yaroslav needed from various commercial sources.

He did not see Abu Muhammad again for some time, but Faysal, his number two, and Raheem busied themselves, ferrying information and instructions to him. Faysal was less forthcoming about his technical background, but Yaroslav soon guessed he must have been involved in the oil and gas sector during his time in Iraq.

Yaroslav learned the group had originally come from their base near Marsabar to reconnoitre the south-west. They wanted to assess the oil fields, to explore what might be extracted from them by way of revenue. It was clear they lacked Yaroslav's practical experience and that was why he had been taken. Since Syria and northern Iraq had fallen, they had lost access to the oil revenues they needed to fight their battles and develop their Caliphate. Abu Muhammad's militia had been instructed to seek out revenue from the more remote deserts of Southern Libya.

They had a small drone they used to deliver photographs of sites Yaroslav had previously visited. The photographs reminded him of each location, its capabilities and his conclusions when he had been there.

He sent them out to reconnoitre and photograph certain wells to help assess whether they were working; how well they were defended, the size of the workforce and where they came from. Yaroslav was in his element. They were producing a plan to become an oil business in their own right – just stealing the crude for their own purposes. He found himself becoming more and more enthusiastic about the project and started to amuse himself, modelling likely outputs and constructing a rough financial forecast. He knew the harder he worked, the better his chances were of staying alive. He had seen how little this group valued human life.

At some of the northern wells, he proposed a plan to load the crude into a fleet of tankers, which could shuttle to the coast and back, taking the crude to refineries. There, they would either sell it, via intermediaries, or have it converted into petrol and smuggle it into Egypt or Sudan, for the black market. In Libya, they would just sell it at the pumps, through independent garages that did not care who they bought from.

He had even identified a small primitive refinery, built by smugglers, which produced *mazout,* the heavy oil commonly used to fuel domestic generators. He told Faysal they should just use their muscle and take it. There was good money to be made.

In addition, ISIL had started 'taxing' the production of crude at certain well heads. Faysal told him that, in Iraq, ISIL had controlled the oil fields in the north of the country, producing thousands of barrels of heavy crude oil a day. They had been able to recruit engineers and expert personnel to manage over 200 wells. Yaroslav was impressed, but he thought this opportunity wasted in the hands of a bunch of barbarians. There were times when he had to remind himself who he was and what he was doing. He was a prisoner held in a concrete box, in the eastern deserts of the Sahara.

One night everything suddenly changed. For a day or so beforehand, Yaroslav had been aware of an increase in the level of activity around the camp. There seemed to be a lot of new faces he had not seen before. The technicals were being checked over and large metal boxes of cannon shells, petrol and machine gun ammo were being strapped onto the rear decks. They were preparing to move out.

The morning after, Faysal failed to appear and Raheem was tense. He refused to be drawn about what was happening, but said Yaroslav was to stay in the camp and continue his work. The Russian put the move out of his mind and continued concentrating on the task in hand. Raheem was forever looking out of the doorway, smoking and watching what proved to be the final stages of the preparations.

That night, almost immediately after the sun fell, there was a big commotion lasting for several hours as the fighters started to form up the convoy. Engines fired and there were raised voices, instructions being shouted and the nervous laughter of excited men. Yaroslav could not see anything, but suddenly the engines stopped and the fighters fell silent. He heard a gentle wind rippling the canvas tenting and rustling through the low scrub. He could almost hear the breathing of the large crowd of men, waiting, anticipating. Then he heard the distorted tones of Abu Muhammad ringing around the camp. He had a microphone and some type of portable speaker. The tinny sound echoed around the desert as he led what Yaroslav assumed was the prayer before battle.

"Merciful Father, I have squandered my days with plans of many things … For all we ought to have thought and have not thought, all we ought to have said and have not said, all we ought to have done and have not done, I pray thee, Allah, for forgiveness

"For Your sake, I go forth, and for Your sake I advance, and for Your sake … I fight!"

A loud throaty cheer was followed by the sound of engines and the shouting of commands.

CHAPTER 29
NATASHA BONNICI

SAVIOUR AZZOPARDI'S HOUSE, SOUTH MALTA

NATASHA'S DATE had gone well. As arranged, she had found Savi sitting on the blue bench outside Mario's Café on the promenade at Pretty Bay, a nondescript coastal resort on the south side of the island. Its name was a misnomer, given it was overshadowed by Freeport Malta, the big commercial freight terminal, with its travelling cranes and mountainous piles of stacked containers only an icecream cone's throw from the public beach.

She had to smile when she first saw him. He was sitting on the back of the bench, with his feet on the seat, engrossed in something on his phone. He either had no decent clothes in his wardrobe or had made no effort whatsoever to dress up for the occasion. He wore battered, dirty old jeans, a white T-shirt with some sporting logo and a pair of trainers that must have cost some money when he had bought them, several years earlier.

He was skinny and had shoulder-length, lank, mousy hair that hung limp against the residual acne on his pitted cheeks. Natasha was surprised. He looked very young, though his profile had said he was thirty. She doubted he was any more than twenty-five.

She had sat down next to him on the bench and looked straight ahead, out over the beach towards the fleet of small, multi-coloured fishing boats that gently rocked in the waters of the bay. It was some minutes before he was even aware of her presence. She could sense him looking at her and glancing back to his phone, checking her profile picture on the dating app.

"So, when you've finished playing with your phone, are you going to buy me this ice cream, Savi?"

"Er, yeah, sure. Hi!"

He stepped off the bench, smiled at her and gave a little wave.

"So, you want the ice cream now? This minute?"

"That's what you offered." She smiled sweetly.

"OK. It's yours."

He thrust his hands in his pockets, turned his back on her and shuffled off towards the café.

Natasha shook her head and went after him, walking alongside.

"D'you treat all your girlfriends like this?"

"Like what?"

"Like you don't give a shit about them? I suppose you're shy." She wrinkled her nose as she said it.

"I'm not shy. It just takes me a while to loosen up, that's all."

"Fair enough. OK, so, here it is. I don't really want a bloody ice cream. Do you live nearby?"

"Sure."

"Let's cut the crap and go to your place then."

Natasha smiled at him and put one hand on his shoulder, looking him straight in the eye.

"Do you have clean sheets?"

He stared at her, speechless, his mouth open. She pressed herself lightly against him. They were the same height. Savi took a small step back in surprise.

"Well? Have you got clean sheets?"

"Yeah, sure. What for?"

"For God's sake, I'm not looking for a husband! I use the app for casual sex. Still interested?"

A faint smile crossed his face.

"Yeah, of course!"

"Good. Where's your car then?"

"I've got a scooter."

"A scooter – really? Well, I'm not riding on that. I've got a car, I'll follow. Off you go now."

He started off then turned back, looking at her askance.

"Are you being serious or are you just taking the piss?"

"D'you want to take a chance or should I just leave now and find someone else? Come on, I'm really in the mood."

"OK, let's go. The scooter's parked over there."

He pointed to the end of the promenade.

She watched the boy go to his scooter and then walked back to the BMW SUV, where Simon was sitting in the driver's seat, smiling.

"Not a fucking word!" she warned.

He burst out laughing. Simon looked after security for Marco and her. He was a large Polish man, who spent a lot of time lifting weights, as well as running up and down the long steep hill that climbed to the *castello* from St Paul's. He had messed up badly when chasing Nick Walker across the Mediterranean, during the oil-smuggling fiasco, and had succeeded in losing Marco's million-euro yacht from a marina in Tunis. Ultimately, Marco had forgiven and reinstated him. After all, he trusted the bodyguard with his life – what was the loss of a boat? Natasha knew this man was a total professional and would help her in anything she needed to do.

"Quite a catch, Miss Natasha. Not sure how he'll fit into life at the *castello*!"

She punched him on the arm, hard.

"I said, not a word! Listen, get in the back and keep your head down. I don't want him seeing you."

They followed Savi out of town, Natasha keeping well back just in case she had to stop for traffic lights or at junctions. She need not have worried. The scooter had no mirrors and, as far as she could tell, Savi never turned his head once.

After ten minutes, the scooter pulled up a narrow dirt track and Natasha followed. She nearly swerved off the road when a jet thundered over the car before bouncing down onto the airport runway, only metres ahead of them. It gave her some satisfaction to realise he lived in such an isolated spot.

She said to Simon: "What a convenient place to live! OK, I'll go in first. You wait right outside the door. When I shout, you come in – and make sure you do!"

"How do I know I won't be interrupting anything?" he asked tongue in cheek.

"This is getting really tiresome. We need to ask this boy some questions and, if we don't get the answers I want, we need to persuade him to talk, OK? We don't need to get too rough – just scare him a bit. I can't imagine he's going to be too much of a problem."

"I get it."

"Good. We're here."

Natasha watched Savi park the scooter, remove his helmet and turn to beckon her in. She followed on his heels and drew in her breath sharply as she entered. Then regretted it instantly. Savi lived by himself and he lived in filth. There were flies in his kitchen and open takeaway cartons of food on the unit tops. Juice bottles and beer cans were piled in the sink, alongside stacks of unwashed dishes. His lounge was even worse. The windows had been painted shut and there was no ventilation. Pizza boxes and kebab wrappers had been routinely stuffed under the couch and ashtrays were filled with cigarette butts. Natasha had a thing about cockroaches – they terrified her. With a shudder, she tried to put the thought of them roaming through the filth out of her mind.

The shock must have registered on her face, as he said over his shoulder, "Yeah, it's a bit of a mess – I usually clean on a Friday. Sorry about that.

"My God, Savi, how can you live like this? It's a shithouse. Do you never get ill?"

"Look, I've only got one set of sheets, but I've got a clean sleeping bag. Shall I go and get it?"

He looked at her hopefully.

"No, I'll tell you what, let's talk first. There are some questions I'd like to ask."

"Yeah, cool."

She shouted loudly: "Simon, come in here, please."

The back door opened and the big man walked in, grinning.

"Hi, Savi!" he said. "Good to meet you. Oh, Jesus, it smells in here!"

Natasha wrinkled her nose, this time in disgust.

"It's making me gag."

Savi watched the big Pole as he slipped off his black jacket and started to work his large hands into some tight black leather gloves.

"Who the fuck are you? What are you doing here?"

Natasha sighed and went up close to Savi.

"OK, you disgusting little dirt bag, fun's over. I need to know what you've told the Americans about jacking a container. It's simple – tell me and they'll never know you've talked. Stay schtum and Simon will beat the shit out of you. Then, I'll tell the Americans you told us everything and they'll be pissed off and *they* will beat the shit out of you. Got it, Savi?"

His eyes opened wide, pupils dilated.

"Americans? What Americans?"

Natasha looked at Simon, and pointed at Savi. Simon stepped forward and cuffed him hard across the ear. Savi cringed and wrapped his arms around his head.

Natasha continued.

"Do I really have to spell it out for you? Because I can go away if you want and leave you with Simon for thirty minutes. I'll bet you'll be ready to talk when I come back!"

He did not respond. Natasha picked up her bag and turned as if to leave.

"Wait, I can't tell you what they're up to, they'll kill me! It's the CIA, for fuck's sake."

Natasha turned to look at him.

"If you're clever they'll never even know. Remember who you're stealing from. Make it look like an inside job. Russians stealing from Russians. That happens, doesn't it?"

"What d'you want to know?" he whined. "I'm not saying I've got the answers."

"I want to know all about the ship and its cargo. Its name, when it leaves, and I need to know when it reaches a certain position in the Black Sea. I need to make sure our container is on the top of the stack on that ship and I need it unloading on a certain date, at Constanta, Romania. I need the port authorities there to release the container to our carrier. Oh, and I need some software in place, to remotely open a set of battery-powered actuated valves.

"All stuff you'd be doing for the Americans, if you were going to steal the container in Istanbul – true?"

"No, not true. I won't be able to do all that. I need the shipper's details from the Americans. I need to get hold of a copy of the Bill of Lading and do a switch, then a change of destination. So, I need to get a copy of the email from the shipper of the goods, releasing the Bill of Lading. It's not that easy. And I need to know a lot more about all this."

"OK, good, you're talking. That's a start. There's work to do, we understand that. Get a few things together. You'll be away for about a week, I'd guess. Pack your laptop and anything you need to work."

"Why, what's happening?"

"You're coming with us until this is all done. It'll keep you out of the hands of Mike Lloyd. Yeah, I know who you're dealing with. Go on, get your stuff together and give your passport and ID card to Simon."

The bodyguard followed Savi around the house as he picked up bits of clothing from the floor, several remote hard drives and some notebooks. All he needed went into a rucksack and two carrier bags.

"I don't understand why you're taking me. And where to?"

"Listen, you dolt. I don't want you running off to Mike Lloyd, or whoever else will have you. So, for the time being, you're staying with us. We have a nice place with a TV and some old school DVDs. The WiFi gets turned on when you're working and not when we can't watch you. Now, give me your phone."

As with all younger people, that was like demanding the sacrifice of a limb and his hand instinctively went to his rear pocket. Simon's meaty hand fastened itself to Savi's wrist and Natasha gingerly slid two fingers inside the pocket to retrieve the phone.

"There. Are we all ready? Let's go and see your new home." Casting her eyes around, she said: "It can't be any worse than this shithouse. When it's done, we'll pay you ten thousand euros. That's a lot of money. You could get a cleaner."

She fixed him with a cold stare and waved his passport in front of him.

"If you try and fuck off or screw this up, we'll kill you – you can be sure of that! It's a small island and you're going nowhere, so just bear it in mind."

Savi was cowering. Natasha thought he was about to cry.

"Who are you anyway?" he muttered.

Simon grabbed him by the collar and pulled him towards the door, saying, "Shut up and get in the car."

He bundled Savi into the back of the SUV and then sat next to him. Natasha activated the child locks and drove.

When they reached the entrance to the *castello*'s estate, Natasha drove past the main gate until she found a small farm track that dropped down onto the valley floor. There another rutted, orange-clay track weaved its way westward, through tall clumps of bamboo, towards the coast. Finally, they reached a three-metre palisade fence with a padlocked gate. Behind the fence was an old chapel, dating back to the seventeenth century, set high on the cliff top. It had spectacular views over the ocean, where a blazing pink sun was rapidly falling below the horizon.

"This is it, our family chapel. It's called Our Lady of the Abandoned! Quite apt, in your case.

Savi looked at the building suspiciously.

"There's food, a basic kitchen, water, sanitation, and Simon will come twice a day to let you get some sun and have a wander around. There's just the one stained-glass window and just a single door to the outside, which makes it perfect. But please don't think you can take advantage of that because it also has some underground stone caves, which used to be catacombs. One has an old wooden door and I've fitted it with a very modern lock. Any messing around and we'll keep you down there. You won't like that, I guarantee it!"

"What about Mike Lloyd, won't he want to know where I am?"

"Of course. We'll WhatsApp him and tell him you don't trust him and you're staying someplace safe until this is over. He needs to know you'll still do what he asks and we'll give him your bank account details, so he can pay you too. You could score big time here!"

Savi stared at Natasha imploringly.

"OK, listen, I'll do what you want, no problem. There are no guarantees, though. It's not like boosting credit card data. But, please, I'll go loony in that place." He pointed to the chapel. "At least get me an X-Box, I'll use it off-line, and the latest *Fifa* and *Civilisation VI*. That should keep me sane for a week."

"Oh," said Natasha, "and one more thing … can you remotely access a network and disable the security cameras? I've got the password."

"How come? Is it your house or do you work there or something?"

Natasha just looked at him.

"OK, don't tell me, I don't care. Give me your email address and write down the network password and the date and time you want the cameras disabled. Consider it done. Do you want me to turn them back on again?"

"Yes, forty-five minutes later."

"OK, piece of cake, and I'll fix it so no one can trace the hack back to you or me. Just get me the games."

Natasha looked at Simon, who gave a curt nod.

With that, they locked Savi in the chapel and made their way back to the car. After a minute or so, they saw a glow at the back of the building as the lights came on and illuminated the old stained glass.

Simon smiled: "Looks like the genius found the light switch. Let's hope he's as good at hacking as the Americans think."

"Better," she replied, "because he'll need to keep them convinced he's following through on their plan at the same time as he dismantles it. And if he messes up …"

She glanced over to the cliff edge. Simon stared back at her.

Natasha tilted her head to one side, thinking.

"I haven't decided yet. Maybe he'll turn out to have other uses. Let's see."

Simon raised his eyebrows and she punched him painfully on the arm.

"Definitely not that!"

MIKE LLOYD and Mary-Ann Baker were sitting in the executive lounge of Zurich Airport, waiting for the Aeroflot flight from Moscow to land. Mike was a negotiator at heart and achieved more through his address book than the pen-pushers in Langley ever knew.

He was passing the time by fiddling with his phone.

"I'm telling you, Mary-Ann, turn off your data roaming. This place is the biggest rip off I know. Last time I was here, I got a bill for data for two hundred euros just for downloading a couple of sports pages." Mike nodded to himself. "Yeah, it's true."

Mary-Ann sighed. "Come on, Uncle Sam won't begrudge us a few euros."

"Don't you believe it. The American taxpayer likes to know his dollar is being well spent."

Mike Lloyd was known for being tight with money; his and the taxpayer's.

"So how do you know Petrov?"

"I don't. I know someone who does."

You've never met him or spoken to him?"

"Nope."

"This should be interesting then. He's not gonna be pleased with us."

"He certainly won't be!"

Mary-Ann Baker had been a little concerned about this off-the-books meeting. She found that a lot of what Mike did was off-the-books and worried that one day it could come back to bite him – or, more importantly, her. She was totally unprepared for the meeting and worried that Mike was too. She had no idea what might happen when they met the Russian.

"You don't seem very certain about the play here?"

Mike was reading the sports section of one of the free American newspapers he had picked up at lounge reception.

"I'm not! I'm just reaching out to see what we can do, before the Pentagon and the Russian Ministry of Defence start throwing rocks at each other. Maybe nothing. Could all be a waste of air fare."

He returned to the report on the Virginia Cavaliers' latest basketball game, but noticed the minute Valentin Petrov entered the lounge.

"Game time," he muttered, without looking up from the paper.

Mary-Ann tried not to swivel her head.

"Where?"

Mike turned a page and shuffled in his seat, recrossing his legs to face away from the counter.

"The older, big guy with the silver hair, in the fifty-bucks suit and brown shoes."

Valentin Petrov entered the executive lounge and stood by the reception desk. He spotted Mike Lloyd at a table on the far side, reading the paper. Mike crossed his legs and then uncrossed them again – a signal to show he had been recognised.

Petrov was a commercially minded man at heart, but politics and Russian pride could not be ignored when dealing with the Americans. Lloyd had suggested the meeting, let him make the play.

After the niceties, Lloyd asked about the missing gas specialist.

"So, where's your boy Yaroslav? Careless of him, getting picked up like that."

Petrov smiled and grimaced.

"Yes, poor Yaroslav. Islamic State have him in Chadian desert. There is no recent contact. When we hear, we pay or we exchange for him. He is worth much to them. They are clever – they know his price will be good."

"So why did they grab him anyway?"

"They tell me they drive him around the desert and Yaroslav looks at oil fields for them. Which field is good, which not so good. If you have intel on him, in spirit of co-operation, a call would be appreciated."

"Hmm. That's a reasonable request. I'll bear it in mind."

Petrov leaned back in his chair and crossed his legs. He unbuttoned the jacket of his bird's-eye weave, steel grey business suit. Mike found the cut a bit too aggressive for the Western taste, but he noticed it perfectly matched the colour of the Russian's swept-back hair.

"So, Mr Lloyd, what are you doing in Libya? I am very interested to hear."

"Well, after the bomb in Malta, you basically gave us no choice but to get involved. That was a mistake on your part."

Petrov moved to speak. Mike held up his hand to silence him and continued.

"We won't let Boutros take Tripoli and we're not going to let Libya end up as a satellite state of the Kremlin, on Europe's doorstep. It's only three hundred kilometres from Sicily, for Christ's sake. We're talking Cuba here. Not going to happen. Not on."

Petrov considered this opening gambit.

"So, you are ready for another Iraq, another Afghanistan? How long you plan to stay for this time … ten years … twenty? I do not think we see American boots on ground."

"No, Valentin. This is different. The Libyan people are sick of militias, sick of foreign fighters, sick of ISIL, sick of their country, which should be one of the richest in Africa, getting messed about by foreign interests."

Petrov laughed.

"Sounds same as Iraq to me. Great thinking, Mr Lloyd! So, you will go in, give everyone democracy and sort out all problems?"

"Yeah, we'll do it differently this time. Project Democracy! Quite a good ring to it, hasn't it? Remember, there's no Muammar Gaddafi or Sadam Hussein this time, no figurehead. It'd be low key, apart from taking out Boutros and maybe ISIL. That'll be a big bang! But afterwards, it'll be easier. There's no Sunni and Shia conflict in Libya. One Sunni government, for a Sunni people. We'd tolerate a moderate Islamic government, just a few Muslim Brotherhood, we can live with that. Iraq was Sunni government for Shia people, with Iran shit-stirring on the sidelines."

"OK, all very interesting worldview and I am sure someone has gamed this back in Moscow, so it will be no surprise to Kremlin. Say it all happens this way. What about our pipeline?"

"We'll buy it."

"You can license it."

"No, that means you retain control. We'll buy it."

"What about lifting threat of sanctions on NordStream2 and TurkStream?"

Mike Lloyd glanced up at Petrov, rather too quickly, and mentally kicked himself. So that was what the Russian was after.

"Now *that's* interesting. You hope maybe someone in the US can take the heat off the Europeans, so they can finish their end of the project and grant you the licences?"

Petrov gazed steadily at Mike, as he thought for a few seconds.

"I can see you'd like to get those lovely pipes ashore. How

about that? Not much point having them all under the Baltic and the Black Sea, if they lead nowhere!"

The pipelines from Russia, under the Black Sea to Turkey and under the Baltic into Germany, were designed to supply gas to replace the declining North Sea output and fuel Europe's growing economies. Following the invasion of Ukraine in 2014, and Russia's aggression in the Balkans, the US had threatened European contractors with sanctions preventing the completion of the projects. It was a threat the Russians needed removed, so they could get the pipelines finished and start getting a return on their considerable investment.

"Yes, Mike … I call you Mike, yes? Nearly as useless as having a pipeline on edge of European territorial waters, from big unexploited African fields, with no gas flowing!"

"You've got a point there, Valentin."

They talked for another three hours, neither man taking notes. It became apparent that Petrov's main goal was to secure the supply through NordStream2 and TurkStream, the two new routes that avoided crossing Ukraine. In principle, he thought a sale of the VertWay Libyan-Malta pipeline infrastructure could be arranged, if Mike could put a buyer forward.

Mike was surprised the Russian seemed to be prepared to drop the Libyan project, without much argument, prompting him to wonder whether the whole thing had been designed to bring about this very scenario. If so, it was an extremely expensive geopolitical gamble, but one that seemed to be about to pay off. By threatening to construct a supply route from Libya, the Russians had created another bargaining chip, one they were willing to surrender to secure their real goal – security of supply for their other trans-European pipelines.

Mike was a chess player and Valentin had seized the initiative. Mike did not like that. It left the US with a big job to do in Libya; one that could be seen as an escalation of their involvement in another Islamic, oil-rich nation, which would not play well globally. The VertWay supply had all sorts of benefits for

Libya, Malta and Europe, while pushing the Russians away from the Libyan oil fields. So, it kind of worked all round.

As they boarded the direct flight back to Malta, Mary-Ann noticed Mike was in a contemplative mood and was curious.

"So, talk about putting the world to rights! What are you going to do now?"

"I'm gonna go back to Langley. There are people there I've got to talk to. I also need to speak to some people in the government, plus oil industry players, and I need to know what's happening on the ground in Libya. Can you get me an update on that?"

On the plane, he quickly turned on his phone to check for messages. He was surprised to see one from Savi Azzopardi, under the alias 'Snakehead'. They used an encryption app, so it took a little time before he could read it.

Gone dark until this is all over. Nervous about it. Will work from somewhere I feel safe. Send info when you need action.

Lloyd was surprised, because he did not think Saviour Azzopardi had enough wit to do something like that. It did not seem like him.

CHAPTER 31

GEORGE ZAMMIT
UBARI AIRPORT, LIBYA

THEY HAD ARRIVED in Ubari during the early hours of the morning and the contractors were already busy preparing defensive positions around the airport. Their base was in the terminal building. A long line of Hesco gabions formed a perimeter wall across the main car park to the front and there were protected positions on the apron, to the rear of the terminal building.

George had been nabbed by Sam as he tried to take a nap inside the departure lounge on the first floor of the terminal.

"Hey, soldier, come here. Time to meet your squad leader and get to work."

He had changed out of the *bubus* robe into his camo cargo pants, but had kept the *cheche* around his head, for practical reasons. It kept the dust and sand out of his face and protected him from the worst of the sun. He had acquired a sand-coloured military jacket and, with his growing black beard, was looking more and more like one of the Tuareg fighters. The only problem was that the Tuaregs were used to going a long way on very little fuel, so George's portly physique did not quite complement the look. But with no fridge on hand to snack from and only eating occasional sparse meals, he noticed he had begun to pull his belt tighter and tighter.

Sam marched him out onto the edge of the apron, to a Hesco wall that ran thirty metres and ended in a block structure, to protect those inside from mortar blasts. There was a platform made of wooden pallets, with firing slits for observation and defence.

"OK, we're out on the west flank here, so you've got eyes over a ninety-degree field, from that yellow directional sign on the taxiway over to the beginning of the turn into the apron. That field is your responsibility. Got it?"

George peered nervously out over the runway. Beyond the scrubland, there were some low buildings that he thought might enable would-be attackers to get within a few hundred metres of their position unobserved.

"Yes, I've got it. *Mela,* don't expect trouble, do we?"

"In this job, we always expect trouble.

"You're an assistant machine gunner. Harley will be along soon and he'll tell you what's what. Basically, you feed him ammo but, if you have to shoot, anything in your field of vision could be a hostile, so shoot the fuck out of it. You're four hours on and four off, 24/7. Put a claim in for your overtime when you get home!"

At that moment, Harley ambled into the block. He was tall, gangly and stick-thin, with long white hair tied into a short pony tail behind his head and a white goatee beard. Like all the contractors, he favoured wrap around Oakleys. The contractors all added their own little embellishments to their corporate clothing, but Harley had excelled himself. He had embroidered Confederate flags, neatly sewn onto his tactical vest, and a strip of denim from an old jacket bearing the words 'Filthy Few Forever' on the back. A red and white arched badge proclaimed 'Sacramento' across his shoulders. Below his battle belt, low on his hip, hung a Wild West holster arrangement with a Smith & Wesson revolver and .357 Magnum ammo studded around the belt.

Sam banged knuckles with Harley and said: "Here's the bad

ass Maltese sharpshooter I was telling you about. He's trained with the Rangers and Green Berets, and has shot up a whole load of Taliban!"

"No way? So you're a bad ass dude? Coulda fooled me." His accent was Texas.

Harley cleared his throat and shot a lump of spit over the Hesco wall.

Sam slapped him on the shoulder and said: "I'll leave you two to get on with it. Things to do."

"So it's you and me against the world?" Harley looked George up and down. "You an A-rab? I don't much like A-rabs."

Harley clearly liked to talk and did not care whether anyone was listening or not. As the afternoon wore on, he told George he had left Texas, after some woman trouble, and became a Hells Angel, out of Sacramento. The words 'Filthy Few' meant he had been an enforcer for them. George nodded his head to show he was impressed, as he did for the rest of the time he listened to Harley's endless stories.

George learned that he had been in the Marines, but those guys apparently had not appreciated his free spirit. He did one tour of Iraq, where he had met Sam. He had been with Sam for nearly ten years and had 'seen the fucking world through the eye of an M16!'

By the time the four hours was up and the new crew arrived, George knew more about the brotherhood, their runs, scrapes, bike blessings, drug purchases, motorcycle maintenance and punishment beatings, than he would ever have thought possible. He sloped off into the terminal, his head ringing, in search of food and sleep. He found it no surprise that Harley did not have a designated partner!

A row of plastic chairs had just provided the opportunity for a few hours' sleep when Abdullah appeared behind him.

"Hah! The machine gun man! Are you safe to be firing these things?"

"If I have to, I follow your instructions, Abdullah. *'Shut your eyes and pull the trigger!'*"

"I think maybe now they expect you aim first, no? Anyway, listen, we must be parted for a little while. I am going north to meet old friends in the Nafusa Hills and then I go to Marsabar. We take a small plane and there is only room for Edal and me. This time, Goose must stay on the ground. I will be back here in a few days and then maybe we get the chance to fight together, side by side, like before."

George sat bolt upright.

"You can't leave me here! No, I'm coming with you. They're all crazy here!"

"No, it has been decided – only Edal and I must go. When we go to Marsabar, it will be dangerous, so it is best we Arabic speakers go alone. We will be back soon. You are a soldier now, my brother."

George shook his head and lay back down. Even the plastic ridges on the seats, which dug into his back, could not stop him from falling into a deep and dreamless sleep. The blissful state lasted until he was shaken awake by Harley.

"Come on, shithead, time to go!"

Wearily, George followed him out onto the apron. It was late afternoon and the sun hung low in the sky. He had not counted on it being so low in the west, the glare obscuring his view of the other side of the runway.

As they walked to their emplacement, a small Cessna Skyhawk approached, its high wing tipping and rocking as it came in to land, bouncing along the uneven runway. It taxied around and he saw Edal and Abdullah running from the terminal building towards it. It did not stop. Abdullah managed to clamber inside the open passenger door, but had to drag Edal through the cabin door, his *bubus* rucking up to his waist, as his feet kicked and scrambled for purchase. Then the door slammed shut and, with an increasingly intense buzzing from the solitary engine, the Cessna took off. Its wings rocked from side to side as it climbed into the sky, heading north.

George felt very alone, knowing Abdullah had gone. Harley was telling a story about a bad trip he had had after taking a hallucinogenic drug made from a Mexican cactus. George had zoned out but, while Harley smoked and droned on about mescal tequila, something attracted his attention. He did not know what it was he had seen, but there had definitely been movement. He peered through the orange light of the afternoon, his eyes half-closed, squinting, and saw it again. A small object, maybe a head, but definitely something to the side of some bushes, several hundred metres away, right on the edge of the airfield. Then he saw it again, maybe thirty metres to the left.

Harley was droning on.

"Well, the thing is, when ya do lots, and I mean lots, of Mexican drugs, ya get this kinda mind-bend phenomenon, ya know? It's a crazy ..."

"Harley, shut up. I can see something moving. Look over there!"

Harley dropped his cigarette and picked up the binoculars. He peered through them.

"To the right of them bushes, ya say? I ain't seein' nuthin'."

He went onto the hand-held radio and started the call protocol.

"Cas 2, Cas 2, this is Cas 6."

"This is Cas 2. What've you got, over?"

"Possible movement, western perimeter. Keep eyes on. Over, out.

"OK, George, so we'll keep a look out. Anyway, where was I ... yeah – these Mexican girls, they were hot, you know. I mean, really hot! So they came up to me and I'm thinking, like, wow! But because I was doing all this heavy peyote, it'd given me mind-bend and ..."

The first mortar shell struck the apron twenty metres in front of them. The blast sucked the air out of the bunker and made George's ears ring. Bits of shrapnel tinkled on the Hesco.

Harley leaped into action. He screamed: "Ready the SAW!" and grabbed the radio set.

"Cas 2, Cas 2, this is Cas 6."

"Cas 6. All cool, over?"

"All cool. Incoming mortar from boundary, two hundred metres north of runway threshold. Ready to engage, over. Out."

He then threw himself on his stomach and grabbed the M249 machine gun. George was trying to control his shaking hands, so he could loosen the ammunition from the cloth pouch, to ease the feed. After the explosion, all had gone quiet. George was hoping it was all over and that whoever it was had disappeared back to where they had come from.

But before he could wipe the smile of relief off his face, all hell broke loose. Mortar rounds came whistling in. They had adjusted their range and the shells went smack into the gabions. Several burst open, throwing sand and rocks up into the air. George saw a dozen or so fighters rise from the scrub in his sector and start running towards him. They had used the glare of the setting sun to creep on their bellies, through the long wispy grass on the airfield, towards the terminal, ready to launch their attack.

George was lying next to the M249. Harley, for some reason, was sitting back, resting against the rear of the enclosure. George was in a blind panic. He set the gun to fully automatic fire and, lying face down on the floor of the bunker, started randomly spraying fire across the field, without raising his head. The M249 could expel 1,000 rounds a minute, so he could use a vast amount of ammunition very quickly. As he had been taught at Al-Udeid, he pulled the trigger and counted: 'Fire, one, two, three.' Pause. 'Fire, one, two, three.' Pause. 'Fire, one, two, three.' The gun jumped wildly on its rest, twisting his wrist left and right, his one hand exerting just enough pressure to keep the trigger depressed during the firing sequence.

The spent brass cartridge cases were spinning and clattering around, while the noise of the gun in the confined space deafened him. For a moment, he became aware of the acrid smell of the propellant from the bullets, the smoke from the mortar explosions and the smell of dead, damp earth from the damaged Hescos. He did not realise it then, but it would be the smell that would stick in his memory afterwards; not the noise of battle, the fear, or the sight of the fighters advancing on him, wanting to take his life. It would be always the acrid, pungent smell.

He risked a look out of the bunker, but quickly pulled his head back as he saw more figures creeping to within fifty metres of him. He was shaking wildly. He put the spasms down to the recoil from the gun, but was surprised to realise they did not stop once he had ceased firing. More mortar rounds kept landing and, at some point, he realised Harley must be either dead or injured, given he had not moved since the second mortar blast.

After what seemed like hours, but was probably less than a minute, George risked another glance through the firing slit. He saw that he had hit some of the oncoming enemy. Two or three were lying on the scrub, injured but still moving, while one or two more had obviously been shot and were lying very still. But more of them were out there, some crawling through the grass towards him and close enough for him to see the grim intent in their faces.

He took his position behind the gun, but could not bring himself to fire directly at the oncoming fighters, so he sprayed bullets over their heads, in an attempt to scare them off. He counted again. 'Fire, one, two, three.' Pause. 'Fire, one, two, three.' Pause. The attackers lay flat, with their heads down. After a little more time, he realised the belt of shells was coming to an end.

The radio was crackling and alive with shouted messages and commands that George did not understand at first. He started to hear 'pull back, pull back'. Out of the corner of his eye, he was aware of a single fighter running past his enclosure and getting behind him. At this point, there was little else he could do except wait for a hero's death.

He turned to check on Harley, who lay as dead as dead could be, with his chest soaked in blood. Gingerly, George took the Smith & Wesson out of Harley's holster and flicked out some shells from his belt. He loaded the revolver and shoved it into the hip pocket of his cargo pants. Then, crouching, he made his way along the Hesco barriers, back to the door of the terminal.

George rounded the corner at a trot, intending to access the door into the terminal. Three fighters were trying to get in, ramming the glass with a fire extinguisher. George stood, frozen, trying to make himself invisible. One turned and saw him. For a moment, they looked into each other's eyes. The fighter shouted, causing the others to stop battering the door. One dropped the fire extinguisher and picked up a weapon that was propped against the wall beside him. George took Harley's pistol and pointed it at them threateningly, while backing away. When he had turned the corner again, he started to run. He heard a shout above him. It was Sam calling down to him.

"Other way, go through the stairwell!" He gesticulated, pointing to the far side of the terminal building.

George realised the main force of the contractors was inside the terminal building. He and Harley had been out on a limb, at the end of the western flank.

He went as fast as he could, around the side, his feet crunching on broken glass, aware of smoke from burning vehicles set alight by the mortar rounds. Climbing over a baggage cart, he barged open a swing door into the lobby area of the stairwell – and froze.

In the lobby, there was a crowd of a dozen fighters peering up the stairs. Every few seconds, the crack of a shot came from above, keeping them bunched in the well. George had burst through the door, head first, right into the middle of them. For a moment, they did not realise who he was but, as he tried to back out slowly, he was aware of raised voices and hands reaching out for him. Instinctively, he pointed the revolver and fired three shots, in rapid succession, into the mêlée. The sound ricocheted up and down the stairwell. There were screams and shouts and then he heard a fourth shot go off, which flashed through the side of his *cheche*, jolting his head to one side and grazing his scalp. He ended up on the floor, blood running down his face, with a fighter on top of him, pounding his head against the tiles. He felt no pain as he gradually slipped away into unconsciousness.

CHAPTER 32
MARCO BONNICI
ZONA TORTONA, MILAN

IT WAS early August in Milan and the holiday crowds were in evidence across the city. The clouds were hanging low over the Sacred Mountains to the north and the earthy smell of ozone promised unseasonal rain.

Sitting outside a coffee shop in the Zona Tortona, the formerly run-down industrial area revitalised by the fashion houses of Milan, Marco wondered whether he was losing his grip on things. In the past, he'd had Sergio to fall back on, to provide balance, support his ideas, challenge his judgement. He had always felt he and Natasha were on the same page, co-conspirators, a familial double act. Now, she was making power plays behind his back, Sergio was dead and Camilleri seemed to be busy playing with the Americans. And, to cap it all, Simon was never to be found. Every time Marco went looking for him, he was told the bodyguard was out doing some mysterious errands for Miss Natasha! Buying an X-Box?

Salvatore had asked to meet him, to bury the hatchet. Marco, suspecting this was on instructions from the Wise Men, had agreed. He wanted to explain to the younger man that there was no hatchet, but there could never be any burying of the feelings Marco held for him and certainly no forgiveness. He felt the Wise

Men's solution, allowing them to express their views, had freed them from each other. Like much of what the Wise Men decreed, it had a certain elegance to it.

He had decided Natasha should chair MalTech Energy, the new company formed to manage the gas deal in Malta. It was the right choice; she had earned it. He had not told her yet, but he had an appointment, later that day, with Signor Bruno, to seek his blessing. She would need help in running BetHi, but this was an opportunity he could not deny her. Marco did not have the stomach to take on the job himself. It was a long-term appointment and his lack of appetite to make such a commitment to the project told him that this part of his life was coming to a close.

Increasingly, he thought of his estate on the slopes of the western Serbian mountains. He wondered whether the small team of gardeners there were following his instructions on its upkeep, or whether they had retired to the village, to drink *rakija* and their homemade plum brandy.

It was a huge project he had undertaken, a landscape of over seven hectares. He had themed the estate around the surrounding high plateau; his forest walk was lined with beds of high-altitude flowers, sourced from the Dolomites and Swiss alpine areas. He introduced shrub plantations, which gradually faded into the indigenous forest. At the top of the walk, higher up the mountain, he created giant rockeries from the glacial detritus of sedimentary rocks. There, carefully selected mosses and a profusion of further hardy alpines rewarded those who made the climb up the steep slopes. His mood lifted as he considered what he had achieved in the four years of self-imposed exile; he also pictured what else could be achieved if he gave himself another four.

His mellow moment instantly disappeared when he saw Salvatore moving purposefully towards him through the crowds of tourists and shoppers. He wore his trademark black suit, white shirt and a scarlet tie. Marco looked at him more closely; there was something different about him. He was paler and his hair had lost its usual gloss. His face looked waxy and a little thinner. Salvatore looked ill.

Even so, he retained his old composure and confidence. Before he sat down at the table, he caught the eye of a waitress and abruptly signalled for two more coffees. Marco watched this with amusement as the two tables of tourists next to him had been studiously ignored by the same girl for the last ten minutes.

Salvatore sat down and fixed Marco with a stare. The older man was perfectly able to meet this fierce gaze. After a few seconds, he began: "Salvatore. Where do we start?"

"Marco, I've always respected you and I'm upset that there's bad blood between us."

Marco shrugged, maintaining the eye-to-eye contact.

"Straight to the point, Salvatore – let us not waste time, spit it out! What troubles you? Your conscience?"

"It's strange, but one thing does bother me. You've been quick to blame me, but you've never asked me who ordered Sergio's death?"

Marco relaxed a little and thought about this.

"No, because I do not wish to know the answer. And probably because I can guess it anyway."

"That's no longer acceptable, Marco. You can't go round focusing your anger on me, when you know what happened wasn't my decision."

"Come on, Salvatore. That is the Auschwitz guard's argument. 'I was just taking orders.' You have got to do better than that. Sergio's blood is all over your hands. I cannot forgive you, I will not do it."

"True, and I'm sorry, Marco. I should've said no. But I didn't dare. Maybe I was too ambitious. I thought I'd be proving myself by doing the thing nobody else wanted to. The truth is, I hate myself for it.

"I know what it's cost me. Your friendship … possibly the chance of something with Natasha, who knows? And when I look at myself now, I don't like what I see. I think it's done me more harm than good within the Family too. It wasn't exactly a popular move."

Marco snorted his contempt.

"Well, Salvatore, I am sorry for your pain and your regrets. If Sergio were here, I am sure he would be heartbroken at how it has all worked out for you!

"But I can assure you, that is nothing compared to the loss I feel. So, if this is your apology, I accept it and hope, over time, things will sit easier with you. But do not count on me to help that along."

Marco rose to go but Salvatore got up and put a hand on his wrist.

"You know, it was Signor Bruno who asked me to organise it."

Marco sat back down. He did not know what to feel. He knew the Wise Men; he knew their names, where to find them, who their wives were, but he had also avoided attributing Sergio's death to the decision of any one man in particular. He could not cope with that. He preferred to think that the decision was taken at a higher corporate level, with no one individual leading, or voicing, the instruction. Rather that it had emanated from a collective mind. That was the only way he had been able to continue looking them in the eye. Now, Salvatore had shattered that fragile illusion. To put a face, and a name, to the thing that had hurt him so much, was difficult to bear.

His anger subsided. He felt deflated.

"So, Salvatore, what has this confession achieved? Do you want me to go and kill Signor Bruno now? Have you brought a gun for me to use? Or do you just want more forgiveness, redemption, something to make you hate yourself a little less? What is it?"

Salvatore looked downcast. He took a sip of coffee. Marco was not finished yet.

"You could have had it all, Salvatore. You could have shadowed Sergio for a few years, become a Wise Man, enjoyed friendship, loyalty, respect! Had all the good things that power and money cannot buy. Now, you will always be the boy who killed Sergio Rossi. No one will trust you. You will never sit at the top table because people know you can be turned. You have helped me, Salvatore, you really have. I can stop hating you. From now on, I will pity you instead!"

Salvatore hunched over his coffee cup, head down. The strength he had mustered for the confrontation had dissipated, spilling out of him as he sat there.

Marco threw twenty euros onto the table. Before he left, he said: "Do not try to do this again. You will get no further with me. If we have to do Family business together, I will try. But that is it."

He walked away down the street, hands in the pockets of his baggy corduroy trousers.

He went back to the boutique hotel he was staying at and lay on the bed. Nothing that had been said had changed how he felt about the Family, Salvatore or the direction of his life in general. He had decided he needed to get Natasha established in Malta and complete his legacy by finalising the energy deal. Then, he would sever his ties with the Family and return to Serbia, where a bigger and better project needed his attention.

He felt the tension in his neck and shoulders start to take a grip. He took off his shoes and lay on the bed for an hour, gently dozing, drifting in and out of sleep. At 17:00 the alarm went off on his phone, alerting him to his meeting with Signor Bruno. He was washing his face and generally tidying himself up when he heard the soft buzz of his phone in his jacket pocket.

Marco had a pager app on his phone and it was his emergency red light. When it buzzed, it showed a code, alerting him to ring the sender immediately. Now that Sergio was dead, only four people had the number: Natasha, Simon, his personal lawyer in Valletta and Hugo, who managed the Wise Men's legal affairs.

He wiped the soap from his face and slipped into a shirt, before dialling Hugo's number.

"Mr Bonnici, you are still in Milano? Yes? You are required at Signor Bruno's *palazzo* immediately."

"Hugo, what is this about?"

"Mr Bonnici, Signor Bruno is dead and it's not due to natural causes!"

CHAPTER 33
IVAN KARAVAYEV
GOZNAK PRINTING WORKS, MOSCOW

WHEN A COUNTRY COLLAPSES, people rarely think about the scale of theft that is possible in the aftermath. After Gaddafi was overthrown in 2011, Libya was in a state of complete chaos. In the midst of the vacuum, the Central Bank of Libya struggled to restore the country's crippled banking system. Sanctions and mismanagement of the currency had created their own problems, but the main reason for the crisis was self-evident.

The bank had been robbed of its reserves when Gaddafi's entourage seized between three and four billion dinars in cash and nearly two and a half billion dinars' worth of gold. In addition, the motley crew also plundered two billion US dollars from the sovereign wealth fund, set up from the legitimate proceeds of oil sales. The Panama Papers revealed the whereabouts of only a fraction of this treasure trove.

The only comfort was that the new regime at the bank decided to withdraw the old currency from circulation, making some of the stolen notes worthless. This was not done to frustrate the thieves from the old regime but so as to remove images of Gaddafi, in his trademark sunglasses, and the pre-coup monarchy, from the notes, replacing them with more suitable emblems of the nascent state.

The French printers charged by the Central Bank of Libya with the job of etching the new graphic designs onto copper plates and then printing the bank notes, took over two years to work through the various denominations of bills, finally celebrating the delivery of a stock of new fifty-dinar notes in June of 2013. It was this denomination that Ivan Karavayev was currently watching fly though the old offset printing press at the Goznak high-security printing works, in Moscow.

The paper itself was manufactured at the company's own mills near St Petersburg, where the forests of pine, fir and larch provided plenty of softwood pulp. This was then blended with linen so that the long cellulose fibres would give the finished notes strength. The pulp was then washed, pressed and treated to make top-quality banknote substrate. The large finished sheets were stacked, two thousand sheets high, and taken on pallets to the new print works in central Moscow. The Goznak Print Works were sited behind the original, classically styled, old Mint building, which had been built in 1917. Ivan managed a series of offset presses, each twenty metres long, where thousands of sheets of bank notes rolled by every hour. Multiple processes overprinted colours, embossed and coloured various security features, until the sheets were finished and ready to be guillotined into recognisable individual banknotes.

These were then sorted into stacks of 200 notes and each was bound with a green wrapper and encapsulated in plastic film.

Today, the press was busy with the order for the Eastern branch of the Central Bank of Libya. Ivan Karavayev found nothing strange about a country having a central bank with two branches, each independently operating the same currency. He did not think it odd that one half of the country starved the other half of cash, as an act of war, nor that the Tripoli branch would honour any new notes that Ivan printed on behalf of its adversary in Benghazi. If the government in Tripoli were to dishonour any of these notes, it would ruin the entire national currency and make the ultimate reunification so much more difficult, which-ever side won the current tussle.

Ivan saw dozens of different currencies being printed, given the presses also produced notes for countries in Asia, the Middle East and Africa. As long as they met the strict specifications and passed inspection, Ivan was happy to see them bundled into five stacks of one thousand notes and layered into wooden packing cases containing one hundred thousand notes per case. These would then be weighed, securely sealed, stamped with a refer-ence number and barcoded. Each case was fitted with a location transponder, which would reveal its whereabouts, anywhere in the world, at any time.

Final audit checks would be made and the cases would then be taken to the secured despatch bays, to await shipment. Mistakes were seldom made, but were not unknown. A single packing case containing one hundred thousand fifty dinar notes was worth three and a half million US dollars. For this print job there were enough notes to fill two hundred packing cases: seven hundred million US dollars or one billion Libyan dinars!

Ivan did not see the notes in terms of what they might buy. To him, they were either printed in accordance with their specifica-tion or they were not.

The transport section of Goznak managed the delivery of the goods. The weight of one billion Libyan dinars was over twenty tonnes, excluding packing materials. Such consignments were routinely packed into a standard container, padded with baffles, sealed, tagged and freighted either by road or rail. On this occa-sion, the journey started with a short trip by road to the freight terminal at Moscow Station, where it waited to begin the forty-eight-hour transfer to Novorossiysk, on the Black Sea.

Goznak had long accepted that its customers were reluctant to assume risk and ownership of these valuable consignments, until the goods were outside the Soviet Republic. As Goznak was wholly owned by the Russian state, it was reasonable for customers to expect the Russian government to take the risk of transporting the money to the point of exit from the country, which it did. Once it reached the port of Novorossiysk and the export procedures had been completed, a bill of lading was physically handed over to the shipper and the ownership of the goods, and risk of loss, transferred.

As the battered light green container from the Goznak works sat in a loading yard, waiting for the start of its onward journey, a smoky thirty-year-old diesel train from Krasnodar creaked and clanked into the yard, at the end of its three-hour journey. It slowly screeched to a halt, its linkages jangling and the metal-on-metal brakes sounding like fingernails on a blackboard.

Its consignor was a well-known fruit-juice manufacturer, based on the outskirts of Krasnodar, who regularly filled twenty-foot containers with twenty-four thousand litres of fruit juice, for export to Northern Europe and North Africa. The juice was pumped into giant disposable polyethylene bladders, which, as they expanded, nestled securely against the packing and baffles around the side of the containers. Once they were three-quarters full, they could be jumped and bounced on, like giant water beds.

This particular order had attracted some excitement, as it was for a consignment of half a million litres of juice. The order had also specified the shipper to be used and the ship that was to take the cargo. The purchaser had asked for the identifying codes for each of the containers. The juice supplier had been surprised when a large box arrived with a bespoke set of fittings that had to be attached to each of the valves on the bladders. The purchaser required photographic evidence that each bladder had been fitted with the component. Those on the production team recognised the fittings as some sort of actuator, designed to open and close the valves, on a remote control. They were perplexed, but the instructions were very specific and easy enough to implement.

CHAPTER 34

MARCO BONNICI
PALAZZO BRUNO, BRERA, MILAN

Marco hailed a taxi and went directly to Brera and Signor Bruno's *palazzo*. The first thing that struck him was the silence. No police cars, no ambulances and no people in uniform managing the scene. He had expected the place to be swarming with Servizio di Pronto Intervento. Yet in the street outside the palazzo, life continued as usual.

He rang the bell and, seconds later, the Sicilian driver, Toni, opened the door, his face looking pale and gaunt. For a horrible moment, it occurred to Marco that Signor Bruno might not have died after all, and that this was some diabolical ruse to bring him to the palazzo. He told himself to get a grip.

Toni took him up to Signor Bruno's study. It was in its usual tidy condition. Marco was a little shocked by what he found, having braced himself to see Signor Bruno's bloodied corpse, his office turned upside down, crowds of investigating police and forensic examiners. Instead, he noticed there was a stuffed bin liner and a janitor's zinc bucket with mop, in one corner of the room. The rug that was usually in front of Signor Bruno's desk had been rolled up and placed upright next to it. The Family's Milanese lawyer, Hugo, stood leaning over the desk where another man sat, examining some papers in front of him.

Marco said to the seated man, "What is going on, Signor De Luca?" He nodded to the lawyer. "Hugo, where is Signor Bruno? You said he was dead."

The seated man looked up and took off his spectacles. He was short and portly, in his later years, with a penchant for suits worn with waistcoats and flamboyant silk pocket handkerchiefs. He had a high forehead, surrounded by close-cropped, snow-white hair that grew over his collar at the back. His salt-and-pepper beard was tightly trimmed and covered several of his chins. Gabriele De Luca was a former chairman of a major Italian car manufacturer, who had found life a little difficult following the scandals surrounding Prime Minister Giulio Andreotti in the early nineteen nineties. He had had the sense to withdraw from public life, moving into the shadows and using his money and influence on behalf of the Family until, eventually, he became a Wise Man some ten years ago.

"Marco, Signor Bruno is indeed dead. He was found two hours ago, shot in the back of the head, execution-style. Most unpleasant!"

"What? Shot? I was due to meet him at six. Where is he? And where are the police?"

"He is being properly looked after and we do not need the police. We can deal with this ourselves."

"You cannot just ignore a murder! What about the legalities?"

Signor De Luca huffed and pulled himself up from his chair.

"We have no intention of ignoring his death. On the contrary, the murder of one of the Family is a most serious issue, but legalities are legalities. We have lawyers who can take care of those. So, please, Marco, we ask for your discretion. And it is not just one death, it is two."

"Two? What on earth has happened?"

"Before we get into that, Hugo needs to ask you some questions. We will also need to talk to Natasha as she was here earlier today for the monthly meeting. I understand she has already boarded her flight. I will telephone her tomorrow. We are in exceptional times."

Hugo then questioned Marco about the reason for his meeting with Signor Bruno. Marco was precise and clear in his answers, with nothing to hide. The next question from Signor De Luca was trickier.

"What have you been doing for the rest of the day? I'm sorry, but I need to ask."

De Luca was rather too quick with this question and the flicker of his narrow eyes put Marco on notice that he had better be careful with his reply.

"I had coffee with Salvatore Randazzo. You will be aware that we have had our differences. We were meeting to try and find a way to set them aside, so we can work together in the future. Signor Bruno was aware of our meeting."

"Ah, yes. And did you resolve your differences?"

"That will never be possible, Signor De Luca, for reasons you well understand, but I am hopeful Salvatore and I can work together, when occasion demands."

"We spoke to Salvatore an hour ago. He told us he informed you that Signor Bruno had given him the order to dispose of Sergio Rossi. He said that you then discussed killing Signor Bruno. Shooting him. Is that true?"

Marco sighed wearily.

"We argued, that is all. He taunted me with a fact that I had already worked out for myself – that Signor Bruno had ordered the killing of Sergio. I asked Salvatore what he wanted me to do with the information he had just given me, whether he expected me to go and kill Signor Bruno – it was a rhetorical question."

"Coincidental, though," Hugo interjected, "given that Signor Bruno was shot not long afterwards."

"Unfortunate timing, certainly. But make of it what you will, my conscience is clear. It is plain to me that Salvatore seeks to take advantage of the situation."

There was an uncomfortable silence in the room. Marco was

determined not to waver and be the first to break it. Finally, Signor De Luca removed his spectacles and rubbed his eyes.

"We do not believe this has anything to do with you, Marco, and neither does Salvatore. But we needed to hear your answer to that question."

Marco slumped back in his chair and sighed, shaking his head in disbelief.

"You said there were two bodies? Who else is involved?"

Hugo glanced at Signor De Luca, who waved his hand at him, indicating he should continue.

"Unfortunately, Signor Bruno was involved in relationships with young men. We know who they are. Toni *facilitated* these friendships, it seems. The boy upstairs was one Alberto Fabbri, whose street name is apparently Tesoro. Mean anything to you?"

"Do you really think it likely I would know a youngster by the nickname of 'Treasure'?"

"Sorry, I have to ask. Fabbri was new on the scene. Met Signor Bruno in the Orto Botanico di Brera. Signor Bruno took a daily stroll through the botanical gardens every afternoon, after lunch. He was regular in all his habits. Alas, it seems someone knew this and capitalised on it."

"Was Tesoro shot too?"

"Yes."

"So – what does this mean?"

"Well, according to Toni, he let Tesoro in through the side door at around 16:00, then he immediately went down to the data room as he realised the CCTV wasn't working. He says he keeps out of the way on Monday and Friday afternoons."

"I can understand that, but hardly a professional approach," said Marco.

"The only other thing we do know is that Signor Bruno had a call arranged with a tax accountant at 15:45, which we have confirmed took place. So, Signor Bruno was in his study when Tesoro arrived and the papers on his desk related to the conversation with the accountant.

"We suspect Tesoro must have waited for Toni to leave, then came back downstairs, opened the backdoor and let in the shooter. The pair of them went upstairs to wait for Signor Bruno, but the gunman had a tidy mind and got rid of Tesoro before coming downstairs to shoot Signor Bruno in his study."

"That assumes the gunman could find his way around the *palazzo*?"

"Yes, it seems so, doesn't it?"

Marco looked around the room.

"There must be security-camera footage available?"

Hugo nodded.

"Yes, you would think so. But the cameras on the main door, the lobby, that stairway and in this office were all disabled, somehow. Someone accessed the network, identified the Mac address of the cameras and then launched multiple 'denial of service' attacks against them. They knew what they were doing. That is why we think this could be an inside job."

Hugo then asked Marco: "What can you tell us about Salvatore's manner this morning?"

Marco locked his fingers together in front of him.

"He was unhappy. He felt he had done the Family a service in following through on the order to kill Sergio. He felt unappreciated and that several Family members, me included, were unfairly hostile to him as a result. He felt that Signor Bruno could have been more supportive of him. He said the episode had cost him dearly."

"What did you say to that?" Hugo asked.

"I said, '*Tough!*'"

De Luca cracked a thin smile.

Hugo went on, "He seemed a little disturbed to us."

"I would not have said that. Salvatore is a proud, even arrogant, man and his ambitions have taken a knock, but I would not say he is *disturbed*."

De Luca shifted his weight in the chair.

"OK, Marco, thank you. Can we change the subject? This situation has consequences for Natasha."

Marco blinked, unsure for a second what that meant.

"We will need her here in Milan more often. Weekly, for two to three days. She knows Signor Bruno's work and is the obvious choice to step in and expand her role. He had great faith in her and intended to talk to her about her long-term prospects.

"She can take the chair of the oil and gas business, but she needs to step away from BetHi. To continue there as well would be too much of a burden. Can you fill her in, after Hugo has spoken to her, and ask her to put arrangements in place to ensure continuity at BetHi?"

Marco got to his feet, nodding agreement.

"Of course. Now, if you do not need me further, I am going to my hotel."

He sat in the back of Signor Bruno's 7 Series BMW, in silence, while the hapless Toni made the fifteen-minute drive to the Tortona Hotel. As he stared idly out of the tinted windows, it occurred to Marco that here was yet another situation where Natasha had benefited from the misfortune of another.

She had been in Milan earlier but had declined his offer of dinner, keen to return to Malta for some reason. He had thought it a little strange at the time, as she would usually grab any opportunity to dress up and step out into one of Milan's finer places. He quickly rebuked himself for these dark thoughts, frightened, as usual, of where such thinking might lead. He turned his mind to more practical problems, such as how they would go about finding a replacement CEO for BetHi.

CHAPTER 35

NATASHA BONNICI
CHAPEL OF OUR LADY OF THE ABANDONED, MALTA

Natasha had returned from her usual monthly meeting with Signor Bruno late the previous night. She knew her father was in Milan but, given their conflicting appointments and Natasha's wish not to be away from the chapel for too long, had left for the airport straight after her visit to the *palazzo*.

She and Simon had settled into an easy rhythm with Savi. He had relaxed into captivity and, when not following their orders, was happy to play endless games of *Fifa* and build his empire in *Civilisation*, on the X-Box. In the early evenings, Simon brought him takeaway food, beer and some weed, and they would sit together until it got dark, watching from their clifftop eyrie, eating, drinking and smoking, as the sun slid down the sky and dipped beneath the darkening sea.

Beyond the chapel, waves pounded against a mass of fallen boulders, sheared from the cliff face over the centuries by the action of wind and rain. The chapel had been built as a place of quiet contemplation. The rumble of the sea and the continuous passing of the wind created a backdrop of white noise which, in time, became its own strange silence.

It seemed Savi had become perfectly at ease with the new

arrangement, where he had no responsibility for anything except the two things he loved most: gaming and hacking computer systems.

Simon had worked out that Savi was awake for most of the night and only rose in the early afternoon. He left boxes of crisps and snacks that seemed to keep the boy happy until his pizza, or kebab, arrived in the evening. In reality, there was not much difference in age between the two of them, but Simon could not help seeing Savi as a useless younger brother and, despite himself, had started to feel a little protective towards him.

Savi had asked Simon to get him some clean clothes. It was true, the jeans and sweatshirts he had brought with him were now filthy and stained with slops from takeaway meals and the dirt and dust of the chapel. Simon had looked him up and down and agreed he could do with some new things. He had asked the boy what he wanted. Savi had thought for a bit and chewed on his bottom lip, then said: "What do you think Natasha would like?"

"Natasha? What's it got to do with her?"

"What do her sort of guys usually wear? She must go out with guys. Well, she's hot, isn't she?

"So?"

"Well, I sort of … like her. She was up for it, you know, with me, until you barged in. So … you know? I need to look my best."

"You're kidding me? You don't think for a minute …" Simon was incredulous. He started laughing.

"You can laugh all you want, but I know when someone's into me. I don't see why you think it's so funny."

Simon's peals of laughter echoed around the deserted countryside.

Savi was hurt by this ridicule.

"I bet you I bang her before this is over!"

Simon spluttered, beer spilling out of his mouth.

"Oh, God, stop it, don't say anymore!" He held his head in his hands. "Fantastic, that's a bet I really want to take. Please, please, promise me one thing? You must tell me when you're going to make your move. I can't wait to see it!"

Savi flicked his greasy hair back and, in all seriousness, preened himself, pouting.

"You wait and see. I know how to get what I want from a woman."

Simon collapsed in fits of laughter again.

Apart from fantasising about what he might get up to with Natasha, Savi was busy using his skills, as a hacker, scammer and internet-nuisance, to phish, hoax and impersonate his way around the Novorossiysk shipping agents. Eventually, he got the information he needed about the carriage of the container from a helpful, but gullible, lady at Krasnodar Krai Freight Forwarding Company.

He then used a mobile WiFi hotspot to connect to the server at his home and set up a VPN link into his EDI terminal. EDI was the electronic tool that enabled all import and export operations and cargo movement at the world's ports.

He logged into the shipper's website, bypassing the firewalls and security features, and inserted a virtual network implant, which allowed him to extract the container-release codes for the container in question. This, in turn, enabled him to access the EDIFACT messaging features.

Savi quickly found the shipping destination fields and changed the container's destination from Istanbul to Constanta. He also added the PIN randomiser that would provide Natasha's haulier with entry to the port of Constanta and trigger release of the container. All of this information was programmed to be released at a future date and time that Natasha had yet to give him.

Savi had asked why Constanta, not Istanbul? Natasha had told him to 'just do it'.

On the shipper's server, Savi had found the load plan for the ship, the *Kapitan Markov,* and the departure date in question. The containers were batched and assembled on the quayside for loading aboard the *Kapitan Markov,* in strict order.

The *Markov* was a small unassuming vessel, with its super-structure rising at the stern of the ship, allowing easier access to its deck hatches. She shuttled containers between the Black Sea ports and Istanbul, where they were transhipped to bigger vessels for the more substantial part of their journeys.

The twenty blue containers of juice sat alongside several hundred others, including the solitary pale green container, stuffed full of Libyan dinars, which Natasha had told Savi should be loaded last.

The large container crane slowly trundled back and forth on rails set into the quayside. Like a giant four-legged spider, it negotiated the piles of containers, dropping its cables and spreader beam, hauling the boxes into the air, before lowering them into the dark holds of the *Kapitan Markov.* It was capable of lifting 400 tonnes, but seldom had to bear that amount. Sitting in the cabin, attached to the trolley, the crane operator loaded the containers, strictly following the load plan that had been worked out by planning software previously hacked by Savi.

The purpose of the load plan was not only to position those containers that needed to be unloaded first, but also to evenly distribute weight, so the *Kapitan Markov* would not become top heavy and start to roll and pitch, once at sea. It was crucial to the ship's safety to ensure a low centre of gravity so as to maintain trim and stability.

The blue containers with their load of juice weighed twenty-four metric tonnes each, so the twenty containers, along with the other heavier ones bound for Istanbul, went on first, deep into the holds, while other lighter loads were stacked on top of them. The *Kapitan Markov* was a small vessel, one hundred metres long and carrying only five hundred containers, three hundred and fifty in the holds and one hundred and fifty stacked above deck, so the 'juice' was a sizeable percentage of its cargo capacity.

Novorossiysk was on the north coast of the Black Sea. The passage to Istanbul involved heading directly south-west, to skirt Sebastopol at the foot of the Crimean Peninsula and then across the centre of the Black Sea, into the mouth of the Bosphorus, the narrow channel that linked Russia to the Mediterranean, at Istanbul. With the *Markov* doing ten knots, the trip usually took about two and half days.

The whole exercise had taken Savi a little under two hours. But he remained puzzled.

"How are you going to divert a ship bound for Istanbul to Constanta in Romania – and why would you want to do that?"

Natasha fixed him with a no-nonsense expression.

"We want a head start on the Russians and the Americans. The Russians own the goods and the Americans think you are going to steal them on their behalf in Istanbul. Once our container is off-loaded in Constanta, I want you to go into the system and reallocate its number to another container, and then set up the heist in the same way, but this time in Istanbul."

"Oh, I get it! You nab the real container in Constanta and the Americans end up stealing the wrong container in Istanbul?" Savi scratched his head. Then his expression became one of concern. "Wait a minute … no way! That puts me right in the shit!"

"Why would it? The container will still have the same code attached to it. They won't know you switched them. You've done exactly what they asked. And you'll get paid twice!"

"I suppose … I still don't know how you're going to get the ship to Constanta."

"OK, I'll tell you how. Work out when the ship is at its nearest point to Constanta and then calculate backwards four hours. At that point, send the message to open those actuating valves."

"What the hell for?"

"That gets the ship to Constanta. Trust me! Then, and only

then, activate the EDIFACT message to the *Kapitan Markov* to unload our container at Constanta."

Savi went through the process again and explained to Natasha exactly what he had been doing.

"You're sure everything is going to go through as it should?"

"Yeah, I know my stuff! If you were standing on the dockside at Novorossiysk, you'd see your containers just about to be loaded."

"OK, so in two days' time, it should all be over and you'll have a pocket full of money."

"That's me done? Can I go now?"

"Don't be stupid. I want you here, following what goes on, so if there're any glitches, you can fix them. Two more days, that's all."

"Well, if I've got to stay a bit longer, tell Simon to get me *The Witcher* and *Doom*. I'm sick of winning on *Fifa*."

Simon and Natasha locked Savi back in the chapel and turned the SUV to drive down the track, towards the *castello*. Simon turned to her and asked: "What happens to the little dickhead once we've got the container?"

She thought for a moment and then said brightly, "Throw him off the cliffs. You can do that, can't you?"

Simon looked straight ahead and kept on driving. He was stunned by how casually she could say such a thing. He knew she had a dark side to her character and was fairly sure it had been her who had taken the *castello's* old Land Rover and used it to kill the Albanian in the Aquarium car park. Simon was no angel himself, having served in the Military Gendarmerie, Poland's military police, but he had never murdered somebody in cold blood.

More to the point, the kid did not deserve it. He had done everything he had been asked to. He was no real danger to them, just a stupid boy who liked computers, gaming and smoking dope. He had stumbled into all this and had no idea what he was dealing with.

Well, even if Natasha gave him a direct order, Simon would not do it. Instead, he would try and find a way to get Savi out, so that the boy could make a run for it. If only he knew, his protector thought grimly. While Savi was planning his wardrobe, ready to make an amorous move on Natasha, she was making plans to pitch him into eternity.

THE CONTRACTORS HAD WITHDRAWN to the relative safety of the terminal building almost immediately they realised the scale of the assault. The attackers were lightly armed and Sam had rightly assumed this was a hit-and-run strike, made primarily as a warning to the new arrivals. The machine gun emplacements had served them well and, despite the odds and the loss of Harley, the Maltese policeman had held the western flank, allowing the others time to set up a defence inside the terminal. Sam calculated that they had killed or disabled about thirty fighters, which was about a third of the attacking force. Judging by the position of the bodies, the Maltese policeman was probably responsible for a good number of those downed.

Sam led a party of contractors and Tuareg out to recover Harley's body and generally survey the damage. He had been on the radio and was assured that three platoons of US Rangers would be with them first thing the next day, to resupply them and help strengthen the base's defences. Now their presence was known, there was no secret to protect and it made it easier to fly in materials and supplies.

During the next few days, US Reaper drones from Turkey were due to hit Boutros's airbases in eastern Libya with large and very expensive rockets. It would be the largest drone strike ever mounted and the US intent would be made clear. A-10 Warthog jets had been briefed to hit Boutros's ground forces and part of the 'big bang' Mike Lloyd had alluded to would be provided by four AC-130 gunships, circling over the airfields. These large Hercules planes carried a massive cargo of armaments with huge destructive capabilities. The aim was the complete annihilation of Boutros's airfields and a good percentage of his ground capabilities.

In the meantime, the Maltese policeman was missing. They had searched the terminal building, the scrubland around the runway, the corpses they had piled near the treeline, but the policeman had not been found. The Tuareg had bagged the enemy bodies and loaded them into four trucks, which they took to the mosque in town, laying them in a line in front of a crowd of silent townspeople. An Imam appeared and they handed over to him the responsibility for a respectful Muslim burial. The Americans had learned their lesson in Iraq, where GIs disrespecting the Muslim dead had turned local populations against them and incensed their enemy.

Sam had got a message through to the operational control at Al-Udeid airbase in Qatar. The assumption was that George had been captured and taken hostage. A senior officer had made a call to the Assistant Commissioner of the Maltese police, informing him of the situation, while the Tuareg fighters quickly let Edal Essa and Abdullah know of the attack and George's capture.

———

George's unconscious body had been dumped into the back of a Kia SUV with additional metal plating welded onto it, making it look like an upside-down bathtub. There were no windows, merely slits in the metal sheeting. They had been driving for over an hour before he regained consciousness. He opened his eyes, or rather one eye, and all he could tell was that the sun had almost set and was casting the last of the day's shadows in their direction of travel. He guessed they were travelling east, then he must have shut his eyes for a moment and fallen asleep or passed out because, when he next woke up, it was totally dark and the vehicle was racing through what felt like empty desert.

He stirred where he lay, the truck still bouncing him along the rough unmetalled road. His body did not hurt, but his head and face were agony. The taste of blood filled his mouth and one of his front teeth was loose. A swelling over one eye hung low, obscuring his vision. There was a driver, and a young boy peering over the front passenger seat and pointing a gun straight into George's face. The way he felt, he wished the kid would just get on with it and pull the trigger.

Sensing his movement, the driver slowed and started to pull over. Once the car had stopped, he jumped out and pulled the rear door open. He roughly yanked George from the car, grabbing his wrists and placing them on the roof. George spat a thick stream of bloody saliva onto the ground and rested his aching head against the roof. The car following them pulled in behind, its full beam forcing them to shield their eyes.

The occupants got out and crossed over to them. A hefty young man in a tan camouflage outfit, with full tactical belt, emerged through the glare. He spoke English with that strange London accent. He took George by the collar and turned him round to face the light. A tall, sour-faced man with a long beard, dressed in a calf-length long black tunic reaching to his knees, followed behind. He approached and looked at George carefully. He had something in his hand that he was studying, looking closely at George and then back at what he was holding.

"Get that stupid turban off him."

The hefty young man pulled the *cheche* from George's head and threw it into the dust. He searched him, going through his pockets and patting down his arms and legs.

The tall man in black came closer and looked again at the card in his hand, then back at George, a smile spreading over his face.

"A day of many blessings! You are the Maltese policeman George Zammit, no? It is hard to be sure, with your face as it is – but I am sure it is you."

The tall man pushed George's Pulizija identity card back into his top pocket.

"We have not met, but I know of you. Where is the *shu hayee*, backstabbing Abdullah Belkacem?"

George did not know who this man was or what he wanted with Abdullah, but he guessed it was not a polite enquiry after a mutual friend.

"At this moment, I don't know. Who are you and how d'you know me?"

"My name is Abu Muhammad. I followed you and Abdullah around Marsabar and I cannot count how many deaths you have caused my people. But now, things are different. I will need to know what you were doing in Ubari, with Tuareg and Americans. You will tell me everything. I will enjoy making you."

George swallowed and his heart sank further as he realised the depth of his predicament.

From nowhere, Muhammad's hand appeared and he swiped the back of it across George's bruised and broken face, a large ring scoring a deep line on his cheek.

"We cannot stay here. *Ant kalbi*, put the dog back in the car. The sky has eyes, even at night."

George slumped in the seat, willing sleep to take him away from this nightmare. Unfortunately, the pain and the trembling in his limbs made that impossible. The long cut from Muhammad's ring caused his cheek to bleed profusely and the blood soaked down through his clothing. It took another ten hours to reach their camp.

It was nearly dawn when Yaroslav heard the trucks arrive back. He got up from his mattress and studied the convoy. There were fewer vehicles and many fewer men than had left. He saw

Raheem, in full battle garb, his head hanging low. The body language was one of defeat. Only Abu Muhammad held his head high, quietly issuing instructions, seemingly unfazed by events. There were several injured men being helped out of the trucks, their wounds still untreated and undressed. Yaroslav could only wonder at the consequences of the inevitable infections that would soon develop.

They had also brought a prisoner with them. Yaroslav watched with interest as the man was led to a small stone hut nearby. He was a middle-aged Arab who had been roughed up, his face badly beaten. Yaroslav noticed the new arrival carried some weight but, he thought grimly, that would soon change.

George was led to a low door and pushed through it, into darkness. He fell onto the damp earth, smelling vegetal rot and animal musk. He lay very still, the cool dirt floor providing some relief for his aching head. Sleep came, as did the searing heat of the Chadian desert morning. When he woke up the pain in his head was soon replaced with a painful thirst. His tongue felt swollen and the perspiration was already soaking through his shirt. The sweat in his hair had loosened the dried blood from the cut on his scalp and cheek. When he rubbed his hands across his face, a red stain spread across his features.

It was several hours before the door was yanked open and the Londoner pulled George to his feet. By then, he was barely semi-conscious and all he could think about was water. He muttered the word time and again to the Londoner.

"Water."

"Later."

"Water."

"Later, I said."

Abu Muhammad sat inside his cool tent, on a canvas director's chair, and smiled when George was dragged in, looking very sorry for himself. He was pushed down onto his knees.

A small, pleasant-looking bespectacled man entered the tent. He was bald, a large shiny forehead emerging beneath the black turban that covered the rest of his head. His long, grey beard reached halfway down his chest. He was smiling and had an affable, gentle manner.

"You may call me Faysal. In this camp, I am the only friend you have. You are surrounded by enemies, only waiting for the word to do terrible things to you."

He smiled cheerfully.

In the background Abu Muhammad sat watching, his expression grim and threatening. Faysal continued, speaking in a quiet, almost apologetic manner.

"We are going to talk and you will tell me what I need to know. If you do, you will drink, we will wash and dress your wounds and we will ransom you. If you do not tell me what I want to know, you will not drink and you will be beaten again, not with fists, but this time with metal and wood. Bones will break. And still you will not drink.

"Now, I must know that you understand? Speak."

George tried to open his swollen and cracked lips and remove his tongue from the back of his mouth. He swallowed, but it was only a reflex movement in his throat. There was no saliva to clear.

"Yes. I understand," he croaked.

Faysal went to the back of the tent and picked up a small bottle of water, placing it next to him, within George's view.

"Where is Abdullah Belkacem?"

Without a second's hesitation, George started speaking.

"He's in Marsabar."

"Who is he with and what are they doing there?"

George did not even try to hide the truth. He told Faysal everything he knew: about their trip to Al-Udeid, the alliance with the Tuareg elders, the contractors and the planned air attack by the Americans on Boutros's forces. All the time, he kept glancing at the water on the table next to Faysal. After ten minutes, he was finished and slumped, his head on his knees, prostrate as if in Muslim prayer. He hated himself for his weakness.

Faysal looked at Abu Muhammad, his eyebrows raised. With a flick of his wrist, Muhammad dismissed George, who was taken back to the heat of the searing stone hut, with his bottle of water.

Abu Muhammad and Faysal sat with glasses of tea. Muhammad had been considering the new information.

"It is a good thing the Americans are attacking Boutros. Let them feel the sting of an American air attack. When they are depleted, we can take advantage. What we know of the Americans is that they never stay anywhere for long. I would rather fight them than other Arabs. Americans you can see and hear, a hundred kilometres away. An Arab, though, he can creep up on you while you sleep."

A little later, the padlock was undone and the door opened, a shaft of light falling across George's red and yellow face. An accented voice said, in English: "Oh, I see they beat you. You are not pretty and you smell bad. My name is Yaroslav, they say I must help you."

George could not make out any face as he peered into the direct sunlight that silhouetted the figure at the door.

"I have bucket of water to wash your hands, face and wounds. There is cloth in bucket. The water is not for drink. It is bad water."

George raised himself and, without speaking to the man, plunged his head into the scummy water and drank deeply. The blood and filth from his hair and face mingled with the scum floating on top of the water.

"Ahhh … I said, do not do that! Maybe you choose to die with cholera. They can kill in many bad ways, maybe cholera is not most bad. Sleep, and put water on your head to be cool; it helps. Remember, is important: do *not* drink more water! I will come back. Now, sleep."

CHAPTER 37
ABDULLAH BELKACEM
MARSABAR, LIBYA

THE CESSNA that left Ubari had landed near the tiny mountain village of Rehibat, which served as the Nafusa Hills' only airport, thanks to a mile-long stretch of straight road that acted as the landing strip. Abdullah and Edal had been met by Rania's brothers and had returned to their family home, some fifty kilometres away. The next day, as Abdullah had done seven years previously, they started the job of building a local resistance to the Islamic State-in-Libya of Abu Muhammad and Boutros's encroaching militias.

Abdullah had old Berber allies in Nalut, a village in the Nafusa mountain range, just east of the Tunisian border. Its position as a crossing point made it a key town in the area and its Berber inhabitants were among the first to rise in protest against Muammar Gaddafi. Abdullah and Edal spoke to the elders and showed them photographs of the Americans alongside them in Ubari. They promised them protection and freedom to live how they chose; in return, the elders promised Abdullah men to fight alongside him.

The same thing happened in other neighbouring Berber villages such as Ghezaia and Wazzin. There was no love of the 'Beards' there and, since Abdullah had been forced to flee, there had been no protection from Abu Muhammad, who had terrorised the villages, forbidding the speaking of their old Berber language, taking food and supplies, forcing sharia teachings down their throats at the mosque and persecuting their women.

Such was the hostility to the Beards, the clans of Berbers and Arabs set aside their age-old differences and soon Abdullah found himself with a force of nearly 300 men to arm and train.

At that point, he called in the first team of US Rangers, a dozen of whom arrived during the night from Tunisia, in three trucks, bringing weapons and equipment. For the next two weeks, the hills crackled with gunfire and explosions. Those living in Marsabar heard the sound of aircraft and helicopters flying overhead. Word spread that Abdullah Belkacem was back, hiding in the hills, with at least 1,000 American Marines, if not more, just waiting to drive Abu Muhammad back to the wastelands of the south.

Those of the Beards who had for so long terrified and controlled Marsabar stayed in their camp in the middle of the Nafusa Hills, awaiting further instructions. In the Chadian desert, far to the south-west, Abu Muhammad and what was left of his militia, were licking their wounds and listening intently to news of the developments in Marsabar.

Abdullah took to making staged appearances in the streets of the town and found, each time, a crowd would quickly develop to walk alongside him, asking questions and pledging support. He would gather the small groups in a local square or on a street corner and pledge he had come back to fight and free them from life under Islamic State. He explained he would take a share of the wealth generated from the port and the refinery, giving back cash to health centres and schools. He promised them a better life, such as they had before the Beards drove him away and diverted the money to their own causes. They would cheer and shout, and Abdullah would draw on their energy, while one or two of his clan would move amongst the crowd, taking names and phone numbers of the men they knew to be most likely to commit to him. He walked the streets without fear, daring the local Islamic State fighters to challenge him. And still the technicals, with their black flags and bullying zealots, stayed away.

One Friday, shortly after his re-emergence in Marsabar, Abdullah went to pray at the mosque and then travelled a short distance out of town, to a remote farm. There he met with Sheik Ahmed al Habib, a local teacher and religious leader, who directed such opposition as there was to the IS presence.

He told Abdullah: "It was not so bad at first – they were more with the oil and the port. It was money they needed. They did not trouble the townspeople. But now it has become bad. They come into town more often, looking for 'wives' to marry. We know what that means.

"They preach on the streets, urging young boys to join them as fighters in jihad. Now the Imam has problems. They challenge his teaching. They say he is betraying and dishonouring those who pray in his mosque. They have set up two of their own *madrassas* in town and threaten parents that, if the children do not go to them, they will be taken away, to protect them from false teachings. Always the young – they always want the young."

They sat cross-legged on the *mergoum*, a brightly coloured and patterned traditional Berber carpet, woven in the old way, without synthetic materials or machines. The faint chatter of women came from a nearby room and Abdullah could smell *ftat misrati*, Libyan flatbread, cooking on an iron skillet. He shook his head. It sickened him to hear what Abu Muhammad was doing in Allah's name. They talked for several hours and, although the Sheikh was reluctant to fully commit his support, Abdullah felt he was making progress with the man.

"I understand you do not know me well. But you know I have done good things before and will do them again in the future. I ask you to trust me and give me your support."

The Sheikh smiled at him.

"They say that, four years ago, you ran away and did not stay to fight. They say you left your family and your clan. They say the Americans pay for you to have an easy life in Malta; that you are no longer a true Muslim."

Abdullah knew the Arab love of gossip and he could imagine the naysayers in the cafés: the old men sitting by the dried-up fountain outside the mosque, the youth hanging around with their mopeds in the squares. He wanted them to talk about his return. He wanted them to talk about the evil of IS and their hopes for a free and fair Libya. That was why he paraded around the town – to stir the conversation and talk of a better life. It would be naïve to expect that all the talk would be good.

"Yes, yes, I can understand this being said. But now, I am here. Imam Ali, the prophet's son-in-law, said: *'People are of two types in relation to you, either your brother in Islam, or your brother in humanity.'* I am different because I am both and I am here to turn word into deed."

The Sheikh bowed his head, always finding a well-chosen religious quote persuasive. Abdullah continued: "So, I once went to the Islamic State-in-Libya camp, some years ago. We left the road at Al Jawsh and headed south on a rough track, then up an old riverbed for maybe two kilometres. This led us to a cleft in the rock, high above the town. At the bottom, there was a wide flat area that was Abu Muhammad's camp. You cannot see it from the air, they have hung camouflage netting between the two rock faces. Do you know this place?"

The Sheikh nodded, but said nothing.

"I am guessing this is still their camp. Do they have trucks and fighters there?"

"Yes, they have over one hundred men, maybe two hundred, with weapons and vehicles."

"I live by my word and my deeds. Tomorrow, that camp will no longer exist. Tomorrow, at first light, watch the sky. You will see a bright early sunrise, but from the south, not the east."

Abdullah had asked the Americans for a show of strength

and to hit the camp as part of their 'shock and awe' raids. Thermal imaging surveillance had established the camp was still very much active, a base for several hundred fighters. Abdullah wanted a 'big bang' to help his recruitment drive with the Marsabar locals and to tug on Abu Muhammad's tail!

The white-haired US general in Al-Udeid loved 'shock and awe' as a tactic, so he had authorised deploying a Massive Ordnance Air Blast bomb, one of the most intimidating non-nuclear weapons in the American arsenal, to destroy the camp and half the hillside with it. The enormous bomb would be dropped from a C-130 cargo plane and guided to its target by a GPS system. The tight ravine was perfect to concentrate the destructive power of its blast. This was intended as a huge, expensive statement of US intent to discourage the civil war and the ISIL militias, as well as to send a message to other foreign powers that their meddling would no longer be tolerated.

Abdullah was confident that once the local community saw and heard the blast, proof of American support, he would acquire sufficient fighters to establish a camp openly in Marsabar. Then, the job of properly arming and training them could begin. The general could start bringing in weapons, vehicles and advisers. The port of Marsabar would soon be in his hands and would be the gateway for supplies and all the hardware Abdullah's men would need to secure the district and protect Tripoli's western flank.

CHAPTER 38
CAPTAIN ERIC SOBOLEV
ABOARD THE KAPITAN MARKOV,
BLACK SEA

THE *KAPITAN MARKOV* had left Novorossiysk and was well into her two-and-a-half-day journey across the Black Sea to the Bosphorus channel and on to Istanbul. Captain Eric Sobolev had sailed the route hundreds of times and knew the seasonal moods and temperament of the waters. In winter, the Black Sea was an evil place, with north-easterly Arctic gales and treacherous winds, which whipped up currents and white-topped waves. In spring and summer it became easier sailing, as the tropical air pushed up from the south, reducing the strength of the wind and calming the sea. It was mid-August, so he was expecting a pleasant crossing and there would be little to do until he reached the narrow, thirty-kilometre channel of the Bosphorus.

After a day and a half's steady cruising at ten knots, the *Kapitan Markov* was to the south-west of Sevastopol and due east of Constanta when, deep down, at the bottom of her hold, the battery-powered valves on the bladders of juice, in their twenty containers, began to turn and a trickle of liquid became a steady stream.

For some hours, this unusual occurrence went unnoticed, other than the occasional waft of a zesty orange scent that floated briefly across the deck and off into the stiff sea breeze. All ships are fitted with automatic bilge pumps that get rid of any water finding its way to the bottom. Be it storm water from the deck, condensation, leakage due to corrosion – all ships take in water and need to get rid of it. The *Kapitan Markov* had two pumps; one fore and one aft. Pipework ran from each area to collect the water and pump it out of the side. The pumps could move hundreds of litres an hour, which was enough to cope with the initial trickle, but, as all twenty containers started to pour juice from their bladders in a steady stream, the five hundred tonnes of liquid quickly overwhelmed the pumps.

This had two effects. First, the juice started to slop around the holds of the ship, becoming 'free water', which was highly dangerous. Secondly, the emptying bladders resulted in a redistribution of the cargo, making the ship top heavy and unbalanced.

Three hours after the valves had first twisted open, the helmsman reported to Captain Sobolev that he thought the ship was becoming heavy to handle. The captain himself had noticed the vessel rolling significantly, from one side to the other, and had started to become concerned. He stayed on the bridge for another ten minutes and felt the situation getting worse. He grabbed the chief officer and told him to take the chief engineer and check out the levels in the bilges and ballast tanks and make sure the cargo was secure.

He was horrified when they reported back that there was a large amount of free water slopping around in the holds and they had no idea where it was coming from. The chief engineer told him that if there was a change in the weather and the seas became rougher, the bilge pumps would not be able to handle this volume of excess water. It was likely the ship would capsize.

The only good news he received was that, strangely, the liquid appeared not to be salt water, but orange juice. Captain Sobolev was relieved in one sense – it was not the case that the ship had sprung a catastrophic leak – but he was annoyed and mystified as to how tonnes of free orange juice had found its way into his holds. Nevertheless, he immediately reduced speed and plotted a course to the nearest decent-sized commercial port, where the cargo could be unloaded and the juice pumped out. That was Constanta, in Romania.

Constanta was three hundred kilometres north of the entry to the Bosphorus Straits and had access to the European hinterland via the Black Sea canal, including the one thousand five hundred kilometre route up the Danube River. Traffic from there could also easily join the Pan European highway and rail system that stretched from Dresden in Northern Germany to Istanbul.

An urgent radio request ensured a berth was quickly organised for the *Kapitan Markov*. As soon as the ship docked, Captain Sobolev and the chief officer began unloading the cargo, while powerful pumps flooded the harbour with gallons of foaming juice.

The Chief was so heavily engrossed in handling these problems, he missed the significance of a strange EDIFACT message, which informed them there was a container that had to be unloaded at Constanta and was cleared for release from the terminal. A similar message had been sent to the port's EDI addresses. The green container, conveniently situated at the top of the first stack, was unloaded and dropped onto a trailer, to be whisked away.

It was all so smooth. The driver, a local smuggler, well versed in stealing from the docks and transporting all manner of cargo, owned a garage some five kilometres outside the port. There, he and his brother, removed the transponders from the body of the container. Then, they broke the seals and locks on the container doors and examined the 200 wooden crates inside, removing more transponders, which they gave to a small boy, along with five Romanian leu to take them to a bridge over the Black Sea canal and cast them into the blue and black, oily waters.

The brothers had been told to wear gloves, face masks and visors, as the cargo was a liquid from a Russian chemical plant, ultimately bound for Syria. Once they were sure the container and its crates were clean, they filled the tractor with diesel and set off on the six hundred kilometre drive to a small village in Western Serbia.

As soon as the EDIFACT system sent a message to Savi's EDI terminal, confirming the release of the container from the Constanta terminal, he immediately set about reallocating the container number, so it appeared that the cargo of Libyan dinars was still sitting on the deck of the *Kapitan Markov*.

Two days later, after a quick clean of its holds, the *Kapitan Markov* left Constanta, cargo restacked, trim adjusted and ballast in order, minus the twenty empty juice containers. Savi had swapped the container numbers and told Mike Lloyd the *Kapitan Markov* had experienced some engineering problems but was now underway, and the release of the container to the haulier in Istanbul had been instructed. It was the same process that had happened earlier in Constanta, except the container in question was now a faded red colour, bearing the logo of a global shipping company.

Angry enquiries were made of the consignor of the twenty juice containers that had caused all the trouble, who reported that all trace of their customer had vanished.

Three days after the switch, Mary-Ann Baker took delivery of the faded red, forty-foot steel box at the US Air Base at Incirlik, in eastern Turkey. She had had several agents tail the container for the twelve-hour eastward journey from the port at Istanbul. It was her first solo mission in the field and she was determined not to be involved in a screw up. Inside the small hangar she had requisitioned, they set about opening the doors and removing the large pallets, stacked with cardboard boxes.

She knew something was wrong as soon as she saw the boxes. She climbed into the container and started squeezing and pushing them. They felt too light and insubstantial. She took a knife to the strapping on the first pallet and threw its contents to the floor below. It weighed less than twenty kilos. She did not even bother to open it.

"Drag the rest of the pallets out!"

Soon the floor was littered with boxes as they ripped the pallets apart, hoping that, somewhere, there would be wooden boxes stacked with green fifty-dinar notes. There were none.

In desperation, Mary-Ann took a knife to one of the boxes. Inside were quilted jackets, packed in cellophane bags and tied into bundles.

"Fuck, fuck and fuck! How's this happened? And what the fuck am I gonna tell Mike Lloyd!"

A week or so later, after an extensive search of the port of Benghazi, an official at the eastern branch of the Central Bank of Libya telephoned the Goznak Printing Works in Moscow to ask what had happened to the delivery of one billion Libyan dinars. The Chief Officer and the Logistics Manager of Goznak were extensively, and unsympathetically, questioned by the Russian state police and the Investigative Committee of Russia (the Russian FBI). It was the FSB who traced the container to Constanta, where the transponders on it, and in the packing cases themselves, had been removed and, presumably, destroyed.

A call was eventually made by the FSB to Valentin Petrov, informing him that the monies bound for eastern Libya had been stolen in transit and enquiries made suggested the theft was organised by security forces of the Government of National Accord in Tripoli. Petrov thought about it and decided that was a highly unlikely explanation.

It was stressed to him that nobody stole that amount of money from the Russian Mint and got away with it. This was a question of national pride. The file on the theft was to remain open and enquiries were to continue, until an accountable person was found and punished. He was ordered to be vigilant and to report any suspicions he might have back to Lubyanka Square. Even someone in Petrov's position shuddered at the mention of Lubyanka Square – a heavy-handed reminder to less diligent citizens of what went on in the basements below.

CHAPTER 39

RANIA BELKACEM
NAFUSA HILLS, LIBYA

It had been very early in the morning when Abdullah had woken Rania and they had left her brother's farm, in the dark, to drive the thirty kilometres towards Al Jawsh. The dual carriageway took them east, through the town and up onto the barren sandstone ridge that overlooked the plain running to the coast. Abdullah had chosen the spot carefully. All he had told Rania about the trip was that this day was going to be a new beginning for them. She had begged him to tell her more, but he had tapped his nose, in that annoying way, and said what he always said.

"Allah has a plan for us all! *Inshallah*! Be patient!"

As the sun started to come up in the east, they settled back in the truck and Rania wrapped a blanket around her. She had brought a flask of hot tea that she and Abdullah sipped, to warm them in the chill of the dawn. He had found a patch of flat scrub on the roadside, overlooking the hills to the south, and had used a small compass to take a bearing so he could manoeuvre the truck to point exactly in the direction he required. Rania was puzzled.

"Husband, you have dragged me from my bed before dawn

and brought me to an empty hillside. Now it is time to tell me what is happening. You are scaring me."

"Relax, Rania. Today is the start of a new era. There will be no more hiding. Wait for a few more minutes and you will see something important – no, amazing!"

Rania pulled the blanket up to her chin and snuggled down into it. She felt sleepy and her eyes started to close. Suddenly, Abdullah sat up straight, then leaped out of the car. He pushed his head in through the window and pulled on her shoulder with his hand.

"Get out – come on! There," he pointed skyward, "there, look … listen!"

They could hear the sound of an airplane. It came into sight, emerging from behind the hills to the east, low enough for them to make out its military insignia. It was a lumbering cargo plane, four propellers powering it through the air towards them. Abdullah grabbed some binoculars from the dashboard and trained them upwards. The plane was flying low and seemed to labour noisily over their heads, shattering the peace of the morning. As it did so, Rania could see that the cargo hatch at the rear of the fuselage was open. She was frightened and stood tight against Abdullah, linking his arm.

The plane crossed the valley beneath them. Once it was over the hills to the south, she saw a long cylinder slowly slide out of the rear of the plane. It fell for a few seconds before a parachute opened, silhouetted black against the morning sky. The plane banked to the left and immediately started to gain height. The cylinder swung in the air, suspended by the parachute. It stabilised and hung for a few seconds more. Then, an unseen hand released the cylinder from the chute and it began to fall directly below, gathering speed, ever faster, until it disappeared into the mountains.

A second later, there was an enormous flash of light, as if, through some cosmic miracle, a second sun had instantly been born in the south; then, in a second, it was gone. As sound follows light, there a was low rumble and then a deafening roar as the energy from the explosion ripped its way through every crevice, nook or cave off the ravine where Abu Muhammad had made camp. Anything soft vaporised instantly. The massive force of ten tonnes of explosive material pushed down, deep into the mountainside, heaving the rock, bending the strata and prising open fault lines.

The remnants of the blast wave hit them, even though they were at least ten kilometres from the strike zone. It was a warm wind laden with dust and gravel that flicked at their clothing and lightly scoured their flesh. Rania found herself in pain, but a glance down told her the cause was the ferocious grip Abdullah had on her upper arm.

They stood, transfixed, not sure what to expect next. The earth rumbled and shook beneath them.

Slowly, there was movement on the mountainside, some kilometres away, on the opposite side of the valley. First, a shower of scree rattled down, tinkling in the quiet of the early morning. Then Rania gasped as vertical fissures and cracks seemed to open in the rock face. A slice, maybe several hundred metres wide, peeled away from the mountainside and started to slide smoothly downwards, in one vast piece.

Rania felt that if she could only stand on top of it, she would be lowered gently to the valley floor, where she could hop off in one seamless movement. But then, the huge mass of sliding mountain violently accelerated and smashed against the base of the plain with an angry roar, disintegrating into clouds of dust that mushroomed high into the clear desert sky.

"*Ya 'iilahi*! Oh my God," she muttered, her hands to her face. "What have you done?"

Her husband stood looking at the earth cleaving itself in front of him, a fierce light burning in his eyes. She knew that look, and the fire in his heart that caused it. She had not seen him this way since his return and it frightened her.

"Praise be to Allah, always and eternally. Rania, that was the birth of a new time. This quiet morning, the time of Abu Muhammad is over. That was the first step in our revenge. There is still more to be done, but today is a happy day."

He grabbed her portly frame and held her tight. '*Revenge*,' she thought, '*is that what this is all about?*' But she said nothing.

Abdullah led her back to the truck.

"The explosion has wiped out the valley road!" He laughed manically. "Do not worry, it is not much further to go the longer way."

"Where to now, husband? What further destruction have you planned for us to see? I hope you have prayed hard for guidance on all this. To destroy the world like that is no small thing."

"It is Allah's will, Rania! I know that. I do not need to pray and examine my conscience. By now, the Beards will know if their dreams of *shaheed* have come true – or not! Martyrs? Hah! They are but thieves and murderers. But it is good the roads are clear of their evil and it is safe for us to travel. Now, let us be happy and celebrate!"

They drove back towards Marsabar. The explosion and the shock wave had been clearly heard, and felt, in Al Jawsh and beyond. There was a stream of traffic driving past on the other side of the road, full of people curious to know what had caused the huge vibrations that rattled their china and scared the dogs. Abdullah lapsed into a thoughtful mood and remained quiet until they turned onto the Marsabar road on the coastal plain.

"Where are you taking me?" his wife asked.

"You will see. We will be there shortly."

"You are taking me back to the farm, the homestead? You know it will break my heart. All those memories of the children playing and happy times with Tareq. Abdullah, no. Must we go?"

She risked a glance at him. He had forbidden any mention of Tareq's name. He had said that, until his brother was avenged, he should not be spoken of. Now, Abdullah's eyes remained trained on the road, but there was a faint trace of a smile on his face.

Although she had protested, she did not dare hope it could be true; he was taking her home – back to their farm, destroyed by Abu Muhammad and lying ruined these past four years. No man dared to touch the land that belonged to Abdullah Belkacem.

He had heard the farm had been burned out, but the stone framework of their house was still sound, apart from where the explosions had ripped the side wall down. The blackened shell of his brother's old Mercedes lay in the front yard, stripped back to metal, bare as a picked-clean carcass.

Rania got out of the car and quietly walked about the yard, memories of the past swirling around her. She saw where her mother would sit on an evening; dead now, some three years ago. The scaffold arrangement they had built as a frame for the raised swimming pool, for Jamal's twelfth birthday party, was still there, its planks hanging loose. Remnants of shredded tarpaulin fluttered but were still attached. She heard the cries of the children, playing in the dirt, and the barking of the dogs. The echoes of home sounded powerfully in her ears.

She saw her husband, inside the shell of the house, tearing timber aside and moving rubble.

"Abdullah, why are we here? Do you torture me with these memories?"

"Come here and look."

He stood in what was once the kitchen. There had been looting, but she recognised two of her old saucepans lying amongst the broken tiles and heaps of plaster. She bent to collect them. He was grinning broadly.

"Look at the entrance to the cellar. It is buried and undisturbed! The rear wall has fallen up against the door and buried it. There must be tonnes of stone over the stairway down to the tunnel."

She saw him dare to hope.

They ran back to the truck and he gunned it through the yard, the few hundred metres to the rough shed in the rear field. While they had lived there, Abdullah had wisely built an escape route, through the sandstone, that exited in the old shed. It was through this low, narrow tunnel that Rania and the children had run, terrified and in total darkness, to escape Muhammad's attack, four years previously.

Inside the shed, Abdullah looked around. The door to the rear cupboard hung loose, but the swing panel in the back, that concealed the steps down to the tunnel, was firmly shut. They looked at each other and Abdullah took his cigarette lighter, pulled at the panel to free it, and plunged down the roughly cut stone steps. Rania waited, not knowing what to think. Soon, she heard her husband scrambling back up and then he appeared, cobwebs hanging from his hair and beard, the dust of years over his clothing. He spat some matter from his mouth and then his face cracked into an enormous smile.

"We are truly blessed today, *Allahu Akbar*! The door is locked and has not been opened. If Allah is willing, we will have our gold and money back. We will rebuild the house and we will start again. We will make up for lost years!"

He grabbed Rania, who could not stop herself from sobbing in his arms.

Abdullah had a strong room in his cellars where he had kept gold and bundles of US dollars, earned through migrant trafficking, smuggling and other such enterprises. The door looked like a section of the stone wall and relied for its security on concealment, rather than the strength of its locks.

He rooted around in the shed for plastic fertiliser sacks, emptying the dried pellets onto the floor. From the truck, he took some long, hexagonal-shaped keys for window locks and a torch. There was a pickaxe in the shed which he gave to Rania.

"I cannot use that!"

"I joke, wife, give it to me. Today, I have the strength to dig a hole a kilometre deep."

Abdullah grabbed Rania's hand and guided her down the narrow stone stairs into the cramped, dark passage. She stooped, but Abdullah had to walk bent double. The fear and claustrophobia returned, reminding her of her flight, with the sobbing children, down that passage.

It took thirty minutes for Abdullah to open the door to the small cave he had hacked into the sandstone and fill two heavy-duty fertiliser sacks with gold bars, sovereigns, kruger rands and rolls of dollars, euros and dinars. They dragged the heavy sacks along the tunnel and up the steps, carefully placing them in the back of the truck where they lay in full view. He had scooped handfuls of fertiliser pellets from the floor of the shed to fill the gaps between the tubes of gold coins and rolls of currency and tied the tops of the sacks, tightly, with blue nylon twine.

"If we are stopped, there are only two old plastic sacks of fertiliser in our truck. They will not look further."

"Will we really rebuild our home? Tell me that is true?"

"It is true, Rania, and our happiness will be part of my revenge!"

"But you will leave to find Muhammad?"

"I must leave – I still have work to do. I have promised the Americans. That bomb this morning? It cost a fortune in US dollars. They have kept their promise to me. There is a good chance, by Allah's will, we can live in peace. But first, I must go and find Abu Muhammad: not for me, but for Tareq. When I come back, this house will be rebuilt and you will make it a home I can return to!

"All is well, is it not?"

Rania looked at him and said: "*Mashallah,* thanks be to Allah! Do not fail Him, or me, Abdullah."

CHAPTER 40

GEORGE ZAMMIT
ABU MUHAMMAD'S CAMP, CHADIAN DESERT

GRADUALLY, the effects of the beating started to subside and the swelling on George's cheek and above his eye turned from red to blue to yellow. The terrible bouts of stomach cramps, diarrhoea and vomiting brought on by the filthy water he had so readily drunk, finally stopped. The effects of the sickness left him exhausted, sore and dehydrated. He slept for most of the day, only to wake at night shivering and trembling under the thin, ragged blanket Yaroslav had thrown into the hut.

George had lain semi-conscious, in his own filth, for four days. His clothing was sodden and soiled, flies and mosquitoes swarming around him. By the third day, he was barely conscious, gripped by fever. He had dreamed of Marianna at the door, shouting at him to come for dinner, kindness in her voice. He had tried to answer, but could not get his words out. Another time, he was back home, at Gina's party, in full dress uniform. Camilleri was sitting in the armchair in the corner of the lounge, with his service medals pinned on his chest, running his white-gloved hands up the leg of Madam President, who sat on his knee like an oversized cat, her skirt pulled up high.

On the fifth day, Yaroslav found George awake. He was naked, covered in his own excrement, his skin red and scabbed where he had scratched at the mosquito bites that tormented him. He was crouching in the corner of the hut, his beard now fully grown and his hair matted, wild and starting to knot. He looked as though he had just spent the last year as a castaway on some faraway island.

At first Yaroslav thought George had lost his mind but, after speaking softly to him and establishing his sanity, he had gone to fetch him a bucket of water, some new clothes and a shovel. Once George had rinsed the worst off himself and put on the T-shirt and loose black cotton trousers, he took the shovel and slowly scraped the top layer of earth out of the hut and relaid the floor with fresh dirt from outside.

The pain in his face was now equal to the pain in his stomach, as his abdominal muscles ached from the vomiting and retching. Little by little, he started to eat, the meagre ration of lentils and bread more than satisfying his appetite. He was weak and miserable, but marvelled at the reduced size of his paunch and the sagging skin that hung from under his jaw.

At least he was receiving a plentiful supply of clean water, in unopened plastic bottles. During the daylight hours, his door was left open and he was free to sit outside the hut. The first day he sat and watched the September clouds start to build – plump white pillows in the clear blue sky. Back home they called them the 'back to school' clouds, as they appeared every year, before the start of the new school year, causing every child's heart to sink.

On the evening of the fifth day, he sat with his back resting against the still-warm blockwork, talking to Yaroslav and thanking him for his care.

The Russian laughed and said: "I am not becoming nurse after that. So, now you better, *da?* How come you get into this mess?"

"Oh, I don't know. I'm a policeman and I've got a damn' fool boss who sent me here to babysit my crazy Libyan friend." George shook his head, asking himself the same question. "My friend has dreams of raising a private militia to settle old scores against IS-in-Libya and stir up trouble for Boutros. I shouldn't say too much."

"So where were you captured?"

"We were digging in at the airfield in Ubari when they hit us. We weren't quite ready for them. One more day and it would have been different."

"I hear you are machine gunner. Ubari, is that south of the Sharara oil fields?"

"*Mela*, for God's sake. I'm a policeman, not a soldier. They gave me the gun but I was terrified, even though I did stop a few. The people I was with are interested in the oil fields, sure."

"In this country that is true of everybody! So, how is it you need airfield?"

"We're working with the Americans and they're airlifting supplies in for us."

Yaroslav's head flicked towards him and his expression told George he had just done what he had decided he would not do – revealed too much. He hastily tried to move the conversation away from what he was doing in the deserts of Libya.

"So, anyway, tell me, who did you meet when you were in Malta? Cheer me up, let's talk about home!"

They talked about his island and Yaroslav told George he had been sent to explore some business opportunities there, but nothing much had come of them. He then went through a list of names – government officials, politicians – while George told stories and made derogatory remarks about each and every one of them. Yaroslav decided not to mention the fact that he had had lunch and several meetings with Assistant Commissioner Gerald Camilleri.

Yaroslav was thinking aloud.

"So, who else I know in Malta? Oh, *da!* There is family – they have *palazzo* up on hill, the Bonnicis. The old man is Marco and the daughter – oooh, a beauty! – is Natasha. For one night, I would pay everything I have. Everything!

George laughed.

"I know her. She's a looker alright!"

Interesting, he thought, the old policeman's instinct returning to him; he knows the Bonnicis.

"I thought Marco Bonnici had left the country and was living in the Balkans somewhere?"

"Maybe. Now he come back. I met the two, the father and the daughter. Nice people. Especially the daughter … oomph!"

George got up and started to walk the stony ground in front of his hut, stretching his limbs and looking around the camp. He smelled earth, diesel and, from somewhere, the faint aroma of spice. Little pleasures were important. Yaroslav looked around and checked him.

"Hey, stay close, two metres! Or they will shoot you!"

The English jihadi, Raheem, had already told George to stay within two metres of the hut, otherwise the guards had permission to fire on him.

"Why would they do that?"

"Because some do not like you! You machine gun their relatives and friends at Ubari! Because Raheem, he say, Americans drop a 'Mother of All Bombs' on their camp in the Nafusa Hills. Everyone there is killed. Many men, their comrades. Someone makes a lot of trouble and we make sure, not trouble for us. *Da*?"

"How many were killed?"

"They say, everybody in camp. Plus, all transport and many weapons destroyed. What you see," Yaroslav looked around him, "is all of Islamic State-in-Libya! Good job done, I say."

"Oh! Was it the Americans? Are Abu Muhammad and Faysal angry?"

"Oh, yes, and they are shocked. It is only Americans have bombs so big. That is why they locked us up. They have been thinking on other things and that is dangerous for us. So, you stay two metres of your hut, because ground is hard and to dig two-metre-deep hole for you is much work."

Yaroslav looked around, to make sure they were not being

watched.

"Listen, big English guy – Raheem – he says they move out soon. He says they will move us to a safe base in Sudan. I beg cigarettes and he talks to me."

"Is that good news?"

"Every day we are alive is good news! Do not think they will not kill us. That would be very stupid."

Yaroslav pulled half a cigarette from his top pocket and lit it. He muttered to George: "Be quiet, here comes Faysal."

Muhammad's deputy walked with a slight waddle and was rocking his way across the rough ground of the camp towards them. He usually had a smile on his face although this evening his expression was anything but friendly. George noticed the change of demeanour and kept his eyes on the ground. Faysal squatted on his haunches in front of them.

"You're both lucky. It's Allah's will that you're not to be killed. I would've shot you both. It'd be a fitting response for what you've done in Nafusa. But others persuaded me to exchange you for prisoners held by Boutros in Benghazi."

Yaroslav scrutinised Faysal as he spoke.

"Tomorrow we'll give you some water, food and a tarpaulin for shelter. We'll drive you into the desert and take co-ordinates, to give to the Russians. They can come and collect you. So, when you're dropped, don't move from there. The desert's a big place and a man could easily get lost and die."

Yaroslav was uneasy.

"Where is this drop?"

"Half a day's drive away from the Sirte Basin, where your Volunteers work security at some of the wells."

"What if they think it is trap? What if they do not come for us? I am not a Volunteer and he is not Russian! Why would they come?"

"That's between you and your countrymen. Or would you rather have the bullet?"

George thought about all the possible downsides: what if

Faysal did not ring or got the coordinates wrong or some idiot threw them out at the wrong place? What if there was a sandstorm, or if their truck broke down? He liked the plan as little as Yaroslav did, but a quick exchange of glances between them showed they both understood there was no choice.

———

The next morning, they were given rucksacks and climbed into the back of the faded green Patriot SUV that Raheem and his jihadis had stolen after they had killed Lev and his Volunteers all those weeks ago. Abu Muhammad and Faysal came outside the command tent to watch their departure. Faysal nodded to them while Abu Muhammad glowered, hand on the pistol at his hip.

Raheem was driving. George watched him strap two jerry cans of fuel onto the rear deck. Seeing that partly reassured him they were going to be taken a decent distance north and not just shot once they were out of camp.

Raheem and a second man, wearing a long red-and-white-checked *keffiyeh* slung loosely round his neck, climbed into the two front seats, while Yaroslav and George slid into the back. Yaroslav was quiet and did not say a word after getting into the vehicle. Instead, he crossed his arms, rested his head against the door post, shut his eyes and fell asleep.

George watched and listened to Raheem and his partner, chatting and laughing. After a couple of hours, the guy in the passenger seat started to nod his head as Raheem drove the SUV down a never-ending red, hard-packed desert road that went straight as an arrow towards the horizon.

George was daydreaming, looking out of the window, when he sensed, rather than saw, Yaroslav suddenly lunge forward and grab Raheem under his chin and put his other arm across his forehead, pulling his head back and to the side, with one sharp movement. George heard Raheem's neck snap and he immediately went limp.

Yaroslav then lunged over the front seat, pushing the dead Raheem to one side and grabbing the wheel. The sleeping man, woken by the commotion, leaned over to stop the Russian, who yelled at George: "Pull on his *keffiyeh*!"

George grabbed the ends of the red-and-white-checked scarf and pulled it hard and tight around the man's throat. He leaned back as far as he could, choking him. The man's hands grabbed at the scarf, but he started to kick and twist in his seat, his flailing feet knocking Yaroslav's arms off the steering wheel.

George's eyes were wide with terror. He pushed himself even further away, to avoid the clutching arms of the man in the front seat. The more he leaned back, the tighter the cloth bound itself to the throat of the blue-faced man.

The truck veered off the road and, as it went onto the scrub, there was a jolt causing George inadvertently to release the *keffiyeh*, causing the other man to lurch forward and put his head deep into the front windscreen.

As the truck ground to a stop and stalled, Yaroslav leaped out and went round to the other side, to pull the dazed passenger out through the door. George watched, mesmerised, as Yaroslav grabbed a rock that was lying beside the vehicle and repeatedly beat the jihadi's head. People do not die easily and George had to turn away while Yaroslav hit the man hard, several times.

Finally the Russian lay panting on the sand, laughing.

"*Bot te ha!* I need gym! When I get back, I must exercise." He paused, breathing heavily. "You did good, letting him go like that. Head through window, it is neat trick!"

"Really? It just slipped out of my hands. I didn't mean to kill him, that's for sure. And you didn't need to do that."

George pointed to the mess that had been a man's head. He felt sick and a heave from deep in his gut made him belch.

"We could've tied him up or something."

Yaroslav looked down.

"What? And when he wake up, we keep looking back to see who chase us? No, this way is better."

He put a gratuitous kick into the side of the bloodied corpse to make his point.

George folded his arms onto the scorching roof of the car and buried his head in them for a moment. A wave of dread gripped him and he fought to control his rising panic. It was good, he told himself, it was all good. They had escaped captivity. He promised himself this was the first step to getting home. He was on his way. He had to be.

The truck was fine, apart from the egg-shaped bulge and dense latticework of cracks in the windscreen that was going to make driving tricky. George suggested punching it out, but Yaroslav said hours of driving with the sand blowing in their faces would be worse than peering through the web of glass.

They dragged the bodies away from the road to a small depression and took their cigarettes, money and the passenger's bloodied *keffiyeh*. Yaroslav wrapped this around his fair hair and white brow, leaving only his eyes unveiled. These he covered with Raheem's sunglasses.

"You already look like Arab. Me, I must try harder."

Together, driving their battered truck, they could easily have passed for a pair of Libyan labourers.

The drive was a torture. Yaroslav had to keep his head about half a metre to the left, to see the road round the enormous dent in the screen. By the time they had driven into Bayda, many hours later, he was sure his spine was permanently deformed. They turned up at the Volunteers' compound, exhausted, hungry and feeling terrible. There was no one there that Yaroslav knew; his people were all out driving around the desert, with fifteen IS prisoners, trying to find him and his companion. The exchange had been for real.

What came as more of a surprise to them was when they were immediately grabbed by a couple of Volunteers and thrown in a locked room, apparently for screwing up the prisoner exchange!

They had clean mattresses to sleep on, a tepid shower, a hot meal of chicken sausage and grain, and even a good measure of vodka from a more understanding Volunteer, who had heard what had happened. George's head swam with the alcohol and sleep came quickly; as did their release, early the next morning.

He rose to find Yaroslav arguing with a group of Volunteers in the large dining hall of the makeshift barracks. They were planning to pull out of Libya as soon as they could. Boutros's air support had taken a beating from the American airstrikes. The US planes and Reaper drones had destroyed the UAE-supplied fleet of ten Chinese Wing Loon drones and six ancient MiG jets – which was Boutros's entire air force. Word had it that he had also run out of cash and promised wages were not being paid. The militias were thinning out as fighters drifted off home with empty pockets.

On top of all that, the Americans had also hit an IS base in the Nafusa Hills and totally demolished an area the size of Gorky Park. With one blow, they had wiped out Islamic State-in-Libya! It was time to leave – none of them got paid enough to fight such odds.

George had to turn away to hide his triumphant expression. He clenched his fists in excitement at the thought of soon being on his way back to Malta.

Yaroslav looked at him, trying to decide what to do with him. After a moment, he turned and spoke to one of the Volunteers. The man left the room, to return with a bundle of dinars. Yaroslav gave George the money, a 9mm Makarov pistol, and threw him the keys to the Patriot SUV.

"Go, my friend. It is one thousand kilometres to Tripoli. You drive, do not stop, you do it in a day and a half, if militias do not kill you. Good luck!"

George was shocked, but realised it was a better outcome than he could have expected. He reached over and took Raheem's sunglasses off Yaroslav's face and the soiled red and white *keffiyeh* from around his neck.

"I'll need these. I'm punching that windscreen out."

CHAPTER 41

NATASHA BONNICI
OFFICES OF THE DEPARTMENT OF ENERGY, AUBERGE D'ALLEMAGNE, VALLETTA, MALTA

THE KNIGHTS HOSPITALLERS came into being as a medieval Catholic medical order, which later turned into a significant naval power that went marauding across the eastern Mediterranean, to the annoyance of the Ottomans of Istanbul. In the early sixteenth century they had made Malta their home. The island's history is still defined by their presence, in particular the Great Siege, where the heavily outnumbered Knights defeated the Ottomans in 1565. Learning from their near defeat at the hands of the Turks, they built the fortified city of Valletta on the high peninsula that juts out between the Grand Harbour to the south and Marsamxett Harbour to the north.

The Knights themselves lived together, by nationality, in monastic palaces called *auberges*, the most famous being the Auberge de Castille that today houses the offices of the Maltese Prime Minister.

The little-known Auberge d'Allemagne, tucked away on the north side of the narrow peninsula, had been left derelict and ignored for centuries. Its shallow steps, leading to the columns that supported the portico, were originally designed so that knights in full armour could ride their horses into the *piano nobile* – the floor where the knights conducted their business. In the nineties it had been rediscovered and refurbished, and today it was home to the Department of Energy. Natasha had just finished her first formal meeting there as chair of MalTech Energy, the joint venture company in which the Family had invested over two hundred million euros.

It had been agreed that MalTech Energy would buy gas from the Libyan wells and operate the receiving plant in Malta. It would on-sell the gas, via a consumer division, to the entire population of the island. In addition, it would lay the pipeline to Sicily and make further sales of gas to the European transmission companies. It was a bold plan – and Natasha sat at the head of the top table, where she felt she deserved to be.

Once the meeting had finished, she asked for the use of a private office and settled down with her phone. She rang a number with a Gibraltar prefix. The call went unanswered. Not fooled, she sent an SMS.

Pick up Nick.

She rang the number again.

"Natasha. What can I do for you? You want another story planting?"

"Nick, hi. No, not this time. I've got something entirely different to talk about."

BetHi had originally been Nick Walker's brainchild. When Marco and Sergio had bought the company under its original first name of BetSlick, it was with the express intention of funnelling millions of euros of the Family's illicit earnings through the operation.

If Natasha were to fulfil her ambition to rise to the top rank of the Family and get close to the seat of power in Milan, she had to find someone to run BetHi for her. Who better than Nick Walker?

She explained the deal to him.

"Come on, Nick, there's nothing to discuss, surely? The whole operation is almost legitimate these days. Crypto has sorted a lot of the problems and, once we get the cash, we roll it through the gaming systems. If there are winnings, we repay them as clean cash to our accounts, and the losses we keep as profits. It's a lot less risky than it used to be."

Nick had yet to be totally convinced.

"It's not every day someone rings you up and offers you the CEO job at one of the biggest gaming platforms in Europe!"

"I don't know, Natasha …"

"Look, you can keep the Gibraltar operation going as insurance. BetHi is so big it nearly runs itself."

"Well, why do you need me then?"

"Come on, Nick, you know why. We need eyes and ears. We need our person on the inside, we …"

"Exactly! You're asking me to put myself back into an exposed position I've been trying to avoid for the last four years!"

"Look, I know the Gibraltar business hasn't exactly thrived. No fault of yours, but you haven't got the cash for TV and sports advertising. The game has moved on and you can't do it your way anymore. Come on, come back and make some serious money."

There was a short silence while Nick pondered the unpalatable truth of what Natasha had said.

"OK, let's just say I agree to think about it, it has to be strictly business. No wider Family involvement and there's no you and me. That wouldn't be good for either of us. Agreed?"

She was silent for just a second too long.

"Agreed. Absolutely. It didn't exactly end well last time, did it?"

She struggled to control her irritation at his insistence on making the point. Who was he to decide a thing like that? She ran her hand over her head and, through the thick mass of hair, felt the scar on her skull made by the Murano glass vase Nick had used to strike her. Then he had left the island without a further thought. He had been a bastard. No one had ever treated her like that. She conveniently overlooked that she had been carrying a gun at the time. Now he had the cheek to say a thing like 'no you and me'! Who did he think he was? She pulled herself together.

Nick said: "Is Camilleri still onside?"

"Of course. Gerald is part of the furniture."

"Does Marco still hate me?"

Natasha forced a laugh.

"Probably. But you know Dad, he's the forgiving sort. Anyway, he's leaving the Family. He's going back to Serbia, for good."

"No way!"

"Afraid so. Come on … what d'you say?"

"I'll think about it."

"No, I haven't got time for that. I need to know now."

"Patience! Twenty-four hours?"

She sighed.

"OK. Twenty-four hours. I'll ring you."

As she descended the steps from the Auberge de d'Allemagne, swapping her spectacles for sunglasses, her mood changed. She had one more unpleasant job to deal with, which was resolving the problem of the overgrown child currently locked up in the family chapel on the cliff top. On the one hand, Savi had done everything she had asked of him; on the other, he knew far too much about her affairs and that was always a worry. She wondered about retaining him, paying him money to sit in the chapel forever, with unlimited supplies of pizza, beer and computer games. She actually thought he might not even notice that his captivity had been indefinitely extended.

She rang Simon and told him to meet her at the chapel.

HASTINGS GARDENS SIT on top of St John's Bastion and St Michael's Bastion, formerly the western defences of Valletta. From the gardens, visitors can look out over the four-metre-thick walls to the pointed church spires of Floriana, the contemporary high rises of Sliema and the marinas of Marsamxett Harbour.

The minute Marco saw Mike Lloyd steaming in through the gate, flanked as usual by his security detail of look-alike night-club doormen, he knew there was something on Lloyd's mind.

"What the fuck, Marco?"

The American's tone was loud and belligerent.

Marco sighed.

"Good morning, Mike, how are things?"

"I was expecting three-quarters of a billion US dollars and ended up with some fucking jackets! I look like a major dick, that's how things are!"

"What, you stole the wrong container?"

Marco did not understand what had happened.

"No, we got the container alright – the right container – but it was full of jackets – dick-licker puffer jackets! This was supposed to be an off the books job, but now it's all round the Firm and I'm a laughing stock!"

Marco felt on safe ground as he had genuinely had no idea of the particulars of the American plan to steal the notes.

"You must have got the wrong container. Anyway, what has this to do with me? I did not even know for sure you were going to steal it."

"Listen, Marco, you tipped me off about the notes, yeah? Someone has been fishing upstream. You're the only other people who knew about it. We had it all sorted. We wait in line and the system magically delivers a container, out the air, like the stork, dumps it on our trailer and, if everything matches, the port gates swing open and we drive out. Well, it's the right container – except it's full of fucking jackets!"

Marco was speechless. He had no answer and could not begin to work out what had happened.

He shrugged and held up his arms in surrender.

"Nothing I can say. I honestly know nothing. You have the Russians involved; the Libyans knew the cash was coming – could have been anybody. I do not know why you are pointing the finger at me. Maybe the Russians have the cash and you messed up?"

"Well, we won't know that until the damn' boat arrives at Benghazi. Then Petrov might be good enough to tell us he's been shafted too.

"OK, Marco, here's how it is. I'll level with you. I was using this guy, IT contractor, skateboarder-hacker type, to pull off the heist. He went dark on me. Not like him. He's as dumb as shit, would never think of doing something like that. So, I set the technicians onto him – they monitor internet traffic and all that clever stuff. They get a ping. A faint ping and only the once, but it's enough. And guess what? It came from right on your doorstep, near some closed-up chapel. So, I'll ask you once more. What the fuck?

"If you're pissing with me, Marco, I'll make sure there're consequences. I'll screw your pipeline deal and to hell with the blow back. This is personal. I can't stand being made to look like a turkey."

It took a few seconds for what had been said to register with Marco. Then, as the possibilities dawned on him, he tried desperately to hide his shock. He did not blink or change his facial expression but, involuntarily, put a hand to his head and ran it through his hair. He should not have done that.

Calmly, he said, "Mike, this one is down to you. I do not have a clue what went wrong with your operation."

Once Lloyd had calmed down, he returned to sit next to Marco and they talked about the purchase of the VertWay pipeline from the Russians by an American consortium, and the gas supply contract to MalTech Energy. The London and New York lawyers seemed to be producing thousands of pages of incomprehensible documents which, Mike complained, he was actually expected to read!

"OK, let's leave that to one side. You probably heard – the military side is going like a dream. We hit the rebels and IS with some big airstrikes and, man, was there some damage! If our boys and the militia guys on the ground can follow through, we'll have made significant progress on the mission soon.

"But once we get control of the western desert and the Marsabar and Az-Zawiyah refineries, you've got to be certain you've the muscle to keep those assets safe."

Marco nodded in agreement.

"My daughter has spent a lot of time working on that side of things and she says she has a plan to tie things up. I will keep you in the loop," he promised.

"Hmmm. That should be interesting. And, by the way ..."

"Yes?"

"If I ever catch you, or any of your crew, with bundles of Libyan dinars sticking out of your pockets, I promise you, you'll learn the meaning of US black ops!"

"Charming!"

"See you, Marco."

Mike Lloyd strode away, his black-suited bodyguards to left and right of him, the three of them swaggering off through the tranquil gardens.

Marco smiled to himself, watching their departure. The smile soon faded as his thoughts returned to the missing money and Mike Lloyd's reference to the chapel on the cliffs. He thought about the young hacker and then Simon, with his recent out of character errands to purchase computer games. He considered the theft of the dinars and Natasha's cryptic comment about tying things up in Libya. His heart sank and he walked wearily back to his car.

He had not really felt in control here since his return. It was as if he only ever knew a piece of what was going on, never the whole picture. He wondered whether it was him. Had he lost his edge during the time he had been away? Was he too slow to spot the angles, anticipate events? Or was Natasha pulling his strings? He could not disagree that she was growing into a formidable operator – who would not want that for their son or daughter? But her methods and her ruthlessness both shocked and frightened him. He did not want to find himself unable to trust her, but he feared that was already the case.

He went back to the car park and drove up through the central belt towards the hilltop town of Mdina, the old capital. Behind the Silent City, he joined the maze of rural back roads that crossed the less frequently visited north-west of the island. Leaving the road, he drove the Range Rover along the rutted, unmetalled farmer's track that ran alongside his small vineyards and fields of potatoes, cauliflowers and cereals. He wanted to approach the chapel from the south, to avoid being seen heading down the long track from the *castello*.

He needed to know if there was anything in Mike Lloyd's suggestion that the hacker kid had been held in their family chapel, under Marco's very own nose!

As he turned a blind corner on the track, where a high bamboo thicket blocked the driver's view of oncoming traffic, he nearly collided with his own black SUV, being driven by Simon. Marco had to stare hard through the glare of the windscreen to be sure that it was Natasha sitting alongside the bodyguard. Both vehicles skidded to a halt on the dirt road and Simon got out first.

"Boss, what are you doing here, I nearly hit you?"

"Get in my car, Simon, and take it back to the *castello*. I need to talk to Miss Natasha. I will see you later."

CHAPTER 43

ABDULLAH BELKACEM
THE FARMHOUSE, MARSABAR,
LIBYA

THE REPERCUSSIONS of the American bomb on the Islamic State-Libya camp and the destruction of Boutros's air support proved to be a turning point in both conflicts. Not only were the attacks totally unexpected, they also brought a whole new degree of chaos to the east of the country and threw the rebels into disarray. The Russian Volunteers were pulling out and Boutros's long-promised cash had failed to arrive, more or less crippling his progress on Tripoli. The sudden and unexpected involvement of the Americans caused the UAE, Turkey and Egypt all to pause, trying to make sense of the new realpolitik.

Abdullah's militia had taken Marsabar without a bullet being fired, as those few IS fighters still left alive in the Nafusa Hills fled south to try and rejoin Abu Muhammad in Chad or Sudan. The Tuareg had expected this and moved several hundred well-equipped militia men of their own from Ubari to establish road-blocks on the routes to the south and east. Little mercy was shown to the fleeing militia.

As he had expected, Abdullah's reinstatement was cause for great excitement within the town and he was overwhelmed by masses of eager young men, all keen to join him, crush the threat of IS and push back Boutros once and for all. The Americans were as good as their word and material was flown from the Middle East bases into Ubari, which was now a secure location with a series of berms and bunkers for planes, ammunition and other equipment.

The Americans established a one thousand kilometre safe corridor, from Ubari in the south, through the Sharara oil field, to Marsabar on the coast. Their idea was to ensure the safe, uninterrupted supply of oil and gas from the largest Libyan fields to the Marsabar and Az-Zawiyah refineries in the north, which could then be piped or tankered by ship to Europe. Abdullah's idea was to have a local Libyan militia, under his command, large enough and well enough equipped to take over the security of the corridor once the Americans pulled out.

Until they could open the port at Marsabar, daily convoys arrived from Ubari with weapons, ammunition and other equipment. Once Marsabar was secured, the US Navy supply ships would be free to dock and the heavier weapons and supplies could easily be unloaded. US advisers had arrived as well, men with expensive sunglasses and pristine desert camouflage fatigues. Abdullah noticed these were regular US military and not the rough and ready contractors he had experienced at Ubari.

Abdullah had also made good on his promise to Rania, who had persuaded him to start the rebuilding of the farmhouse immediately. Cannily, he had invited the US advisers to join him and use the compound and surrounding area as their base. Lines of large command tents formed accommodation for Abdullah, the advisers and the army of recruits that were to become his militia.

It turned out the Americans had a knack for being able to source almost anything and have it brought into Marsabar. Rania was thrilled by the range of Italian tiles and bathrooms, air-conditioning units and UPVC double-glazed windows that magically appeared, every time a convoy of trucks rolled up the dirt road.

Local builders worked the stone and rebuilt the farmhouse

around the door and window units that arrived from Italy. They installed the new services, while Rania took over the planning and set about modernising the finishes inside.

Abdullah had noticed that the US advisers had learned their lessons from Iraq and Afghanistan. They no longer shouted and screamed at the recruits, like West Point drill sergeants, but embraced the Arab values of respect, honour and reputation. They talked of responsibility, teamwork and accepting the word of a superior. When it was time for prayers, a break was scheduled and the advisers withdrew a respectful distance away. They worked closely with the men, identifying leaders and teaching what had basically been an enthusiastic mob to become a paid, well-organised and equipped battalion-sized combat unit of just under one thousand men. It was a level of organisation the Russian Volunteers had never even tried to achieve with Boutros's ragtag Libyan National Army.

One evening, when peace had descended after another hectic day of training, building, shooting and praying, Abdullah was walking between the lines of tents, when he noticed the most senior of the Rangers, Major Floyd Hamilton, sitting in a khaki canvas chair outside his tent. He was holding a book and had a bottle of Coke by his side.

Abdullah liked Floyd, whom he considered a patient and thoughtful man and, he guessed, probably a religious one as well. Abdullah lit a cigarette and squatted down in front of him.

"So, General Floyd, my brother, what do you read when the work is done and the evening is upon us?"

Floyd smiled and put the book down.

"Hey, Abdullah, don't call me General – you'll put a jinx on my chances! A soldier's work is never done, man, and this is my sort of work." He offered the book to Abdullah. "It's *The Seven Pillars of Wisdom*, by a hero of mine, a Brit called T. E. Lawrence. Have you heard of him?"

"Yeah, I have heard this name. He was a friend of the Arabs in Jordan and is long dead?"

"Yeah, he was a British officer – an adviser – like me, I suppose! He stirred up an army of Arabs to beat the Turks in 1916. He respected the Arab people and tried to live like one of them; no air-con, no Coke, no Land Cruisers. You know, just camels and tents – the real deal!"

Abdullah nodded sagely at the major and waited for him to continue.

"He promised them that after the war there'd be an independent Arab nation. But he got pissed on by the English and French governments. Lawrence wanted a democratic state for the Arabs, on the land that's now Iran and Iraq."

"Aha! So, he wanted what ISIL want … but maybe less Shia! A Caliphate on the old lands. But did he know how much oil there was in the ground there?"

"No, probably not."

"And where were the Americans? If there is only the smell of oil, you appear like cats to a roasting chicken."

Floyd smiled.

"It was before our time. Anyway, Lawrence didn't get what he wanted and he was so ashamed that he'd broken his promise, he went and tried to kill himself!"

"A man of his word! Rare in an Englishman. So, what promises can you give me? The smell of oil in Libya is strong." Abdullah held his head up and breathed in deeply. "You can smell it too, no? You Americans are here so we can be free? Are you men like Lawrence, eh? Or is it because we have the oil?"

Abdullah smiled at Floyd, who took the jibe in good humour.

"That's politics, Abdullah! I am just a soldier, but one day soon you gotta think about these things." Floyd paused and looked at him intently, to let Abdullah know he was being serious. "If the rebel wins, the time comes when he's gotta take control and try to do a better job than the other guys."

"Yes, I have been waiting for someone to tell me what is expected of me, if that time comes."

"Ain't no one going to tell you what to do, you know. You gotta work that out for yourself."

"Easy for you to say. But I can do nothing without this!"

Abdullah gestured to the military set up behind him.

"Well, sure. But you've still got choices. Taking the refinery at Az-Zawiyah shouldn't be a problem. The gas gets pumped up here and down the pipeline to Malta and everyone's happy. I bet you could get very rich, offering protection to politicians and the oil guys on the Sharara."

Abdullah lit another cigarette and listened attentively. He wondered whether this was just a man speaking his thoughts or whether these were the instructions he had been waiting for. Floyd continued.

"Or you could become a politician yourself – move on to Tripoli and take power. That's a possibility, too. The government here's weak, getting weaker by the day. The UN has no love for them." He paused. "And we don't like them much, either. Too friendly with the Muslim Brotherhood.

"Boutros and IS-in-Libya have been hammered. This is a real opportunity for you, especially if we agree to help you. You could unlock its resources and do good for your country. All big questions!"

Abdullah was squatting on his haunches, poking the ground in front of him with a stick, deep in thought.

"I hear all this and I know, in every country the Americans take over, they find someone like me and put me in a businessman's suit. Then you say: *'We did it for the people.'* But it is the oil that is your real interest, no?"

Floyd remained still as Abdullah continued speaking.

"Me? I want my town to be safe and my family to live in peace. I do not give a pickled fig for the rest of it. Allah has a plan for me and it is not to be another Gaddafi! That is not the will of Allah!"

"No, Abdullah, I can't see you becoming another Gaddafi. I wouldn't let you!"

Floyd laughed.

"Still, Mr US Major, I mean no offence and maybe I will read your book. I would like to understand an Englishman who thought he was an Arab!

"So, when will we be ready to leave for Az-Zawiyah?" He gestured to a group of young men, kicking a football, tripods of automatic rifles standing in for goal posts. "They are looking good, no?"

Floyd shook his head.

"I'd like to have them for another six months, if it was up to me. You can't build a soldier overnight. But we need to strike while we've got the advantage. I think we're going to have to move out in about ten days."

"Allah be praised! This is good news."

Abdullah suddenly sensed a change in Floyd Hamilton's demeanour. Looking over Abdullah's shoulder, he had seen something. His body had tensed and he jumped to his feet, his hand unclipping the holster of his side arm. He kicked back the canvas chair and pushed himself in front of Abdullah, raising the gun.

A short but trim figure, with a long straggly beard and a stained red-and-white *keffiyeh* wrapped around his head, was walking directly towards them, at speed. He padded up the dusty white path that had gradually appeared between the tents. Even though it was nearly dark, he wore a pair of wraparound sunglasses, a crumpled collarless shirt that had once been white, and baggy black cotton trousers.

There was a sense of purpose in his approach that Floyd Hamilton did not like.

"Stand back!" he shouted, raising his gun.

Abdullah looked on in shock as he suddenly realised who it was coming towards him. He placed a hand on Floyd's arm and gently pressed it.

"All is well, Mr Major. This man means us no harm."

The man stopped three metres away and put his hands on his hips.

"So, is this the famous Berber welcome I get?"

"*Mashallah*, as Allah has willed it!" Abdullah beamed and rushed to meet the visitor, wrapping his arms tightly around him. Not breaking the embrace, he shouted as loud as he could: "George is back! George has returned! Give thanks!"

To say Natasha had got a shock when her father's car had appeared around the bamboo was an understatement. There was no chance of fabricating an explanation. She realised the truth had to come out at some point, but the abruptness with which they had been discovered caught her out, making her breathless and momentarily light-headed.

"So, Natasha, you have truly excelled yourself this time. You know that you have crossed the line. You are on your own from now on. I am going back to Serbia, as soon as I can, and I will leave you to finish whatever it is you are up to.

"I will sort things out with the Wise Men and then I am out. I cannot stand what is going on here. You want to make a play in the big game, go ahead, but do not count on me to stand behind you.

"I think now is a good time for you to move back into the apartment at Portomaso. I assume you have kept the lease on?"

Natasha was stunned. She believed some things in life were a given and had thought she could always rely on her father's support. The fact it was conditional and could be withdrawn had never occurred to her.

"Dad, how can …"

"Shut up, Natasha. I fear for you, I really do. If I can see straight through your dealings, so can others. Some ugly things have happened, not just recently but back over the years, and your fingerprints are all over them."

"Dad, I …"

"I have kept quiet for a long time, about a lot things, but I cannot ignore them any longer, especially as you seem happy to put me at risk, whenever it suits your purposes! I have just been protesting that I knew nothing about the stolen money and listening to Mike Lloyd's threats about what he would do if he found out I was lying."

"Please Dad, let …"

Marco put up his hand to stop her.

"Be quiet. Now, tell me, where is the kid Mike Lloyd was using? Locked up in the chapel still? You kidnapped him and have been keeping him there, yes? You stole the Libyan dinars from the Russians, under Mike Lloyd's nose, goodness knows how. Where is that money?"

Natasha was shocked that her father knew so much, but did not let her expression betray it.

"Yes, you're right. The money's in Vlado's uncle's woodyard, in Užice."

Užice was the town nearest to Marco's estate in Serbia and Vlado was one of his foresters, who had taken a shine to Natasha when she had visited her father there.

"It'll be perfectly safe until we need to move it. Vlado thinks it's equipment for the next stage of your project. It won't be there for long."

"My God! You are hiding the money in Užice? If the Americans or Russians track it there, they will assume it was I who stole it! Do you not realise that? Or do you just not care?"

"I've just said, it won't be there for long."

"I do not know what you are planning and I do not want to know, but move that money today, or tomorrow at the latest, do you hear me? Do you seriously think you can outsmart both the FSB and the CIA? Who the hell do you think you are?"

"I'll move it. Soon."

"Good to hear! Now, we are going to see this guy back at the chapel and you can explain to me exactly what you did."

"We can't, he's not being co-operative at the moment. In fact, he's not there. It seems he made a run for it this morning. Broke the roof tiles and climbed out."

"Where do you think he is now?"

"We've no idea."

Natasha was unaware when she said this that it was not strictly true.

———

Simon had gone to the chapel, very early that morning, at first light, and climbed onto the roof with a large hammer and a steel bar. A few hard blows and the thin, brittle stone slabs that rested on wooden corbels, forming the chapel's roof, had easily cracked and broken. It was the only credible way he could think of to fake Savi's breakout.

As chunks of shattered limestone fell to the chapel floor, Savi's frightened face peered up at him from beneath the hole. The kid was dressed in the new gear that Simon had bought him from some crazy shop in Hamrun: voluminous baggy jeans that hung round his hips, branded unlaced trainers and an oversized, brightly coloured hoody that reached to just above his knees.

Simon lowered a wooden ladder that he had taken from the *castello* and shouted down: "OK, let's go. I'm getting you out of here."

"Hey, wait a minute. What for?"

"Savi, don't fuck around, we've got to go – *now*."

"No, no. I'm cool. I'm happy here for a bit longer. It's OK. I haven't had a chance to, you know, show Natasha my new gear?"

"Savi, you fool, she's not going to shag you, she's going to kill you! She wants me to throw you off the cliff."

"Nah! No chance. You're messing with me."

Savi had a stupid half-smile on his face, but suddenly felt his confidence desert him.

"Yes, of course I'm kidding!" Simon told him sarcastically. "Think about it. You're no more use to her and you know too much. You're a dead man if you don't come with me. Now do as I say and climb the fucking ladder!"

Savi reluctantly loaded his laptop and X-Box into his rucksack, put on his new baseball hat and came up the ladder.

"Really? You being serious? She really asked you to do that? I don't get it. You're not going to, are you?"

"I will if you don't hurry."

"Wait a mo'! How am I going to get paid?"

"Money's no good to you if you're dead. Let's go."

Simon had an on–off girlfriend whom he knew from back home and had set up in a flat in Sliema. Given his work at the castello he did not see a lot of her, but he figured she owed him a favour or two. He had told her to expect a guest for a couple of days and to make sure he stayed put. Danka was a stocky, well-muscled woman with cropped, dyed-blonde hair and a body adorned with tattoos she had designed herself. Her impressive physique came from her work as a kettlebell fitness coach, at her own studio in a converted garage, just off the Sliema promenade. Simon had also seen her in a boxing ring and was not certain, whether he would be able to get the better of her, if they ever got into a full-on fight. Not that it would ever come to that, he was far too fond of her. But he had no doubt she could handle Savi.

He dropped the boy off and had to hurry straight back to the castello to pick up Natasha. Danka, meanwhile, made Savi take a shower and showed him to a small box room that was to be his bedroom. She threw him a can of Coke and locked the door on him. Once he had finished beating on the door and cursing the block of a woman who seemed to be his new gaoler, he reached for his laptop. He might as well finish building the last bit of his empire on *Civilisation*. But, before that, there was something he needed to do …

In the car with Simon, Savi had been thinking about how to get himself out of this mess. His first step had to be to make peace with Mike Lloyd.

Using a pocket-sized wireless modem and his encrypted email service, he routed his VPN through a series of servers in London, Thailand and Johannesburg. Then he sent an email from his Snakehead account.

Mike,

Sorry about the double, i was made to do it. If i tell who forced me, will we be cool? I have insurance so don't come after me. Snakehead

Mike Lloyd authorised the opening of the strange email and, once he had cleaned up the coffee he had spilled over his desk, screaming and shouting about the treacherous nature of human beings, he realised he had no choice but to reply.

He and the hapless Mary-Ann Baker, who still had not recovered from her own humiliation and the recriminations about what had happened in Turkey, sat down at Mike's screen.

He typed: *Who did it? Tell me and I won't break your skinny neck. Promise.*

The reply was almost instantaneous.

Some woman called Natasha and her security guy Simon. Kept me in an old church place. But Simon's a good guy. He bust me out. Can I get paid money for expenses?

As a matter of professional pride, Mike Lloyd needed to know if he had been lied to.

Ever meet or hear them talk about a guy called Marco?

No. Just the woman.

OK. Turn up at the guardhouse at the embassy. There'll be an envelope with $5000 with your name on it. Keep quiet about this or I'll come for you. I mean it.

Don't get heavy. I get it.

Mary-Ann Baker said to Mike: "You're paying him, after what he's done?"

"If he's stupid enough to turn up, which he is, there'll be a standing order for the marines on the gate to grab him."

"What about the Bonnicis? What's the play there?"

Mike went to the window and looked over the embassy's extensive car park, towards the trees of the Ta'Qali parkland.

"I can wait a couple of weeks. You know what they say about revenge. I'll think of something. They're not getting away with this."

When Mike walked to the coffee machine, he passed the team noticeboard, where some wag had pinned a mocked-up advertisement: *SALE! Guys' Black Puffer Jackets – going cheap. Unwanted stock. Ask Mike.*

CHAPTER 45
GEORGE ZAMMIT
ABDULLAH'S CAMP, MARSABAR,
LIBYA

GEORGE HAD LET himself be led through the camp by Abdullah, who had one arm around his shoulders, while holding a pistol in the other, which he fired into the air in celebration. This act brought a dozen Rangers rushing towards them, with M-16s pointing directly at their chests!

After the excitement had calmed down a bit, Rania insisted they sit down to eat. Under the awning of their tent, there was a green plastic table and chairs. From the top of a single gas ring, she produced a large tagine of spiced rice and chicken, studded with chickpeas, apricots, crumbled cinnamon and livid green coriander leaf. George took one look at it and said to her: "Tonight I'll eat everything you can spare, then I'll eat your husband's share because it's his fault I am so thin and hungry!"

Rania laughed.

"And eat you will! You have come back half the size of the man who left. You must excuse Abdullah; he is a terrible man. Everywhere he goes there is trouble and suffering! Tonight he will fast until you have eaten your fill. Then we will see what is left for him."

Abdullah slapped the plastic table.

"No, woman! You will feed me so I have the strength to hear

George's story." He turned to his friend. "Now, you start from the moment I left the airfield and you will not miss one moment!"

So George started to tell his story. He told him about Harley and the attack on the Ubari airfield, then his kidnap and time as a hostage with Abu Muhammad. Abdullah laughed and clapped his hands enthusiastically as the tale of the battle unfolded. During George's description of his spell in captivity, Abdullah held his head low and studied the ground beneath his feet. However, when George recounted his escape, Abdullah leaped up and roared in approval.

"Rania, he killed them with his bare hands! No gun, no knife – just his hands. How I wish I had been there! Strangled him with his own *keffiyeh*!"

Abdullah laughed heartily.

"It wasn't funny! I never meant to kill the man, it just happened that way. In fact, I didn't finish him. The Russian did."

George sighed at the memory. He had examined his conscience time and again, to assure himself he did no more than he had to, in order to escape.

Just as George was set to continue, a beaming Sam, the muscle-bound Texan contractor, stuck his head under the awning.

"Excuse me, folks, but I heard he was back and I just had to see for myself. George the Maltese Machine gun, that's what you're called now! You saved our necks, buddy! You saved our necks! I've gotta give you a man hug!"

Sam pulled George out of his chair and dragged him into a tight embrace. He then held him at arms-length and said: "Thanks, man, from all of us."

Sam turned to Abdullah.

"You know what this guy did? He emptied over a thousand rounds into Johnny Jihad, took down twenty or more, gave us a chance to get into defensive position so we could stop them getting into the terminal. Fucking amazing, man!"

Abdullah glared at Sam and Rania lowered her head.

"Sorry, ma'am, language. But the best bit …"

"Sam, you know that's not quite right."

He grabbed George by the shoulders.

"I couldn't believe it … the weekend-warrior here, he chases a group of them into a stairwell lobby and unloads a Magnum into them, at point blank!

"Blam! Blam! Blam!" Sam made his hand into the shape of a pistol and mimicked the shots, pointing around the tent. "Takes down six more of them – incredible! That's how he got captured! No shame, man, he fought to the last, and then some!"

Abdullah watched, shaking his head in amazement.

"The Maltese Machine gun! I have seen this man do these things before!" Abdullah pointed two fingers back at himself. "With these eyes!"

"Please, come on, Sam, don't make too much of it. I was terrified. I was just trying to get back into the terminal building, so I could hide!"

Abdullah was bursting with pride in his friend and more than willing to believe anything he was told about George's 'heroics'.

"He says he is no hero; he says he is not brave; he says he is just afraid and does not know what he does … phaa!"

Sam shook his head.

"Oh, no! He knows what he's doing alright!" He turned to address George directly. "Some of the boys want you to come round to the tents tonight. We've a little Jack Daniel's, to show our appreciation."

Abdullah raised his hand.

"No, my friend! I do not like to spoil parties, but you know, we do not have alcohol here. It is *haram* – forbidden – so, I think I have not heard that. Anyway, George must rest, he still has important work to do."

"OK, man, whatever you say. But, George, if you ever want a job, you can come and work for me. It's good money and you see the world and get to die young! See you around."

Sam laughed out loud as he made his way back between the tents. George watched him go, then turned to Abdullah, stony-faced.

"What important work have I got to do?"

"We will speak of it tomorrow. Tonight we eat and talk!"

"Abdullah! What important work do I have to do?"

The arrival of Major Floyd Hamilton saved Abdullah from having to provide an answer. The officer shook George's hand vigorously.

"Well, when I heard you're the Maltese Machine gun, I just had to come round and say hi, apologise for the welcome I gave you! You've made quite a name for yourself. They're talking about you in every US base in the Middle East!"

He looked around at the laden table then pulled a phone from his pocket, saying: "Sorry, folks, I don't mean to disturb dinner, but this is important. It was sent to me a few days ago, in case you showed up here. It's a privilege to be able to play it for you, Superintendent."

He gave George his phone, on which he had a saved video message. An image of Sergeant Mario Barrasso, from the training camp at the US Air Base Al-Udeid, stared out at them. Had George been standing, he would have involuntarily taken a step backwards. The unsmiling man took a sheet of paper from his breast pocket and began to speak.

"Superintendent George Zammit of the Malta Pulizija, it was my honour to conduct your induction training on the Desert Warfare and Survival course at the US Army Al-Udeid training facility. It is with great pride that I can inform you that, following reports of exceptional bravery in the field of battle, you have been recommended for the Army Distinguished Service Cross, the highest military honour that can be awarded to a non-US citizen. Congratulations. We salute you. God bless the United States of America!"

The sergeant briskly saluted and the screen went blank.

The major lead a smattering of applause and said: "They tried to get him to record another version, where he smiled a little, but you know how these hard-ass sergeants can be. Anyway, I'm just glad it will not be awarded posthumously!"

Floyd then told him there was an opportunity to repatriate him to Malta the next day, if that was not too soon.

George said it was not a moment too soon.

After Floyd left them, Rania glanced over at George and said to Abdullah: "He must rest, do not talk of more work. Has he not done enough for us?"

Abdullah threw his napkin onto the table.

"I see we will have no peace until I tell you. I am pleased you can return to Malta and see the lady wife and family. That is the right thing to do. But then your policeman boss, the old policeman, will speak to you and there is something we need from you. It is easy and has no risk, but it is very important. But do not worry now. Eat and tell us more of the story – I am enjoying it very much!"

"I suddenly don't feel hungry. I thought I was finished here and was going home to stay? I've been away for nearly four months. My wife won't ever let me leave again; she'll divorce me if I try!"

"Hah, the lady wife will be very much pleased you are coming back a hero, with more medals. She will have her picture in the paper again and she will like being the wife of the Maltese Machine gun."

Rania looked at her husband disapprovingly.

"What, woman? Why do you look at me like that?"

"George, we will have coffee and then you will rest. Abdullah, George is tired, he has had many troubles. Not like you, who only eat, talk and sleep. George, sleep well tonight and the good news is – tomorrow you go home!"

While Rania made them espressos with a small machine she had been given by the Americans, Abdullah leaned across the table and whispered to George.

"Listen, brother, we are close to finishing our journey. We

have taken our town and the refinery, and the pipeline will make this country rich. Soon, we will move further east and get rid of the corrupt and useless government. By then, there will be no Boutros, no Abu Muhammad and no slippery toads sitting in Tripoli, getting fat on the people's oil money. The Libyan people can return to peaceful living and there will be money to be spent on schools and hospitals and there will be work. To do this, there is one more job I need you to do for me. I can only send someone I would trust with my life."

Abdullah explained what it was he needed. George sighed deeply.

"*Mela,* I'll do it, but then I'm going home and I'm going to stay there. You can continue your revolution without any help from me."

————

George's trip home the next day was direct and very expensive, but the bill was taken care of by the US military. A Super Huey army helicopter landed in the morning, kicking up a storm of dust, and whisked him south to the airbase at Ubari. There he boarded a twin-prop Beechcraft, an executive transport plane. He relaxed into the well-worn but comfortable leather seating, and enjoyed coffee and pastries. It was wonderful to be able to eat, any time he wanted to, an experience he had not enjoyed for many weeks.

Within three hours of leaving Marsabar, George found himself in one of the US Embassy's long sedans with tinted windows, giving the driver directions as it squeezed through the busy streets of Birkirkara.

It occurred to him that, following his arrival at the camp the previous evening, he had not spoken to Marianna to tell her he was coming back. He hoped there was somebody in at home and he would not be left sitting on the doorstep.

Before his departure, Rania had ordered him to the toilet

block to shower and change his clothes. She had given him some of Abdullah's underwear, one of his calf-length, white *djellabas* and a bottle of beard oil, so George could tame the ferocious growth on his jaw that, by now, was nearly touching his chest.

It had been weeks since he had washed properly and the shower tray in the communal toilet block ran brown, black, red and brown again, as the caked filth and blood was loosened. Under the filthy *keffiyeh*, his hair was knotted and wild. After washing, he had used the beard oil to smooth the tangled mass back off his brow and plaster it tight to his head. His hair was long, well over his collar.

He stared at his own image in the mirror and the tanned face that looked back at him was not one he immediately recognised. His cheeks were sunken and his cheekbones more prominent. The oiled mass of hair and beard seemed to make his eyes burn more brightly. There was a long white scar on one cheek, where Abu Muhammad had raked a ring across his face. When he smiled, there was a gap where Muhammad's fighters had pummelled his face and a tooth had fallen out. He looked down at his flat midriff and saw his feet, in plain view – a sight he had not enjoyed for some years.

As the embassy car pulled away, leaving George on the doorstep, his worst fears were realised. The house was empty. He had been dropped with no key, no phone, and no money. All he had were the clothes Rania had given him. His hair she had tied back in a small ponytail that he flicked over his collar.

Rather than bother the neighbours, he sat on the front step that gave directly onto the pavement. He enjoyed watching the local people passing in front of him, going about their business. Some he knew, so he gave them a cheery wave and a smile. But none were returned.

After a few minutes of watching people, he noticed a coldness in their stare. A group of youths he had known since they were children, passed him and stopped their chat to look down with disdainful expressions. An elderly woman, Mrs Gauci, who lived some houses away on George's Street, came past, pulling a shopping trolley. She seemed to cross the road to avoid him, even though George knew her house was on his side of the street. He was musing on the nature of prejudice and exclusion when he heard two familiar voices coming from the top of the street.

He watched Marianna and Gina come into view, shopping bags and packs of bottled water in hand. He had never thought about how his wife, who did not drive, managed the shopping and felt a stab of guilt. Suddenly, Gina saw him sitting on the step and grabbed her mother's arm in alarm. The pair of them stopped and stared at him for a moment before Marianna started walking purposefully in his direction.

Gradually, she realised the disreputable-looking foreigner she was frowning at was actually her husband of twenty-two years!

"George, my God!"

She rushed up to him and dropped her shopping, fumbling in her bag for her keys.

George stood there with an inane smile on his face and his arms wide open. Marianna took him by the upper arm and moved him briskly up onto the front step.

"Gina, quick, help me get your father inside, before somebody sees him looking like this!"

CHAPTER 46

NATASHA BONNICI
PALAZZO BRUNO, BRERA, MILAN

THE EXECUTORS of Signor Bruno's will had told the Wise Men they had no immediate use for the *palazzo* in Brera, although they were quick to have the property valued. More out of sentiment than for any other reason, the Wise Men agreed to pay a commercial rent to Signor Bruno's estate for a lease of the *palazzo*, so as to maintain a working base in Milan. This pleased Natasha, who loved to spend her days in the heart of the bustling city, which was always a welcome change from the small, sometimes claustrophobic, island of Malta.

To the rear of the property there was a self-contained flat that had recently been renovated. Although many original features had been preserved, there was modern recessed lighting, underfloor heating and brand-new bathrooms, as well as a contemporary kitchen. The flat enjoyed its own entrance from the turning circle to the rear of the *palazzo* and had a balcony with views over the enclosed private garden. Natasha was immediately taken with it.

She did not like thinking that it might have been for the use of Tesoro or his friends, but it seemed that no one had been there for some time. She had a quiet word with Hugo, who confirmed it had been prepared for a live-in housekeeper, but nobody had been hired and it had never been occupied since the renovations. Natasha telephoned Signor De Luca and suggested it would make a perfect home for her during her stays in Milan and that she would much prefer it to living in a hotel. Signor De Luca had no objection to the arrangement, so it was agreed.

Her new work was fascinating, not from a technical perspective, but for the window it opened onto the extent and variety of the Family's activities. Running through the accounts and company records, she realised the Family had interests in European commercial property and forestry, Argentinian vineyards, Middle Eastern pharmaceutical companies, hotel chains and franchises, quarries and cement works, waste-disposal businesses, a fleet of Rhine barges, numerous prized works of art and a portfolio of properties in the 6th arrondissement of Paris. That was on top of their interests in banking, oil, energy and i-Gaming, which Natasha already knew about. Putting a value on it all was impossible, but it probably meant the Family was one of the wealthiest groups of individuals on the planet, a thought that made her tingle with excitement.

The beneficial ownership of these assets and interests was carefully concealed through a network of trusts and offshore companies that it would be Natasha's job to manage. She realised, with some satisfaction, that the Wise Men had let Signor Bruno create a web of ownership that, at the time of his death, only she and he understood – a dangerous strategy for a group of octogenarians!

It was on her second trip to Milan in her new role that a meeting appeared in her electronic diary between her, Salvatore and Signor De Luca. Its purpose was an update on the energy deal in Malta and the wider distribution arrangements Salvatore was managing, on mainland Europe.

Since Signor Bruno's death, several weeks previously, she had studiously avoided mentioning the investigation or the friction between her father and Salvatore. She was there solely to do the job she had been recruited for and did not want to be seen using her new position to go fishing for information about things that should not concern her. Obviously, she was acutely interested in both matters, but thought an air of studied indifference would be the fastest way to gain the confidence of Signor De Luca.

It had seemed before this as though there had been some tacit agreement to keep her and Salvatore apart, so this appointment came as a surprise to her. They met in Signor Bruno's old study, with Signor De Luca sitting in the place of honour behind the large, antique Tuscan desk. Natasha was shocked by the change in Salvatore's appearance. Although his clothing was immaculate, as usual, the man inside the suit was a shell of his former self. His face had a sickly pallor to it. He had missed his regular fortnightly haircut. His hair was untidy and looked unwashed. He was anxious and stammered through parts of his presentation to Signor De Luca – even calling him Signor Bruno on one occasion. He never stopped fidgeting and, at times, his foot nervously tapped a beat on the tiled floor.

On the way out of the meeting, he grabbed Natasha by the wrist.

She glared at him, aware that she remembered enough of her judo to break his grip, unbalance him and put him on the tiles in seconds. A few years ago, she would not have hesitated.

He saved himself by releasing her and saying: "Sorry, I didn't mean to alarm you. I'm a bit edgy today."

"I know, I can see. You look like shit, by the way."

"Thanks! I feel like shit. I'm not sleeping, I ache and I've been vomiting for the last two days. I can't stop worrying. Can we get a coffee? I need to talk to you."

They walked out onto the street and crossed over to the Palazzo Citterio, an eighteenth-century gallery with a coffee shop in its central courtyard.

"So, what's turned the handsome, assured, self-confident Salvatore Randazzo into a walking zombie? Tell me."

He stirred his coffee, not making eye contact with her.

"Don't you think it's strange that there's been no mention of

Signor Bruno's death? Not from Hugo, Toni, De Luca? Nobody's saying a word."

"Yes, but I've been ignoring it. They like to keep up appearances. But why's that bugging you?"

"I think I might be next. I think someone's poisoning me, but I don't know how. In fact, they may already have done it – I feel terrible."

He hung his head and cast down his eyes. There was not an ounce of fight left in him. Natasha looked at him and noticed his laboured breathing.

"Why on earth do you think that?"

"I'm being followed, for one thing. If the Family have now started murdering their own – first Sergio, now Signor Bruno – I've offended Marco and a few other people, so maybe I've become more trouble than I'm worth? Nobody's telling me anything and it's driving me mad!"

"Calm down, Sal. Why do you think you're being followed?"

"I've had a feeling, several times, and someone's been in my flat and left me a message. There was a dead rat on top of the kitchen worktop. I took it to a private forensic lab and they said it'd been poisoned. I'm telling you, it's a message."

"Really? Have you been tested?

"No, not yet. Maybe I should. Look, if you knew anything about this, you'd tell me, wouldn't you?"

She looked him straight in the eye.

"Yes, Sal, I would. I can see how upset you are. Have you spoken to the Wise Men?"

"I've spoken to Hugo. He says nothing's going on, that I shouldn't worry. But, listen, I've been down to see Tesoro's friends who hang around the Central Station, to see what they know. Apparently, Hugo and his police connections have been all over them, but one of them did say something interesting. Tesoro had been seen with a short, stocky guy with long grey hair. Might have had a Sicilian accent. His friend said this guy had given Tesoro a lot of money, but he didn't think he was a punter. What do you make of that?"

Natasha stopped stirring her coffee and looked at Salvatore closely.

"You can't be serious! You're asking me to believe in ghosts?"

"No, but you can see why I'm jumpy."

"I'd forget about it, if I were you. But, yeah, I can see that it's got you spooked. If I can help, of course I will. All I can do is keep my ears open."

"One more thing – please don't tell Marco this. I wouldn't like to give him the satisfaction of knowing I am slowly going mad!"

"You can forget about my dad – he's backing out of Family things and will soon be rolling boulders around the estate in Serbia. I'm afraid it's me in charge now."

She smiled and flicked back her hair.

"Come on, relax, it's not as bad as it seems. But you need to see a doctor – you look awful – and, remember, there's no such thing as ghosts! I'll pay for the coffee."

They left. Salvatore barely made it to the end of via Brera before he succumbed to another bout of retching, behind an overflowing green dumpster.

Back in her apartment in the *palazzo*, Natasha went out onto the balcony, taking out a burner phone that she kept at the bottom of her wardrobe.

Her call was answered on the third ring.

"He's on the run and looking shocking. He's suspicious and one of the male hookers ID-ed you to him. I've got to say, the thing with the rat was a bit much! He's had it tested and he knows somebody is onto him. So, if you're going to finish it, now's the time."

There was a deep cackle of laughter from the other end of the call.

"I would've paid serious money to have seen his face! OK, message received."

Before hanging up, Natasha said: "Listen, I'm going to Libya for a bit. I haven't told anyone yet, but I need to get that end of things buttoned down."

"*Sì.* Be careful, it's *una lotta tra cani* over there."

"It's a dog fight everywhere! Why should Libya be any different? But, before I go, I think it would be a good idea for us to wind up our business in Milan. Don't you agree?"

CHAPTER 47

NICK WALKER
LUQA INTERNATIONAL AIRPORT,
MALTA

A WARM, south-easterly wind blew fine red dust across the tarmac. As Nick Walker walked around the wing of the BA aircraft, he felt the familiar, dry salty taste of Malta in his mouth. The airport sat on a plateau at the southerly end of the island and, when the wind blew in the right direction, the fine sands of the Libyan desert were carried to it.

His decision to return had not been taken lightly. Natasha had tried on several occasions over recent years to lure him back to BetHi, but he had always managed to persuade himself that, having escaped his ties to the Family, it would be foolish to offer himself back up. He knew what joining them again would involve and, although he was not averse to cutting corners and a little financial gamesmanship himself, the Family operated in a different league altogether.

If he looked hard enough at himself, Nick had to acknowledge his return was largely due to his enduring fascination with Natasha Bonnici. He had not been able to get her out of his system, even after four years, so he reasoned he probably never would. He had had relationships with women on Gibraltar, but Natasha was always there in the background, whispering in his ear, sowing the seeds of doubt, offering herself in comparison.

Although there were a million reasons to avoid her and the Family, he had accepted he was a moth to her flame.

He had no doubt she could be ruthless in her treatment of anyone who stood between her and her ambitions. Having worked on the pieces of the puzzle many times over the past four years, he was convinced she had engineered his exit from BetHi so she could take the CEO job for herself. Few people knew her as well as he did. She had tried to frame him for theft and, that fateful night, he had caught her stalking him around Villa Bianca, barefoot for silence and with a gun in her hand. He would never know what she was really up to. He had panicked and struck out at her with a nearby glass vase. It was a miracle she had not died. The sickening sound the heavy glass made as it hit her skull, and the feel of it as the impact reverberated against his arm, still resonated in his mind. For a while, he had sought to escape both her and the Family, yet here he was, back on the courtesy bus, heading towards the customs desks. Her last message had said the keys to his old home, Villa Bianca, had been hidden under the potted oleander tree to the left of the front door.

Natasha had told him she would be in Milan when he returned, but someone would meet him in Arrivals to take him to the villa and settle him in. He went from the relative calm of the baggage collection carousels, out through the sliding doors, into the noise and chaos of the Arrivals Hall. Dozens of couriers waved signs with hotel logos. VIP drivers, standing a step or two back, brandished the names of visitors from around the world.

For a moment, he thought he had been forgotten, but then he noticed a familiar figure, hunched over a newspaper, wearing a cardigan and some corduroy trousers despite the thirty-degree heat. At first, Nick thought he would slide past, to avoid any confrontation, then realised this was probably no accident. So he went and stood beside the man, who continued to stare at the newsprint.

After a moment or two, Nick said: "Marco? Hello – it's been a long time."

Marco looked up at him with a half-smile.

"Nick Walker. Well, I never thought I would see the day!"

Marco Bonnnici stood up and they exchanged a brief hand-shake, for the sake of good manners.

"Yes, Nick, a lot of water has passed under the bridge, but Natasha tells me you are back and all fired up to run BetHi?"

"Yes, that's the plan."

Marco nodded.

"I thought we should meet sooner rather than later. Give ourselves a chance to chat. So, hand me your bag and I will give you a lift to the villa."

They sat in the white Range Rover, the same car Natasha had arrived in when she had returned to the villa after their quarrel, that fateful night, four years ago. Nick looked out of the window, the high plateau giving him a vantage point over the urban sprawl that comprised the south-east of the island. He started counting the number of tower cranes projecting above the skyline, but stopped when he reached thirty.

"I'm surprised there is any land left to build on!"

"The building is relentless. A lot of it is poor-quality apartments for the rental market. There will be a price correction soon, the market is far too hot," Marco replied, "So, how did she convince you to come back? I thought you had fallen out with us?"

"Well, yeah, but let's say time is a great healer. Gibraltar was fine, but the business never really got to the size I wanted. I hadn't the budget to compete with the big players and I didn't want to sacrifice my independence. This way, I can grow the business in Gibraltar with overflow from BetHi and still get the chance to be CEO of one of the biggest i-Gaming platforms in Europe."

"What about Natasha?"

"I'm looking forward to working with her."

"That is not what I meant."

Nick laughed and shook his head.

"Look, Natasha and I have had our chances, but this is just about work, Marco. Nothing else, honestly."

Perhaps it was the corrupting air of the island, but Nick was shocked by how easily the lie came out of his mouth.

"OK. I think that is very wise."

Marco took his eyes off the road for a second to share a smile with his passenger.

"Listen, I'm sorry about selling the *Blue Cascade*; it's just that I was desperate …" Nick blurted.

"Forget it. That is in the past. None of us behaved well at that time. I should not have deceived you by moving Natasha into the housekeeper's apartment at the villa, to keep an eye on you. I was at fault too.

"How much did you get for the boat by the way?"

"A hundred thousand euro."

Marco laughed.

"Jesus, it was worth ten times that!"

"Not for same-day cash it wasn't – believe me, I tried!"

"Anyway, I have bought a new one. She is a beauty. If you do not steal any money or attempt to kill my daughter, I might take you out in her."

"I promise, none of those things'll happen and I'll look forward to it!"

Nick smiled. He watched the urban landscape flash by as they took the main regional road to the north. The new overpass at Marsa had been completed and it seemed that most of the roads had been resurfaced. A lot had changed in the four years he had been away, yet much of what he saw felt very familiar. He was disappointed Natasha was not going to be there when he arrived at the villa, but checked himself; he had to put those thoughts out of his mind.

"Natasha tells me you're planning to return to Serbia in the near future?" he addressed Marco.

"Yes. Since the death of Sergio, the fun of it all has gone for me. You will find Natasha has her own way of doing things these days. I do not think she needs me around, so I am happy to step back again. I am talking to Milan and completing one or two things here, then that is it, I am done. I will let you young blades take over."

"I've told Natasha, I'm purely here to run BetHi, I've got no interest in any of the other businesses. I'm a civilian. That's our deal."

"Make sure you stick to it – it is a sensible approach. Things are different from how they were four years ago. The game has become a lot rougher than you might imagine."

Nick looked at him, waiting for him to go on, but Marco kept his eyes on the road and his mouth shut. Nick sensed something was not quite right, but did not want to push too hard. Marco seemed absorbed in his own thoughts.

Eventually he said: "You think you know Natasha, but I do not think you do. She has changed – well, maybe not changed, but now she has power, it makes her more ... shall we say, up front. And she can sometimes make decisions that are ill considered. I worry someday she might find herself in serious trouble."

He paused before saying, "After I have left Malta, if ever you need to talk to me, please feel free to do so. I will make sure you have my current number. I suspect you always have her best interests at heart. As do I, of course."

Nick looked at him, trying to understand what had just been said. He was confused by this conversation. He thought Marco was the last person he would ring for advice. Then it occurred to him that was not what Marco had meant. He was asking Nick to keep an eye on Natasha.

The car swung off the coast road and into the drive of Villa Bianca, standing alone on the rocky hillside. In front of them stretched the blue waters of the Mediterranean, a distance of one hundred kilometres to the southern Sicilian coast. Urgent, incoming waves burst on the rocky limestone platform, throwing white plumes of spray high into the air. Nick took a moment to reacquaint himself with the familiar place. The wide deck and pool had been cleaned and the new season's striped cushions put out onto the sun loungers. The polished, stainless-steel banisters and fittings gleamed brightly, yellow and white and hot to the touch in the reflected light. The outdoor kitchen had been swept clear of leaves and the villa's long windows opened, so the salty, iodine-scented sea breeze could run through the rooms, tugging at the voiles and gently shaking the fronds of the potted ferns.

Nick exhaled deeply; he was pleased to be back. He entered the house and, with a smile, went to settle the query that had been on his mind since he had accepted the offer to return to the villa. He opened the light ash door into the lounge and looked towards the console table, positioned against the back wall. There, standing fifty centimetres tall, with the swirling colours of cupric, cobalt and chrome inside its glass body, was the thin-stemmed Murano vase he had used to hit Natasha. He picked it up, to feel its weight and remind himself how well it balanced in his striking hand.

CHAPTER 48

HUGO, TONI AND SIGNOR DE LUCA

LA SCALA, MILAN

MILAN WAS a city familiar with violence. From the mid-nineteen-seventies to the end of the last century, the Red Brigades, Prima Linea, Unità Comuniste Combattenti and other leftists, and Neo-Fascists, had bombed, assassinated and fought each other in the streets of Northern Italy. The last car bomb of the era to explode in Milan was in July 1993. It went off in via Palestro, by the Galleria d'Arte Moderna, some eight hundred metres from Signor Bruno's *palazzo* on via Brera. Whether or not he heard the blast would never now be known.

On that occasion, the bomb was set, not by the warring political extremists of left and right, but by Cosa Nostra as an act of criminal terrorism. It killed three firemen and a security guard who were investigating a Fiat Uno with smoke issuing from under its chassis, prior to it exploding. The fifth death was that of Driss Moussafir, a Moroccan migrant, asleep on a nearby bench, torn in two by a sheet of spinning metal.

Since that time, car bombs had been absent from the city centre, certainly in the vicinity of La Scala, the eighteenth-century opera house, referred to as the heart and soul of Milan. The great and the good of the city gathered there throughout the season, cheering and applauding singers of works by Verdi, Rossini and

Puccini amongst others. Tonight there was to be something different – a performance of Wagner's *Tannhäuser*.

La Scala's *loggione*, the six tiers of boxes above the stalls, were known to seat the most exacting of audiences. For a singer to appear before them for the first time was a baptism of fire. And among that audience, none was more critical than Signor Gabriele De Luca.

He knew opera, meaning – for him – purely Italian opera. In fact, he was of the opinion that any libretto in a language other than Italian did not have the right to call itself opera. He was president of the Amici della Scala, an old-established, elite group of supporters of the opera house. They promoted music, art and culture in Milan and the wider Lombardy region. The Teatro alla Scala was their main and constant point of reference, and he saw himself as the leader of the *loggione*.

It was to him that they would turn after a performance for an indication of whether they should applaud, remain silent or, in extreme cases, boo and catcall. Visitors who attended La Scala in a spirit of reverence, noted that the Milanese treated it as if it were their own private drawing room, where they felt free to behave in any manner they saw fit. It was Signor De Luca who, in 2006, had instigated a show of disapproval so intense that it led tenor Roberto Alagna to flee the stage, in the middle of a performance of Verdi's *Aida*.

That night, the role of Tannhäuser was to be sung by an exceptional young German tenor, who had never before performed at La Scala. Signore De Luca intended to make his debut memorable. He hated Wagner, the Germans, and especially *Tannhäuser*, with its themes of moral laxity and repressed sexuality. He had pleaded with the programme director not to include it in the current season, but without success. So he was now intent on leading the *loggione* in a show of disapproval nobody would forget.

Fortunately, or unfortunately, it was not to be. As usual, Toni was driving the black 7 Series BMW down via Giuseppe Verdi, towards La Scala, where he intended to drop off Signor De Luca and Hugo before returning to the *palazzo*, a few blocks north on via Brera, to wait until the event had finished. At the junction with via Andegari, Toni stopped the car at the pedestrian crossing, blanking the man who tapped on his window, offering flowers for sale.

At that moment, a signal was received that led to a flash of white light, directly underneath the vehicle. It lifted the car vertically, two metres into the air, throwing open its bonnet and blowing its windscreen outwards. With a crash, the car fell back into position in the queue of waiting traffic and bounced on its suspension, onto the bonnet of the car behind it. This coincided with a dull thud as the explosion's sound wave hit the shocked pedestrians, who cowered or lay injured on the pavements.

Then, for the next thirty seconds, onlookers heard the rattle and tinkle of a million pieces of glass falling from the sky in a sparkling shower, as shop windows blown out by the explosion rained back down to earth. Gradually, high-pitched human screams and cries mingled with car and shop alarms that whooped and wailed. Shortly afterwards there was a second explosion, more of a yellow light this time, that engulfed the car in flames, black sooty smoke beginning to plume into the city sky.

As well as the three in the car, later identified as a retired industrialist, his lawyer and driver, seven others were killed, including, ironically, a Moroccan migrant, Saad Kharbouche, a roadside flower seller, plying his trade by the pedestrian crossing.

CHAPTER 49
GEORGE ZAMMIT
GEORGE'S HOUSE, BIRKIRKARA, MALTA

THE FIRST THREE hours after his return home were a blur of chatter, barbering and clothing alterations. While Gina trimmed George's beard and hair, Marianna rummaged through his wardrobe to find clothes that could be cut and cropped to accommodate his considerably slimmer physique. She sliced along seams, took in waistbands and bored new holes in places on his belt that had never been near the buckle.

She watched a new man emerge from this grooming process. As he had to return to Libya, he had decided to keep the beard, now trimmed closer to his face. The desert tan and collection of facial scars from the beatings he had suffered, lent him a rough and rugged look. His hair was brushed back off his forehead and fell over his collar. George sat quietly in a chair, letting his daughter fuss over him. Marianna noticed the new width to his shoulders and the strength in his arms as he sat shirtless at the kitchen table. His flabby pale midriff and pronounced paunch had disappeared and there was now a tanned hardness to his torso. She sensed a new strength and confidence in him, and felt a little flushed around the neck at the thought that they would lie in the same bed together that night.

It did not take long before there was a knock on the front door to disturb the makeover. Gina broke off to answer it. Assistant Commissioner Camilleri popped his face through the kitchen doorway, sporting his best attempt at a sincere smile.

"George, George, how wonderful to see you back! Marianna, I will not disturb the homecoming, but I do need to talk to him for ten minutes. Then, I promise, he is all yours."

George sighed, stood up, grabbed his shirt, brushed the piles of hair off his lap and wiped his face with a towel.

"If we need to talk confidentially, Gerald, we can go outside. Marianna will just listen behind the door if we talk in here."

Outside on the street, Camilleri lit a cigarette.

"So, George, well done! Stories have been getting back to me and some, frankly, I have found hard to believe. The Maltese Machine gun – really?"

"Yes. I've had some astonishing experiences, but don't believe everything you hear. There're some ridiculous exaggerations flying around."

"That is a relief – I was getting quite worried about some of the stories and this 'new' man who was returning to us."

"Listen, I know what you're going to say and I've agreed with Abdullah Belkacem I'll do this one last trip, then I'm out. Finished. I've had enough. I want to go back to real old-fashioned policing. I've done my share of this sort of stuff. From now on, I want a good old boring life, doing the job I enjoy. I know you can fix it and I deserve it after what I've been through."

"George, we can talk about that when we have finished the task in hand and you are well rested. I can understand you are feeling … well, a bit tetchy at the moment."

"Feeling a bit tetchy! Have you any idea what I've been through? I was held for weeks in a concrete box by crazy Islamic terrorists, in the middle of a desert. Those bastards behead people like me. Look!" George grimaced at Camilleri, to show him the gap in his teeth. He pointed to the white scar running from under his eye across his cheek, and the graze from a bullet on his scalp. "I've been beaten, shot, starved, have lived in fear for weeks on end – all for a policeman's salary! And I bet you didn't turn up for Gina's party!"

"George, George, calm down! We'll talk about this later. I am sorry, I never thought it would turn out like this."

Camilleri glanced nervously up and down the street.

"Look, I need you on the Croatian border with Serbia on the E70 at Batrovci, at 18:00 hours, the day after tomorrow. Fly to Trieste, then the Italian police will lend you an unmarked vehicle to escort a wagon, carrying precious cargo, down through Italy to Malta.

"I do not expect any trouble but, just in case, you will need to be armed. So bring the firearms certificate for your weapon and pack the ammunition separately for the flight. It should be straightforward. There will be about thirty hours' driving back from the border to Malta, so take someone with you. Someone experienced and handy with a gun, not a friend to chat with."

George shook his head and went back into the house. He decided the best way to handle the situation with Marianna was to come straight out with the fact he would be leaving the next day. He explained it was just to finish off what he had started before he was taken hostage, and tempered the blow by telling her and Gina that, once he was back, in a couple of days, they would book a holiday to Spain. He told them to have a look for a nice place and work out all the prices. He knew that would keep them busy for the next week, at least.

———

As Camilleri had requested, two evenings later, George and Sergeant Major Chris Grima of the Maltese Pulizija, Rapid Intervention Unit, stood on the Croatian side of the border crossing with Serbia. George had picked Grima because he was known as a competent marksman and a fitness fanatic. He had boasted to George he only needed four hours' sleep a night, so George thought he would be the perfect partner. He was a little alarmed, therefore, when Grima slept all the way through the six-hour drive from collecting the car at Trieste's Friuli Venezia Giulia Airport, to arriving at the Batrovci border between Croatia and Serbia.

The E70 on the Croatian side of the crossing cut through wide swathes of arable farmland, which changed to dense undeveloped deciduous forest as soon as they had crossed into Serbia. What was common to both sides was the kilometres-long lines of trucks and private cars, queueing for hours to present papers to get in and out of the European Union. George had fixed the blue light to the roof and cruised past the lines to get to the border terminal buildings.

The allotted time of eighteen hundred hours had come and gone and they still could not see the yellow, curtain-sided, eighteen-tonne *Jami-Volet*- branded wagon that was carrying a load of two hundred wooden packing cases. Grima stood on a viewing platform on the roof of the building and looked down with a pair of high-powered binoculars at the row of trucks inching towards the crossing point. Eventually, he turned to George, who was absently gazing at the landscape, and gave him a thumbs up. The truck was heading towards them.

The rest of the journey down through Italy passed without incident. The speed limit of seventy kilometres-per-hour felt intolerably slow to George, sitting at the wheel of the Italian police Alfa Romeo Giulia, which could easily cruise at three times that speed. They by-passed Rome on the Grande Raccordo Anulare ringroad, just before the early-morning traffic, and hit Naples' infamous Tangenziale by mid-morning. In the late afternoon, they were queueing for the ferry at Reggio Calabria, to cross the narrow Messina Straits into Sicily, and by nine o'clock that evening, they were the last two vehicles to squeeze onto the late sailing of the *St Jean de Valette* hydrofoil to Valletta, Malta.

Once on the island, George phoned Camilleri and was instructed to meet him at the Freeport in the south of the island.

The yellow *Jami-Volet* wagon pulled into the security check at the entrance to the port and George watched, as Camilleri and six heavily armed officers from the Rapid Intervention Unit surrounded it. George turned to see if Grima was inclined to join them, but he had fallen into another of his deep, hours-long sleeps.

The wagon was escorted by the officers into a closed warehouse, a few dozen metres along the dock. George drove the Alfa Romeo into the building and the large sliding doors were closed behind them. Some dock workers appeared with a forklift. They pulled back the curtain sides of the lorry and lifted the cargo of substantial wooden crates, with Cyrillic script down the sides, onto waiting pallets. Other workers set about securing the crates to the pallets with strong nylon banding.

Camilleri raised a hand and halted the work so he could walk round each crate, inspecting seals, and then gave one of the port workers a case of small plastic nodules, which were attached with electric screwdrivers. George assumed these were transponders of some sort.

He stretched and yawned. Then, he casually walked over to Camilleri, who, having finished his inspection, stood a little apart, watching the proceedings.

"What's in the crates, Assistant Commissioner?"

George did not expect to be told, so was surprised when Camilleri said: "Money, George. Lots of it. That is why you and these officers are going to accompany it all the way to your friend Mr Belkacem. You are going to Tripoli, though nobody needs to know that except the skipper and you. I have checked the seals, so you and I can both confirm the money is intact at this point. Please, George, make sure it stays that way."

He looked at Camilleri aghast. Further explanations were curtailed by loud banging on the large metal sliding door to the warehouse. The armed police immediately drew their weapons and fell to their knees, covering the entrance. Grima, who by this time had woken up, walked over to the door and slid it open slightly, peering out.

A shapely leg, in tight jeans, appeared through the gap and its owner squeezed in at the narrow opening. She strode into the unforgiving high-bay lighting that bounced off the blue gloss resin flooring.

George could not believe it was her – Natasha Bonnici, coming towards him. She walked across and stood beside them as the police officers shouldered their weapons and work recommenced on securing the crates to the pallets. Even from two metres away, she seemed to project an allure, a scent, a cloud of pheromones, that woke George from his lethargy and had him stealing glances at the woman standing beside him.

"Well, well! Inspector Zammit – or is it Superintendent Zammit? Whichever, I'm sure this will all be safe in your hands. I hear you are quite the soldier!"

George gaped, but could find no words to reply.

Natasha continued: "I expect I'll see you on the other side of the water. Be vigilant, Superintendent. Libya's full of crooks."

Even Assistant Commissioner Camilleri could not help but raise an eyebrow at that remark. Natasha turned to him.

"And, Gerald, you're certain nobody else knows about this shipment? No Russians or Americans?"

"No, Miss Bonnici, certainly no Russians and I have said nothing to our American allies. George, you had better be aware: the existence of this cargo is known only to the three of us here and to Abdullah Belkacem. It absolutely has to stay that way."

———

Later that evening, the eighty metre long, one thousand and five hundred tonne general cargo ship *Lorelei* left the Malta Freeport on a charter passage to the Port of Tripoli, Libya. The cargo was a modest load of wooden crates and a passenger manifest of seven heavily armed Maltese policemen. The charter price offered was the equivalent of a full load of general cargo, so the ship's agent had no qualms about accepting the job. There were no customs formalities and no documents or notices to be filed with the port authorities at either end. The trip took thirty-six hours and proved uneventful.

CHAPTER 50
SALVATORE RANDAZZO
ISOLA, MILAN

THE AREA CALLED Isola was in the northern part of Milan and had become one of the city's trendiest neighbourhoods. It had seen the development of a new district, Porta Nuova, that had changed the city's skyline with its avant garde skyscrapers, such as the Bosco Verticale, where Salvatore had his apartment.

The balcony, along with most others in the so-called Vertical Forest, was festooned with climbing plants that draped the sides of the entire building, to form spectacular green walls. The building was an architectural triumph - not that this mattered to Salvatore who lay dead in his austere, unadorned bedroom, on top of a two-metre square bed.

The murderer had injected ricin powder into a number of coffee capsules that stood in a chromium rack next to the espresso machine in the kitchen. While Salvatore sipped coffee and fretted over his declining health, the cup before him held the seeds of his destruction.

It was a sad truth that he had had no family left alive, nor close friends to whom he could turn as his illness progressed. As his condition worsened, Salvatore had called his doctor, who was confused and worried about what he had found. The doctor had, in turn, called an ambulance whose crew was waiting in the entrance foyer of the block at the moment the poison completed its job of destroying the cells that formerly comprised Salvatore Randazzo.

In due course, the Milanese *polizia giudiziaria*, the investigating authority, realised they were managing a murder inquiry and, once they had examined his phone, found a series of unanswered calls to a Maltese number belonging to one Natasha Bonnici. When questions were asked as to what the purpose of the calls might have been, she told the prosecutor, through the office of Assistant Commissioner Camilleri of the Maltese Pulizija, that Randazzo was an old boyfriend who had started pestering her and she had thought the best policy was to ignore the calls that had become increasingly annoying. Other than that, she had nothing to say.

CHAPTER 51
ABDULLAH BELKACEM
MARSABAR, LIBYA

As HIS MILITIA started to make their way towards Tripoli, in trucks and technicals, Abdullah's thoughts were embroiled in Libya's rancid pit of politics and proxy wars. He dreamed of a free and peaceful Marsabar, without foreign threat or interference. He knew that would never happen while he had the Americans for friends, the Turks on his doorstep and the likes of Abu Muhammad and the southern Islamic militias yearning for their Caliphate. Those seeking power, governance and riches had torn Libya to pieces, and now those pieces were being snatched at and picked over by a pack of vicious street dogs.

On the ground, Abdullah had just over 1,000 men, but in the air he could not be matched. Abdullah's friends had brought the mountain down on the hopes of a Caliphate in Libya and chaos had flowed through the valleys of Nafusa. Boutros's Chinese drones and Russian MiGs were burned shells on their runways and global TV coverage had ensured there could be no pretending otherwise.

The Russians were quietly planning their departure, while the Emiratis kept their money under their long white *dishdashas*. The Sudanese units headed south for home, their pockets empty of the dinars currently sailing across the sea in the general cargo ship *Lorelei*.

At the farm outside Marsabar, the tents had started to come down and the number of advisers and contractors was beginning to thin out. Abdullah knew it was time for them to leave, as it had never been part of the deal for an American army of occupation to remain in Libya. Air support was to be continued and he had now acquired three drones of his own, which gave him sharp eyes and fierce firepower. A small team of specialists, based somewhere in Arizona, were allocated to pilot the lethal machines.

Abdullah had spoken, along with Major Floyd Hamilton, via conference calls, to representatives of the Tripoli government and had agreed to flush out the remnants of Boutros's forces that lurked to the east of Tripoli. As he had done in the past, he would take responsibility for the security of the Coastal Road, from the outskirts of Tripoli to the Tunisian border. The lands to the south of it, including the Nafusa Hills, up to the borders with Algeria and Niger, would also be his to secure. The dispute between Tripoli and the rebels in the east, and the arguments about the type of Islamic government the country should have, was pure politics. Abdullah decided there was nothing he could do about that. It was for others to resolve.

The Americans also agreed to honour his promises to the Tuareg and allow them to create a semi-autonomous province in the south, which they would control, again in exchange for them helping to secure the southern desert borders. That way, the Americans and Europeans hoped to stem the tide of displaced migrants on their way north. Whether they would be able to stop the rising tide of refugees from the Sahel was a question for another day.

Abdullah would retain his base at Ubari and provide security for the oil and gas operations in the Sharara oil and gas fields, as well as the pipelines to the refineries at Az-Zawiya and Marsabar. He could charge the Libyan Resources Corporation,

96

who controlled the sale of all Libya's oil and gas, for protecting their assets, allowing him to collect sufficient money to provide local services to the people – and get rich in the process. In short, he had got just about everything he had wanted when he had set off from Malta all those weeks ago.

Apart from the head of Abu Muhammad.

CHAPTER 52
GEORGE ZAMMIT
FREEPORT MALTA, MALTA

BEFORE THE *LORELEI* had set sail from Freeport Malta, Natasha, Camilleri and George gathered in the small office that sat high on a gantry, overlooking the floor of the warehouse. Natasha took the seat behind the desk and was scrutinising George. Without breaking her gaze, she said: "How much does he know?"

Camilleri replied: "Nothing."

Natasha nodded and gave George her most winning smile. He felt himself start to blush.

"OK, George, we've been speaking to your friend Abdullah Belkacem about our business in Libya. Basically, the oil fields and pipelines that're going to deliver the oil and gas to the refineries at Marsabar and Az-Zawiyah need protection and Abdullah and his militia will provide it. The LRC and the government in Tripoli have promised us the earth but, as you know, their promises are worthless. We must look after this ourselves.

"So, in the crates you're carrying, there's a huge amount of money, in Libyan dinars. In fact, one billion dinars. Over six hundred and thirty million euros."

George's eyes grew wider and his mouth opened slightly.

"Yes, it's a lot, isn't it? For that money, we expect our interests to be safe and secure, at least until the oil revenues start to flow and we can replenish the funds. Your warlord friend should be able to buy himself a decent army for that amount of cash. We want you to make sure he doesn't just run off with it."

"Me? How am I going to do that?"

"You'll control the cash. Audits, authorisations, accounting – all that boring stuff. I'll set it up and we'll have accountants to service it here in Malta and in Tripoli. You'll operate the account established by the Central Bank of Libya, in Tripoli, deal with requests for cash and recommend the release of funds. You'll deliver the cash and authorise payment of local expenses. Once money has been released, you'll ensure it is spent correctly and account to me for any discrepancies. More importantly, Belkacem trusts you. He'll do as you say. There's a bond between you. And, even more important, I trust you."

George was confused and worried; he did not like this suggestion at all.

"But ... can this be done from Malta?"

"Of course not! We need eyes on the ground, in Libya – we'll build you a nice house somewhere in Marsabar."

"*Mela* ... You can't do that! I'm not living in Libya. I'm going on holiday to Spain – I've promised the family! My wife won't agree to move ... no, this isn't going to work at all."

Camilleri stood and reached across the cramped office to put his arm around George's shoulder, who flinched and looked imploringly at his boss.

"George, this will make you a rich man. It is a big responsibility and I am sure it carries a big salary. Also, I have authorised a large bonus for you and an enhancement to your pension pot! How about that?"

George was even more confused.

"What d'you mean? Am I being fired?"

"I am sorry, George. There has not been time to talk about this. But, in your absence, there was a small departmental reorganisation and, in the interests of cementing links between the Pulizija and key parts of the Maltese economy, I am seconding you out of the department for a while – national interest and all that. It is splendid news! This is truly an excellent opportunity and has arrived at just the right time for your career development."

"But I don't want to do it. I want to go back to my normal duties!"

"Sorry, not possible just at the moment. The country has greater need of your unique experience and skills. We are all here to serve. You can return to being a policeman once things settle down in Libya and we can find something more suitable and less … stressful for you. In the meantime, you will work for MalTech, as their Libyan Security Liaison Director. I think that is the right title, Ms Bonnici?"

Camilleri smiled triumphantly.

"Oh, I nearly forgot – I have told Marianna you have been unavoidably delayed for a few more days."

Natasha looked across the table at George.

"Welcome aboard, *Mr* Zammit. It's all worked out well for everybody. You come highly recommended. Don't let us down."

She opened her briefcase and gave him an A4 envelope.

"Here are your instructions about what happens when you reach Tripoli and my letter of authority. Don't be bullied into any nonsense by Abdullah. Remember, this is our money and you're responsible for it. If any goes missing, we're not talking about slapped wrists. You understand what I'm saying?"

George swallowed hard and nodded his head.

———

Once the ship had set sail, he found a spot on the deck of the *Lorelei* and watched the lights of Malta fade to pinpricks, then disappear into the enveloping blackness of the night sea. A warm wind cut through his thin jacket as he huddled up against the steel plating of a hatch cover, his knees drawn up to his chest.

He could not believe he was no longer a policeman, even if

temporarily. The Bonnici woman had called him *Mr* Zammit, not Superintendent; he did not like that one bit. A senior police officer was all he had ever wanted to be. He was proud of his rank, the respect it afforded him. And what would Marianna say? Would there be any more invitations to the senior officers' garden parties and the Commissioner's Christmas drinks? Now he was expected to live in Libya … she would not stand for it.

It seemed that he had already accepted the new job, even if he had not said as much. Natasha Bonnici and Camilleri just assumed he was now working for MalTech Energy, whether he liked it or not. It was all a bitter disappointment.

He did not know what the job was, how much he would be paid or even if there was a uniform. All he knew was that he had a billion dinars to look after. They would be unloading it in twenty-four hours and he had to get it into an account with the Central Bank in Tripoli.

He stayed on deck for an hour, until the weariness of three days of travelling drove him to his narrow bunk. The noise and vibrations of the engines shook the ship from top to bottom, but such things rarely bothered George Zammit, who escaped his troubles by falling into a deep and dreamless sleep.

CHAPTER 53

NATASHA BONNICI
PALAZZO BRUNO, MILAN

Natasha had returned to Milan, having watched the *Lorelei* sail from Malta Freeport, bound for Tripoli. She was in her apartment, applying makeup and preparing for a meeting downstairs in Signor Bruno's office. Following the bombing that had killed Signor De Luca, Toni and Hugo, she had telephoned the third Wise Man, Signor Massaro, asking him to come to the *palazzo*. She could sense his hesitation so deliberately dropped all pretence of deference and framed the invitation almost as an instruction. Signor Massaro had asked if Marco would be attending the meeting and she had told him her father had asked her to confirm his retirement from the Family, with immediate effect, and to thank them for the generous retirement benefits.

There had been a long silence on the other end of the line. Natasha did not push things but gave him time to work out how the chips were falling. Eventually, Signor Massaro had said he too had been thinking of retirement for some time now, as his health had not been the best. In the circumstances, he asked to be excused attending and enquired about the retirement package on offer.

Natasha told him she would send him a proposal for his retirement, so he would not be left wanting any comfort he currently enjoyed. She also said that delivery of the retirement package was conditional on his not contacting Herr Schober who, as Natasha reminded him, was the only other Wise Man still left alive.

If he did all this, Massaro had her assurance that he would live to see out his remaining years as a rich man and leave a sizeable legacy for his family.

Herr Schober was not so easily persuaded and demanded to know what the hell was going on and who she thought she was to be telling him what to do? Natasha calmly replied that she was prepared to explain it all to him in person at the *palazzo*. He huffed and puffed and finally agreed to meet with her.

In good time for the meeting, she went down to the study and arranged the seating. Simon had accompanied her from the *castello*. As Marco was making preparations for his permanent departure, he was happy to surrender the Pole's services and she had now officially appointed him her head of security. She had told him to come well prepared and Simon had packed a heavy-duty handgun. He had also hired extra security in the form of three ex-military bodyguards from a Serbian agency, operating in Belgrade. They would be armed but would stay out of sight, in the small room behind Signore Bruno's former office.

Herr Schober turned up fifteen minutes late to the minute, which made Natasha laugh because it was so obviously calculated. He entered without knocking and was accompanied by three suited men who stood at the back of the room.

Natasha smiled sweetly.

"Herr Schober, please, there is no need for muscle in this room. Kindly ask them to wait outside."

Herr Schober looked at her for a minute and then nodded to one of the men, who left with the other two trailing behind him. Outside, they found Simon and the three security hires, waiting with guns drawn. They were swiftly disarmed and Simon disconnected the earpiece and microphone that kept Herr Schober in touch with his detail.

Natasha watched the immaculately dressed, elderly Austrian financier, sitting erect in his chair, his pale blue eyes unwavering. In the nineteen sixties, he had been asked by his government to lead a commission charged with restoring Jewish assets, looted by the Austrian SS, to their rightful owners. Unfortunately, Herr Schober had taken the view that some priceless pieces of art deserved special care, and these were transferred to the vaults of his ancestral home, amongst the vineyards of Burgenland. There, he held secret viewings for 'specially chosen art aficionados from across Europe. Word got out and his subsequent fall from grace was inevitable. It was then that he rekindled his family's long association with the Family in Milan, bringing a harder edge to their financial and banking activities. He had the reputation of being the hawk amongst the Wise Men and Natasha treated him with caution.

"So, Herr Schober, your colleagues Bruno and De Luca are dead. Hugo and Salvatore as well. My father has retired, along with Signor Massaro. I'd say that leaves an opening for some new blood, wouldn't you?"

"You obviously think you have pulled off some sort of coup – and I am as impressed as I am shocked. What do you intend to do with it all? You obviously know all about our financial arrangements, as Signor Bruno made the mistake of trusting you implicitly. Does your father know you are a serial killer? Marco always struck me as a decent man."

Natasha smiled as she went to the burled walnut credenza and poured two cups of coffee.

"Cream?"

He smiled faintly.

"In the circumstances, I think I will decline, thank you."

She made a show of deliberately drinking her coffee, then said: "Why did you come today? You know you're going to take the money because you know there's no alternative."

"I am curious. I want to know who else is involved. I want to know who killed my friends. Because I know it was not all your doing. You could have made yourself invaluable to Signor Bruno and, in time, would have earned a promotion. But there is some-body else involved, who is taking this very personally and is in a hurry. And I repeat, that is not you."

"Yes, you're right. All of that's true. So, are you going to take the money and leave?"

Herr Schober sat impassively, his hands clasped together in his lap.

"You are asking me to walk away from a lifetime's work without understanding the reason why. So no, not until I know who is behind this."

Natasha leaned forward and pressed a button under the desk and then sat back in her chair, arms folded. A buzzer sounded in the next room and the door behind Natasha swung open. A short, stocky man appeared. He was dressed in a blue-grey suit, with an open-necked white shirt beneath. There was a wide beaming smile on his face.

"Wolfram, *ciao*! *Sorpresa!*"

Herr Schober froze in his seat. It took several seconds for him to process what or who had just appeared.

"Surprise indeed. Now I see … It all makes perfect sense."

Natasha stood up and said: "Well, now you know, I'll leave you two to catch up."

She waited in the next room.

The grey-haired man walked behind Herr Schober and placed his hands on the back of his chair. He brought his mouth close to the old man's ear.

"I know it was you, you old fuck! You never could stand me. Even as a boy, you despised me – I got up your stuck-up nose, didn't I? None of the others would've had the guts to make the call. Even if Bruno passed on the message to Salvatore, it was you behind it. So, well done for that. I'm sorry, Wolfram, but you won't get to enjoy your retirement package!"

Herr Schober tried to swivel in the chair but the wire garotte around his frail, wrinkled neck tightened and cut into his thin white skin, a line of dark blood starting to flow down under his collar and soak into his vest. It took less than two minutes before Herr Schober was limp and lifeless in the chair.

Sergio Rossi looked down at the old man's body in disgust. All Sergio's adult life, Schober had treated him with contempt -- be it for Sergio's lack of sophistication, his Sicilian background or for generally not being 'one of them'. Sergio had qualities Schober never recognised, the strongest being his sense of loyalty to those who trusted him. But equally prominent in his character was the Sicilian need to avenge himself on those who disrespected and betrayed him.

CHAPTER 54
MARCO BONNICI

CASTELLO BONNICI, MALTA

MARCO WAS in the process of getting ready to leave. There was no rush, he was having one or two farewell dinners and putting his affairs in order. He had directorships to resign, financial matters to organise and he had decided to put the *castello* onto the market. His time in Malta was over and he needed to sever all links with the island. For as long as he had the house and, more importantly, the garden, part of him would always be connected to it.

Disposing of valuable artefacts, accumulated over centuries by his family, took time and dealers told him he would swamp the local market if everything arrived in the auction houses all at once. Accordingly, the more valuable pieces and collections went to Rome, Milan and Madrid; the pieces with local appeal to the auction houses in Sliema and Valletta. The books in the library he donated to the Bibliotheca, the National Library of Malta in Republic Square, Valletta.

The farmland he planned to lease on favourable terms to some of the long-serving workers, and he set about establishing cooperatives for the winery and olive presses.

He also needed to find some way of resolving his differences with Natasha. They had not had a meaningful conversation since their falling out. He had no doubt as to the gravity of her behaviour and knew he would never feel the same about her again. Nevertheless, he could not contemplate moving to the Serbian estate without a word of farewell.

However, when news filtered through from Milan about the killings of Salvatore, Signor De Luca and Herr Schober, Marco simply refused to believe it. He thought it was some ridiculous rumour. Only when his phone calls to the Wise Men in Milan were not returned did he start to worry. He phoned Natasha, who said she believed the rumours to be true, but was staying in her flat in Portomaso and waiting to see what the outcome might be.

The news was finally confirmed by Signor Massaro, who had telephoned, weeping, to tell Marco of the murder of his fellow Wise Men, saying they had been cut down in cold blood, in Mafia-style executions. He was seeking help and protection from Marco, saying he feared for his life.

He went on to say he held Natasha responsible for the deaths and that she had more or less demanded his retirement as the price for his life. Marco felt an icy chill run through him, as every fear and doubt he had ever nursed about his daughter came flooding back, to hollow him out. His knees felt weak and he closed his eyes. The room started to sway back and forth. He grabbed a chair with his hand and put the phone down on the table. He tried to steady himself, but sent the chair sliding away from him, while Signore Massaro cried and pleaded from the telephone speaker.

Doing his best to gather himself, Marco told Massaro to stay calm and keep safe. He said he would talk to Natasha and find out from her what was happening.

He was totally adrift; not knowing which way to turn. He felt the panic of a swimmer, way too far from shore, who realises he has neither the strength to return to land, nor the energy to keep his mouth above the waves surging around his face. His hands shaking and his legs unsteady, Marco dialled his daughter's number.

"You'd better tell me what is happening in Milan. What the hell have you done?"

"I've done nothing that didn't need doing, Dad." Natasha's voice was flat and cold. "But there's someone you need to see. He'll arrive in Malta tomorrow and I'll bring him up to the *castello* late morning. We should've had this conversation before now; it would all have made more sense to you then and would probably have saved you a lot of worry. I'm sorry for that."

"Nothing about what I have just heard will ever make any sense to me, if it is your doing. Answer me one question: am I safe?"

"Dad, how could you even ask? I promise it'll all make sense when we meet tomorrow. Please, trust me and don't worry."

The next morning, instead of heading out onto the terrace, Marco took a seat in the formal drawing room, an overly elaborate space that was seldom used, but afforded views down the short drive to the main gate. He sat and looked out of the window. He could not read or work. Instead, he just sat watching the gates, in a semi-trance. Katia, the housekeeper, brought breakfast, then later his coffee, and finally asked him if he wanted his lunch served there as well.

He was about to reply when he saw the three-metre steel-plate gates before the house start to move. He abruptly dismissed Katia and hurried to the front door, to watch Natasha's sports car pull up under the portico. She stepped out, took off her sunglasses and looked at him with a peculiar expression on her face. She did not approach him or come towards the front door, but stepped back and to one side. He saw a figure awkwardly lever itself out of the low seat on the passenger side of the car.

When the figure turned to face him, all the breath left Marco's body. He had expected something out of the ordinary this morning and his imagination had taken him to strange and unlikely places, but never had he contemplated this encounter. It was too much for him to comprehend. He walked towards the man in silence. The visitor had a rueful smile on his face, his eyes glistening with tears. Marco was shaking with emotion; the visitor could see the shock and pain of this unexpected reunion written all over his face. Marco had adopted the gait and posture of someone ten years older. He shuffled his way to the inevitable embrace.

Natasha watched from a distance. She slowly got back into the car and left the two of them together, arms around each other. As she drove away, she saw her father in the side mirror, watching her as the gates swung shut.

The two men automatically walked onto the rear terrace, where they had always sat. Sergio had his arm around Marco's shoulders as he struggled to bring his emotions back under control. They sat down in easy chairs and Katia appeared at the terrace door, tray in hand, her face as white as a sheet.

"Yes, Katia, it is him, Lazarus himself. You had better bring us wine. Let us see if ghosts can drink!

"OK, Sergio." Marco exhaled deeply. "Start at the beginning. I cannot wait to hear this."

"Marco, I'm sorry for the deception but they tried to kill me. I didn't know who to trust and I didn't want them to know I was alive. At least, not until I was ready! I didn't want to drag you or Natasha into this or make it your fight.

"I only just escaped … it was blind luck. There was a limo at the gates when I was released, with two Neapolitans in suits. I thought they were drivers, but they were assassins."

Sergio gulped his wine and sighed, gathering himself to tell the story.

"They gave me champagne and I finished it in the car. Then, I realised what was happening. We were in some woods. They opened the door and I charged at them. I threw the bottle; one of the idiots fired, just as the bottle hit him, and the bullet hit his *amico*. Can you believe it? A million to one chance!

"I knew then I could survive. I got the shooter's gun and

finished him. The second guy had a bullet in the leg, but he spilled the beans. I put the first guy in the car and burned him, taking photos as proof of death. I made the second guy send the photos to Salvatore. Then, we drive in their escape car to Le Vele di Scampia – you know, the big block of flats shaped like sails, on the outskirts of Naples? There, I pay some Camorra youths I know to kill him and get rid of the body and the car.

"Lucky? Yes, very. But after that, it's been purely about patience. Marco, they ruined my life, destroyed my marriage …" Marco raised his eyebrows slightly. "Well, she divorced me when I was in prison, which was no big deal, but that bastard Salvatore was fucking Carlita … now *she* I was fond of!

"Anyway, they left me flat. All those promises about a nest egg waiting for me – lies! They let me rot for four years and had no intention of doing the right thing when I got out. There was never any doubt in my mind, Marco, that they'd pay for what they did. You understand that, don't you?"

"I can see it perfectly, Sergio. And I do not blame you. How did Natasha become involved in all this?"

Now the shock was wearing off, Marco was beginning to recover some of his composure.

"I was watching Signor Bruno's *palazzo* from that café across the road, and she saw me. Simple as that. I told her not to tell you because I didn't want you to try and stop me, or get involved. This wasn't your fight, Marco. I told her my plan; she told me how upset you'd been and how you'd distanced yourself from the Family. She offered her help, I'd be lying if I said otherwise, but I did all the wet work!

"But now," he leaned closer to Marco's chair and grabbed his wrist, "*we* can be the Wise Men working with a Wise Woman! How many times have we dreamed of that? Since we were boys in Bologna … remember those times? The way's wide open – we've destroyed all the others. Think about it. The things we can do, you, me and Natasha! What could be better?"

"To live peacefully and quietly, Sergio. Or should I call you

Signor Rossi? And I do not want Natasha tied up in any of this madness."

"It's a bit late for that now. Signorina Bonnici's officially head of the Family! That was her price for agreeing to help me. I came round to the idea pretty quickly. She's got the brains, you know that. She understands all the financial stuff and she's ruthless." Sergio paused and deliberated for a moment. He continued: "I've known that, ever since she pushed Sophia down the staircase."

There was silence between them until Marco said softly: "You knew?"

"I guessed. It was a long time ago. Natasha was very young, Marco."

"She was five years old and she killed her pregnant mother in a fit of jealousy. I knew she had done it but there was no proof. What was I to do then? Sometimes, you know, it has been hard to love her."

"No, she is what she is. We're not going to change that part of her – ever."

The two men looked at each other.

"Anyway, that's why she needs you. That's why I need you. The three of us – we complement each other. Listen, setting the past aside, I'll take back my old job as head of operations; watch Natasha's back and hold a seat as a Wise Man. I'm happy with that! But we need you, Marco. You'll bring stability and experience. Natasha needs and respects you. She's still young."

"She does not need me. She does not tell me what the hell she is up to. She stole a fortune from the Russians, under the nose of the Americans, and they accused *me* of the theft. She even hid the money near my place in Serbia! She and Simon kidnapped a young guy and held him in the old chapel. I swear to you, she would have killed him if I had not stumbled across them. She has left a trail of wreckage behind her these last few years and I worry about her. She is reckless."

"I knew about some of it. Stealing the Russians' cash was a genius operation!"

"What? You knew about it and did not stop her?"

"Well, I thought it was a good idea. The money always had a purpose, that's why she stole it! She's using it to buy an army in Libya, to secure the oil and gas deal."

"For Christ's sake! Does nobody tell me anything? This is what I mean by reckless!"

"No, it's actually very clever. She's got a ruthless streak, I grant you, but that makes it all the more important that you watch over her, no?"

Marco sighed and decided to change the subject.

"Anyway, where did you get the ricin from? That had me really scared, I had no idea what was going on! And, seriously, giving it to Salvatore like a KGB assassin? Did it really have to be that way?"

Sergio laughed.

"Oh, yes, it absolutely did! You wouldn't believe how that bastard wound me up while I was inside. To her credit, Natasha refused to have anything to do with that side of things. I bought the stuff from Danylo – the Ukrainian, you remember? We washed his money, until there was that incident where it seemed Walker had been on the take. Danylo got it from some Russian ex-military type. We owe him a favour for that, by the way."

"Yes, it figures. But no, Sergio, I owe him nothing. I am out of this. You and Natasha can rule across half of Europe, for all I care. You two have changed the rules by killing your own; you have behaved like the Mafia. I am so glad to see you still alive, Sergio, but I cannot be part of the new regime. Why not get an Uzi and shoot up the next person who upsets you when you're driving? This is not us! It is not what *we* do."

"*Sì, sì, hai ragione*, I know. But I needed to make a statement and clear the way for the future – our future. And it felt good to get those old fuckers back for what they did to me!"

"Not my future, Sergio. Not mine! Come on, drink some of this wine. It is last year's and rather good."

"No!" he howled. "Please, not your wine! Haven't you got

anything better to offer a friend who has just returned from the dead?"

"No! Drink it as punishment then, for all the upset you have caused me." They touched glasses, smiling.

"Good to have you back, my old friend," said Marco.

"It's good to be here again, it's been far too long."

They sat on the terrace together, talking in low voices, while Katia set the table for lunch and then approached them to say it was ready to be served. There were grilled prawns since she knew they were Signor Rossi's favourite. For a few hours it felt almost as though Sergio had never been away in prison or taken his bloody revenge after being released. Almost. But each man privately acknowledged that the repercussions of Sergio's return from the dead were unlikely to end here.

CHAPTER 55
NATASHA BONNICI

OFFICES OF BETHI, PACEVILLE,
MALTA

PACEVILLE IS the brash centre of Malta's so-called entertainment district; that is, if your idea of fun centres around gentlemen's clubs, dancing with drunken local teens or squeezing up and down the slimy St Rita Steps, a thoroughfare of greasy, broken tiles onto which the area's bars and fast-food outlets spew spilt liquor, discarded pizza slices, drunken Maltese youths and wasted tourists. The B&Bs, hostels and cheap accommodation house a young crowd of travelling fun and sun seekers, for whom the party never stops. Every day from May to September, the bars pump out music and exhausted clubbers lie on the little patch of man-made beach, like a colony of skinny, multi-coloured seals.

Natasha was oblivious to it all. The offices of BetHi were on the upper floors of a fifteen-storey tower block, which put them out of reach of the smell of fried food and pizza toppings. Driving down from the *castello*, she wished she could have sat in on the two men's reunion. Sergio had promised her he would convince Marco to join them and take the Family through the next stage of its journey. The three of them, working together, an invincible trio, bound by blood loyalty and the fun of the game. She had gone along with him, confident that the last thing her father would do was follow her lead as the new head of the Family, a position she had no intention of relinquishing – not even for him. She had got what she wanted by doing what she had to do. It had taken nerve but, amidst the wreckage Sergio and she had created, she had seized control of one of the most powerful business organisations in Europe.

There were others in the Family, of course, who needed managing; she and Sergio had met or spoken to several of them over the last few days. A mix of fear, bribery and charm had been sufficient to bring them into line. She had convened a wider ten-person council, to sit every other month, to whom she would report. This enfranchisement of the Family's more senior members was well received and lent substance to her claim that this revolution was not a putsch against the Wise Men, but a justified reaction against a small, secretive, self-protective group of octogenarians, who had been reluctant to share power or knowledge in an era that demanded more openness and transparency.

Her long-term strategy was to move the Family away from some of the more troublesome areas of its business, where it bumped up against the traditional organised crime groups, such as waste disposal and construction, and focus more on big ticket, more stable income-generating projects in infrastructure, finance and energy.

Sergio did not really understand the change of strategy, but that did not bother Natasha unduly. He either did or he did not, it did not matter to her. She knew he would always defer to her and be totally loyal; that was just the way he was. Her father was a different matter. She knew he would always doubt her at every turn.

These thoughts ran through her head as the car descended the ramp to the underground parking at the BetHi offices. She had a MalTech appointment that afternoon and, as the new prestigious offices in St Julian's had yet to be opened, had arranged to meet in her old office in Paceville.

The meeting was with the deputy editor of the *Malta Telegraph*. Amy Halliday wanted to do a profile piece on Malta's up and coming new businesswoman. Such PR pieces were usually anathema to Natasha. However, with MalTech being what it was, her new PR agency had told her she needed to start to engage more with the press and develop a personal profile, so, with a resigned sigh, she had agreed to the interview.

The two women met, shook hands and then Natasha directed Amy to the low sofas, set either side of a glass coffee table, from which there were panoramic views over St George's Bay.

They chatted generally about Natasha's background, being brought up in the *castello*, her education on the island and, later, in Italy and in California. Amy pushed her on what it was like to be a woman in the upper echelons of commercial life in Malta and whether she had experienced sexism or unfair treatment at the hands of men. Natasha made some bland statement about the gallantry and good manners of Maltese gentlemen, which she hoped did not sound too patronising.

Then the conversation started to take an awkward turn. It seemed Amy was interested in the origins of the Bonnici family and how it had made its money.

"So, the Bonnicis … it's rumoured you go back a very long way – what can you tell me about that?"

Natasha blagged her way through the family's history, careful to recount how its wealth had all been lost after the First World War, until her grandfather had restored their fortunes in the post-Second World War era of reconstruction.

"Well, yes, but the Bonnicis have invested hundreds of millions of euros in MalTech. Where did that sort of money come from?"

Natasha was ready for the question, but knew she had no convincing answer available.

"Well, we haven't invested quite as much as that – I wish we had!" She laughed. "There's a syndicate of investors, which we're a part of. But, yes, it's a considerable amount of money."

"It's an unprecedentedly large amount for a group of private investors. Don't the Maltese public have a right to know who is behind the supply of their gas?"

"All I can say is, it's a group of private, and I stress *private*, investors. The source of our funds has been checked out by the regulators and the Department of Energy. Everyone's happy with the participating investor group."

"Well, Natasha, that's not true, is it? The investors hide behind a British Virgin Island trust, and those trusts are notorious for their lack of transparency. My research also tells me this company, BetHi, one of Europe's biggest i-Gaming companies, also hides behind a BVI trust. Why is everything around your business so secretive?"

Amy Halliday pushed and probed and Natasha batted away the enquiries. She could see the shape of the piece that would emerge. Eventually, she said: "Can we talk off the record for a minute?"

Amy turned off the digital recorder and smiled sweetly at her.

"Look, I can see where this is going, but the reason our affairs are so complicated is that, after World War One, as I've said, the family were nearly wiped out. My grandfather was determined that would never happen again, so he created a protective structure over the family's assets, which my father continues to use."

Amy nodded along, encouragingly.

"Now, I accept times have changed and so we're looking to move to a more transparent arrangement, but I can't tell you how complicated that is. Don't give me a hard time about it. Malta is a small island and I need friends like you. Can we be friends?"

"I do hope so, Natasha, but I'm going to have to touch on this issue – public interest and all that. Can I say you're looking to simplify …"

Suddenly, Natasha jumped in.

"No! Please, you can't say anything about the money. I don't want you setting hares running, do you understand? You do that and you'll be frozen out of every MalTech press conference, you'll never get a press release and you'll find some new members on your board of directors who won't take kindly to your unsupportive tone. Now do you understand me?"

Gobsmacked, Amy fell back in the sofa.

"Wow! Interesting. You *have* got something to hide!"

Natasha was furious with herself for losing her temper.

At that moment, the door opened and in walked Nick.

He hesitated, hand on the door handle, sensing the atmosphere in the room.

"Natasha, sorry to interrupt. I heard you were in and I thought …"

She stood up, composing herself instantly.

"Nick, nice to see you, come in. This is Amy Halliday from the *Malta Telegraph*, she's here doing a profile piece. Amy, I think you've probably got everything you need?"

Nick smiled at Amy and glanced at Natasha. He had spoken to Amy anonymously, when they were planting stories about the Russians, but they had never met.

Amy started to gather her things. She had been thrown out of better places than this. Interesting, though, how she had touched a raw nerve in Natasha during the interview.

Amy ignored the blatant attempt to get her out of the room and turned to face the newcomer.

"So, Mr Walker, how're you settling in? You were at BetSlick, weren't you? Welcome back. Actually, now I have you, maybe we could arrange to meet up so I can do a profile piece on you, too? New man at the helm of BetHi and so on. I'm sure the gaming community would be really interested. Exciting!"

Nick shrugged.

"Yes, of course, why let Natasha have all the action? It's good to be back, actually, I missed Malta. Gibraltar is small and very parochial – even compared to Malta!"

"Oh, so that's where you've come from, Gibraltar?"

"Yeah, I was there for four years – but anyway, we can talk about that later."

It did not take Amy more than a few seconds to connect his English-accented voice to her tip-off caller. So, Nick Walker was the source behind the leaks about the Russians and the VertWay pipeline. She had noted the Gibraltar international dialling code on one of the incoming calls. And standing behind him, scrutinising her very carefully, was Natasha Bonnici.

Well, these certainly would be interesting profile pieces.

Natasha suddenly walked towards her, arms outstretched, and launched into a display of sisterhood.

"Well, so great of you to come, Amy, many thanks and I can't wait to see the draft!"

Amy hung back, avoiding the attempt at an embrace.

"I'm afraid I don't work like that, Natasha – but I'm sure you'll love the piece once it's in print!"

Natasha dropped her smile.

"I can't wait."

The door shut behind Amy while Nick and Natasha turned to face each other. She was silent, her face fixed, unsmiling.

"She's trouble, that woman. She was fishing."

"She's a journalist, for Christ's sake, that's what they do! Your problem is, you're just too used to ordering people around and getting your own way."

"Maybe, but I lost it with her. I've got to sharpen up. I can't go round being bettered by the likes of Amy bloody Halliday. And you be careful with her, I think she's worked out you were the mystery caller."

"Really? Maybe I shouldn't have mentioned Gib."

"Just avoid her and don't do the profile piece. We don't want the whole oil-smuggling thing being brought up again."

Nick flicked back a lock of his blond hair.

"You're just jealous!"

Natasha smiled at him. Being with Nick always improved her mood.

"Please, she's old enough to be your mother!"

"Yeah, but she's kept herself in good shape. Anyway, come on, welcome me back, have a drink with me. Let's slum it in Paceville!"

"OK. Oh, by the way, I've got news."

"Yes?"

"Sergio's back!"

Nick stopped in his tracks.

"What? You told me he was dead?"

"I know. I was wrong."

As Nick stood there, flummoxed, Natasha grabbed her bag and headed out. Nick's good mood started to ebb away. He saw Sergio as an uncultured, Sicilian Mafia boss and had not been upset when Natasha first told him he was dead. But she had been 'wrong', apparently. Natasha Bonnici, who never made the same screw-ups as ordinary mortals. The first feelings of anxiety about his return to Malta started to pump through Nick's veins.

As Natasha entered the ladies' cloakroom, her phone buzzed in her handbag. It was Camilleri.

"I have some information for you. You asked me to find out the whereabouts of Saviour Azzopardi. I think I have been successful."

"Gerald, how clever of you! And where might I find the little squirt?"

"Well, he's obviously turned over a new leaf. We found him trying to lift kettlebells in a no-nonsense gym off the Sliema promenade. Apparently, he is friendly with the owner, a Polish lady, Danka Bijak, and is tucked up in her flat around the corner. I will text you the address."

She pondered this for a moment, gazing at her phone, then went to her contacts and set up a meeting with *Il-Barri*.

CHAPTER 56
GEORGE ZAMMIT
MARSABAR, LIBYA

GEORGE CLAMBERED down the steep gangway from the *Lorelei* onto the quayside in the Port of Tripoli. The waters of the port were an oily green colour, thick with plastic waste, discarded packaging and, to his disgust, a bloated, dead sheep, its four legs poking upright, the gas in its swollen belly providing buoyancy. The papers Natasha had given him contained a map, which pointed out the silver domes on the top of the brick-red towers of the Central Bank of Libya, visible from the quayside, on the other side of the busy road that ran along the coast.

The sun was up and the heat was already building, lifting the fetid aromas off the greasy dock. He wished he was standing back in Malta's Grand Harbour, which was fresh as a mountain lake by comparison. The port was quiet, with a few small container ships and a bulk carrier moored along the wharfs. Some local fishing boats were unloading the morning's catch. The only other activity centred on the travelling crane that had set about the relatively small job of lifting the pallets of wooden packing crates from the *Lorelei* onto the wharf.

There, a forklift waited to load the crates onto two curtain-sided wagons, their drivers chatting with a security guard and smoking cigarettes. The whole atmosphere was totally relaxed; the only person showing any sign of tension was George.

Natasha Bonnici's instructions clearly said that, on arrival, he had to ring the Central Bank and three armoured trucks would be sent, with an armed escort, to transport the crates the short distance to the bank premises. Only then could unloading from the ship begin. He had made the call, but the crates were already being lifted up and out of the holds and dumped onto the quayside.

The contingent of armed policemen who had accompanied George were watching proceedings from the ship's rail. They had been ordered not to go ashore in Tripoli and to maintain security from the ship.

George was starting to panic when he heard a voice behind him.

"Relax, my brother! You look like you have robbed a bank! Be calm. How are you, my friend? It is always good to see you."

George spun around.

"What are you doing here?"

Nothing in the papers had said Abdullah would meet them on the quayside. His friend wandered over to him, cigarette in hand and looked thoughtfully at the cargo.

"I thought there would be more. Bigger boxes. More boxes. You know? Are you sure that is all there is?"

"No, there was a lot more, but I stopped in Lampedusa and took half for myself. Is it every day somebody gives you a billion dinars?"

"Shhh! Be quiet!" Abdullah pulled a warning expression. "It is a cargo of guns and parts for the Toyotas – that is what I have told them." He nodded towards the drivers. "That is why there will be no worries, no gossip and no trouble!"

"So, you know what we are doing with it? Why are those trucks there?"

"Hah! Now that is a better question!"

"You know we are putting this money in the bank?"

"No, I think not. You remember Gaddafi's family stole billions of dinars from the Central Bank in Tripoli? That bank." Abdullah pointed to the imposing building in the distance. "So I know that place is not safe."

"Then if not the bank, where?"

"Caves!"

"No, no, no! Abdullah, no!" George pulled his friend towards him, by his sleeve, and whispered, "It's a billion dinars – you can't keep it in a cave! I'm responsible for that money. I've got my instructions and that money goes into that bank."

"Yes, that is why it is such a good thing you and I are brothers, because you know I am right about this. Look, if Boutros takes Tripoli, or somebody else, where is the first place they will go, eh?

"Yes, to the bank to steal my money! No, we go to the caves in Nafusa Hills and my brother-in-law will keep it safe."

"It's not your money," George hissed. "It's available to you, but it's not yours. If you like, it's my money – and it's going into the bank. A billion dollars will earn a lot of interest. You can't earn interest in a cave!"

Abdullah was shocked.

"You cannot do that, it is *riba, haram*! Muslims do not do this!"

At that moment, four armoured trucks drove through the port gates and made their way towards the *Lorelei*. George heaved a sigh of relief.

"Take your trucks and go. That money goes to the bank!"

Abdullah cursed and grabbed him by the shirt.

"You are mistaken, my friend. This is not wise. If this money is stolen, then a great opportunity will be lost."

George brushed his hand away.

"There's a bigger chance it'll be lost if you hide it in the hills. It's your job to defend Tripoli. That's how you stop the money being stolen – not by hiding it in a cave!"

Abdullah cursed and glared at him.

"In front of the bank there," he pointed to the left of the bank building, "is the Saraya Lake. It is in a park where you can sit and cool your feet. On the south side, there is an icecream seller. I will meet you there, after you have given my money to General Boutros."

George sighed.

"OK. But it'll take the rest of the day for them to count the money and sign all the papers."

It did take the best part of the day for the thirty tellers at the Central Bank of Libya to run twenty million individual fifty-dinar banknotes through the electronic money detectors and counting machines. Ivan Karavayev of the Goznak Print Works, Moscow, would have been pleased, as all bar two dozen of them were accepted. All twenty million notes, less twenty-four, were rebound in paper wrappers of 1,000 dinars, replaced in their wooden cases and wheeled into the bank's underground vault.

George signed the paperwork and smiled to himself, as he realised he was now the signatory to one of the biggest bank accounts in the world! It did not quite work so simply, of course. There was a complex authentication and second authority process to follow before any money was released, but the thought amused him.

Given it was now evening, he was surprised when he entered the grounds around Saraya Lake, to see Abdullah squatting on his heels, chatting to the icecream vendor.

"Have you been waiting all this time?"

"No, I have just arrived. I have been shopping. There are many exciting shops in Tripoli! I paid a little baksheesh to the bank security guard and he called me when you left. So, we must hurry or we will be late."

"Where're we going?"

"I will tell you on the way! You will be very happy."

Abdullah threw a backpack at George. He looked inside and saw his laundered long blue Tuareg robe, a *cheche* turban and a pair of sandals.

"There is a toilet over by the gate. The floor is swimming, but you can change quickly in there."

"Where're we going, Abdullah? I don't work for the Malta Pulizija anymore – I don't have to take instructions from you, Camilleri or anybody except Signorina Bonnici. So tell me!"

Abdullah looked hurt.

"I have a special trip planned for us both, to be together as brothers – and you say you will not come?"

"Not unless you first tell me where we're going."

"We are going to kill Abu Muhammad! Just you and me. To make things right, *Inshallah*."

George could not believe what he had just heard. They argued and they fought, face to face, showering spittle over each other as they batted words backwards and forwards.

Eventually, after twenty minutes, Abdullah fell silent for a moment, his eyes cast down, before saying, "I will go alone then. Even though, without you, my plan is no good. But if you refuse to help me, I will still go and maybe die trying, because it must be done – finished!

"If I die, then you will have failed me and your people in Malta. Who will protect the oil then, eh? Who do you trust, eh? Who will fight the Beards and look after the people in Marsabar? You?

"You go and tell everyone that now they must trust the government to protect them, *Inshallah!* Please, you leave and tell Rania I have gone and tell her why you are not with me, as I promised her you would be! Go!"

George slumped against the wall of the walkway around the lake. Without looking back, Abdullah started walking down the path to the park exit. George watched him go. With a shake of his head, he set off in the other direction.

CHAPTER 57

ABDULLAH BELKACEM
JEBEL UWEINAT MOUNTAINS,
SOUTH-EAST LIBYA

It had taken Abdullah several days and nights to skirt the northern sands of the Sahara and drive the 2,000 kilometres from Marsabar to the mountains that straddled the border of Libya, Egypt and Sudan. There were easier routes but, in Libya, to head east was to head into trouble, so Abdullah drove south to Ubari, where they rested. Then onwards, west, parallel to the border with Chad. On arriving in the Jebel Uweinat Mountains, he drove through a volcanic landscape with alternating bare rocky plateaux and rolling sandy plains. The land was sparsely populated: harsh, arid and inhospitable.

At times, the Land Cruiser had struggled with the extremes of the journey and George had regretted every minute spent inside it. Back in Tripoli, he had got as far as the park's northern gates, at which point he had turned around and jogged back to find Abdullah. The one thing he had not been able to face was going back to Marsabar and telling Rania he had let her husband go alone to confront Muhammad. He knew Abdullah had pulled a dirty trick, but it had worked.

He hated having allowed himself to be manipulated in this way and thought about his own family. Marianna had been expecting him home days ago, but she had been told George had been asked to stay on to help devise policing strategies in Tripoli. She would have been horrified if she had known half of what was happening.

It seemed to him that what they were doing was pointless. If Abdullah knew where to find Abu Muhammad, why not get the Americans to bomb him in the same way as they had hit the camp in the Nafusa Hills? When asked this, Abdullah had merely said that would be dishonourable and it was better done this way – whatever *this way* turned out to be!

George did not want to think of the treatment they would receive if Muhammad got his hands on him for a second time. He remembered the beatings and the concrete box they had kept him in, to freeze him at night and cook him during the day. He had decided he would rather kill himself than go through that again. This prompted him to ask Abdullah for a side arm, which was kept in the dashboard compartment. In the hours of darkness, when his mood was at its lowest, George wondered if he would have the guts to use it against himself, should the time come.

He had tried to persuade Abdullah to turn back, on several occasions, but was met with a silence as profound as the emptiness of the desert they were driving through. He was scared and exhausted. Jolting over the rough terrain had battered and bruised him, his teeth were on edge, and the few hours of sleep they had snatched had made them both bad-tempered and irritable.

Abdullah had refused to discuss the plan with George, which had wound him up even more and thrown him into a prolonged sulk that had already lasted several days. They spoke little, each passing the indeterminable hours daydreaming and watching the bleak, windswept landscape change from rock to sand and back again.

Abdullah seemed to be following some coordinates on a GPS, not a map, so George did not really know where they were, although he believed they should be somewhere near the

Sudanese and Egyptian border. He was not wrong. When he saw high mountains appear in the distance, he guessed they must be the Uweinat Mountains, which rose to 2,000 metres above the Western Egyptian desert.

That night, they stopped early and Abdullah made them change out of their robes and turbans into desert camouflage jackets and trousers. He threw a brown and tan net over the Land Cruiser and announced there would be no hot food that night as tomorrow they would put the plan into action. He told George they were close to Muhammad's camp and would have to be careful from now on. Abdullah pulled a long rigid metal case from the boot and put it in front of George, who was sitting in the dirt, leaning against a dusty tyre.

"You look inside and do what you have to do."

George watched Abdullah stalk off, then turned his attention to the case.

He opened it and saw that it contained an M24 Army sniper rifle, with hollowed out, large-calibre shells. There was also a small tablet containing a US Army Sniper tutorial, that helped shooters calculate and set up the gun to account for elevation, spindrift, wind speed and air density, to get the perfect shot.

George looked at Abdullah.

"*Mela!* What am I supposed to do with this?"

His friend came over and squatted down in front of him.

"Every morning at daybreak, when the air is still and before the heat builds humidity, Muhammad leaves his tent to pray. He looks north to the *qibla*, towards the city of Mecca. To the north-east of him there is a ridge." He turned and pointed behind them. "From there, it is a clear shot for a man with a good eye and a steady hand.

"It will be your honour to kill him for me and avenge Tareq, *Inshallah*. And I shall be forever grateful to you."

He looked George straight in the eye as he spoke, and George realised this was the plan and Abdullah would not deviate from it.

"You are joking? How far is it from the ridge to the prayer mat?"

"It is less than a thousand metres."

George gasped.

"A thousand metres? I can't do that! Are you crazy?"

Abdullah held his gaze.

"You have the eye. You have the gun. And you have Allah's blessing. You cannot miss!"

"And you, a Muslim, are happy that we shoot a man at prayer? That's the plan?"

"Prayer will not draw Abu Muhammad closer to God. That man lost Allah's love many years ago. I have prayed on it and I am certain."

"If you say so. Seems wrong to me. Say I hit him – which is very unlikely – what happens then? We get chased across the Sahara for a thousand miles by a mob in technicals?"

"No. You kill him then this happens."

From a canvas holdall, he pulled out a short stubby weapon with a shoulder stock.

"It is a laser sighting gun. It paints the target for the Warthogs. They will come immediately and bomb the camp. Tomorrow morning, either way, Muhammad's jihadis will die. But Abu Muhammad himself must die by our hand."

With that, Abdullah got up and walked a little way away, squatting on his heels in the way he did. He lit a cigarette, lost in his own thoughts.

George took the rifle, with its over-long barrel and rest, out of the case. He fitted the scope and spent the rest of the evening reading from the tablet and making necessary adjustments to the scopes and the set up. A ballistic calculator had already prepared the settings for a one thousand-metre shot, in a light northerly wind, medium humidity at an early-morning temperature of ten degrees centigrade. George read from the program that, to compensate for air density, gravity and humidity, he would, in reality, be aiming the shot some ten metres above

Muhammad's head and relying on these calculations to make the bullet's trajectory fall nicely in line with Abu Muhammad's skull.

The bullets were a larger calibre than George had seen before, as a longer shot needed more propellant. He lay on the stony ground, loaded the weapon and checked the balance and the fit of the stock to his shoulder. Then he stripped the rifle down, removed the cartridge, cleaned and oiled the gun and replaced it in the carrying bag.

He walked across to where Abdullah was chewing on a supper of bread and goat's cheese.

"Abdullah, I think it's one chance in a hundred I can hit a man at a thousand metres. You'd better make sure your painting thing has a full charge; we're going to need it. If we're going to do this, we'll need to be there before first light to get set up."

Abdullah smiled grimly. "You hit him first shot; if not, the second or the third, and you will go on until there are no bullets left. It is Allah's will. You will hit him, I am sure of it."

George looked at him doubtfully. Abdullah said: "Listen, the prayers before sunrise are called *Salah*. It starts and Abu Muhammad will stand and bring his hands to the level of his ears. Like this." Abdullah demonstrated the posture. "This is when you get ready. This is the *Takbir* and it lasts maybe five to ten seconds.

"Next, he will recite longer verses and will become more relaxed. This is the *Qayum*. He will cross his arms over his chest and breathe deeply." Again, he demonstrated the position. "This he will hold for forty to sixty seconds, depending on how fast he speaks. This is when you take the shot. After this, there are many ups and downs and it is no good for the shooting.

"So, I will watch through the binoculars and I will say, '*Takbir*', and you will get ready. Then I will say '*Qayum*', and you have thirty seconds to kill him.

"Then I will paint the site with lasers and we will run down the mountain, happy and joyful. *Inshallah!*"

Abdullah smiled widely and grabbed George by the shoulder.

"It is good to be with a brother on this day."

George had to turn away. He had gone pale and felt a little faint. This was cold-blooded murder, even though Abdullah was completely oblivious to the fact. George had no love for Abu Muhammad and had wished him dead many times during his captivity in the Chadian desert, but this – this was too much. He tried to convince himself it was just another competition on the range in Pembroke and that there would not be a man in his sights, only a paper target, but he felt his hands start to shake.

———

In the early hours, the two men started the scramble up to the ridge. Abdullah had said there were no lookouts at night as the militia relied on the remoteness of their camp. Had it not been for surveillance drones operating out of Ubari, they would probably never have found it.

Abdullah had a thermal imaging monocular that he used to scout ahead of them, but everything was still and calm, apart from the noise of their footsteps sliding on the loose rocks. They climbed slowly for some hours. There was no path and Abdullah stopped frequently to check his GPS then disappear for minutes at a time, to find a way around cliffs and steep ravines.

The first light was only just starting to bring definition to the landscape when Abdullah turned and beckoned George to get down. He checked the GPS for the hundredth time and, after moving some metres to the west, nodded to his friend and shed his pack. George looked down over the top of the ridge and into the valley, where he could just make out the shape of a dozen tents shrouded in darkness, nestling in the ravine like small black boxes.

He felt calm and steady of hand as he opened the bag containing the long-barrelled rifle and assembled the firing system. He fitted the ten times magnification scope, set up the tripod and ensured the gun was correctly levelled and balanced. There was a grey foam mat to lie on and a desert-coloured camouflage net to put over himself and Abdullah, to break their outline and prevent sudden reflections from the metal objects they were assembling around them.

As the light of morning intensified, shapes started to emerge from the gloom. Black mounds became low-lying bushes and deep wedges of shadow morphed into rocky outcrops. George kept an eye on the shrubs and thin reedy grasses, to watch for any sign of an early-morning breeze but, as the instructions had assumed, everything was still.

There was no sign of his nerves of the previous day. He had settled into a comfortable position and surveyed the camp through the scope. Abdullah was lying next to him with his eyes pressed to the binoculars. He was mumbling to himself.

"What are you saying?"

"Hush! I am doing *Salah*, it is sunrise, I am praying."

"We are about to commit murder and you think that will do you any good?"

"The best revenge is to improve yourself. That I have done, then we will kill him. It is allowed. Now let me finish my prayers."

George shook his head.

"If you're sure."

It was only a few minutes later that the tents started to empty and Muhammad's men drifted out into an empty space in front of them. Some urinated against the nearby rocks, others lit cigarettes and talked in small groups. The tall, rangy figure of Muhammad was clearly recognisable in his long waistcoat, baggy white cotton trousers and pakol Afghan hat. Over the waistcoat, he wore a quilted jacket, to protect him from the morning chill.

They lay very still, facing to the south-west. Down below, the men formed up in lines, looking north-east, towards them and the *qibla*, the sacred building at Mecca, to which Muslims turn at prayer. Muhammad stood in the first line, giving a line of sight and a clear shot. Not for the first time, George realised a lot of thought had gone into this strike. He saw the fingerprints of Major Floyd Hamilton all over it.

George quickly settled down and adjusted his breathing. Abdullah whispered, "They will start soon."

George had checked his set up a dozen times and knew there was no more to be done and no time to do it anyway. It was down to him: his eye, his ability to control his heartbeat and his breathing.

He did not take his eye off the scope for over five minutes and was in an almost serene state of mind. He had decided his strategy last night and had come to terms with his decision. His conscience was clear.

Muhammad started the prayers. His voice was faint, but they could hear the rise and fall of his intonations. Given how few of them there were, he was not using a microphone and speaker.

George watched Muhammad raise his hands to either side of his head.

Abdullah whispered: "*Takbir!*"

George did not move, but kept his eye looking down the scope. Muhammad's voice continued until George saw him pause and drop his arms and fold them over his chest.

"*Qayum!*"

He watched, saw Muhammad bow his head and the top of his pakol fell into the crosshairs of the scope. The adjustments had been made for the bullet drop, for a shot of 1,000 metres. George took a last short breath through his mouth, held it and squeezed the trigger. As he did so, the first finger of his left hand twitched ever so slightly, enough, he hoped, to send the shot over the head of Muhammad and out of harm's way. He could not commit cold-blooded murder. Let the Warthogs flatten the place, Abu Muhammad deserved that, but not to die at George's hand while he was at prayer. He could not do it.

A bullet from an M24 travels at a supersonic speed, even after racing 1,000 metres through the atmosphere. This means it arrives at its destination before the sound of the shot is heard.

Muhammad heard nothing as the bullet ripped through his pakol and spun into his brain. Those behind him would not even have realised what had happened, until the crack of the shot echoed around the stillness of the valley. George looked up, shocked and open-mouthed. He lay frozen, watching while a crowd gathered around Abu Muhammad's prone body. Abdullah, a satisfied smile on his face, dropped his binoculars and coldly pointed the laser at the camp, dispersing the red dots around the tents.

Then he turned to face George.

"My brother, this is a wonderful moment and I am in your debt forever. It was the will of Allah, but it was by your hand!"

George was speechless as Abdullah shouldered the M24 rifle and pushed a pistol into his friend's hand.

"Now we must move quickly or this happy day could end badly!"

Above them, they heard the distant sound of aircraft approaching. They leaped to their feet and George followed Abdullah, who was scampering down the rocky ridge back towards the Land Cruiser. They had not gone far before the first explosion sent vibrations up through their feet and loosened a rockslide behind them. More explosions followed. Behind the ridge, smoke and dust started to rise as the two Warthogs screamed away into the distance.

Abdullah whooped and laughed, jumping from rock to rock. George was leaner and fitter than he had ever been, but this was a descent for youths and goats, not forty-five-year-old policemen. After thirty minutes, they rested and Abdullah scoured the mountainside through his binoculars for any sign of pursuit. Satisfied they were not being followed, he fell to his knees and prayed again, in thanks for their good fortune.

The first shock of seeing Muhammad hit was over. George

had tried to pull the shot, but the twitch of his finger against the barrel had just served to correct some miscalculation in the targeting. Knowing he was relieved of responsibility for the hit, he should have been pleased with himself, but could not shrug off the fact that he had just gunned down a man at prayer.

Abdullah, on the other hand, was euphoric, but in a world of his own. He prayed, he ran around like a child, he hugged George, he shouted into the sky, and then sat smiling, reliving the moment when a wait of four years had finally ended and he could begin to be at peace with himself.

CHAPTER 58

NATASHA BONNICI
INTERNATIONAL GARDEN HOTEL,
TRIPOLI, LIBYA

As GEORGE and Abdullah were racing back along the southern Libyan border with Chad, chased only by the cloud of dust and the hail of stones the Land Cruiser was throwing high into the air, the great and the good of Libya's new energy sector were meeting in the banqueting suite of one of Tripoli's five-star hotels.

A host of lawyers from London and New York had prepared a dozen trestle tables, piled high with documents dealing with all the legal elements of the transactions. Many long days and nights had been spent bringing the parties to this point but, finally, the completion meeting was underway. There was a strict timetable for when each of the parties had to present themselves and the agenda for the meeting ran to thirty-five pages.

The Russians, represented by Valentin Petrov, were selling the assets of the companies that owned VertWay to a syndicate of American oil companies, funded by a host of international banks. Mike Lloyd was supervising some US Federal officials who were there to sign papers, waiving sanction regulations.

The Libyan Resources Corporation was signing supply agreements with the American energy companies and MalTech Energy. The bankers and the financiers, who represented the investors, were there to ensure the creation of legal securities and to organise the transfer of funds. The Maltese government were represented and formally delivered the permits and agreements to enable MalTech to bring the gas onshore.

Various accountants presented sets of numbers and financial documents that people signed, initialled, verified and authenticated. Gradually, the assembled parties worked their way through the paperwork.

Natasha sat to one side, having finished a mammoth signing session, speaking to no one but her British lawyer or else looking at her phone. Once Mike Lloyd had put his pen down and pushed a pile of twenty documents back to his attorneys, Petrov had sidled across to him and the pair of them walked to a corner of the banqueting suite, Mike rubbing his aching wrist.

He spoke first.

"I hate Tripoli, it's a shit house."

"Then you have never done business in Baku, Iraq or Syria. I tell you, here is like paradise!"

"You've got me there. Maybe someday I'll have the pleasure. So, I hear you've lost a lot of money recently."

Petrov looked around the busy room, avoiding eye contact with him.

"Do you have it?"

"No, money is one thing we're never short of. But I know who does."

"Really? You surprise me. That would be a very interesting thing to know, but why would you tell me?"

"I'm just that sort of guy. And d'you know what? I want nothing for the information, except your future goodwill."

"Well, the future depends on what you do today. So, you should tell me: who would steal money from Mother Russia's Mint? Who would risk her anger?"

Mike turned to look at Natasha, dressed in a white pant suit, with black patent heels, sitting quietly in a corner, avoiding all eye contact behind her large sunglasses.

Valentin Petrov said nothing for a while.

"Hmm. Her? I will consider this allegation and see if I believe it to be true. You know, if I think you are right, someone will learn a hard lesson."

"Don't upset the apple cart, Valentin. Remember, we're all gonna leave here as winners. And that's the sign of a good deal all round. No need for nastiness."

"Maybe, but this is not up to me. For me, the price has been too high. First, we are thrown overboard as partners, then they steal money from our Mint, taking us for fools. I cannot let us be treated in this way, no? I also think that you, too, want to see me make a punishment. Because, if not, why are you so helpful? Are we such good friends? I think not."

Mike Lloyd smiled, turned and casually walked over to where Natasha was sitting. She watched his approach from behind her sunglasses. Mike sat down on a chair next to her. Her lawyer discreetly rose and moved to another part of the room.

"Well, Ms Bonnici, you've done well for yourself. Congratulations! In the next year or so, I'll be seeing you in the Forbes Rich List. Camilleri said you were smart, but I don't think you're as clever as you'd like to believe."

Natasha took off her sunglasses and started cleaning them with a white silk handkerchief. She turned to Mike and smiled sweetly, ignoring the insult.

He had not even started.

"So, tell me about your little friend, Saviour Azzopardi?"

Natasha hesitated for a second before resuming the job of cleaning the sunglasses, still saying nothing.

"I can't work out how you found out about him, but I know you did. Your father knew we were going to steal the Russians' cash, so you had Savi hatch a plan to cut in and grab a load of Libyan dinars for yourself, to further your interests here."

Natasha looked at him and said: "I've no idea what you're talking about."

"You took Savi to that little church place, locked him up, fed the dumb fuck pizza and *pastizzi*, and put the squeeze on him. He fed me a load of bullshit, making me look like a jerk, while you diverted the ship to Constanta and grabbed the cash. Savi, God bless him, switched the container codes and, in Istanbul, we picked up a metal box filled with cheap men's coats. I became a laughing stock. So far so good?"

Natasha looked across the room, avoiding eye contact, and remained silent.

"No need to confirm it. I know what you did and I'm pissed. And you know what? I'm not half as mad as my friend Petrov over there."

Mike Lloyd glanced in Valentin Petrov's direction and Natasha saw the Russian acknowledge the look. Petrov then turned towards her and his icy stare made her realise what Mike Lloyd had done.

She could not breathe for a moment and felt herself start to shake.

"You fool, Lloyd! Don't you know what those people are capable of?"

"Sure I do. I see their work on mortuary slabs from time to time."

Natasha jumped up, grabbed her bag and hurried out of the room.

AMY HALLIDAY WAS AN ACCOMPLISHED JOURNALIST; in fact, she
often thought her forensic approach to her work would have
been better suited to the courtroom rather than a newspaper.

She was back in the office where she had interviewed
Natasha Bonnici, only a week before. Amy admitted to herself
she was excited and onto a good story. She knew there was something about Natasha, or the energy deal, that had spiked American interest. Mike Lloyd, she knew, was far too big a fish to be
interested in a petty case of Maltese corruption. What it involved,
exactly, she could not quite put her finger on.

Despite Natasha's warning, Nick had agreed to the interview
with Amy Halliday, partly due to vanity, partly to raise his business profile – and partly to show Natasha he was his own man
and would not be pushed around by her.

Nick had spent an hour talking about BetHi and his CV in the
gaming industry. As far as the previous iteration of the business,
BetSlick, was concerned, he had brushed aside the subject of its
closure, saying he had learned some important lessons in staff
supervision and systems of control, but had refused to go
further.

Amy braced herself for the next part of the session.

"Who actually owns BetHi? Do you know?"

"No, not in detail, but it's privately owned."

"Do the Bonnicis own it?"

"They've got an interest, which is why Natasha took the CEO role, but I don't know the details."

"It's well known the Bonnicis have far-reaching cash-generative business interests in many parts of Europe. Do you think that's compatible with owning an i-Gaming business, which is an industry closely linked to money laundering?"

Nick laughed and slapped his knees.

"You really expect me to give an answer to that? Come on!"

"No, it's true. The Bonnicis, your friends and employers, are just about to take a huge stake in an international energy deal while, only four years ago, they were implicated in smuggling oil from Libya and your business was closed down as part of an anti-money-laundering operation. So I think I'm entitled to ask you, what's going on now?"

Nick brushed back his hair with his fingers and reclined against the sofa.

"Boy, you've got a head of steam on! I don't really know what you're driving at. I'm the CEO, I operate the day-to-day activities and report to the Board monthly. It's my job to run an efficient and compliant company and that's what I do. I can't help you with the rest of it."

"Hang on, you were the source who phoned and emailed me last year from Gibraltar, giving me information about the Russians' involvement in the Libyan oil and gas deal. Information you received from Natasha Bonnici, who wanted to switch out the Russians and bring in the Americans. I'm guessing you two have a more than a professional relationship. Am I right?"

Nick's expression froze and he felt his mouth dry up, making him incapable of speech. He hesitated for a few seconds, then jumped up and clapped his hands together.

"OK, we're done here, Amy. I've got nothing more for you. Please don't print any of this stuff – it'll only cause big trouble."

He walked to the door and held it open for her, a stiff smile on his face.

Amy gathered her bag and walked to the doorway, where she paused.

"Nick, it's not going to go away. When you're ready, ring me, please. I know I've got a story here. It's in the public interest for people to know what's going on with this gas deal in their own country. You seem like a decent type, don't let Natasha Bonnici drag you down."

After he had taken Amy to the lift and they had said curt goodbyes, Nick retired to his office and closed the door. He leaned back on his chair and put his feet on the edge of the desk, closing his eyes. He was not dozing, he was trying to decide what he should do next. His heart was beating quickly and his shirt was damp with sweat. It was only a matter of a week or two since his arrival back in Malta and already he could feel a steel trap closing in around him.

THE IMPLIED THREAT from Petrov had badly scared Natasha. She went back to her room at the hotel, as quickly as she could, alert to possible threats around every corner. Her imagination ran riot. She feared poisoned umbrellas, toxin-coated door handles, lethal coffee capsules and much worse. She knew how easy it had been for Sergio to get the toxins that had killed Salvatore. It had taken only a matter of days to arrange for a local hoodlum to plant the bomb in Signore De Luca's car. These people were very security conscious and, still, they died.

Her first call was to Sergio, who tried to calm her down. He said he would speak to Petrov and offer some form of compensation. He assured her that if it was a question of an insult, that could always be sorted with money. It would be very expensive, but perhaps a cut of the profits from the gas sales into the EU system might do it. It would have to be more than a gesture, but he agreed it had to be done and quickly.

He suggested returning the dinars, but Natasha refused. She was adamant the cash was central to making their security arrangements in Libya work.

She said Sergio should make contact through Yaroslav, now he was back in Malta from Libya, and persuade him to take a longer-term view of things. He was a negotiator by nature and the obvious intermediary to placate Petrov and his damaged pride.

Natasha fell back onto the bed, relieved that there might yet be some way out of the mess she had created. Her next call was to Assistant Commissioner Camilleri, asking him to keep a special eye on Marco. She told him that she had received some serious threats from a Russian organised crime group and feared her father might be at risk. She asked him to place security at the *castello* and to suggest a replacement for Simon, who was now working exclusively with her. The Assistant Commissioner made all the right noises, but spent some time wondering how all this could have come about without him even being aware of it.

Natasha also wondered what she could do to teach Mike Lloyd that she was not a person to be messed with. The more she thought about Lloyd, the angrier she got, until the fury became unmanageable. She had to do some exercise, shower and force herself to calm down. There were still things to do that day.

A few hours later, in the middle of the afternoon, Simon came to get her for the trip to Marsabar. She had insisted that she wanted to see the oil and gas facility and meet the people in whom she had invested so much money. She had dressed in a two-piece, full-length, embroidered black kaftan, secured at the waist by a broad silk belt. She wore a black headscarf, wrapped loosely around her head and shoulders.

Simon raised an eyebrow when she left her room and joined him in the hotel corridor. She saw him looking her up and down as he took her luggage.

"Like it?"

"Yes, very suitable. Should be interesting to see what the helicopter downdraft does to it!"

"OK. I hadn't thought of that."

The black government limousine bullied its way through the chaotic afternoon traffic on the Second Ring Road to the Tripoli National Football stadium, that doubled as the government's heliport. Simon ensured the pilot did not start the engines until Natasha was onboard and then, with an unbelievable racket, the machine rose over the port and the old town, before turning west, into the sun, towards Marsabar.

Within twenty minutes, it was touching down at the Marsabar Industrial Complex, where she was met by the Chief Executive Officer, Adel Abu Khader, who ushered her and Simon into a freezing cold, brand new Mercedes SUV for a tour of the complex.

The process was complicated and Natasha did her best to follow the workflow and ask intelligent questions. Adel Abu Khader had little idea who she was or why she was visiting. He had received a message from the Libyan Resources Corporation with instructions to host a VIP visit, but that was all. He was perplexed about why she would even be interested in the facility, but did his patronising best to push on through the tour, without so much as stopping the Mercedes.

After fifteen minutes, Natasha asked the driver to pull up and go with Simon for a walk down the two-kilometre loading jetty. Khader was taken aback, not used to being ordered about in his own facility, especially by a woman.

"So, Mr Khader, is production running smoothly now?" she asked.

"Yes." He smiled broadly. "Many thousand barrels of oil and gas. Good production numbers."

"Well, just so you know, that's because my company, MalTech Energy, pay Abdullah Belkacem to protect your oil fields and your distribution pipelines. I've bought the rights to transport my product through the VertWay pipeline and the Malta Spur. I now buy all your gas and want to buy more.

"How has it been for the last four years, with IS in Marsabar interfering in the oil fields? How were production numbers then?"

He turned to look at her, any trace of a smile gone. The hardened face of an experienced oil man showed itself.

"Not good. In fact, very bad!" He shook his head. "Very bad! Why do you come here? You know the numbers; you know what we do, you know the problems. So, you think you and Abdullah Belkacem can fix Libyan problems?"

"No, not Libyan problems, but we can fix Marsabar problems and the problems of this complex and the Waha and Sharara oil fields. We want the same thing, Mr Khader. We want the gas to flow north through VertWay. I'm paying you and Abdullah Belkacem to make sure it does."

"You're paying me?"

"Yes, I know who you are. I know about your successes in the Niger Delta and in Venezuela. You're not some lazy government lackey; you can make this complex very successful, if the politics and security issues are managed. Leave those matters to me and Abdullah Belkacem. You concentrate on pumping oil and gas, lots of it. Someone will come to see you shortly and make sure you have enough money to forget about even receiving your government salary. Forget the local bribes and dealing with the oil smugglers. It's a new world, Mr Khader. I'll send people in to help you. If you need anything, you tell me. But you won't remain in post if the numbers fall or even stay the same – then, Libyan Resources Corporation or not, you'll be out. Work hard and enjoy it. Cheat me, Mr Khader, and you'll only ever do it once. This is to say hello!"

She handed over an envelope containing fifty thousand dinars in brand new, green fifty-dinar notes.

"Now, ask your driver to take me to the American camp. There'll be some security vehicles waiting for us at the gate."

HAMRUN WAS a crowded inner-city suburb of Malta, just west of Valletta. Its narrow streets were a mix of two- and three-storey housing, food and clothing shops, hairdressers, florists and motor repair shops. In short, everything you could possibly want was tucked away in those congested back streets. If a business needed more space, or a larger access, then the front of a house was demolished and the dining room became, say, a butcher's shop or, in the case of Charles Buttigieg, a garage for the repair of marine outboard motors and mopeds.

What Buttigieg did not realise was that the competent and industrious Syrian who worked for him in the afternoons, while he rested upstairs, Jehad Al-Hafez, also used the space, and Buttigieg's tools, for the assembly of bombs. It was not a high-volume enterprise but, occasionally, local criminals or Italian Mafia types needed to settle scores and Jehad was the man to go to.

His time with the Syrian Army, in bomb disposal, had not only taught him how to clear vacated rebel towns of booby traps and roadside explosive devices, but had also given him valuable insight on how to construct the things in the first place.

It had been his handiwork that had scattered the body parts

of the US Chargé d'Affaires over St Julian's. Yaroslav had come across him through a Russian military acquaintance who knew Jehad to be a competent and discreet explosives man. The Russian had been impressed with his work in St Julian's and had no hesitation in using him again.

Yaroslav had no intention of handling the package personally, but had to visit the shop to pass on two envelopes. One contained money, the other a set of instructions and a photograph of Marco Bonnici.

Petrov did not intend to harm Natasha, as she could be valuable in the future, but Yaroslav had confirmed her father was less of a player these days and of little use, other than acting as the vehicle of their displeasure.

Once Jehad Al-Hafez had finished his shift with Charles Buttigieg, he waved a cheery good night and drove his scooter the short distance to an area of the Grand Harbour, near the defunct Marsa power station, called the South West Extension. Here disused, rusted iron structures and dilapidated buildings sat alongside moribund barges, tugs and small rusted tankers, awaiting the scrapman's blowtorch.

Across the wharf, a set of roller-shutter doors concealed a stainless-steel fabricator and pipe fitting shop, that was set into the limestone cliff face. Two old school friends had run the business for years, but were happy to undertake additional work, including the placing and detonation of explosive devices. Jehad Al-Hafez banged on the pressed aluminium slats of the roller door and, once it had squeaked and creaked upwards, handed over the envelope containing their instructions, together with half of the cash, to one of the brothers. He put the envelope with the remaining cash back into his pocket.

Having done that, he mounted the scooter and drove off to have his dinner in a small Lebanese café he knew in Hamrun.

CHAPTER 62
GEORGE ZAMMIT
THE AMERICAN CAMP, MARSABAR, LIBYA

FOLLOWING the shooting of Abu Muhammad, it had taken George and Abdullah four long days to travel west along the back roads and tracks of southern Libya, before they felt safe enough to find tarmac and turn directly north. Abdullah was in a good mood throughout the journey, telling stories of his childhood and great Berber heroes of the past. He promised that, one day, children would talk of the great Maltese hero who had helped liberate Libya and how Allah himself had taken his hand and guided the shot that miraculously destroyed the face of evil itself!

"It is true, my friend, I saw it with my own eyes! I will fight anyone who says it is not true. The shot was over two thousand metres – never has there been such a shot! And there was wind, I felt it. The air was like molasses – thick with dew – slowing the bullet, but still it flew, fast and true, then dropped like a stone, into his head. I saw it myself!"

As they drove through the desert, the distance of the shot increased, the conditions worsened, the light dimmed and the hand of Allah became ever larger. George told Abdullah the death of anybody was no laughing matter and begged him to keep this between themselves. Abdullah swore at him, saying great stories such as this had to be told and the only way to silence him would be to rip out his tongue. By the time they drove into the camp, exhausted, filthy and hungry, a crowd was awaiting their return.

Abdullah went to Floyd Hamilton and embraced him, grinning from ear to ear.

"Thank you for the planes. The sound of the bombs falling on Muhammad's camp echoed around the mountains. I will never forget it. For me, it was a beautiful moment! It made everything perfect. Now we can get to work, making Marsabar a better place."

Floyd Hamilton turned to George, who was standing next to Rania.

"So you got him? With one shot? Hell, the Maltese Machine gun goes sniper! Amazing."

George said: "He was at prayer, Floyd. I shot a man at prayer. I can't say I'm proud of it and would prefer for it not to be mentioned too widely."

"Don't worry, George. I thought about that as well when we put the plan together. I know you had right on your side, and think of the lives you've saved. I'm thinking how many American lives you've probably saved. Good shot – that's what I say!"

Then Abdullah began telling a group of sceptical US Rangers his embellished version of events, until the major called a halt.

"OK, guys, I get it! I get it! Listen, you better go clean up. You've got a private visitor tonight. We thought you'd be back sooner, so I'm sorry it's a bit of a rush. Some Maltese VIP is calling in. Mrs Belkacem is making dinner and a chopper is coming to take her back to Tripoli at 22:00 hours."

"Her? A private visitor, to see us? Who is she?" asked George.

"Ms Bonnici. You know her, don't ya? She seems like a big deal."

George sighed.

"*Mela*, she is a big deal. And coming here? She's my new boss."

George and Abdullah went down to the shower block to

clean up. George decided to put on a clean robe and cloth turban and continue dressing in the local style. His dark beard was now thick and trimmed evenly across his face. He belted the robe with a canvas web military belt on which he hung his side arm. He remembered Harley telling him that army-issue nylon belts made you sweat. George had not been on a set of scales for some months, but he could tell he had lost even more weight and was not displeased at the tanned, scarred, chiselled face that stared back at him from the showerblock mirror.

It was dark as the Mercedes and the SUVs moved down the track between the tents. The Rangers stuck their heads out of the flaps to see who the VIP might be. Abdullah and Rania went to the awning of their tent, ready to greet the arrival.

The Mercedes stopped and Natasha stepped out into the dim lighting of the camp. George hung back, letting Abdullah take centre-stage and formally welcome his guest.

Natasha looked a million dollars in her black kaftan, but later Rania whispered to George: "She looked like a wanton widow at a funeral feast!"

Abdullah stepped forward and offered his hand in greeting.
"*Salam alaikum.*"

And she responded in Arabic.
"*Wa-alaikum salam.*"

Even though they were in a military tent in the middle of hectares of rough scrub, Natasha took off her shoes before stepping onto the ground sheet.

George watched Abdullah and Rania warm to her respectful manner. Abdullah's youngest son appeared with a bowl of water and a towel over his arm. They stood in silence as Natasha rolled up her sleeves, revealing bare arms devoid of her usual expensive watch and gold jewellery, and carefully rinsed the water over both hands and wrists. She took the towel and dabbed her hands and arms dry, returning the towel to the boy with a smile.

Only after completing the ritual did she sit on the canvas chair at the flimsy folding table, buckling under a huge bowl of couscous and diced vegetables. George appeared from the shadows and she flashed him a smile and a nod. He briefly plunged his fingers into the bowl of water and shook the drops onto the floor.

Natasha enquired about Abdullah and Rania's family, their children's health and education. Rania spoke at length, in good English, something George had not heard her do before in these situations. Abdullah was happy to allow it and smiled along, interjecting to keep the conversation going.

Natasha ate the couscous with a spoon, avoiding the high-risk alternative that Abdullah employed, of scooping up the grains with bread. She waited until everybody had finished before accepting the meat in gravy. It had taken George some time to learn Berber manners for family meals, but Natasha had taken care to come well prepared.

They spoke about the shop in Birkirkara, which Natasha knew, and they joked about how a shopkeeper could suddenly become such an important person! Abdullah replied that being a shopkeeper was an important job and that, without him, no houses in Malta would ever have been built and then where would all the children have lived? The meal had been a great success. When nobody could manage any further food, Rania left a bowl of fruit on the table and took the dishes back to the cook house, to wash up, leaving Natasha with the men. Abdullah lit a cigarette and watched her through a cloud of exhaled smoke.

"So, I thank you for your visit and your respect. It is good to know we work with someone who understands our ways. I know what it is you expect of me and I will act wisely for the people I have to serve, to make sure the oil and gas goes into the refinery and under the sea to Malta. You will not be disappointed in me."

"I do hope not. George is your friend, but you must listen to him because he'll be my voice. The money for the protection of the gas is safe and George controls it. It's not your money -- do you understand that? There'll be an office in Tripoli to help us look after our financial affairs. You must respect their instructions. When you need money, you ask, you don't just take. That's how you show respect to me.

"At any time, if you decide you don't like it, you can always go back to selling brushes in Birkirkara and your family can go back to hiding in the hills. I'll find somebody else to help me and you might not like who that is. Am I clear?"

Abdullah had the fierce pride of a Berber clan leader and was not used to being spoken to like that, especially by a woman. It was his country, his people, his fight. He lit another cigarette and glared at Natasha. George looked at him and caught his eye. The questioning look on George's face told him a response was required.

Abdullah made an effort, calmed himself and visibly relaxed in his chair.

"Yes, I understand, and I thank you for the chance to right the many wrongs that have happened here. I can do that, and I can get you your oil and gas as well. George will make sure everything is good!"

Natasha heard the helicopter chattering in the distance and rose, extending her hand to Abdullah.

"*Mashallah*," he told her. "Do you know what that means? It translates as 'what Allah has willed has happened'. Every time I pray, I thank him. And now, I thank you."

Natasha smiled.

"I'm so glad we got the chance to meet and that we now understand each other. Please, have your son fetch Rania. I can't leave without thanking her for the wonderful meal."

Abdullah shouted for the boy, who flew off down the track to fetch his mother.

Natasha took George by the arm and made it look as if he was leading her out of the tent. She spoke quietly in his ear.

"Desert life seems to be suiting you, George. You look like a different man, if I may say so! But, please don't get used to this and go native on me. Remember who you work for and what's at stake. I expect to see you back in Malta next week. Please wear a suit."

With that, Natasha walked off after saying a brief farewell to Rania, who had hurried back to the tent. The whole camp heard the sound of the chopper landing, its red flashing strobe and landing lights silhouetting the small group of people waiting in the scrub. Natasha met Simon at the stairs of the helicopter to help her aboard, holding her scarf and the back of her kaftan to avoid any embarrassing moments.

Abdullah watched the helicopter go. After the downdraft had calmed and the dust settled, he turned to George.

"So, she is not married?"

"No, she's not."

"That does not surprise me. She is a mantis; she would pull the head off a husband after mating."

CHAPTER 63

MARCO BONNICI
CASTELLO BONNICI, MALTA

MARCO HAD BEEN busy with the team from the auction house, sorting and packing items from the library to go to the Bibliotheca. The dust from age-old books and the smell of leather and tobacco had irritated his airways, making him sneeze and cough. The afternoon was hot and humid. Usually, the heat did not bother him, but the library was full of still air and his long-sleeved cotton shirt was damp with sweat.

He found it hard to believe that not only would he be leaving the *castello*, but the building itself was to be sold. It looked like a consortium of hoteliers would go ahead with the purchase, and the estate, as well as the castle itself, would be changed for ever. The building would be released from its role as an ancestral family home and freed to adopt a showier, more contemporary style.

He needed some air and walked out onto the terrace, to take in the view over St Paul's and beyond the escarpments, to the island of Gozo. As the time for his departure drew nearer, he was conscious of putting together a bank of memories: of the *castello*, of Malta and the people who had been around him here for so many years. It was something he could draw on in the future, when the *castello* was a hotel, spa and nine-hole golf course, and his terrace was littered with cheap metal tables, sporting branded parasols.

Sergio had been staying for over a week now, and was sitting on the terrace, working on his laptop, a neglected beer beside him. The pair had reconciled and enjoyed a few evenings to themselves, bringing each other up to date on what had been happening in their respective lives. It had not taken them long to re-establish the friendship that had endured for so many years.

Eventually, Sergio announced he needed cigarettes and rose from his chair, cracking his knuckles and stretching his arms high above his head.

"I do enjoy it here. I can't bear to think of this place not being yours! I'll miss it. I suppose I'll have to go back to Milan in a day or so, but thank you, as always, for your hospitality."

He looked at Marco.

"You know I think of us as brothers? We were twenty years old when we first met. D'you remember that day on Zio Nico's terrace? It's good to be back with you. You and I being apart was one of the hardest things about the last few years."

Marco laughed.

"Stop it, Sergio, or next you will start weeping. Go, get some cigarettes."

Marco reached into his pocket and threw him the keys to the white Range Rover. "If you are passing the garage, do me a favour and put some petrol in it, will you? It's running on fumes."

Sergio nodded and went out to the garages to find his friend's white Range Rover, whistling to himself as he went.

Marco went back to the library and found himself browsing through an original 1796 manuscript of the first ever Maltese-Latin-Italian dictionary, written by the father of the Maltese language, Mikiel Anton Vassalli.

He was soon immersed in the book, but raised his head when he heard a dull crump from outside on the road. He thought little of it and resumed his reading until Katia came dashing in, white-faced. The fact she said nothing but stood staring at him, speechless, told him something terrible had happened.

Marco dropped the priceless manuscript, ran out of the front door and through the open gates. In the ditch on the left-hand side of the road, totally engulfed in flames and blazing furiously, was the Range Rover. Marco went round to the driver's side of the vehicle, feeling the intense heat. He raised his arms to protect his face, but the hairs on his arms singed and he drew back a step or two, realising going any nearer to the inferno was futile. To his horror, he saw a blackened shape, slumped over the wheel, rocking gently back and forth as the flames sucked out whatever combustible fuel there was left in Sergio's body.

Still shaking, Marco pulled out his phone and rang Camilleri. He asked for help in finding Natasha, as soon as possible. Camilleri told him that he was on his way, but Natasha was in Libya, in the middle of the desert somewhere. He would contact her later, at her hotel.

Eventually, the Civil Protection teams extinguished the flames, took the shell of the car away. But not before the paramedics had gingerly removed what was left of Sergio's body. Camilleri supervised the process and, once the ambulance had disappeared down the hill, went into the *castello* to find Marco, who was sitting in the study with a brandy in his hand. Camilleri found the decanter and poured himself a drink.

"I have never seen you drink before," said Marco.

"I have never had a day like this before. I am sorry, Marco. This is a terrible thing. Especially cruel after his recent reappearance.

"I do not wish to state the obvious, but you do realise that little present was meant for you? Natasha rang me only hours ago. She said there was trouble brewing with our Russian friends. She asked me to put a guard on the *castello* and find you a new head of security. I am sorry, the warning came too late. Do you know what this is all about?"

Marco was slumped in his chair, the balloon of brandy cradled in both hands.

"I can guess. She stole the Russians' money, double crossed the Americans and got to their asset, Saviour Azzopardi. Somehow, the Russians have discovered her involvement."

"Yes, so I gathered. I assume she was also involved in the reorganisation of affairs in Milan?"

"I think that was mostly Sergio, but she was involved, yes."

"I cannot protect her if she carries on like this, Marco. She tells me nothing and then expects me to clean up her messes. She is out of control. She needs speaking to."

"Then you will have to redefine your relationship with her, Gerald. She does not listen to me anymore."

Gerald Camilleri did not do full on anger. He did not shout and rage, but developed deep and visceral hatreds that smouldered with all the intensity of hot coals. At that moment, this was the feeling he felt for Petrov, Yaroslav, and all things Russian. In fact, he could easily have let it spread to the ill-mannered Mike Lloyd, but subconsciously he realised he had to contain the parameters of his anger, to concentrate it, focusing it on the people who deserved to feel it the most.

Camilleri telephoned his office and the Pulizija posts at the airport and ferry terminals. He knew Valentin Petrov was in Libya, Natasha had told him as much. That left Yaroslav Bukov. This had to be his work. Malta was a small island, with complex webs of loyalties, stretching across families and communities. This could make police work infuriatingly difficult but, on this occasion, it could work to his benefit; there would be no vows of silence to protect a murdering Russian FSB officer.

He ordered calls to be made to the hotels, the casinos and the better restaurants. He wanted forty-eight hours of total dedication to finding Yaroslav Bukov. Nothing less. Every hooligan, miscreant, career criminal, was to be bullied and harangued. They were to be beaten, bribed, granted favours … whatever they wanted. Camilleri wanted Yaroslav Bukov and he gave himself just forty-eight hours to find him.

There were not many people in Malta who knew how to put a car bomb together and the name of Jehad Al-Hafez was soon mentioned. The Rapid Intervention Squad blocked both ends of the street where Buttigieg's Garage was situated. They entered, crashing back the doors, wearing full riot gear, guns pointing. Jehad was changing the fuel pump on a Honda outboard engine.

He was promised immunity and freedom from arrest, in exchange for information. He quickly told them what he knew and mentally started planning to leave the island as soon as he could. They demanded to see the papers and the cash Yaroslav had left in payment. Jehad had handed the instruction papers over to the brothers at the docks, but gave the Pulizija what little there was left of the cash in the second envelope.

Yaroslav's one mistake had been to use an envelope from the stock of stationery left on the dresser in his hotel room. How such an experienced professional failed to notice the name of the hotel on the back of the envelope was a mystery Camilleri could not fathom.

SAVI AND DANKA were in the middle of a two-player mission on the latest *Call of Duty* game, enjoying a couple of cans of lager and the excitement of the action. It was mid-afternoon and Danka was relaxing before the after-work crowd arrived for the early-evening sessions at the gym. She still had her training gear on from the morning sessions and her tattooed arms rippled with muscle from six hours a day of strenuous upper-body exercise.

Savi had been staying with her for the last few weeks and the pair had started to enjoy each other's company. Danka saw Savi as an overgrown child, the antithesis of the muscle-bound, macho types she worked with at the gym. He sometimes joined her classes in the studio and greatly amused Danka with his half-hearted attempts at working out. He always chose the heaviest kettlebells and desperately tried to follow the exercises, his face twisted in pain as his skinny white arms strained and heaved, while Danka shouted instructions and counted repetitions. She noted he had showed no sign of making any moves to leave so far and Simon had merely shrugged his shoulders when she asked him what plans he had for the boy.

Savi suddenly paused the computer game and turned on the

sofa to look at the door, listening intently. He put his finger to his lips.

"Did you hear that? There's someone shuffling around outside."

The pair of them stopped and listened. There was nothing audible, until somebody tapped lightly on the door. They glanced at each other and Danka said, "Go see who it is."

She picked up a three-kilogram dumbbell that lay next to her on the sofa and absent-mindedly began doing some bicep curls.

Savi had barely turned the latch when *Il-Barri* shoulder-charged through the doorway and stumbled into the room, knocking Savi backwards off his feet. The smell of gutted fish and sweat followed him. He snorted at Danka and grunted "Stay!" while pulling a short knife from the back of his jeans. Savi scurried across the floor towards Danka, on his hands and feet, like an upside-down crab, as *Il-Barri* lumbered towards him, holding the knife dagger-style.

What the hitman had not taken into account was that Danka was not the sort of woman to shy away from a fight. With a roar, she leaped up from the sofa and collided with the brute, swinging the weighty dumbbell against the side of his head. Dazed and semi-conscious, he lay on the floor, wondering what had hit him.

Danka stood over him, dumbbell raised, daring him to make another move.

Gathering such courage as he had, Savi approached and gave *Il-Barri* a tentative kick in the pelvis then quickly stepped back. Danka took two handfuls of *Il-Barri*'s denim jacket and heaved him to his feet, putting one hand tight to his throat. He did not look at her but stared beyond her, off into the middle distance. She noticed, with disgust, the glistening fish scales in his short, sweat-plastered hair.

She said to him: "You get out of here, now! If you think I'm tough, you wait till you see my boyfriend. You're lucky he's not here, he would've killed you! Now go. And if I see you here again, I'll make an even bigger fool out of you."

Savi added from a fair distance away: "Yeah, you go. Fuck off or there'll be more trouble."

Danka bundled him out of the door and double locked it, propping a dining chair against the handle.

Savi sat back down on the sofa and picked up the X-Box controller, saying: "Phew, what the hell did he want? We showed him – yeah? So, what's his problem? You owe him some money or something?"

Danka replied, "Fun's over, Savi. You'd better think about finding somewhere safe to hide. That guy was serious and it was you he was after."

He paused the game and looked at her.

"Shit, you think so? What've I done?" He ran his fingers through his lank, stringy hair. "I suppose I do know what it's all about. There was this woman … we had a bit of a thing. She's just mad I skipped off and left her without a goodbye or anything. Are all women like that?"

Danka looked at him for a moment, in disbelief.

"You can't be serious?"

Savi played his game for a few seconds, then hit pause again.

"You know, I've been giving the future a lot of thought. It's time for me to make some big moves. I've been thinking about a university in England. There's a computer-science course that looks kinda cool. I've got money put by and the CIA guy promised me five grand. It's waiting for me at the embassy and now, I suppose, all this trouble should give me the motivation."

"Savi, you don't really think they're going to hand over five thousand dollars to you, after what you did to them, do you?"

He looked at her for a moment and shrugged.

"Yeah, suppose you're right, they're probably pissed off with me. Just hoped he might … you know? Anyway, I can always make some cash online. I'll get my shit together and move out. I don't want to be a hassle to you guys – and I definitely don't want to be here by myself, in case he comes back, you know? Next time, I might not be able to hold back and someone could get hurt.

"Can you ask Simon to come down? I'd like to say thanks to him as well, for sorting me out. I think it's going to be all good from now on."

It was a great plan, but there was a problem with it. In fact, there were quite a few problems with it. Savi had left school when he was sixteen. In the May he was due to sit his 'O' levels, Rockstar Games were stupid enough to release *Red Dead Redemption*. What could he do? It took him the full two weeks of the exam timetable to complete the game. He never did return to school and had no qualifications. Still, he would work something out.

Danka went across the room to a drawer in a sideboard and took out a white A5 envelope.

"Before you go, Simon said you might find this useful."

"What's that?"

"Your passport, your ID card and two grand of Simon's own money, to help you on your way."

"Oh, yeah! Cool. Thanks a lot. No hurry though, is there?"

CHAPTER 65

MIKE LLOYD
EMBASSY OF THE UNITED STATES, MALTA

TWO MONTHS LATER

IT WAS JUST into the New Year and unseasonably warm when, for the second time in his life, George found himself being honoured with a medal for his courage and bravery. George, Marianna, Denzel and Gina, plus her fiancé Giorgio, were seated in the front row of the huge Reception Room of the purpose-built US Embassy, on land adjacent to the old World War II airfield at Ta'Qali. George was to be formally presented with the Army Distinguished Service Cross, the highest honour awarded to a non-US Citizen.

The event was not as grand as the presentation in the Throne Room of the Grandmaster's Palace in Valletta, where he had received his first medal, four years ago, but Marianna and Gina had behaved as if they were guests of honour at a White House reception. The purchase of new hats, shoes and handbags had been endlessly debated, and finally, the ladies had decided they needed to visit the outlets of Catania, in Sicily, to find suitable outfits. Denzel, meanwhile, looked smart in his Pulizija dress uniform.

The top people from the Embassy were present and they had

brought in Major Floyd Hamilton and, for some reason, Sergeant Mike Barrasso, from the Al-Udeid desert training camp. The sergeant looked over at George, all buffed up with his new suit and shiny beard. He caught George's eye and, while his poker face remained unchanged, gave him the slightest of winks.

The Maltese government was represented by the Deputy Prime Minister, the defence minister and numerous other officials, enough to fill one side of the hall. American diplomats in suits, led by Mike Lloyd, and military representatives in uniform, took up the other side of the aisle. The new Chargé d'Affaires conducted the ceremony and started by praising George's work, as a former police officer, in responding to the bomb attack on his predecessor.

The story of Abu Muhammad's IS assault on the airfield was recounted, as was George's heroic one-man defence of the terminal, a selfless stand that put his life in mortal danger but saved many Americans. At that point, the Chargé d'Affaires handed the podium over to an unsmiling Sergeant Barrasso who explained that George had been a successful candidate on his Desert Warfare and Survival course. His performance on the shooting range had been exceptional and he had acquired all the skills necessary to execute missions in a hostile desert environment.

George could not help but lower his head to hide a smile as he remembered the disastrous weeks he had spent being shouted at and abused by this man. When the sergeant stiffly left the podium, face expressionless, to come and shake George's hand, he smiled broadly while Barrasso's mouth twitched.

George was now a civilian and Head of Libyan Relations for MalTech Energy, so he wore his new blue business suit, with his police medals pinned to his left breast. He sported a brilliant white new tooth, to replace the one lost in the beating at the air terminal, implanted at the cost of the Maltese government. His beard and hair were trimmed and oiled, in the style Abdullah favoured. Rania and Marianna had both told him, in no uncertain terms, it would be a shame if his waistline went back to how it had been before his desert adventures.

On his return to Malta, he and Marianna had cleared out his old clothes and George had joined her and Gina on the shopping trip to Catania, where they had fussed around him, putting together a new wardrobe of slim-fitting suits and on-trend casual clothes. When Denzel saw the purchases, he told his father that he looked like a nineteen nineties golfer!

Once the ceremony had finished and an excited Marianna had sat down to fan her flushed face, the first people to approach him were Barrasso and Floyd Hamilton, the pair laughing with each other. Barrasso, still grinning, came up close and looked around to make sure nobody was listening.

"Zammit, you're a piece of work! I was telling the major here what a useless piece of crap you were and how I wanted to send you home! Then, I get this call about you getting the ADSC and I had to do that video. You know, that medal says 'For Valour'! I say, no way, he's a pussy! Now, the major tells me, not only are you the Maltese Machine gun," he wrapped the phrase in inverted commas by flicking the first two fingers of each hand in front of him, "but you took out a Mooj at one thousand metres. That true? That's some shot!"

George shuffled uncomfortably.

"I can't deny I did it, but I never thought it would happen. I'm not sure I could do it again!"

The sergeant grinned and offered his hand.

"Well, you did it when it counted, buddy. Put it there, Zammit! But," he put his face close to George's ear and glanced around again, to make sure they could not be overheard, "I'll tell you now, if I ever see you lining up for one of my courses again, I swear, I'll fucking kill you myself!"

Barrasso and the major giggled like schoolboys.

George joined in the laughter, but his attention was diverted. He looked over towards the buffet table, where Marianna and Gina were enthusiastically engaged in conversation with the

Chargé d'Affaires and some Maltese government ministers. He realised he had better check to make sure his wife was not getting too carried away by the occasion.

As he approached, he heard her saying: "I just love America – all that countryside. It's very like Malta, from what I've seen, which is only on the television, of course."

The group laughed kindly and the Chargé d'Affaires said: "Well, when you come to visit, and I hope you do, you'll find America a whole lot bigger than Malta, that I guarantee."

George arrived just in time to divert the chat and steer Marianna and Gina away from the buffet table. Gina took her father's arm.

"Dad, he's very nice, the man in 'charge of the affairs'. He told us we should look him up when we visit. Do you think we can go to America? Do you know where he lives?"

"Let's start with Spain and we'll take it from there, don't you think?"

Marianna and Gina were glowing from all the attention, the occasion and the chance to parade in their new outfits. George smiled to see them so happy. He had been away for a long time and, now that he was making regular trips to Libya, it felt good to be home and see them happy, all together as a family.

In the corner, Mike Lloyd was talking quietly and earnestly to Gerald Camilleri, who subtly beckoned George over. George sighed.

"I was talking to Mike about that very unfortunate car bomb that killed your new employer's associate."

"*Mela*, but it wasn't unfortunate, was it? It was murder."

Mike Lloyd glared at George.

"Precipitated by the theft of a shit load of money by your new boss!"

Camilleri sighed and shook his head.

"Nothing to be gained by going down that road again, Mike."

"Well, how about my new posting then? Lima! What a shithouse! To avoid me 'rubbing certain people up the wrong way', I was told. That your doing, Gerald? Or maybe Lady Natasha whispered in the State Department's ear? Langley think it's hilarious. Serves me right for doing an off the books mission. Doesn't look good on my record, boys. Thanks!"

George could not help himself from replying.

"We all know who goes round whispering in people's ears, don't we, Mr Lloyd? That was what got Sergio Rossi killed, and remember who the actual target was! So, no, as far as my employer is concerned, Lima isn't far enough away for you. It's just a shame we couldn't get you to Lagos!"

Camilleri glared at George.

"That is enough!"

George reined himself in.

"Oh, I'm sorry, Gerald. Tell me, when did I start working for you again?"

Satisfied the point had been made and feeling pleased with himself, George turned and walked off to round up the family. He had booked a table for a late lunch at a restaurant overlooking Spinola Bay and his rumbling stomach told him to get out quickly, otherwise he would be at the buffet table and his new waistline would be under serious threat!

Camilleri had picked up Yaroslav Bukov at his hotel in St George's Bay, just as he was checking out. Moments later he would have been whisked off to the protection of the Russian Embassy, to await a flight back to Moscow, via Vienna.

As Yaroslav languished in Corradino Correctional Facility, a Victorian hell-hole of a jail, near the docks, Camilleri had telephoned Valentin Petrov, who took the call whilst at the prestigious White Rabbit restaurant, on the sixteenth floor of the Smolensky Passazh, in central Moscow. Petrov was being entertained by visitors from Baku and the conversation was just getting interesting, so he wanted to wrap things up quickly and get back to the table.

"Make it quick, Assistant Commissioner, it's not every day a humble government servant gets to take lunch at the White Rabbit."

"A deal, Mr Petrov, one in everybody's interest. Leave the Bonnicis alone. You have spilled blood, that is enough. This needs to end. If you agree, I will put Mr Bukov back on the next plane and relations between Malta and Moscow can continue as before while you can get back to your lunch.

"Say 'no' and I will bring Mr Bukov to trial and drag out the whole sorry mess, for the delight of the international press. I have nothing to lose. I can also inform you the government of the Republic of Malta will, as a matter of course, refuse permission for any of your naval vessels to refuel in Maltese territorial waters and we will embargo any bunkering vessels from refuelling on the Hurds Bank shallows."

That was a real threat. There were limited places the Russian Navy could refuel in the Mediterranean and, as Malta was a non-aligned country and not a member of NATO, it had, on occasion been able to help them out discreetly.

There was a pause as Petrov lit a cigarette and inhaled deeply. Camilleri could almost hear his thought processes at work and smiled to himself. There was only one sensible answer.

"Put him on a plane. You have your deal. Tell the Bonnicis never to visit Moscow."

"I doubt it is in their plans, but thank you. And enjoy your lunch."

TWELVE MONTHS LATER

NATASHA BONNICI WAS TIRED. It had been a long and difficult year, during which she had achieved all her goals and more besides. She was still young, fabulously successful, publicly feted and potentially richer than Forbes, or any of the other wealth lists, could ever guess. She had become the face of the European business world and it was only shortage of time that stopped her from capitalising on all the opportunities presented to her.

MalTech Energy was going from strength to strength and, soon, the VertWay spur would trigger the start of a five-year project to convert every home in Malta to natural gas. The Family's acquisitions in the Maltese construction sector meant there were few infrastructure projects in which they did not have a direct interest.

The on-sale of gas to the European distributors had been negotiated by Salvatore before his death, and revenues would soon start to flow. The fact that the Family had acquired large stakes in the distributors themselves meant that they had a double benefit from the arrangements!

The situation in western Libya was stable and Abdullah

Belkacem had proved to be a reliable partner, securing the supply from the on-shore oil and gas fields, whilst ensuring political stability through his control of the southern borders by a well-funded militia that maintained order. The port of Marsabar had been expanded and oil was being tankered out of the refinery in unprecedented volumes.

The success of the Tuareg in policing Libya's southern borders had led to a decrease in the numbers of migrants making the perilous journey through Libya to Europe. But, just as water finds its own course, so the traffic from Tunisia and Morocco had increased and the spotlight had noow fallen on Spain, rather than Malta or Italy.

Adel Abu Khader, at the Marsabar Industrial Complex, had proved himself to be an astute operator and, as promised, had improved production markedly and made himself rich in the process. In a country, and an industry, renowned for corruption, Khader had told Natasha she could count on his honesty, if she gave him what he asked for. She had recognised that he was as good as his word and, on several occasions, George had been required to authorise the transfer of large amounts of money to Khader's new account with Antalya Bank's branch in Cyprus. It did not take the Family long to make the Libyan Resources Corporation an offer that they could not refuse for the whole of the Marsabar refinery and industrial complex

She was returning from Milan to Malta, after a meeting with the new Family Council, on the Dassault Falcon jet, a luxury, but one she thought she deserved. As with all new groupings, there had been arguments and egotistical tantrums from some members, so Natasha had had to stamp her authority on proceedings,

She often wondered why men – it was always men – had to be so difficult. She had never expected to find friends or allies on the Council and had understood it would take time to build trust and for everybody to take the measure of her. Sergio was dead and Marco had been as good as his word, formally retiring from the Family. She spent a lot of time alone or travelling these days.

In Malta, there was Refalo who, in fairness, helped manage the rat's nest that was the MalTech Energy Board, while in Milan, strictly behind her back, she was called the 'Black Spinster' who, they said, had single-handedly wiped out the Wise Men, bombed her uncle's car and exiled her father, to complete her rise to absolute power. If that was how they saw it, then Natasha was happy to let them believe it.

The only person she had in her life, with whom she could relax and be herself, was Nick, and even he kept her at a distance. She had only managed to lure him to a hotel room once, since his arrival back on the island. Even then, she had to break down his resistance with expensive champagne and Jack Daniel's. It did not matter; the sex had not been great, as he had been too drunk. She had stayed awake and watched him sleep, stroking his head, while he snored gently into his pillow.

Simon, Natasha's head of security, had hated Nick Walker since he had tricked him at the Gammarth Marina in Tunis, while on the run in Marco's stolen boat several years earlier. He was aware that Natasha was still fond of the man, so it had given him some satisfaction to mention casually to her that her reluctant beau had been seen having dinner with Amy Halliday, at the Waterfront in Valletta. He had added that he had been told they seemed very cosy together.

Natasha had thought nothing of it at first, but like all worms, it started to grow and grow, twisting itself around inside her stomach. She could not help herself; she had never known jealousy before and, over the course of a week, it had begun to consume her. She found herself dwelling on why Nick would prefer a saggy-breasted older woman, like Amy Halliday, to her.

Eventually, she could stand it no longer and asked Simon to follow Nick, to see if there was anything in the relationship. Simon had gone to the basement of the BetSlick offices and it had been easy enough to put a tracker on Nick's car. He did not go to

Amy's apartment and she did not go to his. He had told Natasha, in passing, that Amy was divorced and lived by herself in a new-build apartment, overlooking the entrance to Marsamxett Harbour. That should have satisfied her, but the poisonous thoughts continued.

When she was alone in the apartment in Milan, or at her flat in Portomaso, she would torture herself with visions of Nick and Amy in a hotel somewhere, in each other's arms, making love, holding one another, night after night. She imagined Amy stroking his smooth pale body and running her fingers through his fine blond hair. It was ridiculous, Natasha knew, but she could not stop the thoughts and it was driving her mad.

She started to think how easy it would be to get rid of Amy, how Nick would turn to Natasha for comfort as he mourned her passing. Natasha even went as far as finding Danylo's phone number and ringing him. He was the Ukrainian who had supplied the ricin that had killed Salvatore. He knew exactly who Natasha was and assured her, if she wanted to do business, he was happy to help. It was only Nick calling, to arrange to meet with her, that saved Natasha from ordering the poison.

Nick had invited her to a small underground bar in Valletta, famous for its cocktails and whisky collection. She was nervous and dreaded what he might say to her. She fussed with her hair, her outfit, her makeup and, at one point, was horrified to realise she might actually be late! What if she turned up and he had been and gone?

She need not have worried. As usual, when she had a meeting, she was punctual. Within minutes, Nick started telling her about Amy and relief flooded through Natasha, to the extent that she was nearly tearful.

"Listen, I've had a couple of dinners with that journalist over the last few months, Amy Halliday – you remember her?"

Natasha remembered her. She had thought of nobody else for weeks.

"It's pretty clear she's out to get you. She's digging around for information and has somehow found out about what happened between us in the villa."

"What? When you brained me with that vase and stole my jewellery and Dad's boat?"

"Oh, please, let's not go through all that again."

She laughed and reached across the table, taking his hand.

"I said there was nothing to it – but she's onto you. She says there's something 'off' about you popping up from nowhere to become one of the richest people in Malta, if not Europe, when a few months ago, nobody outside the gaming industry had even heard of you.

"She also thinks it's weird that BetSlick was closed down due to allegations of money laundering, with the Bonnici name being mentioned, then, weeks later, BetHi pops up with a Bonnici sitting in the big chair! She asked me how I felt about it?"

"She's still banging on about that? What did you say?"

"I said I needed a new challenge; the time was right for me to leave Malta, so I took an opportunity offered to me in Gib.

"Anyway what do you want me to do about Amy now? Keep having the occasional meet, to see where she's at, or just drop it?"

Natasha pulled on his arm, dragging him across the table towards her.

"I don't care either way, Nick. I don't want to have to get you drunk, every time I want to go to bed with you. So forget that old bitch -- I need you to come with me, now."

Nick was bemused.

"I thought we said …"

"Right now, I don't care what we said. Just come with me!"

CHAPTER 67
MARCO BONNICI

ZLATIBOR ESTATE, UŽICE, WESTERN SERBIA

To THE WEST of the market town of Užice, held tight in the valley of the Đetinja river, are the hills of Zlatibor. The region has high mountains, pine forests and alpine meadows that extend westward, all the way to the border of Bosnia and Herzegovina. The sub-alpine climate and the fact it is only a five-hour drive from Belgrade, mean visitors arrive here each summer, to escape the hot, muggy air of the capital.

After treeless Malta, Marco revelled in the cool, minty-smelling coniferous forests that covered the one thousand metre high plateau. There were a hundred days a year here when the high ground was covered in snow, which provided a new aspect to his life. His wardrobe was now filled with fleeces, expensive overcoats of breathable fabrics, as well as technical boots with high ankles and fancy lacing.

The land's limestone base was familiar to him but, rather than the stripped, pitted rock surfaces of Malta, here there was topsoil, foliage and water courses. He had caves, ravines and underground rivers that ran across his estate. During the winter months, he had set himself the task of designing a detailed tourist map of the area, to help visitors navigate and fully appreciate the landscaped features. He had become engrossed in the project; a seemingly simple ambition that had become a major undertaking.

He had a basic plan of the estate, but needed to develop the way the elevations, gradients and depressions were portrayed. He used an engraver's pen to draw the hachures, the parallel lines used in hill-shading on maps, their closeness indicating the steepness of gradients. He carefully washed areas of the map different shades of green or brown, to represent lower- and higher-lying ground. Benchmarks and features were identified and marked. His plantings were also identified and an index, written in a calligraphy font on a side box, described the most notable features. He realised that, given the size of the estate and the variety of the landscape, he had enough work ahead of him to see him through to the spring.

He had tried to fill his time, to be busy and not to brood. His departure from Malta had been a rushed and unpleasant affair. Camilleri had assured him an accommodation had been reached with Petrov so he no longer needed to be looking over his shoulder. He had met once more with Nick and reminded him to keep an eye on Natasha and ring him if he ever felt she was in trouble. Nick had wisely said that Natasha would probably always be on the margin of trouble, but never in it. Marco had only met with her once since the bombing, at Sergio's funeral. She had phoned him after the bomb and Marco, in a state of shock, had assured her he was all right. In fact, as he recovered his senses, he had realised he was very far from being all right.

Sergio's ex-wife had been indifferent to the news of his death. As far as she was concerned, he was already dead to her. The funeral they had endured, six months ago, was quite enough for a man such as him. She did politely enquire whether anything of value had been found that properly belonged in his estate.

Sergio Rossi's second burial was held on a stinking hot morning at the Neo-Gothic Santa Maria Addolorata Cemetery, on the outskirts of Valletta. Monumental tombs and family crypts lined the hillside as far as the chapel at the top of the hill. Addolorata was a true Gothic city of the dead. Marco had bought a suitably large and extravagant tombstone, surrounded by statues of angels, in bronze and marble. Natasha thought the flashy Sicilian would have appreciated the memorial. It had occurred to her that there could not have been too many people at rest in Addolorata who also had a similarly ornate tomb in the Cimitero Monumentale, in Milan!

Marco, Natasha, Camilleri, Nick, Katia and some of the *castello* staff had attended the funeral and there was no reception afterwards. To Marco's surprise, Sergio's daughter had turned up; a plump, busty young woman, with heavy eye makeup, tight black clothing and an air of confidence beyond her eighteen years. Natasha had spoken to her, but Marco only had the chance for the briefest of words, before she told him she did not blame him for what had happened and that she hoped this was the last funeral she would have to attend for her father – two were sufficient for anybody. She had then closed down the conversation, climbed into a waiting car and mysteriously disappeared. Marco had stayed behind at the grave and, as the others drifted off, removing their jackets and fanning themselves in the noon heat, Natasha chose that moment to approach her father.

"When do you go?"

"Soon."

"I'm sorry for this. I never …"

"No, you did not think, did you?" Marco snapped. "You can add Sergio Rossi to the list of people who have died as a result of your behaviour. I never thought I would have a murderer for a daughter."

He looked at her with resignation in his eyes.

"You have what you want now, all of it. It should have been me in that hole, not him. How would you feel then? Probably no different to how you feel now. You are cold and calculating. I am sorry for you. Now, go away and leave me alone. You have broken my heart too many times."

Natasha left Addolorata without another word, her face white and pinched.

Simon had found out the times of the two-hour flight from Malta to Belgrade and told her the date on which Marco had reserved a seat. On the morning of his departure, she had driven to the viewing layby on the road that ran around the airport perimeter, and had sat in her car, watching, as Marco's plane slowly processed from the apron to the end of the runway and then, its engines racing, accelerated until it rose and swept away, over her head.

She had briefly felt a sense of loss, but it was a shallow emotion, not one that burned away inside her, like the jealousy she had felt for Amy Halliday. She wondered if she would ever see her father again, whether he would someday return to Malta. The sale of the *castello* had gone through and Marco had been pleased at the speed with which the transaction had completed and at the price that had been achieved. He had also been surprised that the purchaser had offered to buy the entire contents apart from the valuable antiques he had already sold.

The eventual purchaser turned out not to be the consortium of hoteliers he had expected.

Natasha had set up a company, owned by an offshore trust, to buy it. She could not let part of her past disappear. It was the only remaining link she had to her father and her childhood. The plans to lease the estate lands to the famers and establish co-operatives went ahead and Natasha retained Katia. The *castello* remained cared for, ready for Marco's return, should he ever choose to come home.

CHAPTER 68

GEORGE ZAMMIT
ABDULLAH'S FARMHOUSE, MARSABAR, LIBYA

It had taken a little time, but the farmhouse was eventually finished and it was beautiful beyond Rania's wildest dreams. Not only was there air conditioning in some of the rooms and a small pool for the children, but the tiled Italian showers and modern fitted kitchen were of a style and quality rarely seen outside the cities. Abdullah had urged caution.

"We do not want to make the family jealous and the neighbours covetous!"

But it was too late for that!

Abdullah had insisted on full terraces around the outside of the house, so they could move their seats around to enjoy the morning, afternoon and evening, while keeping a watchful eye on anyone who came within two kilometres. The building had a full range of security features and stood inside a secure perimeter, with a gate house and twenty-four-hour guards.

Abdullah had never forgotten the view from the hill to the south, over five years ago now, when he had seen the smoke rising from his brother's burning Mercedes and had to stand by and watch his home being violated by Abu Muhammad, while Rania and the children had scurried like rats through the escape tunnel. He would do everything he could to ensure nothing like that ever happened again. But he also understood that in this life there are no guarantees; Allah had a plan for everybody.

He and George were lounging in two deep wicker armchairs, on the western side of the house, watching the sun set while they drank tea. The children were enjoying the last of the evening. Abdullah's eldest son, Jamal, was kicking a football around with a group of local kids, who arrived every day, after school to swim in the pool and play football on the small Astroturf pitch Abdullah had laid behind the house, for exactly one hour and thirty minutes. At the end of the allotted time, the minibus that had, in earlier years, transported sub-Saharan migrants across Libya's deserts to Abdullah's compounds by the coast, collected the children and took them home. Jamal then had to do school-work. Abdullah amused George with his lectures on the virtues of education.

George came to Libya every two weeks and spent at least two days with Abdullah and two days in Tripoli, at the MalTech Energy offices. The minute he arrived in Tripoli he would change into a long, cotton, hooded *djellaba* and open-toed sandals. In town, he would wear the traditional Berber flat cap, the *shashiyah*, but when he went into the country, he would bind his head in a Tuareg *cheche*.

Abdullah was looking at George and examining his dress. He could not fault it – he did not look like a tourist or a European in fancy dress – but he did wonder why his friend bothered.

"Well, of course, it's more comfortable and when I come here, I prefer to look like a Libyan and think like a Berber. If people see me in a Western business suit, will I see all I need to see, or will they hide things from me? Looking like this, they'll think I am just another Berber!"

"No, my brother, you are wrong. Everybody knows who you are. You see nothing unless I want you to see it! Everything else, I tell them to hide!"

They laughed.

"There's something about wearing these clothes that makes

me feel as though I belong here. I'm not just George Zammit, former policeman, but George Zammit, Berber. Is that possible? Can I be Maltese and also come here, put on a *djellaba* and become a different man?"

"Yes, it is possible. Because I know this man! In Malta, the lady wife is the boss and he must do her bidding and speak only when spoken to. The old policeman, Camilleri, tricks and deceives him. Now, he is slave to the Lady Mantis and must be watchful, otherwise she will pull off his head!"

"Don't call her that! She's my boss," George laughed.

"Ah! But, here, he is different. He is brave and courageous; he can shoot a man at three thousand metres. He can tear a militia of Beards to pieces with any weapon you give him – a technical with cannon or a pistol. He is a soldier, with many medals for his bravery!"

Abdullah tapped his nose with his forefinger.

"I have seen this man do all this, with these eyes!"

George smiled at his antics.

"Be quiet! You don't know what you're saying."

Abdullah pointed two fingers towards his eyes.

"These eyes do not lie!"

"Drink your tea."

Abdullah laughed along with him.

"At least the lady wife is kind, forgiving and is a good cook. Unlike the Lady Natasha. So how long will you work for the mantis?"

"Hmm. I don't know. Until you've spent all the money, I suppose."

"So that could be a long time? That is good. Maverick needs his Goose." Abdullah looked at George, slyly.

"So does the Lady Mantis make you rich? You have to look after yourself. The Prophet said it is a duty to seek lawful earnings. He is never wrong. May peace be upon Him."

George looked across the coastal plain, towards the refinery some ten kilometres away. The flare stack glowed with an orange corona from the burning gases and the waste white steam rose vertically into the still evening sky.

"*Mela*, I'm as rich as a policeman could ever be, which is good, and despite your efforts to put me in an early grave, I'm still alive, which is even better. I take every day as it comes. Marianna is content, for the time being, and the children are healthy and happy. Who could wish for more?"

"My friend is always wise. May Allah always bless you with health and happiness."

Abdullah poured more green tea into the glasses and heaped his with three spoons of sugar. George smiled, refusing the sugar, patting his newly flat stomach.

He did not know how being with MalTech Energy would work out for him in the long term; at the moment, he was happy to be helping Abdullah. In addition to his substantial salary, Natasha had promised him a large bonus, conditional on him staying for two years, to see the 'project' established. George planned to put the cash to one side and make sure Marianna did not find it! When the time was right, it would be enough to buy a good-sized apartment for Denzel and one for Gina.

Evening was coming and the sparse fields were lit ßby a low sun. In the distance, Marsabar's dogs barked and howled the news of the day to each other.

George had been called upon to endure the privations of captivity. He had suffered beatings and illness. There had been no choice but to be subjected to periods of fear and panic. He had lost the security and comfort of his home and family. Out of it all, the loneliness had been the hardest thing to bear. None of what had happened to him was his choice or by his design.

At home, he was sent out for shopping. Marianna and Gina chided him and complained endlessly at his lack of practical skills, his inability to cook a meal, operate a washing machine, and the way his dinner always ended up on his shirt. Denzel humiliated him on the *bocci* pitch and called him 'old and square'.

By choosing to wear the *djellaba* and the *shashiyah* beret and oil his long beard, George felt he was taking back some control of who he was and how others saw him. He ceased to be George, the Maltese ex-policeman, husband and father, becoming Juriege the Berber, wingman of Maverick, eyes and ears of Lady Mantis, doer of daring deeds in the deserts of Libya!

There, he was respected. Doors were held open for him; cars waited, engines running, ready for his instructions. His best friend was one of the most powerful people in the country. His immediate boss was another. He had authority over enormous sums of money, he signed contracts, dispensed cash and, when his trips were urgent, was allowed to commandeer the Dassault Falcon – the private jet!

He would never choose one over the other, but to be able to be both was indeed a blessing! *Inshallah*!

EPILOGUE

AMY HALLIDAY SAT SLUMPED, looking at the screen in front of her. Today, she had received another fifteen emails from the lawyers concerning the thirteen different cases, currently running against her and the *Malta Telegraph*, in the Maltese courts. That was not an unusual number. In fact, it was lower than she normally had to deal with. The subject of the legal actions were her articles and investigations into BetHi, MalTech Energy and the Bonnici family.

It seemed that every legal office on the island had been instructed by someone connected with Natasha Bonnici to bring a claim designed to censor, intimidate, or silence her and the paper, by burying them in a morass of legal proceedings, claiming criminal defamation, libel and actions to protect reputation.

In fact, there were so many firms of lawyers working for the Bonnicis and their companies that the *Telegraph* found it hard to engage anyone with any specialist knowledge in that area of law to act in their defence. She was told those doing the suing never expected to win the cases, but the so-called 'strategic lawsuits against public participation' – SLAPP actions – involved so much work and expense that most defendants found it impossible to contest them and inevitably sought terms of settlement.

The *Telegraph's* board of directors had already told Amy to back off the stories, to give them space, so they could try to get an agreement to withdraw the raft of frivolous claims that had been brought against them.

At first, she argued that the SLAPP lawsuits proved she was onto something important. Then she argued that the newspaper's duty to its readers was to refuse to be intimidated. Finally, she tried to defend the proceedings herself, acting without a lawyer. The harder she tried, the more applications, petitions and requests for further information piled up in her in-tray. Papers arrived by email and by post to her home. She was served notices and requests for information in person, in restaurants and in shops. It was so intense, she could almost believe there was a personal motive behind it all. She found most of her days consumed in pointless legal process which, of course, was the sole aim of SLAPP proceedings.

She was scared, exhausted and financially ruined. At the request of MalTech Energy, the courts had issued precautionary warrants, freezing the forty thousand euros savings in her bank accounts, as potential damages in defamation actions brought against her. Eventually, the *Telegraph* had washed its hands of her and formally warned her that, if she insisted on stirring up any more trouble, they were going to have to ask her to leave.

Her profile pieces on Natasha Bonnici and Nick Walker had been the first to attract legal proceedings. Attempts by her to name Nick as the whistle-blower on the Russian energy deal, were met with similar SLAPP proceedings. Her investigations into the source of monies used by MalTech Energy and its investor group to establish itself, met with more proceedings. An exposé centred on the Bonnicis' involvement with the oil-smuggling case of four years ago prompted a similar response.

None of the stories had ever appeared in print, but one or two blogs had started to circulate, suggesting that Natasha Bonnici was being heavy-handed in her attempts to silence the print media. Those journalists, too, had found themselves dragged into the courts and, despite their protests, their days became filled with endless legal work and their purses were emptied by the lawyers.

It had been a long day. At seven in the evening, Amy walked down to the badly lit underground car park, alone and despondent. Her white Nissan stood alone in a corner. She looked around and noticed there were no other cars on this level. It was getting late. Somewhere, she heard the echo of a loud metallic bang, as a steel fire door slammed shut on an upper floor of the car park. She opened the door with her remote and threw her bag, stuffed full of the day's legal papers, onto the back seat.

Wearily, she slumped into the driver's seat, checked her hair in the mirror, put one arm onto the top of the passenger seat to prepare to reverse and turned the key in the ignition.

ABOUT THE AUTHOR

AJ Aberford is a former corporate lawyer who moved to Malta several years ago. He is enthralled by the culture and history of the island that acts as a bridge between Europe and North Africa. Its position at the sharp end of the migrant crisis and the rapid growth of its tourist and commercial sectors provide a rich back-drop to the Inspector George Zammit series.

To keep up to date on AJ Aberford's fiction writing please subscribe to his website: **www.ajaberford.com**.

Reviews help authors more than you might think. If you enjoyed *Bullets in the Sand*, please consider leaving a review.

You can connect with AJ Aberford and find out more about the upcoming adventures of George and Abdullah, by following him on Facebook or, better still, subscribing to his mailing list.

When you join the mailing list you will get a link to download a novella, *Meeting in Milan*, a prequel to the Inspector George Zammit series.

ACKNOWLEDGMENTS

The Inspector George Zammit series is my debut work and I have too often been blind to my many mistakes. I thank my wife, Janet, for gently pointing them out, the time she has spent working on the various drafts and for her encouragement and support. I also thank my editor, Lynn Curtis, who has worked patiently with me, giving sage advice, steering the plots and refining the prose.

THE GEORGE ZAMMIT CRIME SERIES

Meeting in Milan (short-story prequel)

Bodies in the Water
Bullets in the Sand
Hawk at the Crossroads

MEETING IN MILAN

Short-story prequel available for free: www.ajaberford.com.

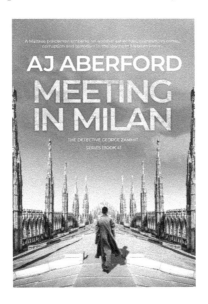

What is a family?

Two very different cousins, one from Malta and one from Sicily, are brought together to embark on their university studies in Bologna.

While spending time with their uncle and dying aunt in Milan, they learn some truths about themselves and realise that family is not what it seems.

In the space of a few short weeks, they have a decision to make. It is a choice that could change their lives forever and, once made, there will be no going back …

HAWK AT THE CROSSROADS

George Zammit returns in *Hawk at the Crossroads*

Pre-order now.

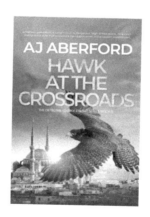

Turkey is the new powerbroker in the eastern Mediterranean and The Hawk sits in Istanbul, pulling the strings. But why should any of this concern a Maltese policeman?

Inspector George Zammit, of the Maltese *Pulizija*, receives a phone call from an old friend in need, the Libyan militia leader, Abdullah Belkacem. As a result, George and Abdullah are catapulted into an adventure, taking them from disputed Greek Islands to war-torn Libya, in a journey that tests their friendship to the limit.

As an arch manipulator and power broker, The Hawk plays his cards close to his chest. But, with one daring move, he turns the politics of the eastern Mediterranean upside down, making a powerful enemy.

Natasha Bonnici is now the head of a mysterious organised crime family, based in Milan. She and The Hawk circle each other, as the biggest game of all plays out.

Can lowly Inspector George Zammit face these forces and restore order, before the s slips into chaos?

If you like Henning Mankell's *Wallander* books, or those of Michael Dibden's *Aurelio Zen*, you will love *Hawk at the Crossroads*, with its unique blend of humour, drama and adventure. George Zammit is to Malta, what 'Montalbano' is to Sicily or Donna Leon's 'Commissario Guido Brunetti' is to Venice.

Here follows a taster …

O. R. TAMBO INTERNATIONAL AIRPORT – JOHANNESBURG

SANT'AGATA PRISON, AVELLINO, ITALY

South African diamonds are legally exported in secure containers with specifically numbered and government-validated certificates. This regulates the trade in stones mined in the warzones of Africa that have caused misery to so many, for so long. It's for good reason that such stones are often referred to as 'blood diamonds'.

Christina Cassar had passed through the security scanner of O. R. Tambo International Airport, overseen by a lethargic, slack-jawed woman whose glazed eyes only occasionally drifted towards the screen in front of her. Christina gathered her blue cabin bag, cosmetics, jacket, and slipped her feet into her expensive sandals. She took the soiled grey plastic tray and headed towards the stainless-steel packing table. They were in no hurry, having plenty of time left before their fifteen-hour flight back to Malta, via Amsterdam. She and her boyfriend, Nick Walker, had spent the last week at an industry conference at Sun City, the large resort 140 kilometres to the north-west of Johannesburg.

There, Nick had attended a relaxed programme of presentations and workshops, meeting colleagues and friends from the world of online gaming. During the day Christina read at the poolside, and when Nick was free, they had visited the Madikwe

Game Reserve, played golf and enjoyed the resort's spas and pools. At night, they dined, took in shows in the big hotels, and Nick took Christina onto the gaming floors of the casinos, explaining why it was odds-on she would never get her money back once she had converted it into chips.

He was at an adjacent security scanner, putting his belt back through his trouser loops and re-packing his laptop, when he noticed a group of four Hawks walking slowly down the security hall. South Africa's Priority Crime Investigation brigade, the Hawks were a much-feared branch of the police and their appearance usually meant trouble for somebody. They wore black berets, short-sleeved blue shirts, stab jackets, and their trouser legs tucked down inside high, black lace-up boots.,

Christina's cabin bag had glided through the scanner. She hadn't noticed the security woman, apparently watching the endless parade of personal items passing before her, signal to a colleague with a nod. He had helpfully corrected the position of the blue cabin bag on the conveyor belt and, in doing so, deftly slipped a paper envelope into one of its external pockets.

When diamonds are traded in Amsterdam, Surat in India or even Kinshasa, it is traditional to package them in a small paper envelope with a waxy blue interior finish. *Briefke* is the Flemish word for this envelope, and it is used by everybody in the diamond trade. Christina didn't realise it, but the *briefke* inside the front pocket of her cabin bag held about 1,000 carats of diamonds, or 240 grams, with a retail value of over $1 million US for accredited stones.

Nick saw the Hawks looking over at the scanner where Christina was fussing, repacking her cosmetics. He zipped up his briefcase and noticed one of the policemen tap a colleague on the arm and point in Christina's direction. Two of them walked slowly towards her, their thumbs tucked under the shoulder straps of their stab jackets. One was smiling and started engaging her in conversation. He watched as she produced her passport and boarding pass, which the Hawk took from her and inspected. Nick smiled to himself. He knew Christina had nothing to fear, but she would be petrified by the big, intimidating police officers in their military-style uniform.

Nick was walking towards her when the second officer started gathering her things from the packing area. He took her cabin bag, her purse and her jacket, while the first man laid his hand on her arm. Nick was becoming concerned. He arrived in time to hear his agitated girlfriend saying: "What are you doing? Those are my things."

The first officer put her passport and boarding pass into the pocket of his stab jacket, then looked at her with an expression that had curdled.

"You must come with us."

Christina saw Nick approach and stepped towards him, fear on her face.

"Nick, they want to take me with them. They've got my things."

Confused, he spoke to the officer who seemed to be in charge, noticing the sergeant's stripes on his epaulettes.

"Hey, what's going on? You can't take her away, she's done nothing wrong."

He'd made to take her hand and pull her towards him when the two Hawks who had initially stood back quickly moved in and grabbed his arms, roughly pulling them behind him. The man with the sergeant's stripes spoke loudly in his ear.

"Who are you to her? Are you two travelling together?"

"Yes, we live together. Now let us go! Get off me!"

There was a brief scuffle as he tried to shake himself free, until he realised he was making things worse for both of them. He forced himself to relax and turned to Christina, saying, "Let's go with them and get this sorted out – whatever they think it is."

Turning to the sergeant who was holding him, he said: "It's OK, we're coming with you."

The police officer relaxed his grip and said: "Sensible of you. We go this way."

He nodded to his colleagues and they set off. Christina grabbed Nick's hand and the pair of them were marched, closely surrounded by the four Hawks, through the endless corridors of the airport. Heads turned and people sidestepped as the Hawks paraded the couple through the terminal to the airport police station. There they were split up and held in separate, stifling interview rooms.

The sergeant interviewed Christina first, after placing her cabin bag at his feet. He looked at her for a while then said: "Is there anything you want to tell me?"

"No. I don't understand what this is all about."

With a shrug, he reached down to her bag and slipped his hand into the front pocket.

Christina gasped in horror and put her hand to her mouth when he produced the white *briefke* and let a small stream of glittering stones tinkle onto the metal table between them. His gaze met hers as, without a word, he slowly gathered up the stones and put them back into the envelope.

The sergeant sighed deeply and closely studied the shocked and tearful young woman, sitting shaking on a wooden chair bolted to the floor. She was a pretty, slightly built woman, with short, pixie-cut blonde hair, clusters of freckles on her cheeks and piercing blue eyes. Tears had smudged her mascara and reddened her lids. Her tip-tilted nose was running slightly. She looked and felt very small in the presence of the bulky law-enforcement officer across the table from her.

Sergeant Enzokuhle Lubanzi was not a man given to pity. He had seen too many tears and heard too many cries of innocence. If he had any sympathy, it was for those who were forced into wrongdoing by threats from organised-crime gangs or else by desperate poverty. He'd seen plenty of that, but here sat a well-dressed white woman, returning from a week in Sun City, with a business-class ticket to a destination half-way across the world, smuggling what could be a million dollars' worth of blood diamonds. If compassion had been in his makeup, he wouldn't be wasting it on a person such as this.

He said: "You won't know this, but the nickname for the Women's Correctional Facility in Johannesburg is also Sun City. Ironic, hey? You won't see much sun, but there is gambling and the inmates are very like the wild animals on the Madikwe Reserve.

HOBECK BOOKS – THE HOME OF GREAT STORIES

We hope you've enjoyed reading this novel by AJ Aberford. To keep up to date on AJ Aberford's fiction writing please subscribe to his website: **www.ajaberford.com** and you will also be able to download the free novella *Meeting in Milan*.

Hobeck Books also offers a number of short stories and novellas, free for subscribers in the compilation *Crime Bites*.

- *Echo Rock* by Robert Daws
- *Old Dogs, Old Tricks* by A B Morgan
- *The Silence of the Rabbit* by Wendy Turbin
- *Never Mind the Baubles: An Anthology of Twisted Winter Tales* by the Hobeck Team (including many of the Hobeck authors and Hobeck's two publishers)
- *The Clarice Cliff Vase* by Linda Huber
- *Here She Lies* by Kerena Swan
- *The Macnab Principle* by R.D. Nixon
- *Fatal Beginnings* by Brian Price
- *A Defining Moment* by Lin Le Versha
- *Saviour* by Jennie Ensor
- *You Can't Trust Anyone These Days* by Maureen Myant

Also please visit the Hobeck Books website for details of our other superb authors and their books, and if you would like to get in touch, we would love to hear from you.

Hobeck Books also presents a weekly podcast, the Hobcast Book Show, where founders Adrian Hobart and Rebecca Collins discuss all things book related, key issues from each week, including the ups and downs of running a creative business. Each episode includes an interview with one of the people who make Hobeck possible: the editors, the authors, the cover designers. These are the people who help Hobeck bring great stories to life. Without them, Hobeck wouldn't exist. The Hobcast can be listened to from all the usual platforms but it can also be found on the Hobeck website: **www.hobeck.net/hobcast**.

OTHER HOBECK BOOKS TO EXPLORE

The Rock Crime Series by Robert Daws

The magnificent Rock crime series from acclaimed British actor
Robert Daws – includes free bonus story *Echo Rock*.

'An exciting 21st-century crime writer.'
Peter James

'A top crime thriller.'
Adam Croft, crime writer

Detective Sergeant Tamara Sullivan approaches her secondment
to the sun-soaked streets of Gibraltar with mixed feelings.
Desperate to prove herself following a career-threatening
decision during a dangerous incident serving with London's
Metropolitan Police, Sullivan is pitched into a series of life-and-
death cases in partnership with her new boss, Detective Chief
Inspector Gus Broderick. An old-school cop, Broderick is himself
haunted by personal demons following the unexplained
disappearance of his wife some years earlier. The two detectives
form an uneasy alliance and friendship in the face of a series of
murders that challenge Sullivan and Broderick to their limits and
beyond.

The Rock crime series transports readers to the ancient streets of the British Overseas Territory of Gibraltar, sat precariously at the western entrance to the Mediterranean and subject to the jealous attention of neighbouring Spain. Robert Daws shows his mastery of the classic whodunnit with three novels rich in great characters, tense plotting full of twists and turns and breath-taking set-piece action.

The Rock

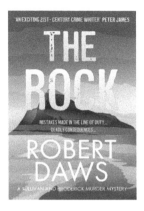

Exiled to Gibraltar from London's Metropolitan Police after a
lapse of judgement, DS Tamara Sullivan feels she's being
punished – no matter how sun-kissed the Rock is.

But this is no sleepy siesta of a posting on the Mediterranean.
Paired with her new boss, DCI Gus Broderick, Sullivan will need
all her skills to survive the most dangerous case of her career.

A young constable is found hanging in his apartment. With no
time for introductions, Sullivan and Broderick, unravel a dark
and sinister secret that has remained buried for decades.

Are they prepared to face the fury of what they are about to
uncover?

Poisoned Rock

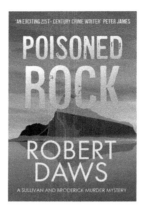

As the bright lights of a Hollywood movie production shine into the dark recesses of Gibraltar, murky secrets emerge from the shadows of the Rock's past.

It seems the legacy of wartime spying, sabotage and treachery runs deep on the Rock.

Past and present collide plunging detectives Tamara Sullivan and Gus Broderick into a tangled web of intrigue and murder, and their skills and uneasy working relationship are about to be tested to the limit.

Killing Rock

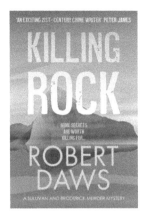

A wealthy household massacred in Spain.

Unidentified mummified remains found at the foot of The Rock.

A US Congressman's run for President hangs on events in Gibraltar.

What's the connection?

Detectives Tamara Sullivan and Gus Broderick face the most dangerous and elusive murder investigation of their lives, and for Broderick, it's about to become all too personal, with his career in real peril as his past comes back to haunt him.

Will Sullivan and Broderick's partnership survive this latest case, as killers stalk the narrow streets of Gibraltar?

Lightning Source UK Ltd.
Milton Keynes UK
UKHW010701301222
414627UK00001B/206

9 781913 793739